# THE DRAGON'S GOLD

## JUMPSTART DUCHY
### BOOK 2

## STEFON MEARS

Thousand
Faces
Publishing

# Also by Stefon Mears

**The Rise of Magic Series**
*Magician's Choice*
*Sleight of Mind*
*Lunar Alchemy*
*Three Fae Monte*
*The Sphinx Principle*
*Double Backed Magic*
*Mercury Fold (coming soon)*

**Cavan Oltblood Series**
*Half a Wizard*
*The Ice Dagger*
*Spells of Undeath*

**Power City Tales**
*Not Quite Bulletproof*
*No Money in Heroism*

**Standalones**
*Between the Cracks*
*Sects and the City*
*Prince of a Thousand Worlds*
*Devil's Night*
*Portal-Land, Oregon*
*Stealing from Pirates*
*Fade to Gold*
*With a Broken Sword*
*Twice Against the Dragon*
*The House on Cedar Street*
*Sudden Death*
*On the Edge of Faerie*

**Short Story Collections**
*Spell Slingers*
*Twisted Timelines*
*Longhairs and Short Tales: A Collection of Cat Stories*
*Confronting Legends (Spells & Swords Vol. 1)*
*The Patreon Collection, Vol. 1-8 (Vol. 9, coming soon)*

**Nonfiction**
*The 30-Day Novel and Beyond!*

**Spells for Hire Series**
*Devil's Shoestring*
*Zombie Powder*
*Spirit Trap*
*Dragon's Blood*

**The Telepath Trilogy**
*Surviving Telepathy*
*Immoral Telepathy*
*Targeting Telepathy*

**Edge of Humanity Series**
*Caught Between Monsters*
*Hunting Monsters*

**Jumpstart Duchy Series**
*Into the Torn Kingdoms*
*The Dragon's Gold*
*The Gift Castle*
*The Deadly Feast*
*The King's Test*
*Triumph in the Torn Kingdoms*

Published by Thousand Faces Publishing, Portland, Oregon

http://1kfaces.com



Front cover image © Fedbul | Dreamstime.com (File ID: 160376698)



Hardback ISBN: 978-1-948490-44-3

Paperback ISBN: 978-1-948490-27-6

# THE DRAGON'S GOLD

# FOREWORD

The man known as Aefric Brightstaff was not born on Qorunn. He was born on the distant world of Earth, where he went by the name Keifer McShane.

On Earth, he knew the world of Qorunn only through *The Torn Kingdoms*, the setting of his favorite roleplaying game. His primary source of joy and solace, following the untimely death of his wife, Andi.

When a Jumpstart crowdfunding campaign for the next edition of *The Torn Kingdoms* offered him the chance to become a duke in the world he loved, Keifer pounced on it. Imagined they would send him a patent of nobility. Ask his opinion about the non-player character who'd bear his name and title. Perhaps even allow him to include Andi as his duchess, when the books went to print.

He couldn't wait to become a part of the world he loved so well.

But he mistook it all for make-believe.

Keifer didn't expect the great Mage of Marrisford himself, the one and only Kainemorton, to show up on his doorstep.

Keifer didn't expect to be transported to Qorunn, where he would start life anew as an orphan boy on the streets of the fabled city of Sartis. That shining beacon on the southern sea.

Now known as Aefric, he grew into a powerful adventurer. Widely believed to be a wizard, he is in fact the first of the dweomerblood. It is said that magic itself flows through his very veins.

As Aefric, he mastered the fabled Brightstaff. He fought in the Godswalk Wars, and saved countless lives at the Battle of Deepwater, in the kingdom of Armyr.

In gratitude, King Colm of Armyr named Aefric Duke of Deepwater. And no sooner had Aefric taken possession of his duchy than he prevented an invasion by Armyr's southern neighbor, Malimfar.

Keifer McShane. Aefric Brightstaff.

One man who has lived two lives.

This is book two of his story…

# 1

———

Aefric Brightstaff reined in near the brown, rocky crest of the ridge where he would soon overlook the path leading down into the Dragonscar. A vast chasm, well over a hundred miles long and at least a score of miles across, the Dragonscar formed the northern border of his duchy.

It was almost midday, and almost midsummer. A lazy, sultry day. But high on this ridge, with the vast beauty of the Risen Sea scarcely a mile to his left, the whipping wind cooled the day's heat quite well.

So well, in fact, that he took advantage of the pause to draw a leather thong from his belt and tie back his long blonde hair. As he did, he stared off into the sea.

No ships in sight, and he wondered if there should be.

His brilliant black stallion, Windsong, stamped eagerly, and snorted. Irritated, perhaps, that Aefric had reined in where he had, instead of beginning his descent into the chasm.

An impressive steed, Windsong. He'd been a gift from Queen Eppida herself, on the day Aefric was made duke of Deepwater. And Aefric had never known a horse so eager to run. His stamina seemed endless, at times.

But if Aefric rode down into the chasm before any of his soldiers or guards checked it out, he'd never hear the end of it. Not from Ser Beornric Ol'Sandallas, the captain of his personal guard. And especially not from his general, Ser Yrsa Azenai.

Ser Yrsa, who still had not quite forgiven Aefric...

Aefric had done many things right, during his first days as duke of Deepwater. But he'd committed one major faux pas.

He'd sent his armies south to aid his neighbor, the duchy of Merrek, under the command of his new countess, Faenella.

He hadn't given command to his own general. Hadn't even consulted with her. Hadn't even informed her of what he was doing.

And the mere fact that he hadn't yet been to his ducal seat at Water's End, or even known he *had* a general, was really no excuse.

She'd been furious. And like the woman herself, her fury was no small matter.

Aefric was tall. Ser Yrsa was taller.

Aefric's blonde hair was sandy. Hers had red undertones that always made Aefric wonder if they came from the blood of enemies that she'd just never bothered wholly washing out.

Despite the fact that she was a good decade older than Aefric, she moved about in full plate armor with more agility than he felt in his riding outfit, which today consisted of a quilted tunic of Deepwater gray, and leather breeches.

And she fought with those huge twin maces. Those vicious, ridged things should have been top heavy. But he'd seen her practice with them. She whipped them around like they were wands.

Aefric had grown up living the hard, dangerous life of an adventurer. And though he relied more on his magic than the sword at his side, he knew his way around personal combat.

But watching Yrsa on the training ground always made him feel as though he'd lived a soft life of physical ineptitude.

Dear gods. The strength in that woman's hands and wrists. She could probably tie horseshoes into neat little bows with no more effort than Aefric needed to lace up his boots.

She might have tried tying Aefric into a neat little bow, when they finally met. Except that Aefric had been both sincere and effusive in his apologies.

It probably helped that Ser Beornric — who'd gotten to know Aefric well over the previous aett or so — had taken her drinking, and had a long talk with her.

That was a season ago. When Aefric had first arrived at Water's End and met the woman who had served as his predecessor's general for more than five years.

But Aefric could tell he was far from forgiven.

They were catching him up now, Sers Beornric and Yrsa. Along with the six knights of his personal guard.

All eight of them looked irritated, though Ser Beornric, at least, looked to have some humor about it. A smile hid beneath that bushy new mustache of his.

Ser Beornric had been a knight of the king during the Godswalk Wars, and he had the rough features and old scars to prove it. But he had been at the Battle of Deepwater, and was one of those who called Aefric that battle's hero, and sworn he would follow Aefric into any of the thirteen hells, if asked.

The man was maybe ten summers shy of twice Aefric's age — this summer would make an even two dozen for Aefric — with more salt than pepper in his short hair and mustache these days. For all that, Ser Beornric was still quite fit. And even had he not been, his knowledge of Armyr, its history and its politics had proven invaluable to Aefric as he settled into his duties as duke.

Ser Yrsa, though, saw nothing funny in the situation.

"Might I remind your grace," she said through gritted teeth, "that the *purpose* of riding with his soldiery is to keep him safe? Even the finest soldiers in Qorunn cannot protect their duke *if he insists on leaving them behind.*"

Ser Yrsa had several degrees of anger, and Aefric had learned to discern most of them by watching her major scar. All of his knights had scars, of course. He had several himself.

Ser Yrsa, though, had taken a sword blow to the face at some point. The scar left by that sword started from the middle of her forehead, and carved a shallow groove down through her left eye all the way to her chin.

The effect should probably have been disturbing. But she wore that scar as well as she wore her armor.

A healer had at least restored her vision, though the eye was not ... as it had been. Her right eye was a dark gray, but her left eye was red. A pale red where most would have white, and a dark red for the iris.

The pupil, at least, remained black.

At the moment, her scar had darkened from its stark whiteness against her natural tawny coloring, but was not yet approaching purple. Aefric knew from that that she was irritated but not yet *angry*. And that, at least, was a good thing.

"Ser Yrsa," Aefric said, "you may remind me of anything you wish. In fact, I've encouraged you before to speak your mind."

"You have," she said, while the knights of Aefric's personal guard took up positions around them. "Many nobles say such things, your grace. Few understand what they're really saying. Fewer still mean it."

"I both understand," Aefric said, "and mean what I've said."

"Then *stop being a damned fool!*" she barked, making Aefric's guards wince.

Ser Yrsa held off further words, as the two score soldiers they'd brought along moved past them and began setting up for the lunch break.

The soldiers were all clad in chainmail and steel half-helmets, and wearing tabards of Deepwater gray, bearing the Deepwater device: the image of a lake, with a sword sticking up, hilt first.

The company consisted of a two dozen pikemen, a dozen archers, and four scouts.

She lowered her voice as she continued.

"I know you've been an adventurer," she said, showing more patience than Aefric expected. "But you're not riding like an adventurer right now, are you? Did you once check your perimeter? Did you once worry about what might be *just past* that ridge ahead?"

Aefric opened his mouth to answer. She didn't let him.

"No, you did not. I know body language, and you rode up here like a man out for a jaunt to the tavern, along heavily guarded streets." She shook her head. "But we're not on streets. Or roads. And the guards were behind you."

"I'm not entirely incapable myself," Aefric said.

"No," Ser Yrsa said, keeping her voice low. "Which makes it all the worse. You *know* better. But you're relying on your ability to counter-strike. On the speed with which you could conjure a defense, should an unexpected attack come. *Which is no excuse not to be aware when that attack comes.*"

Ser Beornric drew breath to say something. Ser Yrsa raised a hand to stop him. The hammer of her gaze continued to pound Aefric.

"We approach the Dragonscar," she said. "A questionable place unto itself. But more than that, the border with Silverlake."

"Are you expecting Duke Wylyn to ride against us?" Aefric asked, honestly curious.

"No," Ser Yrsa said, shaking her head once without ever moving her gaze from his. "But during the Godswalk Wars, Silverlake was attacked from below by the dybbungstad and their demon twins. What if the dybbungstad established a base here in the Dragonscar? They might remain still."

"We've had scouts in the area since before I was made duke," Aefric said. "If there've been warning signs, I haven't heard of them."

"And none of our scouts have gone *into* the Dragonscar, because their primary job has been to watch Silverlake. Which they can do by spyglass across the ridge. True they reported no signs of activity in the Dragonscar, such as fires. But I've never heard of the dybbungstad cooking their meat. Have you?"

"No," Aefric said, shaking his head.

"In fact," Ser Yrsa said, lifting an eyebrow. "Do you have any experience fighting the dybbungstad?"

Did he? A complex question.

As Keifer McShane, who knew Qorunn through his *Torn Kingdoms* game books, his characters had faced the dybbungstad in a series of adventure modules. *J1-6,* collectively called *What Price Honor?*

But from his lived experience here in Qorunn...

"No," Aefric said. "I'd almost come to regard them as myth, before the Godswalk Wars. And I never got far enough north to fight them."

"Nor did I," she said, with a nod. "And I do not wish to learn about them through the death of my duke."

Aefric felt as though she'd thrown cold water in his face.

He nodded. "You're right. I'm sorry. I wasn't thinking."

"You were caught up in the gorgeous skies and the wondrous sight of the sea," she said, that raised eyebrow now carrying some accusation to it.

"I was," Aefric said. "But I was also giving Windsong his head for a bit. I didn't want him too excited when we start the descent."

"Fair enough," she said. "But what would I have asked of you, had you sought my opinion first?"

Interesting. She didn't ask what he *should* have done, but what *she would have asked him* to do.

"To at least warn you and Ser Beornric, so the two of you could ride with me."

"Thank you, your grace," she said, bowing her head. "Now, if you will excuse me, I shall make sure our men don't slack in setting up their perimeter."

"Of course," Aefric said. "And thank you."

Ser Yrsa frowned a moment, on hearing Aefric thank her after the way she'd taken him to task. She snorted softly, then shook her head.

Finally, just before riding off, she looked back over her shoulder and said, "I heard about the tactics you employed while working with those eldrani archers, down in Kesh. That was good work."

She turned and rode off then.

"Was that a compliment?" Aefric asked, astonished.

"I believe so," Ser Beornric said. "Perhaps she's finally warming to you."

"I just had to let her know she could yell at me?"

"Only when you do something stupid, your grace," Ser Beornric said with a quirked half-smile.

"So, what," Aefric said, "I should expect her to yell at me now once or twice an aett?"

"I'd never have suggested such a thing myself, your grace," Ser Beornric said. "But I wouldn't accuse you of being wrong about it."

Aefric had to laugh at that, and when he did the knights of his personal guard joined in.

They were laughing with him, though. At least, he hoped so.

They were still laughing when the warning whistle came.

---

THE SOUND OF THE WARNING WHISTLE CUT THROUGH THE WHIPPING OF the sea winds.

Danger nearby, not yet imminent.

Aefric swore. Ser Yrsa had been right. He'd been getting too used to the softer life of a duke. The day's beauty had lulled him into foolishly assuming he was safe. A mistake he resolved not to make again.

All seven knights around Aefric — Ser Beornric included — donned their helmets, and closed their visors. They drew their weapons and closed ranks about their duke.

Aefric drew the Brightstaff from the sling attached to his horse's saddle. Carved from a six-foot branch of white thunderwood, the powerful staff had a brown, leather-wrapped grip, and a yellow diamond embedded into its top.

Up ahead, he could see his soldiers taking up positions along the brown rocks of the ridge.

The dozen archers were already on down on one knee, arrows ready to draw. They sighted their longbows down the path into the Dragonscar.

Behind them, the soldiers with pikes formed ranks, while Ser Yrsa, still ahorse, took a report from two of the leather-clad scouts.

"Let's go," Aefric said, impatiently.

"Your grace," Ser Beornric said, "proper form says we should wait for word from Yrsa."

"But—"

With Ser Beornric's visor down, Aefric couldn't read his expression. Yet somehow that visor spoke volumes.

"Fine," Aefric said, letting out an explosive sigh. "But if any of my people get killed, when I could have prevented it, she'll find out why she should worry about *my* anger, for a change."

Ser Beornric said nothing. Only nodded once.

And Aefric had to fight down the tension that was locking up his shoulders and churning his empty stomach. He never did well, trying to hold back when action was coming.

No. That wasn't true. He could set an ambush and wait with the patience of a hunting cat.

But that was waiting with a plan. This was waiting for others to *bring him into* the plan. When he didn't even know what the threat was, yet. Could have been soldiers. Could have been bandits. Could have been dybbungstad, for all he knew.

And for him to sit, waiting, felt most unfamiliar. And most unfair.

The yellow diamond atop the Brightstaff began to glow. Not because Aefric deliberately called forth light, either. Which meant that he was leaking magic a bit.

He'd never met anyone else who'd had that problem. But then, he'd never met another dweomerblood, either.

He forced his mouth closed tight, and flared his nostrils in deep breaths of sea air. Focused on the whipping wind against his face.

He could wait. He had to wait. He *hated* it. But he would do it.

*Finally*, the scouts gave Ser Yrsa the battlefield salute — the right fist, palm side forward, raised to shoulder height instead of to full extension as a normal salute would be — and trotted back to Aefric.

They gave their duke the same salute. He returned it.

"Your grace," the lead scout said. She was a wiry woman, and both she and her partner had smeared their tanned skin, their short-cropped hair, and their leathers with brown dust to blend in better against the rocks. "Unknown armed party at the bottom of the pass.

They have lookouts watching the approach, but I do not believe they spotted us. Two of our number remain below, keeping watch."

"How many in the unknown party?"

"Close to fifty. They have the sea-worn look of sailors, but there are no signs of shipwreck. Some of them have leathers, but the rest wear no armor. For weapons they have swords and clubs, mostly, but they look to have a few short bows."

"Which means they may have a wizard?"

"Unknown at this time, your grace."

"How well ensconced are they?"

"Very well, though they lack enough missile weapons to fully exploit their positioning. And they do not seem to be expecting trouble. Nevertheless, they've set up among the rocks, and they have their backs to a cave."

"Lousy fighting on horseback," Ser Beornric said, "weaving among rocks."

"True," Aefric said. "What's the ground like?"

"Rocky," the scout said, "and where they set up, largely unstable enough that horses will not do well in a skirmish. There is a smooth line of approach along the rock wall from seaward, but getting to it would be tricky."

Aefric nodded.

"You said there's a cave behind them," he said. "So some could be in hiding? There could be more than fifty?"

"No, your grace," she said. "It's a shallow cave, and full of crates."

"Pirates or smugglers then," Ser Beornric said.

"So said General Yrsa," the scout said with a bow of her head.

"What is her plan?" Aefric asked.

"To ride down the pass herself, with two dozen pike, and demand their business. If they give a satisfying answer, she will report it to your grace. If they do not, she will give the signal. The archers will loose and begin the battle. She will take as many captives as possible."

"And she expects me to sit idly by through this, does she?"

"Your grace," the scout said, squirming a bit under his glare, "she requests that you and your guards hold in reserve, to support as needed."

"Is *that* what she requests?" Aefric asked sharply.

The path down to the chasm floor was likely at least a hundred and fifty feet. And likely steep enough that the horses would have to watch their footing.

Not exactly an ideal cavalry charge.

"It is, your grace." The poor scout sounded as though she'd rather have been back down below, keeping an eye on all those potential enemies than here, than telling her duke something he didn't want to hear.

"Very well," Aefric said with a nod and a smile. "If she wishes us to remain as support, that is what we shall do. Please, tell General Yrsa that I intend to comply with her request."

"Thank you, your grace," the scout said, giving Aefric the battle-field salute even as she bowed, and she and her partner scout quickly hustled back over to Ser Yrsa.

Ser Yrsa gave Aefric a nod, then turned, gave her orders, and started leading the two dozen pike-wielding soldiers down the pass.

"So, your grace," Ser Beornric said casually. "What loophole do you intend to exploit?"

"Loophole?" Aefric asked in barely disguised mock innocence.

"Yes, your grace" Ser Beornric said, patiently. "I have no doubt that you intend to comply with the letter of Ser Yrsa's request, while still managing to do exactly what you wish."

Aefric chuckled. "I believe you're getting to know me too well, Beornric."

"Thank you, your grace."

"Don't worry though," Aefric said to his guards. "I don't intend to leave the rest of you out of the fun."

———

Brightstaff in hand, Aefric crouched at the edge of the rocky ridge, overlooking the Dragonscar down below.

He smiled into the wind. From where he crouched, he could see most, if not all, of those ... pirates, smugglers, or whatever they might have been.

He had control of himself again. The yellow diamond atop the Brightstaff remained unlit. Of course, he also held it back from the edge, so its glint in the bright sunlight wouldn't be seen from below.

To Aefric's right, his dozen archers, with their longbows ready. To his left, Ser Beornric and the half-dozen knights of his personal guard. They too had their bows ready, though theirs were recurved, rather than traditional longbows.

Aefric could feel all of the archers gauging the strong, salty sea wind as they picked targets down below.

The scouts had been right. The sailors might all have been armed, but they didn't look ready for a fight. They were watching the sea, not the land around them. Even those who looked to be standing watch scarcely look away from the sea.

Clearly they were expecting a ship soon.

It occurred to Aefric that a ship might be able to sail up close to the foot of the Dragonscar. There was little beach, where the sea met the land, but the curve of the land might form a decent natural harbor. Assuming there were no dangerous reefs to worry about...

Aefric dragged his attention back to the sailors below him. He knew that the others were picking their targets now, but Aefric had to wait for that.

One or more of those sailors might be a wizard. Likely only one, but the chance of a competent apprentice was not worth discounting.

Had he been closer, he could have felt the magic of any spell-casters, as well as any enchanted items, should they have any. But from here, spotting them would require a spell. A spell they might detect.

So instead, Aefric held his eyes slightly unfocused so that, at the same time, he could watch the movements of all the sailors he could see. He wanted to know the instant any of them made for a wand — certainly none of them carried a staff or a rod — or began casting a spell.

Commotion down below. Their scouts must have spotted Ser Yrsa, approaching with the foot soldiers.

The sailors drew and readied weapons. Focused their cover on the direction of the path down from the ridge. One moved about, giving orders. He was a big man, the sort who had rolls of muscle hidden under rolls of fat. Black shaggy hair and beard, though he was dressed no better than the others. They were all in roughspun clothing, mostly tunics and breeches.

"Dibs on the fat man," Ser Beornric said, and one of the archers swore.

"In this wind?" Aefric said. "Anyone who calls dibs must hit their target on the first shot, or buy all the other archers a drink when we next reach a town."

"Agreed," Ser Beornric said, his wolfish smile visible because — like the other knights — he'd raised his visor for this.

The others all echoed his agreement. And to Aefric's amusement, they all began calling dibs on one target or another.

"I reserve the right," Aefric said, "to attack any who show themselves to be spellcasters. Be they dibsed or not."

They were smart enough not to object.

Ser Yrsa came into view. She still sat her horse, and Aefric noticed that she had no weapon in hand. The foot soldiers fanned out around her, pikes ready.

The ground beneath her was solid enough, if rocky, but the scouts were right. Where the sailors had set up, there were any number of cracks that could steal a hoof, and possibly part of a horse's leg.

Even fighting on foot among those rocks could be tricky.

Ser Yrsa started saying something. Aefric could tell that much. But damn the wind, he couldn't hear her words. Only the commanding tone of her voice.

He couldn't understand the answer called back by the fat man, either. It didn't sound very respectful though. And the gesture accompanying the response was clear enough.

*We've got you outnumbered.*

And they did. They had numbers on their side — about two-to-one, down there — and a slight edge in the terrain. On the other hand, Ser Yrsa's soldiers were likely better trained. And she had an advantage the sailors hadn't spotted yet.

She called back to them once more. Likely an order to surrender.

The fat man gave the attack signal for her.

Aefric's archers had been told to wait for one of two things. Either Ser Yrsa would wave, or the sailors would shoot.

Their four bowmen shot.

The archers on the ridge unleashed.

Ser Yrsa leaped down from her horse, and led the foot charge. Aefric could hear their roar over the wind.

The first volley of arrows from the ridge was still falling when the second volley was loosed.

There.

Back beside the fat man with the shaggy hair and beard. A slight man had emerged in dirty, sea green robes. He had short, greasy hair and pale, blotchy skin. And he looked as though he disdained all of this.

But he lifted his hands and began to cast a spell that would have loosed an explosive ball of fire. Had he gotten the chance to finish it.

Aefric didn't let him.

Froze him like a human statue, right where he stood.

Most of the first arrows from the ridge struck their targets, including Ser Beornric's. Though the fat man must've had decent armor under his clothes, because the arrow stuck behind his shoulder without doing him much apparent harm.

He looked up, though and began calling a retreat.

Didn't help. The second wave of arrows began hitting their targets.

Then Ser Yrsa was among them, breaking limbs and ribs and jaws with every swift strike of her maces.

There was something hypnotically deadly about the way she moved when she was fighting. Every strike led to the next. Her momentum shifted with every blow. Sometimes accelerating in the direction she was already moving, other times reversing direction.

The foot soldiers worked in pairs, to take advantage of their weapons' reach. Each pair coming around both sides of a rock at once, stabbing with their pikes at foes who'd thought themselves safely shielded.

Between the archers, Ser Yrsa, and the organized attack of the foot soldiers, the sailors were falling quickly.

A fact that wasn't lost on them.

They threw down their weapons and surrendered before the fourth volley of arrows was loosed.

Ser Yrsa whistled a rising note.

A scout poked his head around the corner of the pass.

"Your grace," the scout said, "General Yrsa asks that you join her below."

THE RIDE DOWN FROM THE RIDGE WAS ACTUALLY MORE PLEASANT THAN Aefric expected. The path zigzagged its way down, and the walls rose gradually on each side, so there was a view of the chasm below and the sea to the west for at least the first third of the way down.

Though that did mean that the hundred fifty feet of direct distance was more like four hundred fifty feet of riding.

So he felt all the better about not waiting for some sign from Ser Yrsa that he was supposed to lead a supporting charge. That would have made no sense ... at all...

Just what *had* she intended? Had she simply told Aefric that he and his knights were being held in reserve to *placate* him while she took care of the problem herself?

He didn't like that idea. Not one bit.

Down at the bottom, Ser Yrsa had things well in hand. Two of his soldiers had taken arrow wounds. One, only the tip had gotten past the links in her chainmail, so her chest wound was hardly more than a scratch. The other had been caught in the arm, just below the end of his chainmail sleeve.

Punched right through his forearm. The arm was wrapped and in a sling by the time Aefric saw the man. Aefric would have to say something to him, and perhaps to the others who'd taken nothing more than minor cuts and bruises, after they finished dealing with the sailors.

Most of the foot soldiers were busy keeping the surrendered soldiers under guard. Aefric could see the pile of the sailors' weapons, well behind Ser Yrsa.

A couple of his soldiers were limping. Likely turned ankles during the fight, thanks to those cracks in the rock floor.

The sailors were in a bad way. Fully a third of their number were dead. Another two dozen were down with arrow wounds. Of the others, only a few had escaped the battle without a scratch, and that didn't seem to endear them to their many wounded colleagues.

The fat man with the shaggy black hair and beard had one of Ser Beornric's arrows in his forearm. He was clutching the arm, and panting open-mouthed as he glared first at Ser Yrsa, then at the knights, then at Aefric, then back at Ser Yrsa and around again.

"I hit the green robe. I *know* I did." This from lean, dark-skinned Ser Temat, pointing at the unbroken arrows at the feet of the frozen wizard. "His corpse should have a scar like mine."

Aefric understood the sentiment, but there was no way an arrow could cause a scar as wicked as the one crossing Ser Temat's neck.

"It was my spell," Aefric said. "He can't be harmed in his current state. Any more than he can *cause* harm."

"So long as all agree I don't have to buy drinks," Ser Temat said, and Aefric dismounted and left the knights and archers to the debate.

He approached Ser Yrsa.

"Well done, your grace," she said, approvingly. "Exactly the kind of reserve support I had in mind."

Aefric tried to conceal his frown of puzzlement behind a nod, but he thought he saw amusement in Ser Yrsa's eyes that suggested she knew exactly what he'd been thinking.

Not that this was the time and place to discuss it.

"Did that one" — Aefric nodded toward the fat man — "even give you a name before he called the attack?"

"I said," the fat man said in a voice used to hollering orders, "she wants my name she can suck it from my—"

"Yes, yes," Ser Yrsa said. "We all heard your attempt at wit."

The fat man eyed Aefric. "Goes for you too, pretty man."

Aefric shook his head. Why they bothered putting up fronts like that he never understood. What did this man think his bluster would earn him? Respect?

Ser Yrsa raised an eyebrow at Aefric. He nodded. She could take the lead for now.

"If you don't have a name," she said to the fat man, "I'll call you Dog. Who's your master, Dog?"

"I'm my own master," he sneered.

Ser Yrsa and Dog went back and forth a couple of times, getting nowhere, while Aefric looked over the other sailors. None of them looked happy about the current arrangement. And not only that, he got the impression that not all of them were happy with Dog, either.

"All right, all right," Aefric said, waving his hands to stop the pointless back-and-forth.

Ser Yrsa frowned at Aefric. He sighed.

"Look," he said, with a shake of his head. "It's obvious that the man won't tell us what we want to know. And I don't fancy wasting my time, any more than I fancy torture."

Dog's eyes flared with triumph. He must've thought Aefric was an easy mark. What with his finery, and letting Ser Yrsa handle the questioning.

Aefric smiled.

"I am Aefric Brightstaff," he said. "Duke of Deepwater. You and yours attacked my soldiers without provocation or anything like a rational excuse. As duke, I have the right to regard an attack on my soldiers as an attack on my person. And since I also have the right of high justice, I might as well just execute the lot of you right now, and commandeer your cargo as payment for the harm caused to my people."

"No!" one of the sailors yelled. He clutched a broken right arm, likely the work of Ser Yrsa's maces. He was deeply tanned and sun-wrinkled, and kept his hair cropped close. He had three gold earrings dangling from his left ear.

"I'm Mavash," he said, stepping forward. "Second mate aboard the *Swift Wave.*"

The fat man whirled and grabbed Mavash by the collar of his undyed roughspun jerkin.

Before the fat man could finish growling his threat, Ser Yrsa smacked him across the back of the head with a mace.

He thumped to the ground, unconscious.

"Continue," Aefric said.

Mavash cleared his throat.

"Brusi there," — he pointed to the fallen fat man — "he's our captain all right. But we sail under..." he looked around at his companions. None would meet his eye, though they were all shaking their heads.

"We serve the pirate queen Nelazzi."

Nelazzi. Scourge of the Risen Sea. Aefric knew that she'd caused problems for his predecessor, Duchess Arinda. And as Keifer, she'd been one of his favorite villainous non-player characters from the *Torn Kingdoms* sourcebooks about Qorunn.

His favorite appearance by her had been in adventure module *O3: Sea Devils and Sea Dogs*, where she could be persuaded to aid against the sea devils, but was likely to betray the player characters and steal the adventure's treasure...

"Well," one of the other sailors grumbled, "if we weren't dead before, we are now."

"She won't blame us," Mavash said, pointing at Brusi. "She'll blame *him*. And she'd be right to."

"You're the one, said her name," one of the other sailors said.

"Only because Brusi was too stupid to lie to them as wears a tabard. And insulting *these two*? What was he thinking?" Mavash grimaced, then ducked his head to Aefric and said, "Begging your pardon. Your highness. My life ain't worth much. But if tellin' truths now will spare it, I'll tell all I know."

"Address him as 'your grace,'" Ser Yrsa said, sidestepping the question of his fate. "And clearly Captain Brusi challenged me because he thought he had the advantage."

"No excuse," Mavash said, shaking his head. "Bribed or lied. Only way with them as wears tabards. Anything else leads to, well…"

Mavash gestured to the current state of the sailors.

"Where's the *Swift Wave*?" Ser Yrsa asked.

"Holding anchor," Mavash said. "Safely away from here. You've got us. And I'll tell you whatever you want to know. But I'm not giving up our ship. Not even if you kill me."

"Who'd you steal that cargo from?" Ser Yrsa said. "And where was it bound?"

"Begging your pardon, Ser," Mavash said, ducking his head at Ser Yrsa, "but we didn't steal it from nobody. Know the right people in the right place to buy it for the right price. We smuggle, I don't deny it. But we ain't pirates."

"And yet," Ser Yrsa said, one eyebrow high in disbelief, "you serve a pirate queen."

"Only 'cause she needs smugglers sometimes." He hissed in a breath and blanched at a flare of pain from his broken arm. "Wouldn't happen to have a healer handy, would you?"

Ser Yrsa shook her head.

"Tell me about the other ship," Aefric said. "The one you're waiting for."

Mavash paled, as did several of the others.

"That…" Mavash clearly didn't think well under pressure. "That would be the *Swift Wave*. Uh. Due to pick us up…"

"Appallingly bad liar, isn't he?" Aefric asked Ser Yrsa.

"An embarrassment to liars everywhere," she agreed. "Especially for a man who offered to buy his life with the truth." She leaned closer to Aefric. "What do you think?"

"I think I have a plan," Aefric said, with a smile.

---

A SHORT TIME LATER, EVERYTHING WAS IN PLACE.

The fallen sailors had been taken to another nearby, shallow cave, found by the scouts.

The surviving sailors had been stripped to their undergarments, gagged, hobbled and bound together back at the base of the pass, where they would be out of sight. Their wizard stood among them in his sea green robes, still frozen in place by Aefric's spell, as Aefric expected him to remain until sometime past the next dawn.

The wizard had been carrying a bronze pendant that held a spark of magic. Aefric now had that pendant in his pouch, pending further study and a determination of what to do with it.

The prisoners were kept under guard by a few of the more injured among Aefric's soldiers.

The archers had retreated back up to the ridge, where they set up once more. The knights of Aefric's personal guard — with Ser Beornric — were up there as well, sighting down and waiting for targets for their arrows.

Aefric himself was up there with them, over his own objections. He'd wanted to remain below for the coming fight, but both Ser Yrsa and Ser Beornric insisted — with the other knights of his personal guard echoing their complaints.

If he would be down there, risking his life, then his guard had to remain down there as well. Part of the price of his position.

He knew that. Intellectually. It was just one of the parts of being a duke that he was ... less fond of.

The remainder of his soldiers were down below. They'd shed their tabards and their half-helms, and thrown the sailors' roughspun clothing over their chainmail. They carried the swords and clubs of the sailors — nicely visible to anyone on approach — but kept their pikes on the ground at their feet.

Ser Yrsa was down with the soldiers, of course. She hadn't bothered with a disguise. She had arranged for a stack of the heavy crates to be moved slightly. Just enough to give her space to hide.

One of her lieutenants would be calling the strike. Unless, of course, Aefric himself started things. Which was certainly possible.

If only because he knew his soldiers wouldn't pass for the sailors.

Not up close. They didn't have the weathered look. Their posture was too good. And their chainmail would *clink* when they moved.

He could only hope that whoever was coming in would buy the deception long enough to land their boats and approach.

For the moment, he could only wait.

This was the good kind of waiting though. His empty stomach felt the right kind of tension. His muscles sang with readiness. A dozen spells danced on his fingers and his lips.

This kind of waiting he'd done countless times over the years, and he knew how to do it well. There was a trick to when and how to make little movements that kept his muscles ready, without any of them falling asleep or starting to cramp.

Finally, a ship weighed anchor in the distance. Aefric raised his spyglass. Couldn't read the name on the side. It was too far away for that. But he could tell it was a big, two-mast ship kitted for battle. Right down the vicious ramming prow in the front.

The ship was launching four smaller boats that were far more crowded with people than he expected.

Four boats. Easily fifteen to a boat.

But ... they'd kept no empty space for the crates of cargo they surely intended to pick up.

For that matter, where was their own illicit cargo, to trade?

Then the truth ran cold down his spine.

Each boat had two rowers, and three with naked steel in their hands, watching the other ten. Who were tied together.

Slavers.

That ship out at anchor. It couldn't be allowed to leave. There might be more slaves aboard.

But the slavers on that ship would be watching the shore, through their own spyglasses.

When fighting broke out, what would they do?

They had no more launches. They couldn't support their troops on the ground. Not unless they wanted to bring their ship all the way to shore, which might not be possible.

They might already be as close as was safe, for a ship of that size.

They'd watch their people lose. See them taken prisoner.

They wouldn't stay. No percentage in it.

By the time Aefric could get sea support from the port city of Ajenmoor, to the south, that slaver ship would be long gone.

No.

He almost took off right away. But he couldn't do that. He was a duke. He had responsibilities. And he also had the power to do this the right way.

He cast a sending spell then, which would carry his words to someone he knew well. In this case, the message was for his old friend and ducal wizard, Karbin.

"Karbin, contact Ajenmoor and have them send three ships to the Dragonscar. Might be a fight. Definitely pick up prisoners and cargo. Hurry. Slavers."

Some variations on that spell would allow for a response. The one Aefric used did not. He didn't have time for back and forth.

"I'll be back," he said to Ser Beornric, and before the knight could raise an objection, Aefric was already flying.

He flew swiftly, low to the ground, south for a distance, before turning west over the shore. He stayed low. Low enough that the spray and lick of the waves wetted him down.

If that water made him cold, he didn't feel it. He burned with anger.

He flew that way out across the sea until he was well west of that slaver ship, though he kept it in sight the whole time.

Then he ascended to a greater height, hundreds of feet above the sea, and eased his way closer to the ship.

No one would see him here. Not while they were all watching the shore.

Well, surely whoever sat their crow's nest kept his lookout for other ships. But he wouldn't see Aefric either. Not at Aefric's height.

He needed the spyglass to watch the launches approach the shore. Muscles tensed and ready, he forced himself to wait while they beached.

As the offloading began, Aefric put away the spyglass and called forth the magic of the Brightstaff. White fire coruscated along the length of the thunderwood, passing over Aefric's hands without harming them, and circling the yellow diamond embedded in the staff's top.

Then he struck. Calling forth mighty strokes of lightning from the Brightstaff, he dealt the slaver ship two vicious blows.

His first bolt struck the mainmast at its base. His second, the mizzenmast, the same way. Both snapped and burned.

Fire spread quickly. Along the deck, but more so along rigging and the sails.

Panic ensued. The sailors not caught in the lightning or the first burst of flames began struggling to put the fires out.

If Aefric left them to it, they might succeed. But he couldn't take the chance that they'd fail. Not if there might be more slaves in the hold of that ship.

So he drew from a small sheath at his belt the wand Garram, a gift from the king himself. The wand had served King Colm's great great grandfather, King Iounn Stronghand, and Aefric had come to master its powers over ice and fire.

He used the wand to extinguish the flames.

The slavers might have oars, though from his current position, Aefric couldn't see them. Even if they did, though, they'd never achieve any speed now. Not without their sails. They might try, but they wouldn't get far before support arrived from Ajenmoor.

His work here was finished. For now.

Of course, chances were that sailors on that ship had spotted him by this time. Surely someone had wondered where lightning had struck from, out of a clear blue sky.

Well, that was fine with him. He was too high up to worry about arrows. And if they had a wizard who wanted to come play, well, Aefric was more than happy to face him.

That no wizard flew forth disappointed Aefric.

He flew back to see how Ser Yrsa's half of the battle had fared.

With the strong, sea wind at his back now, Aefric flew down out of the bright afternoon sky toward the mouth of the Dragonscar. Even before he landed, he was able to get a good sense of the situation.

The slavers had been defeated handily. Of the twenty slavers, half were dead. The other half had clearly surrendered — and weren't happy about it. They'd thrown down their weapons and were being corralled by Aefric's soldiers.

Ser Yrsa was overseeing the unbinding of the slaves.

Forty slaves, dressed in sack cloth belted with rope that had doubled as wrist bindings.

Aefric landed near Ser Yrsa, who spared him a cold glance.

"It is a strange thing, your grace," she said in tones that could freeze lava. "I would have sworn that not an hour past, you and I had discussed what it means for a duke to travel unguarded. Does my memory fail me?"

"It does not," Aefric said. "But this is hardly the time and place for this discussion."

"So long as your grace understands that this discussion is coming."

"Oh, I have no doubt of it," Aefric said, drawing a sharper glare because he sounded unrepentant. "And I have no doubt that Ser Beornric will have words to contribute to the conversation."

"Presuming he does not simply resign his post," Ser Yrsa said, "I should think so."

She drew breath to say something else, but Aefric mouthed *later*, and she grimaced, but nodded.

Speaking of Ser Beornric, Aefric could hear him, as well as the other knights of his guard, thundering closer from the pass. Aefric turned, watched them approach, and before any of them could open their mouths, said, "Ser Yrsa and I have already agreed to discuss the matter later. There is much to do right now."

Ser Beornric frowned, but nodded and dismounted, with the other six knights of Aefric's guard following suit.

A short time later, the slavers were contained, and the slaves freed. Two of the scouts were keeping an eye on the slavers' ship, and the other two were watching the Dragonscar, to make sure no one else approached.

For the time being, the slavers and the smugglers were kept separate. The smugglers likely knew that Aefric's party had taken the slavers captive, but the slavers might not have known that the smugglers were prisoners as well.

Which was how Aefric wanted it.

He did check his freezing spell, to make sure that the wizard in green remained locked in place, unable to do more than breathe. So far all was well.

Ser Yrsa had already called for food from their supplies, for the poor souls who had been enslaved.

They were a mixed group, with no particular attributes in common. Forty in all. Thirty of them human, of a variety of ages, physical conditions, and backgrounds. Twenty of them women, but ten of them men.

Five were eldrani, and even in their captive state, the beauty of their people shone out. Three of them were women, and two were men. Including, in their number, two dark-skinned eldrani. One man, one woman.

Dark-skinned eldrani were quite rare in this part of Qorunn. Aefric couldn't remember seeing them before, on this side of the Risen Sea, where their pale kin were far more common.

Of course, these two had all the stunning beauty of their people, and in their case it extended beyond their sharp features to their hair, the dark purple of latest sunset, and their eyes the yellow of flame.

Of the other former slaves, three were derekek, all male. Derekek stood about the height of humans, but were thicker through the limbs and torso. Their flesh was always some shade of green and they tended to wear their hair in spikes.

All three of these derekek had the same coloring — a dark, mossy green — and somehow even managed to keep their hair spiked through their captivity, which surprised Aefric.

He'd always thought they spiked their hair with grease or fat or something. But perhaps their hair simply grew that way.

The remaining two were borogs. Bigger than humans, though smaller than na'shek, they had heads like rhinos, with horns and skin to match.

"Your grace," Ser Yrsa said, leaning close. "The troops are nervous about the borogs, and I can't say I blame them. Should we bind them as well?"

"No," Aefric said, just as quietly. "The Godswalk Wars are over, and these two aren't under the influence of the Flayer. I won't treat them like they're guilty unless I'm given a better reason than their race."

Louder, to the group, he said, "Do all of you understand the common tongue?"

The humans all spoke assent, along with one of the pale eldrani men. This one had short hair of vivid blue. He spoke up to say, "These four" — he indicated the other eldrani — "have no common tongue. Neither speak the derekek or horn-noses."

Aefric almost corrected that last, but it wasn't intended as a derogation. Well, it *was*, but only in the sense that the eldrani word for borogs was *shissnatach*, which translated to the common tongue as horn-noses.

"All right," Aefric said. "What's your name?"

"Ulltruchu," he said, bowing his head in a very human gesture of respect.

"*Well, Ulltruchu,*" Aefric said in High Eldrani, "*I will ask you to translate for your fellows of the True Race*" — which was actually how eldrani referred to themselves, despite being a relatively young people — "*while I do my best to translate for the others.*"

Ulltruchu bowed his head again.

"All right," Aefric said. "You are all free people. Let me make that clear. I will do my best to return you all to your proper homes as soon as possible."

Aefric had just begun translating that into Dreykeke, the

language of derekek, when one of the human women raised her hand.

"Please allow me to finish translating first," Aefric said, "or this will take forever."

She nodded respectfully, and Aefric continued his translation.

Dreykeke was a language he was pretty good at. Helped that the language only had one main form, and that regional variations were mostly in colloquialisms.

As he finished with the first translation, the derekek frowned and two of them looked at the other, who wanted to say something.

Aefric asked him, as well, to wait.

Borog, alas, was a language he didn't know much of. He knew full well that what he said came out no more coherent than, *"You whole."* Borogs didn't have a word for "free" but considered captivity a kind of injury. *"Me run you to clan."*

The Borog language, as far as Aefric understood it, didn't differentiate between subject and object when it came to pronouns. *"Me"* — *uruk* — stood for both "I," "me," and "my."

The borogs' eyes narrowed in shock. They both snorted. The bigger one started to speak.

*"You hold fire,"* Aefric said, not knowing any other way to ask them to wait. *"Others shoot first."*

That one snorted. Which Aefric hoped was agreement.

Aefric turned back to the first woman who'd raised her hand.

"We're refugees, your grace," she said with a shaky bow. "None of us — well, I don't know about the greenies and" — her gaze flicked to the borogs — *"them,* but the rest of us have nowhere to go."

Everyone who could understand that was nodding agreement, with Ulltruchu agreeing for the eldrani.

Confirming that the derekek were in the same position was easy enough. And while the larger borog said a lot, Aefric was able to understand just enough to know that they were refugees too. They had no clan to return to.

With that established, the next question was the one Aefric considered most immediately important.

"Are there any other slaves on that ship?"

None of them seemed to know of any, so likely not.

From there, a quick series of questions and translations determined that almost all of them were from south of Armyr, the region around Kesh, and the Free Baronies of Olwich.

The two dark-skinned eldrani, whose names were Li'nasachal and Li'sheneesha, had been captive the longest, and were taken much further to the south. In the outskirts of Sartis, on their way to that great city.

The borogs were another matter. Aefric went back and forth with them a few times, trying to find the right words for his question and trying to understand their answers.

The closest he could come was that they'd been taken recently, near great mountains. Which could have been any of a dozen mountain ranges that Aefric could name.

Unfortunately, the others had all been kept in the hold, and had no idea where they were when the borogs were brought aboard.

"Your grace," one of the scouts interrupted then. "The ship is moving."

"Rowing?" Aefric asked, looking up and checking through his spyglass.

Sure enough, it had oars in the water.

And it was trying to escape.

"No," Aefric said, lifting the Brightstaff and ready to take to the air.

Ser Yrsa grabbed him by one shoulder, and Ser Beornric grabbed him by the other.

"They'll get away," Aefric said.

"They won't get far," Ser Beornric said. "I heard you tell Karbin to send for ships."

"*I* didn't hear that," Ser Yrsa said archly, "but either way, if they escape, they escape."

"But I could—"

"Does your grace know the penalty for slaving in Armyr?" Ser Yrsa asked.

"No," Aefric admitted. "Though I have a few ideas—"

"*Neither* do they," Ser Yrsa said. "But in many places, it's death. Which means those sailors will fight to the death. And if it's just you out there fighting them, one of them might get lucky."

Aefric flared his nostrils in a quick, deep breath.

"One is all it takes," Ser Beornric said. "And you'd be out there alone. Dying. With no aid anywhere nearby."

"Fine," Aefric said, though he hated saying it. "If they get away, though, I'm taking it out on the mayor of Ajenmoor."

"Your grace," Ser Micham said. Ser Micham was the only one of Aefric's guards who had enough of a sea-worn look to pass for a sailor. But that was because he'd grown up the son of Ajenmoor's mayor.

"Micham," Aefric said. "I know he's your father. But still—"

"Did you tell him about the slavers?"

"I told Karbin to tell him, yes."

"Then the ships will be here with all speed," Ser Micham said confidently. "Father *hates* slavers."

"Well," Aefric said, watching the slave ship depart. "He better hurry."

---

Aefric couldn't simply stand there and watch, while the slave ship escaped. And there was nothing he could do, from where he stood on the shore, in the mouth of the Dragonscar, to prevent it.

So he turned back to the people who had been the slavers' cargo.

"All right," he said. "None of you have homes? Well, if you want one here in Deepwater, you have it. If you have someplace else in mind, tell me where and I'll get you there. On my word."

He was only just starting to translate that for the derekek — over the bubble of excited conversation from the humans and eldrani — when Ser Yrsa started talking to him.

He couldn't both translate and listen at the same time, so he made her wait until he'd at least finished telling the derekek what he'd told the others.

"Your grace," she said in a low voice. "Your offer is most generous, but the borogs... Would you even be doing them a favor? It's not as though they'd be welcomed here."

Aefric gave her a flat look. "If they want to live here, I'll find them a home and work. And I'll do my damnedest to make sure people learn to live with them."

He did his best to translate for the borogs. Which came out something like. "*You run with me clan? You choose. Run other clan. Or ... outcast... No. No outcast. But ... outcast?*"

He shrugged hopelessly. The closest he could come to telling them they could make their own way was the Borog word for "outcast."

The borogs spoke to each other for a moment. Then the big one said, as near as Aefric could understand, "*You order kra naruk me choose gron kraknon ortok nak kor run with you clan?*"

Aefric shrugged helplessly.

"*Speak it humanway,*" the bigger borog said.

"You two are welcome to live and work in my lands. If you choose."

The borog snorted. Said something to the smaller borog. They spoke for a moment.

"*You, me and me,*" the bigger borog said. And there was a difference in those two "mes," but Aefric couldn't quite pick it out. He shrugged.

"*You,*" the borog said, pointing at Aefric. "*Me,*" he — Aefric was pretty sure it was a he — pointed to himself. "*Me,*" he said in that slightly different way, indicating the smaller borog.

Aefric nodded.

"*What humanway speak you, me and me.*"

"Us," Aefric said. He pointed to the two of them, and then himself. "Us."

The bigger borog snorted, then forced himself to make a slow nod. "*You speak, me and me choose, me and me run with us?*"

*"Yes,"* Aefric said.

*"You human. Me and me borog."*

*"You choose,"* Aefric said.

The borog snorted. *"Me and me speak. Answer soon."*

Aefric nodded.

"I think this is a mistake," Ser Yrsa said softly.

"Wouldn't be my first or my last," Aefric said, just as softly. "While they consider the offer, let's talk to the slavers."

Their captain was a hard, scarred woman who looked as though her gray-streaked black hair had been on fire when sections of it were hacked off to save the rest.

"Don't bother, pretty man," she said as Aefric approached. "Won't talk just 'cause you know a trick or two."

"Do you know what the punishment is for slavery, here in Armyr?" Ser Yrsa asked.

"Death, I imagine," she said, as though it didn't matter. "Don't give us a lot o' incentive to wag our tongues. Do it?"

"It's an interesting law, actually," Ser Beornric said. "King Colm's great, great, great grandmother, Queen Celia Stronghand, thought it up. If you took slaves from Armyr, well," — Ser Beornric smiled that wolfish smile of his — "you didn't, so I'll leave that part to your imagination. But if we find out where you took your slaves *from*, we'll return you *there* to face justice."

"Really?" Aefric asked, while his smile spread out slowly. "The Free Baronies of Olwich take their *free* part very seriously, you know."

"Oh, indeed they do," Ser Yrsa said. "I understand that they execute slavers publicly, and they have to start each execution at dawn or the slaver might not be dead before dark."

"Are you suggesting we might face justice here?" the hard captain asked.

"Well," Aefric said, hazarding a guess, "the law does differentiate between unrepentant slavers and cooperative *former* slavers."

"Everyone deserves a second chance," Ser Beornric said. "Assuming they show remorse."

"That part *is* important," Ser Yrsa said.

"And how do we know you wouldn't just kill us here and be done with us, once you have your answers?"

"You don't," Aefric said. "But it seems to me that a quick death here would be preferable to what they'd do to you in Olwich."

"I'll think about it," she said, but Aefric thought he saw hope in her dark eyes.

"Offer goes for all of you," he said. "Doesn't have to be the captain, speaking up."

"Any of you speaks up," the captain said, "you better hope they kill you before I do. Because what I'll do to you will be nastier than anything Olwich can dream up."

"She might believe that," Aefric said. "But doesn't mean you should. Your lives are on the line here too."

Aefric turned away then, and Ser Yrsa told the soldiers standing guard to call out if any of the prisoners wanted to talk.

Aefric and Sers Yrsa and Beornric went over to talk to the smugglers then. Turned out he had to renew his freeze spell while he did, because the wizard in green had almost gotten himself free.

"Not bad," Aefric said. "You've been held by a spell like this before, then."

The wizard in green couldn't answer, of course.

"Guards," Aefric said, "if he shows any sign of movement before I've released him. Anything at all, even a blink. Don't hesitate. Kill him."

When his guards nodded, Aefric wondered if they were more pale because of their wounds, or at the thought of killing a prisoner.

Wouldn't matter. If the wizard in green got free, he'd kill them as fast as look at them. And if the choice was a wizard who was a pirate and smuggler — as well as a *slaver* — or even one of his soldiers, Aefric knew which he'd choose.

"Your grace," Ser Beornric said softly. "Unless you know something I don't. He's just a wizard. We could knock him out and tie him up safe enough."

"Can't knock him out while he's held by my spell."

Ser Yrsa cleared her throat and drew a mace.

"Fair point," Aefric said. Odds were that wizard wouldn't get a spell off in the time it took Ser Yrsa to knock him out. "Fine then."

Aefric stepped up to the wizard in green, while Ser Yrsa took up position behind him.

Aefric held up a sharp dagger to get the wizard's attention.

"I'm going to hold this to your chest. And then I'm going to release my spell. I strongly suggest not doing anything I might misinterpret while we tie you up."

The wizard in green couldn't respond, of course.

Aefric didn't actually put the dagger to the wizard's chest, just in case. He turned the point away as he released the spell.

Ser Yrsa swung her mace, fast as a stroke of lightning, and the wizard in green fell like a ship's mast.

Two of Aefric's soldiers bound and gagged the wizard tightly.

"All right, Mavash," Aefric said turning to the smuggler he'd spoken with earlier, who'd watched the interplay with wide eyes. "You knew that was a slaver ship coming, don't try to deny it."

Mavash hung his head, but nodded.

"And I bet you heard what we were saying about the punishment for slavery."

"But we ain't never carried no slaves!" Mavash insisted. "Wouldn't be doin' it now. But you can't say no to the pirate queen."

"So you insist you've never carried slaves before," Aefric said.

Mavash nodded rapidly, still looking down.

"There's only one way you can prove that," Aefric said. When Mavash looked up, hope in his eyes, Aefric continued, "Give us the *Swift Wave*. If you're kitted to carry cargo, not people, should be easy enough to tell."

"*I* could tell, your grace," Ser Micham said, confidently. "If I saw her hold."

Mavash shook his head.

"Give us the *Swift Wave*," Aefric said. "Or we'll have to assume you're refusing because a search of that ship would prove that you're slavers too."

"We ain't slavers," another of the smugglers insisted. "Give 'em the ship, Mavash. You given 'em everything else already anyway."

"I give you the ship, no one will ever sail with me again," he said.

"If you don't," Aefric said, "you could be looking at a life so short it wouldn't matter."

For a moment the only sounds were the whipping of the sea wind and the distant, excited conversation of the refugees.

"Don't matter where they are now," Mavash mumbled, sounding defeated. "They'll be back for us at dusk. You can take 'em then."

"Which way will they be coming?" Aefric asked.

"South," Mavash said, sounding thoroughly miserable. "You could hide your ships here in the cove. *Swift Wind* wouldn't see 'em before they're in shooting range."

"Is there a reef to worry about?" Aefric asked.

"Ain't no reef, yer grace," Mavash said. "We don't bring the ship to shore while sun's up 'cause it'd draw eyes to us."

"Your grace," one of the scouts called. "Three ships incoming, from the south. Warships. Three-masted frigates. Flying Deepwater and Ajenmoor flags."

"I can signal them, your grace," Ser Micham said. "There's a code. Send them after the slave ship."

"Do it," Aefric said. "But make sure at least one ship comes back here."

"Yes, your grace," Ser Micham said, giving a battlefield salute then running toward the shore.

The man ran well, if noisily, in full plate armor.

"All right," Aefric said, turning back to Mavash. "Tell us everything we need to know about the *Swift Wave*. Complement. Armament. Everything."

Mavash sighed, and began to talk.

THERE WAS PROBABLY SOMETHING AEFRIC HATED WORSE THAN LETTING others do his fighting. In fact, there were probably several things he hated worse than that.

Slavers, for example.

But letting other people go and fight slavers on his behalf, while he remained behind, waiting. Surely that was the worst feeling in the world.

His empty stomach seethed. He paced in the hot afternoon sun, just to give his tense muscles something to do. But the problem was that even pacing seemed to remind him what he was not doing.

The sound of his boots and the butt of his staff on the hard, brown rocks of the Dragonscar sounded to him like the clash of battle. The cool, salt sea wind in his face called him to take to the air and chase down that slaver ship.

Intellectually, he knew that remaining with his troops at the Dragonscar was what he needed to do. Sers Yrsa and Beornric were right. He wasn't just an adventurer anymore, free to risk his life every time it suited him.

He was a duke now. He had responsibilities. Even if they felt abstract, compared to a ship full of enemies.

Nevertheless. This was a battle he could, in theory, leave to sailors who had their share of experience fighting the likes of pirates and slavers. They could handle chasing down one, mastless ship. Especially a ship that was already short its captain and nineteen others from the fighting members of its crew.

"You should eat something, your grace," Ser Beornric said. "You haven't eaten since your morning toast and bacon."

Aefric hadn't seen the knight approach. Been too wrapped up in what he wanted to be doing.

Now he looked up to see Sers Beornric and Yrsa standing side by side, not five paces seaward of him. Beornric looked sympathetic, and offered an apple with one gauntleted hand, and some jerked deer with the other.

Ser Yrsa's look was more gauging. Or perhaps irritated. She had something of a scowl going, and the area around her main scar was darker than its usual tan.

"I couldn't eat right now," Aefric said. "Not until we're done here."

"Then perhaps it's time for that conversation," Ser Yrsa said.

"Fine," Aefric said, and the three of them moved deeper into the Dragonscar. Farther from the rest of both troops and prisoners, and forcing two of the scouts to move deeper in as well, to maintain their watch.

The rock walls of the Dragonscar were jagged, and many shades of brown and dark red. Legend claimed that one of the last of the great, giant dragons had died while flying above the valley that was now the Risen Sea. That the dragon had crashed to the face of Qorunn and, in so doing, torn its way through the cliffs as it died.

The displaced rock and dirt was said to form the Threepeaks Mountains, though they were too far south — nearly twenty miles — for that to be a serious possibility.

Still. Looking up at the walls of the chasm, Aefric could almost believe it. The walls were jagged as though ripped up by violence, but their edges had been rounded and worn through the centuries since whatever had happened to them.

Of course, given the width of the Dragonscar, that dragon would have to have been *immense*...

"Don't try to tell me you're scouting dangers," Ser Yrsa said. "Body language is all wrong. I can tell you're wondering if the legends are true."

"I'm still inside the area declared clear by the scouts," Aefric said, turning to his general. "So I felt comfortable enough to wonder."

"Fair enough," Ser Beornric said, looking back and forth between the other two.

"I did not rush headlong," Aefric said. "When I went after that slaver ship. I did it right. I approached from a blind angle, and struck from outside their range. I did the damage I intended, and stopped before fire could consume the ship."

"And flew back directly over that ship," Ser Yrsa said, and smiled viciously when Aefric's eyes widened in surprise. "I had the scouts watching for you."

"I was outside bowshot," Aefric said. "And I admit I was trying to draw out any wizards they might have had. And before you ask, I was confident that they didn't have any *exceptional* wizards, because an exceptional wizard would have detected me, and possibly stopped or diverted my second strike."

Ser Yrsa sighed.

"The point is," Aefric said. "You asked me not to act impulsively and foolishly. I didn't. I went after the slaver ship the right way. With caution, then speed. I did not expose myself to undue risk."

Ser Yrsa raised her eyebrows at Ser Beornric, who gave a heavy sigh.

"Yes, your grace," he said. "You did. Because we already had their captain, many of their fighters, and most if not all of their cargo. There was no pressing need for you to risk yourself at all."

"I couldn't chance their getting away, in case they had more slaves aboard."

"Yes," Ser Yrsa insisted. "You could have. And not the least because you had already summoned aid."

"That aid was *hours* away."

"*You cannot save everyone.*" Ser Yrsa stepped in close, staring Aefric in the eye. "I understand that you wish to. And I respect the desire. Even admire it, after a fashion. But if you continue to *act* like an adventurer, you will meet the *untimely fate* of an adventurer."

"By all rights," Ser Beornric said, "you should have died at Frozen Ridge. And you know it. Only the actions of a god spared your life."

Aefric opened his mouth to deny that — after all, he had been the only witness, and he'd not been in a coherent frame of mind at the time.

But he closed his mouth and frowned, instead.

Even standing here in the Dragonscar, a full season later, he could still see that flash of silver eyes. Feel the press of those lips to his forehead.

Aefric nodded.

"Tell me which god saved you," Ser Yrsa said, one eyebrow high, "and I'll light a candle to him—"

"To *her*," Aefric said softly. "It was Kalinda, the new goddess of magic."

"Then I'll happily make offerings of thanksgiving at her temple," Ser Yrsa said. "For saving the life of my duke. But only a fool would count on such a thing happening twice to the same person."

"You've done well as a duke so far," Ser Beornric said. "You have your vassals working together, all save Count Ferrin of Motte. And you're bringing him to heel."

"He's right," Ser Yrsa said. "Your intercessions are going to help Deepwater recover faster from the Godswalk Wars than either of your peers in Silverlake and Merrek."

"And even Merrek would be far worse off, if not for what you did at Frozen Ridge. And Duchess Ashling knows it. Those three ships she gave you were a *princely* expression of thanks. And even so she said there would be something more to come."

"All right," Aefric said, raising his hands in surrender. "I get your point."

"You don't," Ser Yrsa said with penetrating confidence.

Aefric opened his mouth to object, but Ser Beornric cut in quickly.

"*The point*," Ser Beornric said, "is that your life is no longer yours alone to risk."

"You belong to all of us now," Ser Yrsa said. "To your vassals, through your oaths, yes, but to the peasantry as well. And to your soldiers. And your merchants. All of us."

"We all have a stake in what happens to you," Ser Beornric said, and Aefric began to wonder if they'd rehearsed this. "And we will all suffer if you fall."

"This is why we will lay down our lives for you," Ser Yrsa said. "And why, when the time comes for that sacrifice, *you must let us*."

"I will not throw away the lives of my people."

"And no one is happier to hear that than I am," Ser Yrsa said, not so much as blinking at Aefric's protest. "But we're not talking about throwing lives away. We're talking about our roles in life. *Soldiers* fight. *Knights* fight. *Dukes* rule their lands."

"I am also a knight," Aefric said. "King Colm knighted me before he elevated me."

"The point remains," Ser Beornric said. "If you are willing to fight, should war come, so much the better. You will inspire your troops, and they will love you more and fight all the harder for it."

"And you've already proven you'll do it," Ser Yrsa said. "You proved yourself before you ever had the title."

"But not every squabble and skirmish is worth risking *your* life," Ser Beornric said, pointing at Aefric for emphasis.

Aefric realized he'd been holding a breath, even as he'd been holding onto an objection.

He let both go slowly, turning away and looking up into the clear blue sky of midsummer.

"Ser Beornric is right," Ser Yrsa said. "You're off to an excellent start as a duke. Especially for a man not born to his title. But you must accept *all* of your role or you will end up chipping away even the gains you've made."

"If your vassals learn that you continually risk your life," Ser Beornric said, "they'll stop thinking of you as their duke. In their minds you'll become nothing more than the man sitting regent for the next to hold the title. You will lose their trust and confidence. They will feel they have no choice but to work and plan for themselves."

"Your knights and soldiers will feel that you do not trust them to do their jobs, and they will lose faith in your leadership."

"*All right,*" Aefric said sharply, turning back to face the united knights. "I get your point. And I acknowledge that you're right. Now hear *my* point."

Ser Yrsa blinked in surprise, but Ser Beornric only frowned and nodded.

"There will come times when I must be the one who acts. Because there will be times that I can do something that none of you can do."

"Including Karbin, your ducal wizard?" Ser Yrsa asked.

"Perhaps," Aefric said, grimacing as he acknowledged her point, but pressing on all the same. "But the actions will be more powerful coming from me. More meaningful."

"Motte," Ser Beornric said, thoughtfully. "When you blasted your way into Castle Kirandai and challenged Count Ferrin before his court."

"Exactly so," Aefric said. "There will be times to remind everyone that I am not only a duke. That I am a force to be reckoned with on my own."

"Perhaps," Ser Yrsa said, grudgingly. "But will you at least agree to consult with Ser Beornric or myself before you take such an action? Or at least your ducal wizard? Will you allow one of us to determine if there might be another way of accomplishing your goal, before you charge into the hazard?"

"You do have advisers for a reason, your grace," Ser Beornric said softly.

Aefric considered that through a long, slow breath.

"Very well," he agreed.

"Thank you, your grace," Ser Yrsa said meaningfully, and even added a bow, for good measure.

Ser Beornric joined her in that bow, and Aefric began to realize that they hadn't just been angry at him, for what he'd done in assaulting that slaver ship.

They'd been worried. Honestly worried.

He wasn't used to people worrying about him.

He'd have to think about that.

***

As part of trying to take a more hands-off approach — as well as letting his people do their jobs — Aefric left the rest of the guarding to Ser Yrsa. He'd allow her to handle any further interrogations, as well, should any prove necessary.

In the meantime, there was something he *could* do, and he was determined to do it.

He went back to see the refugees.

They'd split into three groups. The humans and eldrani in one group, the derekek in another, and the borogs slightly to one side, on their own.

Aefric found it odd that the derekek were being left to themselves. Prejudice against the borogs, well, that wasn't surprising in the wake of the Godswalk Wars. But the derekek had fought alongside the humans and eldrani. And alongside the kindaren, for that matter.

But then, perhaps this wasn't a matter of prejudice, but a simple matter of communication, because none of the others seemed to speak any Dreykeke, and the derekek didn't speak the common tongue or High Eldrani. Or, apparently, Low Eldrani, for that matter.

As Aefric approached, Ulltruchu stood and came up to him, smiling.

"*Your grace,*" Ulltruchu said in High Eldrani, with a bow. "*I am pleased to be the one to tell you that both my people and the humans have all decided to remain here in Deepwater. I have begun compiling a list of the skills we have among us.*"

"Excellent," Aefric said. "*I'll want to hear more about that. But if you'll excuse me, I need to first find out what the derekek and borogs have decided.*"

"Your grace," Ulltruchu said softly — and perhaps a bit chidingly — in the common tongue. "Surely you make not the same offer to *them* as you make us."

"They are refugees," Aefric said. "The same as you are. And they have lost their homes, the same as you have. So yes, I mean to make them the same offer."

"Your grace is most generous," Ulltruchu said, then switched back to High Eldrani. "*But surely servants of the Flayer would sow only sorrow in your lands.*"

"*The madness of the Flayer has gone from their hearts,*" Aefric said. "*I will give them the chance to show they are people, not weapons.*"

Ulltruchu might have said more, but Aefric turned away and moved on to speak to the derekek.

"*Wish you to remain here? Or make new homes elsewhere?*"

*"Here is where the winds have blown us."* The speaker was the same one who'd spoken for the three derekek before. *"Here is where we will build a home. If we are welcome."*

*"You are."*

*"We are sailors and traders. We worked the rivers, but know the seas as well."*

Hardly a surprise. The derekek were known for their sailing.

*"You will have your choice,"* Aefric said. *"We need sailors on both. And I know where others of your people dwell and sail in my lands."*

When the derekek had finished offering their thanks, which took a moment because all three wanted to wish Aefric long life, good health, and good winds, he moved closer to the water to speak with the borogs.

*"Your clan ereh tok me and me,"* the big one said, before Aefric could begin.

*"Me no ... ereh tok?"* Aefric gave an exaggerated shrug.

Both borogs snorted at that.

"Us no," the big one said, then switched back to his own language. *"You clan ... speak ... me and me ... outcast."*

*"Me speak, you choose, you run with me clan."* Aefric stomped his foot the way he'd seen a borog chieftain do after making a decision.

The two borogs snorted, then conversed quickly and quietly.

*"Kora?"* the big borog said.

Aefric frowned. He'd heard that word before. He knew it. But what could it mean? What had it meant then?

Wait.

He had to be asking *why*. He wanted to know *why* Aefric made this offer.

Aefric frowned, trying to think of the right words to come at least close to saying what he needed to say, in Borog.

*"Speak it humanway,"* the big borog said.

"Wait," Aefric said. "Do you understand the common tongue?"

The big borog snorted, and this time Aefric thought there was something more to that snort. As though the big borog was admitting something he'd wanted to keep close to the chest.

Which meant he'd been listening to what Aefric had told everyone else. As well as what all the humans had been saying, both the refugees and his own troops.

"Look," Aefric said. "The wars are over. The gods have gone back to their heavens and hells. And they've left us to clean up the mess. I know my people blame yours for what your people did while in service to the Flayer. But can you tell me that yours don't blame us for what we did for our gods?"

The borog made a show of slowly shaking his big head.

"Now," Aefric said. "We can hold on to old grudges and prejudices forever. Or we can learn to move past them. To see each other as people, not enemies. I don't know about you, but I'd rather live in a world where we all learn to get along, than one where we're always at each other's throats."

"You ... people..." the big borog said, haltingly, and his voice seemed to have to grind out his words. "...never ... for-give."

"They'll learn."

"What ... us ... do?"

"Borogs are said to be great miners," Aefric said.

*"And the dark swallows all."*

Aefric had to shake himself, hearing a borog proverb that was their way of saying something was so obvious it didn't need to be said. But he'd been in such a literal conversation, that for a moment he'd forgotten he was hearing a saying.

The big borog snorted, and this time there was amusement in it.

"Our mines also have na'shek," Aefric said. "Not many, but a few."

Both borogs lowered their horns. Enmity between the borogs and the na'shek went back centuries. Perhaps further.

"You want to be accepted?" Aefric asked. "You and the na'shek will have to learn to live and work together too."

*"Mar kon nokka ton,"* the big borog said.

Aefric didn't know the literal translation for that one, but he knew it amounted to saying something was impossible.

Aefric sighed. "Well, that'll be harder. I was hoping you'd be able to work in the Threepeaks Mountains, maybe in the gold or silver mines. But I couldn't guarantee that you wouldn't run into any na'shek. There aren't many there, but—"

"Dig ... gold?" the borog asked, then used the Borog word for gold, seeking confirmation. *"Aur?"*

"Yes," Aefric said. "You would be mining gold for me, and paid for your efforts."

The smaller borog stomped and scraped his — or maybe her — feet over and over, one after the other. Aefric wasn't sure, but he thought that was an expression of excitement.

"Yes," the big one said. "Us ... dig gold ... for you."

"You're sure?" Aefric said. "Even if there are na'shek?"

*"Aur ke na tak,"* the bigger borog said. "Gold ... god metal."

"Holy?" Aefric asked.

Both borogs snorted.

"Bigger ... than clan," the big borog said.

"Well, perfect then," Aefric said, smiling. "I'll make the arrangements."

**2**

———

THOUGH THE WAITING DID SEEM INTERMINABLE, IN TRUTH, THE SUN WAS not that much lower in the skies above the Risen Sea when the three frigates from Ajenmoor returned with the slaver ship in tow.

By that time, one of the slavers had cracked and poured out his information to Ser Yrsa. Or, at least, he pretended to. When Ser Yrsa had gone over the information with Aefric, she'd sounded skeptical that he'd given her more than the absolute minimum.

Certainly his captain didn't look nearly as upset about the proffered information as she should have, if it were all real and useful.

So the chances were that he'd lied about their base, or their normal routes, or the contacts he'd named, or perhaps all of the above.

The captains from all three Ajenmoor ships came to shore in the same launch, and Aefric was surprised to see who had come with them.

"Karbin!" he said, happily.

As always, Aefric smiled at the familiar sight of his old friend and mentor, now ducal wizard. Karbin had been a wizard for a long time before Aefric had first met him, well over a decade ago, but the man's appearance hadn't changed by the years. His blue-black skin still radiated the youth and vitality of a man of only thirty summers.

But then, magic-users often found ways to stretch their youth well beyond reason.

Karbin continued for favor the colors of sand and dusk in his clothing. He wore robes, today, with high boots of hard leather, and carried six wands on his belt, along with that obsidian rod he favored.

"Couldn't let you take on slavers all on your lonesome, your grace," Karbin said, stepping out of the launch and onto the rocky shore of the Dragonscar.

"Oh, too late to stop his grace from that," Ser Beornric said lightly, getting a frown from Karbin.

"We've already had that talk," Aefric protested, but Karbin's frown deepened as he stood to one side and let the captains come ashore.

Two of the captains were men, and one a woman. All three were human, and all three were about Ser Beornric's age, though the years at sea had played them harder. All three were lean, and looked tough enough to hammer in nails with their fists alone.

Of the three of them, the woman — Captain Coral — was senior, and did their talking.

"Funny thing about that ship, your grace," she said once the introductions were done. "By the time we caught it, it were already two masts light, and fire'd played hell across the decks."

"Yes," Aefric said, "well, I didn't want it to get away."

Captain Coral nodded. "Guess you didn't at that. Well, most of the fight was gone from 'em when we caught up."

"Were there more slaves aboard?"

She looked over at the refugees. "Got forty over there, do you? Your grace?"

"Yes."

"Then you got them all but for the poor young man we found chained up in the captain's cabin."

"Ser Yrsa," Aefric said. "Bring the good captains here up to speed."

"Yes, your grace," she said, and stepped up to do just that.

While she went over what Aefric and his people had learned, Aefric spoke quietly with Karbin.

"Should've known you'd be coming. I said the magic word."

"Slavers," Karbin agreed. "Not that I was left much to do."

"I'm not sure about that," Aefric said. "The pirate queen Nelazzi's involved. And there's still the question of where the slavers were taking those refugees."

"I can't think of anywhere that slavery is legal these days," Karbin said. "Not formally or informally."

"Neither can I," Aefric admitted, "but a lot may have changed with the Godswalk Wars. Some may be looking for an edge over their neighbors, even if they don't admit to it openly."

"It's possible," Karbin said. "Want me to look into it?"

"After we know all we're going to learn from this."

With that, Aefric and Karbin turned their attention back to Captain Coral, who was just sending her rowers back to her ship to retrieve a healer, to see to the wounded. First among Aefric's troops, and then among the prisoners.

"If Nelazzi's involved," Captain Coral said when she turned back to Aefric, "this is a big deal. Too big for us. We've got our hands full, just keeping the seaways safe around Deepwater."

Aefric drew breath, but before he could make his observation, Captain Coral hurried along to make it for him.

"And I can see that even then we've had blind spots. Never thought anyone'd be daft enough to use an unfriendly spot like this for smuggling. But now we can keep an eye on it."

"And I assume you can start today?"

"Oh, don't worry, your grace," she said with a grin wolfish enough to give Ser Beornric a run for his money. "When that smuggler ship comes a-calling at dusk, we'll be ready for it."

"Good," Aefric said, then lowered his voice. "Our informant, Mavash, wouldn't tell us where the *Swift Wave* is currently. That says to me that it's at harbor someplace they want to continue to feel safe. I want to know where that is."

"You and me both, your grace," she said widening her grin. And close as she was right now, Aefric could smell the salt fish on her breath.

Perhaps everyone had eaten lunch by now but him.

Still. Even his empty stomach wasn't desperate enough to rumble at the odor of salt fish breath.

"All right," Aefric said. He looked over at the cargo the smugglers had been hiding in the cave. "Those crates contain varieties of seed, mostly, as well as various grains. And it saddens me that these things are fodder for smugglers these days. The other crates house art objects, likely looted from fallen castles, mansions and the like."

He sighed. "Tell me truly, captain. Is there any hope of getting that cargo back to the people it was stolen from?"

"If the smugglers stole it themselves, your grace, there'd be a chance," she said dubiously. "But the long odds say they bought it from those who bought it from the original thieves. Whatever's in those crates was likely moved first when it was stolen, then each time it's been sold since."

She shook her head. "Better chance of asking the sea to stop licking the shore for a day or two."

"All right," Aefric said, shaking his head. "Will you need all three ships to handle the *Swift Wave*?"

"Without its captain and most of its fighters?" Captain Coral spat. "Hardly a challenge for one of us, your grace, let alone three."

"Fine then," Aefric said. "Then you can spare a ship to gather up the refugees and cargo and sail them up the Searun to Water's End."

"Begging your pardon, your grace," Captain Coral said, "but these ships are too big for the Searun River. They'd have to go all the way south and come up the Haven to Behal. Faster to put in at Ajenmoor and have a smaller ship or two take the refugees and cargo to Water's End, if that's your will."

"It is, and that's fine," Aefric said.

"See three of those refugees are derekek," Captain Coral said. "We've a few among our crew, and most of us speak some Dray-keki," — a common mispronunciation of Dreykeke — "they're free to join up, if they want. Always use a good hand."

"Ask them," Aefric said, "but make clear that it's just an option. Those three are used to working the rivers, and they're free to continue doing so."

"I'll ask," said one of the other captains, who then hustled off to do so.

"What about the hulk?" Captain Coral said, gesturing to the slaver ship. "Still holds water, but won't be easy, cheap or fast to get it back in sailing shape."

"Your grace," Ser Micham said, "if I may."

"Go ahead," Aefric said.

"Father has spoken before about wanting to use a ship in the harbor as a jail. But it didn't seem a good use of resources." He nodded to the slaver ship. "That would be perfect for what he has in mind."

"Sounds fine to me," Aefric said, then turned to the captain. "Bring it back to Ajenmoor, then. Waste not, want not."

"Aye, your grace. Shall we do that with the *Swift Wave* as well?"

"I'll want Karbin to search it first. He knows what to look for. Otherwise, whatever you'd usually do with a captured ship is fine."

"Happy to have him along," Captain Coral said, giving Karbin a smile that was downright saucy.

"All right," Aefric said. "Then the prisoners are yours as well, to bring back to Ajenmoor for trial. I'll write a letter to accompany the refugees and cargo to Water's End, and dispatch a pair of soldiers to come along deliver it. Otherwise I think we're done here."

Captain Coral nodded agreement, and went over some of the details with Sers Yrsa and Beornric, while Aefric found a decently flat rock and wrote out a letter for his seneschal at Water's End, including a list of the refugees and a detailed cargo manifest.

Not a letter most nobles could write. But most nobles hadn't enchanted their own quill pen to write in steady lines without the need for ink, sand or a blotter.

He sealed it in wax with both his ducal seal — the image of a lake with a sword sticking out of it, hilt first — and his personal seal — the image of a staff with two bolts of lightning coming from it, upwards to the left and right.

Once this was done, the two soldiers Ser Yrsa had chosen stepped up to receive it. Aefric noted that both had sustained injuries during the skirmish with the smugglers.

They'd been healed, but he could see the bloodstains on their tabards. One at the shoulder, one at the hip.

Aefric was almost ready to hand over the letter, but then a thought occurred to him.

"Ser Micham," he said, and that knight stepped forward. "I'll entrust the letter and this mission to you, and these two worthies will serve as your escort."

"Your grace," Ser Micham said, trying to hide his frown. Either at being used as a messenger, or at having two soldiers come along as escort.

"You know Ajenmoor," Aefric said, reassuringly. "And you know ships. You know what we need and who to talk to, to get both the refugees and the cargo to Water's End as swiftly and securely as possible. Which makes you the best person for the job."

"Thank you, your grace," Ser Micham said, a little more easily.

"And," Aefric said, softly, "if this affords you a moment or two to greet your father, so much the better."

"Thank you, your grace," Ser Micham said, smiling now.

Aefric watched the knight take charge of getting the refugees and cargo loaded, commandeering the longboats from the slaver ship, in the process.

"That was kind of you, your grace," Ser Beornric said softly. "He hasn't seen his father since before you arrived at Behal this past spring."

"That's part of the reason," Aefric said, just as softly. "But it also occurred to me that since I have yet to visit Ajenmoor, their mayor might've taken it as an insult, if I commandeered a couple of ships with only soldiers carrying my words."

"A fair thought."

"Well," Aefric said with a half-smile, "it seems to me that someone's been encouraging me to act more like a duke."

While Ser Beornric laughed, Aefric turned to Ser Yrsa.

"General? Shall we get back to the Dragonscar?"

ALAS, GETTING BACK TO EXPLORING THE DRAGONSCAR WAS NOT SO EASY as that. Aefric, himself, was ready. Hungry still, but eager to see more of this chasm while he still had a few hours of afternoon sun.

True, the chasm had been absorbing the summer heat, and the sun would be in the sky to their backs, but it did form a lovely tunnel for the whipping sea wind, keeping things relatively cool.

Ser Beornric and the knights of his personal guard — short of Ser Micham — also looked ready to get back to the reason they were out here.

Ser Yrsa, as well, seemed just as ready. And yet, it was she who pointed out that they couldn't leave yet.

"I'm sorry, your grace," she said with some chagrin. "But it would not be wise to depart until sailors from the Ajenmoor ships have taken charge of the prisoners. And with Ser Micham taking up the launches with refugees and cargo, that may be some time."

Aefric sighed. Turned to Ser Beornric. "You said something of food?"

"At once, your grace." Ser Beornric signaled to one of the soldiers, who fetched some jerked deer and an apple.

Aefric had just taken his first, crisp bite of the sweet, red fruit, when he heard an argument behind him. And one of the voices was Ser Micham's.

He was still turning when Ser Yrsa said, "Please, your grace. Let me."

Aefric didn't want to. He wanted to go back and handle the argument himself. But he had the distinct impression that Ser Yrsa was making a point, so he bit down on his frustration and the apple at the same time.

"Elbar's Blood," she shouted, striding toward the problem. "What is it now?"

Aefric barely tasted his apple, even though he finished it faster than he expected. He was trying to hear what was going on behind him. And Ser Beornric must've known it, because he started talking.

"Not sure I believe a dragon *caused* the Dragonscar," he said. "But I have heard tell that the bones of one of the great wyrms still lie at the other end. Hope we see them."

Curiosity warred in Aefric. He still wanted to listen in on the argument — sounded like it was between Ser Yrsa and one of the captains now — but he was more than a little curious about the dragon bones.

Aefric had been involved in exactly *one* fight against a dragon. Triskarathrax, it was called. Big as a decent-sized keep was Triskarathrax, with scales so black they shimmered all colors during the battle.

Aefric had gone into that fight along with more than a dozen others. All heroes in their own right. All fighting to save the small town of Merin's Stand, which was being punished for refusing to the pay the tribute demanded by the dragon.

Aefric wouldn't say he *won* that fight. But he did survive it. And so did the dragon. Though Triskarathrax never came back to Merin's Stand. Not that Aefric had ever heard.

"They say," Ser Beornric continued, "that the skeleton's still intact. That some've tried to pull bones and teeth from the remains, but couldn't do it."

"Your grace," Ser Yrsa called, and Aefric turned that way at once.

There she stood by the water, with Ser Micham and the two soldiers, facing down one of the captains. Aefric didn't remember the man's name.

Refugees had been loaded into the launches once more. All except for the two borogs.

Aefric growled and threw aside his apple core. He had the distinct feeling he knew what the problem was.

He forced a deep breath, and strolled casually over to the argument. His head held high. As though he didn't have a care in the world.

When he reached the standoff, he made a show of sighing.

Both the captain and Ser Yrsa started talking at once.

"Silence," Aefric snapped, and both the captain and the general not only stopped talking, they each fell back a step.

"I believe my orders were clear enough," Aefric said. "So would someone mind telling me why two of the refugees have not been loaded onto boats?"

"Well," the captain said, "they're *borogs*, your grace."

"Now, I realize, captain, that we have only just met," Aefric said. "And I realize further that you may have heard any number of things about me. But I must ask you..."

Aefric leaned a little closer, and snapped his next words out sharply.

"*Do you think I'm blind or stupid?*"

The man's mouth started moving, but no words came out.

"Certainly you cannot believe that I didn't *know* they were borogs when I gave that order. Or did you simply *overlook* the fact that *I* was the one addressing them in their own language?"

Poorly, in Aefric's opinion, but the point stood.

"Begging your grace's pardon," Captain Coral said, pushing her junior captain back a step and taking his place in the discussion. "We didn't think you meant them to be counted as refugees. Because they're borogs. And what you do with borogs is kill 'em. Figured your soldiers would handle that while we handled our part."

Behind her, her junior captain nodded rapidly.

"A poor assumption," Aefric said. "And now you know better. Shall I consider this matter resolved?"

"Wish I could say so, your grace," Captain Coral said. "But if we take borogs into Ajenmoor, they won't leave alive."

Aefric was about to say something very nasty about that, but Ser Micham spoke up.

"Begging pardon, your grace."

Aefric gritted his teeth, but nodded.

"During the Godswalk Wars, Father put a bounty on the heads of any and all borogs. No questions asked. That bounty's likely still in place."

"It is," Captain Coral confirmed.

"Why didn't you mention it before?"

"I should have, your grace," Ser Micham said with a bow of his head. "But as I was acting on your orders, I felt confident that I could keep them safe. Maybe use it as an opportunity to mention to Father that you wouldn't approve of that bounty still being in effect."

"Typical knight thinking," Captain Coral said with a grimace.

Ser Micham's head snapped up. His eyes blazed and he visibly checked his hand from reaching for his sword.

"Don't mean offense," Captain Coral said in tones that suggested to Aefric that she didn't actually care if Ser Micham felt offended. "But your grace's orders won't stop panic on the docks at the sight of them horn-noses. And they won't stop the dock patrol — or any nearby as has a bow or crossbow — from taking a shot at getting that bounty."

Ser Yrsa leaned in closer to Aefric.

"I hate to say it, but they're right," she said softly. "Some would shoot for public safety. Others hoping for a pouch of coins. But they'll shoot. And if the borogs don't go down right away, they'll fight back. It'll get ugly."

Aefric sighed.

"Captain Coral, apologize to Ser Micham for the offense you've given him."

"Your grace," she started but before she could finish her objection, Aefric spoke over her.

"His thinking may have been in error. But if that is cause for insult, I should insult you and your captains for thinking I'd treat those borogs as anything less than refugees. Which is what they are."

Aefric let those words hang for a moment. "But further insults will accomplish nothing. You were in the wrong. Apologize."

She frowned, but nodded.

"Ser Micham," she said, "I wronged you more than you deserved. I apologize."

Not a great apology, but at the moment it would do.

Ser Micham gave Captain Coral a stiff nod that suggested he didn't consider the matter settled. Well, that was fine. As long as he didn't interfere with everyone doing their job today.

"Now," Aefric said. "As I have no wish to see those borogs murdered for no crime greater than being borogs, they will accompany us into the Dragonscar. I *trust* that resolves this issue?"

"Completely, your grace," Captain Coral said, and from the way she was looking at Aefric, he suspected she was questioning the wisdom of having pissed off the new duke.

"Ser Micham," Aefric said, and waited until he had the knight's full attention to continue. "Please give your father my regards. And inform him that I wish him to rescind all bounties set upon members of any race."

"Does your grace," Ser Micham said, his expression pained, "include the sea devils in that list?"

Aefric checked his initial response. He wanted to say *yes*, out of spite. But the truth was, even before the Godswalk Wars, he'd never heard of those strange fish-lizard humanoids known widely as "sea devils" so much as *speaking* with the land-borne peoples.

They raided. They made war. They stole young men and women for breeding purposes. And Aefric had never heard of them doing *anything* else.

Even their wars didn't seem to be for land or resources, but merely ways of murdering many at once.

This behavior had led to most scholars arguing that the sea devils weren't people at all, the way most used the term. That they didn't have art or culture or values. That they were monsters, pure and simple.

Aefric didn't want to believe that. But he'd never seen evidence to the contrary.

And if he asked a port city like Ajenmoor to rescind a bounty on sea devils, they'd consider him a fool. He'd make enemies he didn't need.

"No," he said with a sigh. "I'd like to think we'll know peace with the sea devils one day, but I'll need to see some kind of proof before I'm willing to go *that* far."

Ser Micham, Captain Coral, and the other captain all heaved relieved sighs at the same moment.

Had all three been holding their breath? Really?

Well, maybe that was a good thing. Let them wonder about Aefric's priorities.

"I'll leave you to it then," Aefric said, and walked over to the borogs.

"Me hear," the big borog said. "Us ... run with chief." He pointed at Aefric. "Keep chief ... safe."

Well. At least it sounded as though *somebody* approved of what he was doing.

---

THE BIGGEST PROBLEM WITH JERKED DEER, AEFRIC DECIDED, WAS THAT it stayed with you all day. He'd eaten only two decent-sized pieces as part of his late lunch, back by the shore.

And yet, here it was. Hours later. And he could still taste the salty tang of it on his tongue. Still burped it, too.

And frankly, this batch was too gamey.

The afternoon's ride hadn't been nearly as interesting or eventful as the lengthy midday pause had been.

True, there was some beauty to the Dragonscar. A simple, stark beauty, but beauty nonetheless.

So far it was all rock. Shades of brown and red, mostly, but some were pale enough to qualify for an interpretation of beige.

The chasm walls were jagged here and there — though those jagged edges had been worn by time and winds until they were more rounded than edgy — and in some places the ground had been unstable enough that they'd had to walk the horses past cracks and fissures.

No signs of life down here, though. Nothing growing, that Aefric had seen so far. Even some moss would've been a pleasant change.

No, the most interesting thing they'd seen so far had been caves. Lots of them. Most of them shallow, but a few here and there looked to go back a ways. Even down.

Those caves that had potential to be more than shallow indentations got marked on the map that the scouts were putting together.

There would be no spelunking. Not on this venture.

Oh, Aefric wanted to go into those caves. He hadn't gone exploring an unknown cavern since ... had to be three years or more since he'd found that cave system down southeast a ways.

But that was not the purpose of this venture. He was here to *see* the Dragonscar. To make sure there were no threats to his duchy *coming from* the Dragonscar.

He hadn't brought enough food, or the right equipment, to start exploring every cave they found.

More was the pity.

And now, the sun was setting, and they'd made camp for the night. The fire was going, and the soldiers who'd been designated as cooks were making a savory stew of roast chicken and root vegetables.

Aefric sat on his blanket, sharing a cup of beer with his knights while the two borogs sat nearby.

The borogs hadn't done anything to attract attention to themselves. Not since Aefric's party left the sailors behind. Aefric and his knights had been riding their horses at a walk — Ser Beornric to his right, Ser Yrsa to his left, and the other five fanned out around him — and the borogs had kept pace easily, flanking the knights with room to spare.

They'd been quiet, and Aefric had the impression they'd been watchful.

As the hours passed, the knights came to accept the presence of the borogs. Even now, as they sat talking about the battle that was likely happening back at the shore between the ships from Ajenmoor and the *Swift Wave*.

The borogs sat silently. Watching. Not accepting any beer. And not sitting on the blankets.

"You're welcome to sit closer," Aefric said. "We'll make room."

"No," the bigger borog said. He pointed to Aefric. "Chief." He pointed to the knights. *"Glukrar."* Aefric frowned, then realized he *did* know that word. It meant blooded warriors. "Me and me ... new clan."

He snorted, and the smaller borog snorted a moment later.

"They want to prove themselves first," Ser Beornric said, looking surprised. "I can respect that."

The other knights nodded, and seemed to regard the borogs a little better after that.

The borogs did eat, at least, though not nearly as much as Aefric expected, given their size. Of course, that was for the best, since they'd only brought so much food, and the hunting here didn't look good.

After dinner, Ser Arras stood and sang for a while.

She didn't sing often, which Aefric considered a pity. Her voice was as beautiful as her face, and she had the looks to give credence to the rumors that she was Duchess Arinda's bastard child, conceived and born while Arinda was traveling abroad.

She tried to minimize the comparisons by keeping her own black hair cut short. Though from what Aefric had been told, the hazel of her eyes was almost identical to that of the late duchess.

The song she sang was one Aefric had never heard before. It told the story of a dragon that had come to Deepwater through the lake, from the other side of the world.

It was a dragon with sixteen legs and four wings and eyes like crescent moons.

The dragon perched on the Threepeaks Mountains and cried a challenge to all comers. Threatening to raid if not satisfied in battle.

The way Ser Arras sang the tale, scores of knights and wizards tried their best, but all fell before the beast.

But then a young squire, the bastard son of the king, went up to the dragon on his own. No weapon in hand. No armor to protect him.

He climbed the mountain not to fight the dragon, but to sing to it.

The young man, it seemed, had a voice whose beauty would make the stars weep. And he sang to the dragon of his people. Of their goodness. And of how they loved life.

The dragon was smitten. Fell straightaway in love with the young man.

The young man stayed up there with the dragon, and sang to it every night. He lived on food brought up by others and left as offerings.

For decades, the man sang to the dragon every night. But men live shorter lives than dragons. And one day, the man sang no more.

The people who lived at the foot of the mountain where the dragon had made its home, they shook with fear when they heard silence one night where they'd expected the echoes of the man's songs.

They began to send messengers to the nobles, begging for warriors and wizards to come and save them. For surely now that the man was dead, the dragon would come for them.

And the dragon did come.

After three nights of silence, the dragon took to the air and swooped down on its four mighty wings.

But the dragon did not come to raid. The dragon flew past the village, out over Lake Deepwater and set the dead body of the beloved man gently on an island in the delta where the lake flowed into the river Haven. And then the dragon went back into the lake, and was never seen again.

But the man was buried where the dragon set him. And a castle was raised on that spot. And a city built around the castle.

Both city and castle were named for the man.

Behal.

When she finished her song, Ser Arras sat again. But the smaller borog stood and sang.

Aefric couldn't follow the song. Didn't speak enough of the language. But it sounded poignant.

He was trying to puzzle together what he could about it, when he felt a ringing sensation through his bones, and an urge to turn his head to the side.

The sensations of an incoming message spell.

A moment later, he heard Karbin's voice.

"*Swift Wave* secured. Few losses. Second wizard captured. Wizard in green was passenger, not crew. Still investigating. Will update tomorrow."

A passenger. Why would smugglers carry a passenger? And why would a passenger have been ready to cast exploding fire in defense of a smuggler crew? Why not simply surrender and claim innocence?

Nelazzi. The wizard in green had to be a connection to Nelazzi. Maybe along to ensure they did her bidding?

Aefric found himself contemplating different possibilities there, as he drifted off to sleep that night.

But he was dreaming of Princess Maev when the call to arms rang out.

---

IN AEFRIC'S DREAM, MAEV'S LARGE, SOFT GRAY EYES WERE SMILING down at him. The curve of her lips and set of her fine jaw looked smug.

He'd been out hunting in the woods near Water's End. Separated from his guards, as he'd crept along a deer trail.

Which, of course, was when Maev had pounced on him.

He hadn't known she was there. No surprise. She wasn't just any scout, but a fully trained forester, comfortable in any remote environment.

She was good enough that he could have been standing right next to her, and never seen her.

Instead, she and her forest lynx, Sylkanis, jumped down from the branch of a tree. Sylkanis landed beside him, but Maev tackled him to the ground. Knocked the bow from his hands, and pinned his wrists to the pine needles and dirt beside his head.

She was wearing her buckskin clothes, which in the dream hugged her slender curves even more than they did in waking life. And Aefric was very aware of how she sat astride him.

"Caught you at last," she said, voice teasing. "Right where I want you."

Aefric was pretty sure he'd been about to say something about how glad he was to be caught, but his guards must've seen her take him down, without recognizing their princess.

"To arms!" someone shouted. "Wake and ware! To arms!"

Wake and ware? Why would...

The dream dissolved into the starry sky and brisk cold of night in the Dragonscar. The air still smelled of the sea, and of the roast chicken stew they'd had for dinner.

The fire burned low, but shed enough light for Aefric to make sense of the commotion he heard.

Knights donning armor. Soldiers grabbing pikes.

The clash of weapons.

But something sounded wrong. Not the clash of metal on metal. More like metal on ... stone?

No. That didn't make sense. He must still be sleep-addled.

Aefric kicked aside his blankets and came to his feet. He still wore that quilted tunic of Deepwater gray, but beyond that he had on only undergarments. And he didn't want to waste time putting on pants.

The Brightstaff leapt to his hand.

"Guard your eyes," he yelled, and flared the yellow diamond atop the Brightstaff to light up the night like daytime.

He heard hisses and groans from a few others, who hadn't looked away in time. But that was a small price to pay for the chance to see what was going on.

The camp was under attack. And the defense wasn't going well.

Already he could see six of his soldiers on the ground, wounded or worse. While others were doing battle with...

Four men.

No. Not men. They were simulacra of men, formed from the same brown rock as much of the Dragonscar. Like statues, given life.

And the pikes of his soldiers were doing nothing to them. Neither were the arrows shot by the archers, kneeling to the sides of the fight.

Aefric took to the air, seeking a better vantage point for his part of the battle.

Just then, the two borogs charged.

They were unarmed and unarmored. In fact, they wore nothing more than that sack cloth with rope belts that the slavers had made them wear. And yet, they'd split off to opposite sides of the camp, lowered their horns, and charged.

They charged the same simulacrum. Hit it from both sides with their horns.

Chips of stone flew. The simulacrum hit the ground.

Aefric blasted it with lightning from the Brightstaff.

The simulacrum barely looked scorched, and didn't so much as slow its movements.

This wasn't good. His soldiers couldn't hurt those things. The borogs had done some damage, but not much. The one they'd taken down was already rising to its feet. Fists raised to do battle.

And two more of his soldiers had fallen, while Aefric had accomplished nothing himself.

Fear gripped his guts. Not for himself. No. The fear he felt was for his soldiers. Flinging themselves into the hazard, while their comrades fell about them, and their own weapons seemed to do nothing.

Those men and women would all be dead soon. Unless Aefric thought of something.

But what?

The attackers were made of stone. Maybe if dropped from a great height, they'd shatter.

Aefric reached out with magic to grab one of the simulacra and yank it into the air.

He tried.

He strained.

No good.

The spells that made those things also bound them to keep contact with the chasm floor.

And while he wasted effort, more soldiers fell before the fists of the simulacra.

Damn it! There had to be a way.

But trying to move those things with magic was like trying to move the chasm itself.

Wait.

Like trying to move the chasm itself.

And striking those things. That was like *striking* the chasm itself.

What if that was the answer?

These were creatures of stone. In fact, from the look of them, creatures of the very stone of the Dragonscar, where they were fighting. Perhaps they couldn't be defeated while touching the stone from which they'd been forged?

But his magic couldn't pry them loose.

Perhaps an impact could?

*"Throw to sky,"* Aefric yelled, in Borog, which got a snort from both the two borogs currently locked in a kind of boxing match with one of the simulacra, and not doing well.

The two borogs fell back several steps, each to the opposite side. The simulacrum turned to go back to fighting easier prey — the soldiers.

The borogs charged again. But this time, the small one came in low and the big one came in high.

The simulacrum turned back at the sound of the charge. Faced the big borog. Lowered its weight, and spread its arms in challenge.

The borogs struck.

The simulacrum grabbed the big borog by the waist, even as its feet came up off the ground.

The big borog snapped his horn up, and the simulacrum lost its grip.

The simulacrum went airborne.

Not by more than a few feet. And it was already reaching out for the big borog.

But Aefric was ready.

This time his bolt of lightning blasted it apart.

"Get them off the rocks!" Aefric called down. "Get them airborne! They're vulnerable when they're airborne."

Before he was finished talking, he heard the hoofbeats of a charging horse.

Ser Yrsa. She blasted three notes on a whistle, and all the soldiers before her parted like a crowd making way for the king.

She lowered a pike as though it were a proper lance. Caught a simulacrum in the head.

The pike snapped. But chips flew. And so did the simulacrum.

Aefric blasted it.

Two down, two to go.

Whoever built the simulacra hadn't designed them to adapt to changes in their enemies' tactics. Once the other knights grabbed up pikes and made their own mounted charges, the battle was over in moments.

Still, it had lasted too long. Ten of Aefric's soldiers looked dead, and at least six more were wounded. Aefric suspected that the borogs were wounded as well. But they weren't bleeding, and they refused to acknowledge anything worse than being winded from the effort.

Whoever created those stone simulacra had a lot to answer for. And Aefric knew just where to start looking for answers.

---

THE SMELL OF THE MIDNIGHT SEA WIND WAS TOO CLEAN. TOO CLEAN for Aefric's mood. It should have smelled of death and decay, to reflect the soldiers who'd died at the hands of the simulacra.

He couldn't allow himself to become distracted by such thoughts. He had work to do, and time might be of the essence.

Aefric left Ser Yrsa to sort out the troops while he went over to inspect the remains of the simulacra.

By the light of his Brightstaff's diamond, the bits of shattered simulacra looked almost identical to the rocky floor of the chasm. Even their shapes were harder to discern now. They looked less like pieces of sculpture and more like bare rock.

Fortunately, he could still feel the magic that had given them something like life.

With that sense of lingering magic to guide him, he waved his hand and gathered the bits of fallen stone men together.

So much easier to move them that way, now that they weren't up and fighting. No active spell to overcome.

And the traces of that spell that lingered were already starting to fade.

Aefric stood the Brightstaff in place, its yellow diamond still turning the nighttime to false morning. With a stick of red sealing wax in one hand and flame in the other, he dribbled a circle around the components, then sealed it with a word of power.

The red wax kindled with ghostly white flames.

Those flames trapped the fading magic within the circle. It wouldn't escape him now.

With another wave of his hand, Aefric brought his pack winging to him through the air, high enough that it wouldn't get in anyone's way.

He dug out a blank sheet of parchment. He fed it a small pulse of the power that flowed unendingly through him.

The parchment quivered. Quickly, Aefric slid it through the ghostly flames and into the circle, so that the parchment was bathed by them on its way in. Purifying the little dribble of power Aefric had given the parchment.

Once it lay flat on the ground among the fallen bits of simulacra, Aefric began his working.

This was not some quick spell, to be over and done with a word or a gesture. Or even a properly channeled thought.

This was his own spin on the technique taught to him by that order of wizard-knights known as the Iron Wands.

All magic came down to three elements: an understanding of the interrelationship of forces, applied logic, and a touch of artistry.

The technique in question, as the Iron Wands performed it, never worked for Aefric. Their approach relied on the laws and logic of magic. Which might have been fine for wizards.

But though most of the world thought him a wizard, Aefric was a dweomerblood.

The logic side of magic often failed him in ways that had driven to distraction his wizardly teachers — including Karbin and the great Kainemorton himself.

But Aefric had an artist's flare with magic, in ways they would never understand.

So where the Iron Wands would have sifted and strained the dregs of a spell to distill what they could about the magic-user who'd cast it, Aefric instead whispered magic to those dregs.

He offered them the coherency they craved, and the perfection of completeness.

And so the dregs of the spells that had given life to those simulacra came together on that piece of parchment in patterns of lines, curves and colors.

They did not form a symbol or sigil, such as the Iron Wands would have produced.

Instead, the results of Aefric's working had produced a pattern that would evoke a sense of identity in him when he regarded it.

He broke the circle then, and took up the parchment.

The magic-user had been a wizard, as opposed to some other kind of spell-slinger. The work was too technical for ... say ... a warlock.

The spell was not more than a year old, at the most. Possibly had been cast as recently as two seasons ago, which would have been wintertime.

That was all Aefric could tell right then. But if he ever met the wizard, or saw another of that wizard's spells, he would recognize them at once.

Aefric was still studying his interpretation of that wizard's identity when Ser Beornric brought him pants and boots.

Oh. Yes. That brisk, midnight wind was cold, wasn't it? Aefric realized he was shivering, and his bare legs were covered in gooseflesh.

He donned his leather pants and the boots, and as he finished tying the laces, Ser Yrsa approached as well.

"Final count," she said grimly. "Eight dead. Three who might not live to see sunup. Four who will, but won't be leaving this chasm under their own power. Six more, mobile, but hurt too bad to fight again anytime soon. And maybe a dozen others took a few lumps."

"More than half our soldiers gone in ... what ... a few minutes fighting those things?" Ser Beornric shook his head. "What were they, your grace?"

"More important," Ser Yrsa said. "When should we expect more of them?"

"They were creatures carved from stone and given a semblance of life by magic," Aefric said. "Got to be guarding something, but I don't know what. Or where they came from."

"*Aur*," the smaller borog said, but the big borog snorted aggressively.

"*Grek*," the smaller borog said, apologizing. "You chief. You ... speak."

"Go on," Aefric said. "What do you mean about gold?"

"Me..." The smaller borog turned to the larger one and they exchanged a few Borog words faster than he could follow.

The smaller one pointed to his — her? — horn.

"Me ... nose taste ... gold."

"Smell?" Aefric asked, then made a show of flaring his nostrils wide in a deep breath.

The borogs both worked at nodding.

"You can smell gold?"

They nodded slowly again. As though not sure they were doing it right.

"I'm sorry," Aefric said, kicking himself for not having done this sooner. Apparently he had habits of bias that he wasn't aware of. "What should I call you?"

The bigger borog stomped his foot. "Ge'rek."

The smaller borog stomped his or her foot. "Po'rek."

"And, Po'rek, are you telling me you smell gold? Right now?"

"*Kre*," Po'rek said, by way of agreement. Pointed farther down the chasm and to the right. "Much."

"Hard to be certain," Ser Yrsa said, "but I'm pretty sure that's the direction the stone men came from."

"All right," Aefric said. "So it sounds as though someone's found gold, and doesn't want anyone else finding it."

"So someone's watching us?" Ser Beornric said, trying to spot a lookout.

"Possibly," Aefric said. "But more likely, we're within range of a warding's detection."

"We've been here for hours," Ser Yrsa said. "If we tripped an alarm, we should've known before now."

"Not necessarily," Aefric said. "Too many factors. Could be a time-of-night issue. The stone men didn't need light to see. And afterwards, if they'd won, anyone looking down from the ridge above would never have seen the aftermath of the slaughter."

"They'd've seen the bodies come morning," Ser Yrsa said. "No way our scouts would miss them."

"They might," Aefric said. "If they were more interested in watching the ridge on Silverlake's side than in looking into the chasm itself."

Ser Yrsa opened her mouth to object, but Aefric pushed ahead to finish his point first.

"Besides," Aefric said. "We don't know the full orders those stone men had. They might haul away bodies, leaving only blood. And since they bludgeon instead of carving up their enemies, the slaughter might not leave enough blood to attract a scout's attention. Especially if seen through a spyglass."

"Fair enough," Ser Yrsa said. "And it's not as though anyone casually comes down here." She nodded. "I'll gather some of the troops and check it out."

"No," Aefric said, then raised both hands before his knights could object to what they had to know was coming. "Yes, I'm going. No, you can't talk me out of it. Magic's involved, and I'm the only one of us who could sense it, let alone defeat it."

"You're not going alone," Ser Beornric said with an air of finality.

"No," Aefric agreed. "Of course not. You two will come, and the knights, and Po'rek and Ge'rek, if they're willing."

"You chief," Ge'rek said simply. "Us come."

Both borogs stamped their feet.

Aefric suspected that the right thing to say in response would be, *"And the dark swallows all."* But he couldn't bring himself to say those words. Not even in Borog.

At the moment, they sounded too much like prophecy.

———

AEFRIC'S KNIGHTS WERE SO EAGER TO COME ALONG TO INVESTIGATE THE source of the stone men, they might've gone even had Aefric stayed behind.

He suspected that they were disappointed to have missed most of the fight against the stone men. It was over before most of them had their armor on.

The soldiers had been standing guard, not the knights. The right of rank, Aefric supposed. And the soldiers had slept in their chainmail. Habit of campaigning, most likely.

Those details had left the soldiers doing the fighting. And the dying.

The first part of that, Aefric was proud of. His men and women hadn't hesitated. Not even in the face of an inhuman enemy that they couldn't seem to hurt.

But the latter part. That he hated. Good men and women had died that night. And more good men and women might die from their wounds, before he could get them to proper aid.

"We do something like this again," Aefric said, gesturing to the Dragonscar at large, "we bring a healer next time."

"Yes, your grace," Ser Yrsa said. "I've had the same thought. It's just that healers are in short supply right now. And I'm afraid I honestly expected this trip to be uneventful. I'll know better in the future."

Ser Beornric said something quiet to her, and Ser Yrsa snorted a dark laugh and thumped him on the shoulder.

Aefric suspected he didn't want to hear that joke.

With the knights and the borogs gathered, they set out, with Aefric's staff providing light.

They didn't have to go far. Not more than a few hundred feet father down the Dragonscar were another set of caves. Not mere indentations, either. Three deep-looking caves on the south side — the Deepwater side — and two others on the north, Silverlake side.

Po'rek and Ge'rek both pointed to the middle cave on the right-hand side.

"Much much gold there," Po'rek said, then pointed to the first cave on the right. "Much gold there." Po'rek turned and pointed at the righthand cave on the Silverlake side. "Gold there too."

Aefric looked at Ge'rek for confirmation, but Ge'rek snorted.

"Po'rek ... smell ... strong."

Two of Aefric's knights snorted a laugh at that, but he didn't bother looking to see which ones. He even understood the joke. The musky smell of the borogs was strong, if dry, even when they were left to their own devices. But these two had been imprisoned on a ship for some time.

They were more than a little rank. Fortunately, the constant sea wind had helped Aefric ignore that fact much of the time.

The point was made anyway. Po'rek had a better sense of smell than Ge'rek.

"Take up guard positions," Aefric said. "I'm going to see if there's any magic here."

The knights and borogs surrounded him, but leaving Aefric

enough room to maneuver. He hoped they weren't watching. They'd be disappointed. There wasn't much to see.

All he really did was shift his attention to that part of him that could detect the presence of magic. He'd had that ability as far back as he remembered. Didn't take any effort, really. In fact, if there was anything *obvious* coming from the area, he'd know it already.

There wasn't.

But there might be something subtle. And that required focused attention.

So Aefric relaxed. And he breathed. And he stretched out with that part of himself that could detect the presence of magic.

Nothing.

Nothing.

Something.

It wasn't much. Just a faint tingle. And it was coming from the cave of much much gold, according to Po'rek.

Aefric gently reached out with his awareness toward that cave.

He quickly determined three things.

First, that there was a ward of detection at the mouth of that cave. Second, that the ward had been part of a bigger spell, the rest of which had been collapsed. And third, that the ward had been cast by the same wizard who had created the stone simulacra.

The collapsed spell had been a larger detection spell that triggered a response. That had to be the stone men, and their attack.

But that wouldn't make sense. Why attack people who had yet to discover the gold? That would just be telling them there was something down here worth defending.

"How sure are we that people don't come down here?" Aefric asked.

"Reasonably," Ser Yrsa said. "Every scouting report I've seen that detailed the floor of the Dragonscar was more than a century old. And as I said before. None of the more recent scouts along the ridge ever spotted activity down here. So apart from whoever created the stone men, we might be the first ones in this part of the Dragonscar in ... fifty years? A hundred?"

"Beg pardon, General," Ser Wardius said, "but I've been down here before."

Everyone turned to look at him.

Although all of Aefric's knights had scars, none were as scarred as wiry Ser Wardius. And not just the jagged scars on both cheeks. He was missing the tip of his nose and the small finger of his left hand. And when he wasn't wearing his gauntlets, his hands showed more scarring than they did tanned skin.

"Oh?" Ser Yrsa said, in tones that implied Ser Wardius better have an excellent explanation.

Though whether the knight had to explain why he'd been down here or why he hadn't mentioned it before, Aefric wasn't certain.

"I grew up in the town of Greatcatch," Ser Wardius said, then shook his head. "Sea devils wiped it out during the wars, but it used to be only an hour south of the Dragonscar, as you ride along the coast."

Ser Wardius looked lost in memory now.

"To us kids growing up in Greatcatch, the Dragonscar was the most haunted place in the world. Used to dare each other just to set foot in it. The braver of us, we'd come up here in twos and threes with some food, have a little picnic down near the water. Shelter in a couple of those hollow dents some might call caves.

"Always had to be the best, in those days," he said, shaking his head. "That was me. Certain I'd live forever. So I got me a pliant horse and all the food I could carry. And I rode this old Dragonscar from one end to the other."

"I suppose you're going to tell me you plucked a bone off the dragon's skeleton," Ser Yrsa said.

"No, ser," Ser Wardius said. "I wasted a good day and a good knife trying, but those bones wouldn't come loose. So instead I climbed up the ribs and pissed off the skull."

Even the borogs laughed at that, and borog laughter was a chuffing kind of sound.

"So you've been through here," Aefric said, "but all alone."

"Yes, your grace," Ser Wardius said. "I'd've told you before, but I didn't think it mattered. When I came through last time, I didn't meet anyone or anything. I livened up the story for my friends, of course. Talked about ghosts and running from borogs."

He looked at the borogs. "No offense."

They didn't even acknowledge the statement, which demonstrated that it didn't bother them.

Ser Wardius shrugged. "Truth was, it was a boring ride, last time. Figured it'd be the same this time."

"Hmmm," Aefric said. "Could be that no one else's done it since—"

"Oh, another dozen kids did it, your grace," Ser Wardius said. "Likely more. Once I came back alive. Became a right of passage."

"But Greatcatch is gone," Aefric said. "So likely no one's made that ride since it fell."

"If I were those smugglers," Ser Beornric said, "I'd want to ride at least a day's travel into the Dragonscar. Maybe two or three. Make sure there weren't any surprises waiting for me."

"How many would you send?"

"Handful, at most," Ser Beornric said quickly. "Hug one side of the chasm, to keep from getting spotted."

"I agree," Ser Yrsa said. "No way those smugglers, or some other sailors, haven't been here. Might even have been the ones casting the spell."

"That wizard in green," Ser Beornric started to say, but let his words trail off when Aefric shook his head.

"No," Aefric said. "I'd've recognized his magic. So, that detection spell. It couldn't have triggered for the smugglers, or they wouldn't be using this place."

He snapped his fingers. "Numbers. Has to be a numbers game. We came through here with more than forty."

"You think they weren't worried about anything less than a small company of troops?" Ser Beornric asked.

"I think they were worried about enough people to set up a first mining foray," Aefric said. "Someone doesn't want anyone else digging up that gold. The question is *who*?"

Once back at camp, Aefric took time to honor the dead, and talk to the wounded. He did what he could to ease their suffering, as well as thank them for their quick rallying to the defense of the camp.

But there was more. Aefric wanted to make sure his troops understood that their duke's top priorities right now were to get the living back alive for healing, and to bring the dead back for burial.

And he wanted them to know that, once those things were accomplished, he intended to find out who had been behind that attack, and make them pay for the lives they'd taken.

Not just words, either. Gold was a good discovery, but Aefric didn't like the price he'd paid for that discovery.

He *would* find the source of those stone simulacra. And he would make that person pay. And anyone else who'd been involved.

After he'd given every wounded soldier some of his time, Aefric gathered with his knights again at the edge of the firelight to discuss what needed to be done. The two borogs lingered nearby, listening.

"We have no choice but to turn back," Ser Yrsa said.

"I agree," Aefric said. "We have too many dead already. I have no desire to see our wounded add to that number. We leave at dawn."

"What about the gold?" Ser Beornric asked.

"We'll have to come back for it," Aefric said, "when we can."

"But if the stone men's master knows we've been here, they may do something else. Set up an even deadlier trap."

"We could leave the scouts," Ser Yrsa said. "They could watch from up on the ridge, and they're good at living off the land. They'll get word to us if there's a problem."

"Us stay," Ge'rek said.

"By yourselves?" Aefric asked in disbelief.

"God metal," Ge'rek said with a snort.

Aefric was starting to think there was a whole portion of the Borog language that could only be spoken by someone with a nose capable of such expressive snorting. They seemed to use snorts to mean at least a dozen different things.

"Chief speak us dig god metal," Po'rek explained. "God metal here. Dig here."

Both snorted.

"But you have no tools," Ser Beornric said. "I mean, we can give you a couple of camp shovels, but they're hardly—"

They snorted again, and stamped their feet.

"We can't leave you much food," Ser Yrsa pointed out.

More snorting and stamping.

"I won't have you starve to death," Aefric said. "Not in my service."

The borogs spoke quietly to each other for a moment.

"What ... starve?" Ge'rek asked.

"Starving is dying because you don't eat," Aefric said.

The borogs chuffed laughter.

"Us dig," Ge'rek said. "Find food."

"You're sure?"

"*And the dark swallows all,*" Po'rek added, and Ge'rek stomped for emphasis.

Aefric wanted to ask for confirmation one more time, but after hearing that borog saying, he knew there was no point.

"All right then," he said, and led them back toward the caves, with the knights in tow. He lit the way with the yellow diamond atop his staff, but he kept its shine down to the dim glow of candlelight for now.

He pointed to the first cave on the righthand side, where Po'rek had said there was "much gold."

"You start digging there," he said.

He pointed to the second cave, where Po'rek had said there was "much much gold."

"Do not dig there until I say dig there. Do not even enter."

The borogs hesitated, so Aefric stamped his foot.

They gave their shoulders a quick duck in submission.

Ge'rek pointed to the first cave and said, "Us dig there. Not dig other caves."

"No," Po'rek corrected. Pointed at the first cave. "Chief say dig there. Us go there. Dig. When chief say 'dig there'" — Po'rek pointed at the second cave — "us go there. Dig there. When chief say."

"Let's stick to that for now," Aefric said, and both borogs snorted agreement.

"Us dig tonight," Ge'rek said. "Sleep when fire eye high."

*"Kre,"* Po'rek said, by way of agreement, and they both started into the first cave.

"You don't need anything else first?" Aefric asked. "Some sleep? Some food? Anything?"

They both made a show of slowly shaking their heads, then turned and went together into the first cave.

"They must know what they're doing," Ser Yrsa said, sounding as amazed as Aefric felt, at least.

"They are noted for their mining," Ser Beornric agreed. "Perhaps they're more comfortable in the caves than they are out here."

"Perhaps," Aefric said. "But I won't leave them here alone. I still want those scouts on the ridge as soon as possible, keeping an eye on things. And I want regular reports."

"Of course, your grace," Ser Yrsa said quickly.

"All right," Aefric said. "Have I missed anything?"

"One thing I can think of, your grace," Ser Beornric said.

Aefric nodded for him to go on.

"One of those caves that smell like gold..." He shook his head. "Just saying that sounds wrong. But if they're right, and we're assuming they are—"

"What if they're not?" Ser Yrsa said, and several of the other knights nodded, as though they'd wondered as well.

"What do you mean?" Aefric asked.

"Well," Ser Yrsa said. "They say they smell gold. But how do we know they do?"

"Why would they lie about something like that?"

"They know they're only here and alive on your sufferance, your grace. Maybe they want to dig their way back underground. Maybe find tunnels that lead to other borog clans. Gods know, since the wars, we're more likely to find borogs underground than aboveground."

"Are they?" Aefric asked. "Only alive on my sufferance?" He looked around at his other knights. "Am I the only one who noticed the way they fought alongside us? Without armor or weapons, they threw themselves into the hazard."

No one answered. Most of the knights tried to look anywhere else.

"I was up and fighting while the knights of my personal guard were still donning their armor." Aefric held up his hands to stop their objections. "Don't try to tell me I should've waited. You knew I wouldn't, and you know I won't. Don't blame me for that any more than I blame you for wanting armor between yourselves and danger."

A few of them looked as though they wanted to say something. Before they could, Aefric spoke again.

"Have Ge'rek and Po'rek proven *nothing* so far to *any* of you?"

"They've proven themselves to me, your grace." That was from Ser Vria. At least a head shorter than the rest of his knights, and the only one of them with eldrani blood. And the eldrani loved the borogs not much better than the na'shek did.

The others began uttering their own words of agreement.

"Good," Aefric said. "That's a step. Now. It's a simple enough matter to see if they're right about gold."

"Please tell me your grace doesn't intend to go caving here and now," Ser Yrsa said, sounding pained.

"Not at all," Aefric said. "I intend to do my best to get a few hours sleep before sunrise. Much like I hope the rest of you do."

Ser Beornric got it first.

"Ah," he said. "You figure if the smell of gold is that strong to them, then they may dig some up overnight."

"Exactly," Aefric said.

"And if we check in the morning and they're gone?" Ser Yrsa asked.

"Then they're gone," Aefric said with a shrug. "I meant it when I said they were free to choose where they wanted to go. If they want to dig their way back to some underground society, then I'll wish them godspeed."

Aefric smirked. "I admit, though. If they can smell gold — and maybe other precious metals — they might be handy to have around. Even the na'shek can't do that."

"Bed then?" Ser Yrsa asked.

"Bed," Aefric said, and they returned to camp and made ready to get at least a few hours sleep before sunrise.

Aefric hoped he'd be able to return to that dream about Maev. Or perhaps one of Byrhta. He hadn't seen her in at least three aetts. He hoped she and Vercy were doing well down in Riverbreak.

And Maev. He hadn't heard from Maev in almost as long. She was still off in the kingdom of Varondam, forging an alliance. Possibly through marriage. That was certainly her father's plan, and undoubtedly Varondam's plan as well.

It wasn't Maev's plan, the last Aefric had heard. What was it she called King Dalius in that letter? Ah, yes. A fop, with fewer scars than she had.

Made Aefric wonder about Maev's scars. He'd never seen any that were more significant than a couple of scratches on the back of her left hand. And she didn't have any scars at all on her face, or neck, or arms...

Aefric smiled, imagining getting the chance to go looking for those scars as he shifted about in his bedroll, seeking more comfort. It could be fun for the two of them to take some time and really explore each other's scars...

He felt guilty about his feelings there. Maev was a princess. Her marrying King Dalius — fop or not — would be good for Armyr. A solid alliance that would functionally surround the kingdom of Malimfar, who'd already tried to invade Armyr once this year.

Truth was, the marriage might be good for Maev, as well. She would be queen of Varondam. And from the way she spoke of King Dalius, she could probably become the true ruler of that country.

It was an excellent opportunity for her.

But as he fell asleep, Aefric found his thoughts turning not to the women in his life, but to the other thing he'd learned tonight. Quite possibly the point Ser Beornric had intended to raise, before the conversation ran away from him.

One of those caves where Po'rek had smelled gold had been on the north side.

The Dragonscar was edge of Aefric's land. North of the Dragon-scar was the duchy of Silverlake.

If Po'rek's nose was right about the gold, did Aefric have the right to mine that north side cave? Did he have a responsibility to discuss the matter with Duke Wylyn of Silverlake? Did he need to present the question to King Colm for judgment, before taking action either way?

Considering the possibilities there kept him awake much longer than he wanted to be...

DAWN IN THE DRAGONSCAR THE NEXT MORNING DIDN'T PROVE TO BE much warmer than the previous midnight.

That wind from off the Risen Sea never let up down here. It had become such a constant that Aefric had begun noticing secondary smells, underneath the sea smell itself.

Dust. Aefric was definitely beginning to notice the smell of dust from the chasm. But nothing green, and nothing pleasant.

Well, the smell of that roast chicken stew being heated up for breakfast was pleasant.

In general though, between the constant winds, the stark rocks, and distinct lack of green, this would truly be a miserable place to live.

He hoped that the miners would find some way to mitigate those problems, when the time came.

As for himself, Aefric knew he couldn't dress for the wind today. By midday they'd be back up on the ridge, dealing with the midsummer heat. So from the limited selection of clothes he'd brought along, he chose a navy blue linen shirt. Same leather pants, though.

He chuckled as he realized he'd been thinking that his leather pants needed cleaning. Truly, he was thinking more like a duke than like an adventurer these days.

Time was, he'd only have thought about how his clothes needed cleaning if he were going to enter a town anytime soon.

He donned the same calf-high leather boots, of course. Even as a duke he didn't see the point of lugging along extra footwear on a trip like this one.

But the cloak that had served as his extra blanket last night, that he packed in Windsong's saddlebags, as he prepared his horse himself that morning.

As Aefric looked around at his knights, tending their own horses, he realized he'd never seen any of them attended by squires.

Of course, with the exception of Ser Yrsa, they were all knights of his personal guard. Perhaps that role was one that forbade squires?

Perhaps. But if so, that didn't explain why Ser Yrsa didn't have a squire out here.

He'd have to remember to ask about those things later.

Once breakfast was finished, and the company packed and ready to move out, Aefric double-checked the final preparations.

The nine dead soldiers — eight who'd died in the battle and one who'd fallen to his wounds overnight — were loaded aboard two horses. Five aboard Aefric's Windsong, and four aboard Ser Yrsa's white mare.

That left six too wounded to walk. They were strapped to makeshift litters, made with blankets and headless pikes. The litters would be pulled by the horses of Ser Beornric and the other knights.

Aefric and Ser Yrsa would lead their own horses. The others would be led by the six soldiers who were mobile, but too wounded to fight.

There was only one last thing to take care of, before they left. Aefric and Sers Beornric and Yrsa walked back to the cave where the borogs were mining.

As they approached the cave, Aefric realized he kept expecting to hear the sounds he associated with mining. The *clang* of a pick. The grind of a shovel. The sharp *thump* of a hammer striking rock.

But the main thing he heard was the whip of the wind.

"Perhaps they took off after all," Ser Yrsa said.

"Ge'rek! Po'rek!" Aefric called into the cave, without entering it. The early dawn's rays barely scratched the surface of the cave's gloom.

By the time he heard their footsteps, Ge'rek and Po'rek were coming into view.

That was disturbing. Ge'rek was taller than Aefric by half a head, and at least twice as broad. Po'rek was only about Aefric's height, but at least half-again as broad as he was.

He would not have expected them to move so quietly on the rocks. Certainly they hadn't seemed all that quiet out in the chasm...

"Chief," Ge'rek said, and made a clumsy attempt at a bow, the way he'd seen the humans do it.

"Chief," Po'rek said, and his or her bow was slightly better.

"We're going to leave soon," Aefric said. "Is there anything more you need from us, before we go?"

"*Notek,*" Ge'rek said, and Po'rek snorted agreement.

Aefric shook his head. Started to ask what that meant, but didn't get further than, "I don't—"

"It's like a blessing," Ser Yrsa said. "You're their chief, and they're laboring in your name. They want your blessing, for want of a better word."

Aefric gave Ser Yrsa a flat look.

The look she returned would probably have been innocent on anyone else. But that scar on the left side of her face kept her from pulling it off.

"You speak Borog," Aefric said.

"Better than your grace does, I'm afraid," she answered, not sounding at all apologetic.

"And you didn't mention this because..."

"Your grace wished to handle the matter himself. And honestly, did quite well."

"We're going to discuss this later, you know."

"I never doubted it, your grace."

Aefric noted, and not for the first time, that Ser Yrsa tended to address him much more formally when she was doing something she knew would aggravate him.

And that it happened often enough that he'd *noticed* it more than once just made it more irritating.

No doubt about it, though. That woman could hold a grudge.

Aefric frowned, but asked her, "Is there a standard blessing?"

"Speak from your heart," she said. "If you can work in what you want for them and from them, so much the better."

Aefric transferred the Brightstaff to his left hand, and raised his right in benediction.

He drew a deep breath, and thought about everything he knew about borogs and borog culture. Sadly, doing so did not take long.

"As you labor in my service, dig well, dig deep, and gather honor and *aur* in my name."

"For chief!" Ge'rek said, and stamped.

"For chief!" Po'rek echoed, and stamped.

They both pumped their arms, and thumped each other's chests.

"God metal for chief!" Ge'rek bellowed so loudly it must've echoed up and down the Dragonscar.

Aefric expected Po'rek to repeat the bellow, but no. Instead, Po'rek turned and went into the cave. He or she came back a moment later, carrying two handfuls of gold nuggets that looked as though they'd been professionally cleaned.

Not so much as a speck of dirt diminished their sparkle. And if there were any impurities in the gold, Aefric couldn't see them.

Po'rek dropped to both knees with a loud *thump*. Head bowed, he or she offered the nuggets to Aefric.

The eight nuggets looked light in Po'rek's hands, but when Aefric took them, he realized they had to be at least a pound each. Of pure gold.

And this had come from two borogs, digging without tools for only a few hours. From the cave that smelled to Po'rek as though it had the lesser of the two veins on this side of the chasm.

There might be more gold down here than in all the Threepeaks Mountains.

No wonder someone was willing to set traps and kill strangers to protect this discovery.

---

Aefric stowed those gold nuggets in a special sack he kept tucked deep inside his backpack. The sack was a wonderful bit of magic, and one he hadn't mentioned to anyone since his days of traveling with Karbin's adventuring company, the Last Sons.

Aefric still didn't understand exactly how the magic of the sack worked. Not truly. And certainly not well enough to try to create such a thing himself.

No, that sack was an intricate marvel of subtly woven planar workings, creating within a single, apparently normal canvas sack, a seemingly endless series of other sacks, organized by the magic of the sack itself.

Aefric had only to place those nuggets in the sack, and they were gone. Irretrievable to anyone else, so long as the sack was keyed to him. Which, of course, Aefric had done properly, because he'd used the long, slow method to investigate the sack when he first obtained it, rather than the quick-and-dirty solution most adventurers relied on.

Aefric's personal fortune, or at least, what he'd accumulated through years of adventuring, was hidden away in that sack. Along with certain important trophies, and other objects that others ... did not need to know he had.

Aefric didn't use that sack often, and almost never when there was a chance of anyone seeing what he was doing. He'd only brought it along now out of the hope of leaving with a bone from the rumored dragon skeleton at the end of the Dragonscar.

But with those gold nuggets to bring back, he was glad he had it.

Once that was done, he diverted the subject from gold by turning to Ser Yrsa and saying, "Now, about your command of the Borog language."

Ser Beornric and the other knights paused their final preparations to listen in on the conversation. And Aefric was pretty sure his nearby soldiers were doing the same thing.

"Yes, your grace?" Ser Yrsa said, doing a poor job of hiding a smile in her eyes.

"I want the real reason you didn't tell me," Aefric said.

"As I said, your grace," Ser Yrsa started, but Aefric cut her off with a quick wave of his hand.

"No games," Aefric said. "I want the truth."

"I don't mean that as a game, your grace," Ser Yrsa said. "When your grace endeavors to handle something himself, it is not my place to supplant him."

"So," Aefric said with a nod that was anything but approval. "You withheld information from me on a technicality, and left me in a position where I might have stumbled into creating a problem where there didn't have to be one. Is that it?"

"Well, your—"

"*Is that it, General?*" Aefric asked, now standing eye-to-eye with her.

Ser Yrsa looked away first.

"Not entirely, your grace," she said, and met Aefric's eye again, with a little more defiance. "I have not your grace's trusting nature. I felt that, if they believed no one present had a good command of their language, Ge'rek and Po'rek might reveal something they intended to keep hidden from us."

"Tell me, *General.* Just what exactly is it that you expected them to be hiding? *Keeping in mind* that until today they'd been captives of slavers, on their way to a lifetime of service. Before *we* rescued them."

"We don't know what they were doing before they were captured. For all we know, they might have been advance scouts for an invading army. An army coming this way."

"And for all we know," Aefric said, "every other captive on that ship was a spy or assassin in disguise."

"Yes, your grace," Ser Yrsa said. "A concern I shared with Ser Micham, before he left with them on his mission. And as for the time before that..."

She called forward two archers. "Caul, Aleand."

They stepped forward and saluted.

"Tell the duke the orders I gave you, just before we freed the slavers' captives."

"Yes, General," Caul said, speaking for both men. Caul was a thin, sallow man for a soldier, but he had a quick eye and quick hands. "You told Aleand and me to find a vantage point to keep an eye on the slaves, nock arrows, and wait for your signal."

Aefric looked at Ser Yrsa in amazement.

"You were ready to shoot down unarmed, defenseless captives?"

"No, your grace," she said firmly. "I was ready to shoot down spies or assassins who might be here to attack my duke. Or perhaps men and women driven mad by captivity. Or any at all who would dare raise arms against my duke, whatever reason they might have in their heads."

"And you expected that to happen?"

"No, your grace," she said. "My job is to make sure it *doesn't* happen. My job is to consider all of the nasty possibilities of life, and to make sure *you* survive, if any one of them should happen to come to pass."

"I must say, your grace," Ser Beornric added quietly, "that some men and women are broken by captivity. Makes 'em do strange things, once they get free. Violent, sometimes. Seen it myself."

"All right," Aefric said, knowing he'd heard of things like that before, in another life, even if he'd never encountered them himself.

He turned back to Ser Yrsa. "All right. So. You understood every-thing Ge'rek and Po'rek were saying, even while I was flailing about like a fool, trying to make myself understood."

"Not like a fool," Ser Yrsa said, just as firmly as she'd insisted on her other points. When Aefric frowned at her words, she continued,

"Your grace has a love and respect for life and freedom beyond anything I have seen in a noble, myself. You showed those borogs a level of consideration they've likely never gotten from a human before. There's nothing foolish about that."

"And yet," Aefric said, "I could easily have made a critical error."

"No, your grace," she said, with a single shake of her head. "I would have stepped in, had that happened. But until then, I had to put your safety ahead of your intentions. And that meant listening in on their conversation while they didn't know I could."

"And? Did you learn anything interesting?"

"So far as I can tell, your grace, they are as they present themselves. Including that they appear to be devoted to you as their chief. Which was why I finally admitted my understanding of Borog. They deserved the *notek*, and you deserved a chance to give it to them."

Aefric sighed. "I should still be angry at you, you know. For holding back that information, and making the decision without consulting me."

"Your grace certainly has that right," Ser Yrsa said, straightening, to stand at attention. "If your grace wishes to punish me, I stand ready to receive my punishment."

Aefric cocked an eyebrow, curious. "Anything you'd like to say in your defense?"

She didn't even hesitate.

"The nature of my position as general is such that I must make decisions in your grace's name on a consistent basis. I must always do so with the utmost integrity, and the intention to safeguard your grace's person and interests in all things.

"This requires me to act on all information available to *me*, and not necessarily all information available to your grace. This includes instances when a situation arises in which I possess critical, time-sensitive information that I must act on, without the opportunity to first share that information with your grace."

"In other words," Aefric said. "You didn't tell me you spoke Borog at the time because it would ruin your stratagem, but if I were to have asked at any point, you would have told me?"

"Exactly so, your grace," Ser Yrsa said. "And I regret any undue embarrassment or other feelings your grace might have experienced in the process."

Aefric chuckled.

"Damn it," he said, still chuckling. "I was all ready to be mad at you."

"I apologize for failing you in that, your grace. I shall endeavor to give you proper reason to be angry with me at my first opportunity."

Aefric opened his mouth to object, but then he saw the laughter in her eyes.

"Don't you dare," he said, clapping her on the shoulder and sharing that laugh with her.

"As your grace commands, of course," she said, giving Aefric a mischievous look.

And with that, they set out to leave the Dragonscar.

**3**

———————

TRAVEL BACK FROM THE DRAGONSCAR WAS A SLOW AFFAIR. WITH everyone afoot, and too many injured, speed wasn't even a consideration.

Well, that wasn't entirely true. Aefric worried about speed all the time. He worried that they weren't moving fast enough to get the worst off of the injured to healers before they suffered permanent damage, or died from their wounds.

He also worried that even their slow pace might be too fast. Might jostle their wounds in ways that would only make things worse.

But nothing could be done about it. The wounded had received the best field care they could get without a true healer. And Aefric had no magical way to get them to help sooner.

Even if he could fly with so many — which he could not — he couldn't guarantee them any smoother a ride than they'd have strapped to those litters.

At least the whole company had enough food for the trip, even at this speed. They'd brought enough to see them through the Dragonscar, which meant they had enough food to last at least another aett out here in the wild.

Which was just as well.

With the four scouts having been left behind on the ridge, watching the chasm and — Aefric hoped — making sure nothing bad happened to Ge'rek and Po'rek, there would be no target-of-opportunity hunting along the way.

The healthier and more mobile among the archers handled the scouting duties, but they were under strict orders not to draw unless attacked.

Ser Yrsa had explained that if they were given leave to hunt, they might pay more attention to scouting food than danger. They simply weren't trained to do both and do them well.

Most of their archers could hit a moving squirrel on a branch at two hundred paces. But in so doing they'd overlook a tarok, standing at the base of that tree.

Training. A simple matter of training.

And given the state of their party on the march home, Aefric agreed that having those on scout duty focus on seeking out dangers was far more important than the possibility of fresh meat for dinner.

They'd be eating fresh meals soon enough. Even if the hike, itself, seemed to take forever.

Didn't help that they'd had to return to that first pass, down near the mouth of the Dragonscar, to make their way back up to the ridge.

Oh, the scouts had found another way up that was much closer to the caves with the gold. Unfortunately, though, until stonemasons and engineers came down and worked that route into a proper pass, it would only provide access to those who were hale and healthy, and on foot.

Great for getting the scouts into position atop the ridge quickly. But not an option for Aefric's party on the return trip.

Backtracking to near the mouth of the Dragonscar had cost them most of their first day's travel.

Aefric did reach out to Karbin by message spell, as they had neared the water. But Karbin was off investigating a lead he'd found aboard the *Swift Wave*, and nowhere near any ships or healers he could send.

And so the march continued.

The land between the Dragonscar and Lake Deepwater was good, arable land. Fine fields, broken up only by small hills and occasional groves of trees. Mostly maples and oaks.

Oh, there'd be more than enough farmland up here to support a mining town or two. Especially around Lake Dragonskull and the Elquill River. That was good.

Possibly too good. Aefric found himself wondering why no one had settled up here before. A river and a lake, and no town or city nearby?

Isolation was one possible answer. The Elquill flowed down out of the Threepeaks, and didn't connect to any larger rivers. So no water traffic.

Still. Aefric's old adventuring instincts wondered if there might be a more sinister reason no one lived between the Threepeaks and the Dragonscar...

Aefric shook himself out of his musings. He had more than enough worries before him already. He didn't need to go hunting for more. The question about settling that area could wait for now.

He shifted his attention to their travel. He didn't expect to run into any trouble, but until he learned who had created those stone simulacra, he couldn't afford to assume safety.

Still, it was a hot day in the seventh aett of summer. Just past the midpoint, and the heat would stick around for some time.

There was some breeze, yes. But as he hiked along, belly full of yet another bowl of that roast chicken stew, Aefric found his thoughts wandering away from the clear skies and waving grass and nearby small pack of birch trees.

Could one of his lers have been responsible for those stone simulacra? They would have had to find and hire a fairly powerful wizard to handle those spells, but some of his lers had money.

Lers were technically nobles, but they were not considered *ranking* nobles. The true ranks of nobility started with the barons. Lers were more like knights who didn't take up arms.

Possible. It was *possible* that one of his lers was behind whatever was happening in the Dragonscar.

Aefric tried to remember if any of his lers oversaw lands in this part of his duchy. Didn't seem likely, given the lack of settlements. Some might control lands nearby, though, closer to Lake Deepwater.

If so, one of those lers might be trying to angle for a promotion to barony. Perhaps hoping to be allowed to hold some or all of the land between the Threepeaks and the Dragonscar in Aefric's name.

Certainly he'd mused more than once during the hike home about the possibility of elevating a baron to look after the people who'd end up settling between the Threepeaks and the Dragonscar. Assuming the king gave him permission to create a new baron, of course.

But he couldn't remember which lers held land where.

The question would have to wait until he returned to Water's End. Which felt like a lifetime away.

It wasn't that bad, of course. "A lifetime away" was how he thought of Oregon these days, and Portland. Of lost Andi, and role-playing games, and tight matches on park basketball courts.

"A lifetime away" was the world where he'd been born as Keifer McShane, before he'd backed a Jumpstart for the next edition of the *Torn Kingdoms* campaign setting, and learned that the duchy he'd "bought" with his support was more than just a piece of paper.

He still thought about his life in Oregon once in a while. And Andi, whom he'd loved so well he'd thought he'd never love again. But his memories of her now were sweet, not painful. And his memories of Oregon brought no longing for those simpler days.

Aefric liked the man he'd become. And the truth was, he was sure Andi would have approved. Not least because she'd always liked his hair long, and she'd love the scars he had these days.

No, Water's End was not "a lifetime away." But it was farther than Aefric wanted it to be.

On the way up, Aefric's party had needed just under a day and a half to reach the Dragonscar from their final civilized waystation, Lachedran.

The large town of Lachedran sat at the northern tip of Lake Deepwater, right at edge of the foothills which led to the Threepeaks

Mountains. No further from Water's End than an hour or two by ship.

But slowly as they had to go, the hike back from the Dragonscar to Lachedran would take them almost four full days.

***

After four long days of marching, Aefric was only too glad to be met by outriders from Lachedran as he approached the crest of one of the larger — if gentler — hills in the area.

The outriders approached in a pack of six, leather clad and armed with both crossbows and either longswords or maces, by their preference.

Their horses had been chosen for speed, and as soon as they confirmed Aefric's identity and the extent of the situation, they sent two of their number riding back at a gallop, seeking healers and wagons.

For his part, Aefric didn't really want to stop. Unless his eyes deceived him, over the tops of those elm trees on the next hill along, he could see signs of smoke. And with a few quick, deep breaths, he was pretty sure he could detect the *scent* of woodsmoke as well.

Late afternoon woodsmoke meant cooking fires.

And if Aefric was right that he could hear the faint sounds of cattle lowing and sheep bleating, they had to be close to the outskirts of Lachedran's surrounding farms.

The town couldn't be far, now.

His feet itched to keep moving. To cover that last distance, whatever it turned out to be.

The last thing he wanted to do was stand here and wait. The breeze had faltered and quit at least an hour ago. He was hot, dirty, sweaty, and more than ready to take a bath. Perhaps sit in a chair, and eat a meal that didn't involve either roast chicken *or* stew. Perhaps not root vegetables either.

And certainly not jerked deer or apples. He'd had enough of those things to last him through the summer.

Still. Aefric held his tongue, and stayed where he was.

Stopping was the right thing to do.

Too many of their number were wounded too badly to take risks. Calling for the healers to come deal with them here was faster and safer.

Of course, not all of the troops were badly off... Some had come through unscathed, and even those who'd suffered only minor bumps and scrapes had recovered well during the hike.

The real concern were those in the litters, and a handful of others. But did that mean *everyone* had to wait here?

Aefric almost suggested sending the healthier troops ahead, so they could get settled and have something fresh to eat. But he knew what Ser Yrsa would say, without even asking.

*Send the troops ahead while your grace remains behind? Does your grace want to insult them?*

Fortunately, the healers and wagons didn't take long to arrive. Only two healers, but several wagons.

The troops then moved the dead — who were as well-preserved as Aefric could make them with the wand Garram and such ice spells as he knew — into one of the wagons, while the healers tended to the living.

At least the two healers the outriders had brought were good ones. Both in the yellow robes and bearing the hand symbol of the goddess Nilasah, goddess of compassion, and patroness of the Guild of Healers and Physickers.

Both healers were dark-skinned humans. The man older — going gray in his black curls and showing smile lines about his mouth — and the woman younger. She wore her long black hair knotted behind her head.

They both had the fitness and vitality that Aefric always imagined indicated they were in good standing with their goddess.

The healing took time. There were only the two healers — quite likely the only true healers in the whole town — and they had to work through their examinations before beginning their prayers. Then came the chants and incense and more.

After all. Those in the litters were in bad shape.

Well, no. They'd been in *bad* shape after the fight with the stone simulacra. At this point, they were in *terrible* shape.

Days of dragging them across the hills and plains of northern Deepwater had not been salutary.

In fact, those men and women needed more treatment than the healers could handle with their travel packs. Those soldiers would need to be in the care of healers for days before they could even recover enough to move about on their own, much less return to Water's End.

But thanks to the efforts of those healers, all six would live. And that was the most important thing. In fact, as Aefric checked on each of them, he saw that festering wounds had soothed and closed, and fevered skin had returned to normal colors and temperatures.

Some of them had begun to smell like death. Now they just smelled like days of effort and travel.

All six were breathing easier, and sleeping. And for the first time in days, their sleep looked comfortable. Almost untroubled.

Nevertheless, the healers kept all six strapped to their makeshift litters as they were moved into wagons for transport.

Of the others who'd been mobile, but too injured for further fighting, they were handled easily enough, once the healers got to them. Splinted breaks and deeper hurts of muscle and sinew were handled with quick prayers and a liniment that smelled like orange blossoms.

Hardly seemed like effort, after the long chants and incense and such that the healers had needed for the others.

And yet with those quick prayers and liniments, the healers mitigated those broken bones and other wounds. Stopping those injuries from getting worse or treading water, and boosting them on the path to becoming whole again.

Even poor Filsan, whose left forearm had been broken in three places, was smiling and rolling his wrist as though the whole arm were a new toy.

It was enough to make Aefric smile.

The sun had been hovering about mid-afternoon when the healers had arrived. It was close to setting by the time they finished, and Aefric's party was ready, at last, to continue on.

---

WITH THE HEALERS HAVING DONE SUCH WORK AS THEY COULD DO OUT here among the hills outside Lachedran, it was finally time to see about going into the town itself.

By this point, the sun hung low in the western sky, and the worst of the day's heat was behind them.

Aefric still felt baked and dirty and smelly, and more than ready to find fresh food, and rest.

Fortunately, the returning outriders had brought drays and wagons enough that none of the troops needed to hike the rest of the way, while Aefric and his knights were now free to ride their horses again, for the final approach.

The outriders split into two groups of three, one group up front to lead the way, and the other group spread out and handling rear guard. And then the whole gathering got underway.

Aefric hadn't paid very much attention to Lachedran, when they'd come through on their way north. His thoughts had already been racing ahead to the Dragonscar. But now he found himself curious about his northernmost settlement.

If any strange and unusual forces kept people from settling the area around Lake Dragonskull and the Elquill River, those forces must never have bothered the people of Lachedran. Not any more than the Godswalk Wars had, and the wars had left the town itself untouched, even though some of its people had died in the fighting.

As the town had grown, they'd never added a second wall around the newer settlements. Certainly they had the money to build one, so Aefric presumed that they hadn't built a second wall because they'd deemed it unnecessary.

Not even so much as a watchtower.

In fact, the defensive fortifications of the farms out here extended only as far as rail fences intended to keep their sheep and cattle at home for the night.

The roads of packed dirt he rode on now were wide, and fairly straight, leading directly towards the town ahead.

They passed a couple of checkpoints — no fortifications there, either, just a couple of guards with spears and a signal horn — on their way past the farms, and then they started onto the cobblestones of the outskirts of Lachedran.

Single-story houses, and occasional two-story buildings out here, all built from wood. Though it did look as though they used stone for their foundations.

The wall surrounding Old Lachedran looked old, but strong. It was made entirely of wood, as well, and stood perhaps thirty feet high. Though Aefric didn't spot anyone patrolling up there.

Definitely not a place used to trouble.

The gates were open, and the spearmen standing guard waved Aefric's party through as though expecting them. Which they probably were.

Here in Old Lachedran, the roads were fire-hardened brick, and a good deal more stone had gone into the construction. Though wood had certainly been used to turn some one- and two-story buildings into two- and three-story buildings.

There was a good deal more activity in this part of town. Out beyond the wall, Aefric hadn't seen many people moving about, or heard all that much activity. But here, barely twenty yards inside the wall, he could hear music and laughter and all the indications of a thriving inn and tavern community.

In fact, he noticed that his soldiers perked up immediately, no doubt hoping to investigate those noises. As well as the delightful smells of roasting mutton and beef and more.

Wasn't just the taverns and inns, either. Aefric could see more people out on foot or ahorse, on about their business even as the sun was setting.

But then, Lachedran *was* a large town, with a good-sized population. No doubt that, like the cities of Water's End and Behal, activity did not stop here just because the sun went down. Already he could see lamplighters igniting oil lamps at intervals along the streets.

Oil lamps instead of torches. Very fashionable of them.

Interesting, though, that the area outside the wall seemed so much more provincial. Was that because the denizens came into Old Lachedran for their nightly affairs? Or did that wall represent a sociological dividing line between the peoples of Lachedran?

Aefric wondered about that as he looked about, riding through the town. Whenever a group of people saw their duke notice them, he got bows or doffed caps and waves, and often wishes of long life or good health.

Aefric's party passed through an open area in the town center that looked as though it were being set up for a market, which was interesting. Most farmers and peddlers markets, of course, began with dawn, not dusk. Which meant it was likely another kind of market entirely...

This was where the healers departed for their temple, along with their charges. Before they left, they promised once more to send regular reports to Water's End, about the soldiers' recuperation.

Aefric's thoughts went back and forth between his wounded soldiers and that strange market setup as they passed further along through the town, to a second, smaller town square, closer to the water.

Here, they came to stop before a pair of three-story buildings, joined by what looked to be a single enclosed hall on the second floor, supported by a pair of pillars down below.

This, Aefric remembered from the trip up. The right-hand house, painted a pale blue, with its mural of flowers surrounding the bottom, was the mayor's house. And the left-hand building, painted Deepwater gray with navy blue trim, housed the mayor's office, as well as the city council, the town historian, the tax assessor, and other important governmental functions.

The mayor, surrounded by servants and aides, stood outside his house, waiting.

The mayor of Lachedran, one Brangton Couglas, had held his

post for more than thirty years. About half his life, to judge by looking at him, but it had been a good life.

He was a heavy man, dusky-hued, with wavy, gray hair and beard, both neatly trimmed. He wore robes in a checked pattern of soft yellows bordered by dark browns, which called attention to his medal of office, which was bigger than Brangton's good-sized fist, and hung from a thick, twisted chain of gold.

"Your grace," he called out in a strong voice. "I've only just heard. What befell you? Is there anything I can do?"

Aefric felt that Brangton was pushing the definition of "just," but let that go.

"Nothing that threatens Lachedran," Aefric said.

He'd already discussed the matter with Sers Yrsa and Beornric, and they'd agreed that the best path here was to hold back what they'd learned in the Dragonscar.

"We fought both smugglers and slavers," Aefric continued. "But they've been dealt with. As for what you can do for me—"

"Of course, your grace," Brangton said. "You and your men need food and rest. I'll see to it at once."

He raised his hands, but before he could clap them, Aefric spoke.

"I appreciate the offer, Mayor Brangton. But what I need from you is to get word to the *Calming Influence* that I'm here and ready to go. It should still be at harbor here, waiting for me."

Brangton frowned, and smoothed the front of his robe. He sounded less pleased when he said, "Forgive me, your grace. I meant only to offer you hospitality. I know you have had a hard march from the Dragonscar, made all the harder for your hurts and losses."

Aefric forced himself to draw a deep breath through his nose, without letting show what he was doing. If the mayor saw that sigh, he might take offense.

And apparently, Aefric had already offended him. A man who'd handled his city for longer than Aefric had been alive.

Politics. He had to remember to balance speed with politics, in all things.

"The error is mine, Mayor Brangton," Aefric said, sliding down from his saddle and stepping up to kiss the man's hand.

Brangton made a surprised and pleased sound, which was what Aefric was hoping for. The kissing of hands, that was to be done for lesser nobles. Brangton, for all his authority as mayor, as not a noble. Not even a ler.

In kissing his hand, Aefric was paying the man a mighty compliment.

"The road overwhelmed my thoughts," Aefric said with a smile, "as it no doubt overwhelms my smell. There is nothing I must do at Water's End that cannot wait until morning. And surely I and mine would benefit from your hospitality not only in body, but in spirit."

"Thank you, your grace," Brangton said, and pressed his forehead to Aefric's knuckles, as though the man actually were a noble.

And with that, Aefric suffered another delay in getting back to Water's End.

As it turned out, there was a special set of chambers on the third floor of the mayor's house set aside for the duke or duchess, when they visited.

The chambers were set at the back of the house, and had a stone terrace overlooking the docks and the lake. Large panes of impressively thin glass, fitted and fixed in place well enough to keep the winds out, when closed.

Despite the hour, a good many boats and ships were out on the water. Including the *Calming Influence*. The great, three-masted warship cut an imposing presence, out in the harbor.

The stone floor of the chambers had clearly just been swept, and the air smelled sweet from the fresh rugs of woven rushes. The rooms were lit by oil lamps, hanging from hooks at intervals on the ceiling.

The furniture was of birch. In the sitting room, there were padded, comfortable couches arranged around a low coffee table.

Seating for six, eight if they got cozy. An armoire contained a selection of cloaks and hoods and boots.

Aefric was impressed at the masculine cut of the cloaks and design of the boots. He hadn't stayed here before, which — he'd expected — meant that everything in here was likely as it had been when Arinda Soulfist was duchess.

And yet, just like at Behal and Water's End, it seemed as though an advance troop of tailors and cobblers had come through, making sure that Aefric had clothing that fit him well.

Kainemorton's work, no doubt. The Mage of Marrisford had likely magically taken his measurements some time ago, and simply passed them along to all interested parties, once it was announced that Aefric would be the new duke of Deepwater.

Speaking of clothing, in the bedroom proper, Aefric found an armoire with a selection of clothes and underclothes that all looked as though they'd fit him.

The furniture in here was beech as well, including the large, comfortable looking bed, with its thick bedspread that would no doubt be too hot as the warm night wore on.

But then, the bedspread was likely there for its look. It was made from soft, padded linens of Deepwater gray, with the Deepwater sigil done large in navy blue.

The bedframe had posts, and a canopy, with gauzy cream-colored fabrics hanging down. At the base of the bed was a chest, currently empty. It had a lock, and the key was in the lock.

Convenient. He put his backpack in there and locked it, pocketing the key.

In one corner of the room was a small altar, with a cabinet underneath that likely held candles, incense, and perhaps a few statues or symbols of the different gods they might expect their duke to revere.

Beside that was a stand with a copper basin and three ewers of water. But the cleaning Aefric needed went beyond what a basin could provide.

No. What he needed was that copper tub over by the fireplace, with water heating for his bath.

Even now a pair of servants — young women, both, wearing simple bodices and skirts in the brown and gold colors of Lachedran — were preparing that bath for him. Aefric smiled as he remembered quipping about his own smell.

Well, if his joke had ensured he'd get a bath before dinner, he'd choose self-deprecation every time.

The fire was a bit much, though, so Aefric said to the servants, "I'll be in the next room. Please call me when the bath is ready."

Both women looked to be fighting against excited giggles as they smiled and bowed and said, "Yes, your grace."

Aefric shook his head. After spending so much of his life as an adventurer — treated hardly better than a mercenary in most places — the idea that he was a kind of celebrity now still took getting used to.

He wandered back into his sitting room, to see that Sers Yrsa and Beornric had arrived. And apparently, while Aefric had been looking around, a servant had brought in a selection of sliced cheeses and meats, and set them on the coffee table with a cut crystal jug of wine, and a set of four cut crystal wineglasses.

"Shall we?" Aefric asked, pointing at the assortment and setting the Brightstaff to stand beside him as he eased down onto a couch with a grateful sigh. His two knight-advisers did the same, on the couch facing him.

He wasn't used to hiking that far anymore. Too much time either flying or riding or sailing. His legs were tight and sore along muscles that felt neglected by his new lifestyle.

After each had partaken of some sliced chicken and a good, sharp cheese, as well as a few sips of crisp, light white wine, Ser Yrsa began the conversation.

"Your grace," she said, "I forbade the troops from carousing tonight."

"Why?" Aefric asked.

"They have fought three skirmishes since we last left Lachedran. They've seen their fellows get wounded or killed. The first chance they'll get, they're likely to overindulge, grateful to be alive and largely intact. I don't want them doing that here."

"Drunk men keep few secrets," Aefric said with a sigh.

"None at all, in my experience," Ser Beornric said. "Which is why I'm very careful when and where I choose to drink more than a touch."

Ser Yrsa snorted. "What you consider a 'touch' is enough to put most folks under the table."

"But I never lose command of my faculties," Ser Beornric said, smiling, and taking a sip of wine to prove his point.

"All right," Aefric said. "There are two servants in the next room, working on my bath. So let there be no spilling of secrets in here either."

"I think you made the wise move," Ser Beornric said. "Staying here tonight. Though you may be paying for that hand-kiss for a while. He's likely to expect it now."

"I did it to prove a point about my apology," Aefric said, raising an eyebrow. "Not to promote the man. He can hope, but he's not likely to get it again anytime soon."

"For the best," Ser Yrsa said softly. "It's no secret that he covets nobility. That gesture may make him an eager servant at a time when we definitely benefit from his good graces."

Aefric held up a hand for silence. He cast about with his focus to make sure he sensed no magic he didn't expect.

All clear. He nodded, and lowered his hand.

"You think he might be involved?" Aefric asked softly.

"Do you want to rule him out?" Ser Beornric asked, and now all three of them were leaning closer and speaking in hushed voices.

"No. He might be the closest person in a position of power, and thus, a likely suspect. No. Keep your eyes and ears open. See what you can find out. But I still intend to be back in Water's End before noon tomorrow."

"Why the hurry?" Ser Yrsa asked.

"I need to know how things went in Ajenmoor," Aefric said. "I want to see to the welfare of those captives. And I want to send a few rika birds, as well as check the most recent news."

"Plans?" Ser Yrsa asked.

"Not sure yet," Aefric said. "Too many variables. But I need to know who the closest lers in question are, and what their standing is. I need to research ... something as well."

He mouthed, "North side cave gold."

Ser Beornric frowned, nodding agreement. Ser Yrsa, apparently, hadn't considered the political implications of that particular gold vein. She blinked rapidly, and took a sip of wine as she considered.

She opened her mouth to say something, but Aefric mouthed, "Not here."

She nodded.

"Your grace?"

Aefric looked up to see one of the servants who'd been preparing his bath, smiling at him from the doorway. The two of them looked enough alike to be sisters, but this was the one with darker brown hair, while the other had hints of auburn in hers.

"The bath is ready for you, your grace," she said with a bow.

The young woman really seemed to relish saying "your grace." She put more feeling into those two words than any others.

"I'll see you both at dinner then," Aefric said to his knights, as he stood.

"Yes, your grace," they both said, before Ser Yrsa added, "Sers Arras and Temet will be on duty this evening."

"Very good," Aefric said, then wandered back into his bedroom, while his knights departed.

The two serving girls were kneeling on a carpet of rushes, beside the tub. They looked from him to the Brightstaff in his hand — a touch of wonder in their eyes as they regarded it — and back.

"You said the bath is ready, yes?" Aefric asked.

"That's right, your grace." This from the one with darker hair, who'd called him in to his bath. "And we're ready to assist, of course."

"May we help your grace out of his clothes?" the other serving girl asked, sounding hopeful and not being very subtle about the way her gaze moved over him.

When he was growing up, Aefric had never thought of himself as particularly attractive. Not in this world, or the other. But he had to admit, since he'd become duke, that belief was being sorely put to the test.

But all he wanted right now was a bath.

"I've been bathing myself since I was a small child," Aefric said. "I think I can handle it."

"Are you certain, your grace?" This from the one with darker hair. "We'd both be most eager to assist."

The one with hints of auburn in her hair nodded rapidly.

"I'm certain," Aefric said. "And I'm sure you both have other duties. Thank you very much."

The one with auburn in her hair looked as though she wanted to say something, but the other one quickly squeezed her forearm, and shook her head.

They both bowed and accepted their dismissal.

Alone at last, Aefric stripped and sank gratefully into the steaming water of the bath.

Already his sore muscles started to thank him.

———

SCRUBBED AND CLEAN, AEFRIC FELT ALMOST LIKE A NEW MAN. HE EVEN smelled like a new man. The soap he'd found had been crafted with bits of lavender in it, which was a much better smell than days of travel.

And Aefric'd had time to think, while in the tub. Too much time, in fact.

He'd come up with at least a dozen reasons why Mayor Brangton couldn't have been behind those stone simulacra. And at least as many reasons why he was a likely suspect.

This was always the problem with speculating when he didn't

have enough information. But if there was a secret to *stopping* himself from speculating at such times, he had yet to discover it.

At the moment, he was leaning towards considering the mayor a likely suspect. The man was situated relatively closely, geographically. He had money, possibly enough to hire the kind of wizard he'd need for those spells.

Probably not enough money to keep such a wizard on retainer. But that only made Mayor Brangton more likely. After all, keeping the wizard around after the spells were cast only increased the chance of discovery.

Most of all, Mayor Brangton aspired to nobility. It was all too easy to imagine him trying to parley the discovery of multiple rich veins of gold into a barony. Say, covering the area from Lake Deepwater to the Dragonscar, and from Lake Dragonskull to the Risen Sea.

*Very* easy to imagine.

But, as always, Aefric found himself coming once more to the place these speculations always seemed to break down.

First of all, if Brangton knew about the gold *and* the simulacra, why hold his silence when Aefric and his party passed through on their way to the Dragonscar?

That was a hard one to overcome. Unless he'd either hoped the simulacra would kill *all* of them — which didn't make sense if the end goal was a noble rank — or he thought they'd be interrupted on their way and have to turn back.

If *that* was the case, then Mayor Brangton knew about the smugglers, and possibly the slavers.

Aefric hoped not. Because if Brangton was working with smugglers and slavers, Aefric would soon be looking for a new mayor of Lachedran.

Further, if Mayor Brangton had discovered the gold, why keep it a secret? Especially why use magic to protect that secret? Why not just come running to Water's End with the discovery?

Surely that would be a faster path to nobility.

Which would mean — if Brangton was the culprit — that nobility alone would not be his motivation.

Unless he'd thought of a different path than going to his duke...

No. That seemed too unlikely to consider. His only other options would be going directly to King Colm, or hoping for support from Duke Wylyn of Silverlake.

King Colm was far too happy with Aefric to support taking land away from him. He'd even expanded Aefric's demesne by the barony of Netar, after Aefric had saved Armyr from invasion this past spring.

A good barony, too. Distant from Aefric's ducal lands, but on the Maiden's Blood River, down near Armityr.

So if nobility alone was not the goal, that begged the question of Mayor Brangton's motivation. Which would start the speculations all over again.

And, alas, much as Aefric might wish to sit in his tub and speculate all evening — if only for the peace and quiet — he had to dress and head down to dinner.

He dried himself with a surprisingly soft linen towel dyed navy blue. From the same place he'd gotten the towel — a cabinet near the fireplace — he found brushes and combs to get his long blonde hair back under control.

He dressed in a silk shirt of royal blue, quite nice and long enough to wear over hose. So he donned black hose to go with the shirt. Current fashion demanded a wide belt to go with the shirt and hose, and Aefric found just such a belt. Black leather, which went with a pair of ankle-high, cuffed shoes.

Unfortunately, the belt was too wide for his sword or his wand. He'd really have to have those sheathes set for hooks or clasps. He'd been too used to needing ... less temporary fixings for such things, while adventuring.

Go tumbling down a mountain just once, and say goodbye to any sword or wand affixed only by hooks or clasps.

But Aefric wasn't likely to go tumbling down a mountain anytime soon.

So he forewent his usual armament, beyond the Brightstaff itself, which went everywhere with him.

He did tie a small pouch of coins and gems to his belt. He wasn't likely to need them, but the habit of making sure he had money on his person was too old to argue with.

He donned a ring woven from sixteen different shades of gold, that featured a large emerald. A gift from the queen. To complete his ensemble, he added a small necklace. A thin gold chain, and featuring only a small sapphire.

A simple necklace, but he liked it, and it worked well with the shirt and his eyes.

He checked himself in the mirror that was mounted near the bath, to make sure that he hadn't committed any fashion sins that could be considered too egregious.

Good enough.

He then put his sword and the wand Garram into the chest at the foot of the bed. He locked the chest, first with the key — which he then put into his pouch — and then with magic.

It wasn't likely anyone would try to steal from him here. But he wasn't willing to chance being wrong.

Finally, feeling ready, he took up the Brightstaff and went into his sitting room. He opened the hallway door to tell his guards to call for a page, but found a servant already waiting with them.

The servant was a young man who couldn't have seen more than fourteen summers, this one included. He was dressed in a simple brown linen tunic and hose that had been dyed a dull golden color.

"Your grace," the servant said with a bow.

"Are you here to escort me to dinner?" Aefric asked.

"Yes, your grace." Poor kid sounded half-scared to death.

"Have I kept you waiting long?"

"Of course not, your grace," the servant said, though when Aefric glanced at Ser Arras, she wiggled her hand to indicate *yes, but not too long.*

"I can assure your grace that they will hold dinner for him as long as he likes."

Wow. This kid was good. He knew the formal forms of address better than Aefric would have expected from a servant in the house of a commoner.

"What is your name?" Aefric asked.

"Edric, your grace," the servant said. "Edric Ol'Nia. Son of Ler Osvalt Ol'Nia."

"Osvalt... Osvalt," Aefric said. "I don't remember your father. Where are his lands?"

"Forgive me, your grace," Edric said. "My father died during the Godswalk Wars. Our land was at the foot of the Threepeaks, on the east side of Lake Deepwater."

"Was?"

"Our lands were destroyed, along with my family, around the Battle of Deepwater, your grace. When I come of age, with your grace's permission, I am to inherit what remains of them."

"Of course you would," Aefric said. "Who suggests you might not? For that matter, who stands regent for those lands right now?"

"No formal regent was assigned, your grace. Duchess Arinda was already dead, and so far as I know the matter was never broached with Prince Killian, when he sat in ducal regency at Water's End."

"No *formal* regent," Aefric said. "So who watches over your family's lands *informally*?"

"Mayor Brangton took on that duty when he took me in."

"And made you a servant," Ser Temat growled.

Aefric forgot sometimes how intimidating Ser Temat could be. First because of his size, for the man was certainly big and strong. And then again because he'd survived that blow that had left a wicked scar across the dark skin of his neck.

Aefric also suspected that his habit of keeping his head shaved contributed as well. Added a hint of scoundrel to his aspect.

Edric paled under Ser Temat's growl, and a bead of sweat trickled down the side of his face.

"Ser Temat," Aefric said softly.

Ser Temat nodded an apology to Aefric, then crouched down to look Edric in the eye.

"I'm angry *on your behalf*, boy," Ser Temat said. "You should be a page in a noble household, learning what it means to be an Armyrian noble. You shouldn't be dressed as a common servant, and you shouldn't be working here."

"Mayor Brangton has been training me as a page," Edric said, showing a fair amount of spine on behalf of his master.

"Mayor Brangton has never had that training himself," Ser Arras said. "So how could he train you properly?"

"That's enough for now," Aefric said, as the poor lad looked too caught between loyalties for further discussion. "Take me down to dinner."

It might just turn out that Aefric had more to discuss with Mayor Brangton than he'd thought.

THE DINING ROOM — *ROOM, NOT HALL, AEFRIC NOTED* — SAT AT THE back of the Mayor's house, on the first floor.

One wall of that room consisted entirely of large, bay windows, and gave a marvelous view of the docks and the lake beyond.

Of course, it also gave a view of the mayor's guards, because there was no wall surrounding the house. So, it seemed, he set a wall of guards outside those windows, because this would be the easiest possible room to break into.

At least, that was the reason Aefric assumed. He didn't intend to ask.

Either way, they were positioned at the bottom of the steps down from the patio outside those windows. Likely so they didn't obscure the view.

The stone floor of the room was entirely carpeted in rugs woven from rushes. And from their sweet smell, they must've been freshly woven.

The long wall facing the windows featured large portraits. Half of that space was dedicated to portraits of the mayor throughout his life, and one more recent portrait, life-size, of the mayor himself and his family.

The other half of the wall featured portraits of past dukes and duchesses of Deepwater, with a space conspicuously left unfilled.

The short walls featured flags. On one side was the Deepwater banner, and on the other, the brown and gold checks of Lachedran.

A pair of large oil lamps hung from the ceiling, providing a warm, yellow light.

The dining table, in the center of the room, was a vague rectangle that looked to have been carved out of a single beech trunk. Though Aefric had never seen a beech tree grow four feet wide.

There was enough room at the table to seat at least twelve, but only half that many chairs and place settings were arranged, leaving the long, middle part of the table empty of seating. It did have a low, fragrant display of colorful zinnias.

Odd, that Mayor Brangton wouldn't invite prominent merchants or others of local importance, to share a meal with their duke. Suggested he had business he wanted to discuss...

Sers Yrsa and Beornric were already present and waiting when Aefric arrived, both dressed casually in tunics of Deepwater gray and hose of navy blue.

The mayor was waiting as well, and smiled broadly as Aefric entered, flanked by Sers Temat and Arras, in their plate armor.

Brangton was dressed as Aefric had seen him before, but this time, on his arm, was a very pretty woman who couldn't have been older than Aefric himself.

She had the pale skin so favored by nobility in Armyr, which went well with her gown, the color of marigolds. She wore her pale blonde hair up in a complicated arrangement, with exactly two strands dangling down to tickle her bare shoulders. Around her long neck she wore a gold necklace studded with diamonds.

Given the gold wedding ring on the middle finger of her right hand, this woman could only be the mayor's most recent wife.

"Most recent" because Aefric knew from the family portrait that the mayor had two adult children — a man and a woman — who looked to be a good ten years older than this blonde woman.

Of course, she was in that portrait too. Seated in the position of the spouse, while the children all stood.

All told, by Aefric's guess, this woman was at least the mayor's *third* wife, because she was too young to have given birth to the other three children present in the room.

The oldest of these children was a black-haired boy of maybe fourteen summers, and the younger two might've been twins. Both girls, both blonde, and both had seen about as many summers as Edric...

Oh. Of course. Mayor Brangton no doubt intended one of those girls to fall in love with Edric and marry him, gaining nobility in his family line at last.

One other person was present in the room, who was clearly not part of Mayor Brangton's family. Or at least, she wasn't in the portrait.

She *looked* to be about as old as the mayor, though her long hair was more of a steely gray, and his more storm cloud gray. She had the thinness that comes with age sometimes, and age spots visible where her arms extended beyond the sleeves of her black silk gown.

Many would mistake her for being about the mayor's age, but Aefric knew better. This woman was a wizard. Competent, to judge by the feel of the magic that hung about her, but not particularly impressive.

Still, competent enough that she probably knew the spells that slowed aging. Which meant either she was much older than she looked, or she eschewed those spells. Something few wizards would do, less out of vanity — though that certainly motivated some — but because the additional years would lead to deeper understanding of the arcane arts.

And though the woman, herself, might not have been too impressive a wizard, she did wear a necklace tucked under her gown that had some sort of noteworthy enchantments laid on it.

"Your grace," the mayor said with a smile, bringing Aefric's attention back to him. "May I present my wife Leca."

Aefric noticed that Leca almost raised her hand to be kissed, but instead curled that hand into the skirts of her dress.

He made no move to kiss her hand, of course. Instead, he smiled and paid the appropriate, expected compliments.

"It is always a pleasure to meet a woman of such beauty and grace."

Leca beamed under Aefric's praise, and bowed at the compliments, though the mayor almost frowned. He got his smile back in place, though, quickly enough that Aefric could pretend to have missed the shift.

"My children, Somfort, Ula and Lila."

"Such fine children," Aefric said, giving them smiles and saying something quick and pleasant about each of them in turn, before gesturing to the adult children in the picture. "Where are the other two?"

"Scilla," Mayor Brangton said with a sigh as he pointed to his eldest daughter's image, "has chosen the life of a merchant sea captain. And she's quite good at it, I fear, so there's no way of telling when I'll see her next."

He pointed at the image of his son.

"Brangford, though, is in Ajenmoor, handling some trade matters for me. He's due back around the end of summer."

Trade matters. A simple phrase to cover a multitude of possibilities...

"Last," Mayor Brangton said with a smile, "but certainly never least, may I present our town wizard, Sufidia."

"Your grace," she said with a weak voice but a deep bow. "I have heard tell of the spells you wove to defeat Malimfar's armies at Frozen Ridge. Your work is a credit to our profession."

"You are too kind," Aefric said, and at last the children were escorted away, and the adults were seated. Aefric at the head of the table, with Ser Yrsa at his right hand and Ser Beornric at his left.

Mayor Brangton sat at the foot of the table, with his wife at his right hand, and Sufidia at his left.

This looked more like the arrangement of a business meeting, than a dinner, to Aefric's way of thinking. Or perhaps a war council.

Aefric wondered which it would be.

———

The six of them were only just seated at opposite ends of Mayor Brangton's dinner table when a lute player came in, and set up in the corner.

She began softly strumming out sweet tunes, while servants brought in the meal.

And Mayor Brangton did not skimp on the meal.

The dinner was a full five courses, six if Aefric counted dessert, which he did. And each course allowed Mayor Brangton to say something about his town.

The salad was a mixture of tossed greens that had been crossbred locally with certain peppers to lend them a little crunch, and a touch of spiciness.

The salad was followed by a light soup featuring three varieties of lake fish that swam close to Lachedran.

Next came a second salad, of mixed citrus fruits, of which Aefric only recognized oranges. Or maybe they were all oranges, merely different varieties. Aefric was more interested in the palate cleansing sweet tastes than Mayor Brangton's story about their local origins.

The citrus salad was followed by a spiced sausage filled with both beef and pork, spiced with a variety of peppers, and a touch of a creamy cheese that lent a delightful surprise to the occasional bite.

The sausage, the mayor explained, was from a local recipe even older than Lachedran itself, going back to the days when this whole region north of the lake was pasture land for peoples who were said to have made their city inside the nearest of the Threepeaks Mountains.

The main course was a rack of lamb, prepared with rosemary and mint, in addition to more local peppers. Delightful.

Finally, the dessert course was a blackberry pie so good Aefric was actually interested when the mayor was talking about the blackberry brambles that grew wild among some of the nearby hills.

Beyond the food, Aefric tried to focus the conversation on

Lachedran, its history, its current state, and any issues Mayor Brangton wanted to raise.

Aefric kept thinking that this arrangement at the table was much too formal for a dinner of this sort. There was too much empty space between the mayor's side and his.

It made the center of the table feel like a demilitarized zone. That the two parties were set up like opposing sides, either in a negotiation or a confrontation.

He kept waiting to find out which. And he expected that continuing to ask questions about Lachedran would bring out the answer.

But if Mayor Brangton had any problems, he pretended otherwise over the course of that dinner. To hear him tell it, everything around Lachedran was wonderful. The people were all happy and well-fed. There were no disputes worth mentioning, and hadn't been in over a hundred years.

Aefric hadn't been a duke very long, but he'd been one long enough to know that *no place* was *that* free of problems.

Which made him wonder all the more what the real story was here. The mayor was clearly hiding something. The problem was, there was no way to tell if what he was hiding had anything to do with what was going on in the Dragonscar.

Frustrating. And to alleviate his frustration, Aefric continued to ask questions that would give Brangton the opportunity to discuss any issues he had that might need assistance.

The man was having an extended, private audience with his duke. Surely he wanted to use it to seek *some* kind of aid. Everyone else always did.

Unfortunately, Brangton kept trying to steer the conversation to Aefric's journey into the Dragonscar. He seemed quite curious about those smugglers and slavers, and the battles that had taken so sharp a toll on Aefric's party.

And whenever he asked about those things, Leca would shiver as though such topics might make her faint.

That behavior tested Aefric's patience. It seemed too much like pretense, as though claiming so delicate a constitution should make her more appealing.

Perhaps that appealed to the mayor, but Aefric preferred his women strong.

He did use her reaction, though, as an excuse to stay away from details. Instead, every time the mayor turned the subject towards Aefric's skirmishes, he replied in the same way.

"The matter has been handled, for now. And Ajenmoor will see to it that neither smugglers nor slavers return anytime soon."

"But they must've been well-fortified with magic," Sufidia said, the third time Aefric gave that response. And she did so before Aefric could turn the topic back to fish, or shipping, or anything else local.

"Not fortified with magic," Ser Yrsa said, "but with surprise. They'd dug in, in a way I hadn't thought they'd have time to prepare. We dug them out well enough though, thanks in no small part to his grace."

"There are more than enough accolades to go around, for the way we survived that battle," Aefric said. "Every one of my soldiers and knights fought fiercely. I may have turned the tide, but they bought me the chance to do so, and their efforts won the day."

"No doubt your grace is too generous," Leca said. "His puissance in battle is well known."

"No battle is won alone," Aefric said, though gently, so she wouldn't feel that he'd taken her words wrong. "Even the most decisive single maneuver is only possible because everyone else did their job and created the opportunity."

"What magic did you face?" Sufidia asked.

"The threat was physical," Aefric said, staying just on the proper side of the line of truth there. Because though the stone simulacra had been created through magic, the blows they struck were purely physical. "As my general observed, the primary advantage our adversaries had was surprise."

"I have never stood to battle, myself," Sufidia said, sounding regretful. "My spells are all those that aid us here in town. Assisting construction, shipping, little twists to the weather here and there. Hardly anything worth noticing."

She shook her head and gestured to the Brightstaff where it stood beside Aefric's chair. "I doubt I could call so much as a puff out of a weapon like that."

"You aren't without your resources," Aefric said, then tapped his collarbone to indicate her necklace.

Her cheeks colored with embarrassment.

"Forgive me, your grace," she said, bowing her head. "I wouldn't have carried an item of magic into your presence, save that I forgot I was wearing it."

"That's fine," Aefric said with what he hoped was a reassuring smile. "So long as you don't intend to use it against me or my knights."

"I ... wouldn't know how, your grace." Her cheeks were almost as dark now as the rich wine they drank. "It's ... it provides me with Moleund's Gift. I ... doubt I could even remove it safely, at this stage of my life."

Moleund's Gift, the formal name for the spells that extended youth. Aefric had never heard of those spells being placed on a necklace. But accusing her of lying would take this meal in the wrong direction.

He could try to sense the magics of the necklace more clearly, but not without her noticing...

No. There was no need to accuse her of lying here and now. And anyway, he could tell she wasn't the wizard behind the simulacra. He would have known in an instant if she were.

Instead he turned the conversation back to Lachedran, and asked to hear more about the trade deals Brangford was negotiating.

The more he could get Mayor Brangton talking about what he was doing for Lachedran, the more likely he'd slip up. If he turned out to have been behind those stone simulacra.

After all, he hadn't invited any other advisers to dinner this evening. Only the town wizard, who clearly had not cast the spells Aefric had found in the Dragonscar.

What better way to allay suspicion than to invite the wrong wizard to dinner?

-------

By the time Aefric returned to his room that evening, he was tired and frustrated.

Dinner hadn't answered any questions for him. He felt no nearer to determining the mayor's guilt or innocence in regard to what was happening in the Dragonscar.

What was more, he found himself concerned over whatever issues the mayor had been trying to hide from him.

True, those issues might have been minor things. Perhaps small points that would have been embarrassing to the mayor, should his duke learn of them, but otherwise unimportant.

But Aefric couldn't dismiss the possibility that those issues might have been large, important things that the duke of Deepwater would need to know.

And since Aefric only knew of two such issues, he kept finding himself thinking of them over and over again, during course of the evening: the Dragonscar, or the boy Edric.

Aefric couldn't raise the issue of the Dragonscar, because he didn't want to tip anything there himself. He certainly didn't need to either alert an enemy about what he knew, or — potentially even worse — arouse the interest of a previously ignorant party.

The last thing Aefric needed was for the mayor to send a scouting expedition into the Dragonscar.

As for the boy Edric, perhaps Aefric was simply irritated with the mayor, but he kept suspecting the man of either trying to marry a daughter to the boy, or directly trying to steal the boy's inheritance.

In fact, no fewer than three times over the course of the meal, Aefric had considered raising the question of Edric and the future of the boy's lands. Just to get the question out into the open.

Each time, he had bitten down the desire to do so. Forced himself to delay that question, for one simple reason.

If Aefric's suspicions proved to be correct, it was a topic to raise *before he left*, not a topic to address while he was enjoying the mayor's hospitality.

Forcing a confrontation about a legal matter over dinner, well, it was the sort of thing that would give Aefric a reputation as a bad guest.

And everyone, from Ser Beornric to his seneschals at both Water's End and Behal, had taken time to make clear to Aefric that proper behavior as both a host and a guest was *critical* to keeping noble society moving.

Much as he wanted to raise the issue of Edric, doing so at dinner would have been wrong. No matter how frustrated Aefric felt at the time.

Ah, well. The most important part of the evening was that Aefric had survived dinner without committing any major gaffes. He'd made it back to his rooms in one piece, and now he could relax. Just sit for a time, looking out over Lake Deepwater and enjoying the momentary quiet.

Perhaps it was better this way. That he'd stayed here tonight, instead of simply boarding the *Calming Influence* and sailing back to Water's End.

Had he done so, he might never have learned of Edric. And since that was true, surely one more night wouldn't make a difference in the boy's future.

Yes. Aefric could handle the Edric matter in the morning. Take the boy along to Water's End, and see him properly fostered.

But then a horrible thought trickled a chill down Aefric's spine.

What if all the servants in this house were the children of lers who'd lost their land in the Godswalk Wars?

How many lers had seen their lands destroyed? How many families, reduced now to one or two heirs who were all but lost to the society that should support them?

How many such heirs might be right here in Lachedran, in the questionable care of Mayor Brangton?

Aefric considered letting that question wait until morning. But then he sighed, because he knew that would be a mistake.

He stood, sighed again, then crossed the sitting room and opened the door into the hall.

"Ser Arras, Ser Temat," he said, for those two knights were still standing guard, and would be until close to midnight. "Would you please have a servant bring me Sers Beornric and Yrsa?"

"Right away, your grace," Ser Arras said, and went to do just that, while Aefric went back into his sitting room to wait.

He found a bottle of brandy, and poured small measures into three glasses while he waited, looking out over the lake and musing about the many ways it seemed that people could fall through the cracks of society.

The knights didn't keep him waiting long, and once all three were seated and had shared a sip of brandy — apple brandy, which was a disappointment — he told them about Edric.

"You think the mayor's making a move for this boy's lands?" Ser Yrsa asked, and Aefric was pleased to note the informality of her tone. Perhaps she *was* finally warming to him.

"I'm not sure if he intends that, or simply to marry the boy to one of his daughters. Either way, I want this Edric coming with us tomorrow. We need to see him properly fostered."

"And you're worried about the other servants now, aren't you?" Ser Beornric asked, proving once more that the knight knew him well. "Whether or not they're all in the same situation."

"No doubt they all talk to each other," Aefric said. "So Edric will know if any of the others are in the same position he is. But if I call him to my room at this hour, my intentions might be ... misunderstood."

"I'll handle it," Ser Yrsa said, rising. "I charged the boy with getting my clothes cleaned. I'll find something to complain about and use it as an excuse to send for him."

"Perfect."

"Is there anything else, your grace?" Ser Beornric asked, and from the way his gaze moved to Ser Yrsa and back, Aefric suspected he'd interrupted the two of them seeking a very pleasant end to the evening.

Well, good for them. Most of his knights were sleeping together in some combination or other. No reason to exclude these two.

"No, that's all for tonight. See you both at breakfast."

They said their goodnights then, and left.

Aefric considered finishing his brandy, but he really didn't want the taste of apple. Not after all the apples he'd eaten over the last aett.

He sat on the couch and sighed, looking out over the lake. Toying with his glass, while he considered the fact that he already had the apple taste of the brandy on his tongue and its scent in his nose, so there really was little to be gained by *not* finishing the glass.

Except that doing so would *strengthen* the taste and smell of the apple brandy. Which would have been very good brandy under other circumstances. If only Aefric were not so very tired of apples...

He was jarred from his musings by a gentle knock on his door.

Aefric sighed, and his shoulders drooped. He felt, in that moment, as though he'd been away from home for half a year, instead of just under an aett.

He should have seen this coming. He really should have. All the signs were there.

The mayor, with his aspirations to nobility. Emboldened by Aefric's regrettable choice to kiss the man's hand, as though he *were* a noble.

Add to that the fact that Mayor Brangton had to have heard by now that the old practice of *leaba* was seeing a resurgence, and Aefric knew exactly who had to be at his door.

Well, not *exactly*. But he had no doubt that it was one of the two young women who'd prepared his bath. Coming to offer him *leaba*.

*Leaba*. Once considered part of hospitality among the nobles of Armyr. It was the practice of offering a visiting noble — a *titled* noble, knights, lers, and others were not included — a bed mate for plea-sure. A volunteer, traditionally a commoner, usually from among the servants.

It had to be offered freely and accepted freely. To coerce someone into participating — on either end — was to commit a grievous wrong.

Aefric didn't particularly want the company tonight. True, he'd felt a flicker of envy when he realized that his two knight counselors had company this evening when he did not.

Still, he had so very many things on his mind. And whoever was standing on the other side of that door, she wouldn't be a woman Aefric could discuss these matters with.

She wouldn't be Maev, or Byrhta.

She would be a near stranger, here only for the bliss moment. Both his and her own.

Were Aefric in the house of a proper noble tonight — one of his barons, perhaps — he could refuse the offer and know that the refusal would be taken the right way.

But for all his aspirations, Mayor Brangton was *not* a noble. Which was why he wouldn't know how to properly foster the child of a ler, like poor Edric. And why Aefric couldn't count on the man reacting properly, should he refuse the offer of *leaba*.

Not exactly *coercion*, but not exactly *free acceptance* either.

Leave it to Mayor Brangton to find a way to put Aefric in an ethical gray area.

The soft knock came again.

Ah well. The one thing Aefric could count on, was that the woman coming to offer him *leaba* would be attractive. Certainly those two sisters who'd been preparing his bath had been most appealing, when he allowed himself to stop and consider them.

He finished off his apple brandy, then called to his knights on the other side of the door.

"Yes?"

The door opened enough for Ser Arras to lean in and speak.

"You have a visitor, your grace."

"Let me guess," Aefric said. "One of the serving women who prepared my bath?"

"No, your grace. The mayor's wife wishes to see you."

---

AEFRIC CONSIDERED JUMPING OUT THE WINDOW AND FLYING STRAIGHT back to Water's End. He could send a rika in the morning. Tell Sers Yrsa and Beornric to bring with them that chest from the ducal bedroom here, along with the boy Edric, and any other lost ler children they might find.

Aefric was a duke, after all. Surely such a thing would just be written off as eccentric behavior. Not a grave insult or anything...

He couldn't do it though. Even if such thoughts weren't more than just a fleeting fancy. Even if he really, really wanted to escape his current situation the old way. The adventurer's way.

He couldn't do it because, right now, Lachedran was too strategically important to what was going on in the Dragonscar. And Aefric needed to maintain good relations here until he both decided what he was going to do about the Dragonscar, and was ready to act.

So he had to deal with the very real fact of a late night visit.

From the mayor's own wife.

Oh, Aefric had known that the man craved nobility, but this. This went well above simple aspiration. Beyond even an improper offer of *leaba*.

This...

One thing Aefric was still getting used to here in Armyr. Among the nobility, sex for pleasure was not only permitted, it was encouraged, whenever there was mutual desire. Even outside of marriage, so long as one or both participants drank the nysta tea, to prevent unwanted conception.

The way it had been explained to Aefric, lust and jealousy had once caused major conflicts, even wars, among the nobles in the early days of Armyr. Problems that had been mitigated, once those nobles were free to share pleasure with any other nobles they found attractive.

As Aefric understood it, the practice had even spread to the common folk, in the trendier of towns and cities.

Socially, the only restriction was that nobles lay with nobles and common folk lay with common folk, with the only sanctioned exception being the practice of *leaba*.

The mayor, for all his dreams of nobility, was of the common folk. And Aefric was a noble. It would be a breach of etiquette for the mayor's wife to come to Aefric to share a night of pleasure.

Technically, Aefric supposed, Leca could offer *leaba*, because she was a commoner. But such an offer still shouldn't, properly speaking, come in this household, because the mayor was *not a noble*.

Frankly, her coming to him this way felt as though she were being prostituted by her husband, in exchange for Aefric's political goodwill.

Easy to imagine. The strong personality of the mayor browbeating the weaker personality of his young wife into coming to Aefric and ... submitting herself.

With that in mind, Aefric shouldn't even let the poor woman into his room.

And yet...

And yet Aefric knew that sending her away would be taken as an insult. Possibly by Leca. Definitely by Brangton. And avoiding that kind of insult was what had led to him staying here in Lachedran for the night in the first place.

Plus, sending her away might even get her punished. Depending on the kind of man the mayor was.

That was speculation, though.

Really, it all came down to this question.

Could Aefric do something personally distasteful, just for his own political ... convenience?

What precedent would he be establishing? That his good graces could be bought with sexual favors?

Or was he overthinking this? Was this part of the gray area of Armyrian sexuality that he just didn't understand yet? Or worse, was this part of some new trend he hadn't heard about yet?

Should Aefric expect to have wives and daughters flung into his bed, anytime he accepted hospitality from some mayor or city councilor or even a major merchant family?

There had to be a limit somewhere, didn't there?

There had to be some—

"Your grace?" Ser Arras prompted, from the doorway.

Aefric forced a deep breath. Tried to relax muscles that had grown quite tense in the last minute or so.

He could at least allow her in. Converse with her for a time. Have a drink. Accept her company. Then, perhaps, he could find a graceful way to avoid accepting ... anything else.

"Excuse me," Aefric said with a forced smile, certain that Leca would hear his words as well. "I was just so surprised by my good fortune that I thought I was dreaming. Please. Do send her in at once."

That smile locked in place, Aefric stood and faced the door as Leca entered.

Her smile was so bright and sincere that Aefric felt his spirits lift, despite himself.

She actually looked ... happy to be here?

Well, at least that alleviated *one* of his concerns.

She wore a soft, dark green woolen cloak, held closed with one hand. Her pale blonde hair was down, loose and bouncing as she padded across the carpeting of rushes with quick steps, while Ser Arras closed the door behind her.

Before Aefric could utter the inane greeting that was the only thing he could think of, she sank to her knees on the carpet before him, head bowed.

"There's no need for that," Aefric said, puzzled, but she didn't look up while she spoke.

"I must thank your grace for receiving me," she said softly. "No doubt your grace believes I should not have come. That because my husband is of common stock, I must be as well."

Aefric wasn't sure what he expected to happen when she came in, but this was not it.

"I ... take it you're not?" Aefric asked, curious now.

"No, your grace," she said, looking up and smiling with both her full lips and her soft brown eyes. She no longer held the cloak tightly closed, and he could see that beneath it she wore only a sheer white chemise.

"My full name is Karaleca Ol'Nara. My brother Morgard and I are the surviving children of Ler Boury Ol'Nara."

Well. This did put things in a different perspective. If she was a noble, her coming to him tonight wasn't a violation of etiquette. And there certainly could be no question of her willingness.

No, from the look in her eye, Aefric could not doubt that this woman was exactly where she wanted to be, doing exactly what she wanted to do.

In fact, her gaze held enough heat to set Aefric's blood racing.

Aefric forced himself to think. To consider her lineage, and what it meant, through a long, slow breath. Put this information in the context of everything else he'd learned since arriving in Lachedran.

For her part, Leca waited patiently, holding his gaze with hers.

"Let me guess," Aefric said. "Your lands were on the other side of the Deepwater, and destroyed during the Godswalk Wars."

"Yes, your grace," Leca said, sounding impressed. "On the northeastern shores of the Deepwater, in fact." A wistful look came over her for a moment. "Wonderful area for freshwater clams and mussels."

"Even so," Aefric said. "Your husband, as you said, is of common stock. Does he not object to ... your being here tonight?"

Leca cocked a pale eyebrow in an expression that showed both more intelligence and more playfulness than Aefric had noted from her at dinner.

"I suspect that my husband would not appreciate my exercising my noble privilege with many. But in your case, he would not object. He is ... *most eager* to make a good impression on his duke." Her smile quirked attractively. "Though he did make sure I drank my nysta tea, before coming here."

Well, there went the last objection Aefric could make. And he had to admit. The woman was really quite pretty.

And he couldn't leave her kneeling like that all night.

"In that case" — Aefric reached down to take her hand — "come join me on the couch."

---

AEFRIC HAD NOT REALLY WANTED COMPANY THAT NIGHT IN LACHEDRAN. He'd wanted time to himself. To savor the peace and quiet, and to consider everything he'd learned on this trip. Both in the Dragonscar, and here in Lachedran.

Still. If he had to have company tonight — and if that company could not be Maev or Byrhta — he could do far worse than Leca. Not only was she quite pretty, with a shapely figure only barely hidden by her thin chemise, but she'd already demonstrated more intelligence and personality than she'd shown at dinner.

Her company might prove more interesting than he expected.

It didn't hurt that she was clearly eager to be here with him.

In fact, the moment Aefric invited Leca to join him on the couch that night, her smile brightened enough to guide passing ships to shore.

"It would be my great pleasure, your grace."

She took his hand, but didn't seem to need it as she rose gracefully to her bare feet. This close to her now, he noticed that she smelled of zinnias.

She raised a bottle she'd held hidden inside her dark green cloak. That wistful look came into her eyes again for a moment.

"This is the last bottle of sharabi I have, from the last vintage produced by our vineyards before the wars," she said. "It would mean a great deal to me if your grace would share it with me."

"I'd be honored," Aefric said, and fetched them two wine glasses from a beech cabinet along the wall.

Sharabi was technically a kind of wine, but Aefric had never himself seen the grapes it was made from. He knew only that it came in several varieties, all of them shades of green.

This sharabi was an emerald green, and had a delicate, almost minty aroma.

"If you've never had the Ol'Nara vintage, your grace, may I suggest that you hold your first taste on your tongue. You will know when it is ready to swallow."

"Very well," Aefric said with a smile. "What shall we drink to. Lachedran?"

"No," Leca said, raising her glass. "We shall drink to your grace. May your firm hand guide Deepwater to new heights of prosperity for all its peoples."

That, Aefric would definitely drink to.

Leca was right about the sharabi. Its flavor was complex. It began as a crisp taste, with hints of mint, but evolved a sweetness the longer it lingered on the tongue.

When he swallowed, it *felt* as good going down as it tasted.

Before the next sip, Aefric raised his glass once more in toast.

"Let us next drink to the Ol'Nara family and lands. May you and your brother restore both, and may your vineyards produce many more fine bottles of sharabi."

"From your grace's lips to the ears of the gods," Leca said, smiling, and they drank again.

That finished their glasses. He hadn't filled them very far, in case the sharabi turned out to be stronger than he expected. But it didn't seem to be any more alcoholic than most light wines.

Aefric reached for the bottle, but Leca interrupted him.

"Now," she said, her voice teasing, "there *is* a way to improve the taste of the sharabi even further. But it's not for everyone."

"I'm willing to try," Aefric said. "What is—"

She leaned in and kissed him. Deeply. Passionately. She kissed him as though she'd been burning to kiss him for hours. Perhaps longer.

Aefric found himself caught up in that kiss. His heart pounded. Need coursed through him. He swept her up into his arms.

Their glasses, forgotten, fell to shatter on the floor. She was in his lap now, whimpering into his mouth as their kiss went on. Her hands roamed over his arms and chest as hungrily as her tongue worked in his mouth.

The presence of her chemise was maddening. Aefric's hands could feel the delightful contours of her body underneath, but already he found he yearned for the sensations of the fevered skin beneath.

It was all he could do not to simply rip the garment in half.

That first kiss finally ended, and Leca's smile made Aefric realize he tasted three things: the mint, the sweetness, and her.

He chuckled breathlessly.

"As I was telling your grace," Leca said softly, her fingers playing in his hair. "The right tongue improves the taste."

"Tell me then," he said, gently stroking her neck and shoulder. "Does anything else improve the taste?"

"I can think of a few things," she said, heat all through her voice now, "if your grace is willing to try them."

He picked her up and carried her into the bedroom.

Leca proved to be an enthusiastic, adventurous lover. Not at all the shy, hesitant woman she'd pretended to be at dinner.

Afterward, as the two of them lay sated for a time, they spoke first of small matters. She asked about his scars, and how he'd come to possess the Brightstaff. He asked about how she'd grown up, and how her life in Lachedran had been.

But then Aefric asked two questions he'd been waiting to ask.

"Who is to inherit your family lands, you or your brother?"

"Morgard is my elder by three summers, your grace," she said. "He would have taken possession of our lands already, but for two things. He needs to be formally acknowledged by your grace, and he needs funds to begin rebuilding."

"Obviously I'll be happy to see to the former. And as for the latter—"

"Oh, he's been working towards it for some time now, your grace," she said, nuzzling Aefric's shoulder. "He works with Brangford, and invests when he can."

"Where is he now, then?" he asked, stroking the soft skin of her shoulder and side. "Here in Lachedran, or in Ajenmoor with Brangford?"

"In Ajenmoor, your grace." She raised her head and gave Aefric an almost fretful look. "It's the first time he's left town on business, and I confess I miss him."

"No doubt he'll return soon."

"I hope so." She walked her fingers across Aefric's chest and smiled. "Distract me, your grace?"

"Happily," Aefric said.

He kissed her, and then they sought deeper distractions together.

When next they rested, savoring languorous contentment, Aefric fetched the bottle and more glasses, and they drank sharabi in bed, speaking of little matters and paying each other little compliments until Aefric asked another important question.

"I am troubled to hear how you and your brother were displaced by the wars. Do you know of any children of nobles in similar situations?"

"Only Edric, your grace."

"That serving boy?" Aefric asked, as though uncertain. "The one who escorted me to dinner?"

"Yes, your grace," Leca said with a smile. "Did he do well? I assigned him the task myself."

"Very well," Aefric said.

"Good," she said, then sighed deeply, which in her current naked and glistening state was distracting. Fortunately she continued speaking before Aefric found himself *too* distracted.

"I'd wanted him assigned to my brother, for proper page training, like Morgard went through when he was young. But Brangton insisted on keeping Edric here in the house. Said he could train the boy just as well."

Aefric frowned and sighed deeply as he shook his head.

Leca's turn to get distracted, watching his chest rise and fall with the sigh.

"So many muscles for a wizard," she said softly, reaching out with her free hand to run her fingers over his chest. Circling the scar on his ribs that had been left by the point of a tarok's spear, long ago.

"I trained as a dweomerblade as well," he said softly. "With the Iron Wands."

"Very impressive, your grace."

Aefric drew another deep breath, enjoying the touch of her fingers, before forcing his attention back to important matters.

"But about Edric," he said. "He really ought to be formally fostered. Trained as a page in a noble household, taught the ways of nobility, and then prepared to inherit and run his family lands, once he's of age."

"I agree, of course," Leca said, then tossed down the last of her sharabi and leaned back to set her glass on a nightstand. Her gaze roved over Aefric's naked body the whole time.

"I'll bring him with me to Water's End, then," Aefric said. "See him placed with an appropriate household."

"That would be wonderful, your grace," she said, stalking closer now on her hands and knees, sleek as a hunting cat.

Leca snatched Aefric's glass from his hand. Poured the last of his sharabi on his chest. It felt cool and sticky against his skin.

She tossed the glass away to shatter over by the hearth.

Aefric tried to make a joke about Leca having to clean that up, but never got the chance.

She pounced, pinning him to the mattress, and started licking the sharabi from his chest.

That was the end of their conversation for quite some time.

**4**

———————

Aefric and Leca were awakened the next morning by the two serving girls who'd prepared Aefric's bath the night before.

Outside, the sky was still dark, with the first hints of the graying dawn on the horizon. What light they had here in the bedroom was provided by candles the servants carried, though they quickly lit the oil lamps, bringing a warm yellow glow to the shambles of the bed.

Aefric shared a good morning kiss with Leca that tasted more of mint than Aefric expected, and came away from it smiling.

"Another blessing of our sharabi," Leca said. "Avoids morning breath."

Aefric chuckled, and started to get out of bed, already thinking ahead to his travel and plans, and certain that Leca would want to begin her own day.

Apparently Leca had other plans.

She grabbed him by the arm and tugged, while lying back among the sheets.

"Are you sure about this?" Aefric asked quietly, gazing into soft brown eyes that definitely *looked* certain.

"Who knows when I'll get to share a bed with your grace again?" she said softly, and gave him an enticing smile. "So I want very much to lie with my duke one more time, before he returns to Water's End. *If* your grace will permit me that pleasure, of course."

"Permit it?" Aefric whispered, smiling despite himself as he looked her over. "Why, I find I'm tempted to insist upon it."

"Clear the room," Leca said to the servants. The moment they were gone she spread her arms, quirked a smile, and said, "I am, of course, *entirely* at your grace's command."

She was a compelling woman, in her way, and far more interesting than Aefric had originally believed.

In that sense, it was probably a good thing she was married. Which was one of the odder thoughts he'd ever had about a woman who was sharing his bed.

But at the moment, far more pleasant facts about her demanded his attention.

Once they were finished, with one more kiss for good measure, Leca donned her chemise and cloak and left with a light step.

As he watched her go, Aefric realized there was one downside to their last hurrah. He no longer had time for a bath.

So while the servants fussed about, he did his best to wash up at the basin, then donned clothes from the armoire. He probably should have had his traveling clothes cleaned, as Ser Yrsa had, but he simply hadn't thought to do it. Not with Water's End so close.

He could have cleaned his clothes with magic, of course, but he wanted to get out of that habit. It was important for the servants to have their work.

He chose soft, brown leather pants that would work well with his usual belt, and let him carry his wand and sword again. For a shirt he selected a soft, red tunic trimmed and embroidered with gold thread.

No jewelry today, though. Not for travel. The jewelry went back into his backpack.

Then, hair combed, he called the Brightstaff to his hand and told the serving girls — who were, at this point, changing the bedding — that he was ready to be escorted to breakfast.

Aefric had been hoping that Edric would be his escort, but the serving girl with the hints of auburn in her hair abandoned the bedding to escort him herself.

This morning Ser Vria and Ser Wardius were on active guard duty, and flanked Aefric as he followed the serving girl back down the stairs to the same dining room for breakfast.

Breakfast was a much more stilted affair. And not just because the children were present, seated in the middle of the table and trying very hard to avoid drawing attention.

They even dressed as though trying to remain invisible. They wore simple outfits of neutral colors that might almost have been chosen for their ability to match the chairs they sat on.

Sufidia was absent this morning. Apparently this meal was only for family and guests.

The mayor was dressed in shades of dark red today that gave him a grand look, going well with both his weight and the medal of office, around his neck.

Leca's burnt orange dress was of a light, summertime weight. Though it was far more covering than what she'd worn the night before, beginning with a high collar and falling as low as her ankles, with hints of red silk showing through slashed sleeves that extended down to her wrists. For jewelry, she adorned only her wedding band and a silver necklace that featured a yellow diamond.

Aefric tried not to think about whether or not that necklace was a specific allusion to the much larger yellow diamond atop the Brightstaff, standing beside his chair.

She didn't help the matter by toying with her diamond once in a while, when he happened to be looking at her.

Mayor Brangton himself seemed ... out of sorts about something this morning.

Aefric devoutly hoped the mayor wasn't having second thoughts about approving Leca's visit to his room. But if so, he didn't demonstrate any displeasure with her, or with Aefric.

It just seemed more that his thoughts were elsewhere.

Aefric was trying to decide how much he could trust his read of the situation. Because if something *was* troubling the mayor, he wanted to know what.

Unless what troubled him happened to be what Aefric and Leca had done last night. And that morning.

Yes. That would be just about the only thing that could make the morning breakfast even more awkward than it felt already.

For her part, if Leca noticed the stilted sense to the room, she ignored it. Or perhaps she was determined to overcome it.

Because she was obviously in a marvelous mood, carrying the conversation about Lachedran mornings, the bustle of the docks and the city and the like.

She spoke enough that no one else really had to, while they all ate oat bread sweetened with honey and a selection of sliced meats, cheeses, and fruits. With the meal, as appeared to be the breakfast custom throughout Armyr, they drank only fresh water.

The mayor seemed to take little interest in his food, and none at all in the conversation, until Leca said, "Oh, and your grace, I've already told Edric to pack his belongings. He'll be ready to leave at your grace's command."

Those last three words. She made them sound so innocent. And yet, from the sparkle in her eye, Aefric suspected those words would forever be a private joke between them.

Before Aefric could follow that thought too far afield, the mayor finally spoke up.

"What's this? What's this about Edric?"

"Oh, isn't it wonderful, Brangton?" Leca said excitedly. "His grace has offered to take the boy to Water's End and see him properly fostered and trained."

"But ... we can handle those things here," Mayor Brangton protested. "Your grace, surely there's no need to trouble yourself about the boy."

"There's every need," Aefric said, softly but firmly. "As the merchants, sailors, farmers, miners and other common folk must know that they have their duke's love and support, so too must the nobles know this."

"But—"

"Edric is the son of a ler. And I understand he is the inheritor of his family's estate. As his liege, it is my responsibility to see to it that he is trained and prepared to handle his duties. Fosterage, and page training, are only the first steps."

"And yet your grace never had such training—"

Leca dropped her fork. Ser Beornric slammed down his water glass. Ser Yrsa threw down her knife.

All three glared at Mayor Brangton.

Apparently making such a statement about one's duke was even more of a breach of etiquette than Aefric would have thought. Which, in its way, might have been proving the mayor's point.

Ser Beornric and Ser Yrsa both drew breath, likely to say something scathing.

Leca spoke up first.

"Your grace," she said, rapidly and urgently. "Please forgive my husband for his poorly chosen words. Clearly his love for the boy has made him *forget himself*."

Mayor Brangton still looked as though he wanted to argue. Started to say something, but Leca didn't give him a chance.

"*Obviously*," Leca said quickly, her gaze shifting from her husband to Aefric and back as she continued, "we are *both thrilled* that his grace takes such an interest in even the least members of his nobility. And we are *both quite pleased* that we have been able to bring this matter to your grace's attention, and to see that Edric's ascension to *his proper role in society* is assured."

During this interplay, Aefric noticed the reactions of the children.

Both Ula and Lila paled and bit their bottom lips to keep from talking. Somfort only expressed himself in the universal language of teenagers.

He scowled.

Finally, though, one of the girls spoke.

"Must Edric leave us, your grace?"

"I'm afraid so," Aefric said gently. "I'm grateful that your family was able to take him in after the wars. But now it's time for him to live with a noble family. And learn what it will mean to serve as steward to lands in his duke's name."

Mayor Brangton bowed his head.

Leca watched him as though not certain she could trust him to speak for himself. But with the silence stretching uncomfortably in the room, she gave him the chance.

Mayor Brangton drew a calming breath, seeming to put himself together as he did. He ran his hands down the front of his robes, and touched his medal of office, and those actions seemed to help.

"My dear wife is quite correct," he said, then smiled. "As she so often is." He drew another breath and said, "Please excuse my ill chosen words, your grace."

"Think nothing of it, Mayor Brangton." Aefric smiled, and assisted Leca's effort to help the mayor save face. "I know you've come to love the boy. You are free to write, of course, and he to visit, in time. But this really is what's best for him."

"Of course, your grace," Mayor Brangton said, and the man's smile looked strained.

"Can we write too?" one of the girls asked, though Aefric wasn't sure if this was Ula or Lila. Either way, the other nodded her head rapidly.

"Of course," Aefric said. "And if you wish, in time, you might be allowed to visit him as well."

Aefric doubted that very much, but the poor things looked too heartbroken already.

"But I must ask, Mayor Brangton," Aefric said. "If you have not been troubled this morning over thoughts of missing the boy when he leaves, what then troubles you so?"

"Oh," Mayor Brangton said. "Forgive me, your grace. I've just had a rika from my son. Negotiations in Ajenmoor ... are not going well."

"I'm sorry to hear that," Aefric said. "May I ask what the matter is? I might be able to assist."

"Your grace is most kind and generous," Mayor Brangton said, sounding much more himself. "But this is a simple matter of business. And as the business is personal, not that of the town, I would not feel right about exploiting your grace's generosity for my personal gain."

Leca's eyes actually widened in surprise for a moment, before she caught herself and put her smile back in place. But when she met Aefric's eyes, he had no doubt.

The mayor was lying.

The only question was, about what?

---

Aefric had originally intended to board the *Calming Influence* at about dawn, and be back at Water's End by midmorning.

He should have known that leaving Lachedran would not be so simple. He really should have. A full season now, he'd been a duke. He'd had plenty of time to adjust to the realities of travel as a noble, compared to travel as an adventurer.

The problem was that for the last several days, he'd been living like an adventurer again. Out in the field. Handling his own backpack. Camping every night.

Old habits of thought and expectation had come back quite easily.

When Aefric had been traveling on his own, or with an adventuring band, leaving anyplace was rarely more complicated than gathering together his pack, and either setting out on foot or ahorse.

As a duke, nothing was ever quite so simple.

First, it was expected that he wouldn't gather his own possessions, for travel. He was supposed to *send* someone for them. Of course, given that Aefric's backpack was sitting in a chest *locked by magic*, this was not an option.

And yet, explaining this fact to the mayor's majordomo took longer than Aefric would have needed to just retrieve the backpack himself in the first place.

Didn't help that the majordomo, Pleton, was an officious, furtive little man in black velvet, who seemed to look more and more ratlike, the longer Aefric had to deal with him.

Likely that was just Aefric's irritation.

Likely.

Even after the backpack issue was resolved, Aefric *still* had to wait while his clothes and other belongings were fetched by servants. Because that was how things were done.

And then the majordomo *smelled* those clothes with his twitching little nose, and took his servants to task for not having had their duke's garments cleaned the night before.

A high-pitched tongue-lashing that might have gone on for some time, had Aefric not, finally, cleared his throat loudly.

Even then, Aefric had wasted more time explaining to the majordomo that no shame would fall on the mayor's household if their duke returned to Water's End with a pack full of smelly clothes.

The majordomo refused to believe this, until Aefric finally *insisted* that he did not have time to wait while his clothes were cleaned.

At that point, Leca had to step in and speed up the process. The mayor himself was busy, though whether that was with town matters or personal matters Aefric didn't know.

Once Leca became involved, the leaving process accelerated. She clearly knew how to run the household and the majordomo. She even made sure that Edric was dressed in a fine tunic and breeches for the trip. And he carried the rest of his belongings in a small, brown canvas pack. His wide eyes looked torn somewhere between terror and excitement.

Nevertheless, even with Leca's aid, it was almost midmorning by the time Aefric got to say his goodbyes to the mayor — who would not miss his duke's departure, of course — Leca, the children, and Sufidia.

Aefric's knights and troops — along with Edric, and a covered cart carrying the soldiers who fell in the Dragonscar — were gathered on the cobblestones outside the mayoral buildings. Ser Yrsa had already reported that all were present and accounted for, save the six who were in the healers' care. Further that all of Aefric's people had reported being fed and treated well during their night in Lachedran.

It was already a warm morning, and the fresh smell of the lake was calling to Aefric. As he mounted Windsong and took his place flanked by Sers Yrsa and Beornric near the head of their procession, Aefric started to believe he might get back on something like a reasonable schedule.

If the winds were fair. And from the snap of his banner, held aloft by the soldier riding behind Aefric, the winds showed promise.

The delays, however, were not over.

Aefric had raised his hand to give the order to move out, when the majordomor cried, "Wait!" and came running up, waving his little hands.

The man really should have had a tail to stroke nervously.

Before Aefric could even ask, the reason for this delay became apparent.

Mayor Brangton, Leca, and Sufidia came trotting up on dappled geldings, with the children following behind, on ponies.

"Come, your grace," Mayor Brangton said with a smile so bright that Aefric immediately felt suspicious. "Let us see you to your ship."

Spear-carrying town guards walked ahead of the procession, ostensibly to clear a path.

A task that became necessary sooner than Aefric would have believed.

The area of that small square in front of the mayoral buildings had been kept clear, it turned out, while most of the population of Lachedran had been working their way down towards the docks.

Some on foot, some riding, and some in carts and wagons. But they were all coming to the docks. And had been, for quite some time. And it didn't look as though any of them had come for their usual daily work.

No. Aefric had the building suspicion that the better part of Lachedran's population had gathered down by the docks, for no other reason than to see their duke on his way.

In fact, there were already food peddlers moving among the crowd to sell their wares.

And that wasn't all.

The docks of Lachedran were made from pale wood. Likely

beech. And every so often, at the base of the piers, raised platforms had been built, where fish were sorted. And possibly sold.

Once such platform had been cleared of fish. Recently, by the smell. And a small brass band had set up in one corner.

The brass band started playing a fanfare as Aefric and the others approached.

Aefric once more considered simply taking to the air and flying back to Water's End. Surely no one could blame him...

No. No. No point in offending an entire town. Whatever was coming, he could handle it.

And so, a short time later, he found himself *standing* on that platform, along with Sers Yrsa and Beornric — with Edric half-hiding behind Ser Beornric — the mayor, his wife, his children, and Sufidia.

The town guard had tried to form a ring at the bottom of the platform. Aefric's knights and troops handled it themselves.

The midsummer sun had started beating down heavily now, and the day would be hot already if not for the building westerly wind. Which was in Aefric's face as he looked over the crowd.

Aefric had to swallow his frustration, though. Because when he looked out over the crowd, he saw eager faces gazing up at him. Some of them were calling his name or wishing the gods' blessings on him. Others were praising him as the Hero of Deepwater, or the Hero of Frozen Ridge.

Suddenly he realized that this little bit of ... pageantry was important to the *people* of Lachedran, not just their mayor.

Aefric felt his stomach twist into knots.

All these people. He'd never meet most of them. Not personally. He'd never know their names. Never know if they had good, happy lives or sad, miserable lives. Most of them would live — however long they lived — and never even see him again.

And yet, every day he made decisions that affected them. From little things like the details of trade agreements he brokered or arranged, to taxes and construction efforts, to the potentially large things like that gold in the Dragonscar.

Every one of these people would flourish or suffer by what he did as duke. And not just them. Thousands and thousands of others, all across his lands. And their children and grandchildren.

All these people, smiling and waving and wishing him well. They were missing work for this. For some of them, this would be a moment they talked about later. The day they saw the duke.

They would remember what he wore. How he behaved, up here on this stage before them.

Aefric owed these people the best he could do for them.

And right now, that meant smiling and waving. Meeting eyes where he could.

"Good people of Lachedran," the mayor boomed out, and at his words the crowd grew quiet to listen. "Thank you all for taking time out of your busy days for the unexpected blessing of our duke's presence. His grace returns to us after facing horrors on our behalf."

A gasp from the crowd.

"His grace personally stood to battle with smugglers."

A few outcries from the crowd, likely from merchants.

"His grace personally stood to battle with *slavers.*"

At that, the whole crowd seemed to call out their anger with one voice.

"And yet, through the grace of the gods, the magic of his calling, and the strong arms of his warriors, our duke returns to us triumphant!"

The mayor gave the crowd a moment to cheer their duke.

Aefric did his best to keep his smile in place. Inwardly he hoped no skald started calling him the Hero of Dragonscar or similar rubbish.

Frankly, talking about those fights just made Aefric wonder how Karbin was doing, tracking the slaver ring. If the refugees had been given homes and work yet. How Ge'rek and Po'rek were doing up in the Dragonscar...

"His grace will now return to Water's End," the mayor continued. "But I knew that before he left, his people here in Lachedran would wish to convey their thanks for all he has done for them."

The cheer that followed was embarrassingly loud.

"And now," the mayor said, giving Aefric a smile, "perhaps his grace would be so kind as to favor us with a few words about his battles, before he leaves?"

Aefric stomach sank and his mouth went dry.

Yes. He definitely should have just flown back to Water's End.

---

SOMEHOW THE MORNING SUN, HERE ON THIS FISH-SMELLING PLATFORM above the Lachedran docks, felt hotter than it had a moment before.

The wind was blowing. Aefric knew that. He could feel it on his face. But he couldn't hear that wind to save his life. No. His ears were far too busy listening to the rush of his racing blood.

Compared to that sound, the huge crowd gathered here on the pale wood of the docks seemed to be completely silent. Waiting to hear their duke ... what?

Give them a speech? About battles?

What in the thirteen hells had the mayor been thinking? Asking for Aefric to "say a few words" about battles against smugglers and slavers.

And yet, Aefric had to say ... something.

He found himself remembering his life a world away. A life in which he was known as Keifer, and lived in a country where leaders were elected, not born or made.

A world where those leaders had to win favor with speeches. Interviews. Debates.

As Keifer, he had heard the words of politicians on many occasions. And a key point that had frustrated him then might be of use to him now.

Those politicians, they never answered questions. Not really. Instead, they simply took the opportunity provided by a question to talk about whatever they wanted to talk about in the first place.

The mayor wanted Aefric to give the people of Lachedran a brief speech? Well, fine. He could do that. And he didn't have to talk about anything as ... distasteful as recounting a battle.

Aefric smiled as he stepped forward. He gave a quick nod to the mayor and his family — getting bows from them in return — then turned to the crowd.

He raised his free hand. He was tempted to call light out of the Brightstaff in his other hand, but given the strength of the morning sun, the effect wouldn't be very impressive anyway.

"Good people of Lachedran," Aefric said. "It brings me great pleasure to be among you today, after spending the night in your delightful town."

There was a burble of approval from the crowd, so Aefric waited a moment for it to die down.

"I even got to partake of some of your marvelous cuisine. Your delicious spiced greens, your lake fish and lamb. And perhaps most important, the very variety of sausage made in this area since before there was a town."

The townsfolk's approval was louder this time, and full of pride.

"I found the local fare clever, with strong roots, and a hint of spiciness," Aefric said. "Rather like the people, I expect."

That got him some cheers.

"Would that I could pass a full aett here in Lachedran, getting to know your town and its people. But an aett would not be enough. I would need at least a season. And still I would fall short."

Aefric hadn't planned to pause after that line, but the crowd didn't give him any choice. They cheered louder yet.

"But as your duke, my first thought must never be of my own desires and pleasures, but the duties that I owe to my people. And so, much as I might enjoy staying here all the way through the harvest festival, I must set sail this morning for Water's End. Duty calls, and I must answer."

Mixed response to that one. Some were cheering, but others actually called for him to stay.

"As your mayor mentioned, there have been problems with smugglers and slavers. I would see those problems ended. And that's not all."

They were quiet now, listening, and Aefric let them wait just a moment before he continued, in somber tones.

"We saved refugees, in those battles. People just like yourselves, save that they were displaced by the Godswalk Wars. Destitute, they wandered, seeking new lives, new homes, only to find themselves *snatched up* by slavers."

The crowd began to jeer the slavers. Aefric spoke louder to be heard above them.

"*I won't have it.* I will find homes for those refugees, here in Deepwater. I will find work for those refugees, here in Deepwater. And I will work to find all the people *of* Deepwater, commoner and noble alike, who were displaced during the wars. And I will see them *restored.*"

The crowd roared its agreement.

"Now, I know this is a large task," Aefric said. "And I know that I will need the help of many to see it through. But the process must begin *somewhere*. And the process must begin *sometime*. And I say that this process will begin *today*. Right here in Lachedran!"

The crowd's approval bordered on frenetic.

Mayor Brangton began to step forward, as though Aefric were giving him a cue.

Aefric gestured to the mayor and said, "Now, I know that Mayor Brangton would be only too happy to undertake this task on my behalf."

The mayor started to raise his hands to speak. But Aefric kept talking.

"But I also know that Mayor Brangton keeps a very busy schedule just looking after the interests of this marvelous town. And this is not a town matter. This is a duchy matter. I would not steal your mayor's time for my own project."

The mayor frowned, but lowered his hands.

"And so," Aefric said, "I would charge his wife, Karaleca Ol'Nara, with this task. If she is willing."

Aefric turned and looked at Leca.

She looked astonished, but the smile she gave Aefric was both sincere and determined.

She stepped forward.

"Your grace," she said in carrying tones, "I would be both pleased and proud to see to this task. I will form a committee and begin the process this very day!"

The crowd cheered.

"Then I am twice blessed that I came to Lachedran," Aefric said, addressing the crowd. "And I may leave you now, confident that Lachedran will lead the way once more, and help me help those who believe they have lost everything. Good people of Lachedran, I thank you."

As the crowd cheered, Aefric turned to Mayor Brangton and Leca.

"Mayor Brangton, I thank you again for your hospitality. You have an excellent town here, and I know that you will continue to steer it in the right direction."

"Thank you, your grace," Mayor Brangton said, and bowed.

"Leca, thank you for agreeing to be part of my vanguard in this. It's important to me that we find all those displaced by the wars, and I know that you will do the job well."

"I am grateful for the opportunity, your grace," she said with a bow. "I will find all those who have been lost."

"I'll want you to coordinate with my historian, as well," Aefric said. "She has all the records, as well as copies of all the patents of nobility. After all, there might be those who try to fake their way to an elevated status. I won't have that either."

"I will be careful, your grace."

"I know you will." Aefric turned to the town wizard. "Sufidia, it was a pleasure to meet you. Perhaps next time we can discuss arcane matters."

"Nothing would please me more, your grace," she answered with a creaky bow.

"And now," Aefric said, turning to Sers Beornric and Yrsa. "Can you get us to the ship?"

"I'll see to it at once, your grace," Ser Beornric said.

Good. Because the morning grew later, and Aefric still had much to do.

———

AT LONG LAST, AEFRIC STOOD STOOD ABOARD THE *CALMING INFLUENCE*, right at the bow of the ship. So close that he could touch the figurehead, if he had any interest in touching a representation of a water nymph. Which he did not.

The great, three-masted warship weighed anchor, turned its sails to the wind, and began cutting water on its way out of the harbor.

The winds out here kept the worst of the morning heat at bay, as the *Calming Influence* built up speed, moving past the local fishing boats, as well as trading vessels, pleasure cruisers and others.

Sers Beornric and Yrsa joined Aefric here at the bow, where the captain had assured him that they would not be in the way, and could speak without being overheard.

Of course, given the number of knights, soldiers and horses traveling on this ship, Aefric sincerely doubted that at least *some* of them weren't in the way.

Oh, well. Couldn't be helped. At least the sailors would be too busy to care about their duke's secrets anyway.

"I've left young Edric in Ser Vria's care," Ser Beornric said.

Ser Yrsa chuckled. "Should have seen the boy staring at her. Like he'd never seen a half-eldrani woman before."

Likely true. There weren't very many eldrani men *or* women in Deepwater. So likely the lad had never seen such beauty before in his life.

"Ought to be careful with that," Aefric said with a smile. "Might start him into puberty early."

"Might," Ser Beornric said. "But she's good with people. She'll get him talking. Give him something to think about other than walking away from everything he knows, for the second time in his life."

"You think I made a mistake?"

"Not at all, your grace," Ser Beornric said. "It's a good thing you're doing."

"Doesn't make it any easier on the boy though," Ser Yrsa said. "Hope you can find him a gentle household."

"I'll see what can be done," Aefric said, then sighed. "Assuming we can confirm that he *is* the son of Ler Osvalt."

"I saw his patents," Ser Yrsa said. "He showed them to me this morning like they were the most precious thing in the world. Told me he used to carry them in his shirt, tied to his belly. Before he came to live with the mayor." She shrugged one shoulder. "Look authentic to me."

"Good," Aefric said. "The historian will have to confirm them, of course, but that shouldn't be a problem."

"What about the mayor?" Ser Beornric said. "Do you think he'll be a problem?"

"Maybe," Aefric said. "I can't help thinking that he wanted to keep the boy there."

"You think he'd try to steal the Ol'Nia lands?" Ser Yrsa asked. "Maybe not kill the lad for them — well, *maybe* kill the lad for them, I've seen worse the gods know — but just force his stewardship and become a ler in fact, if not in title?"

"I don't buy it," Ser Beornric said. "That man practically found release when you kissed his hand. He wants a title."

"I don't think he wanted to steal Edric's lands," Aefric said. "I think he wanted to marry the boy to one of his daughters, and leave his grandchildren a noble legacy."

"Never happen," Ser Beornric said. "A ler, marrying some mayor's daughter?"

"Might," Ser Yrsa said. "If that ler was raised to think like a commoner. Marry for love, not advantage."

"Moot point now," Aefric said. "At least in Edric's case."

"You think there are others," Ser Yrsa said. "Lost children of petty nobles."

"I know there are at least two. Leca, and her brother Morgard. She told me last night that they're the children of Ler Boury Ol'Nara."

"*That's* why she looked so familiar," Ser Yrsa said, thumping a fist on the rail. "It was driving me mad."

"You knew Ler Boury?" Aefric asked.

"Haven't thought about her in years. Didn't know she was dead. But yeah. She used to come to Arinda's court every midwinter. And she brought the best mussels I've ever tasted. And don't get me started on the sharabi."

She sighed at the memory, then shook herself and nodded.

"And sure enough," she continued. "Ler Boury had the same hair, same eyes, and same cheekbones as the mayor's wife."

Ser Beornric swore softly. Aefric frowned puzzlement at him.

"Excuse me, your grace," Ser Beornric said, somewhat chagrined. "Just making the connection that she told you that *last night*. Which means she *did* come to your room last night." He shook his head. "Means I owe Wardius dinner."

Ser Yrsa chuckled. "I can't believe you took that bet."

"Not that I doubted your grace's charms," Ser Beornric said quickly. "I just … didn't think her husband would be too keen on the prospect."

Ser Yrsa snorted. "I wouldn't be surprised if he opened the door and shoved her in there. Anything to get his grace thinking of the mayor as a noble."

"In any event," Aefric said. "Her brother Morgard is the elder, and should already have assumed his lands. He should have come to me by now for confirmation."

"So the question is, why hasn't he?" Ser Yrsa said, frowning.

"The answer I was given," Aefric said, "was that he's needed to amass money to rebuild."

"And asking his duke for aid was a foreign concept?" Ser Beornric said drolly. "How refreshing."

"He's been working closely with Brangford, the mayor's son. And right now they're both in Ajenmoor."

"Where the mayor is having problems with a trade deal," Ser Beornric said.

"Where the mayor *says* he's having problems with a trade deal," Ser Yrsa corrected.

"Morgard is unmarried," Aefric said. "Which means that if anything *happens* to him in Ajenmoor..."

"Leca inherits," Ser Beornric finished.

"And the mayor has no doubt set aside money to rebuild," Ser Yrsa said.

"Some of my major points of concern," Aefric said. "I'll want to summon Morgard from Ajenmoor as soon as we dock."

"And you gave the task of finding more lost nobles to Leca, not the mayor," Ser Yrsa said.

"Nobles *and* commoners," Aefric said. "I meant that. I know that there are people out there in bad shape, and I want them found and helped."

"I think Yrsa's point stands," Ser Beornric said. "You trust Leca to handle this, but not the mayor."

Aefric frowned. "Was I that obvious?"

"You gave a good excuse for public ears," Ser Yrsa said, "but you didn't fool anyone on the stage. I think the only question in the mayor's mind is, did you give Leca the job because you don't trust him, or out of ... a surge of generosity after last night?"

"The only thing Leca did last night that got her this job was prove that first, she has a brain in her head, and second, she cares about people."

"I'm not sure your grace is entertaining women correctly," Ser Beornric teased.

"She was happy to tell me of Edric's lineage, and honestly thrilled when I offered to see him fostered properly. She said herself that she'd wanted Edric assigned to her brother, for page training, but the mayor overruled her."

Ser Yrsa snapped her fingers. "Of course he did. The mayor *does* want Edric thinking like a commoner. Wants his wife thinking like one too. That's why he didn't introduce her as Mistress Karaleca, as he should have, but only by a nickname. Leca."

"More reason to think he didn't want her going to your grace last night," Ser Beornric said.

"What would he say?" Ser Yrsa said with a sneer. "You think he'd try to forbid her? She's not like Edric. She was raised knowing who and what she is, and what it means to *be* who she is. If he tried to deny her the noble privilege, she might just leave him. Try to convince the dashing young duke with the good heart to give her a place at his court."

"It's a wonder she married a mayor in the first place," Ser Beornric said. "Beauty like her, and a noble to boot, and he an old man and a commoner."

"Beauty," Ser Yrsa scoffed. "If beauty were enough for nobles, every king and prince across the face of Qorunn would be throwing themselves at the feet of Byrhta Ol'Caran and begging for her hand. And every queen and princess would be doing the same with her brother Taeric."

"And they have a younger sister, too, don't they?" Ser Beornric said, grimacing. "Poor Count Cyneric, trying to find them all marriages, after what the wars did to Goldenfall."

"The same thing the wars did to the Ol'Nara lands," Aefric said. "So it wasn't as though Leca had a dowry to offer. Might have married Mayor Brangton just to build a life for herself and her brother."

"But once her brother is ler," Ser Beornric said, "with lands again—"

"Then she'd still be the former wife of a commoner," Ser Yrsa said. "Mayor or not, the man's still a commoner. And this Morgard would have to offer one impressive dowry to get anyone to forget that. *If* Karaleca was willing to leave her husband in the first place."

"I can't help thinking about the mayor's Ajenmoor connection," Aefric said, trying to get them onto more important topics. "And those slavers and smugglers."

"You think the mayor's involved?" Ser Yrsa asked.

"Don't know one way or the other. I doubt, at the moment, that he's involved with ... the other thing we found. But he did seem *awfully* interested in ferreting out details about the smugglers and slavers we fought in the Dragonscar."

"If he's involved with slavers..." Ser Yrsa let those words hang.

"If he is," Aefric said, "Leca will be a widow, and Lachedran will need a new mayor."

"Any word from Karbin?" Ser Beornric asked.

"None," Aefric said. "I hate to reach for him by message spell when I don't know what he's up to. If I distract him in the middle of something important..."

Aefric shook his head.

"No. The man's known what he was about since before I was a street rat in Sartis. He'll contact me when he's ready."

"I'll check for a Dragonscar report from the scouts as soon as we dock," Ser Yrsa said. "First report should have reached us by now."

"Good," Aefric said. "There's too much going on, all at once." He shook his head. "Makes me think it's all tied together, somehow."

Ser Beornric chuckled.

Aefric frowned at him.

"Your grace has asked me to tell him when he's thinking like an adventurer." Ser Beornric clapped him on the shoulder. "That's *just* what you're doing."

"He's right," Ser Yrsa said, giving Aefric a lopsided grin that made her major scar look sinister. "Perhaps when you were adventuring, the matters you dealt with were small enough that they could all be tied together. But politics is a massive knot, your grace. And though the strands of that knot might look as though they all come from the same rope, untie them, and you'll find scores and scores of ropes."

Aefric sighed, and nodded, and hoped devoutly that his knight-advisers were right.

WATER'S END. THE SECOND LARGEST CITY IN ARMYR, BEHIND ONLY THE royal capital at Armityr. It sprawled up and down the western shore of reputedly bottomless Lake Deepwater, and extended outward farther every year, from what Aefric had been told.

And the anchor point of the city, the jewel atop the crown, was the namesake castle. From what Aefric had been able to figure out, somewhere beneath the gleaming, shimmering surface of those walls — as perfect a navy blue as the center of the lake itself — was actual good, solid granite.

But four generations of dukes and duchesses Soulfist had cast and expanded on the spells that had overlain that granite with what seemed to be perfect, pure, elemental water, stilled within a single moment.

If that were true — and Aefric felt he would know for certain once he managed to puzzle through Duchess Arinda's old family notes and grimoires — it was one of the most amazing feats of wizardry Aefric had ever encountered.

And he'd traveled with the great mage Kainemorton for close to five years.

With such a magnificent surface, Water's End would have been a wonder, even had it stood only a few stories tall.

But no. The tremendous main keep itself stood more than a *dozen* stories tall, and featured a huge, stained glass dome over the main hall.

And up above the keep itself rose many spires and towers, including the Seven Great Spires of Water's End, which reached hundreds of feet into the air. Six of the seven great spires, the outermost, were connected together by a web of arching bridges. Like jets of water, connected by sprays.

The seventh, that central tower called the Spike, stood tallest, and alone.

The view from atop the Spike was dizzying, but glorious.

And every inch of that castle, including the hundred-plus-foot walls surrounding the keep and environs, was covered in that wondrous, shimmering substance.

The castle moat was cut from the lake, of course, but Water's End didn't sit on a preexisting island, the way the ducal keep at Behal did.

Which was just as well. Water's End was too much a part of the life and business of the city for that.

Just seeing that grand castle — *Aefric's* castle — always gave him a lift. And sailing toward it that late morning, at speed, was no exception.

Home. His beautiful, glistening home.

Oh, if only he could take the day to himself to enjoy coming home. Rest. Walk in the gardens. Perhaps enjoy a pleasure cruise, or explore yet more of the castle — he hadn't seen more than ... perhaps a third, at this point. If that.

But no. Once more, his feet would have to be moving when they hit the docks.

Ah, the docks. They completed the image of Water's End as part of the lake itself. The docks looked to have been shaped from smoothed coral, in dark shades of greens and browns and reds.

The port was busy that day. The harbor had a reef, and local pilots had to guide ships in to the dock. As the *Calming Influence* approached, Aefric could see that dock traffic was backed up with dozens of one- and two-mast ships waiting out in the harbor, beyond the reef.

Traders and the like, all coming into Water's End to do their business.

One advantage to being the duke, though. Aefric didn't have to wait in line. Didn't even need to wait for a pilot. The moment the *Calming Influence* approached the port, the local pilots saw the duke's banner and made room.

The *Calming Influence* glided safely through the reef, and docked at the duke's personal pier.

Aefric's seneschal, Kentigern Ol'Klimath, stood waiting down on the docks. He was wearing a padded doublet of royal blue, trimmed in silver, with hose the color of dark mustard, and those low, soft leather boots he favored, because they had silver thread among the black, turned-down cuffs.

Kentigern was the fourth Ol'Klimath to serve as seneschal at Water's End, and even though he'd seen only perhaps a dozen more summers than Aefric, the man was a veritable sapphire mine of knowledge about the duchy and its people.

But right now, his tanned face was frowning into his heavy, dark brown beard, and he wore that black velvet cap over his thick, dark brown hair. Never a good sign. Aefric would have sworn the man only wore that cap when he had bad news.

Of course, Aefric's conclusion here might've had something to do with the two dozen soldiers — the remainder of his personal guard — standing at hand, in formation.

"All right," Aefric said to Sers Yrsa and Beornric, while the ship put in and made ready for him to disembark. "Looks as though I'm going to need to walk in. Possibly while getting harangued. No reason for you both to put up with this. Beornric, organize the knights and the boy."

"Of course, your grace."

Aefric turned to Ser Yrsa. "Bring the horses with you, and see to getting the troops squared away and the dead prepared for their rites. And I think it's better if the living don't talk about their trip yet."

"I agree, your grace," she said. "And I'll bring you a report from the scouts as soon as I'm able."

"Excellent. Thank you both."

Then it was time, and Aefric hefted his backpack. Though he left the rest of his gear and clothes in Windsong's saddle bags, for the servants to handle.

That wasn't easy for him, but it had to be done.

Even so, he was only halfway down the gangplank to the apparently green coral of the pier when Kentigern started in.

"Your grace!" He said, in that dramatic, skald's voice of his. "Thank every god that you're alive. When I'd heard reports about you fighting smugglers and slavers and worse, well, I didn't know what to think."

"You knew full well that I was alive," Aefric said, walking straight past him to address his personal guard next. "Some of you argued that I should have brought you with me on this trip. I'd thought you could use the time off instead."

"Your grace..." Kentigern started, but Aefric ignored him.

Kentigern was an excellent seneschal. However, he seemed to consider it his duty to try to run his duke's life for him, and Aefric wouldn't have that. So he was forced to use little displays of power to remind the man of his place.

As he was doing right now.

"Instead, I faced a deadlier threat than I expected," Aefric said, still addressing the soldiers of his personal guard. "I cannot deny that. Still. If more of you had come, some of you might not have come back."

Aefric drew a deep breath. "But I must admit that the risk to me would have been lessened by your strength of arms. And I know you all well enough to know that only makes you more eager to come along next time."

Nods and grumbles of agreement from those soldiers.

"Your grace..." Kentigern started again.

Aefric gave his seneschal a forestalling hand, and his personal guard a nod.

"Next time I do something like this," he said, "I shall allow you all to come along. And know that I thank you for your diligence."

"*Your grace,*" Kentigern insisted.

"Yes, Kentigern," Aefric said, moving the Brightstaff between himself and his seneschal, to maintain a little distance. "I know. I worried you. That was never my intention. Please do excuse me."

"I don't like to hear about these things through rika birds from a mayor," Kentigern said, and Aefric began to wonder if some of his seneschal's irritation might not be with his duke. "Such a grasping man, that Brangton Couglas. Ought to be retired, and a new mayor installed."

"I would have been here last night," Aefric said, and started walking, allowing the knights and soldiers of his personal guard to fall in around him, while Kentigern and Ser Beornric walked alongside him. "But when the mayor of Lachedran offered hospitality, accepting seemed..."

Aefric frowned and stopped walking, halting the whole procession.

He turned to face Kentigern.

"What do you mean you heard by rika bird? You didn't hear about those skirmishes from Ser Micham himself?"

"Ser Micham, your grace?" Kentigern asked, frowning in puzzlement. "Ser Micham left with you."

"Yes," Aefric said, impatiently. "And he returned days ago by ship from Ajenmoor, along with thirty-eight refugees, quite a bit of cargo, and a letter I wrote to *you*."

Troubled understanding spread across Kentigern's expressive face.

"No, your grace," he said softly, but firmly. "No he did not."

Ajenmoor was no more than an hour away by air...

No. That was not the way to handle this. And Aefric made himself draw a slow, deep breath to force himself to focus.

"Kentigern," Aefric said, "you're riding double with me." He turned to Ser Beornric. "We'll need the horses, and the boy rides double with you. And the moment we reach the castle, I want you... Wait."

Aefric turned back to Kentigern, who was wide-eyed with worry, but not interrupting for once.

"Is Ser Deirdre still at court?"

"Yes, your grace."

"Good." Aefric turned back to Ser Beornric. "Get the whole of my guard ready to travel no later than" — Aefric gauged the sun's position to be no more than an hour before true midday — "an hour past midday. Preferably midday itself."

"We'll be ready by midday, your grace," Ser Beornric said with a short bow. "If I have to drag every one of them out myself, we'll be ready."

"Good. Find Ser Deirdre as well, and..." Aefric blew out a breath. He could command her to come. But with Deirdre, that would only make her drag her feet. "Tell her I have a mission for her, if she thinks she can handle it."

Ser Beornric's mustache broadened with his wolfish grin. But then, he knew Ser Deirdre at least as well as Aefric did.

"So she's to be ready to go as well?"

Aefric nodded, made a fist and clasped that wrist in the traditional salute of a noble to a knight.

Ser Beornric bowed, and left to be about his orders.

Aefric turned back and bellowed over the restless crowd.

"General Yrsa!"

"Your grace," she called, and, hearing the urgency in his tone, ran forward. She stopped before him and bowed.

"We have to accelerate our timetable. After you deal with this lot, I want another ... two hundred soldiers armed and ready to travel, and enough ships to carry us all — including every knight and solider of my personal guard. And I want this all ready by midday."

"Then they will be ready by midday, your grace. Where are we bound?"

"Where are we bound?" Aefric asked in disbelief. "I'm going to find out what in the thirteen hells is happening in Ajenmoor!"

---

A SHORT TIME LATER, AEFRIC SAT AT THE DESK IN HIS ... TERTIARY office? He thought that was right, but he had official rooms and offices all throughout this immense castle. He'd have to go over the list again, to be sure which one this was, in terms of priority.

In terms of location, just now, this was his most important office.

This was the office on the bottom floor of the castle, nearest the docks. It was a small, understated office compared to ... at least two others Aefric could think of.

This office had only the one desk, no view — light came in through slits high in the walls, with more added by candles on the desk — only three cabinets, and no rug on the red maple floorboards.

Of course, the desk and the cabinets were still of rare red calinwood, which was notable for its dark beauty even when raw, but when finally polished — as the furniture in here was — it shone with almost an inner light. And there were still the flags of Armyr and Deepwater on the soft, gray, plastered walls, as well as a recent portrait of Aefric himself.

Aefric's enchanted quill pen scratched quickly as he finished writing out his orders and letter of authority for Ser Deirdre, while Kentigern, standing on the other side of that desk, rocked back and forth with worry.

The man could have sat. There were two chairs for guests, both finely carved calinwood. But at times like these he preferred to stand. And rock.

Meanwhile, poor little Edric Ol'Nia tried very hard to hide in a corner.

As soon as Aefric waxed and sealed both letter and orders, Kentigern spoke up.

"Really, your grace. I must object." For the ... seventh? Yes. Seventh time so far, by Aefric's count. "Your grace cannot simply *charge off* after every problem. Whatever is happening in Ajenmoor—"

"Whatever is happening in Ajenmoor," Aefric said, "has delayed a knight of my personal guard *and* a ship full of refugees and cargo. *All of whom should have been afforded every assistance because of letters in my own hand.*"

Kentigern sputtered for a moment. Aefric kept talking.

"I've yet to visit Ajenmoor," Aefric said, standing, and leaning closer to his seneschal, across the desk. "I need to let their mayor and his people see my face. I need to find out who or what *dares* delay *my* knight on his duty, and I need to get that — and possibly a handful of other matters — straightened out. Today."

Where it stood beside the desk, the Brightstaff began to glow from the yellow diamond atop it.

In the corner, Edric gasped.

"Is. That. Clear?" Aefric asked Kentigern.

"It is clear, your grace," Kentigern said with a bow. "I mean no offense. I only—"

"You only wish to assist," Aefric said, waving a hand to dismiss the concern. "I know this, of course. Just as I know that you are the finest seneschal I could hope for. But there are some things I must do myself, and this is one of them."

"Thank you, your grace," Kentigern said, sounding somehow both mollified *and* hesitant. "And I understand and appreciate your grace's point. What I meant to say, however, was that I only wish to inform you of other matters right here at Water's End that can only be dealt with by your grace, himself."

"Oh?" Aefric asked, straightening up, and allowing the Bright-staff's diamond to dim again.

"There are reports from your vassals—"

"Those can wait."

"There are personal letters from Princess Maev, Mistress Byrhta Ol'Caran, and Mistress Vercy Ol'Karmak."

Aefric frowned. "Shouldn't you refer to Byrhta as 'baroness regent?'"

"It's clearly a private letter, your grace, not Riverbreak business." Kentigern lowered his voice. "It smells of her perfume, your grace."

Ah, the spicy, exotic scent of Byrhta's perfume. Just the memory of it made Aefric's heart beat faster.

He shook his head, as much to clear it as to go with what he said next.

"Nevertheless," Aefric said. "Those letters will have to wait until I return."

Aefric started to turn away.

"There's more," Kentigern objected. "Even more important matters. An emissary from Duchess Ashling of Merrek arrived three days ago, bearing a message for you. And she says her message must be delivered into the hands of the duke himself."

Aefric sighed. "Oh, gods. If it's an invitation, I'll have to go, and I don't have time right now." He shook his head. "Please extend my regrets, and inform her that the matter I deal with today is most urgent. The emissary is to be made welcome, and assured that I shall return as soon as possible, and receive her then."

Kentigern sighed. "Your grace..."

Aefric held up a forestalling hand. "I assure you, Kentigern. This can't be helped."

"Very well," Kentigern said, heaving an even more dramatic sigh.

There was a knock on the door.

"Come," Aefric said, and the door was opened by Ser Beornric.

"Your troops and guards just about ready to go, your grace," Ser Beornric said. "And your fresh clothes have arrived as well."

Aefric frowned. He had at least two more matters he wanted to deal with before leaving. But leaving as soon as possible was more important. One of those matters could keep, and he'd see to the other right now.

"Excellent," Aefric said, strapping on his backpack, an action that made Kentigern grimace.

"Your grace, really—"

"Edric, come forward," Aefric said.

The boy showed impressive courage. He was clearly frightened by everything happening — and Aefric's fierce urgency wasn't helping — and yet he immediately stepped forward and bowed.

"Your grace," Edric said.

"Kentigern, this is Edric Ol'Nia, son of—"

"Ler Osvalt Ol'Nia," Kentigern said, nodding. "You have your father's look, Master Edric."

Edric fought down the smile, but lost his fight against the blush.

"Confirm his identity and his patents with the historian, and then see about getting him fostered." Aefric leaned closer to his seneschal. "A gentle house, if you could. He's had a hard life."

"Of course, your grace," Kentigern said.

"Edric," Aefric said, "this is Kentigern, my seneschal. Trust him in all things, and do as he says."

"Of course, your grace," Edric said with another bow. Clearly Leca had been tutoring him, because that bow was more precise than any bow Aefric had seen from Mayor Brangton.

Aefric took the Brightstaff in hand and turned to Ser Beornric. "Let's go."

"But *your grace*," Kentigern said.

He sounded frantic enough that Aefric turned to hear the rest of what he'd say.

"There's... I just..." Kentigern shrugged helplessly. "Princess Astrid of Malimfar is here."

Of *Malimfar*? Impossible. Malimfar tried to invade through Merrek this past spring. Only Aefric's magic had stopped Malimfar's armies before they stormed Armyr's half of the Indecisive River Valley.

Aefric frowned. "I don't think I heard you right."

"You did, your grace," Kentigern said, sounding as uncomfortable about this as he looked. "Princess Astrid, the crown princess of Malimfar herself, arrived by ship yesterday, seeking an audience with your grace."

"Did you inform the king?" Aefric asked.

"I sent a rika at once. Should arrive at Armityr by tomorrow."

"How did she arrive?" Ser Beornric said. "Full entourage?"

"No," Kentigern said, sounding upset about that. "Only four knights. Two ladies-in-waiting. A handful of others, and hardly enough luggage to last her an aett."

Ser Beornric shook his head. Said to Aefric, "That's the royal equivalent of traveling with nothing but the pack on your back. Maybe you should..."

He trailed off when Aefric sighed and shook his head.

"She'll just have to wait as well."

"But she's a *princess*," Kentigern said. "By protocol alone, you must see her before you leave."

"We're all but at war with Malimfar. The usual protocols don't apply."

"Not so," Kentigern said firmly. "At times like these, the protocols are more important than ever. They are all that prevent the sort of incidents that turn 'all but at war' into 'at war.'"

"Nevertheless," Aefric said, "I can't chance it. For all I know, she's here to challenge me to a duel, to restore her father's honor. And I don't have time for it. If she wants to try to kill me, she can wait until I come back."

"But she's—"

"*Kentigern*," Aefric said sharply. "You will *make excuses*. And you will *tell her* I will be happy to *receive her* when I return from *pressing business*. If you must, you may tell her that lives hang in the balance, because they do. But you *must* do this. Am I understood?"

"You are understood, your grace," Kentigern said, and though his voice sounded sour, he bowed. "I ... will think of something."

"Thank you," Aefric said. "I know this isn't easy for you. But believe me. What's going on in Ajenmoor right now is *very* important."

"I understand, your grace," Kentigern said.

He didn't sound as though he understood at all. But he did sound as though he'd extend doubt's benefit to his duke for the time being. And he clearly expected to understand everything by the time Aefric returned, or shortly thereafter.

No one should be able to express so very much with four words and the right tone of voice. Kentigern really would have made an excellent skald.

But for now, Aefric had to be about business every bit as important as he claimed.

And for the sake of Ajenmoor, every one of those refugees — and Ser Micham himself — had better be alive and intact when Aefric arrived.

***

THIS SHOULD HAVE BEEN A PLEASURE CRUISE. A HOT, MIDSUMMER DAY with a bright, clear sky. Cool winds and fresh spray from the lake. And Aefric seated aboard his large, comfortable wooden chair on the afterdeck, enjoying his lunch, with the Brightstaff standing tall beside him, and Sers Yrsa and Beornric sitting nearby, on folding canvas chairs.

And Aefric did sit in *his* chair. The ship he sailed was the *Duke's Hand* (renamed from *Duchess' Hand,* after Arinda's death), which

normally served as the duke's pleasure craft. And the afterdeck —
apart from the ship's wheel, of course — was entirely his domain.

Today, the *Duke's Hand* was merely the most convenient ship for
him to use, to lead the caravan of five other ships — all of them two-
masted schooners, like the *Duke's Hand* — north up the lake to the
Searun River, and from there to Ajenmoor.

Of course, with the wind in their face today, they'd be rowing, not
truly sailing. Already the great drum beat low and heavy, setting the
pace for the rowers.

But once they hit the Searun they'd have the river's flow to help.

His luncheon that day was simple fare, though excellent, and had
been prepared by the castle cook just before he left. Trenchers of hot
roast beef with melted cheese and broccoli. To drink with it, a light,
pale red wine that seemed to bring out more flavor in the beef and
the cheese.

Over the meal, Ser Yrsa went over the first report from the scouts
up at the Dragonscar.

Not that there was much to report. Everything was so quiet up
there that the scouts weren't even sure the borogs were still down
below, much less mining in that cave.

Aefric considered that quiet a good thing, though. No doubt Duke
Wylyn had scouts watching the Dragonscar from time to time, and
the less Aefric's own scouts would hear — while knowing what to
listen for — the less chance of Silverlake's scouts figuring out what
was going on before Aefric was ready.

As they finished eating, and savored an extra glass of the fine, pale
wine, Aefric explained the basics of his Ajenmoor plan to his knight-
advisers.

Doubtless with Ser Deirdre lurking somewhere nearby, hoping to
overhear.

But Aefric's seat was at the back of the ship, and he made sure he
and the other two kept their voices down. He doubted she heard
anything. And if she'd tried to use magic to eavesdrop, well, she wasn't
good enough at that sort of magic to do so without Aefric noticing.

"There are many ways this could go wrong," Ser Yrsa said, when Aefric was finished. "People see their duke arriving with a force this size, it'll make them edgy."

"Edgy people make mistakes," Aefric agreed. "But they tend to make mistakes that align with their activities. The innocent will be frightened, until they see what I *do* with those troops. As for the guilty, well, let them react and we'll deal with them."

"Hardly the way things are usually done," Ser Beornric said. "Usually everything you're talking about would be handled with a messenger delegating these tasks to the local mayor."

"I tried that already," Aefric said. "Now it's time to get involved myself."

"What about Ser Deirdre?" Ser Beornric asked. "What's her role in all this?"

"Good point. Summon her for me, will you?"

Ser Beornric went to the edge of the afterdeck and called down. "Ser Deirdre, your duke awaits you."

She must've been lingering nearby all right. Hardly a dozen heartbeats passed between the time that Ser Beornric called her and the time Ser Deirdre climbed the ladder to the afterdeck and somersaulted forward to one knee before her duke.

Like Aefric, but unlike every other knight on this ship, Ser Deirdre did not wear full plate armor. Instead she favored leathers of a deep maroon red. Hardly two shades darker than the hair she wore in a long braid down her back.

At her belt, she wore a rapier and a dueling dagger, and both almost hummed with the magic of her calling.

Ser Deirdre was a true dweomerblade. A warrior who found magic through the arts of battle, focused mostly through her weapons.

Some dweomerblades that Aefric had known, back with the Iron Wands, had been ... explosive in their skills and magic. Ser Deirdre was far more subtle in hers.

Aefric trained with her sometimes. And though he could do more with magic than she ever would, when it came to melee combat, she was the best he'd ever seen.

And yet here she was, kneeling before him again. A sight that made Ser Yrsa grumble.

Aefric was not the king. No one was expected to kneel before him save vassals, and even then only during the oaths of vassalage.

Ser Deirdre had sworn herself to Aefric's service nearly a season ago. And yet, she insisted on kneeling every time she was called before him.

At first, Aefric had stopped whatever he was doing at the time and *insisted* on her coming to her feet immediately. But that seemed to please her. And it didn't stop her from kneeling the next time.

So he stopped reacting. Pretended to treat her behavior as his due. On the theory that she knelt to him just to get a reaction, such as Ser Yrsa was giving her right now.

But that didn't seem to stop her either...

Ser Deirdre, on one knee before him, there on the afterdeck of the *Duke's Hand*, spread her arms out low and wide. Her smile was wry. Her green eyes taunting. But her tone almost respectful as she said, "You want me, your grace?"

"I told you I had a mission for you, if you could handle it."

"I'm sure I can handle anything your grace has for me."

"When we dock at Ajenmoor, I need you to find someone. Morgard Ol'Nara. Bring him to me. On my ship is fine, if I'm still in Ajenmoor. Otherwise, bring him to me at Water's End."

"Have you a description, your grace?"

"No," Aefric said, but Ser Yrsa spoke up.

"I've seen him, your grace," she said. "Though not in at least a decade. Hair pale as sunshine, like his sister. Probably tending towards slender. Probably dressed like a merchant."

"Not much to go on," Ser Deirdre said. "Especially in a place as big as Ajenmoor."

"I know," Aefric said. "But I have every confidence in you. Morgard will be working with Brangford Couglas, son of—"

"Son of that foul old mayor in Lachedran," Ser Deirdre said with a sneer. "I've had the displeasure." She sighed. "More than enough to go on, then. I know the sorts of places Couglas haunts."

"What sorts of places?" Aefric asked, then finally gestured for her to rise.

"Couglas tried to impress me once by telling me he could get me Kefthali leather," she said as she came smoothly to her feet.

"He does business with *Kefthal?*" Sers Beornric and Yrsa said at the same time.

"Kefthal," Aefric said, trying to recall. "Kefthal."

His eyes widened, as information read in a book a world a way surfaced in his head, meshing with rumors he'd heard during his travels across Qorunn.

"Not that place ruled by a council of necromancers," he said.

"That's Kefthal," Ser Yrsa said, and Ser Beornric nodded.

"The Nine Beyond Death," Ser Deirdre said with a grimace. "And yes, your grace, they still hold Kefthal in their bony clutches."

"Which is why *civilized* people don't do business with them," Ser Beornric said.

"The point is," Ser Deirdre said, "if Couglas has contacts that deal with the likes of Kefthal, then I'll know where to find him in Ajenmoor." She nodded. "I'll bring you this Morgard Ol'Nara, your grace. Wrapped in a bow, if you like."

"There's no need to go *that* far," Aefric said with a smile. "But thank you, Ser Deirdre."

"Am I to arrest him?"

"If necessary," Aefric said, "but I'd rather you didn't. I want him to come to court so I can see him formally acknowledged as ler of his family lands. But I need him to come now, because I suspect a plot to steal those lands."

Aefric shook his head. "He doesn't need to know about the plot. All he needs to know is that he's summoned to my court at once, and he's not allowed to refuse."

"He's in danger here, isn't he?" Ser Deirdre said, her lips twisting in that wry smile again.

"I believe so, yes."

"Oh, your grace does know how to show a girl a good time."

"I can assign you some soldiers to assist, if you like."

"Please, your grace," Ser Deirdre scoffed. "I work best without an audience."

"All right then," Aefric said, chuckling. "Here are your official orders, and a letter of introduction, in case you need it."

"I won't," she said, taking the papers, "but it's best to be safe."

He gave her the knight's salute then, and she bowed and took her leave.

"You realize she might just cut a bloody swath through Ajenmoor," Ser Beornric said.

"No," Ser Yrsa said, watching Ser Deirdre's departure. "Not if she doesn't have to. Not while working in his grace's name."

"Think that'll make a difference to her?"

"Oh, yes. I don't doubt it," Ser Yrsa said, then turned to Aefric and raised an eyebrow. "But there's another matter we should discuss."

Aefric, whose thoughts were already at Ajenmoor, gave her a blank look.

"Princess Astrid of Malimfar."

"You really ought to have received her before leaving," Ser Beornric said.

"I told you," Aefric said, shaking his head. "If she wants to duel me for her father's honor, she can wait until we get back."

"Two problems there," Ser Yrsa said. "First, she's a princess. She shouldn't have to wait."

"Lives hang in the balance," Aefric started, but Ser Yrsa cut in.

"*Commoner* lives." She shook her head, and she was so agitated that the skin around her scar was darker. "And not even the lives of your own people, but refugees."

"They're my people," Aefric said, matching her tone, "because they've chosen to be."

"I hate to say it," Ser Beornric said, "but Yrsa's right. They're still commoners, and Astrid's a princess."

"Not just any princess, either," Ser Yrsa said, tone becoming more heated. "A *crown* princess. You just told the future ruler of Malimfar that she has to wait, because you have *more important matters to attend to.*"

"*And I do,*" Aefric said.

Ser Beornric cleared his throat.

"That's adventurer thinking," Ser Beornric said, voice impressively calm, as he poured them each a fresh glass of wine. "Expected ducal behavior here is for you to give priority to the visiting royalty. Assign someone else to handle whatever other business is so pressing."

"No," Aefric said, shaking his head. "I'm sorry. But I'm not going to put pleasing some uninvited guest — even a royal guest — ahead of saving lives."

"And if this leads to Malimfar harassing our shipping?" Ser Yrsa asked. "Fighting with us out on the sea lanes, where we're only just starting to rebuild?"

Aefric drew a long breath, and thought about those poor refugees. Only saved from a life of slavery because Aefric had wanted to see the Dragonscar.

He shook his head.

"I stand by my decision. For all I know, going to Ajenmoor myself, today, may mean the difference in stopping countless innocents from falling prey to those slavers."

Ser Yrsa opened her mouth, likely to say something scathing. But Ser Beornric touched her shoulder. She frowned and turned her head away.

"All right then," Ser Beornric said. "Done is done. Now let's discuss the possible ramifications from this decision."

That discussion went on for much longer than Aefric expected.

---

By the time the *Duke's Hand* approached Ajenmoor, Aefric found himself accepting that, yes, in fact, he probably *should* have delayed sailing for an hour or two, while he dealt with that princess from Malimfar.

If he'd counted correctly, and he feared he had, there were at least *sixty-eight* ways his declining to receive Princess Astrid himself that day — even if he sailed shortly afterwards — could come back to haunt him.

And those were only the ways that Sers Yrsa and Beornric could think of as they made their way down the Searun River in the hot afternoon sun.

But now, at least, he could set those worries aside for a time, and focus on others.

For they were at last approaching Ajenmoor.

Now that he could see it — or at least the beginnings of it — Aefric had to admit that Ser Deirdre was right. If all she'd had to go on was a vague description, she would never find Morgard in a place that size.

The city of Ajenmoor started with a thirty-foot-high wooden wall, on both sides of the Searun. And Aefric could see the edges of a thick chain dipping into the water on both sides of the roughly five-hundred-foot width of the river. Likely they could cut off access here, as well as in the harbor.

The city was impressively big. Larger than Behal, certainly, though smaller than Water's End.

It descended towards the docks in large hemispheres the locals called "rings." From what Kentigern had told Aefric previously, the lowest ring was for the docks and the offices of associated businesses.

The second ring up was for the wealthy, with land values and ... associated qualities descending further with each level from the third to the fifth.

Apparently, there was heavy traffic in riverboats going from the docks to the fifth ring, both bringing sailors to cheap entertainment and ferrying locals down to their work on the docks. Faster — and less likely to lead to being stopped by the city watch — than taking the sloping roads that ran from the wooden wall down to the docks.

It was a busy city. They were still passing the fifth ring, and already Aefric could hear and smell and see the sounds of bustling city life all about him.

His caravan of ships no longer had the waters to themselves. Two merchant vessels were working against the river's flow to make their way to smaller towns along the Searun and, eventually, Lake Deepwater. Several smaller craft plied the waterways as well going back, forth, and across.

Of course, all these ships and boats were smart enough to clear space for the caravan flying the duke's banner.

Aefric was less interested in the river traffic, though, in those first moments of entering Ajenmoor, than he was in what he was smelling.

On the voyage here, he'd been smelling mostly the clean smells of the river since they'd left the lake.

But now, sailing into another city, part of Aefric — the part that had grown up in another world — once more found the smells ... almost sanitized.

The aromas of cooking and baking, and the stench of hard work, the odors of fish, and the sea. Those were all present, and to be expected.

But as they'd been everywhere else so far, the rank tangs of dung and urine were missing.

The part of Aefric that had grown up in Sartis understood the absence. That the means of waste disposal here were just a part of life. But there was a touch of magic to those means, and the part of him that had grown up in Oregon — on a world called not Qorunn, but Earth — kept expecting the lack of technological sanitation beyond aqueducts to mean more than it did here.

It was a habit of expectation. Though the habit, by now, was stronger than the expectation itself.

Every town, every city so far, had all been free of those smells. And yet, Aefric still found himself checking the air every time he entered a new place. Just to see if this one was different.

But even here among the fifth ring, those odors were absent.

So Aefric chuckled at himself, and turned his attention to looking out over his port city.

Ajenmoor. The largest of that scant handful of settlements that had survived the Godswalk Wars, here along his coastline.

Ajenmoor was old, and as he sailed towards the docks, Aefric could see that best in the buildings of the fourth ring. The fifth ring, that had been all wooden construction, and much of it recent, and cheaply made. The roads were hard-packed dirt, and muddy in places.

But the fourth ring was where some of the older buildings were visible that hadn't gotten the ... care of buildings farther down. Certain larger temples that had fallen from favor, and old guildhalls, for guilds whose power and influence had waned.

The stone of those buildings looked worn, cracked and tired. And though the roadways here in the fourth ring were cobbled with stones from the river, they were ill-matched, and missing in places.

The third ring stood in sharper contrast. The people here dressed better, carried themselves straighter. The cobblestones of their streets were smoother, more regular. Their houses and buildings were painted, and in good repair. And some of them even took note of the passing ducal caravan, and doffed hats or waved, or held their right fists high in salute.

The second ring looked finer still. More of the houses and buildings had glass in their windows. The streets here were tiled, not cobblestoned, and lined with bright flowers, or leafy trees, or both.

More silks and velvets and jewelry for the denizens of the second ring, and those who took note of Aefric's ship did not wave or salute, but nodded. Some as though considering what the duke's visit might mean for them, personally.

The mayor's house would be somewhere in that second ring.

Finally, Aefric's ship reached the lowest ring, and the docks.

Aefric had been getting used to the docks of Water's End, and come to think of them as large. But sailing into Ajenmoor that day, he had to laugh at himself.

The docks at Water's End could handle two dozen, perhaps two score ships at a time.

But the massive docks and piers of Ajenmoor looked as though they could handle ten, perhaps twenty times that many.

They weren't. At the moment, they looked to have no more than thirty ships at dock, and another ... half-dozen out in the harbor. In fact, the docks here at Ajenmoor had probably not seen full usage since before — or at least sometime during — the Godswalk Wars.

Out in the harbor, a series of ancient stone posts had been installed, with heavy chain links dipping from them down below the water line. And, yes, Aefric could spot the chain towers, at the edges of the harbor.

Those chains might have been sagging at the moment, but those towers could pull them tight to raise either a chain or a net or similar, and close the harbor.

Good.

Aefric looked out over the ships both at dock and in the harbor. Shook his head.

"I don't see the ship Ser Micham took," he said. "At least, I don't think I do. Though I see four that look rather like it. What about you two?"

Ser Beornric frowned so hard his bushy mustaches almost drooped past his chin. Shook his head.

"To be honest, your grace," Ser Yrsa said, "I wasn't paying much attention to the details of the ship he took. I think I know which four you mean, but if any of them are that ship, I couldn't pick it out."

"Ah, well," Aefric said with a sigh. "Didn't expect it to be that easy."

But then he spotted a ship at anchor in the harbor. A familiar looking ship, without any masts at all.

Aefric nodded. At least *some* of the ships from the Dragonscar had returned then.

As planned, the *Duke's Hand* sailed into dock and prepared for debarkation. The other five ships sailed out into the harbor and spread out.

The *Duke's Hand* was still settling in when a dozen members of the dock patrol showed up — wearing chainmail and carrying crossbows — flanking some kind of functionary. A dusky, older man dressed in dark velvets and hose.

"Are you the harbormaster?" Aefric called down.

"No ... your grace?" the man said, caught somewhere between a sentence and a question. "I'm—"

"Ser Deirdre," Aefric said, over whatever the man had been about to say.

"At once, your grace," she said and dove over the side of the ship, somersaulted twice in the air, and was running as soon as her boots hit the docks.

The city watch lost their formation then, as some of them looked as though they wanted to pursue her, or shoot their crossbows at her, but weren't sure whether or not they should do either.

Just then, the boatswain blew the disembark, and the gangplank was lowered. The dock patrol turned all their attention back to Aefric and his ship, though they were smart enough not to raise those crossbows.

Nevertheless, the soldiers and knights of Aefric's personal guard put themselves between those crossbows and their duke.

General Yrsa stepped onto the gangplank.

"I am Ser Yrsa Azenai, general in charge of the armies of his grace, Ser Aefric Brightstaff, Hero of Deepwater, Hero of Frozen Ridge, Baron of Netar, and Duke of Deepwater. And if you are not the harbormaster, who are you, to meet your duke with *weapons drawn?*"

The dock patrol immediately started slinging their crossbows on their backs once more, as though ordered. Which flustered the man in velvet.

"I am Nashen Ol'Nashek," he said, bowing. "Chief assistant to Harbormaster Jojen Ol'Talas. And, having seen the duke's standard flying above this ship, which I recognize of course as the *Duke's Hand,* I have come to greet his grace on this most unexpected visit. Those about me are nothing more than a guard of honor."

Ser Yrsa began walking slowly down the gangplank, followed by Aefric, Ser Beornric, and Aefric's guards.

"And *why*," Ser Yrsa said as she walked, "does this Jojen Ol'Talas not come greet the duke himself?"

"Forgive him, your grace," Nashen Ol'Nashek said, addressing Aefric now, not Ser Yrsa. "He is in a meeting with the mayor and city council."

"I presume," Ser Yrsa said — and Aefric could tell by the way Nashen Ol'Nashek paled that she'd arched the eyebrow above her scarred, red left eye — "that I'll be given the same excuse if I ask why the *mayor* did not come to greet his duke?"

"Alas," Nashen Ol'Nashek said, "I have no other reason to provide."

"I am disappointed," Aefric said. "I was already displeased with Ajenmoor when I arrived, and this does nothing to improve my disposition."

"Your grace," Nashen Ol'Nashek said, bowing even deeper. "What may I do to improve your grace's humor?"

"You may take me to this so-important meeting at once," Aefric said, then smiled as he heard a loud, metallic creaking sound coming from the harbor behind him.

"The chain," Nashen Ol'Nashek gasped.

"Yes," Aefric said, pleased that Ser Deirdre had gotten the first part of her job done so quickly. "Until I have the answers I seek, this port is closed."

He leveled a glare on Nashen Ol'Nashek.

"Pray I get my answers quickly."

---

AEFRIC HAD TO ADMIT. THE CITY COUNCIL BUILDING REALLY WAS QUITE pretty. Its stonework was overlaid with a mosaic of tilework in blues and greens, to represent the seas, and dark yellows and browns to represent different trading lanes.

It was a three-story structure, though each of the second and third levels were half the size of the level below them, and seated at the back half of the building, which was at the very edge of the second ring and right above the buildings and warehouses of the docks below.

Two guards stood at the double-doors, spears in hand.

Despite the presence of Nashen Ol'Nashek, they crossed their spears over the doors as Aefric's group approached.

Aefric fought down a sigh. He didn't have the time or the patience for this. The day had been long already.

He was hot. He was irritated that he had to be here at all, and every minute he was here and not back at Water's End likely increased the amount of offense he'd given the *crown princess of Malimfar*.

And now there were guards standing between him and where he needed to go.

With one spell he could blast those guards aside and open the doors at the same time.

It'd be quick. It'd be easy. And in the mood Aefric was in, he had to admit, he *wanted* to do it. To take out some of this frustrated anger on at least *one* of the obstacles in his path.

Of course, if he did cast that spell, chances were, the guards would not survive. And if there was anyone in the room on the other side of those doors, they'd be in for a world of hurt as well.

The guards didn't deserve to die. Not because their duke was hot, tired, and frustrated. And if there was anyone on the other side of those doors, well, they deserved death even less. They weren't even trying to bar Aefric's way.

Ah, well. Maybe the guards were smart enough to recognize their duke, and open the way for him with just a word?

It was worth a shot.

"Open the doors," Aefric said.

The guards took in the crowd. Aefric, with the Brightstaff in hand. Seven knights, all bearing the ducal sigil on their tabards. Twenty-four soldiers, also wearing tabards with the Deepwater sigil.

Oh, and the chief assistant to the harbormaster, along with a dozen members of the dock patrol who looked very much as though they'd rather be anywhere else.

And yet, the guards held firm. Because *of course* they did. Because *of course* it couldn't be that *freaking easy* just this once.

And the worst part was, Aefric had to admire their devotion to duty, even in the face of nobility and overwhelming odds.

"The council is in session," one guard said, in reply. He looked about a decade older than Aefric, and from the scars on his hands — and the one on his cheek — he'd seen his share of fighting. "No one may enter."

"You are addressing his grace, the Duke of Deepwater," Ser Beornric snapped.

"Then I must beg your grace's pardon," the guard said, bowing — and his younger, shakier partner bowed as well — "but I have my orders, and I'm not to admit anyone."

Ser Beornric started to say something, but Aefric stilled him with a raised hand.

"What is your name?" Aefric asked the guard.

"Delif, your grace," the guard said.

"Well, Delif, I commend you for your diligence. However. Allow me to ask a question. From whom did these orders come?"

"From Sijen, the Mayor's Right Hand, your grace."

"Mayor's Right Hand is a formal title, your grace," Nashen Ol'Nashek said quickly. "She sees that the mayor's will is carried out."

"So," Aefric said. "Ultimately, your orders come from the mayor. Is that correct?"

"Yes, your grace."

"And I *outrank* your mayor. Don't I."

Nothing about Aefric's words or tone could have been mistaken for a question.

Delif opened his mouth, but hesitated.

"After all," Aefric said. "This is Ajenmoor. And Ajenmoor, last time I checked, was part of the duchy of Deepwater. *My* duchy. I'm correct about that, am I not, Ser Yrsa?"

"You are, your grace," Ser Yrsa said, her voice low and dangerous.

"Then I must assume that your mayor shows me proper obedience," Aefric said, "and will allow me to overrule him in this matter."

Aefric took a step closer to the guard.

"That is," Aefric continued, allowing his own voice to become low and dangerous, "unless you believe Ajenmoor would *defy* its lawful overlord. There's a word for that, I believe…"

"Ajenmoor does not defy our duke," Nashen Ol'Nashek said, practically stumbling over both his words and his feet as he rushed forward and shoved those spears aside. "You will open these doors for his grace *at once*, or I will see you both *punished severely*."

Delif looked at his partner, sighed, and pulled a key from back behind his belt. He unlocked the doors.

"By law," Delif said, sounding defeated, "no one is allowed to come armed into a council meeting. But I imagine your grace intends to overrule that as well."

Aefric didn't bother answering. He nodded at Ser Yrsa.

Ser Yrsa kicked the doors open.

⁂

THOSE GREAT, HEAVY MACES IN HER HANDS, SER YRSA KICKED OPEN THE double-doors of the Ajenmoor city council building.

Shocking the dozen or so clerks who likely had been working very hard before an angry, scarred knight burst in with murder in her eyes.

One of them — a man who had to have seen fifty summers — fainted dead away.

Ser Yrsa actually looked about for threats before lowering her maces and stepping to one side. She announced in a loud, clear voice, "His grace, Ser Aefric Brightstaff, Hero of Deepwater, Hero of Frozen Ridge, Baron of Netar, and Duke of Deepwater."

The clerks were quick to gather themselves enough to bow as Aefric entered. Though they looked more than a little frightened by the number of knights and soldiers who followed their duke in and up the wide, tiled stairs.

More guards at each of the next two floors. The first set just stood aside. The second set were sweating and unsteady, but didn't look willing to yield the door to the council chamber.

"Your grace?" Ser Yrsa said, and Aefric knew that tone. She was more than willing to take them both down.

"Just announce me, for the moment."

Ser Yrsa announced her duke through those closed double-doors. And this time she did it loud enough that Aefric was pretty sure she could be heard everywhere in Ajenmoor.

The doors were opened with impressive speed by a puzzled-looking young clerk.

Ser Yrsa entered first, slow and angry. Ser Beornric and the knights of Aefric's personal guard followed, after making sure that the door guardians and their spears were well back.

Aefric entered next, followed by the two dozen soldiers of his personal guard, who fanned out behind him.

The council chamber was squared on the wall where Aefric had entered, but ended in a curved wall, mostly of glass, giving a wonderful view of the harbor and afternoon sky.

On the tiles of the floor was a mosaic map featuring the sea lanes and ports connected with Ajenmoor. Or at least, those which *had* been connected with Ajenmoor before the wars. Aefric couldn't know how many of those other ports yet stood, let alone how many were trading these days.

A long table followed the curve of the room, even though it looked as though it had been carved from a single trunk. Had to have been made by shipwrights. No one else was so good at smoothly curving wood.

A half-dozen clerks flattened against the side walls, trying very hard to stay out of the way while looking pale and shocked at the presence of armed knights and soldiers.

Aefric ignored the clerks.

Fifteen men and women sat at the table, every seat full. All of them well dressed, and many of them with the weathered look of those who had worked ships or docks themselves, to one extent or another. And all of whom looked offended at the presence of weapons.

Interestingly, three of those at the table were derekek, two males and a female.

But Aefric's attention went straight to the mayor. He had the look of Ser Micham. Not just in the brown of his hair and beard — though the mayor's hair grayed at the temples — but in in the shape of his chin. He looked as Ser Micham might look in another ... twenty years, if he stayed in shape.

The mayor was dressed in greens, both velvet tunic and hose, and his gold chain of office, of course, though a rust red watch cap sat before him on the table. Likely removed because the room was practically baking in the afternoon heat.

In fact, Aefric could smell that the meeting had been going on for some time.

"Your grace," the mayor said, scraping his chair backward so he could stand and bow. And just like that, the whole room was filled with the sound of scraping chair legs, so the whole of the council — and their clerks — could bow to their duke before the council reclaimed their seats.

"If I might ask your grace," the mayor said, once he was seated again, "to what do we owe this most unexpected ... and martial ... pleasure?"

"You may recall, about an aett ago, that my court wizard, Karbin, came to you for ships."

"Oh, of course, your grace," the mayor said, and other members of the council nodded agreement. "We were most happy to provide those ships. And I understand their mission was quite successful."

"*Mostly* successful," Aefric said. "But I sent your son, Ser Micham back to Ajenmoor, with two soldiers to aid him. His mission was to see a ship full of refugees and recovered cargo brought back to Water's End."

Aefric wasn't sure what reaction he expected from the mayor at that moment, but anger wasn't it.

"My *son?*" the mayor snapped at a man down at the end of the table, to Aefric's right, who looked unhappy at the revelation.

"Imagine my surprise," Aefric continued, "when I returned to Water's End to find none of these things waiting for me. Not Ser Micham. Not the two soldiers. Not the *thirty-eight* refugees. And not the cargo."

"Well, your grace," the mayor started, his tone seething, but Aefric could tell the anger was not directed at him. "That ship has sat in the harbor since its return to Ajenmoor. Would you care to tell *our duke* why that is, Galdiff?"

Galdiff, the man the mayor had snapped at before, drew a steadying breath through a narrow nose. He was a tall, slender man, but tanned and weathered. The sort who was probably stronger than he looked. Like a rigger.

His tunic and hose were both a dark brown, and his balding pate still hung on to some of its black hair. Many men would have grown a beard, or at least a mustache, to make up for the lack on their heads, but Galdiff did not.

He steepled his fingers, which had the effect of showing off that he was missing half a small finger, on his right hand.

"Your grace," Galdiff said, inclining his head. "That the current situation has imposed on your time and expectations is regrettable. However, there are matters of *law* and *custom* that must be addressed and must *not* be ignored."

"Oh, do go on," Aefric said, attempting to convey with his tone that he was only too happy to provide this man with extra rope, that he might hang himself.

"The ships that answered your grace's call to arms were mine," Galdiff said. "And I was most happy to provide them, and to serve my duke in his time of need."

Galdiff raised one eyebrow at the mayor.

"However, both law and custom make the matter of spoils quite clear. My ships answered the call. My ships stood to battle. My sailors faced the hazard. The spoils belong to my company."

"Under normal circumstances, yes," the mayor started, but had the good sense to stop talking when Aefric raised a forestalling hand.

"And what spoils do you believe you're entitled to?" Aefric asked Galdiff with an insincere smile.

"All spoils from that day, your grace," Galdiff said easily. "The mastless ship. The *Swift Wave*. Along with any booty recovered and any and all bounties and rewards due for prisoners taken."

"I see," Aefric said, and now his tone was getting a worried look from Ser Beornric. "And do you count those refugees as booty?"

"Of course not, your grace," Galdiff said. "Any more than I count this Ser Micham, or your two soldiers. However, as *some people*" — here Galdiff glared at the mayor — "refuse to acknowledge what is mine by right of both law *and* custom, the ship, and all aboard, will not dock until the matter is settled."

"I see," Aefric said, and Ser Beornric took a step closer, as though to hold Aefric back, if needed.

"I'm glad your grace understands the situation better than ... certain others."

"Oh, I understand the situation quite well," Aefric said. "I'm afraid, however, that you are in error, regarding the facts of what transpired that day. As you would know, if Ser Micham had been allowed to dock and present the letter I prepared for the mayor."

Galdiff frowned, but checked himself from interrupting.

"What you refer to as 'booty,'" Aefric said, "was stolen, smuggled cargo that *I and mine* recovered. In the Dragonscar. With no ships around. Every crate of it aboard your ship out there in the harbor is only aboard your ship because *I* commandeered it for the task of transport."

Galdiff frowned.

"Now," Aefric said, thoughtfully. "I believe we've covered Ser Micham, the soldiers, the refugees and the cargo on that ship in the harbor. That brings us to the mastless ship."

"A ship chased down, recovered, and brought back by my ships and sailors," Galdiff said. "Surely your grace won't dispute that point."

Aefric favored Galdiff with a smile that made the man wince.

"Do you know why that ship lacks even a single mast?" Aefric asked. "Because *I* destroyed both its mainmast and mizzenmast myself. And though your ships did chase it down as it tried to row away, its captain and the core of its crew had already been defeated and taken captive by my knights, my soldiers, and myself. Your ship and crew never truly entered the hazard in dealing with those slavers."

"Well—" Galdiff tried, but Aefric kept talking.

"Therefore," he said, "by your own laws and customs, that ship is *mine* to dispose of. Not yours."

Galdiff frowned, but said nothing.

"And I," Aefric said, "give it to your mayor on behalf of his fine city."

"Thank you, your grace," the mayor said, sounding amazed.

Aefric gave him a smile. "Ser Micham tells me you've wished for just such a ship to use as a floating jail. Ajenmoor now has one."

"Your grace is too kind and generous," the mayor said happily. "I hope he knows that all the resources of Ajenmoor are his to command, if ever he has need."

"We'll return to that, I'm sure," Aefric said, turning his attention back to Galdiff. "Now. I believe that brings us to the question of the *Swift Wave*."

"Surely your grace does not contest that it is mine by right of conquest," Galdiff said, sounding desperate. "My ships captured it."

"I certainly *could* dispute the point," Aefric said. "Its captain and most of its fighting crew were captured by myself and my knights and soldiers. Further, *my* court wizard assisted in the capture of the ship itself. In an ambush made possible by *my* previous actions."

Aefric shook his head. "Nevertheless, I will not make these disputes."

"Thank you, your grace," Galdiff said, dipping his head in a bow. "The *Swift Wave* will serve well as—"

"Instead, I shall take it from you as punishment for interfering with my knight, in the performance of his duty in my name."

"Your *grace*," Galdiff said, but Aefric spoke over whatever the man was going to say next.

*"Pray I consider that sufficient punishment,"* Aefric said. "And that you do not give me cause to punish you further."

Galdiff frowned, but checked himself from speaking.

"Ser Micham was about *my* business. And you have needlessly delayed him — not to mention those poor refugees — for nearly an aett. I will not have it."

Galdiff bowed his head. "Yes, your grace. I ... am sorry, your grace."

"Very well," Aefric said, nodding. "Now. Despite your ... ill-considered actions in that matter, I will concede that your ships were timely, and your sailors a help to me. In light of that, I will allow you to keep any and all bounties and rewards due for the smugglers and slavers captured that day."

Galdiff blinked in surprise. "Thank you, your grace."

"Are you certain, your grace?" the mayor asked, perhaps hoping to direct those monies into his own pockets. "That's not an inconsiderable amount."

"He and his answered the call quickly and effectively, and were ready to face the hazard, if needed. That should not be overlooked or forgotten," Aefric said, then hardened his voice. "Though what followed was inexcusable."

"I understand, your grace," Galdiff said, frowning in thought. "And I will remember, for the future."

"Good. See that you do." Aefric turned to the mayor. "Now let us see about these ships."

***

APPARENTLY, THE QUESTION OF THAT SHIP FULL OF "BOOTY" OUT IN THE harbor had been the sticking point in that council meeting. Because once Aefric resolved that issue, the council was more than ready to gather their papers and end the meeting.

Then again, the presence of so many armed knights and soldiers might have contributed to their eagerness to be elsewhere.

Once the others and their clerks had cleared out, the only council members remaining were Galdiff, the mayor — whose name was Vagran Ol'Talas — and the harbormaster, Jojen Ol'Talas, who turned out to be the mayor's second son.

Jojen Ol'Talas had the same hair as his brother and father, though his eyes were a lighter hazel, and his chin and lips would make him pretty, rather than handsome.

Of course, age might've been a factor there. Because if Jojen Ol'Talas was beyond the age of majority, it couldn't have been by more than a single summer. Two at the most.

Aefric found himself feeling pity for Nashen Ol'Nashek. Having to obey the orders of a man a third his age.

Speaking of whom, the chief assistant to the harbormaster was waiting for them when Aefric and the others emerged from the council building.

"Harbormaster," Nashen Ol'Nashek said, giving the younger man a shallow bow, "you should know that his grace has ordered the harbor chained and closed until ... well ... I confess I am uncertain of the circumstances that will allow its reopening."

Jojen Ol'Talas looked ready to argue as he turned to Aefric. But then, so did the mayor. Galdiff, meanwhile, looked amused at their discomfort.

"I'll reopen it soon," Aefric said, before any of the others could voice an objection. "When Ser Micham is continuing on his assigned task once more."

"But surely, your grace—" Mayor Vagran started, but Aefric silenced him with a wave.

"I have verbal agreements to my rulings," Aefric said. "Nothing more. And under the circumstances, I'll see my orders *enacted* before I allow the harbor to reopen."

The mayor visibly swallowed his objections, and looked as though the words had given him indigestion.

Aefric cocked an eyebrow.

"All the more reason to see matters settled quickly," Aefric said. "Would you not agree?"

Holding his lips shut tight in a line, the mayor only bowed. His harbormaster / son looked even more furious, but at a signal from his father, bowed as well. If that quick, jagged movement could be called a "bow."

As they all made their way down the broad, tiled road toward the docks — on foot, at Aefric's insistence, given the crowd — he asked the mayor about those prisoners.

"Several of them were known to us already, your grace," Mayor Vagran said, sounding more comfortable on this subject. "Wanted on charges of smuggling and piracy, mostly, but those are high crimes here in Ajenmoor."

"They are indeed," Galdiff said happily, rubbing his palms together. "Including two known cronies of Nelazzi herself."

"He's right," Mayor Vagran conceded reluctantly. "Those taken today included both Captain Brusi and *Gwawl*."

Captain Brusi? Interesting. Apparently Mavash had held some information back while he was supposedly telling all...

Galdiff actually started chuckling with pleasure.

"Who is Gwawl?" Aefric asked the mayor.

"Gwawl," Mayor Vagran said with a sigh, "is a highly placed wizard in the service of Nelazzi. Your grace might've noted him as favoring green garb. Gwawl's wanted for a *list* of crimes." He shot Galdiff a dark look. "And the reward for his capture..."

"Will, when added to the others — especially the slavers — be almost enough to make up for the loss of the *Swift Wave*," Galdiff said, and bowed to Aefric again. "Thank you again, your grace. Rest assured that I and my ships will ever sail in your service."

Aefric nodded slowly. On the one hand, keeping Galdiff and his ships readily available had been the half the point of allowing him to keep the bounties and rewards.

On the other, he looked far less chastened by the whole experience than Aefric liked.

"So long as you remember..." Aefric said, letting his words trail off to see how Galdiff finished his thought.

"Of course, your grace," Galdiff said quickly. "I assure your grace that never again will I or mine impede those about business in his name. Why, I will even swear here and now to render all your grace's future messengers and agents such service as I and mine can provide."

Galdiff was saying the right words, but the way he said them still made Aefric uncomfortable, so he acknowledged those words with a nod, but nothing more.

"I take it," Aefric said to the mayor, "that this Gwawl will provide information useful to finding and stopping Nelazzi?"

"Oh, your grace," the mayor said, frowning. "We have nowhere near the resources necessary for such an undertaking. Not unless your grace intends to grant us significant aid."

"What about the slavers?" Aefric said. "Tell me at least that you're getting information that will help shatter this ring of slavers that dared operate on *my* lands."

"Well, your grace," Mayor Vagran said slowly, "these things take time. If you were to rescind Duchess Arinda's proscription against torture—"

"I will not," Aefric said.

"Then, alas, getting such answers will not be swift, nor easy."

"Perhaps," Aefric said, confident that the prisoners would provide *something* that would become useful, once Karbin returned.

Which made Aefric wonder how his old friend and mentor was doing...

Meanwhile, all about them, the late afternoon streets were mostly clear. At least, for the block or so nearest. People could be spotted watching from the safety of distance, or windows — especially on second and third floors — but no one tried to approach.

So. It seemed that Aefric's marching through the streets accompanied by a small force of knights and soldiers was causing some consternation.

That was fine.

Word would get around about *why* Aefric had arrived in force — especially once word spread about the soldiers on ships in the harbor — and that might make life easier for his future messengers and agents.

"Although," Mayor Vagran said, frowning in distaste, "on the subject of prisoners, I fear I must ask. By any chance did your grace recover a certain ... pendant or amulet from Gwawl? He's been complaining for want of it. Claims it was taken from him by a man with a staff."

"Yes," Galdiff said quickly. "As property of a prisoner I am to receive credit for, by right of law and custom that item should be mine."

"I do have it," Aefric said, though he'd forgotten all about that bronze pendant with its spark of magic until this very moment. "Though I intend to hold onto it."

"But your grace," Galdiff said, greed in his voice, "by right of *law and custom*, that amulet should be mine."

"And it is your intention to assert that law and custom be followed in this matter?" Aefric asked.

"Of course, your grace," Galdiff said with a bow. "After all, without law and custom, we're no better than borogs."

Aefric had *almost* felt bad about what he was about to do. Until Galdiff said that about borogs.

"Very well, then," Aefric said. "I shall follow law and custom in the matter of Gwawl."

"Thank you, your grace," Galdiff said eagerly, visibly restraining himself from holding out a hand. "Does your grace have the amulet with him?"

"It was my spells that stopped Gwawl and brought him into custody," Aefric said, "and I can provide witnesses if desired."

"I witnessed," Ser Beornric said.

"As did I," Ser Yrsa said.

All around them, Aefric knights slapped their hilts in agreement.

"As such," Aefric said, "I assert that Gwawl is my prisoner by right of law and custom. General Yrsa, we'll be taking him back to Water's End."

"Yes, your grace," Ser Yrsa said, giving Galdiff an evil smile.

"I'll see that his things are made ready, your grace," Mayor Vagran said, smiling at Galdiff's clear discomfort.

"But..." Galdiff said, paling. "But your grace said that all the prisoners ... that..."

"Such was my intention," Aefric said. "Not because I felt they were your due by action, nor by law and custom. But as a gesture of gratitude for the speed with which your ships and sailors came to my aid."

Aefric shook his head. "But for all I know right now, that pendant may be the key to taking down Nelazzi, the slavers, or both. And I'll not surrender it. Which, it seems, requires me to keep Gwawl as my prisoner."

"Perhaps, your grace, we could—"

"We cannot," Aefric said, then arched an eyebrow at Galdiff, who'd begun sweating now. "I trust, Galdiff, that if I find I require other information or possessions from the remaining prisoners *in order to stop those who prey on our sea lanes*, that there will be no dispute?"

"None, your grace," Galdiff said, swallowing.

Aefric clapped him on the shoulder.

"You do not yet know me here," Aefric said. "But I assure you. I claim that pendant not for greed or power, but because I may need it as I pursue the slavers and Nelazzi."

"Your grace truly intends to take down Nelazzi?"

"I don't like pirates. I don't like smugglers. And I *especially* don't like slavers. And she works with all three. She must be stopped."

Aefric shook his head with a sigh. "Or at least, she must be *hampered*. If I cannot stop her, I'll at least make her turn her eyes away from our lands and ships."

Galdiff shook his head, looking at Aefric as though he'd said he'd make the sun rise in the west.

He swallowed his words, though, frowning in thought as he looked out into the distance.

"Though something Galdiff said has reminded me," Aefric said to the mayor. "About your bounty on borogs..."

---

THE REMAINDER OF THAT AFTERNOON WAS ONLY ABOUT ONE PART interesting for every three or four parts dull, in Aefric's mind.

It seemed that taking possession of the *Swift Wave*, transferring ownership of the mastless hulk, taking custody of Gwawl and the like all involved paperwork.

Lots of paperwork.

But the good moments made even the tedium worth enduring.

The sheer relief of the refugees on seeing Aefric again, and being told they'd soon be taken to Water's End.

Those poor people had looked stressed and exhausted almost beyond endurance, but they broke out into smiles and a ragged but honest cheer all the same.

That alone was almost worth the risk of war with Malimfar.

Almost. Aefric knew all too well that the *thought* of war and the *fact* of war were very different matters.

Nearly as good was getting to see Ser Micham greet his father and brother.

Ser Micham tended towards being reserved, when about his duties. But he hefted both his father and his brother into the air in one great, shouting, joyful bear hug.

He quickly recovered himself, bowed to Aefric, and began apologizing for failing to complete his task, but Aefric wouldn't hear of it. And he insisted his knight take some time to greet his brother and father properly.

The *Swift Wave* was *just* small enough for the voyage up the Searun, so Aefric had Ser Micham, the refugees, and the recovered cargo all transferred aboard it for the trip to Water's End.

The *Swift Wave* needed a crew, of course. But among the six ships

Aefric had brought with him could be spared enough sailors to see that ship safely about such a short voyage.

The mayor, his harbormaster, and Galdiff had all visibly paled at the sight of Aefric's five ships full of ready soldiers. But when the mayor finally managed to sputter a question about them, Aefric wasn't very reassuring.

"I didn't know what to expect in Ajenmoor," he said, "or why my knight had been delayed on his mission. I was ready to ... ensure compliance, if there were those who thought they could take advantage of the new duke."

The implications were not lost on any of them.

Most of all, Aefric had to devote a good deal of the rest of his afternoon to waiting. He was tempted no less than fifteen times to simply fly back to Water's End.

Ultimately, he chose not to. He didn't like setting the precedent of flying someplace *just* because royalty was waiting on him.

It reminded Aefric of what Karbin and Kainemorton had always said about teleportation — if the nobles could simply pay for it, wizards would have time to do nothing else.

Not that many wizards could teleport reliably and safely. Aefric himself didn't even know the spell...

The sun was setting by the time the paperwork was finished, everything that needed to be moved had been moved, and even the *Swift Wave* was ready for its trip up the Searun.

Unfortunately, by then, that was a trip the *Swift Wave* could no longer make on its own. The wind had shifted, and was supporting the river's flow. And as the mayor, the harbormaster, his chief assistant, and Galdiff all insisted, that meant oars were the only way up the Searun that night.

The *Swift Wave* didn't currently have enough crew to man the oars, and Aefric refused to have the refugees pressed into service.

"Best to wait until morning, your grace," Mayor Vagran said for the fourth time. "Dark has already begun to fall. Please. Allow me the honor of hosting you tonight."

On the one hand, the mayor had a point. The sun was setting over the Risen Sea, and already they'd called dock patrol out with lanterns to ensure enough light for the final stages of preparation.

In fact, the city itself was coming alive with lights. Streetlamps were lit along the docks and the second and third tiers. None yet on the fourth and fifth tiers, but they'd probably be lit up soon.

On the other hand, though, Aefric was keeping a *princess* waiting back at Water's End. Delaying his return trip until morning might be the worst thing he could possibly do...

He sighed. Clapped the mayor on the shoulder.

"Normally, I would be quite happy to accept your fine offer of hospitality," Aefric said. "And I'd like to spend some time here in Ajenmoor actually seeing the city, instead of rushing about on business."

He shook his head. "But alas, right now, matters are waiting for me back at Water's End that must be dealt with before morning."

Galdiff — who still hung about, though his business was long-completed — snapped his attention to Aefric.

"Anything I could be of assistance with, your grace?" he asked, a little too eagerly.

"No," Aefric said, forcing a smile. "Some things a duke must do for himself. But it means we must sail up the river tonight."

"Night sailing on a river is never entirely safe at the best of times," Mayor Vagran said. "But with the wind *and* the river against you?" He shook his head. "You won't get there any faster, your grace, if you run aground."

"Well," Aefric said with a smile, "the river, even I cannot help. But I have learned to make the wind serve me, when needed."

A spell he'd learned from Sirondfar, court wizard to Duchess Ashling of Merrek, after the Malimfar business this past spring.

A spell he'd learned ... but not had a good excuse to use yet.

"But your grace would be sailing away from the setting sun," Mayor Vagran said, reasonably, "and into darkness."

"Oh," Aefric said, allowing the yellow diamond atop the Bright-staff to begin to glow, "I think I can handle that."

"Your grace is determined then?" Mayor Vagran asked.

"Your grace really ought to consider staying here in Ajenmoor tonight," Galdiff said suddenly. "The people should have a proper chance to meet their duke."

"And they will," Aefric said. "When I return for a proper visit. At which time, I will also wish to discuss with the council the state of trade and trade routes, and what can be done to improve both."

"I'm sure that could be arranged for the morning," Galdiff said, getting a strange look from the mayor. "Or perhaps even over dinner..."

"It will wait," Aefric said. "Other matters take precedence right now, and those matters demand that I sail for Water's End. Tonight."

Galdiff opened his mouth to say something else.

"The question is decided," Aefric said, arching an eyebrow.

Galdiff nodded and bowed.

Aefric and his knights and soldiers boarded the *Duke's Hand* — save Ser Micham, who stood aboard the *Swift Wave* — while the mayor and the others watched from the docks, waving their goodbyes.

Then, with a smile, Aefric lit up the night with his Brightstaff, and conjured a wind to carry his ships up the river and back to Lake Deepwater.

This was no simple spell, though. It required nonstop focus and attention, for the duration of the trip.

But to be honest, Aefric found the effort exhilarating and fulfilling in a way that most of his ducal duties simply were not.

Plus, the need for concentration kept him from worrying about what might be waiting for him at Water's End.

## 5

―――――――

By the time the *Duke's Hand* was in Lake Deepwater once more, the dark skies were bright with stars, the moon rode high, and Aefric was exhausted, and damp with sweat.

What a day he'd had, starting before even that speech in Lachedran, then sailing to Water's End, then on to Ajenmoor, and all that had happened there.

Add to all that, the spells he'd worked to call enough wind to propel five ships upriver swiftly from Ajenmoor into Lake Deepwater.

Spells that were more taxing than Sirondfar had led him to believe.

But then, Sirondfar wasn't just a wizard, he was a *ventavis*, which meant he specialized in the magic of birds and weather. Perhaps, for him, these spells weren't taxing at all.

Of course, practice might've been a factor.

Oddly, Aefric felt more than just the mental effort of all that spell-work. His muscles ached. As though he'd been holding his arms, legs, and back tense for...

Oh. Yes. He probably had. The entire way. Something else to keep an eye on, in the future.

In the meantime, he called for water, and sat, panting, on his wooden chair on the afterdeck.

"You know," Ser Yrsa observed, from a folding, canvas chair to Aefric's right. "He could probably have stopped his spells the moment we left the Searun. Rather than keeping them going halfway down the lake."

"True," Ser Beornric said, from a similar chair to Aefric's left. "But when does our duke make things easy on himself?"

"Really?" Aefric said, accepting a skin of water from the captain's cabin boy. "That's the first thing you two have to say to me? Not 'impressive work, your grace,' or 'could we fetch you some food, your grace?' You have to point out that I could have stopped sooner?"

He drank deeply from the waterskin. But his question went unanswered.

"He's less winded than I expected," Ser Yrsa said to Ser Beornric, and the smile in her eyes — which did not reach her lips — said that she was enjoying their teasing.

"Even magic that drains him never seems to do so for long," Ser Beornric said to Ser Yrsa. "His recuperative powers are quite impressive."

"I'm sure the ladies of his court—"

"Are you two quite finished?" Aefric asked.

"Please," Ser Yrsa said, and now that smile twitched at her lips, "excuse us, your grace. We'd grown quite accustomed to your not hearing us over the last couple of hours."

"Made for some very interesting conversation," Ser Beornric added, hardly able to hide his smile, even under that bushy mustache.

"Still," Ser Yrsa said, her eyes practically twinkling with mirth now, "such magic, you performed. It was impressive work, your grace."

"Indeed," Ser Beornric agreed. "Could we fetch your grace some food?"

Aefric started laughing. And the moment he did, they laughed even harder.

"Let me guess," Aefric said, once he controlled his laughter enough for words. "You thought some mirth was in order?"

"It's been a very serious day," Ser Yrsa said. "And the evening doesn't look likely to get any lighter. It's never a good idea to go into a battle tense."

"And from your posture at the moment," Ser Beornric said, "you look almost dangerously tense."

"Fair enough," Aefric said, then frowned. "You think I'm going into battle?"

"You face the unknown in this princess," Ser Yrsa said. "And politics can be a battle as fierce as any fought in the fields of this world."

Aefric wasn't sure he agreed with that point, but his knight-advisers were right that he did need to relax.

He flared his nostrils, going for a deep breath...

...and failing.

Apparently the muscles through his torso were so tense that he couldn't take in half the air he was used to, even when trying.

He closed his eyes. Rolled his shoulders and neck. Focused on starting his breath as low down in his belly as he could imagine.

He tried to suck in a deep breath.

Twitching cramps raced around from his collarbone to his hips.

Aefric coughed out that failed breath. Rolled his shoulders and neck again. Rolled his hips next. Tracked his eyes up into the night sky, where the stars seemed almost to dance, and the moon was about halfway toward full.

He tried for that deep breath once more. Slowly.

Finally, he managed to fill his lungs and diaphragm with air.

He held that breath for several heartbeats, against muscles that wanted to force it back out and grab more air quickly.

He exhaled just as slowly and smoothly as he could.

He made himself draw six more deep breaths that way. Inhaling slowly, filling his lungs and diaphragm, then holding that breath, until he slowly let it out once more.

"Better?" Ser Yrsa asked.

Aefric nodded.

"Good, because we're coming into port."

Aefric shook himself. They were indeed.

The city of Water's End was a busy place even at night. The streets lit up not by the canted yellow light of oil lamps, but brighter white light of spells attached to poles by Aefric's predecessors.

The docks bustled with ships being loaded in preparation for leaving in the morning. The streets were alive with people, both those seeking entertainment at the end of their work day, and those whose work began with the setting sun.

Even as the *Duke's Hand* sailed the safe route through the reef, Aefric could hear the distant strains of music and shouts of laughter.

He imagined he could smell all sorts of wonders cooking and baking, but that might have been the fantasy of his empty, rumbling stomach.

He distracted himself from such thoughts by gazing at the castle itself, which was lit up by more than just the windows, and patrols atop the walls, and parapets.

The walls themselves sparkled by night, as though they were part of the lake, reflecting the stars.

A beautiful sight. And he could hear cries of wonder from the refugees aboard the *Swift Wave*, which followed the *Duke's Hand* through the reef ahead of the five ships carrying soldiers.

Kentigern was already waiting on the duke's pier, oil lamp in hand and surrounded by a handful of pages.

Aefric was tempted to ask how his seneschal knew to be there, waiting, for surely the man had not been standing there all evening.

Likely there was a perfectly reasonable explanation for Kentigern's seeming prescience about his duke's movements. Perhaps a signal system from the ships to the docks.

Aefric wouldn't ask, though. He liked the mystery of it.

The ship was barely in dock, and the gangplank lowered, before Kentigern started in.

"Your grace," he said. "Dinner has already been served, but—"

"The ship behind me is the *Swift Wave*," Aefric said, coming down the gangplank. "It's carrying refugees, cargo, and Ser Micham. He already has a letter for you, detailing these things and what I want done with them."

Aefric, now on the smoothed coral of the dock, with his knights and guards falling in around him, raised his hand to stop Kentigern's question.

"Add to those orders," Aefric said, "that I want those refugees fed at once, and lodged in the castle tonight. We'll meet about them in the morning."

"Yes, your grace," Kentigern said, and opened his mouth to say more. Before he could, Aefric continued.

"There's also an itemized manifest of cargo recovered from the smugglers I mentioned previously." He shook his head. "I've been told we'd never be able to find its proper owners. Nevertheless, I want you to go through the art objects. Look for anything that might be special or irreplaceable or otherwise significant, and set it aside. Most of it, though, is either seed or grain of some variety, and that needs to be sent where it will do the most good. Much of it to Goldenfall, I imagine."

Kentigern bowed acknowledgment, frowning a frown that Aefric knew well. It was the frown that said Kentigern had something he needed to say, but that he knew he'd have to wait until Aefric was finished before he could talk.

"Now," Aefric said, "I've also brought back a prisoner. Gwawl. Apparently he's a crony of that pirate queen Nelazzi."

Kentigern's eyes rounded wide. Nelazzi's raids on and around Deepwater's coastline had caused serious problems for Duchess Arinda a few years back.

"He's also a wizard, so he'll need an appropriate cell. I assume we have one?"

"We have several, your grace," Kentigern said, gazing back toward the incoming ships. "First installed ... five generations ago, and kept ready at the insistence of the Soulfists."

"And they were right to do so." Aefric shook his head. "There's more to talk about, about Ajenmoor and a few other things, but they'll keep until morning."

"Did your grace accomplish all he needed to in Ajenmoor?" Kentigern asked, showing surprising patience.

Perhaps his news wasn't all that dire?

"Not remotely," Aefric said, arching an eyebrow. "There are still answers I need, but I assumed it would be better if I returned tonight, given the presence of a certain princess?"

"Two princesses, your grace," Kentigern said, apparently caught between amusement and exasperation. "Princess Xenia of Caiperas arrived this afternoon."

AEFRIC WALKED QUICKLY ALONG THE DUKE'S PIER TOWARD THE CASTLE at Water's End, with Kentigern to his right, and Ser Beornric to his left. The four of them trailed a cloud of pages, and were surrounded by the knights and soldiers of his personal guard.

Ser Yrsa followed behind, organizing the debarkation of ships full of soldiers and refugees, and the offloading of the recovered cargo.

Ser Yrsa had been right. Aefric's night didn't look to be any shorter or easier than his day had been.

"Caiperas..." Aefric said, thinking. He'd never been there. Not as Aefric. But as Keifer he'd read of it in *Torn Kingdoms* sourcebooks. He knew he had. But in the moment he couldn't recall anything important about anyplace called Caiperas.

Well, he could remember that it was the setting of adventure module, *T2: The Keep on Windy Hill*, but that was hardly politically relevant.

"I don't recall it," he said. "Remind me."

"Caiperas is the kingdom east of Malimfar," Kentigern said quickly, — possibly before Ser Beornric could — "and south of Rethneryl. Its border touches Armyr only slightly, among the royal lands near Armityr."

"We've long had peace with Caiperas," Ser Beornric said. "Though they're old enemies of Malimfar. Their border disputes go back centuries. Maybe further."

"Caiperas has been making overtures to King Colm," Kentigern continued, "ever since the Battle of Frozen Ridge. Angling for a formal alliance."

"Great," Aefric said. "So this Princess Xenia is here to what ... help solidify that alliance?"

"The oldest way possible," Kentigern said, nodding. "Or at least, that's my guess. She arrived with a full entourage, as though expecting to stay a while."

"Why here? Why with me? Surely Prince Killian would be a more fitting pursuit for her."

"In that they are both royalty and of old families, yes," Ser Beornric said. "But Armyr, even after the wars, is still a rich, powerful kingdom. While Caiperas..."

"Is a darling place," Kentigern said, "by all accounts. But it's ... small, your grace. And not especially wealthy, or well-located, strategically."

"If Queen Eppida gives the king another son," Ser Beornric said, "Caiperas might be able to arrange a marriage to *him*. But to the crown prince?"

Both Ser Beornric and Kentigern shook their heads.

"Your grace, on the other hand," Kentigern said, "holds the largest duchy in Armyr, and has significant power of his own."

"What he's saying, if he ever gets around to it," Ser Beornric said, giving Kentigern an amused look, "is that in the eyes of many, you're practically a prince. Especially in terms of marriage eligibility."

Practically a prince...

Would that make Aefric a fit match for Maev after all?

Dangerous line of thought. By now, Maev might already be promised to Varondam's King Dalius.

Aefric shook away the thought, and asked a different question.

"How did that Malimfar princess, Astrid, react to Princess Xenia's arrival?"

"Her highness welcomed her highness like a sister, of course," Kentigern said, as though the answer should've been obvious. "Mind you, I don't doubt that privately she's furious. Especially since she'd gotten here first, but has yet to meet your grace. But she'll never let any of that show in public. She's royalty."

"Not necessarily the best indicator of self-control," Ser Beornric said. "I've personally witnessed royal anger in public settings on more than one occasion."

"Of course," Kentigern said, as though speaking to someone slow. "But always when there's a point to be made. It would have served Princess Astrid nothing to express her anger then. She'll show it when she'll gain something by it."

"Well," Aefric said with a sigh. "I have yet to eat any dinner. So, I guess I should invite both princesses to join me?"

"That will insult Princess Astrid," Kentigern said. "After all, she arrived first. No doubt she expects to be received by you first, and to have her say before Princess Xenia gets her turn."

"So I should invite Astrid to join me for dinner, and Xenia to join me for breakfast?"

"*Princess* Astrid and *Princess* Xenia, your grace," Kentigern said. "I know we're only speaking among ourselves, but your grace must not be overheard taking familiarities he has not been permitted."

"Thank you," Aefric said. "I'll watch that."

"Your plan, however, will insult Princess Xenia," Kentigern said, patiently. "After all, she's a princess, and will expect to be received properly at the first opportunity."

Aefric shook his head. "But she already knows another princess is waiting, and arrived first."

"And your grace is quite droll to suggest that will matter," Kentigern said, quirking a half-smile.

"Worse," Ser Beornric said. "Because Malimfar and Caiperas are traditional enemies, if you do anything that either can construe as showing favor one way or the other, they will take that decision as a political statement."

"So whatever I do, I'm insulting somebody," Aefric said, frustrated.

"Well, to be frank your grace," Kentigern said. "The insults began this afternoon, when Princess Astrid's people learned that you had docked here briefly, but did not receive her before setting sail again."

"And did you inform her of the reasons?"

"The reasons your grace gave me made little difference to Princess Astrid, I'm afraid," Kentigern said with an expressive grimace. "I believe the reference to lives hanging in the balance was taken as an excuse, not a reason."

Aefric stopped walking, forcing the whole procession to stop with him.

"All right," Aefric said. "This is what we'll do. I'm going to fly up to my rooms, to clean up and change. After all, I have royalty to greet."

"Your grace," Kentigern started, but stilled when Aefric raised a hand.

"Now, I want the refugees and cargo — and the prisoner — brought in as we discussed. But I want the soldiers of my personal guard acting as escort. And, Kentigern, I want you choosing a route that will make sure they're seen, but not as though we're trying to *make* them seen."

"Ah," Kentigern said, smiling. "I know just the route, your grace. I can ensure that both princesses hear about it from their own people."

"Good," Aefric said. "You are, of course, to personally oversee this, by my order. Take as much time as you need to, to make sure that word gets back to both princesses before you go to them. Then tell them I'm back, and have rushed to make up for my inexcusable tardiness in meeting them."

"May I use those words, your grace?" Kentigern said, smiling wider.

"You can tell them they're my words, if you think it will help."

"It's even true," Ser Beornric said with a chuckle.

"Please also tell the princesses that the day has kept me so busy that I've barely eaten."

"Also true," Ser Beornric said with a sigh. "Though you could have eaten in Ajenmoor."

"Not while we had so much going on," Aefric said. "No, not even when matters were slow."

Aefric turned back to Kentigern.

"Tell them then that I require a late supper, and that I wish to invite them both to join me in my private dining room, so that we may all meet in mutual friendship, and enjoy an evening's company before politics rears its ugly head."

"Your grace," Kentigern said, grimacing. "That's hardly—"

"No," Ser Beornric said, smiling. "It's clever. Think who's saying it, and what they know about him."

"Exactly," Aefric said with a smile. "I've been an adventurer most of my life, and a duke for a little more than a season. Surely they won't be expecting me to be politically adroit enough to see the insults they might take at being greeted together."

"Perhaps," Kentigern said, tugging at his heavy, dark brown beard. "They *might* even be willing to accept your grace's ... unorthodox idea for the evening. If I make sure to seem frustrated by the phrasing."

"Which you are," Aefric said, smiling and clapping Kentigern on the shoulder. "Come now, Kentigern. Surely I've given you a *wealth* of frustration to draw on, over the past season."

Kentigern arched an eyebrow. "I'm sure I don't know what your grace means."

Aefric started laughing, and Kentigern's eyes sparkled with mirth.

"Well," he admitted, smiling, "perhaps a *little*." He nodded. "This might work, your grace."

"It's worth a shot, at least," Aefric said. "Anything else before I fly?"

"A thousand things, your grace," Kentigern said. "But none of them more important than two princesses."

"Then here we go," Aefric said, and took to the air.

---

The summer night was warm, but felt much cooler as Aefric soared through it on his way to his ducal apartments.

His personal apartments in the Castle at Water's End stretched across three floors, high up in the main keep. The lowest section included his personal dining room and sitting room, a solarium, a music room, an art gallery, a war room, and a couple of other rooms besides.

All the areas that the "public" might have access to were on that bottom floor of his apartment. The public part was only theoretical, of course. Although he was considered available when in one of the rooms on that floor, the truth was that even most of those who lived and worked in the castle would never set foot in one of those rooms.

The second level up included the duke's bedroom, a secondary, more private sitting room, his closets, his personal library, his bath room, garderobe, and similar. He also had another solarium on this floor, as well as a meditation chamber.

The third level included his study, magical library, and laboratories for magic and alchemy.

And the right word was enough to light most of these rooms with soft, apparently sourceless white light, generated by the spells of Aefric's predecessors.

He landed on the small balcony of the second floor, outside the glass doors and between the intricately carved greenwood furniture.

The magic lock on the door opened at his touch, and he entered the secondary sitting room.

Dajen, his chief evening valet, waited, standing tall and straight in livery of the Deepwater colors. As though he both knew Aefric was arriving, and *how* he would arrive.

Impressive.

But then, Dajen had to have been approaching his sixtieth summer — though the only signs of his age were in the halo of snow white hair around his bald head, and the few wrinkles gracing his face — and had served the dukes and duchesses of Deepwater his whole life.

Aefric was hardly the first Duke of Deepwater to arrive at his rooms by landing on the balcony.

Dajen not only had a better understand of color, texture and fabric than Aefric ever would. He could recount every major fashion trend of his lifetime, and more minor trends than Aefric cared to think about.

The man knew his business.

"Your grace," he said with a bow. "I have taken the liberty of having a bath prepared, and clothes for the evening laid out." He raised one snow white eyebrow. "I presume your grace has foregone eating again?"

Aefric — a man who had faced death in countless ways over the years — nodded, embarrassed. Something about the way Dajen carried himself made Aefric feel like a guilty schoolboy, caught out by a favorite teacher.

"Will your grace be dining alone?" Dajen asked, taking Aefric's cloak and backpack. "Or will the visiting princesses accompany?"

"Don't you know the answer already?" Aefric asked, stripping down as he made his way into the bath room.

"It is polite to ask, your grace," Dajen said.

"Then yes, the princesses have both been invited. Though I don't know if both will accept."

"They will, your grace. If only out of curiosity."

Aefric's bath room here was done in patterns of white marble that showed veins of silver and gold. And the matching marble bathtub itself was immense. Easily big enough for eight to bathe together, and enchanted to keep the water at just the right temperature.

Which made Aefric wonder if he just happened to enjoy the same heat in his baths that Arinda had, or if the spells detected the perfect temperature for the bather, and accommodated.

If so, would that change the temperature if Aefric had company in the bath?

But he had no time for such questions now. Nor to soak in the tub for as long as he liked, enjoying the smells of the excellent herbal concoction Dajen had arranged for him.

Today that combination was one Aefric couldn't quite place. Something woodsy, though. Maev would've been able to pick out the details.

*Ah, Maev. Two princesses visiting him tonight, and neither of them the right one.*

Worse the right one was likely off getting married. And Aefric himself might be pressured into taking as a bride one of the two princesses he'd meet tonight.

Then again, perhaps not. Arinda had always made clear that she would plan her own marriage, when the time came. Though she'd died unmarried, and without acknowledged issue.

Both details the sort that might make King Colm pressure Aefric not only to marry, but to marry a woman who would bring advantage to all of Armyr.

If so, which way would the king lean?

Towards Princess Astrid, the crown princess of a country Armyr had so recently been in conflict with? A match with her might ease tensions and forge a more lasting peace between Armyr and Malimfar.

Or would he lean towards Princess Xenia? A princess — though likely not a crown princess or Kentigern would have said so — from a country Armyr traditionally had good relations with.

Or at least, a country they hadn't been in active conflict with. Either way, a country not important enough to marry the king's own children to, but possibly important enough to pressure a duke into marriage...

Ah, well. Aefric could worry about that if and when King Colm made his wishes known.

And all of that was assuming that Princess Astrid wanted to *marry* Aefric. Kentigern and Beornric seemed to think she would. Aefric, though, still considered the possibility that she was here to challenge him to a duel or something.

And Princess Xenia. Both Kentigern and Beornric seemed to think it was a foregone conclusion that she'd want to marry Aefric. But what if she was counting on that assumption? What if she was actually here to negotiate some kind of trade deal, and counting on the possibility of marriage to bring her more favorable terms...

Aefric sighed, as he scrubbed. Too many variables.

Especially since Aefric had to consider the possibility that he was manufacturing these other outcomes to avoid considering the most likely reason that they'd come here.

Marriage. To a rich and powerful duke, who had the favor of his king.

There was no denying that Aefric was the second most eligible bachelor in Armyr, after only Prince Killian.

Until he committed himself to one marriage or another, visits from hopeful noblewomen, even royalty, might be a fact of life.

Still. Such visits from noblewomen made sense. But princesses? That seemed odd. After all, he might be a fairly powerful and influential duke, but he was still a duke. Not a prince.

Which meant that, if they were here for marriage, they saw more advantage in that match than just his lands and title. Could they covet his coastline? His magic? Something else besides?

Thoughts like those kept his mind busy enough that Dajen had to noisily clear his throat to make Aefric realize he was clean and had been delaying.

He accepted the towel then, and dried off.

To wear, Dajen had laid out clothing that emphasized Aefric's background as a magic-user.

Hose of silver, with a velvet tunic of deep, midnight blue. Occult symbols had been embroidered all over the tunic, in silver thread. Nothing significant, of course, but they looked good.

The belt was a sash of cloth-of-silver, that would never hold a sword or even a wand sheath.

Aefric cocked an eyebrow at Dajen.

"Your grace's ... affectation of carrying the Brightstaff notwithstanding, certainly he does not expect to meet royalty while armed."

Aefric sighed. "I suppose not."

It did, at least, have a loop for the dagger that all nobles were expected to carry on their person.

Once Aefric's blonde locks were brushed out, Dajen offered him the ducal coronet.

Aefric frowned at it. It seemed too much. Hammered gold, with a large sapphire in a central triangle, and smaller rubies and emeralds alternating around the rim.

"In meeting royalty," Dajen said softly, "one is expected to wear one's coronet."

"Fine," Aefric said, and put it on. And he put on the emerald ring Queen Eppida had given him. And the gold brooch, studded with sapphires, that Duchess Ashling had given him. "But that's enough."

"I still think," Dajen started, holding up a gold necklace, but Aefric shook his head.

"I'm wearing more than enough jewelry."

"Your grace knows best," Dajen said, sounding as though he meant those words without a trace of irony, which Aefric found hard to believe.

Aefric studied himself in the full-length mirror. He felt gaudy, but Dajen nodded as though the look was right. And Dajen knew fashion better than Aefric could ever hope to.

"Would your grace care to wait in his study until the princesses arrive? I've set out a book of kindaren poetry. I think your grace will appreciate the author's views on power and beauty."

"That does sound tempting," Aefric admitted. "But I'll wait for them in the dining room."

"But your grace," Dajen said. "These are your lands and your castle, and they the visitors. They should be seen to wait for you."

"Normally, perhaps," Aefric said. "But I've given out all the royal insults I intend to today. I don't mind waiting for them, if it might be taken as eagerness to meet them, or some other kind of compliment."

"Then I shall hope they take it thus," Dajen said, dusting Aefric's shoulders and straightening his belt, before nodding. "In any case, I shall have the servants send word that your grace awaits their pleasure."

"Thank you, Dajen," Aefric said, taking the Brightstaff in hand.

At least, if all this came out wrong, he'd have *one* weapon at the ready.

AEFRIC STILL HAD TO SMILE SOMETIMES, AS HE WALKED AMONG HIS apartments.

He'd thought his rooms at Behal Castle had been spacious to the point of excessive. And yet, they were tiny and cramped beside what he had at Water's End.

And the duke's personal dining room was a perfect example.

At Behal, when dining in private, Aefric sat at a table in his sitting room. At one end of that sitting room, true, but still in the same room. And the table had seating for eight.

But here at Water's End, when dining in private, he had a room for just that purpose.

A room whose white maple floorboards were covered in rugs that emulated the look of Lake Deepwater, and whose walls had been plastered and painted a soft, sky blue.

The walls were also covered in rich tapestries depicting pleasant floral scenes. Though a soft, yellow, painted sun peeked out from its hiding place on one wall, behind a tapestry.

The closest any of the tapestries came to depicting violence was the handsome young hunter who'd been surprised in the woods by a leaf-clad forest nymph riding a unicorn. And his bow dangled forgotten in his hand.

Large windows along one wall looked out past the wide balcony, over the castle walls, and gave a view of the lake beyond.

Soft yellowish light came from spells on the unlit candles of the chandelier that hung above the dining table.

Tonight, the dining table was small, though it, and its three chairs were ornately carved from deeply polished calinwood.

The table had come from a separate room, tucked away behind a tapestry, which held a variety of tables and chairs, depending on the duke's need on any given night.

Much the same way, a secondary kitchen hid behind another tapestry, where even now cooks were busily making sure that every part of that night's meal would be served at just the right cook and temperature.

In one corner of the room, two musicians — a pair of married kindaren, noted for the sweetness of their harmonies — finished tuning their lute and bodhrán.

Two knights of Aefric's personal guard stood in the hallway outside the room. No doubt the princesses would bring their own guards, but by keeping his own guards in the hall, theirs would have to remain there as well.

The illusion of privacy, given the coming and going of servants. Also, the fewer swords in the room that evening, the better, far as Aefric was concerned.

He sat at the head of the small table, with the Brightstaff standing beside his chair. He kept his thoughts busy by trying to guess which princess would arrive first, and which would be the one wishing to arrive last. Either to make an entrance, or to keep him waiting.

Even though doing so would mean giving her rival — political rival, at least — the first chance to speak with duke.

In the end, neither arrived first. They arrived together. Which meant that the poor page at the door likely had to make the choice of which one to announce first.

Aefric stood as soon as the door was opened.

The page, a fragile-looking youth, bowed and announced. "Your grace, may I present their highnesses, Astrid Eadredsdottir, Crown Princess of Malimfar, and Xenia Zaredes, Princess of Caiperas."

Ah. Of course. One was a crown princess, and one was not. At least that made the page's job easier.

They came into the room together, and though both had the pale beauty that all nobles seemed to have in this part of Qorunn, otherwise they couldn't have been more different.

Princess Astrid was a tall, slender woman, with high cheekbones, creamy skin, and long blonde ringlets. She wore a dress of vibrantly purple taffeta, high at the throat, but with slashes at the sleeves and skirts that showed off red silk. She wore bracelets of gold on each wrist, rings on three fingers of each hand, and a brooch with gold worked as rays of the sun, and a large carnelian in the center.

Atop her ringlets, she wore a gold diadem that featured a ruby, surrounded by small diamonds.

Princess Xenia was shorter, and curvaceous, with a heart-shaped face, skin like a late-season peach, and dark brown hair woven into braids down her back. She wore a low-cut gown of ice blue velvet crisscrossed with cloth-of-gold weave. For ornamentation, she wore only a single gold ring on each hand, and a gold necklace that ended in a unicorn whose horn had been expertly carved from diamond.

A blue diamond was the star of Princess Xenia's gold diadem, surrounded by smaller diamonds, rubies, and sapphires.

Both princesses came in wearing only a little magic. One ring each, worn on the index finger of the right hand.

"Your highnesses," the page said, bowing low to them, "may I present his grace, Ser Aefric Brightstaff, Duke of Deepwater and Baron of Netar."

Now came the bows. Kentigern had gone over them. Dajen had gone over them again. Just to make sure.

Because Aefric was the host, the foreign princesses had to bow first, in the order they were announced.

Then, because they were princesses and he only a duke, Aefric had to bow *lower* to them, than they did to him.

Unfortunately, both princesses bowed deeply. In fact, unless Aefric was mistaken, they seemed to be competing for which of them could bow lower.

If it *was* a competition, Aefric's money would be on Princess Astrid. She could bow all the way to the rug without the risk of falling out of her dress. Princess Xenia ... would be relying on the skills of her dressmakers.

Fortunately, they stopped short of any wardrobe malfunctions.

Unfortunately, they'd still bowed so low that Aefric practically had to touch the rug with his forehead to bow lower. But he managed it. Though he did have to catch his coronet to keep it from falling off.

And when he came up, they both seemed...

...Well. To be honest. Aefric couldn't tell what they were thinking. Princess Astrid held close to a completely blank expression, while Princess Xenia looked amused. But then, she'd looked amused since they came in.

"Your highnesses," Aefric said, "would you care to join me at the table?"

"That would be lovely, your grace," Princess Xenia said with a smile. "Thank you."

"Would it?" Princess Astrid asked, but not as though she expected an answer. "I can't help but wonder why we were *both* invited to your table tonight, your grace."

"Come now, Astrid," Princess Xenia said, while they took their seats. "You arrived scarcely a day before I did, and we both know our dear duke here has been quite busy in the interim."

She turned to Aefric. "Lachedran, Water's End, Ajenmoor and back to Water's End in one day, your grace? Do I have that right?"

"You do, your highness," Aefric said with a smile and a deep breath. "I confess. I'm exhausted. But I couldn't keep such important guests waiting for a little matter like sleep. And with you both here, I feared that inviting one and not the other might be taken as a statement."

He shook his head. "I'm quite new to politics, I'm afraid."

"I understand your grace left with six ships this afternoon but came back with seven," Princess Astrid said. "A feat of magic quite useful for a duke with such a long coastline."

"Hardly a feat of magic," Aefric said. "The seventh ship was taken from smugglers."

Aefric then told them an expurgated version of what happened in the Dragonscar, omitting any mention of mines, borogs, magic pendants, specific names of prisoners, and the like.

As he did this, the first salad course was served. A mixture of greens, along with a variety of savory mushrooms that grew under the docks, and three kinds of peppers. All with a light oil sauce.

To accompany the salad, a light white wine.

Without appearing to give the movements much thought, each

princess passed her right hand over her plate of food and goblet of wine. As each did so, the ring on her index finger flared green.

Of course. Poison detection. Green would mean that the food and drinks were safe.

"I must confess," Princess Astrid said, after Aefric's tale was told. "We've had our troubles with smugglers and slavers as well." She shook her head just enough to make her ringlets dance a little on her shoulders. "The aftermath of the wars, I fear. And we're in a worse position to fight them off than we were in the spring."

"Yes," Princess Xenia said, "well, when one attempts to invade another country, one must be prepared to pay the price."

"The price was disproportionate to the invasion," Princess Astrid said, dropping her silver fork and narrowing her eyes.

"Malimfar brought quite an army to our doorstep," Aefric said softly. "I did what I had to do to drive it back. Nothing more."

"It may be that your grace sees things that way," Princess Astrid said. "But the fact remains that our army has been decimated. Our lands ravaged by an unseasonable blizzard and plundered by mercenaries—"

"Mercenaries *your father* hired," Princess Xenia observed.

"—and to top it off, our largest remaining port city after the Godswalk Wars, Kivash, was *stolen* by the armies of Armyr. Now I ask your grace, does that seem like a just 'price,' considering that our armies never even crossed the border into Armyr? Let alone made war?"

"Your highness should not pretend to be the wronged party in this matter," Aefric said. "Malimfar's armies might not have begun their work, but the invasion was already underway. I would remind your highness that in my duchy alone, Malimfar had agents working to sow dissension and foment rebellion among my vassals. I will be dealing with the aftermath of Malimfar's efforts for years to come."

Which reminded Aefric he needed to check the latest reports about his county of Motte.

"If your grace believes that then he has been misled," Princess

Astrid said, haughtily enough that she might have believed it. "Malimfar does not employ such base methods. Perhaps—"

"The information was gained from Ser Grud Ol'Garan, Knight of the Garnet, and confirmed by the king's justiciar, who operates under the auspices of Taesark."

It was said that those who served Taesark, the god of justice, could ferret out truth even from those who had been fed only lies.

And Princess Astrid's eyes had widened slightly at Aefric's mention of Ser Grud. Only a flicker of a reaction, true, but enough to show that she knew the name.

The musicians began to play then, a slow, soft love song that felt entirely inappropriate. Though it did sound beautiful.

---

THE SECOND COURSE OF DINNER THAT NIGHT WAS A LIGHT VEGETABLE soup served in a savory broth, with slices of a local yellow cheese sharp enough to pierce the hull of a ship.

Princess Astrid was quiet during the soup course. She maintained her pleasantly blank expression, but Aefric had no doubt that her thoughts whirled.

It could be that she was ignorant on the subject of Malimfar's espionage. But then, she certainly couldn't deny a report that came from a justiciar of Taesark.

Of course, it could also have been the case that she knew exactly what Malimfar had been up to in Deepwater, and was trying to figure out some new way to spin it.

Either way, the result was that she ceded the conversation to Princess Xenia, who filled the time with questions about Deepwater that were clearly intended to flatter Aefric.

She wanted to hear about the beauty of his coastline, the richness of his farms, the production of his mines and quarries. Even topics that might have involved trade interest, or similar, were phrased in such ways as to focus on complimentary aspects.

For example, when asking about the ring Queen Eppida had

given him — which was woven from sixteen different shades of gold, she'd phrased the question: "Such a lovely ring, your grace. Tell me. Was it fashioned entirely from your grace's own gold mines? I've heard it said that the mines in the Threepeaks are rich enough that your grace could build a keep entirely of gold."

Aefric scarcely recalled later how he'd answered such questions, save that he'd erred on the side of self-effacing, and always tried to turn the topic around.

Though asking about Caiperas was not so easy, when he knew so little about it to begin with.

Princess Astrid finally rejoined the conversation between courses, while the kindaren musicians were singing a ballad about lovers lost in a forest, only to be guided to each other by friendly animals that served Halstaffur, the Green Lord.

"Your grace must forgive my silence—"

"Must he?" Princess Xenia asked, clearly enjoying Princess Astrid's discomfort.

"—but I have found his suggestions most troubling. Malimfar has always upheld the strictest rules of honorable warfare—"

"I beg to differ," Princess Xenia said archly.

"Of course you do, Xenia," Princess Astrid said breezily. "Begging comes easily to you. As I'm sure his grace will learn soon enough."

Princess Xenia dropped her fork, put her hands on the table and began to rise, glaring at Princess Astrid.

Princess Astrid returned the glare, and matched the movement.

"Your highnesses," Aefric said, "I will not have violence descend on my dinner table."

They held their glares.

"I believe Princess Astrid had a point to make. I'd hate to see that point get lost."

The glares continued.

"*Enough*," Aefric said. "I will not have the conflicts between Malimfar and Caiperas turn my castle into a war zone. If the two of you must fight, have a duel and be done with it. Otherwise, control your tempers or leave my duchy."

Both glares turned into surprised looks at Aefric.

"You would require us to leave?" Princess Xenia asked. "So soon? Both of us?"

"What choice do your highnesses present me?" Aefric asked. "If your highnesses cannot share a private dinner without incident, how can I trust their behavior in front of my court?"

He shook his head. "No. This must end. If you must fight, have your duel and let that be the end of it. Otherwise, I would have your highnesses' promise of peace for the duration of their stay."

"I'm not at all certain your grace has the authority to ask that of us," Princess Astrid said.

"I have the right of high justice," Aefric said. "If I have the power to take a man's head, I have the power to swear two princesses to peace."

"Not quite the same thing, your grace," Princess Xenia said softly, as though hesitant to correct Aefric. "This is not a matter of law, but of rank and authority."

"And without a royal writ or decree to support him," Princess Astrid said, "your grace lacks sufficient standing to compel us."

On this, it seemed, they were united.

"These are my lands," Aefric said. "This is my castle. You are my guests. If you will not respect your host enough to behave yourselves during your stay, then I will regard you as poor guests and require you to leave."

Aefric was gambling now. The host-guest relationship was critical to noble society. He knew that much. But he was still learning how it worked. He *might* be right about what he'd just said — that they'd be behaving as bad guests — but in truth he might be the bad host for asserting himself above his rank.

If that was what he was doing.

Either way, he could only watch as they digested his words.

Princess Xenia rolled in her lips as she looked back and forth between Princess Astrid and Aefric.

Princess Astrid retreated behind her pleasantly blank expression, but Aefric could practically hear her thinking quickly.

These two hated each other. That much was clear. But was their hatred more important than whatever mission brought them here?

Because certainly they couldn't doubt that, right or wrong, Aefric meant what he said, and he *would* have them removed from his lands. If he had to.

"Very well," Princess Astrid said. "For the sake of improving relations between Malimfar and Armyr, I shall set aside any ... disagreements with Xenia, save for those that merit a challenge."

"And in the spirit of the love that Caiperas and Armyr have always held for one another," Princess Xenia said with a smile, "I shall likewise set aside any disagreements with Astrid that do not merit a challenge."

"I thank your highnesses," Aefric said.

The second salad course came next. A mixture of crispy vegetables served with a tangy sauce that went quite well with the slightly stronger white wine served with that course.

During that course, the musicians sang a song about a shipwrecked sailor whose life was saved by a mermaid. Sadly, the mermaid's heart was broken when the sailor was later rescued.

Their final verse was a two-part lament, of how the mermaid would pine for the sailor, and how the sailor would pine for the mermaid. With the end suggesting that to this day they searched the seas for one another.

While enjoying that course, Princess Astrid resumed what she had been saying before.

"Your grace's suggestion about the use of agents to sow dissension and foment rebellion," she said between bites. "That is contrary to the way Malimfar has always conducted warfare."

"And yet," Princess Xenia said, "Malimfar thought nothing of massing its forces and hiring mercenaries in support of an attack without first declaring war."

"Only a fool declares war before fighting," Princess Astrid said. "Wars are declared once they are fact, not theory. Anyone with any knowledge of history knows this."

Sadly, Aefric couldn't deny it. In his experience, invasions tended to precede formal declarations of war.

Turning back to Aefric, Princess Astrid continued.

"Our scouts watch Armyr, as we assume Armyr's scouts watch us," she said with an elegant, one-shoulder shrug. "If we managed to amass a major force without Armyr noticing and assembling a force to match us, then the error is Armyr's. Not Malimfar's."

"So," Princess Xenia responded, "you postulate that every country should keep a weather eye on every country that borders it, or they deserve to be invaded?"

"This is the way warfare has been conducted since time out of time," Princess Astrid said with another slight shrug, then turned to Aefric. "Please forgive Xenia her ignorance in these matters. She had no head for strategy."

Princess Xenia tried to say something then, but Princess Astrid spoke faster to get the rest of her point out.

"Naturally, Father expected an emissary from Armyr to come ask about the massing armies, and negotiate a peace without bloodshed. Instead, King Colm took the coward's way out and sent a wizard to rain down ice and snow."

She quickly raised a hand in a gesture that came close to apology.

"I mean no offense to your grace's skills. But armies expect to be matched by armies, with wizards playing their proper roles, and no more. To attempt to shortcut the whole process with spells that not only slaughtered many, but ruined the land beneath for years to come. Well. That was ... excessive."

Of course, the land she spoke of was hardly rich farmland...

"An interesting point," Aefric said. "May I retort?"

"Please do, your grace," Princess Astrid said, and honestly looked interested in Aefric's answer.

"I shall begin by addressing the issue of Malimfar's massing forces, and the response from Armyr. I happen to know that Duchess Ashling of Merrek, whose duchy forms much of Armyr's border with Malimfar, was aware of the massing forces, and was building her response."

"Wise of her," Princess Astrid said, while Princess Xenia frowned. Perhaps feeling left out of the conversation.

"However," Aefric continued, "your highness suggests that Malimfar was massing its forces openly. And that's not entirely true. After all, half of the Indecisive River Valley belongs to Malimfar. And yet its forces were not massing on Malimfar's side of the river, but up above the ridge beyond, where their numbers could not accurately be gauged.

"Further," he continued, "the ridge hid from Armyrian sight the presence of those mercenary companies. Scouts from Merrek would have been hard pressed to assess the strength of Malimfar's forces accurately to within ten thousand soldiers. To say nothing of the siege engines I myself saw while flying."

"The key," Princess Astrid said, "was that we were not hiding what we were doing. Withholding information about the extent of our resources was simply good battlefield management."

"Hardly the same thing," Princess Xenia said.

Princess Astrid visibly checked herself from loosing an insult there, so Aefric hurried into the conversational gap.

"Perhaps. However, it does not address the larger point. Malimfar sent agents into Armyr aetts, perhaps a whole season in advance of assembling its armies. Agents working to turn my vassals against each other, and against me, before I'd even arrived in Deepwater. And these agents did their work in such a way as to try to shift the blame for their Deepwater activities to Merrek."

"Well," Princess Xenia said. "That would make invasion easier, wouldn't it? I mean, perhaps I don't have Astrid's 'head for strategy,' but it seems to me that getting the nobles to squabble among themselves would soften Armyr up for invasion. And getting one duchy to blame another, well, that would split forces. Wouldn't it?"

Princess Astrid tried to say something, but this time it was Princess Xenia pushing ahead to finish her point.

"It seems to me that this is hardly a shining example of the honorable warfare Malimfar *claims* to uphold."

Princess Astrid frowned. Turned her attention to Aefric.

"I know that your grace is convinced that Malimfar has done this thing," she said. "And I know that speaking even unintentional untruths to a justiciar blessed by Taesark cannot be done, let alone deliberate lies."

"Does make the evidence rather damning," Princess Xenia said with fake sympathy.

"And yet," Princess Astrid said, "I would swear before your grace here and now, that if such activities were commissioned on *behalf* of Malimfar, they were done without the *knowledge and permission* of Malimfar."

She shook her head. "I know my father would never countenance such a thing."

"Perhaps you know strategy, but not your father," Princess Xenia said.

"Do you *want* that challenge, Xenia?" Princess Astrid asked. "Because if you do, I'll forgo a champion if you will."

"Your highnesses, please," Aefric said, making calming gestures until both eased back in their chairs again. Then, to Princess Astrid, he said, "Whether King Eadred knew or not, the fact remains that the blame for the activities of Ser Grud and his agents belongs to Malimfar. And I fear that if you cannot accept that, we will have difficulty finding much to discuss profitably."

Princess Astrid considered that, while the three of them finished their salad.

---

The main course of the meal that night in Aefric's private dining room was a fivefin shark steak, served with a rich sauce that brought out the subtleties in the shark's flavoring. It paired well with a crisp white wine that seemed to add dimensions to the taste of both the shark and the sauce.

It was served with a small side of mussels, a soft, chewy bread, and asparagus spears.

Through the main course, Aefric started to believe that the

princesses were willing to be on their best behavior for the rest of the meal.

They didn't bicker. They didn't discuss sensitive subjects. Both seemed happy to discuss the positive aspects of their respective countries, and to ask for tales of Aefric's adventuring days.

In fact, Aefric found himself relaxing. Enjoying their company even. Both princesses could be quite charming, when they wanted to be. And whether Princess Xenia was telling of a misadventure on horseback while riding with her maids, or Princess Astrid was recounting entertaining mistakes she made while learning to sail, both seemed content to settle into allowing themselves to be pleasant company.

In fact, it wasn't until the dessert course — a mixed berry compote, served with fresh, whipped cream and a sweet white wine — that Princess Astrid finally addressed an uncomfortable topic.

"Your grace," she said. "I know that the history between Malimfar and Caiperas has been ... difficult. With poor decisions made on both sides."

"I can accede to that," Princess Xenia said with a nod.

"But before this past spring, there had been peace between Armyr and Malimfar for close to a century. And even then, our last dispute was what had led to us sharing the Indecisive River Valley in peace and comity ever since."

"Well," Aefric said, "'ever since'..."

"The words were poorly chosen," Princess Astrid said. "But the fact remains that, for the most part, relations between Malimfar and Armyr have been pleasant."

"I'm afraid I'm too new to Armyr to speak to that," Aefric said. "I'd have to consult my historian."

"I would take it as a kindness if you did," Princess Astrid said. "So that your grace would know that I do not exaggerate."

"She's telling the truth," Princess Xenia said, reluctantly. "Though we've had our problems with Malimfar since time out of time, their relations with Armyr have traditionally been frustratingly good."

"With that in mind," Princess Astrid said, "and in the spirit of past good relations, I will reveal one truth I need not reveal, make to your grace one promise, and ask of your grace one boon."

"All ... right..." Aefric said, while Princess Xenia frowned as though Princess Astrid were doing something clever and unexpected.

"The truth I need not reveal is this. Ser Grud of the Garnet is known to me. He did, in fact, spend much of last year at court in the capital at Svarturvigi."

Aefric had already guessed as much from a hint she gave earlier, but said nothing.

"The promise I make is this," she continued. "I shall investigate the actions of Ser Grud and such others as might have been involved, and find their source. For I know that it could not have been my father. He would not countenance so cowardly an act."

In another world, the part of Aefric known as Keifer would have referenced the common term "plausible deniability." But he wasn't sure the phrase was known here in Qorunn.

"What will you do when you find this 'source?'" Princess Xenia asked.

"We are speaking of wrongs committed in Malimfar's name. I shall turn the guilty party over to my father, of course, to see justice done." Princess Astrid turned to Aefric. "And then I shall return here and bring you a full report of my findings. And, if my father is willing, the perpetrator's head."

"The head will not be necessary," Aefric said, "but I would be curious about the report."

"Then you shall have it, your grace," Princess Astrid said, smiling now. And there was such purpose in her smile that it made her prettier.

Interesting.

"And the boon your highness would ask?" Aefric asked.

"It is of two parts, your grace," she said. "But they are related. First, I would ask that your grace pardon my behavior earlier, especially the ... vehemence of my insistence that Malimfar had been the wronged party in the events of this past spring. I lacked critical information to judge the situation."

Princess Xenia managed to convey sheer disbelief while doing nothing more than exhaling.

"Would it help if I requested a copy for your highness of the justiciar's report regarding Ser Grud?" Aefric asked.

"It would. Thank you, your grace," Princess Astrid said with a smile. "And the second part of the boon I would ask is this. I am well aware that during your grace's tenure as duke, he has had good reason to think ill of Malimfar. I would ask that he keep an open mind regarding my kingdom ... and its royal family."

Her smile took on a shy quality then that was simply devastating. Aefric's heart lurched, despite himself. He had to swallow before he could speak.

"I have learned since the Godswalk Wars that many previous assumptions must be reexamined. I can attempt this with Malimfar as well."

Of course, keeping an open mind was no promise that he would forget what had gone before...

"Your grace is most kind," Princess Astrid said, holding that shy smile.

"Fortunately," Princess Xenia said quickly, "I need ask no kindness in regard to the history between Armyr and Caiperas, which has always been good. However, in the spirit of the evening, I too would be willing to offer a truth I need not reveal, make your grace a promise, and ask of your grace a boon."

Princess Astrid's turn to give her counterpart a slight frown.

"First the truth," Princess Xenia said. "When I was young I tried to study magic with the hopes of becoming a wizard." She sighed deeply. "Alas, I had not your grace's gift for it. Though I do retain a few modest skills."

With one hand raised and a look of intense concentration, she managed to make her dessert fork wobble on the table for a moment, then rise hesitantly into the air a few inches, before falling back to the table.

A bead of perspiration ran down the side of Princess Xenia's face, and she was breathing hard, as though she'd run up a dozen flights of stairs.

"Hardly much of a secret," Princess Astrid said, arching an eyebrow. "Your father sent far and wide for tutors for you."

"Yes," Princess Xenia said, getting her wind back. "But his grace wasn't likely to know. And it's hardly the sort of thing one admits to an accomplished wizard such as his grace."

Aefric would never have said so, but he knew Xenia for a failed apprentice the moment he met her. Training at magic leaves its mark upon a person.

Which was part of what frustrated him about certain eldrani "spells" like the Cat's Eyes. They didn't *feel* like magic, but what else could they have been?

Maev knew the Cat's Eyes — the only human he'd ever met who did — but she carried no sense of magic-user about her...

"Please," Princess Astrid said dismissively, and pulling Aefric's attention back to the conversation. "You only did your little party trick as an excuse for heavy breathing in that—"

"And what of *your* secret?" Princess Xenia asked. "From the moment his grace mentioned the name Ser Grud, it was quite obvious that you knew the knight. Really, you *must* learn to school your reactions if you would pretend to hide such information."

Now *that* was interesting, and a truth Princess Xenia might not have realized she was revealing. Because until that moment, Aefric had considered her the more visibly responsive of the two princesses.

But if she considered Princess Astrid's momentary flinch a large reveal, what did that say about her own apparent reactions? Were they all affectation? Done in the service of a desired outcome?

A disturbing thought.

"For the promise," Princess Xenia said then. "It was obvious from your grace's tone earlier that he hates slavers. Well, we of Caiperas hate them too. And I promise to make contact with all our trade agents and gather such information as I can for your grace about these slavers that trouble his lands."

"Trade contacts from a landlocked kingdom," Princess Astrid

said, practically rolling her eyes. "I'm sure the information you gather will prove *invaluable*."

"Did I interrupt *you*, Astrid?"

Princess Astrid raised her hands, conceding the point, and gestured for Princess Xenia to continue.

"And the boon?" Aefric asked.

Did these women *train* in shy smiles? The one Princess Xenia turned on Aefric then was at least as powerful as Princess Astrid's.

"I was hoping that, before I return to Caiperas, his grace might be willing to show me some of the magic I have heard so much about."

"I don't see why not," Aefric said.

"Oh, thank you, your grace," she said, smiling broadly.

Princess Astrid took that as an opening to turn the topic back to Aefric and his magic, his training and the like, which topic lasted through the end of dinner.

* * *

DINNER, AT LAST, WAS ENDING, AND AEFRIC LOOKED FORWARD TO seeing the two princesses on their way so he could have a little time to himself before bed.

At least they weren't Armyrian noblewomen. He didn't have to worry about their personal rivalry bringing them to his chambers that night.

At least, he didn't *think* that would happen...

No. Someone would have warned him.

No, soon they would return to their own rooms, and he could finally take time to read his letters from Maev, Byrhta, and Vercy. And then there were reports that he really ought to go over before his morning meeting with his advisers.

He might even try to contact Karbin by message spell. He'd expected to hear from his old mentor well before now, and he was starting to become worried.

He didn't believe there was a *true* need for concern. Karbin had pulled himself out of tighter scrapes than a simple investigation into a ring of slavers. Hells, the man had once fought his way back from the Abyss itself.

Still. Odd that he hadn't reported in yet.

Aefric was just saying his goodbyes to the princesses, near the door of the dining room when Princess Astrid turned, a thoughtful look on her face.

"Your grace," she said. "As I must leave for Malimfar in the morning, to begin my investigations properly, might I have the honor of sharing a last drink with you on the balcony?"

"Oh," Princess Xenia said, turning. "That sounds like a lovely idea. It's such a pleasant evening."

"Oh, that's right," Princess Astrid said, and she smiled the way a cat smiles when it corners a mouse. "I imagine you'll need to leave for Caiperas first thing tomorrow. Won't you, Xenia?"

"Well, I—"

"After all," Princess Astrid continued, "you did promise to use Caiperas' *extensive* network of trade contacts to aid his grace's search for those slavers. And surely that cannot be done from here by rika bird."

"Well," Princess Xenia said, frowning, and visibly trying to find a way to counter Princess Astrid's logic.

"Although, from here," Princess Astrid said, "it might be faster to travel to those port cities in person for your share of the investigation. Caiperas is *such* a long way from here by horse."

Princess Xenia opened her mouth to say something, but this time Princess Astrid didn't even let her say "well" before pouncing.

"And you *did* promise his grace, didn't you."

Aefric had witnessed many duels in his day.

Duels fought with spells, swords, axes, daggers, maces, bows, crossbows, *hand* crossbows, even one ill-advised duel fought with ballista. But rarely did he see so one-sided a duel as the verbal takedown of Princess Xenia he'd just witnessed.

Princess Xenia sighed, and said, "You're right, Astrid. I really should begin at first light."

"In that case," Princess Astrid said, "I cannot object if you wish to join us. Should his grace be willing to share a drink and conversation with us."

"But of course," Aefric said, smiling. And the smile was actually sincere. After all, they were both leaving in the morning. And neither one had so much as *hinted* about marriage.

Well, all right. They'd hinted a *little*, but in such a roundabout way that Aefric felt he could be excused for ignoring those hints completely.

And in the morning they'd be *gone*.

Oh, they'd come back. That much was certain as well. But one thing Aefric had learned in his years of adventuring — focus on the problem at hand first. Tomorrow's problem could wait until today's problem left it enough room.

So tonight, a drink.

The balcony on the public floor of his apartments was wide and broad enough for a decent-sized party. Which probably meant that Aefric would be expected to throw parties here from time to time.

Again, that was a future problem.

Right now, he had two princesses, settling onto comfortable, padded greenwood chairs on that balcony that gave them a wonderful view of the lake. On a clear night like this one, they could see the lights in towns all around the lake.

Even, only just barely, the lights of Behal, away to the south, and Lachedran, to the north.

Just before joining them, Aefric called a servant over. A young girl who must've been in training, because he didn't know her name.

"Quick," he said softly. "Run upstairs to Dajen and have him pick out a drink fit for these two princesses, then bring it down with enough glasses for three."

"At once, your grace," the girl said softly, and whisked away up the stairs.

"The drinks will be out in just a moment," Aefric said, coming over to join them.

"The view is magnificent, your grace," Princess Astrid said, getting agreement from Princess Xenia. "Your grace really must visit us at

Svarturvigi. Our castle is not so grand as this one, but we have amazing views of the sunset over the Risen Sea."

"At Reyvenue," Princess Xenia said, "it is our view of the dawn that's the most striking. As it first peeks over the tip of the Demon, our mightiest mountain, it looks as a battle out of the tales of the gods."

"We have both views here as well," Aefric said. "The lake to the east, yes. But also the mountains to the north, and the Risen Sea to the west."

"But surely, your grace," Princess Astrid said, "the Risen Sea is too far for a proper view."

"From the keep, yes," Aefric said, then pointed up. "But from the Spike, which is what we call our central tower, the views cannot be beaten."

The serving girl came out with a bottle and three small, stemmed glasses. Both princesses checked the glasses and the bottle with their poison-detecting rings, then nodded for the girl to pour.

The liqueur was thick, and amber in color, and smelled sweet.

"To friendly relations among all our countries," Aefric said, raising his glass in a toast. The princesses both raised theirs in agreement, and all three drank.

The liqueur was strong, and tasted of honey and caramel. Both princesses made sounds even more approving than those they'd made for the dessert.

"Where did you get this?" Princess Astrid asked.

"I'll have to ask my valet," Aefric admitted. "I let him choose."

"And your grace admits that, rather than take the credit," Princess Astrid said, as though surprised. She raised her glass and smiled. "To an honest nobleman."

"They're certainly rare enough," Princess Xenia said, and raised her own glass in solidarity.

Aefric wasn't sure whether he should raise his glass to the toast, but he did drink with them.

"Oh," he said after the drink. "I promised your highness a display of magic. And if you're leaving in the morning, this is really the only time for it."

"Well," Princess Xenia said, shooting a glance at Princess Astrid. "I'd been hoping for a *private* demonstration—"

"I'll bet you were," Princess Astrid said.

"—but under the circumstances, I suppose we must make do." She gave Aefric a big smile. "Please, your grace."

"All right," Aefric said, setting down his glass. "I imagine lightning is what I'm best known for. And it's certainly showy."

"But potentially destructive," Princess Astrid said.

"I'm sure his grace knows what he's doing," Princess Xenia said, then fluttered her eyelashes at Princess Astrid. "Though perhaps a display of your grace's ice magic prowess—"

"Xenia!" Princess Astrid said, beginning to stand.

"Please, your highnesses," Aefric said, making calming gestures. "We were doing so well. Let us not descend again into pointless disputes."

Princess Astrid resumed her seat, but continued glaring at Princess Xenia, who was doing her best to ignore her counterpart, and pay her attention to Aefric.

"I'm sure whatever your grace thinks best will be more than good enough."

"Lightning it is," he said, calling the Brightstaff to his hand from where it stood no more than two feet away.

Princess Xenia made a small, impressed sound at that, while Princess Astrid rolled her eyes at her.

Aefric took his staff in both hands and raised it horizontally.

He mumbled a few nonsense words for effect, while he focused his will and his skills through the powers of his staff.

White fire began to play along the staff's length. He shifted his grip, and thrust the yellow diamond into the air.

Bolts of lightning shot off into the clear night sky. Yellow bolts at first, then green, blue, indigo, violet, red, orange, and yellow once more.

He thumped the staff on the ground, extinguishing its flames.

Both princesses applauded. Princess Xenia effusively, but even Princess Astrid looked impressed.

Aefric left the Brightstaff standing beside him, resumed his seat, and poured them each a little more of the liqueur.

The conversation was lighter then, but measured. As though the two princesses were still involved in some kind of conversational duel.

If so, though, Aefric couldn't quite follow the strikes and parries. Because they were discussing nothing more significant than ships and horses, weather, favorite meals and places and times of year.

By the time they finally departed that night, each giving Aefric a smile and a kiss on the cheek — which he took as a gesture of friendship — he had the feeling that he'd been involved in one conversation while the princesses were having another.

And he didn't know what it was.

***

With the princesses finally gone, Aefric ascended his carved, curved staircase to the private floors of his apartments.

Dajen was waiting for Aefric in the sitting room, standing crisp and tall at the top of the stairs, as though he'd known exactly what moment his duke would arrive.

Always. He *always* seemed to do that. If Aefric didn't know better, he'd've sworn magic was involved.

"I trust that your grace intends to retire to his study for a time?"

Not just a lucky guess, that time. Aefric had made it an almost nightly habit, before bed.

"I do," Aefric said, then hurried along to cut off what Dajen would inevitably say next. "I do not, however, require a robe, or other lounging attire. What I have on will suffice."

Dajen frowned. "Your grace is certain? He might be more comfortable in—"

"Dajen," Aefric said. "I appreciate your efforts. You must know this. But you must also remember. I used to live out of two or three sets of clothes for aetts at a time. I don't need to change my outfit three or four times a day, the way some nobles do."

"Your grace also often lived on" — Dajen frowned in distaste — "trail rations and the low cooking of the basest inns and taverns. Should I then ask his cooks to refrain from providing him such fine cuisine as he enjoyed tonight?"

Aefric laughed. "Don't you dare."

"I would never dream of providing your grace anything less than the best available of all things," Dajen said, a triumphant gleam in his eye. "And as your grace makes the transition to the expectations of a duke's life, he must consider that there are reasons for all such benefits. Including the changes of clothes."

"All right, all right," Aefric said, raising his free hand in surrender before Dajen started explaining what those benefits were. "I'll keep that in mind for the future. But for now, for tonight, I'm not changing my clothes again."

"If your grace insists," Dajen said with a slight bow. "May I provide any other service?"

"Some water for my study?"

"A fresh ewer and goblet await your grace even now."

"I should have known," Aefric said, shaking his head. "Three other things, then. Send word to my historian that I need a copy of the justiciar's report on Ser Grud Ol'Garan for Princess Astrid of Malimfar. Preferably prepared before the princess leaves in the morning."

"Of course, your grace," Dajen said.

"I'd also like two bottles of that excellent liqueur you chose for tonight prepared as gifts. One each for Princess Astrid and Princess Xenia."

"A fine choice, your grace," Dajen said with a small bow. "I'm pleased that they appreciated the honsach."

"They admired it a great deal," Aefric said. "And for the last thing, please inform my councilors that the princesses depart in the morning, and that our morning meeting will be a breakfast meeting, after I've said a proper goodbye to the princesses."

"I shall see it done, your grace."

Aefric thanked and dismissed Dajen then, and retired to his study, speaking the word that lit the room as he entered, closing the door behind him.

Ah, peace at last.

Aefric's study was one of his favorite rooms in the castle. Possibly because no one would disturb him here short of a pressing need.

But also, he enjoyed the study on its own merits. The cool blues and greens of the painted plaster on the walls. The soft, gray rugs spread out across the black walnut floorboards.

One long wall was covered in a tapestry map of Deepwater, from Kerrik Forest to the Risen Sea, and from border of Merrek to the Dragonscar. But the towns and cities were missing from the map, as were the castles of his vassals.

Instead, only personal residences of the duke himself were marked. The Castle at Water's End. Behal Castle. His hunting lodge in the Forest of Souls. A handful of other properties scattered across the lands held by his vassals.

On the short walls hung four large paintings Aefric had commissioned of views from atop the Spike. The north and east views on one wall, the south and west views facing it.

The other long wall featured windows, for such times as Aefric wished to gaze out over the lake. This evening, he had the navy blue curtains drawn shut. He'd seen enough of the lake today.

He had a large, calinwood desk in the center of the room, with a matching armchair. He also had a place to sit along each of the three interior walls, all of them overstuffed: a navy blue couch before the long wall, and a pair of facing armchairs on the short walls.

In the wintertime, braziers would probably need to be brought in, to drive away the chill. But tonight, the room was pleasant. Not too warm and not too cold. And the air smelled faintly of something floral.

Honeysuckle?

Perhaps. Or perhaps he'd just had Maev on his mind too much lately. That scent he always associated with her.

A small bookcase sat beside the door. Normally, it held only whatever books Aefric himself brought in from his library, for casual reading. Tonight, it held that copy of kindaren poetry that Dajen had spoken of.

The poetry could wait.

On a small, calinwood table on the opposite side of the door sat a chased silver ewer of water, and a matching goblet.

Aefric filled the goblet with water, collected the three letters from his desk — ignored the reports that lay beside them — and lounged on his couch to read. Maev's letter first, then Byrhta's, then Vercy's.

Maev's had been sealed with forest green wax, and her personal device: a bow (usually golden) with arrow nocked.

Aefric broke the seal and unfolded the letter...

---

*My dearest Aefric,*

*I hope you are well, and that the trip to the Dragonscar you wrote of planning was both successful and interesting. Might you have brought me back a piece of the dragon's skeleton?*

*A claw would be appropriate, I should think. Likely large enough to make a good bow. Strictly as a fancy, of course. Something to hang on a wall. For I doubt I should ever be strong enough to bend a bow made from a dragon's claw.*

*Though I would, of course, try.*

*I hope you brought yourself back a bit of that skeleton, as well. Perhaps a bit of spine, that could be sliced into a cross section and fitted with jewels as a proper coronet for a duke such as yourself.*

*And knowing you, you'd find a way to call some magic out of the bones, to make it both a weapon and an ornamentation.*

*I can just picture you wearing it. Shocking and impressing the whole of your court. Why, I bet all the young noblewomen would swoon at the sight of you.*

*The only swooning I might do down here in Varondam would be from the heat. Oh, but the summers are devilishly hot down here, Aefric. Their tailors had to outfit me with a whole new wardrobe.*

*The bright colors are ... pleasant enough, I suppose.*

*But the fabrics, Aefric. So thin! I fear that if I exert myself, my gown will come apart and leave me naked before the whole of the court.*

*Couldn't you just picture that happening to me?*

*Fortunately, they've also provided me hunting garb of appropriate thickness and strength. Likely because I threatened to go kill a stag and make my own.*

*I may anyway. I know you favor the way I look in my buckskin clothes.*

*Negotiations towards this alliance that Father wants are going well. Well enough that I might even be able to escape without a promise of marriage to their King Dalius.*

*It helps, I think, that I'm not what King Dalius had hoped for.*

*Mind you, he would never say any such thing. And he's the sort who believes that alliances are best solidified through marriage and children.*

*So that is working against me.*

*Still. From little things I've noticed here and there, I suspect that he's as disappointed in the fact of me as he was excited about the idea of me.*

*I believe he expected me to be some demure, retiring princess, offering up shy smiles and focusing on looking pretty. Never saying what was really on my mind, except behind closed doors.*

*You're laughing at that description of me. Admit it. Can you even picture me behaving that way? I certainly can't.*

*I know Father wanted me to be "on my best behavior" while I'm down here. But I won't lie about who I am. And if Father believes otherwise, then he's been turning a blind eye to the truths of his daughter.*

*I know he'll be disappointed that I haven't been charmed by King Dalius. But I cannot help that. Charm is not enough for me.*

*If I must marry King Dalius, then I will do so as my duty to Father and Armyr.*

*But it would not be for love, nor the hope that love would grow with time.*

*And if I can escape this wedding, I will.*

*Honestly, Aefric. King Dalius claims to love his hunting, but the man hunts with a crossbow.*

*A crossbow!*

*Certainly he's accurate enough, I suppose, but he takes forever to aim. And between the smells of the oil and the cacophony of that loading lever, he can only find game if others ride ahead and flush it out for him.*

*Plus, he moves through the forest with all the silent glory of an armored knight falling down a flight of stairs.*

*What's more, I think he's jealous of me, if you can believe that. I've told him more than once that I am a fully trained forester. And that I was a lead scout for Father during the Godswalk Wars.*

*I've probably shot more arrows this year alone than he has bolts his entire life.*

*Still. He considers himself a great hunter. And so it seems to prick his fragile ego that during the time he struggles to bring down a single deer, I bring down two or three, depending on my mood.*

*And when needed, I finish them myself with a proper dagger slice across the right part of the throat. Not with the stab of a rapier through the heart, damaging the pelt.*

*The man is good with his rapier. I'll give him that. He may have inherited the surname Swiftblade, but he more than lives up to it. Still...*

*Oh, dear. I've started ranting to you again. I am sorry, dearest Aefric. I know I said I would try to refrain from that. And I certainly would prefer to write to you of happier things.*

*Worse, a page has just come in. I am summoned to court for the presentation of ... some noble or other. King Dalius certainly keeps a large court.*

*And so, alas, I must go and put on some bit of thin frippery that passes for a gown down here. Even though the man I would most wish to see me wear such a thing is hundreds of miles from me.*

*No doubt being courted and seduced by countless noblewomen. Chief among them Byrhta Ol'Caran.*

*I hope they have not driven me from your heart and your thoughts entirely, in my absence. And I hope that Father has not yet begun pressuring you to wed, as he regrets not pressuring Arinda.*

*That really would be most unfair of him.*

*They call me again. I really must go.*
*Sylkanis sends her greetings. I think she misses you as much as I do.*
*Yours most truly,*
*Maev*

---

MAEV'S LETTER SMELLED OF HONEYSUCKLE, THOUGH TOO FAINTLY TO have shared its aroma with the entire room.

And yet, Aefric was sure now that he could smell honeysuckle in the room. Just faintly, but enough that it had to be deliberate.

Interesting. Had Maev commissioned one of his servants to scent the air of his study when he received her letter?

He wouldn't put it past her. And she already seemed to know him well enough to guess that his alone time in the ducal study would be sacrosanct.

If she did arrange that hint of honeysuckle to the air, it was a clever bit of subtlety from Maev, which suited her. If asked, she'd probably refer to it as "leading her quarry," or by some other hunting term.

Was it too much to hope that she'd hold on to a few of those dresses when she left Varondam? Aefric found he was quite curious to see her in such a "thin bit of frippery."

Though she would always look more herself in buckskins made by her own hand than any court dress. The way he'd first seen her. Long black hair streaming behind her as she rode up the road to Behal Castle that day this spring.

She wore her buckskins that day. Possibly to test the reactions of the new duke she'd heard so much about. And it was in buckskins he'd always picture her.

He found himself both happy and sad that she seemed ill-suited for King Dalius. Happy, selfishly, because he considered himself a much better match for her.

Assuming King Colm would even consider letting them marry.

Aefric felt sad, though, because she might have to marry King

Dalius. And she should have a happy life, with a husband she could at least grow to love.

Aefric lay back on the couch in his study, sipping gently from his goblet of water, and read the letter two more times. He was tempted to write back now, but decided to wait. He really ought to read the other two letters tonight, then write back to all three tomorrow.

He set aside Maev's letter and picked up Byrhta's.

It was sealed with blue wax, as most correspondence from River-break was, but the sigil was new.

Previously, Byrhta had had no personal sigil, any more than she had a personal title. She was the daughter of the Count of Goldenfall, but it was her elder brother Taeric who was due to inherit.

And yet, her letter had been sealed with blue wax, and impressed with the image of a harp.

An interesting choice. The harp was an instrument traditionally associated with the eldrani, whose blood she shared.

A fitting device for her.

The sigil, and the scent of her spicy and exotic perfume, left no doubt that this letter was personal, not business.

Aefric broke the seal and began to read.

---

*My sweet Aefric,*

*It feels as though the ages have shifted since last I saw you, though it has scarce been three aetts.*

*Perhaps I was spoiled for a short time this spring, by such steady access to your presence and your bed. If so, let me be so spoiled again sometime soon.*

*I miss you terribly.*

*The noblemen here in Riverbreak all seem to think that the title of ler should impress me. As though, merely because I do not stand to inherit my father's county, I should be excited to have petty nobles pay court to me.*

*As though the prospect of marriage with such as them should thrill me. No matter their age, or meager holdings.*

*They do not seem to realize that my father and my brother both would sooner make me a ler in my own right, than see me married to the likes of them.*

*Worse, I suspect that some of them hope to dazzle me with gifts and promises so that I won't realize they're actually trying to win power and influence over their baroness regent.*

*Fools.*

*Honestly. Because I have a portion of my grandmother's beauty, they seem to think I must be as slow-witted as a brained cow.*

*Of course, that assumption does have its advantages. I've been able to accomplish a good deal for Riverbreak, by manipulating those fools into doing what was better for the barony than for their own pockets.*

*We may double our grain production alone by next year. And...*

*Forgive me.*

*I began this letter as your lover, not your vassal, and it's not right for me to retreat into thoughts of business.*

*It's only that I'm so excited to be doing this work, Aefric. This is the first real chance anyone has given me to do more than play politics and look pretty.*

*Don't get me wrong. My father has always known that I am more than just ornamentation. And during my fosterage with Duchess Arinda, she saw to my education properly, and prepared me in case something happened to Taeric.*

*Arinda taught me so much. I will always be grateful to her.*

*But in the last few years, there has been little to truly engage my mind, and push me to do more than the simple tasks any courtier might do.*

*You are the first to give me such a chance. And it means so much to me that you did so not to impress me, nor to win any favor from me, but only because you believe in me. That I could do this job, and do it well.*

*You looked beyond the beauty that dazzles so many others, and saw the woman underneath.*

*I swear I shall prove that you made a wise choice, and that you are right to have confidence in me.*

*And as for thanking you for the opportunity, well, I promise to continue to do so. Every chance I get.*

*And I plan to get quite creative in how I go about expressing my gratitude.*

*I hope to make it to Water's End for a visit before the end of summer. That will depend on how firm a grip I get on the court here, in the interim, and whether or not Vercy will insist on coming along.*

*She will make a fine baroness one day. She has a good head on her shoulders, and I am training her as Arinda trained me.*

*She needs seasoning, though. Confidence. Too many of her lers and knights have known her since she was a child. And though she demonstrates at times that she can stand up to them, at other times the habit of yielding to her elders is too strong in her.*

*I blame her parents for that. Baron Karmody liked his women submissive, and Baroness Montess played into that. Pushed the idea that a noblewoman should be subtle and yielding in court, and expressive and strong only in private.*

*That might work for an untitled noblewoman, but it's a terrible thing in a baroness.*

*Fortunately, I have no trouble giving her a strong lead to follow. And you yourself have given me the opportunity to show her.*

*Vercy is still smitten with you. She speaks of you often, and in such hopeful terms that I think she truly does aspire to marry you one day.*

*She told me how Arinda "promised" to wed her elder brother Baston.*

*The poor dear. It sounds as though her whole family believed that was a true promise. I could have told them that Arinda made such "promises" only on whims, and never meant them to be taken seriously. They were as fleeting as compliments.*

*I cannot tell her that now, of course. Not after the shame her brother brought on her house. Though at least she accepts that you cannot be held to Arinda's "promise."*

*Though I daresay she still plans to prove herself a fit wife for you. An interesting notion.*

*But now, alas, I must go. Court is to begin soon, and I wish this letter to reach you by evening.*

*Give my best to Princess Maev, for I've no doubt she writes you as often as I do. She and I still need to have that talk she spoke of. Assuming she ever returns from Varondam.*

*Do write me back soon, Aefric. I know your duties keep you busy, but I want to hear all about the Dragonscar, and whatever other adventures you've found yourself embroiled in. I look forward to your letters almost as much as I do to seeing you in person.*

*And now I must say farewell, sweet Aefric. I hope that sometimes as you fall asleep, you think of me. As I think of you.*

*Yours,*

*Byrhta*

*P.S. I hope you like the sigil I've chosen. I don't believe you've ever heard me play the harp, but I'll correct that the next time I see you.*

*And you do know when I most love to sing to you.*

---

AEFRIC SIGHED, CONTENTEDLY, AS LAY BACK FOR A MOMENT ON HIS overstuffed couch, sipping his water and staring at the ceiling of his study.

Maev and Byrhta. Two such very different women. And yet, both held such deep appeal to him.

Interesting that Byrhta should mention the notion of Vercy proving herself a fit bride for Aefric. Vercy had first mentioned that idea back in the spring, just after the justiciar pronounced judgment on Ser Grud, Baston and her parents, for their roles on Malimfar's espionage.

It was expected, of course, that Aefric would marry a peer. A duchess, a rich enough countess perhaps, or even a princess. Or at least a highly placed family member of a peer.

The idea that he would marry a baroness, much less a baroness who was his own vassal, well, that was not an idea he should entertain. Everyone had said so.

But when Vercy put the idea forward, how was he expected to look into her eyes and deny her the possibility?

Of course, in *not* denying her that possibility, he had also opened the door for Byrhta to aspire to marry him as well.

Byrhta, who did not have even a title of her own, much less a dowry worthy of a duke. Until that moment, she'd likely been happy enough to be Aefric's friend and lover. Perhaps get a position at his court. The gods knew she was smart enough to do many jobs well.

But by bringing it up again in this letter, Byrhta was proving what Ser Grey — Aefric's castellan at Behal — had said this spring.

If Vercy had the chance to "prove" herself a fit bride, then so did Byrhta.

Hardly a horrible fate. Byrhta's beauty was famed across half of Qorunn, and she was intelligent, witty...

She wasn't Maev.

But then again, Maev wasn't Byrhta.

Marrying one would always mean losing the other. Which was the saddest part about having to choose.

Though that was a future problem. He certainly didn't have to choose tonight.

No. Tonight he could re-read Byrhta's letter another time or two for pleasure. To contemplate hearing her play the harp and sing. She would be naked, of course. She most loved to sing to Aefric when they were both naked, after lovemaking.

He even allowed himself to wonder just what she had in mind, when it came to expressing her gratitude.

Very pleasant things to think about. And he looked forward to writing back to her as well.

But for now, tonight, there was the letter from Vercy.

Vercy's letter was perfumed as well. Water lilies, if Aefric guessed the scent correctly. She had no personal sigil yet, so she'd impressed the blue wax with the Riverbreak device: an otter, facing to the dexter.

Aefric broke the seal and began to read.

---

YOUR GRACE,

*Do you know what I heard today? Some of my lers feel affronted that you chose Byrhta to be my baroness regent, instead of one of them. Apparently, some of them have taken to grumbling together about it, over wine.*

*The gall. To believe they know better than their duke.*

*Well, in case any of them dare raise such concerns to your grace, allow me to set your mind at ease.*

*Byrhta has been a wonderful choice as regent.*

*I would swear that I have learned more about what it means to be a noble and how to handle courtiers in a single season with her than I ever learned from my mother.*

*To be fair, though, Mother never expected me to inherit the title. She was preparing me to marry a ruler, not become one myself.*

*But Byrhta has been teaching me how to hear beyond what is spoken, and how to read beyond what it written, to ferret out the meaning of what lies beneath.*

*She's so brilliant, poised and beautiful. I hope to be like her one day.*

*Well, more than that. For wonderful as the poor dear is, I shall be a baroness, and she, alas, shall have no title of her own.*

*I do not suppose that your grace could find a title for her? Perhaps the king could be persuaded to grant your grace permission to create her a baroness?*

*She would do quite well for your grace in such a role.*

*But, alas, I know better than to hope for such things for her. Merit alone is not reason enough to raise up a vassal.*

*Perhaps, instead, your grace could consent to help her father find her a fit marriage. Perhaps to Count Draven, who has his holdings among the royal lands. He is said to be quite handsome, and fairly rich.*

*No doubt Draven and Byrhta would make a delightful couple.*

*Perhaps your grace could invite him to the harvest festival at Water's End, and introduce them. I would be more than happy to assist. And I could certainly recommend her to him, if it helped.*

*Not that I want her getting married too soon. That might take her away from me, and I would hate to lose her wisdom and guidance before coming of age.*

*Though, admittedly, to see her happily married, I would accept that fate.*

*Though not all of my ideas come from Byrhta, of course. It was my idea to ride the length and breadth of my barony, letting my people see me, and learning how things really stand among the lands of my lers.*

*Perhaps that is part of the reason for the grumbling. I've seen proof that some have been lying about their taxes, and the treatment of their peasants.*

*Which reminds me. While we were riding my lands, Byrhta spotted excellent conditions for growing nysta. And given the popularity of nysta tea, that means another crop to improve Riverbreak's revenues.*

*Alas, I must go. Court is to begin soon, and I wish to raise ideas to Byrhta about...*

*Well. I shall tell your grace if those ideas bear fruit.*

*I trust that your grace is well, and hope that your grace shall write to me soon.*

*Your faithful vassal, and perhaps one day more than that, I remain*
*Vercy*

---

AEFRIC SMILED AS HE CONSIDERED VERCY'S LETTER. PUSHING TO FIND A husband for Byrhta, was she? He wondered if Byrhta knew of her charge's matchmaking desires, and what she'd say if she did.

Byrhta would probably like the idea of being created a baroness more than she'd like the idea of Vercy hunting up husbands for her.

Of course, if those mines in the Dragonscar proved as rich as they might, Aefric might need to create a baron to handle the lands up there.

Assuming the king would permit it, Aefric could do a lot worse for a new baron than Byrhta...

Of course, whether that happened or not, Vercy might have a point about this Count Draven being an excellent match for Byrhta. But if so, let her father make the arrangements.

Aefric was in no greater hurry to find Byrhta a husband than he was to find one for Maev. For much the same reason.

Which might have been part of Vercy's plan. Trying to remove some of her competition.

Still. Aefric would have to write Vercy back as well. Think of some way to write a letter that was cordial and fitting for a duke writing to a vassal, without being too encouraging about her ... amorous intentions.

He lay back on the soft gray, overstuffed couch and let his gaze run over the huge tapestry of his duchy, while he considered his three letters, and what he might say in response to each.

No, he decided, standing. He had spent enough time on letters and private thoughts. Midnight was not more than an hour or two away, and he would have to rise before the sun if he would see the princesses on their way in the morning.

And he very much intended to do that. Not only because it was his duty as their host, but to make sure they left.

He locked all three letters in a drawer in his desk. He looked at the reports that awaited his attention — left there, no doubt, by Dajen — but shook his head. They could wait.

He finished his goblet of water and opened the door of his study.

Dajen was standing not one step away. Waiting.

"How?" Aefric finally asked. "How could you possibly have known I was just leaving my study? Or have you been standing there this entire time?"

Dajen smiled. "Much as it might please me to lead your grace to believe I would stand outside his study door all night, waiting for him to emerge, your grace is far too aware of the other duties I perform on his behalf, to believe such.

"In fact," he continued, "I should first and foremost wish to assure your grace that the ducal historian has been made aware of his desires in the matter of the justiciar's report, and promised a copy will be ready before Princess Astrid takes her leave. Further, that two bottles of honsach have been prepared, and will be ready for your grace to present to the princesses in the morning."

"Thank you, Dajen."

"Of course, your grace," Dajen said with a bow. "And as to the matter of how I came to be standing outside your grace's study door at just the right moment, well. Your grace must remember that I have lived in this castle my whole life, and that I served both Duchess Arinda and her father, Duke Arallan, in the same capacity that I now serve your grace."

Dajen's gaze wandered about the sitting room and ceiling.

"I know these chambers better than anyone else. And I know their sounds. This gives me an advantage in understanding your grace's movements through his apartments."

"Fair enough," Aefric said, cocking his head to the side and narrowing his eyes. "Of course, that doesn't explain how you knew I'd be landing on my balcony this evening, exactly when I did."

"No, your grace," Dajen said with a smile. "It does not."

Aefric chuckled. Let the man have his secrets.

"All right," he said. "I think I'm ready to retire then, unless there's anything else I need to deal with."

"Only one matter known to me, your grace," Dajen said. "A visitor arrived while your grace was in his study. As I will not interrupt your grace in his study for anything less than a matter of critical importance, I have asked the visitor to await your grace's pleasure in the sitting room below."

"Who is the visitor?"

"Mistress Zoleen Fyrenn, your grace."

"Fyrenn?" Aefric asked for confirmation.

"Yes, your grace. The younger sister of her grace, Duchess Ashling Fyrenn of Merrek, and of her majesty, Queen Eppida Fyrenn."

"Is she the emissary sent by Duchess Ashling? Kentigern mentioned one."

"Yes, your grace," Dajen said. "And she brought with her a package. A gift from the duchess, I believe."

"And here I was hoping that could wait till morning," Aefric muttered.

"I could tell her that your grace is indisposed and not receiving visitors tonight," Dajen offered.

"No," Aefric said. "Better to get it out of the way. Thank you, Dajen."

"Of course, your grace. Will you wish refreshment?"

Aefric frowned. "Isn't there a servant on duty downstairs?"

"Pakel is on duty for the remainder of the night, your grace. I merely wished to be helpful."

"I'm sure if I need anything downstairs, Pakel can handle it. Thank you."

Dajen bowed, and Aefric went back down the curved staircase, glad he hadn't changed into lounge clothing.

---

AEFRIC FOUND ZOLEEN FYRENN IN HIS SITTING ROOM ON THE PUBLIC floor of his apartments.

When he entered, she rose from her seat on a large, padded maroon couch, where she'd been enjoying both a small glass of dark green sharabi and the view of the lake and the night sky.

Aefric would have known her as a Fyrenn even without Dajen's identifying her. Were it not for Maev and Byrhta, the Fyrenn sisters would have been the most beautiful women he'd ever seen.

And Zoleen had all the gorgeous beauty of her sisters. The striking features, the sapphire eyes. Her copper hair worn long in soft, gentle waves.

She was clearly the youngest of the three, right about the age of majority, but she held herself well, and filled out her deceptively complex red dress in ways that no doubt made her dressmakers sigh with joy, at getting to tailor for her.

"Your grace," she said, with a smile and a bow. "Thank you for receiving me at this hour."

"Well," Aefric said with a smile, gesturing to Pakel — a heavyset man about five summers older than Aefric — for a glass of sharabi as he walked toward the couch. "I know you've come on business for your sister Ashling, and I'm glad I don't have to make you wait longer than you have already."

"Hardly a burden to wait on so handsome — and busy — a duke as yourself, your grace," Zoleen said with a smile. "Especially when the waiting is done at so fascinating a place as Water's End. I suspect I could spend an entire summer here and not see even all of the castle, let alone all of the city."

"Too true," Aefric said, inviting her to sit with a gesture as he took his own seat on the couch. "I've been here a season, and I doubt I've seen half the castle myself."

"I have an advantage, though," Zoleen said mischievously. "I'm not constantly barraged by business and demands on my time while I'm here."

"True enough," Aefric said with a chuckle. He accepted his sharabi from Pakel with a word of thanks, and raised his glass in toast. "To finding time for the simple pleasures."

Zoleen raised her glass in confirmation of the toast, and they both drank. This dark sharabi was strong, with a rich taste that made Aefric think of blackberries.

After the toast, Zoleen set down her glass and picked up a small valise. She patted it.

"I have come bearing a gift for your grace, Ser Aefric Brightstaff, Duke of Deepwater and Baron of Netar, from my sister, Ashling Fyrenn, Duchess of Merrek, in gratitude for his efforts this spring in the Indecisive River Valley, not least of which was his stirring victory at Frozen Ridge."

She got all that out in a single breath without sounding rushed. Impressive.

"Your sister has already given me three excellent ships," Aefric said. "I hardly think she needs to give me more."

"She disagrees." Zoleen smiled. "In fact, her exact words to me were, 'Don't let Aefric humble his way out of this, Zolly.'"

Aefric chuckled. "All right then. What is the gift?"

Zoleen opened the valise and drew out two folded pieces of parchment. She unfolded the first piece. It was a sketch of a good-sized keep on a small hill situated near a river and surrounded by a town.

"Oh, what has she done?" Aefric asked breathlessly.

"When Merrek annexed the city of Kivash as retribution for

Malimfar's aggression this past spring, the city was taken intact."

Zoleen unfolded the other piece of parchment, which turned out to be a map of Kivash.

"The forces of Malimfari nobles occupied three castles within that city at the time. They were offered the opportunity to leave in peace, if they surrendered those castles and all properties and goods contained therein. When they realized how badly outnumbered they were, they chose wisdom, and accepted the offer."

Aefric let out a breath. Those nobles must have been screaming bloody murder to their king. Just another thing to upset Princess Astrid.

"The largest and finest of these castles, of course," Zoleen continued, "Ash — I mean, Duchess Ashling — retained for herself. The second largest she presented as a gift to his majesty, King Colm Stronghand, in thanks for his aid and support in driving back the forces of Malimfar, and in capturing the city."

She pointed to a marked spot on the map, down near the mouth of the river and fairly close to the town square on the southern bank of the Indecisive.

"And the third is here," she said. "The keep depicted in the drawing your grace has already seen. This castle and everything within it, her grace, Duchess Ashling Fyrenn, presents to your grace, Duke Aefric Brightstaff, as both a gesture of friendship and a gift of thanks for his quick thinking and decisive actions against the armies of Malimfar on her behalf, and on behalf of Armyr."

"That's too much," Aefric said under his breath.

"The castle is to be regarded as the property of the Duke of Deepwater in perpetuity," Zoleen continued, clearly enjoying Aefric's reaction. "And the castle, the hill it stands on, and the land beneath are to be regarded as part of the duchy of Deepwater, not the duchy of Merrek."

Zoleen put the map and sketch on the table and pulled a soft leather scroll case out of the valise and handed it to Aefric.

"Here is the deed and the formal letter associated with the gift."

Aefric looked at the scroll case in her hand and chuckled breathlessly in disbelief.

"In addition to those ships, she's giving me a castle?"

"A castle," Zoleen said, smiling, "the land beneath, and whatever goods and properties are contained within."

She raised the scroll case slightly, as a signal for Aefric to take it. He stared at it, unsure. It sounded like too much.

"Her grace's soldiers protect the castle right now," Zoleen said. "Keeping it safe from thieves and ensuring that it remains unspoiled until such time as your grace sends his own replacements. Preferably, while taking possession of the castle, and surveying its contents."

"She's too generous," Aefric said, shaking his head.

Zoleen frowned. Perhaps surprised that Aefric not only hadn't eagerly snatched that scroll case from her, but even accepted it at all yet. Her voice was more serious when she next spoke.

"Duchess Ashling is all too aware of how much her lands and people would have suffered, had your grace not stopped Malimfar at Frozen Ridge. Even a military victory would have come at a high cost of life, and done significant damage to both the river valley and Merrek's economy for years to come."

She offered the scroll case again.

Aefric finally accepted it, still shaking his head in wonder.

Zoleen picked up her glass of sharabi. Raised it as though in toast. "All that she has given your grace amounts to only a fraction of what she would have lost."

Aefric raised his glass, and joined her in the drink, still marveling.

---

AEFRIC SAT WITH ZOLEEN FYRENN ON THAT SOFT COUCH IN HIS SITTING room for some time. Drinking sharabi, looking out over the lake by night, and speaking of little more than pleasantries.

But Aefric's day had been long. So after no more than a second slow glass of sharabi, he smiled, stood, and said, "I've enjoyed sitting with you tonight, Zoleen. But I must rise early tomorrow, and so I should probably say goodnight."

"If morning must come early," Zoleen said slowly, while one hand teased along her thigh, "I would be more than happy to help ensure that your grace ... sleeps soundly."

The smile she gave him then left no possible doubt about her meaning.

Aefric looked her over, and had to admit he was tempted. Her beauty was exquisite, and his blood had already been raised by those letters from Maev and Byrhta.

It wasn't as though either of them would object to his taking this young beauty to his bed.

And the release *would* do him good.

Which left only one concern.

"You tempt me, Zoleen," Aefric said, letting his gaze wander over her again. "But I worry that you might be too young—"

"I reached the age of majority this past midwinter, your grace." She smiled and shook her head. "Ash said you would ask my age, if I came to you for the noble privilege. But I didn't believe her."

"Where I grew up," Aefric said, "no one below the age of majority was considered fit to give consent for such activities."

A statement that was both true and not true. It was true in America, where he'd grown and lived as Keifer McShane, but the question was ... much less clear in Sartis and the many lands of his youth in Qorunn, as Aefric.

"Well," Zoleen said, coming to her feet and closing the distance between them. "Then let me lay both those concerns to rest."

She raised up on her toes and whispered her next words scant inches from Aefric's lips.

"I, Zoleen Fyrenn, do solemnly swear on my family's honor that I came of age this past midwinter. And I further swear that I give your grace my 'consent' most freely and eagerly."

Aefric took her in his arms. Tasted the blackberries of the sharabi while they kissed deeply and clutched each other tightly. She whimpered into his mouth as that kiss went on.

The silks of her dress were soft under Aefric's hands. Part of him was tempted to tear them. To rip the dress right off her so that nothing stood between him and Zoleen's firm, hot flesh.

But no. That would be too quick. And Aefric had felt rushed about too many things. He didn't want to feel rushed about sex, too.

So he pulled back from the heat of the kiss, even though Zoleen's panting lips reached for his, for more.

He held up a single finger, and ran it slowly down her cheek. Enjoying the way she shivered in response as much as he enjoyed the smoothness of her skin. He dragged that finger along her chin then.

When that finger reached the tip of her chin, Zoleen dipped her lips and kissed it.

The look she gave him was fiery. Her hands twitched, as though wanting to tear off his clothes. Or at least to continue their explorations of his body.

"I am torn," he whispered. "Part of me wishes to take this slowly, and enjoy getting to know every inch of you. The rest wishes to tear off your dress and take you the first time here on the couch."

"The first time?" she whispered back with a smile. "I thought your grace had an early morning."

"I do," he admitted, reluctantly. "And yet beauty like yours deserves its proper due. I would never be sated after only a single draught."

She tilted her head to one side, and the quality of her smile shifted slightly. "This from a man who has known the charms of Byrhta Ol'Caran? My beauty is nothing to hers."

"Beauty should never be compared," Aefric whispered, leaning in and kissing her long, smooth neck. "Only appreciated. Preferably slowly. And repeatedly."

Zoleen pulled back, smiling with her eyes more than her lips, and put her hands on Aefric's chest.

"Does your grace truly believe that?"

"I do," Aefric said.

"And your grace truly wishes to devote a good deal of time to the slow exploration of my beauty? And to seek the bliss moment with me not just once, but several times?"

Aefric nodded, letting his gaze say more than his words could.

She shivered. "Well. I think that will be worth the wait then."

The wait?

Was she saying what he thought she was saying?

She leaned in, still holding his chest in place with her hands, and began planting small kisses along his jawline.

"Tomorrow night, your grace," she whispered, between kisses. "I shall return. And your grace can show me how so famous an adventurer would go about *exploring* me."

She pulled back and smiled.

Aefric trembled. His hands yearned to clutch her, but it sounded as though she were saying no. That for tonight, at least, nothing more would happen.

He was so ... ready for her. The thought of having to stop now, that was almost physically painful.

But if that was her will, then he would restrain himself.

"All right then," Aefric said, his voice shaky as he brought his hands together in front of the bulge in his hose, one hand clutching the other wrist for something to focus on other than the tempting beauty before him. "I shall ... say goodnight ... and look forward to tomorrow."

"Oh, your grace," she said with a low, throaty laugh. "I would not be so base as to bring your grace's blood to a boil, and then *abandon* him in such a state."

Aefric frowned, now, puzzled.

"Please, your grace, be seated on the couch," Zoleen said, gently turning Aefric so he could do so. "And let me give your grace a goodnight kiss he will not soon forget."

Zoleen knelt on the soft carpet before him and began to pull down his hose. Once that was done, the "kiss" she went on to give him was wondrous bliss itself.

After she finished, she left with a smile and a promise to return the next night.

And when Aefric retired at last, he slept very well indeed.

**6**

———————

AEFRIC AROSE BEFORE DAWN THE NEXT MORNING, BETTER RESTED THAN he'd expected to be. He bathed, was shaved, and dressed that morning in formal Deepwater colors.

His tunic was long, and of navy blue silk, and his hose, Deepwater gray, like his cloak. He wore a leather belt that day, with the wand Garram on his hip, though he eschewed the sword, in deference to the wishes of his guards.

According to Ser Beornric they took Aefric's wearing a sword as a slight on their ability to protect him. It was one thing when he was out and traveling, but another thing entirely when he was home, at one of his castles.

*One* of his castles. How many did he have now?

Four. Water's End and Behal, here in Deepwater. And two more he hadn't even seen yet. The first in his new barony in Netar, and now another, in Kivash.

How his life had changed from the days when he was a simple adventurer who owned little more than he carried with him.

He'd been a landowner as Keifer. In America. In Oregon. But the house he'd owned there would have fit easily inside his ducal apartments here at Water's End, with room to spare.

At least his guards didn't object to the Brightstaff. He'd carried it for years, and had no intention of stopping anytime soon.

Aefric had planned to wear his long blonde hair down and unadorned, but as he left his closets, he found Ocheda, his chief daytime valet, waiting for him, with a hat in hand.

Ocheda was only perhaps a decade older than Aefric, but she had a manner that suggested that she'd lived in Water's End for thousands of years, and knew better than anyone how to tend to a duke.

Everything about her was severe. Her height — she was almost as tall as Aefric. Her thin physique, her sharp eyes, and the even sharper temper she showed to any servants who had not done their work to her satisfaction.

Aefric sometimes wondered how well she and Dajen got along. But then, perhaps there was a reason he never saw the two of them together.

The hat she held was a bycocket, with its body of Deepwater gray, but its turned-back brim — which formed a point in front — of navy blue. The hat also featured a tailfeather from a pyltenius bird.

The pyltenius was sometimes called the false phoenix. For though it had the fiery red and orange coloring of its famous cousin, it had no magic to speak of.

The tailfeather was striking, though. Beginning from a hint of yellow near the quill, through an orange that darkened into a blazing red and finally a deep blue.

"No," Aefric said, shaking his head.

"I told Dajen you would say that," Ocheda, arching an eyebrow as though ready to pronounce doom on either Dajen or Aefric. "He insisted that I offer the hat anyway. He said that hats have been out of fashion too long among nobles. That they are due for a resurgence, and that your grace would do well to be the trendsetter here, and not the follower."

Aefric frowned at the hat. Dajen was right about so very many things...

He shook his head and put it on. "What do you think?"

Even her considering frown looked severe.

"Striking, your grace," she said. "The addition of the feather brings out the reds in your skin tone and the golds in your hair. Most becoming."

Aefric shook his head and took it off. "I used to wear hats, sometimes, when I adventured. I was forever losing them."

"I daresay your grace could afford more hats now, if needed."

He took off the hat and called the Brightstaff to his hand. "Tell Dajen I will think about it. But I'm not wearing it today."

"Would a different cut of hat help, your grace?" Ocheda asked. "This was Dajen's first choice, but I believe he had a couple of others under consideration."

"Perhaps," he said, then shook his head. "I don't know. I'll think about it."

"Of course, your grace," she said with a bow.

"And, Ocheda," Aefric said, turning away, "if this is some sort of game or joke between the two of you, to see if you could get me to wear that hat, I *will* have my revenge."

"Your grace is quite droll," Ocheda said, which Aefric noted was neither an admission nor a denial. Something to consider as he left to start his day.

---

WHEN AEFRIC HAD FIRST COME TO WATER'S END, HE'D WONDERED why the castle stables were at the rear, near the docks. He'd since learned that this was a clever decision by the castle's designer.

There were two ways to depart Water's End. By land along the Kingsroad and by water via the docks.

Because the stables were placed near the docks, Aefric did not have to meet one princess on one side of the castle that morning, and the other princess on the other side.

He wondered just how many incidents had been avoided, because past dukes and duchesses had been able to wish their departing guests farewell at the same time, no matter how they were leaving, rather than having to give one guest priority over another.

And so, it was just as the eastern sky began to gray with the coming sun that, by the light of oil lamps, Aefric met both his departing princesses that morning.

Princess Xenia, who stood with her guards and her cloud of ladies in waiting, while her several carriages and dozens of horses were noisily being readied for their trip.

Princess Astrid, whose guards stood nearby, but whose other retainers, and baggage, had already been loaded aboard her schooner.

The overnight chill was still strong enough that both wore cloaks. Apart from that — and their surprising lack of obvious jewelry — the princesses were dressed quite differently.

Princess Xenia wore riding leathers, and a whip-thin rapier, while Princess Astrid wore a fine dress of sky blue, and no obvious weapon beyond the token dagger at her belt.

Aefric hesitated, uncertain which to address first.

Princess Astrid gestured to Princess Xenia.

"Xenia has the far longer, harder road ahead of her," Princess Astrid said with a straight face. "I would take no offense if your grace said his goodbyes to her first."

"Thank you, Astrid," Princess Xenia said with a smile that seemed to indicate she'd won some kind of point, in the endless game the two of them played.

She stepped up to Aefric and offered him her hands.

He stood the Brightstaff beside him and clasped her hands.

"Thank you, Princess Xenia," Aefric said, "for coming to visit me. And thank you for the aid your highness will give me in hunting down that ring of slavers."

He released her hands, though hers parted only reluctantly. He hoped he hadn't just given insult, but he needed at least one hand free and wasn't sure that letting go with only one hand would have been any better.

He called a servant forward with a gesture.

"Here," Aefric said, "is a bottle of the fine honsach we shared last night. I hope you will enjoy it, and remember the friendship and pleasures of the evening we first shared such a drink."

He took the bottle from the servant and handed it to her.

"Thank you, your grace," Princess Xenia said with a bow. "Your grace has been a most excellent host, and I shall share your grace's generosity with my royal parents, who will enjoy both the gift, and the thought behind it, as much as I will."

She handed the bottle to one of her ladies, because her servants were too busy rushing to prepare to leave.

Aefric took that opportunity to turn to Princess Astrid, which got him a smile from her.

She, too, offered both hands, so Aefric took hers as well.

Meanwhile, Princess Xenia frowned, as though she hadn't considered her portion of the goodbyes finished.

"Thank you, Princess Astrid," Aefric said, "for coming to visit me. I confess that when I first heard tell of your coming, I suspected that your highness' purpose had been to challenge me to a duel, or something similar."

Princess Astrid laughed.

"How amusing, that your grace believes I would challenge him so."

"I believe that your highness would challenge anyone, if she believed she had cause."

Princess Astrid took the compliment with a smile and a slight nod.

"It pleases me to learn that your highness had no knowledge of the ... espionage worked against my duchy and my vassals, and I am gladdened to know that she will help root out the source of this problem, wherever her investigation takes her."

That was, technically, more than she'd promised to do, which Aefric could tell she recognized by the slight narrowing of her eyes. But she didn't correct him.

Aefric released her hands then, and she, too, let go only reluctantly. He called forward another servant with a gesture, and presented her with a bottle of honsach.

"I suspect this gift will not surprise your highness. But I hope that your highness will enjoy it, and remember the friendship and pleasures of the evening we first shared such a drink."

Princess Astrid accepted the bottle with a smile.

"Thank you, your grace," she said. "I have enjoyed my brief stay in your grace's magnificent palace, and hope to return for a longer visit sometime soon. Once I have the answers that we both require."

"To help with that," Aefric said, and gestured to a third servant, "I have here—"

"Wait!"

Around Aefric, three sets of guards turned as though to face down a threat.

But Aefric knew that voice.

Kentigern?

Aefric turned, and sure enough, there was his seneschal. Perhaps a hundred strides distant.

Running Aefric's way.

Running?

In the season or so that Aefric had lived at Water's End, he had never seen Kentigern move at faster than a brisk walk, and even then only because he needed to keep up with Aefric's faster pace.

But there he was, in his black velvet doublet and hose, chain of office bouncing on his chest and as he pounded the tile of the walkway with the soles of his favorite black boots.

Princess Astrid stepped forward, as though to take the justiciar's report from the servant, but Aefric, frowning, took it from the servant himself and held it with both hands.

Princess Xenia said something low to her counterpart that Aefric didn't hear.

"Your ... grace..." Kentigern said, arriving in a flash of sweat and exhaustion. "... must ... wait..."

He put his hands on his knees and fought to regain his breath.

"Fetch him some water," Aefric said to the servant who had held the justiciar's report. To the princesses, he said, "Forgive him, your highnesses, but he never interrupts me without good cause." To

Kentigern, he said, "Find your breath, good seneschal, and tell me what troubles you."

"Pri…" Kentigern panted. Shook his head. Swallowed. "Privately … please … your … grace."

"A moment, if I may, your highnesses," Aefric said, gesturing with the report for the Brightstaff to follow as he took his seneschal's shoulder in hand and steered Kentigern several paces away.

The Brightstaff floated after Aefric, staying close at hand. His guards took up positions between themselves and the rest of the assemblage.

All work of preparing for Princess Xenia's departure stopped, as all of her people turned to watch the spectacle.

"Whatever is the matter, man?" Aefric said, low in Kentigern's ear.

"The … report," Kentigern harshly whispered to Aefric.

"Yes, what about it?"

"*King's* … justiciar." Kentigern forced a deeper breath then. Cleared his throat. Forced a deeper, slower breath, and finished, "Even your grace needs *royal* permission to give that report to anyone. *Especially* a member of the Malimfari royal family."

"She claims ignorance in the matter," Aefric said, "and has given her word to investigate—"

"If you give her that report," Kentigern said, voice low but firm, "without the king's permission, you risk royal censure and punishment."

Aefric sighed and shook his head. He handed the report to Kentigern.

"Thank you, your grace," Kentigern said, relieved. "I shall leave your grace to his goodbyes, and see you at the meeting."

Aefric detached two of his guards to escort Kentigern back to his offices, just in case.

Princess Astrid looked offended when Aefric returned, Brightstaff in hand, though Princess Xenia looked positively thrilled.

"I note," Princess Astrid said archly, "that your grace no longer holds the report from his king's justiciar."

"No," Aefric said with a sigh. "I don't. My seneschal informs me that I need royal permission to share that report outside my own court."

"I trust that your grace would understand if that leads me to question the information I was given about the contents of that report."

"Does your highness accuse me of lying?" Aefric asked, hoping he kept his voice neutral.

"Clearly," Princess Xenia said. "Even unmistakably, I should think."

"I agree that you *should* think, Xenia. It would make a refreshing change," Princess Astrid said, while not taking her gaze from Aefric. "I do not mean to give your grace the lie. Your grace has noted that he is new to politics. I suspect only that others might manipulate the timing and presentation of information to him, to take advantage of his reputation for honesty, while hiding from him certain ... uncomfortable truths."

"Then you accuse my advisers of manipulating me?"

"If your grace must hear it plainspoken, I accuse your king, and his agents, who might hold places in your court. Your grace is new to his duchy, and likely has not had time — to say nothing of the practice needed — to learn the true ebb and flow of the loyalties of his courtiers."

"And of what, exactly, do you accuse my king and his 'agents?'" Aefric asked, and he knew now that he sounded dangerous, because Princess Astrid's guards put their hands on their sword hilts.

"The matter is quite simple," Princess Astrid said. "I take your grace at his word that agents worked within his lands to sow dissension and foment rebellion among his vassals and smallfolk. But as to how this was done, when, and by whom, there might be subtleties to the details that someone new to politics — such as your grace — would not know to look for, but someone who was raised in a royal court — such as myself, or even Xenia here — would recognize in a moment."

Princess Xenia drew breath to retort, but Aefric beat her to it.

"If your highness is willing to take me at my word, then trust my word that the justiciar's report only confirmed what I had already discovered myself."

"I take your grace at his word that he understood the evidence he found as pointing to Malimfar," Princess Astrid said. "And, in the spirit of the friendship your grace has shown me, I shall conduct my promised investigation, and bring to your grace my report. I only remind your grace that he has promised to keep an open mind in regard to Malimfar and its royal family, and hope he will retain that open mind when he reads my report."

"I remember, and will do my best."

"I can ask nothing more," Princess Astrid said, and bowed.

"Then, your highnesses," Aefric said, "I wish you both swift and pleasant journeys."

He bowed deeply to them, and took his leave as the sun began to rise.

---

AEFRIC HAD EXPECTED THAT SAYING GOODBYE TO THE TWO PRINCESSES would give him a lift. A certain amount of relief. After all, now they were gone, and with them the constant pressure to represent not only himself and his duchy, but all of Armyr.

But the issue of the justiciar's report had stolen that relief from him. He kept thinking about the almost greedy way Princess Astrid had reached for that report. What it might mean that she wanted it so.

What might have happened, had he let her take it.

And he wondered what it meant that Princess Xenia — her clear rival in all things — never expressed an opinion either way. Save, perhaps, for words she spoke to Princess Astrid after Aefric took the report himself.

Words Aefric hadn't heard.

It was a long walk, back to his apartments, and Aefric opted to pass through a hidden hallway door and take the servants' backway — a series of concealed stairs and passages that networked much of the castle — rather than risk encountering courtiers he really didn't want to speak to this morning.

This way, with two guards in his wake, he passed only servants, who were quick to make way for their duke.

A smile was too much for him, at the moment, but he gave each servant a word of greeting — by name, where the he knew them — as he passed.

He could afford to. They wouldn't try to interrupt him, or distract his line of thought with demands he didn't have time for.

Back in his apartments, Aefric gave his cloak to Ocheda, who arched a sharp eyebrow as though doubting that Aefric's need for it had passed. Nevertheless, she took the cloak with a bow, but not a single word of complaint or objection.

Aefric then stepped into his bedroom, opened his spell-guarded chest, and retrieved a certain something from a special sack in his backpack.

Finally, he returned to the public floor of his apartments, and entered his meeting room.

In truth, Aefric probably had scores of rooms in Water's End that he could use for meetings. But, by tradition, the duke met each morning with his most trusted advisers in his own apartments, in a room designed for such meetings.

Despite the same high ceiling as most of his rooms, the meeting room felt small. The round, blackwood table in the center had seating for eight, which left the two long walls feeling close.

Probably didn't help that the walls were paneled in black oak, like the floorboards. No plaster in here.

The short walls, in contrast, felt farther away. But not that far, because one was covered in cabinets and shelves — full of maps, books about tactics and strategies, travelogues of nearby countries, written by past dukes, duchesses, and trusted courtiers.

The other short wall, this morning, held a buffet breakfast of fresh fruits, sliced ham and beef, and honeyed oat bread, along with several ewers of water, and goblets.

Aefric's stomach growled almost as loud a greeting to the food as Aefric spoke to his advisers, who were all present and waiting.

Ser Yrsa, his general, who looked battle ready, despite dressing in a dark brown tunic with light brown hose, rather than the full plate armor she favored so often.

Of course, she did still wear both her great maces at her belt.

Kentigern, his seneschal, who hadn't changed his clothes, but had at least cleaned himself up after his earlier exertions.

Ser Calder Ol'Ulith, Aefric's castellan. Nearly three times Aefric's age, Ser Calder still looked as though he'd been forged from even better steel than the excellent broadsword at his side.

Ser Calder wore Deepwater colors this morning, a navy blue doublet over a Deepwater gray tunic, and navy blue hose. His gray hair he wore short and slicked back — as though he might be going into battle any minute.

And, as always, his sharp brown eyes seemed to deduce more from a single glance at Aefric than most could have known after five minutes of conversation.

Elkari Ol'Nuval, Aefric's historian. She had been the chief assistant to the ducal historian until this past winter, when her predecessor passed. After that, she'd served the role of ducal historian in a temporary capacity until the new duke found a replacement.

Although several in his court had suggested that — having seen only thirty or so summers — Elkari was too young for her post, Aefric had needed only one meeting with her this spring to not only confirm her in the position, but name her to his ducal council.

Her command of Armyr's and Deepwater's histories was simply too impressive to risk losing.

Elkari favored breeches and tunic, in browns that went well with the dusky hue of her complexion, and this morning was no exception.

She wore her hair short, and her main adornment was ink stains on her hands.

The other adviser present was, of course, Ser Beornric, who wore his full plate armor, complete with longsword.

One adviser was missing, of course. Karbin. Still on his mission, and still without word.

Aefric stood the Brightstaff beside his chair, then fetched himself a plate of food before taking his seat.

"All right," he said, after placating his stomach with at least a bite of fresh roast beef. "We should probably start with the princesses."

"I do apologize for interrupting your grace this morning," Kentigern said. "But giving Princess Astrid that report would have been disastrous."

"Why?" Aefric said, then, as everyone else at the table started to speak, he held up a hand to make them wait. "I understand that it's a royal report, and that I need royal permission before showing it to anyone. Well, anyone outside this room."

Aefric shook his head. "What I don't understand is why that report must be kept secret. The information was gained under the auspices of Taesark. Its truth is unquestionable."

"But its *information* may not be common knowledge," Ser Calder said pointedly.

"Consider it this way," Ser Yrsa said. "That report contains a good deal of what we know of Malimfar's activities in Deepwater and Merrek. But there may have been other activities not connected to Ser Grud."

"Oh," Aefric said, drawing the sound out. "So you're saying that, in giving the report to Malimfar, we could be confirming for them what we *don't* know of their activities."

"More than that," Ser Yrsa said. "You'd be giving them the opportunity to review what we've learned, and present the same information to us from a different angle. An angle that makes them look innocent."

"Or at least makes Princess Astrid look innocent," Kentigern said. "Which might be important, if they intend to seek marriage between the two of you."

"Plausible deniability," Aefric muttered.

"How was that?" Ser Calder asked.

"Plausible deniability. It's the concept of doing something on someone's behalf, without telling them. So that, if the action fails or has unintended consequences, that person remains ignorant of any wrongdoing. If not necessarily innocent."

"Well, of course," Elkari said. "I confess the phrase is new to me, but the concept is quite old and well-known, your grace. I could provide a number of examples."

"No need," Aefric said. "And remember, Elkari, that I don't stand on formality in these meetings."

"Yes, y—" Elkari firmed her lips and bowed her head.

"What did you think of the princesses?" Kentigern asked Aefric.

"And how did you get rid of them so quickly?" Ser Beornric asked, smiling broad enough to tug at his scars.

"Last night I thought they seemed decent enough, if caught up in their own personal rivalry. But this morning..." Aefric shook his head. "Now I'm not sure they said a sincere word the entire time I spent with them."

"They are princesses from foreign kingdoms," Ser Calder said. "One of a recent enemy, and the other of a tentative friend. They will present you only the face they wish you to see."

"In that," Aefric said, "I think they fell short. Their rivalry was too strong." He sipped some water through a thought. "And I can't help but wonder why Princess Xenia said nothing through the whole question of my giving Princess Astrid a copy of that report."

"If you would do that for an enemy," Ser Yrsa said simply, "how much further would you go for a friend?"

"All right," Aefric said. "As to their leaving, Princess Astrid promised to investigate Malimfar's espionage and give me a report of her findings. She left this morning to begin her investigation. Though it's safe to say her report will present Malimfar in the best possible light."

"Nevertheless," Ser Calder said, "what they tell us will have value, as will what they *don't*."

"And Princess Xenia," Aefric said. "I think she intended to stay for some time—"

"I'll guarantee that," Kentigern said.

"But," Aefric continued, "after she promised to use Caiperas' trade contacts to seek information about the slaver ring, Princess Astrid pressured her into leaving to get started."

"Easy promise to make," Ser Beornric said, running his fingers over his mustache. "Safe, too."

"I know," Aefric said. "But much the same as with Malimfar, what Caiperas doesn't tell us may be as informative as what they do."

"You suspect them of involvement with the slavers?" Elkari asked, sounding shocked.

"At this point I don't rule it out," Aefric said, "but I was referring to the strength and breadth of their trade contacts."

"A good thought," Kentigern said, tugging on his beard. "Does this mean you intend to send her report to his majesty?"

"I intend to send copies of *both* reports to his majesty."

All three knights present knocked the table in approval. And so did the historian.

Aefric had to smile at that. Knocking the table to show approval had been something only his knights had done in previous meetings. Apparently the practice was spreading.

"Now," Aefric said, more seriously. "Speaking of the slavers, I haven't heard from Karbin yet. He hasn't sent a rika by any chance?"

"I'm afraid not," Kentigern said. "Though there has been a rika from Ajenmoor. An official objection from the city council to your bringing armed knights and soldiers into a council meeting."

Aefric frowned puzzlement. "Seriously?"

"Apparently," Kentigern said, frowning as well, "that had not been done in two hundred years. And they ask that, in the future, your grace respect their traditions."

"They have guts," Ser Yrsa said. "I'll give them that."

"Did the mayor sign it?" Ser Calder asked.

"No. There were three names, but not his."

Ser Calder snorted. "Ignore it then. Or perhaps punish them for it, if you feel offended. It's a token objection from the old guard, who are losing power in Ajenmoor to the rising merchant navies. Bet I could even name the signatories."

"Would Galdiff be one of them?" Aefric asked.

"Galdiff Reteka?" Ser Calder asked.

Aefric hadn't caught the man's last name, but Sers Yrsa and Beornric both nodded.

Ser Calder scoffed. "Never. He leads the new guard. And the mayor is caught between both factions."

"I may want to hear more about that later," Aefric said, pulling a heavy pouch from his belt and holding it above the table. "But we have something more important to discuss next."

He dumped the contents of that pouch onto the table.

A single, large gold nugget.

<hr>

For a moment, silence reigned in Aefric's meeting room, as each of his advisers stared at the large, remarkably clean gold nugget on the table in front of their duke.

Sers Yrsa and Beornric had already seen it, of course, and only nodded. Perhaps pleased that they were finally going to discuss this matter.

Aefric passed the nugget around the table, letting each of the advisers inspect it and reassure themselves of its veracity.

While they did, Aefric refilled his plate from the buffet. More sliced roast beef, sharp yellow cheese, and slices of pear and that sweet citrus so popular with sailors for its bite, nava.

He noticed he was the only one eating, but wasn't too surprised. The others had likely taken their normal breakfasts while he'd been down seeing off the princesses.

"I take it," Ser Calder said, after everyone had seen the gold nugget, "that this didn't come from any of your usual mines in the Threepeaks?"

"It came from the Dragonscar," Aefric said, and told them of the borogs, who could smell gold. Of the gold in the caves undeniably on his side of the Dragonscar, and the gold in the north-side cave that might not be his to mine.

"You left borogs mining gold unguarded?" Ser Calder asked, practically radiating disapproval.

"Not at all," Aefric said, turning to Ser Yrsa. "In fact, do you have a report?"

"I do," she said with a nod. "All is quiet in the Dragonscar. Our scouts cannot even tell that the borogs are down there."

"Likely because they've tunneled away," Ser Calder said, "and took the gold with them."

"Enough of that," Aefric said, slashing his hand through the air.

"He's right," Ser Beornric said to Ser Calder. "These two borogs, Ge'rek and Po'rek, clearly consider our duke to be their new chief, and are happy to dig for him."

Ser Yrsa knocked the table in agreement.

"The borogs are not the question before us," Aefric said.

"The gold is," Kentigern agreed. "Obviously, the south side caves are clearly yours, as is any gold you can dig up from them."

"What about the north side?" Aefric asked, turning to Elkari. "Is there any precedent for a situation like this?"

"Not with a chasm such as the Dragonscar," Elkari said slowly, frowning. She twirled the tips of her thumbs and looked at the ceiling as she continued. "Although throughout the history of Deepwater, ownership of the Dragonscar has always been plain, and understood to include its caves."

"*Understood*," Ser Calder said. "Which means it hasn't been tested. And if that north-side cave goes back very far, every foot it travels under Wylyn's land will weaken your claim to the gold."

"What's more, retrieving the gold would involve digging outward *from* those caves," Kentigern said. "If I were Duke Wylyn, I would claim that the north side gold lies under my lands, and therefore is mine."

"He couldn't come into the Dragonscar to mine it though," Elkari said. "He has no right to come into Deepwater to mine."

"So," Aefric said. "Wylyn can't mine that cave because the cave is part of the Dragonscar, which is mine. But I can't mine that gold, because it's under Silverlake and Wylyn's."

"*Might* be Duke Wylyn's," Elkari said. "There's no strong precedent here."

"Duke Wylyn could just mine downward from his own ridge," Ser Beornric said.

"Far more dangerous, expensive and time consuming than using an existing cave," Ser Yrsa said.

"Not if the cave isn't an option," Ser Beornric countered.

"Could be done as a joint venture," Kentigern said. "With the gold being shared between you."

"I like that option best," Aefric said. "But the question is how to begin. I was thinking of bringing the matter to his majesty for judgment."

"Without telling Duke Wylyn?" Kentigern asked, scandalized.

"Well, that was one question I wanted to put before all of you. But before you answer, there's another factor to consider."

Ser Beornric frowned and Ser Yrsa nodded. The others all sat forward, waiting to hear.

Aefric told them how they'd tripped an alarm spell of some sort, and of the stone men who had then attacked.

"So someone else knows about the gold," Ser Calder said. "The question is who."

"The obvious answer is Duke Wylyn," Ser Yrsa said. "So let's add him to the list first."

"For much the same reason," Elkari said, "Countess Briluufa must be considered."

"Who?" Aefric asked.

"Countess Briluufa Ol'Galalifa," Elkari said. "Silverlake is the smallest of Armyr's duchies. Duke Wylyn Stormsent has few vassals, and only a single count. Countess Briluufa, whose lands touch both the shores of the Risen Sea, and a portion of the Dragonscar."

"That's a point," Ser Beornric said. "She might have sent scouts into the Dragonscar and found that gold. Same as Duke Wylyn might've."

"Let us not forget," Elkair added, "that neither Countess Briluufa nor Duke Wylyn has the right to send their scouts *into* the Dragonscar. By both a royal decree going back two-hundred thirty years, and by custom before that, the king's vassals are not allowed to scout beyond their own boundaries, save what their senses can tell them from a border."

"Point taken," Aefric said. "But add her to the list. And what do we know of this Countess Briluufa?"

"She led her troops from the front during the Godswalk Wars," Ser Yrsa said. "Lost a son, who'd be about your age, but still has an heir, a daughter."

"She's aggressive," Ser Calder said. "Arinda used to complain about Briluufa at least once a season."

"Wait," Aefric said. "Her lands reach the north side of the Dragon-scar *and* the shores of the Risen Sea?"

"That's correct," Elkari said.

"You think she knew about the slavers," Ser Beornric said.

"Or at least the smugglers," Aefric said. "If she's as aggressive as all that, how likely is it that she doesn't expect the new duke to be just as aggressive?"

Ser Yrsa frowned in thought. "There's logic to that. Would imply that she'd increase her scouting. Make her likely to have at least *seen* people using the Dragonscar as a transfer point."

"Doesn't mean she's involved," Kentigern said. "She might simply watch, because it's not happening on her land."

"Might watch *closely*," Ser Calder added, "to make sure it *stays* off her land."

"Let me guess," Aefric said with a sigh. "And she wouldn't say anything because why should she?"

"Exactly," Ser Yrsa said. "Not her affair. If asked, she might claim to have assumed they had at least your tacit blessing."

"I doubt she'd have the effrontery to go *that* far," Ser Beornric said.

"You haven't met her," Ser Calder said. "I have. Wouldn't put it past her to test the new duke with a comment like that, and offer a half-hearted apology, if called on it."

"Point is," Aefric said. "Duke Wylyn and Countess Briluufa are on the list. Who else?"

"Mayor Brangton?" Ser Beornric asked.

"Possible," Aefric said, "but unlikely. I still think that if he knew, he would have brought the discovery to me in person, angling to be ennobled and given charge of the land."

"What about Ajenmoor?" Ser Yrsa asked. "Mayor Vagran perhaps, or Galdiff? Enough money passes through their hands to pay for the spells."

"Galfiff certainly seems the type," Ser Beornric said.

"But how would they have discovered the gold?" Kentigern asked. "Ajenmoor isn't noted for overland expeditions."

"Put Ajenmoor on the list, all the same," Aefric said. "Until we can clear them, someone there might be involved. Someone on the city council, maybe."

"That brings us back to Nelazzi," Ser Yrsa said.

"Back to?" Ser Calder asked. "Why might the so-called pirate queen be involved in Dragonscar gold?"

Aefric wolfed down more breakfast while Ser Yrsa caught them up on what they'd learned about Gwawl and Captain Brusi, and Nelazzi's definite connection to the smugglers, and likely connection to the slavers.

"Doesn't make a connection," Ser Calder said. "You had to travel a day into the Dragonscar to reach the caves with the gold, and you only found them because..."

Ser Calder frowned, perhaps unable to finish his sentence.

"Because Ge'rek and Po'rek could smell the gold," Aefric said. "Yes. And why should we assume that there aren't any borogs sailing with Nelazzi?"

"Why should we assume Nelazzi entered the Dragonscar at all?" Ser Calder asked. "If her ship came within a day of Ajenmoor—"

"She wouldn't need to come near us herself," Ser Yrsa said. "Nelazzi has agents in every major port. And we all know it. We also know that if smugglers and slavers intended to use the Dragonscar as an exchange point, *someone* had to explore it first. Likely going farther in than a day's travel."

"And yet," Ser Calder countered, "if all they wanted was a safe exchange point, they'd hardly need to explore every cave. Just make sure no threats were coming out. Ridiculous to think they'd go deep enough to find gold."

"The gold's not that far back," Aefric said. "And no pirate becomes as successful as Nelazzi without caution. I think she'd look at those caves as both potential threats and potential tools. She'd want to know what's in them."

"So you think whoever scouted for the smugglers and slavers might have been the ones to find the gold," Ser Yrsa said.

"It's a possibility," Aefric said. "And since we know the smugglers we caught were working for Nelazzi — albeit under protest, or so they claim — Nelazzi's people might have picked the exchange point. Which means Nelazzi's people might have done the scouting."

"And Nelazzi could definitely afford the spells," Ser Beornric said, nodding agreement. "That does track."

"I still think Duke Wylyn is the obvious answer," Ser Calder said.

"Obvious doesn't mean right," Aefric said.

"Also," Kentigern said, "it must be pointed out that if Duke Wylyn or Countess Briluufa commissioned those spells, they engaged in an act of war against Deepwater."

"Which should have given them cause to hesitate," Ser Yrsa said. "Though that wouldn't trouble Nelazzi at all."

"I doubt it would trouble Countess Briluufa either," Ser Calder said.

"Those spells cost the lives of several of my soldiers," Aefric said darkly. "And whoever commissioned those spells had to know what they would do. I don't know what Wylyn Stormsent has been like since he became a duke, but I know his reputation of old. I wouldn't put this past him. Would Countess Briluufa be as bold?"

"She would," Ser Calder said.

"Well," Aefric said, "whoever did it will pay. I will see to that. In the meantime, the gold and the caves remain an open question. And based on this conversation, I'm tempted to bring this matter to the king before informing my peer."

The three knights knocked the table in agreement. Elkari frowned, looking up.

"Duke Wylyn will take that as an insult," Kentigern said.

"Perhaps," Elkari said, still staring at the ceiling. "But there is precedent for nobles taking claims to the king before pressing them against their neighbors."

She turned her gaze to Aefric. "This sort of claim could be construed as falling into the same category. Perhaps more so, as it involves lands that are indisputably yours, even if it touches on lands that might not be."

"*Might* not be?" Ser Calder asked.

"The caves belong to Deepwater," Elkari said with a shrug. "And what is within the caves has been understood to be *part of* the caves. The question, then, is merely where the cave stops being a cave and begins being part of Silverlake."

"I'll send a messenger to the king about it today," Aefric said.

"You would do better to go yourself," Ser Calder said. "The king favors you."

"A fair point," Kentigern said. "And the king will wish you to see Netar soon."

Aefric's reply was interrupted by the sudden appearance of Karbin.

---

ONE THING AEFRIC HAD TO GIVE HIS KNIGHTS. NO MATTER WHERE THEY were or what they were doing, they were always ready to do battle.

The moment that Karbin appeared in the room — teleporting in, with a skill and precision that Aefric hoped to have one day, if he ever learned that spell — Sers Yrsa, Beornric and Calder were on their feet in a flash, weapons in hand.

"Hold!" Aefric called out, both hands coming up as he stood.

"Good," Karbin said with a weak smile. "I made the meeting."

Karbin looked exhausted. He was clean, of course. No doubt he used small spells he'd learned during apprenticeship to drive away dirt and grime, the same as Aefric did.

But he still wore the same clothes he'd worn in the Dragonscar. Robes of sand and dusk. Hard leather boots that reached the knee. Only five of the six wands he'd started with remained on his belt, but he still had that strange obsidian rod he'd found in the ruins beneath Sulkrekeep.

What was more, his posture told the tale of his exhaustion. So while the others composed themselves after the sudden appearance of the ducal wizard, Aefric saw him seated and fed.

Ser Calder wanted to press Karbin for news immediately, but Aefric wanted to let the man rest and eat first, so he had the others recount the earlier part of the meeting for him.

Once everything had been covered, Elkari raised a point.

"I meant to ask earlier, y—" Elkari checked herself from using Aefric's honorific. "Those spells you encountered in the Dragonscar. Do you know how old they were?"

"Somewhere between two seasons and a year old. Why?"

"No specific reason," Elkari said. "But when I return to my office, I can review what we know of the events of that time frame and look for synchronicities."

"Please do," Aefric said, then turned to Karbin. "So. What news, old friend?"

"The day we took her," Karbin said, "the *Swift Wave* last docked at Redport."

"That's in Countess Briluufa's lands," Ser Calder said sharply.

"It is," Karbin agreed. "But the smugglers behaved themselves in port. In fact, I couldn't find any evidence that they ever conducted any illegal activities there. Seems most likely that it was just a conveniently close port, for the wait."

"You determined that in a handful of days?" Ser Calder scoffed. "Determining that with certainty takes a *season*, at least."

"And if I had a season to spare," Karbin said patiently, "I might have spent it. As it was, I was busy trying to track their movements, and the slavers."

"How did you do?" Aefric asked.

"Well," Karbin said. "I was able to find out that the *Swift Wave* docks at Redport every few aetts, which means it's a regular stop for them."

"As I said," Ser Calder started, but Aefric hushed him and gestured for Karbin to continue.

"While I was there, I also learned that the *Gull's Bride* docked there at least once a season as well."

"The *Gull's Bride*?" Aefric asked.

"Never bothered learning the name of the slaver ship you demolished?" Karbin asked with a smile.

"Did they do business in Redport?" Aefric asked.

"No," Karbin said. "Or if they did, I couldn't find any trace of it before I had to move on."

"Had they been there recently?" Ser Yrsa asked, earning a frown from Ser Calder, likely because she got to ask a question without censure.

"No," Karbin said. "Which was the interesting thing. From what I could learn, the *Gull's Bride* only stopped there for supplies, and always stocked up as though starting a long voyage."

"So," Aefric said, thinking, "they would stock up, go ... gather their slaves, sell or otherwise dispose of their slaves, and not return to Redport until their hold was empty."

"Which means we need to know where they stopped after making their supply run," Ser Beornric said.

"Well," Karbin said, "there's no way to be sure of how many stops they made, especially since we don't know whether they raided for slaves, or simply carried them for other raiders."

Aefric growled.

"But," Karbin continued, "I was able to find at least one other port they'd stopped at in the last few aetts. Kefthal."

"Kefthal?" Aefric said, even louder than the others around the table who'd said the same thing. "How do you know?"

Karbin slapped down a thick, twine-bound roll of pale leather, large enough to make a pair of gloves from. A pair of very soft gloves, if one was willing to overlook the nature of the material.

"Kefthali leather," Aefric said.

"Why do you have that?" Ser Calder said, looking disgusted.

"Two reasons," Karbin said. "The first is proof. The second—"

"Spells can find a connection to someone who carried it," Aefric said. "I thought they didn't sell anything in Redport, though."

"The *Gull's Bride* didn't," Karbin said, smiling. "But one of their sailors did, this past spring."

"Sounds unlikely," Ser Calder said. "Why buy the leather in spring and not do anything with it by summer?"

"Wouldn't be easy or cheap to find a leatherworker willing to work with Kefthali leather," Kentigern said.

"Just so," Karbin said. "The leatherworker more than tripled her price once she saw the material. The customer had spent his days since trying to sell it."

"Get a name?" Ser Beornric asked, bringing the topic back to the slavers.

"No, but they're in Ajenmoor's cells, yes?" Karbin asked. "Not an hour's flight from here."

"Assuming that sailor is still among the living," Ser Yrsa said. "Not all the slavers survived the fight."

"We didn't kill many," Ser Beornric said. "The odds are good."

"There's no tie to Nelazzi in that," Ser Calder said.

"There's a tie to Nelazzi in Captain Brusi and Gwawl," Aefric said.

"Reminds me," Karbin said. "Have you had a chance to investigate that pendant?"

"It's what I plan to do after the meeting."

"Pendant?" Ser Calder asked.

"I took it from Gwawl," Aefric said. "Don't know what it does yet."

"You know who else claims to deal in Kefthali leather," Ser Yrsa said.

Aefric nodded. "Brangford Couglas. Son of the mayor of Lachedran."

"Means he might be tied to all of this."

"Or it might mean there's more of a trade in Kefthali leather than we know of," Kentigern said. "Which is a troubling thought."

"Is all their leather made from human skin?" Elkari asked.

"No," Karbin said, frowning. "They also tan the hides of derekek, borogs, taroks, kindaren ... really, anything they can get their bony fingers on. Especially eldrani."

"All right," Aefric said. "That's quite a bit, my friend, but is there anything else I should know?"

"Yes," Karbin said. "Our good Ser Calder here asked about ties to Nelazzi. Well, I fought one of her wizards down in Wulfport. Didn't catch which ship she sailed."

"Are you all right?" Aefric asked.

"Tired, mostly," Karbin said with a smile. "I'd been asking the wrong questions of the wrong people, in a tavern near the docks. Some hired thugs tried to jump me in an alley after I left, but they were just a distraction while the wizard took aim."

Karbin shook himself. "This was late last night. I fought her off, but she had reinforcements coming. I escaped, then laid a false trail for a few hours. Snatched a quick nap, then teleported here first thing."

"Good work," Aefric said, clapping him on the shoulder. "Get some rest, my friend, before you worry about prisoners in Ajenmoor. In fact." He turned to Kentigern. "Send a rika to Mayor Vagran. Tell him to hold those prisoners until Karbin has concluded his investigations there."

"Hold the..." Kentigern started, then answered his own question. "Oh. Yes. Slavers."

It was a common practice to send captured slavers to the kingdoms where they'd preyed, for punishment.

"Speaking of which," Aefric said, still focused on Kentigern. "Have you had a chance to see to those refugees this morning?"

"Not yet," Kentigern admitted, "though I intend to when we're done here. And I did see Edric fostered to a good ler family just west of Behal. He'll do well there, I think, and they will do well by him."

"Excellent," Aefric said. "Then unless there's anything else pressing—"

"I still think you should take the Dragonscar matter to the king yourself," Ser Calder said. "Your presence will carry more weight. Plus, you can visit Netar while you're nearby, which will please him."

"He may have a point," Kentigern said.

"Perhaps," Aefric said, sighing. "But that's a full aett's travel just going out there. Longer if I go with full retinue."

"Which you should," Kentigern said. "It's only proper."

"I don't know that I have the time."

"You may have to make the time," Ser Beornric said. "You need to visit Netar soon anyway, and Ser Calder is right about the Dragonscar matter. The king will give the issue more weight if you bring it to him yourself."

"Give you a chance to talk to him about the princesses, too," Ser Yrsa said, frowning. "I confess, I don't like the idea of your being away for long right now, but it might be the right course."

"I have to go to Armityr," Aefric grumbled. "I have to go to Netar. I have to go to Kivash." He looked at Karbin. "I'm not sure I did less traveling as an adventurer, and traveling takes longer now."

"Why do you have to go to Kivash?" Ser Beornric said.

Aefric told them about the keep Ashling had given him.

"Oh, she's good," Ser Yrsa said, laughing in approval.

"It's too much," Aefric said.

"No," Ser Calder said, thoughtfully. "Yrsa's right. It's an excellent move by Duchess Ashling."

"In this one gesture, she thanks you and gives you a vested interest in making sure Kivash stays part of Armyr," Ser Beornric said, shaking his head. "*And* she helps ensure that you'll answer, if she calls for help at the border."

"Princess Astrid will throw a fit when she finds out," Aefric said.

"Do you care?" Kentigern asked.

Aefric frowned. "Well. She's a princess. And generally upsetting royalty isn't my best move, yes?"

"Upsetting *Armyrian* royalty isn't your best move," Ser Calder said. "Malimfar's the kingdom whose ass you personally kicked not a season ago. They're already mad at you."

"Ah," Kentigern said, realizing the point of disconnection. "Upsetting and insulting aren't the same thing, when it comes to foreign royalty. Insulting them is a bad idea, but you may have no control over whether or not you upset them."

"He's right," Ser Beornric said. "You don't insult Malimfar by accepting the keep. Doesn't mean they can't choose to be upset by it."

"You *did* accept the keep?" Ser Calder asked.

"Seemed ungrateful not to, so yes," Aefric said.

"Which was the right course of action," Ser Yrsa said. "Don't get me wrong. It was a good move on Duchess Ashling's part to offer it, but it's a good move on your part to accept it. Duchess Arinda always had problems with Duchess Ashling. Be helpful going forward if you have a better working relationship with her."

Kentigern chuckled.

"What?" Aefric asked.

Kentigern suddenly seemed to realize that everyone was looking at him. He smirked.

"Well," he said, "I was wondering why Duchess Ashling sent her sister Zoleen as a mere messenger. I believe now I know."

No one else said anything, but the same idea seemed to flit across all their faces.

Once upon a time, the Fyrenn family counted almost half of Deepwater as part of their lands. Back when it was the principality of Fyr, before the kingdom of Armyr existed.

It was well known that the Fyrenn family wanted to rule those lands again. And marrying into the bloodline of the Deepwater duke was certainly one way to do that.

"All right," Aefric said. "I'm adjourning this meeting before the lot of you start discussing my bridal options. We all have busy days ahead of us. Let's get to it."

With the morning meeting out of the way, Aefric looked forward to doing something that both was productive for him as a duke, and gave him as an excuse to use some of the magic that was both his calling and part of his very nature as a dweomerblood.

He could finally explore the depths of the secrets concealed within the bronze pendant he'd taken from the wizard Gwawl.

While this type of magical investigation could be done almost anywhere — as he'd more than proven over the years — it was immensely easier to do in a properly dedicated and prepared lab.

With that in mind, he left instructions with Ocheda and his guards — Sers Vria and Micham this morning — that he was not to be disturbed, and entered his personal magical laboratory.

Aefric's magical lab was the only room in his ducal apartments that hadn't been plastered. By design. The stone of the walls, ceiling and floor had all been whitewashed, but nothing more.

No windows. No hearth. No tapestries. No soft, plush furniture for lounging.

In one corner, a big, heavy desk with several drawers, but only a simple wooden stool. Six shelves on the walls above it, all of them filled with grimoires. Some found or penned by Aefric, others accumulated over the years by the Soulfists. But most of them had been written by his predecessors to the duchy.

Those last, he had yet to puzzle through. But today was not the day for those. On the walls near the desk, diagrams and sketches on parchment that had been spell-tacked to the walls. Some of them Aefric's. Most of them older.

In the opposite corner, a similar desk, stool, and series of shelves and diagrams, but those were dedicated to alchemy and the skills of potion-making. Aefric knew little of those things, but apparently the Soulfists had known much.

One more set of books to puzzle through, when he had time.

On a table beside the alchemy desk were arranged alembics and burners, mortars and pestles and other tools useful in the practice of alchemy and potion-making. Underneath the table, cabinets full of reagents and more tools.

Aefric frowned at the alchemy setup. Wished he had more time. He'd hardly touched any of the equipment, let alone the reagents, since he first arrived at Water's End.

Made him feel a trifle guilty. He used to dream about having such resources available. Back when he had all the time he wanted, for research.

Now he had the resources, but not the time. Wasn't that always the way?

Along the middle of the room, a series of inset magic circles, along with a triangle, hexagram, and heptagram. All of them of red gold, and each serving a different purpose.

A double-door in the middle of one long wall led into the only closet. Yes, it held braziers and coals, incenses and the like, but it also held those bits of special equipment required by certain kinds of spells and research.

A robe woven in the light of the full moon, from material Aefric himself had gathered with a silver knife. Soft slippers made from a single, blind giant snake whose skin had never known sunlight or moonlight. And a few other items along similar lines. Things Aefric used to keep in that certain sack in his backpack, but now had a special place to keep them.

Aefric's magic laboratory.

At least he made use of the room itself, and its magic circles, if not yet its alchemy equipment.

Here, not only were there no unknown or unexpected magical influences to account for, but he could investigate that pendant within the simplest of his magic circles, where even the ebbs and flows of the natural magic of Qorunn would be filtered and controlled.

It reminded Aefric of listening to music through noise-canceling headphones, in the world where he was known as Keifer. No unexpected distractions.

Aefric entered the lab and stood his Brightstaff just inside the thick, heavy door. As he closed that door, he didn't trigger the room's light spells. Instead he gestured, and a series of large, blocky white candles in sconces along the four walls ignited with small flares.

Candlelight sometimes reacted to magic in ways that the magic-user might need to know. Not important in day-to-day spellcasting, but sometimes crucial to research.

The candles weren't *likely* to react to what he would do today. But if they did, he wanted to know.

He sat cross-legged on the floor in the simplest circle and considered the pendant.

Physically, it did not look all that impressive. Which was interesting. Generally speaking, objects that were to be enchanted were first forged or fashioned to the highest available quality.

Not just a matter of personal vanity. The effort that went into preparing the vessel for spells would be reflected in how well the vessel then *held* those spells.

It wasn't a matter of only the highest quality raw materials, either. The effort, skill and time that went into the design played a major role.

The quality of this pendant's bronze was ... passable. But more important, it had been cast, not forged. Which meant that it had received less individual effort and attention than would have gone into forging the same pendant.

Its shape was that of a sextant, and it hung on a simple leather thong. And because the sextant had not been cast carefully, Aefric could see and feel little areas where more effort should have gone into grinding down excess bronze. Which would have given the sextant a sharper, truer shape.

The pendant looked cheap. The sort of thing one might buy for a few coppers from a street vendor.

Which meant that no one was likely to take an interest in this pendant unless they could sense its magic.

Probably why Gwawl thought he could ask for it back. It had little obvious value, so many captors would simply return it.

And yet, there was magic to it.

Though even the magic of it was not all that obvious. Aefric might have missed it, had Gwawl not shown himself to be such a threat in battle.

Yes, Aefric had stopped the man before he'd had a chance to *cast* a single spell. Still. Aefric had recognized the spell Gwawl *had been* casting. Had that spell gone through, it would have burned many of Aefric's soldiers alive.

So Aefric had inspected Gwawl carefully, and found the spark of magic in the pendant.

Not much of a spark. But then, such a cheap pendant wouldn't likely hold much magic. Not reliably.

Still. It was a clue.

So Aefric relaxed and focused himself. Projected part of his consciousness out of his body and into the through flows of magic inherent to Qorunn.

Within the filtered environment of this permanent magic circle, it was simplicity itself to follow those flows into the pendant, and begin checking into its magic.

Aefric did not need long to discover that the main purpose of the pendant was to give its wearer access to wind spells, similar to those Aefric had used to speed the *Duke's Hand* back from Ajenmoor.

He dug deeper all the same.

He found that there were three such spells within the pendant. All of them incomplete, and requiring the right words and gestures to activate them. Further, the pendant could not power the spells itself. That was up to the magic-user.

The first spell would call winds. The second would still winds. And the third would shift winds.

All three of those were spells Aefric had learned from Sirondfar last spring. Though the approach to them used by the enchantments of this pendant was quite different stylistically from the approach Aefric had learned from Sirondfar.

As different as a jaunty dance tune from a lament.

There might be something Aefric could learn from the design of the spells. If he could figure out how to complete them. But that would take a good deal of study and experimentation. Possibly a full season.

Could be an interesting puzzle. When Aefric had time.

Assuming the spells lasted long enough. Which, given the quality of the pendant, they might not.

Aefric dug in deeper. Tried to find out more about the magic-user who had enchanted the pendant...

Too intricate for a sparker, one of those who'd tried to become a magic-user and failed, but made their living on what little they knew.

Possibly a warlock's work...

Yes. A warlock or a wizard. That much was certain.

Now, to try to dig through until he found a pattern in the incomplete spellwork. Something he might recognize, if he—

What was that?

Could there be another spell ... underneath the wind spells?

Something jarred Aefric back to awareness of the world around him. His legs were asleep, and his back felt stiff. From the burn of the candles, he'd been in here ... most of the morning, at least.

No wonder he felt stiff and sore. He'd have to remember to use one of the stools next time.

But what had pulled him back?

Someone pounded on his door four times.

Oh. Probably that then.

Aefric huffed out an angry breath. Whoever was interrupting him better have a damned good reason.

<hr>

WHILE THE KNOCKING CONTINUED ON THE DOOR OF HIS MAGIC LAB, Aefric tried to calm down through a series of deep breaths.

Didn't work. Not with that knocking still going. His muscles were tense, his jaw clamped tight, and his eyes narrowed.

Fine. Someone wanted his attention? Well, they'd likely be very sorry they got it.

With a gesture, Aefric sent the bronze pendant winging through the air to his research desk as he crossed the room to the door.

He ripped open the heavy door.

"This had better be good," he said.

Ser Calder stood before him, fist raised. Sers Vria and Micham immediately grabbed him and pulled him back. Both looking grim, and ready to do more than put hands on Aefric's castellan.

They looked ready to throw him down the stairs.

Off to one side, Ocheda frowned disapproval at all of them.

"Unhand me!" Ser Calder insisted.

Aefric briefly considered letting his knights throw Ser Calder down the stairs.

Aefric clenched and unclenched his fists. Shook his head as though pronouncing doom on his castellan. Flared his nostrils in a deep breath to get hold of his anger.

He extinguished the candles in his lab with a gesture, took the Brightstaff in hand, and stepped onto the white oak floorboards of the landing, closing the door behind him.

All three knights started talking at once.

Aefric snapped his fingers, causing a small clap of thunder.

"Release him," Aefric said darkly. "For the moment."

Sers Vria and Micham both let go of Ser Calder, but glowered at him, and kept their hands on the hilts of their swords.

"Ocheda," Aefric said, while looking at Ser Calder, "what instructions did I give when I entered my lab?"

"You were not to be disturbed, your grace."

Aefric nodded.

"Ser Vria. Ser Micham. What instructions did I give when I entered my lab?"

"You were not to be disturbed, your grace," they said with impressive synchronicity.

During these questions, Ser Calder was straightening his tunic, and giving dark looks to pretty much everyone. But he'd learned from previous instances of all too similar behavior not to speak until Aefric got to him.

"Was Ser Calder informed of my instructions?" Aefric asked.

"Yes, your grace," the knights and valet answered.

"Ser Calder," Aefric said. "I take it by the pose I saw you in when I opened my door that you were the one who disturbed me with your knocking?"

"Yes, your grace, but—"

"*Ser Calder*," Aefric said. "Is this the first time you have interrupted me against my instructions?"

"No, your grace, but—"

"*Ser Calder*," Aefric said. "Do you remember what I told you the last time?"

"Yes, your grace, but—"

"*Ser Calder*." Aefric continued, "Are we actively under attack? By a dragon perhaps?"

Ser Calder sighed. "No, your grace."

"Ocheda," Aefric said, "from this moment forward, Ser Calder is not permitted beyond the public floor of my apartments for any reason."

"Yes, your grace," Ocheda said with a smile that looked sharp enough to slash Ser Calder's cheek.

"Your grace!" Ser Calder objected.

"You were warned," Aefric said, keeping his gaze on Ser Calder, but talking to Ocheda as he continued. "In the future, when Ser Calder arrives, he is to be told only that I am indisposed. He will then await me in the public floor sitting room. If his matter is urgent, he may present it to the head valet on duty, who will then decide if the matter is important enough to disturb me. Is that clear?"

"Yes, your grace," Ocheda said, sounding happier than Aefric had ever heard her before.

"If, in my head valet's judgment, his news is important enough to disturb me, Ser Calder is then to await me in the meeting room. If it is not, he is to leave, and the head valet will inform me of his message when I am available. Is that clear?"

"Yes, your grace."

Ser Calder looked almost apoplectic, but Ocheda looked thrilled.

"One more thing," Aefric said. "Until further notice, Ser Calder is not to come armed into my presence."

*"I am your sworn knight!"* Ser Calder said.

"Yes, you are," Aefric said. "Ser Vria, Ser Micham, does Ser Calder demonstrate the respect that a sworn knight owes his liege lord?"

"No, your grace," both said, while giving Ser Calder dark looks.

"Exactly," Aefric said. "Ser Calder, when your behavior again reflects the *respect* a sworn knight owes his liege lord, I shall restore to you the right to bear arms in my presence. Not before."

Ser Calder met Aefric's glare for a moment, but yielded with a nod. He unhooked the broadsword from his belt and shoved it at Ser Micham.

"I understand that you think I'm being too harsh," Aefric said, a little more gently. "But you *have* been warned before. And when I'm in my lab, as I was today, interrupting me might be dangerous."

Ser Calder blinked as though he'd somehow never considered that. Even though Aefric was sure he'd pointed that little fact out before.

"Your grace is well?" Ser Calder asked, tentatively.

"Fortunately," Aefric said, "in this case, I was only investigating that bronze pendant."

"Did your grace learn anything useful?"

"Doesn't look like much," Aefric started, then frowned. "I trust, Ser Calder, that you did not interrupt me to ask about the pendant."

"No, your grace," Ser Calder said quickly, adding in a small bow for good measure. "Excuse me, your grace."

"What then," Aefric asked, "was so important?"

Voices downstairs. Some kind of disturbance.

Ocheda immediately swept down the stairs to look into it.

Ser Calder drew a deep breath, and let it out in a rush.

"When Princess Astrid left for Malimfar, it turns out she didn't take all of her retinue along."

"I was told she hardly came with any retinue at all."

"That's correct, your grace," Ser Calder said. "And yet, when she set sail, four of her knights remained behind."

"Odd that Kentigern didn't mention this at the morning meeting," Aefric said.

"Likely he didn't know, your grace," Ser Calder said. "They'd left the castle with the others. But instead of leaving Water's End, they've taken rooms at the Red Branch Inn."

"That's just outside the castle gates," Aefric said.

"Exactly, your grace," Ser Calder said, then shook his head. "Given Malimfar's history of espionage here in Deepwater, I thought you would wish to know at once. But I see now that this information could have waited until your grace emerged."

"It both could have and should have," Aefric said.

"Yes, your grace," Ser Calder said with a nod. Then, with a frustrated look, added, "So the pendant is nothing after all?"

"Your grace," Ocheda said, coming up the stairs with a speed Aefric hadn't realized she was capable of.

"Yes?" Aefric asked giving her his attention.

"There's been a rika. The king is coming. He and Queen Eppida left Armityr with the dawn this morning."

"Then they'll be here in about an aett," Aefric said, and blew out a breath. Too many things were happening at once.

"There's more, your grace," Ocheda added. "His majesty bids you take no action regarding Malimfar or its princess until he arrives."

Aefric thumped his staff on the floorboards in frustration.

"Which means I can't so much as *talk* to those knights until he gets here," Aefric said, shaking his head. Then he looked at Ser Calder. "Which may not have been exactly what his majesty meant, but his majesty likely has reasons for his orders that I do not know. Therefore, as a good vassal to my liege lord, I must err on the side of caution."

"Yes, your grace," Ser Calder said, sounding almost chastened this time. Good.

"I want eyes kept on them, though. They're here for a reason, and I want to know what."

ONCE MORE BACK IN THE PRIVACY OF BOTH HIS LAB AND THE SIMPLEST OF his inset magic circles, Aefric returned to his study of the bronze pendant.

He did not need long to confirm all that he'd learned before. Not just about the low quality of the pendant, but the number, nature and design of the incomplete spells enchanted into the pendant.

In some ways, using a pendant designed along such lines made sense. It would allow a wizard to cast the spells contained therein, but the wizard would have to know they were there, have learned the second half of those spells, and be capable of powering them.

In other words, they made for a perfect charm to be carried by a pirate wizard. Useful by the wizard for any ship at sea, but useless in the hands of most captors.

Not just spite, either, but strategy. If Nelazzi were attacking with not only her own ship, but several — and she was said to often attack with three ships together — and one of those ships were taken, the pendant's spells could not be used to then help capture the other ships.

And yet, Aefric felt certain that he'd found something else buried in that pendant. Just before he'd been interrupted, he was *sure* he'd found something. Perhaps another layer to the spells...

As he always did with this kind of investigation, Aefric proceeded slowly and carefully. Reconfirmed everything that he knew, first, before pushing beyond to what he did not know yet.

And in this case, he might've been wrong. Because everything looked just as he'd expected. With a handful of small, likely temporary spells invested in a vessel that certainly couldn't hold anything more.

Perhaps he'd been distracted by the knock, before, when he'd—

There.

Oh, but it was small. And subtle. And hard to focus on.

What was it?

No. No good.

Aefric returned his thoughts to his body. He frowned at the pendant by candlelight.

There *was* something else going on in there. He felt confident of it now. But it was something hard to see...

Illusion?

Could there have been illusion magic *inside* the wind spells, hiding something deeper?

Aefric rolled his shoulders and hips. Adjusted his position on the stool.

And once more he shifted part of his consciousness into the flow of Qorunn's magic, and again into the pendant.

This time, he sought first and foremost the telltale signs that Kainemorton himself had taught Aefric to look for.

And he went slowly, carefully over all three spells one at a time.

But that yielded no further information.

So Aefric went in at them again, this time as one...

There.

There weren't three incomplete spells. There was one, complete spell. And it had nothing to do with the wind...

Aefric doubled down on his focus. Gave the investigation all the slow, careful attention he could manage.

He found the keystone.

Suddenly, it all made sense.

There were a total of two spells on the pendant. The first was the illusion. The pretense of three incomplete spells that hid the presence of the other, very complete spell.

That second spell, though, was the one that mattered.

That was a passage spell.

The bearer of this pendant could pass through a certain set of magical defenses with impunity. Might even be able to lead others. That was less certain, at this point.

So Aefric continued his investigation. All thoughts of lunch or other business were gone now. He would stay with this as long as he needed...

When Aefric finally opened his eyes, the candles on the walls of his laboratory indicated he'd been sitting there for ... eight hours?

Yes. Eight.

That explained why Aefric's stomach was rumbling louder objections than Ser Calder had been earlier.

But it was worth it.

The pendant could indeed bring more people along, if they were all within a structure. Say, a ship.

Assuming the bearer of the pendant knew the key phrase. Which Aefric now knew was "safe haven."

He chuckled, and dangled the bronze pendant before him. No wonder Gwawl wanted it back so badly. This pendant was the key to entering some secret lair.

Nelazzi's?

No way to tell. Not from the spells. But given Gwawl's connection to Nelazzi, that the pendant served as passage to her secret hideaway seemed likely.

Unless that was just hope talking.

Perhaps he was simply tired and hungry, but something about this didn't make sense. The spell Aefric had found under the illusion, that was a potent little bit of enchantment. Too potent, and too coherent, to survive long in a cheap pendant like this one.

Heck, even the illusion was too much to last long in a pendant like this one.

And yet, Aefric found no signs of decay in either spell.

That ... that didn't make sense.

There had to be something more going on here.

Could the inner spell be the illusion?

No. No, it couldn't. That would require an illusion that was still too high quality for this pendant.

Two excellent spells. Both within a vessel that shouldn't have been able to hold either.

So either Aefric was wrong...

...or there was more to this pendant than there seemed.

Aefric crossed the room on tired feet. He needed rest and food. But at least the stool that had kept him from stiffening up this time.

He opened the door to the landing, where Ser Vria and Ser Micham immediately gave him their attention.

"Ser Calder and Ser Beornric are down in the sitting room," Ser Vria said, "awaiting your pleasure, your grace."

Aefric looked back and forth between Ser Micham and Ser Vria for a moment.

Both were more than attractive enough to draw and hold attention. Though out of their armor, Ser Micham would still be big and tough-looking, whereas Ser Vria, properly dressed, could be mistaken for one of the noblewomen of Aefric's court. Especially with her eldrani heritage...

"How much longer are the two of you on duty?"

"We'd be off duty right now," Ser Vria said, "but we weren't willing to yield guard of the door until your grace came out."

"I think Arras and Wardius are downstairs," Ser Micham added, "ready to relieve us."

"Excellent. And thank you both for your dedication. In fact..." Aefric lowered his voice, and gestured for his knights to lean closer. "I need the two of you to do something for me, if you're willing."

"Anything, your grace," Ser Vria said, while Ser Micham said, "Name it and it's done, your grace."

"I knew I could trust you both," Aefric said with a smile. He held up the bronze pendant. "Once you're off duty, I want you to dress like courtiers, and act like a besotted couple. Take this with you to the finest jeweler in Water's End. Make sure anyone who sees you thinks you're there for a promise ring, but insist on seeing the master jeweler in person, in private."

He pressed the pendant into Ser Vria's hands.

"Once you're alone with the master jeweler, look at some rings. Make it believable. But before you leave, maybe pretending it's an afterthought, ask the master jeweler to inspect this closely. Say it's an old family heirloom that's supposed to be worth something, but looks like dung."

"It does at that," Ser Vria said, then whispered, "Your grace believes there's something more to it?"

"There might be, but right now ... what I'm seeing doesn't make sense. I need to know what a master jeweler thinks of the structure of this thing. And I need this kept quiet."

"We'll handle it, your grace," Ser Vria said, and Ser Micham nodded.

"Thank you. No one else can know you have the pendant, and bring it back to me personally."

"Of course, your grace," Ser Vria said, then frowned. "But if I may ask, why all the secrecy?"

"They say Nelazzi has eyes in every port," Aefric said with a grimace. "Well, I trust my inner circle, but Water's End is still a port city. And I need to keep Nelazzi in the dark."

"No one will learn about this from us, your grace," Ser Micham said.

"Thank you," Aefric said, then started down the stairs, where he was met by Dajen, who had one eyebrow raised as he looked over Aefric's clothing.

"Your grace is rumpled," Dajen said. "And clearly he has been ... perspiring."

Aefric paused. Considered arguing. Sighed. "You want me to change my clothes."

"I desire that your grace only ever presents himself as befits a nobleman of his standing and accomplishments." Dajen smiled. "Though I should also note that a change of clothes can bring a new outlook on the problems a duke may face, as well as providing a fresher, more confident feeling overall."

"He's good," Ser Micham said softly.

Aefric couldn't deny that he'd worked hard that day, and he probably smelled like it.

"Fine," Aefric said. "You win. I'll change."

"I assure your grace that the victory is his," Dajen said, leading Aefric to his closets, where his body servants came to attention. "And he will understand why, once he has changed."

So Aefric stripped down, cleaned up at a basin, brushed out his hair, and dressed in the evening clothes selected by Dajen.

A long silk tunic of midnight blue, subtly embroidered with silver thread, and slashed across the middle by a cloth-of-silver belt. Hose the purple of late sunset. Low slippers of soft, creamy leather that had been dyed to match his tunic.

For adornment, a small platinum brooch that featured a large cat's eye gemstone. And, of course, Aefric carried the Brightstaff.

As Aefric looked himself over in the mirror, he realized he did feel better and more coherent.

He almost said so, but one look at Dajen told him there was no need. The wise old valet already knew.

In the main part of Aefric's public sitting room were a series of plush, well-padded couches and armchairs, that could likely sit up to twenty people. Thirty, if they were all friendly enough.

Most of those seats were empty when Aefric came down the stairs. But more of them were taken up than he'd expected.

He'd been told by his knight-guards to expect Sers Beornric and Calder. But Ser Yrsa had joined them. As had Zoleen Fyrenn, whose slow appreciative gaze made Aefric feel even better about his clothing choice.

All four of them stood and bowed as he reached the foot of the staircase.

Two of the knights were dressed as they had been earlier. Sers Calder and Yrsa remained in their tunics and hose, with Ser Calder also wearing his doublet.

Ser Beornric had changed out of his full plate armor, though, and now wore a russet tunic with pale brown hose.

Sers Yrsa and Beornric were still armed, of course, though Ser Calder, Aefric was pleased to see, was not.

Zoleen Fyrenn wore a complex, eye-catching evening gown that matched the sapphire blue of her eyes.

During the bows, Aefric noticed four pages along the wall, awaiting his attention.

"Wait," Aefric said to the assemblage, raising his free hand. He turned to Sers Vria and Micham. "You've been on duty long enough. Go. Rest. Eat. Do whatever it is you guys do when you have time to yourselves."

"Sparring or sex, most likely," Ser Yrsa said dryly, as Sers Vria and Micham left Aefric's apartments to be about their mission.

Aefric looked over at Zoleen Fyrenn and the three remaining knights.

"Do any of you have anything immediately pressing?"

They all admitted that they didn't.

"Pages first then," Aefric said.

The first page stepped forward, bearing a scroll. He bowed and presented the scroll. "From your grace's historian."

"Thank you," Aefric said, taking the scroll, tucking it into his belt, and dismissing the page.

The second page stepped forward. "There has been a rika from Galdiff Reteka of Ajenmoor, assuring your grace that he has received your grace's court wizard, and is rendering him all assistance."

"Does like his credit, doesn't he?" Ser Yrsa said.

"Thank you," Aefric said, dismissing the page.

The third page stepped forward. "Your grace's seneschal requests a meeting before your grace retires for the evening."

"Very good," Aefric said. "Tell Kentigern I'll see him after dinner."

As the third page left, the fourth page stepped forward, bowed, and said, "There has been a rika from Baroness Herewyn Ol'Norette, of Norra. She invites your grace to the Feast of Dereth Sehk, which is to take place during the last three days of the final aett of summer."

"Has my seneschal already been informed of this one?" Aefric asked the page.

"It was Master Kentigern who bid me deliver this message to your grace."

"Excellent, thank you," Aefric said, and dismissed that page as well, before walking over to join the others on his couches.

"I've never heard of the Feast of Dereth Sehk," Aefric said, standing the Brightstaff beside his chosen seat. He sat, and gestured for the others to sit as well. "Do any of you know what it is?"

"Only practiced in Norra, I believe, your grace," Ser Calder said.

"Well, of course it's only practiced in Norra," Zoleen said. "It was in Norra that the final battle was said to take place. Your grace doesn't know the story?"

Aefric shook his head.

Zoleen smiled, clearly pleased to be the one to tell it.

"Prior to the Godswalk Wars," she said, "only once were the gods ever said to have trod the face of Qorunn. Thousands of years ago. Long before even my ancestors established the principality of Fyr.

"Most of the gods came down for reasons known only to themselves. Though most like to say that they came to bless temples and worshipers, or even just to prove that they existed.

"But when they departed once more for their heavens and hells, it was said that the derekek emperor Orsk Nolekk was furious. He ruled more than half of Qorunn at the time, and had been told by his priests that he was to be taken up with the gods, to join their number.

"But he'd been left behind. And in his fury, swore he would conquer all of Qorunn. If the gods wouldn't take him in, he'd crush all their temples and slay all their priests. If he couldn't be a god, then neither could they.

"War raged across the lands of Qorunn. It was said that the humans and na'shek formed their first alliance then. And that the alliance included even taroks and borogs, in places."

"Don't forget the kindaren," Ser Calder said. "They were part of the alliance too."

"I'm telling this story," Zoleen said, looking very much like her sister Ashling for a moment. She turned back to Aefric and continued.

"I have heard this story since childhood, and studied it myself. *I* have never run across *credible* references to the kindaren as part of the alliance, and believe that their race, like the eldrani, is too young to have been involved. Inclusion of the kindaren can only be a later addition to the story, and not a reflection of true events of the time."

She gave the knights each a look that challenged them to correct her. They allowed her to continue without comment. She turned back to Aefric.

"As would happen thousands of years later with the Godwalk Wars, the final battle took place within the lands that we now know as Armyr. The Godswalk Wars, of course, had their final major battle in your own duchy of Deepwater. But the war against Emperor Orsk came to its conclusion in what we now call the barony of Norra."

Aefric might have disputed that the Battle of Deepwater was the final major battle of the Godswalk Wars. But that point wasn't worth interrupting the story.

"The alliance," Zoleen continued, "under the leadership of a human named Dereth Sehk, met the forces of Emperor Orsk and dealt them a sound defeat that broke the power of the derekek armies.

"It is said that, after Orsk's defeat, the derekek were cursed by the gods to never again form or hold a kingdom. Which is why, to this day, they prefer sailing the seas, lakes, and rivers of Qorunn."

"The last, as I understand it," Ser Beornric said, "is speculation."

"Perhaps," Zoleen said, giving Ser Beornric an arch look. "But I do not believe, Ser Beornric, that you can name any derekek kingdoms that have existed in the last thousand years. Or am I mistaken in this?"

"There are those who dispute that Emperor Orsk was derekek," Ser Calder said. "Some say he was human. Others, a borog. And the name certainly sounds—"

"Naming styles and conventions change with time," Zoleen said, then turned back to Aefric. "We have histories at Fyrcloch Castle that go back almost that far, if your grace would be interested to read them."

"I would," Aefric said, giving her a smile, "when I could find the time." He sighed. "Speaking of which, I suspect that these three good knights have not come to discuss history with me, but have business that requires my attention. Yes?"

Sers Beornric and Calder nodded. Ser Yrsa only gave Aefric a look that said the answer was obvious.

"I thought as much. Why don't the three of you await me in the meeting room, and I'll join you in a moment."

Ser Beornric cleared his throat. "Your grace has not eaten since this morning."

"Nevertheless," Aefric said, though his stomach chose that moment to sound an agreement with Ser Beornric.

Once all three knights were on their way into the meeting room, Aefric smiled at Zoleen.

"You're early," he said.

"Well," she said, giving him a coquettish smile, "your grace has not been seen since the departure of the princesses this morning. I wished to ensure that your grace had not been spirited away by amorous royalty."

Aefric laughed.

"Or worse," Zoleen continued, "forgotten our appointment."

"Impossible," Aefric said. "I have a kiss to return, after all."

"I like the sound of that," Zoleen said, her voice low and warm. "So long as the evening doesn't end with that kiss."

Aefric held her gaze and shook his head slowly. "It won't."

"Then I shall look forward to returning later," she said, then cocked head to one side. "Unless your grace wishes me to await him upstairs?"

"No," Aefric said with a smile. "I wouldn't be able to concentrate on work. Better you return later."

"Until then, your grace," she said, and took her leave.

Once she was gone, Aefric sighed. He'd been warned too many times not to trust Duchess Ashling...

"Dajen," Aefric said.

"Your grace," Dajen said, stepping forward.

"If Zoleen Fyrenn returns before I am ready to retire, have her await me in the upstairs sitting room."

"Yes, your grace."

"She may suggest waiting for me in my bedroom," Aefric said. "But you know only that she was to be admitted to the *sitting room*. Is that clear?"

"Of course, your grace," Dajen said, then frowned. "If I may ask, does your grace feel he has reason to expect Mistress Zoleen to be admitted somewhere without your grace's prior permission?"

Aefric smiled and clapped Dajen on the shoulder.

"Nothing I've seen here at Water's End would make me think so," he said. "But once, in Behal, I found Byrhta Ol'Caran awaiting me in my chambers, when I was not expecting her."

"Was her presence ... unwelcome, your grace?" Dajen asked.

"Not at all," Aefric admitted. "But it was unexpected."

"Yes, well," Dajen said with as close to a grimace as Aefric had ever seen from him. "Your grace must remember that Mistress Byrhta is well known both here and at Behal. Duchess Arinda gave her the freedom of her castles, and ... I daresay that most of the servants will continue to do so, unless your grace instructs otherwise."

"Byrhta told me that night," Aefric said, cocking an eyebrow, "that she thought the servants wanted her in my bed as much as she wanted to be there."

"Well," Dajen said, in the same almost pained tone, though his expression was under control again. "I daresay that many members of the castle staff both here and at Behal would choose Mistress Byrhta as a bride for your grace, had they the choice. She's quite popular."

"She is a charming one," Aefric said.

"And though Mistress Zoleen has her charms," Dajen said, "she is neither so well known nor so well loved here or at Behal as Mistress Byrhta. Your grace should not expect Mistress Zoleen to be admitted anywhere your grace has not expressly permitted her."

"Good," Aefric said, then shook his head.

He was intending to sleep with this woman that night, but he wasn't sure he trusted her.

How strange his life had gotten.

And to see how much stranger it was getting, he went to meet with his knight-advisers.

WHEN AEFRIC ENTERED HIS MEETING ROOM, SERS YRSA, BEORNRIC AND Calder were already standing. As though they hadn't bothered to sit at the table during their wait.

All three knights looked at Aefric, but he lit the yellow diamond atop the Brightstaff to warn them that he would speak first.

"I'm tired, I'm hungry, and I want some fresh air," Aefric said. "Unless any of you have a reason not to, we're taking this out onto the balcony."

For once, all three agreed.

A few short minutes later, all three were seated on the greenwood furniture of Aefric's public floor balcony. Dajen had sent to the kitchens for food, but the conversation couldn't wait that long.

The day was giving way to evening. The sun was setting somewhere on the other side of the castle, and in the distance to the east, Aefric could see the first wink of a star in the darkening sky.

The air was balmy and still. The lake down below was busy with ships and boats, and if Aefric strained a bit, he could just hear the sounds of bells and work down on the docks.

"Your grace?" Ser Beornric asked.

"Sorry," Aefric said, sitting back and rolling his shoulders. "Long day. What news?"

"Those knights I spoke of," Ser Calder said. "I have their names now. Drenger Eyersson, Soren Isarson, Tohr Duisson, and Rafnar Tyyrsson."

"All men?" Aefric asked, surprised.

"Women knights are rare in Malimfar," Ser Yrsa said. "Though they do have the Order of the Shield Maiden, which admits only women."

"All four are young, with no visible scars," Ser Calder continued. "All four have purchased horses and have been heard to talk about hunting."

"Which is what I'd do," Ser Beornric said, "if I was stuck someplace waiting for orders. Gives me an excuse to ride about. See the land. The people."

"The defenses," Ser Yrsa added.

"Exactly," Ser Calder said. "They're being quite open about their presence and activities, but I don't believe for a moment that they're innocent."

"What kind of horses did they buy?" Ser Yrsa asked.

"Decent riding horses," Ser Calder said. "But not battle-trained, and certainly not warhorses. Bought them without haggling, but they did take their time in choosing."

"Where'd they get them?" Ser Beornric asked.

"The new place," Ser Calder said. "Sunrise Stables. Get their horses from Fyretti."

"Well," Aefric said, "do your best to keep an eye on them. But remember. So long as they behave themselves, we can't take action about these knights until we hear from his majesty."

"Any idea why his majesty is coming?" Ser Beornric asked.

"Beyond the obvious?" Ser Yrsa asked. "Two foreign princesses came *here*. Not to Armityr. That'll start rumors that they're seeking marriage with our eligible young duke, even though it might be cover for something else."

"Like what?" Aefric asked. "Beyond Malimfar wanting revenge."

"That's enough for me," Ser Beornric said. "Perhaps we can't arrest the knights, but we can at least invite them to stay here in the castle, where we can be sure they aren't rumormongering in town."

"We can't," Aefric said. "The king's message said to take no action regarding Malimfar. That might count."

"Surely, your grace," Ser Calder started, but Aefric cut him off.

"Yes, Ser Calder? Would you care to tell me how I should interpret the instructions of my liege lord?"

Ser Calder clamped his mouth tight and turned to glare out over the lake.

"Perhaps, Ser Calder," Aefric said, "you should find out what those knights are up to this evening. It would be good to know if they gamble, whore or drink excessively."

"Of course, your grace," Ser Calder said, voice tight. "Shall I be about that at once?"

"Have you other news I should be made aware of first?"

"No, your grace."

"Then I shall leave it to your discretion. You may remain if you can keep your temper. If not, then you have my leave to depart."

Ser Calder drew a long, slow breath.

"I think, perhaps, the day has been overlong for me," Ser Calder said. "I am not so young as I once was. So I shall take my leave with thanks, your grace, and see about the conduct of those knights before I retire for the evening."

"Thank you, Ser Calder," Aefric said. "I do appreciate your service."

Ser Calder visibly checked himself from saying something, but nodded, bowed, and departed.

"Perhaps you should have mercy on him," Ser Beornric said softly. "He's older than both of us put together, and he's a proud, accomplished man."

"That's part of the problem, isn't it?" Ser Yrsa said, surprising Aefric. But he nodded.

"He's been castellan here for a long time," Aefric said. "He's well known and well respected. And he's been testing me. Trying to put his judgment before mine."

"I suspect," Ser Yrsa said, "he feels he was passed over for the duchy."

"Arrogant of him," Ser Beornric said. "He's hardly of noble birth. Son of a tara farmer, I believe."

"That's right," Ser Yrsa said. "And my father was a rigger. Calder and I weren't born and bred for knighthood. We were knighted for excellence in battle. Mine was during the Sea Devils War some twenty summers past. Calder's was during a border struggle with Merrek, even further back. Maybe fifty summers or so."

Ser Beornric looked closely at Ser Yrsa's guarded expression.

"I didn't mean—"

"I know," Ser Yrsa said in the gentlest tone Aefric had ever heard from her. "You may be a fifth generation knight, Beornric, but you've never once lorded your family history or noble relations over anyone that I've seen."

"Once you're a knight, you're a knight," Ser Beornric said. "It's what *you* do that matters, not what your parents did." He turned back to Aefric. "Ranking nobility, though, that's a different animal."

"And yet," Aefric said, "King Colm *did* give the duchy to a man with no nobility in his family history. Ser Calder, at least, was born here in Deepwater. And he was already a castellan here at Water's End while I was still a street rat in Sartis."

"Which is my point," Ser Yrsa said. "Further, Arinda left a lot of the running of the duchy to Calder, so he had the experience. And he's served Armyr and Deepwater well for a long time."

"Well," Ser Beornric said, "let's not overlook the service our duke here did both Deepwater and Armyr during the wars."

"Certainly not," Ser Yrsa said. "Apart from the grumbling of a few old noble families, I don't think anyone disputes the reasons King Colm made his decision. But I think it still rankles Calder, who'd practically been rehearsing for the job for decades."

"Which brings up a supporting point," Ser Beornric said, turning back to Aefric. "Not only did you get the title he wanted, but by actually ruling you've taken away a lot of what he used to do." He shook his head. "Might be why he's so eager to see you go to Netar."

"And part of the reason I can't yet," Aefric said. "Not if I'm going to keep him on as castellan. His place needs to be made clear to him."

"There's Kivash," Ser Yrsa said suddenly. When Aefric looked the question at her, she continued. "You'll need a castellan down there as well. No reason it couldn't be him. And as Kivash is a potential source of conflict, he might get to taste battle again."

"He'd take it as an insult," Ser Beornric said.

The food arrived.

Fresh salmon, fire roasted with herbs and some kind of ground nut, served with sweet corn and spicy ground tara, along with honeyed oat bread.

Dajen had even anticipated Aefric's desires on the beverage front. Beer, from a brewery here in Water's End. A crisp but hearty brew that went well with the salmon, and almost seemed to echo the nuts in the dish.

As Aefric tucked in greedily, Ser Beornric continued.

"You send Calder to Kivash, you're telling him you don't trust him to do his job. Especially if you send him before you restore him the right to bear arms in your presence."

"Not just him," Ser Yrsa said, sighing as she conceded the point. "You'd be telling all of Water's End the same thing. Maybe all of Deepwater." She thumped one fist on the table. "Elbar's Blood, I thought I had it."

"He'll fall in line," Aefric said, "or I'll give him some land to retire on and find myself another castellan."

Sers Beornric and Yrsa discussed other possibilities for Ser Calder while Aefric ate, but none of them sounded likely.

"All right," Aefric said, once his plate was empty. "Enough of Ser Calder, for now. What other news?"

"I was hoping you'd have some for us," Ser Beornric said.

"As was I," Ser Yrsa said. "But I also wanted you to know that Princess Xenia did not stop in Behal, but kept moving."

"Really," Aefric said in wonder. "But she wouldn't find another castle before dark, much less a titled noble to host her."

"Indications are that they may ride through the night," Ser Yrsa said.

"Is this a change from their arrival?" Aefric asked.

"No," Ser Yrsa said, "but they didn't send word ahead of themselves, either. I think they'd wanted to surprise you, so they'd avoided the normal stops for a traveling princess."

"Why, though?" Aefric asked. "Why was surprising me important?"

"A mystery," Ser Yrsa said with a sigh, and hefted her own beer. Her third, while Aefric and Ser Beornric were both on their second. "Much as her purpose here."

"It is odd that she left without ever saying why she came," Ser Beornric said. "I know we're all assuming interest in marriage, but we don't *know* that."

"Testing the waters?" Aefric asked. "Finding out whether or not I'd be suitable first?"

"Or strategy," Ser Yrsa said. "Caiperas and Malimfar both spy on each other, of course, so she likely knew Princess Astrid was coming. Princess Xenia might only have come to counter, and to ensure that Princess Astrid could not pay court to you without Caiperas having some say."

Aefric shook his head. "You sound as though you think she'd marry me if she had to, to keep me from marrying Princess Astrid."

"She probably would," Ser Yrsa said.

"Your grace," Dajen said from the door to the sitting room. "Sers Vria and Micham are here, requesting a moment of your time."

"Excellent," Aefric said, smiling. "Tell them I'll be right in." To Sers Yrsa and Beornric, he added, "I may just have some news for you after all. Wait here for me."

---

WHEN AEFRIC ENTERED HIS PUBLIC FLOOR SITTING ROOM, HE ALMOST didn't recognize Sers Micham and Vria, who stood waiting for him near the couches.

They looked fantastic. Aefric had never seen either of them dressed up before, but he resolved to give them an excuse to dress up again sometime soon. A ball, perhaps.

Ser Micham wore a burgundy silk tunic, dark, mustard hose, and low, soft boots turned down at the cuff.

Ser Vria wore her orange hair down, over a dark blue, velvet gown that was surprisingly low-cut, and slippers that added a little sparkle to every step.

Aefric looked them up and down. Shook his head.

"I really must have the two of you dress up more often," he said. "There'd be no risk of anyone attacking me. They'd be too busy staring at the pair of you."

"Your grace is too kind," Ser Vria said, pleasure evident in her golden eyes, as both bowed to accept the compliment.

Ser Micham looked pointedly at Dajen. Aefric waved off the

concern. There might be spies in his court, but he couldn't believe Dajen was one of them.

Ser Vria pulled the pendant out of her décolletage and handed it to Aefric.

"What did you learn?" he asked, looking over the bronze, to see if he noticed anything different in the sextant shape of the pendant.

Ser Micham leaned in and angled it. Aefric spotted the tiny spark of a diamond.

He looked closer, while Ser Vria spoke.

"The sextant was cast with a small gap in the bronze, which had been filled with something else, and covered over with more bronze. We had master jewel smith, Tayor Sizen, clear away the added bronze to see what lay underneath."

Ser Micham picked up from there.

"Inset into the bronze, it turned out, was a tiny gold vessel fitted with diamonds. Handmade, according to the master, who marveled that anyone had commissioned such painstaking work only to cover it up. He was only too happy to have freed the diamonds and gold again."

"Impressive," Aefric said. He could see the gold and at least a couple of the diamonds now. The whole piece was so small. It must have taken a great deal of time and attention to put it together.

Exactly the sort of thing that could easily have held the illusion and passage spells Aefric had found.

"Even more impressive," Ser Vria added, "when your grace considers that the tiny diamond chips form a shape."

"They do?" Aefric asked, squinting. He could see diamonds, but not a shape.

"It can only be seen under the highest grade jeweler's loop," Ser Vria said. "A capital N."

Nelazzi.

Aefric smiled. "Thank you both. You've just answered two very important questions for me."

"Happy to do so, your grace," Ser Micham said.

"I hope your grace gives us more such assignments in the future," Ser Vria said with a smile. "That was fun. Pretending like that."

"I may just," Aefric said. "But for tonight, the two of you are now *actually* dismissed. Go relax and have fun."

As they left to do so, Aefric took the pendant back out onto the balcony with him. After Dajen brought them another round of beer, as well as a slice each of raspberry tart, Aefric explained to Sers Beornric and Yrsa what he'd learned about the pendant, and what Sers Vria and Micham had just discovered.

"Tremendous," Ser Beornric said, thumping the table with his fist. "This might be—"

"It might," Aefric said. "But we need to keep it to ourselves for now."

"You're worried about spies?" Ser Yrsa asked. She frowned, but nodded. "There shouldn't be any within the castle itself, but ... better safe than sorry."

"Right," Aefric said. "Still. Between this and whatever Karbin learns in Ajenmoor, we might soon be able to strike a meaningful blow against the pirate queen herself."

"I hate to say this," Ser Yrsa said, "but now might not be the time."

Aefric frowned around a bite of tart that *had* tasted perfect. Right until she said that.

"Please, your grace," she said. "Hear me out. We are rebuilding our coastline. We lost so many small villages and towns to the sea devils during the wars. Right now it's in the best interests of pirates to let us rebuild, so there'll be something worth raiding later on."

"Ah," Aefric said. "But if we strike at Nelazzi now..."

"Then we must be sure to crush her and her whole organization in a single swift blow." Ser Yrsa chopped her hand for emphasis. "To do otherwise, while we're vulnerable, is to risk retribution that could destroy everything we've started rebuilding."

"She has a point," Ser Beornric said sourly. "The wars have left us weak on the seas, and all but unprotected along most of our long coastline. We shouldn't go after Nelazzi. Not as things stand."

Aefric frowned. Flared his nostrils in a deep breath.

But then he had an idea.

"Delay might be a smarter way to go, at that," Aefric said slowly. "If I have time with that pendant, I might be able to work through its spells. Learn more about the magic of the caster behind those spells. Because when the time comes, we *will* face that caster. Any edge I can get might make the difference."

He made a connection then, frowned, and shook his head.

"Nelazzi can't be behind the stone men in the Dragonscar."

"Why not?" Ser Beornric asked.

"Because I'd know the work of that wizard again anywhere, and that wizard didn't enchant this pendant. So someone else must have. And *neither* of those spellcasters is Gwawl."

"So?" Ser Yrsa asked. "The Dragonscar could be commission work."

"Powerful magic-users tend to be territorial. Even Karbin. He'd never object to any magic I work for myself, but since I named him my ducal wizard, any magic done for the duchy needs to go through him. If I commissioned someone else to, say, cast wards on the Dragonscar, he'd take it as a personal affront."

"But Nelazzi's a pirate," Ser Beornric said. "For all she gets called a pirate *queen*, she's still not a noble, and her wizards are just hirelings."

"The issue isn't her position, though," Aefric said. "It's the pride that comes with power." He held up the pendant. "This is the work of a master. *I* might not be good enough to cast the spells I found on this thing."

"Could be both are commissions..." Ser Yrsa stopped her own sentence and shook her head. "No. Who would trust a safe passage charm to the spells of an outsider?"

"Exactly," Aefric said. "She's got someone working for her who could enchant this pendant. Which means that if she needed major spells cast in the Dragonscar, this wizard would cast those too. Otherwise, she'd risk offending that wizard, and losing him or her."

"There's one more possibility," Ser Beornric said darkly. "The wizard who enchanted that pendant might've been killed when the work was finished."

"True," Aefric said, frowning. "Though wizards of this power don't slay easily."

"It's not worth gambling on," Ser Yrsa said. "If she failed, she'd have an angry, powerful wizard on her hands. And if she succeeded, she'd lose a useful resource."

"So the Dragonscar question remains," Ser Beornric said. "Too much to hope they were related."

"In the meantime, then," Ser Yrsa said, "ignore Nelazzi and focus on the slavers. The more immediate threat. Act as though your anger about the slavers has made you forget Nelazzi's involvement. After all, she made her fame as a pirate, not a slaver. With time, she'll lower her guard."

"And then, when the time is right," Aefric said, "we crush her."

"Ideally in a single swift, decisive stroke," Ser Yrsa said. "But if not, we'll be in a stronger position for her response."

"Just as well," Ser Beornric said. "With both the king and queen only days away, you don't want to be planning a sea war."

Aefric blew out a breath, then sat up straight.

"Hey," he said. "Would Ser Calder take it as a promotion to be made vassal directly to the king instead of to me?"

"Not at his age," Ser Yrsa said. "Sorry."

"Ah, well."

"Your grace," Dajen said from the doorway. "Master Kentigern is here to see you, if your grace has time."

"By all means," Aefric said, "send him out. And fetch him some beer and tart, as well."

---

Aefric was tempted to conjure up a wind. The balmy, still air of the evening was proving too much, after the long day he'd had.

The level of focus he'd needed to defeat the illusion on that pendant, and then learn all he could from its spells, had been draining. Not so much for his magical reserves, as for his mind.

Didn't help that the greenwood chair he sat on was surprisingly comfortable. Or that he was full after the salmon dinner, and the tart afterwards, and pleasantly relaxed by the beer…

Aefric realized with a start that he'd missed the last portion of Kentigern's report entirely.

"I'm sorry, Kentigern," Aefric said. "I'm afraid I missed everything after the grains report."

Ser Yrsa pulled a coin from her purse and handed it to Ser Beornric.

Kentigern gave them a questioning look.

"The bet was about his grace's attention," Ser Yrsa said frankly. "I was sure you'd notice you lost it before our duke did."

Kentigern huffed and stroked his beard, but then looked sharply at Aefric for the first time.

"Your grace is exhausted," Kentigern said.

"More mentally than physically, but yes," Aefric said. "But I know I need to hear the reports, and I'm sure there are decisions I have to make about them."

"You could hand some of that off to Calder," Ser Yrsa said. "Might smooth things a bit."

"Not until he falls in line," Aefric said, then explained to Kentigern the disagreement with Ser Calder.

"I do apologize, your grace," Kentigern said, bowing his head. "I should have seen this coming."

"You're not his keeper," Aefric said.

"No, but I've worked with the man for years, as my mother did before me. I should have seen his resentment coming, and warned you."

"The actions are his," Aefric said, "and so is the responsibility. I won't have you blame yourself for his behavior."

"Perhaps I could speak to him?"

"No," Aefric said firmly. "He has created the situation for himself. He will either accept his place, or *be* replaced. I will not bow to my own castellan."

"Nor should you," Ser Yrsa said. "And Calder knows that, whether he wants to accept it or not."

"As for the rest of this..." Kentigern said, then shuffled the disturbingly large stack of parchment he'd been making on the table. "Most of it can wait for tomorrow."

"All right then," Aefric said. "I'll get a good night's sleep and spend most of the day tomorrow working through those matters with you. Let's get as much straightened out as we can before their majesties arrive."

"Excellent," Kentigern said, pleased. "Thank you, your grace."

"Otherwise, I should probably call it a day."

"If I might have a little more of your grace's time," Kentigern said. "There are still two other matters I should inform you of tonight."

"And there's still the question of that scroll from the historian," Ser Beornric said. "I can't be the only one curious about it."

Aefric had forgotten about that scroll. He took it from where he'd stashed it at his belt and set it on the table.

"Yours first," he said to Kentigern.

"Thank you, your grace." Kentigern shuffled aside most of the paperwork, and selected a single sheet. "This has a report of the cargo recovered from the smugglers, and my recommendations for redistribution of the grain and seed."

Aefric looked it over. It looked good overall — most of it going to Goldenfall, which had been hit the hardest by the wars, and some to Felspark, which had suffered the second worst. Although Felspark was further along the road to recovery, thanks to those young clerics of the Greenlord, whose services had been provided by Baron Osmaer of Havenford.

Of the rest of the seed and grains, some of it had been marked for distribution to the rebuilding efforts along the coast, but the rest had been marked for trade.

Aefric pointed out that last category. "I don't want those traded, right now."

"Other places need them too, your grace," Kentigern said. "But even you can't afford to supply everyone."

"I don't mean to," Aefric said with a chuckle. "But one area has fallen through the cracks of our rebuilding efforts. My own lands between the lake and the Golden River."

"Ah, of course," Kentigern said, and visibly ran some calculations. "Should be enough there to get the steadings of three or four lers running again."

"We may need to spread it thinner than that," Aefric said. "Getting a dozen of them started is likely better than giving three or four a larger hand up."

"I'll find a way to make it work, your grace," Kentigern said, shifting Aefric's attention to the rest of the report. "I have appraisers going over the various artwork, but it may be some time yet before we have a true sense of the value there."

"Mark any of it you think I should consider keeping, and make the rest available for trade. I like the idea of using any money we get from that cargo to help refugees from the wars. Both those we saved from the slavers, and those here in Deepwater."

"Speaking of the refugees," Kentigern said. "Of the forty, two dozen are farmers."

"Probably best sent to Goldenfall or the lands I just spoke of, I suspect," Aefric said.

"That was my plan, your grace," Kentigern said. "Another dozens are crafters. Woodworkers and stonemasons, mostly."

"The rebuilding projects on the coast?"

"That's what I was thinking," Kentigern said. "But I could redirect some to the lake's east side, if you'd rather."

"No, we have enough local people in need of work to handle that."

"There are the two derekek," Kentigern said. "But all they have to do is head down to the docks and they'll likely have captains competing for their services."

"Fine," Aefric said.

"Which leaves us with two of the eldrani," Kentigern said with a sigh. "They ... declined to name any skills when Ulltruchu organized that list for me."

"Oh?" Aefric asked. "Which two?"

"Li'nasachal and Li'sheneesha," Kentigern read from a list.

"The two dark-skinned eldrani," Ser Beornric said.

"I recall them," Aefric said. "I assume they were told that the list is only being compiled to help them?"

"Ulltruchu and I both told them this. They insist that they will list their skills, and I quote, 'only to the master of the Brightstaff.'"

"Odd way to phrase it," Ser Beornric said.

"It's a translation issue," Aefric said. "One way of showing respect in High Eldrani is to refer to someone not by name or title but by accomplishment."

"So they consider your greatest accomplishment carrying a magic staff?" Ser Yrsa asked.

Aefric chuckled. "Haven't I told you how I got this staff?"

She shook her head.

"I'll have to tell you sometime. But their choice of that honorific suggests that *they* know the story. Which is interesting. All right." He turned to Kentigern. "I'll see them tomorrow as well. Is there anything else for tonight?"

"Nothing pressing, your grace."

"Then let's see about that scroll." He opened the scroll from Elkari.

The wording was dense. And her handwriting small. Aefric had to light up the yellow diamond atop the Brightstaff to read it. And mentally exhausted as he was, he needed three tries to make sense of it.

It was a report of events that took place between two seasons and one year ago that might have involved the Dragonscar. And there was little to it.

The most interesting item on the list was a shipwreck during a major winter storm, where the survivors washed up in the cove at the mouth of the Dragonscar.

Aefric frowned, and passed the report around.

"Looks to me," he said, "as though we might now know when that cove came to the attention of the smugglers, slavers and so on. But I don't see anything there that helps figure out who both found the gold and tried to keep people away from it."

"May I hold onto this?" Ser Yrsa asked. "I'll check it against scouting reports. Maybe something will turn up."

"Please do," Aefric said. "And now, if that's all for today, I'm going to turn in."

Sers Yrsa and Beornric exchanged an amused look.

"Sleep well, your grace," Ser Yrsa said, with barely a pretense of innocence.

Aefric almost said something. But then, what did it matter if they knew that Zoleen would be joining Aefric that night? Those two had pushed him to embrace the noble privilege as part of setting his own nobles at ease.

And quite frankly, after the day he'd had, Aefric thought he deserved a little fun.

---

AEFRIC'S PRIVATE SITTING ROOM WAS MUCH SMALLER THAN HIS PUBLIC floor sitting room, but it was a little more lavish. For example, it was carpeted with rugs thick enough for Aefric's toes to sink into, when he was barefoot.

He wasn't barefoot now. He still wore the same outfit he'd worn when he'd gone downstairs earlier. He'd considered changing — Dajen had seemed to feel that he should — but given the way Zoleen had looked at him in his midnight blue velvet tunic with its silver embroidery, he felt motivated to keep wearing it for now.

Here, there were only two couches and a single armchair facing the large hearth, with the couches angled to make the chair the point of the triangle they formed with the wall.

The hearth was cold tonight. There was no need for a fire, for the late evening chill had yet to descend.

The couches and chair were well-padded enough to sink into, and the couches long enough to sleep on, should Aefric ever feel so inclined.

A triangular table of polished calinwood sat between them.

Opposite the hearth were glass doors leading onto the small, private balcony.

Along one wall were cabinets, beginning near the circular staircase, and doors leading to other private rooms. On the wall opposite, two doors. One leading into Aefric's bedroom, and the other into his closets.

The walls were bare of art that night. Duchess Arinda had kept portraits of herself and her family on those walls, but Aefric had moved those portraits to another part of the castle. They would be part of a more formal display honoring the Soulfist family, and other past dukes and duchesses of Deepwater.

He had yet to settle on what should replace them here.

He was contemplating that very question over a goblet of water when Dajen ascended the stairs and cleared his throat.

"Your grace, Mistress Zoleen Fyrenn has arrived. May I bring her to you?"

"Please," Aefric said, checking himself from standing.

That was one of the harder things he'd had to adjust to, in becoming duke. As Keifer McShane, he'd been raised to stand when a lady entered the room.

Growing up here in Qorunn as Aefric, that habit had remained with him. If anything, it had been emphasized by the fact that he'd been an untitled, itinerant adventurer. In those days, he'd only come into contact with nobility in three circumstances.

The first was when they sought his help with some problem in their lands. At times like those, giving the nobles and royals their social due had helped them swallow their pride in seeking aid from an outsider.

The second was when those problems were resolved, and they wanted to either reward Aefric, celebrate him, or both. At times like those, *not* giving nobles and royals their due was asking for trouble. After all, they no longer *needed* him.

The third, well, was when some misunderstanding had led to them thinking he'd broken a law, or something similar. Times like those, respectful deference was the only way to go.

But now Aefric *was* a noble. And not just any noble. He was a freaking *duke*. People were supposed to stand when *he* entered the room, not the other way around.

For Aefric to stand when anyone less than royalty entered the room, that would be making a statement about that individual's importance to Aefric, personally.

And he'd just met Zoleen.

He did, however, move from the chair to the couch that would give him a better view of the stairs.

Dajen returned shortly, announcing Zoleen as she ascended the stairs. She still wore that complex gown of sapphire blue, to match her eyes.

Aefric found himself glad she didn't just show up in a cloak and nightshirt. That happened once in a while, when a woman arrived for the noble privilege. And when it happened the first time he would sleep with a woman, he found it ... rushed.

"Your grace," Zoleen said with a smile and a deep bow. "I was only too happy to receive your summons. I'd begun to fear that your grace would work through the night."

"Another night, perhaps," Aefric said with a smile. "But how could I focus so on work when I knew that you were waiting for me?"

She gave a small bow to the compliment.

"Would you care to join me on the couch for some sharabi?" Aefric asked.

Zoleen's eyebrows raised a fraction — perhaps surprised that he didn't take her straight to bed — but she smiled. "I'd be delighted, your grace."

Dajen was quick to provide the sharabi and withdraw while Zoleen took her seat beside Aefric.

"To your grace," she said, raising her glass of tonight's pale green sharabi. "May Deepwater know many years of peace and prosperity under your rule."

Aefric raised his glass in confirmation, and they drank together. Tonight's sharabi was light, sweet, and carried a clean, wintergreen undertaste.

They settled back on the couch then, and spoke of small matters for a time, before Zoleen said, "I understand their majesties are coming for a visit. Is this their first visit since you were created duke?"

"It is," Aefric said. "Though I don't think it's as much a formal visit as it is to see about what Malimfar and Caiperas are up to."

"Forgive me, your grace," Zoleen said, "but it's a mistake to think so. They could send an agent for that. If they're both coming, and with full retinue, then this is a formal visit, and quite possibly a check to see how you're doing."

"In what way?"

"Reports," Zoleen said, "can be exaggerated or misstated. King Colm will want to see for himself how things stand here in your duchy."

"You sound as though you don't approve."

"It's not my place to approve or disapprove of the actions of my king," Zoleen said, then shrugged one shoulder. "But I will say that his majesty can be ... more involved in the territories of his vassals than most monarchs."

"Your sister has had problems with him?"

Zoleen curled her lips inward as she smiled, which gave her an appealingly mischievous look.

"My sister is the queen, your grace."

Aefric chuckled. "I believe you knew I meant your other sister..." Aefric cocked his head at her. "Or is this situation more complicated than that?"

Zoleen shrugged playfully and sipped her sharabi.

"Very well," Aefric said. "I'll consider myself warned. Thank you."

"I believe I've had enough sharabi," Zoleen said, playfully, "if your grace would care to express his thanks with more than words."

He kissed her then, and the wintergreen of the sharabi was strong on her tongue, though underneath he could detect the bitter hints of nysta tea.

They kissed there on the couch for a time. Unhurried. Just allowing the passions and pleasures of a new lover build, until they grew heated enough that at last Aefric picked her up and carried her to his bed while Zoleen leaned in and nibbled along his neck.

Aefric's bed here in Water's End was even larger than his bed in Behal. That one could have slept three, giving each of them room to comfortably spread out. This bed, though, could just as easily have slept five. Which made Aefric wonder, once in a while, whether some of his ducal predecessors had preferred their sex as a group activity.

He sat her on the edge of the bed. He reached to run his fingers through her long waves of copper hair, but Zoleen intercepted one of his hands and began kissing his palm.

He leaned in and nuzzled her hair and neck as she did, breathing in her scent, like wild strawberries.

His free hand found one of the ties of her gown and tried to loosen it, but it wouldn't come.

"You can't start with that one," Zoleen whispered, nuzzling his hand. "I'll show you, if you like."

"I have a better idea," he said, helping her stand and getting a puzzled look for his trouble.

Aefric channeled a touch of magic through his mouth and blew a puff of air at her along with the right pair of words.

Every tie and fastener of her gown and undergarments came loose.

Zoleen, surprised, reached to catch the clothes that were now falling off her body, but stopped her hands.

Instead she let her clothes fall and posed for Aefric with her hands on her cocked hips. She gave him a saucy look.

"Your grace knows a spell that strips women of their clothes?"

"Well, sort of," Aefric admitted. "It's really just a first-degree derivation of a spell that undoes ropes, chains and other bindings. Mostly useful for—"

"Your grace knows a *spell* that strips women of their *clothes*."

Aefric shrugged helplessly. What Zoleen was saying was true, technically, but it wasn't as though—

"And does your grace often use magic to render women naked before him?"

"No," Aefric said quickly, getting a little flustered now. She was supposed to be impressed with the little bit of magic, not...

Well, honestly, he couldn't read her reaction through that saucy look she was giving him. And she was, after all, distractingly naked. Even if that *had* been the point.

"How often—" Zoleen started, but Aefric spoke over her.

"I've never done that before," he said, shrugging and sighing. "It's a beautiful gown, and intricate enough that I didn't want to mess it up. Plus, I thought the bit of magic might amuse you."

"It did," she said with a warm smile. "I'll admit I was shocked. But I'll also admit that there's something pleasing about a man so eager to see me naked, and yet still concerned about my gown."

Aefric wasn't sure what to say to that.

"I know I don't measure up to Byrhta Ol'Caran," Zoleen said. "Nevertheless I hope your grace is pleased with the results of his spellwork."

Aefric made a show of looking her over slowly. From her beautiful face and the heat in her sapphire eyes, down her long neck, her supple curves, her lean, shapely legs.

"Very," Aefric said, voice low and throaty. "In fact," Aefric said, stepping closer and taking her face in his hands, "I believe I'm ready to begin the exploration I spoke of."

He kissed her then, and though her mouth met him open and ready, he made that kiss slow, to give her a taste of what was to come. And through the kiss, his hands never left her face. Not even as hers slid around his waist.

When he finally pulled back from that kiss, Zoleen muttered, "One thing."

Aefric raised his eyebrows.

"When the time comes for getting you out of these clothes," — she tugged on his silk tunic for emphasis — "I want to do it myself. No magic."

"I'll look forward to it," Aefric said, kissing her again and easing her back onto the bed.

Aefric did his best to not only enjoy exploring every inch of

Zoleen, but to make sure she enjoyed his efforts as much as he did. Preferably more so.

In fact, that was how the night seemed to go for them. Each of them trying to outdo the other, when it came to bringing pleasure.

But it was a lighthearted competition, one they could joke about as they rested in between. And one that kept them smiling, even when they fell asleep in each other's arms.

**7**

———————

Aefric shared a surprisingly comfortable breakfast with Zoleen the next morning. The meal was crisp bacon served with sliced fruit and honeyed oat bread, along with water to drink. And the conversation was light and easy.

She did tease him a bit about last night's "disrobing enchantment," as she called it, and asked about other "nefarious" uses he'd put magic to over the years. But that only opened the door to jokes he'd played with and on adventuring companions over the years.

Such stories kept them both laughing, even when it came time to part and begin their days.

Once Aefric was bathed, shaved, and dressed — today in a ruby red tunic over dark brown hose, though once more without a hat — he met with his advisers in his meeting room.

Ser Beornric was in his full plate, as he so often was, but this morning Ser Yrsa had chosen full plate as well, because she was due to review troop emplacements near to Water's End and Behal.

Ser Calder favored a tunic of dark yellow-green, with similar hose. Though he visibly chafed at being unarmed, he as wise enough not to say anything.

Both Kentigern and Elkari had chosen dark brown tunics today, with lighter brown hose.

Elkari looked a little more ink-stained than usual, and struggled not to yawn, as though she'd worked a late night.

Once all were seated, Ser Yrsa went first. "I found an interesting correlation between our good historian's report and the scouting reports of the same time frame."

"The shipwreck?" Ser Beornric asked.

"That corresponds as well, of course," Ser Yrsa said, as though expecting the question, "but there's a point of greater interest, during the final aett of last year's summer."

"Oh," Kentigern said, remembering, "the heat wave was bad last year. I cannot tell you how grateful I was when the rains came at last."

"Regardless of the heat," Ser Yrsa said. "Our scouts spotted a large group riding along the ridge of the Dragonscar, on the Silverlake side. Two dozen riders. And it looked as though they were led by a noble."

"Looked as though?" Ser Calder asked. "They didn't know?"

"They weren't flying any banners or flags," Ser Yrsa said. "And yet their formation was, in the opinion of the scouts, typical for a noble riding in company."

"That phrase, 'in company,'" Elkari said, "can mean many things."

"In this instance," Ser Yrsa said, "it refers to a military style of company." She turned back to Aefric. "Fearing that it was the prelude to an attack, our scouts kept pace and watched, but it just looked to be a review of the border."

"By Duke Wylyn?" Aefric asked.

"Unknown," Ser Yrsa admitted. "Might've been the duke. More likely it was a noble of the duke's court, acting on Silverlake's behalf."

"Unless the party originated in Johalan," Ser Calder said. "That's Briluufa's county. Aggressive as she can be, she might have spotted our scouts and used their presence as an excuse to push her scouting outside her county, if not outside Silverlake."

"Possible," Ser Yrsa admitted. "They were first spotted closer to the mouth of the Dragonscar, so that might be."

"What's the correlation with Elkari's report?" Aefric asked.

"The last aett of summer," Elkari said. "That was when our duke regent, Prince Killian, took his court to Norra for the Feast of Dereth Sehk."

"Exactly," Ser Yrsa said. "And I believe he took you along, didn't he, Calder?"

"He did," Ser Calder said with a brisk nod. "He insisted, in fact. Said I never take any time to have fun, and that he'd see to it I did."

"Sounds like Prince Killian all right," Ser Beornric said.

"And I take it," Aefric said, "that Prince Killian made no secret of his plans?"

"He rarely did," Ser Calder said with a grimace. "Even when I asked him to."

"All right," Aefric said. "So, if I'm in Silverlake and I want to check out the Dragonscar, that's not a bad time to do it." He frowned. "But they never went *into* the Dragonscar?"

"Of course not, your grace," Ser Yrsa said, and Aefric suspected that she'd added the honorific to avoid sounding as though she were censuring him. "A party that size in military formation, crossing your border without permission? They'd be taken as invaders. Likely attacked."

"Ah," Aefric said, understanding. "But the big group would keep the attention of the scouts, allowing a *smaller* group to explore the Dragonscar unnoticed."

"Exactly," Ser Yrsa said.

"And before your installation as duke," Ser Beornric said, "Duke Wylyn was petitioning to have his duchy extended south to the Threepeaks."

"Which he might have done anyway," Elkari said. "The dukes of Silverlake have long lamented the size of Deepwater, and lobbied to have the king grant them more land."

"From what I heard around Armityr at the time," Ser Beornric said, "Silverlake was pushing harder than usual."

"And the timing," Ser Yrsa said. "We know that the spells in the Dragonscar were cast between last summer and last winter. Which suggests that, in that time, someone explored the Dragonscar, found the gold, and took measures to protect it."

"Last winter was rough," Elkari said. "Some of the worst storms of the last twenty-five years, even before the snows hit."

"Which suggests," Ser Calder said, "that the spells were cast in summer or autumn." He nodded. "It fits."

"Looks likely," Aefric said. "Or at least likely enough that I need to pay Duke Wylyn a visit. How many days do I have before their majesties arrive?"

"Your grace can hardly go accuse Duke Wylyn of something that would amount to an act of war," Ser Calder said sharply.

Aefric tried to give Ser Calder a patient look, but he was running out of patience when it came to that man. Certainly the rest of the table had fallen silent.

"Ser Calder," Aefric said, and the knight pressed his lips into a line, likely expecting rebuke. "I know you and I do not know each other well. And I know that I've something of a reputation for impulsiveness."

"A reputation that Count Ferrin of Motte would call confirmed," Ser Beornric said softly.

Aefric ignored him and continued speaking to Ser Calder.

"But even I would not go running into the heart of Silverlake to accuse their duke of something unproven."

"Forgive me, your grace," Ser Calder said *just* above a mumble. "It is only that, three times since you were installed as duke, you have flown off to deal with something yourself through swift and decisive violence."

Aefric could think of only two…

"Motte," Ser Yrsa said quietly, "Frozen Ridge, and the *Gull's Bride*."

Oh. Yes. The ship full of slavers.

"Fair enough," Aefric admitted. "But the only one of those that was a political situation was Motte, and I was making a point."

Ser Calder nodded.

"I don't plan on flying into Silverlake. I plan on sending a rika to let them know I'm coming, then sailing into one of his ports and riding to his castle with a small, but reasonable entourage."

"And what excuse will you give for the visit?" Kentigern asked.

"Slavers," Ser Beornric said, as though the answer should have been obvious to all.

"Just so," Aefric said. "And while I'm there, I'll see what I can find out." He turned to his seneschal. "How long do I have before their majesties arrive?"

"They are coming with full entourage," Kentigern said, "which means they'll make all the stops... Certainly at least an aett. Perhaps as many as twelve days."

"It's two days to Castle Stormsent from here," Aefric said. "Two more back. That should give me plenty of time."

"Doesn't track," Ser Calder said. "I'm sorry, your grace, but why would you go yourself to discuss slavers with the duke? Why not send an emissary?"

"Two reasons," Aefric said. "The first is that I've made no secret that the matter is important to me. The second is that Duke Wylyn and I are both former adventurers. He and I can likely understand each other in ways that most nobles wouldn't."

"Not to mention that it'll have more impact if our duke goes himself," Ser Beornric said.

"Will you announce a similar plan to visit Merrek?" Kentigern asked. "To lend more credence to the façade?"

"Don't need to," Aefric said, smiling. "Duchess Ashling's own sister is already here in my court. Certainly it's reasonable that I could expect Zoleen to speak for Duchess Ashling on matters like this."

"Speaking of whom," Ser Yrsa said, then drew a deep breath. "I trust your grace was ... circumspect with her last night? Anything you said to her will likely reach her sister's ears."

"We hardly talked about the duchy at all," Aefric said, "and certainly not about business. And when we did speak of Deepwater, it was only about little things. Water's End. The waters and depth of the lake. The shops and artisans and the like. If you must know, we spoke mostly about ourselves. Personal histories."

"It could be," Elkari said slowly to Ser Yrsa, "that Mistress Zoleen has simply been charmed by our duke. Not to mention that she is of an old and powerful family, and his grace is unmarried."

"When the Fyrenn name is involved," Ser Yrsa said, "caution is the watchword."

"Noted," Aefric said. "And I will keep it in mind. Now. If I plan on catching the evening tides out of Ajenmoor on my way to Silverlake, Kentigern and I have a lot of work to do. Is there anything else pressing?"

A knock sounded on the meeting room door, and Aefric began to suspect that his day would, once again, grow quite long.

***

AEFRIC GIRDED HIMSELF FOR BAD NEWS, AND ANSWERED THE KNOCK BY calling out, "Come."

The door to his meeting room opened, and Ser Arras poked her head in.

"I wouldn't disturb your morning meeting, your grace, save that your ducal wizard has arrived."

"By all means, send him in," Aefric said, while his other advisers discussed something among themselves in low voices.

Karbin looked better rested today, which was good. That meant he hadn't arrived five breaths ahead of disaster.

He dressed in the robes of sand and dusk he so favored, and Aefric wondered for a moment what Dajen would say about the court wizard's habit of wearing the same style of clothing every day.

But then, Karbin wasn't the duke.

Four wands at his belt today, plus that obsidian rod of his. In his hands he carried a blackwood scroll case.

Once he was seated at the table, he said, "I do apologize for being late, but I flew in directly from Ajenmoor."

"You're capable of teleportation," Ser Calder said. "Why not do that?"

"You're capable of running," Karbin said. "Why walk? You're

capable of shouting? Why speak in a regular voice? You're capable of staying awake through the night. Why sleep?"

"Have it as you would," Ser Calder said.

Karbin nodded, then turned back to Aefric.

"First, I must say that Galdiff Reteka is a man I trust not at all."

"Oh," Ser Yrsa said, "I think you'll find you can trust him to act in his own best interests."

"As can be said of many untrustworthy people," Karbin said. "He *was* quite helpful, I will admit. He eased and sped my access to the prisoners, and ensured I had a private room to conduct my interviews."

"With him listening in, no doubt," Ser Beornric said.

"Hardly," Karbin said with a knowing smile. "I ensured personally that my interviews were unheard by any."

Ser Beornric nodded approval.

"From what I could put together," Karbin said. "The smugglers truly don't work for Nelazzi, for the most part. This mission was not one they asked for, and a few of them were relieved to see it end badly. It means they aren't likely to be pressed into another such mission on her behalf."

"Assuming they find work at sea again," Elkari said.

"Oh," Ser Yrsa said, "there's always someone ready to hire sailors. Especially those with certain categories of experience."

"Now," Karbin said, "obviously, none of them wanted to risk angering the pirate queen. So they tried to avoid telling me anything that could link them to her."

"Naturally," Aefric said.

"They were not entirely successful in this, of course. What's more, some of them don't like slavers, and were willing to talk a little more openly. And between what some said, what others *didn't* say, and what I'd already learned from my prior investigations, I was able to put together a pretty good look at their recent routes, which led to some interesting conclusions."

Karbin opened his scroll case and unrolled a map of the Risen Sea.

He traced the typical route of the smugglers.

"That doesn't come near Deepwater," Aefric said. "At least, no closer than Redport."

"Where they conducted no illegal activities," Karbin said. "Exactly. Lends credence to the idea that this was new for them."

"So?" Ser Calder asked. "I thought we were more worried about the slavers."

"We are," Aefric confirmed. "Even Nelazzi herself is less important."

That got him a glance from Karbin, but no comment as his old mentor continued.

"It matters because those smugglers rarely crossed paths with those slavers before. Only six total ports, three of which — here, here and here — aren't anywhere near us, nor any of the places their routes took them in the last two seasons."

"Which matters because..." Ser Calder said.

"Because I could eliminate those ports from the list I already had," Karbin said.

"But why does it matter?" Ser Calder asked. "Why does it have to involve a port known to both? Wouldn't it be smarter for the delivering ship to sail into a new port?"

"No," Ser Yrsa said. "New ships are marked and watched. Known ships are a known quantity. Ports used by the slavers would have a market for their cargo. Ports used by the smugglers would be places they know how to move that cargo."

"And there are only three remaining, known to both," Karbin said. "One, as I'm sure you all expected, is Kefthal."

A general murmur of agreement around the table.

"The other two," Karbin said, pointing to the map, "are here, Redport, and here, Wulfport."

Oppressive silence settled on the room.

Wulfport was in Malimfar, which was bad enough. But Redport, that was here in Armyr...

"I thought you said they conducted no illegal business in Redport," Aefric said.

"The smugglers never did. I'm *reasonably* certain of that. The slavers..." Karbin shook his head. "I got just enough in hints and implications from the prisoners in Ajenmoor to make me uncertain. I need more time to investigate."

"You mustn't," Kentigern said. "Not without permission from the king."

A few mouths opened to reply, but Kentigern got there first.

"If one *duke* investigates another for taking part in a *slavery ring* without first at least *discussing* the matter with his majesty, that duke is asking for censure. And punishment."

"Unless he's right," Aefric said.

"Even then," Kentigern insisted. "Oh, the punishment might be lesser, but that duke would still be guilty of acting above his station. And the only station above the duke is that of the king himself."

"I think we all agree," Ser Beornric said diplomatically, "that none of us want to give the impression that his grace here wishes to usurp royal authority."

"*No way in any of the thirteen hells do I want to usurp royal authority*," Aefric said. "I have plenty of authority right now, thank you. So let's move on past that point, shall we? Redport can wait until King Colm arrives."

"The king is coming?" Karbin asked.

"As is the queen," Kentigern said, "and full royal entourage."

"What about Wulfport?" Aefric asked, bringing them back on topic. "What do we know there?"

"Too much," Karbin said, shaking his head. "I confirmed that Wulfport has been a regular business stop for both the slavers and the smugglers since midway through the Godswalk Wars."

That was a big enough accusation to settle silence on the room for a moment.

"Do you have proof?" Aefric asked.

"Nothing conclusive," Karbin said. "Not at this time."

"But you do," Ser Calder said suddenly.

Once everyone was looking at him, Ser Calder continued, addressing Aefric now.

"When our good court wizard was last in Wulfport, tracing the slavers, he was assaulted by a wizard for asking the wrong questions. Tracing *slavers*, not pirates," Ser Calder said, then turned to Karbin. "I know you said it was one of Nelazzi's wizards who attacked you, but you yourself admitted it was late and you were tired. Clearly the wizard was a contact of those slavers, there to quash an investigation into Wulfport that would yield more fruit."

"That does sound reasonable," Ser Beornric said.

"What made you think of Nelazzi?" Aefric asked Karbin.

"I'd run into the tactic before, when I'd crossed paths with the pirate queen. But I suppose it could have spread by now..."

"Either way," Aefric said, "it's clear that the slaver ring goes through Malimfar and—"

Kentigern cleared his throat.

Aefric sighed. "And I'm not allowed to take any action where Malimfar is concerned." He shook his head. "Fine, then. We'll keep everything about that confined to this room for the time being. But Karbin, I'll want a detailed report to give his majesty."

"And you'll have one. There are a couple of more leads I could check out, if you like. Leads that would not take me into Malimfar or Redport."

"Fine then," Aefric said. "Do any of the rest of you have anything pressing?"

"Nothing yet," Elkari said. "I *may* have found a precedent that might apply to the Dragonscar mine that touches on Duke Wylyn's land. I need more research to be certain."

"Good," Aefric said, and was about to dismiss the meeting when she spoke up again.

"And I've had my assistants compiling a list of lers and territories from before the Godswalk Wars, for comparison with the duchy as it stands, for purposes of aiding the search for missing lers."

"That reminds me," Kentigern said. "I suppose this is as good a time as any to mention that your grace has had a rika this morning from Mistress Karaleca in Lachedran, to say that she's gathered her committee and begun her search."

"She wrote to say that?" Ser Yrsa asked.

"Well," Kentigern said, then pulled out the small, rolled up message itself. "I think it was an excuse to offer her thanks again, and remind his grace that she's doing this."

"Fine," Aefric said, taking the message, but not reading it then. "If that's all, then let us adjourn. We have a lot of work ahead of us."

---

BY MIDDAY, AEFRIC WAS CERTAIN OF THREE THINGS.

The first was that his seneschal deserved a raise. Aefric wasn't sure what he was paying the man, but it wasn't enough.

Over the course of the morning, Aefric, Kentigern, and Ser Calder had gone over a good portion of the things that were involved in running the duchy.

Reports from the vassals about the state of their lands, and their needs going forward.

Reports from the mayors, lers, and landed knights in the ducal lands about *their* status and *their* needs going forward.

Amalgamated reports that gave an overview of the state of production of every single crop grown between Kerrik Forest in the east, the Risen Sea in the west, the Dragonscar in the north, and the Merrek border in the south.

And not just the crops. The mines and quarries, timber and construction. There were similar reports about trade, both overall and by category. The states of the various trades and guilds. And more than that besides.

And Kentigern had organized all of these things. Not just into coherent reports, but he ordered the reports themselves, so that one lead into the other.

By the time Aefric had to make a decision about something, Kentigern had made sure he'd already received all pertinent information.

The man was a gem.

The second thing Aefric had grown certain of was that he had no immediate need to get rid of Ser Calder. While they were working, the man behaved himself, and at least *seemed* to understand that he'd been overstepping his bounds.

The rhythm Aefric established might have helped there. First, he let Kentigern report on a topic. Then he asked Ser Calder for his thoughts, and, where appropriate, a little of the history.

For example, Ler Osgood, whose lands were just west of Behal, was reporting that the hot summer had hurt his production of sweet peppers, and that he would need permission to raise taxes to see his people through the winter if he did not receive ducal aid.

But this was a trick Ler Osgood had played more than once. Kentigern knew that, and had warned Aefric that, after receiving permission, Ler Osgood was likely to report that he'd saved his harvest — but not lower his taxes again.

Still, it was Ser Calder who suggested sending a knight down to investigate. Without warning.

Apparently Duchess Arinda used to respond with a rika suggesting sending someone down to examine his situation, which was usually enough to get Ler Osgood to claim he'd had a breakthrough in irrigation and saved his crop after all. Or something along such lines.

Perhaps, however, skipping the rika and sending a knight down to investigate — undoubtedly proving that the peppers were doing just fine — might put a stop to this trick for good.

"Ser Grey," Aefric had said, smiling, "would be perfect."

"You would send Behal's castellan?" Ser Calder asked, almost sounding offended, but then furrowed his brow as he thought about it.

"Wait," he said. "You want to send someone to show you're taking his cow spittle seriously. If you'll pardon my phrasing, your grace."

"Exactly," Aefric said. "Arinda never actually sent a knight, there's no precedent. So if I start by appearing to take him seriously enough that I send a castellan down to assess how much aid he needs, I have the right to more than a little anger when it turns out to be a false excuse."

"And everyone in the Behal region knows Ser Grey's reputation. He won't dare lie to her face."

"There is always the possibility," Kentigern said, "that he's telling the truth this time."

"Perhaps," Ser Calder said, "but given his history, it's not likely."

"Either way," Aefric said. "If it's an actual problem, for once, and I send Ser Grey, it tells all my lers and my people that I take such problems seriously."

"And if it's *not* an actual problem," Ser Calder said, quirking a half-smile, "you have an indisputable witness when you call him to account. I like it."

By the third time Aefric took one of Ser Calder's suggestions and gave it his own twist, Ser Calder laughed aloud.

"We must play chess sometime, your grace," he said. "From the angles you take on problems, I suspect that you develop your knights and wizards in ways that no one can see coming."

"Whereas you favor bishops and rooks?" Aefric asked.

Ser Calder nodded acknowledgment, but he was smiling. Aefric began to feel that he might be able to work with his castellan after all.

The third thing Aefric became convinced of, as the morning crawled past, was that he would soon need to visit Motte.

He couldn't put his finger on why. But something in the reports from Motte felt ... off. Kentigern couldn't spot it, and neither could Ser Calder, but Aefric couldn't shake that feeling.

And for all that people called him a wizard, properly speaking, Aefric was a dweomerblood. And intuition was as much a part of how he lived and worked as logic and precedent. Perhaps more so.

It felt like the same kind of intuition right now telling him that something was wrong in Motte.

But he didn't have time to check into it. Not right now.

At midday, Aefric took his lunch alone, on his private balcony. That might upset a few people who had hoped for his company, but it was a lovely day — if hot — and Aefric wanted to get some letters written before he left for Silverlake.

The letters to Maev and Byrhta were both difficult, for much the same reason. He wanted to share with both of them all that had been going on. Not just to express it, but to get their opinions.

Unfortunately, he had to be more circumspect than that in letters. Especially when writing to Maev, who was all the way down in Varondam where, for all he knew, they might insist on reading her letters.

So with Maev Aefric spoke of how he missed her, and how, alas, he never reached the dragon's skeleton because he'd been called back from the Dragonscar by business that couldn't wait.

He wrote about fighting smugglers and slavers — and rescuing the refugees — but confined himself to a single line complaining about the politics of his cities.

He couldn't explicitly mention the visit by the princesses. There might be political implications. So, instead, he made a single-line reference to princesses hunting in his lands.

Maev, he felt, would understand that. She always spoke of their feelings for one another as a mutual hunt. The use of the plural would surely catch her attention and convey his meaning.

Aefric did mention the coming royal visit, though. No reason he could think of not to, and it might help make sure she got his message about the princesses.

He did not greet Maev on Byrhta's behalf. If they wanted to send messages back and forth, they could write their own letters.

With Byrhta, his letter covered much the same ground, for Aefric missed her as well. Though he could be more explicit about the visit of the princesses. She might have heard about it by now anyway.

The other letter he had to write was to Vercy, which would likely disappoint her. Because unlike the other two letters, this one wasn't very personal. Aefric covered many of the same events, but from more of a distance, with less of his personal take. And, if anything, less actual information.

Aefric frowned as he read it over. Added a paragraph at the end expressing gratitude about all she was learning and all she was doing both for Riverbreak and all of Deepwater.

He didn't address Vercy's suggestion about a possible husband for

Byrhta, but he did add a personal note about the joys of sailing out on the lake. Just so he didn't come across as too cold or distant.

He didn't want to *hurt* her. He just didn't want to *encourage* her.

Unfortunately, Aefric'd gotten so involved in writing his letters that he needed to bolt down what must have been a very good lunch, while it was hot. It was a meat pie featuring lamb and a mixture of vegetables in a flaky, buttery crust. Even cold, it was still better than a lot of what he'd eaten during his adventuring days.

Then, it was back into his primary office for an afternoon of more reports and decisions.

By the time he was done for the day, Aefric found himself hoping that something attacked them on the way to Silverfall. Just for the change of pace.

---

It was late afternoon that day, and preparations were underway for the *Duke's Hand* to take Aefric and a small entourage from Water's End to Alimar's Launch, up in Silverlake.

At the moment, however, Aefric was letting others see to those arrangements. He was sitting at the red, polished calinwood desk in his ... third? No. Fourth best office, down on the bottom floor of the Castle at Water's End, and close to the docks.

Out of the way, leaning against the calinwood cabinets, stood Ser Vria. Because everyone objected to Aefric taking this meeting without at least one guard in the room, and Ser Vria had the added benefit of speaking at least some High Eldrani.

How much she spoke of that language, Aefric wasn't sure.

Facing Aefric across that desk and seated primly on finely carved calinwood chairs, were Li'nasachal and Li'sheneesha, with their dark, eldrani beauty, their flame-yellow eyes and long, vivid hair, the purple of late sunset. They weren't dressed in rags this time, but in light brown cotton. Li'nasachal in tunic and breeches, and Li'she-neesha in a robe.

Flags of Armyr and Deepwater adorned the soft gray of the plastered walls, but the eldrani looked back and forth between Aefric and the recent portrait of Aefric, before Li'sheneesha spoke.

*"The artist has a feel for the body,"* she said, in High Eldrani, *"but not your soul, Kalifnia."*

*Kalifnia.* Aefric hadn't heard that term since he was last in *Ahlisklasach,* an Eldrani city near Thunderwood. The word best translated as "low king," which might be a reasonable way to refer to a duke.

*"The soul can be a bit much to ask of an artist,"* Aefric said.

*"It is the soul that matters,"* Li'nasachal said. *"Without the soul, a portrait is just a collection of colors. However pretty."*

*"Well,"* Aefric said, *"at least the colors are pleasing then. I understand you would not list your skills for Ulltruchu, nor for my seneschal. You do understand that we only seek this information to help you find homes and work."*

*"We could not trust that information to underlings, Kalifnia,"* Li'nasachal said. *"For if we did, we would never be allowed in your presence."*

"Please step back from the desk, your grace," Ser Vria said, drawing her sword and stepping up beside the desk.

Li'nasachal and Li'sheneesha did not react. They didn't even acknowledge Ser Vria.

*"Your guard illustrates my point,"* Li'nasachal said.

"Your grace, please," Ser Vria said, in the common tongue.

"I don't believe they intend me harm, Ser Vria," Aefric said the same way.

*"Upon our lives,"* Li'sheneesha said in High Eldrani, *"I swear we do not."*

*"A gamble set,"* Ser Vria said in High Eldrani, by which Aefric was pretty sure she meant that their lives were already in the balance.

*"What are these skills?"* Aefric asked, shifting back to High Eldrani.

"From what they've said so far, they can only be *Sinflissacta,*" Ser Vria said, in the common tongue. "Soul thieves."

*"We are not thieves,"* Li'nasachal said, finally looking at Ser Vria. *"Your poor command of the True Tongue shames your family."*

*"Your calling shames yours,"* Ser Vria snapped back, clearly itching to use the blade in her hands.

"Ser Vria," Aefric said sharply, in the common tongue. "Take two steps back and lower your blade. Use it only if they *actually* try to harm one of us."

"Yes, your grace," she said immediately, and did so.

*"She is obedient, at least,"* Li'sheneesha said. *"As one of her station should be."*

There were so many things Aefric wanted to address right then, but he decided to start with this one.

"You understand the common tongue."

"And speak it," Li'sheneesha admitted with a frown. "But there was no profit in admitting so earlier."

"And it is a ... harsh language," Li'nasachal said. "It does not ... *it does not flow as the world flows.*"

"Nevertheless," Aefric said. "No more pretending not to understand it. And I'll have you both apologize to my knight. There may be a misunderstanding, and if so, we shall resolve it. But you've still been rude to her."

The look both eldrani gave Ser Vria didn't help their cause. They clearly looked down on her for not being pure-blood eldrani. Some places cared about that, others didn't. But Aefric wouldn't have it here in Deepwater.

*"As Kalifnia says,"* Li'nasachal said, *"so must we do. I regret my rudeness to you, Ser Vria."*

"As do I, Ser Vria," Li'sheneesha said. *"I shall further say that I have heard tell of your prowess with your blade."*

The compliment was unexpected, but it was a good sign.

"Now," Aefric said. "Clearly I am unfamiliar with the term, so what is a *Sinflissacta*? I know that *sin* refers to the present state of a person's soul, but that's all I recognize of the word."

*"Your command of the True Tongue does you credit, Kalifnia,"* Li'nasachal said.

"We are," Li'sheneesha said, in the common tongue, for a change, "how shall I say? Surveyors of the soul. Assessors. Judges. With the proper rituals, we can look into a person, and know their true nature as it exists in this place at this moment, and even follow that nature forward and backward in time, for a distance."

"Why have I never heard of this before?" Aefric asked.

"It is … a … forgive me," Li'nasachal said, "my command of the common tongue is … lacking. *It is an art long forgotten by all save those of our order. It is little called, and less practiced.*"

"*We were only on this side of the Risen Sea,*" Li'sheneesha said, "*because we had been called to Ahlisklasach to clarify the succession.*"

"And you were taken captive while returning to Sartis, to catch a ship back across the sea," Aefric said.

"*A destiny shifted,*" Li'nasachal said, "*in ways even we could not have foreseen.*"

"But I could send you back across the Risen Sea, if you wish," Aefric said. "We have ships going that direction, I'm sure."

"*Destiny has shifted,*" Li'sheneesha said, as though that should have explained everything, but when it clearly didn't, she continued. "*There are events, Kalifnia, that shift one's destiny. Once such has happened, fighting those events brings only pain.*"

"*We believe,*" Li'nasachal said, "*that you have experience with such an event, Kalifnia.*"

They weren't kidding. It was just such an unexpected shift in destiny that brought him to Qorunn in the first place.

"*We are here now,*" Li'sheneesha said. "*We must follow this strand of the shifting fates. Should the time come to do so, we shall return home.*"

"*Until then,*" Li'nasachal said. "*We are here, and we wish to be of service to you, Kalifnia.*"

"As … *Sinflissacta?*" Aefric asked.

"We are what we are," Li'sheneesha said in the common tongue. "As you must be who you are, until you shift destiny, or are shifted by it."

Aefric needed a moment to shake off the chain of thoughts *that* one started.

"Why do some call you soul thieves?" he asked.

"*Fear,*" Li'nasachal said. "*Ignorance.*"

*"You must understand, Kalifnia,"* Li'sheneesha said. *"When we are called to read a soul, much hangs in the balance. When the reading is poor, some feel that we have stolen their destiny. Given it to another."*

*"Over time,"* Li'nasachal said, *"accusations of stealing destiny became accusations of stealing souls. But neither is true. We cannot touch the soul any more than you might reach up your hand and touch the sun."*

"How could you be of service to me?" Aefric asked. "What could I expect to learn from such a reading?"

"If we understand what role a person is to have in your service, *Kalifnia,*" Li'sheneesha said, in the common tongue, "we can tell you with certainty whether or not that person is right for the position. If they will prosper or fail."

*"The words are imprecise,"* Li'nasachal said. *"It is not only a person's skill that determines their successes and failures, but whether or not they act in accordance with the callings of their soul. These things cannot be hidden from us."*

*"We can hear their soul's song,"* Li'sheneesha said. *"And we listen. The soul sings only truth, and cannot hide behind perceived duty, honor or fleeting needs and desires."*

*"The soul knows,"* Li'nasachal said. *"Always."*

Aefric sighed and shook his head. "That may be, but even your own people have lost faith in your arts, or they would not be forgotten."

*"As Kalifnia says,"* Li'nasachal admitted.

"If I tried to rely on your arts when it came to promotions, or granting offices and the like, it would be seen as though *you* were making the decisions, not me. I couldn't take that risk."

*"As Kalifnia says,"* Li'sheneesha said, *"so we have heard tell before. Sometimes from our own people."*

"Are you certain you wouldn't rather return to your order?"

*"Destiny has tilted,"* Li'nasachal said. *"And it tilts us your way, Kalifnia. Until such time as we rebalance the scales, we must here remain."*

"All right," Aefric said, then stood. "You can stay here at Water's End for now. But we'll have to figure out what to do with you before the end of summer."

*"As Kalifnia says, so shall it be,"* they said together.

He dismissed them then, and as they left, Ser Vria said, "I know you like to help everyone you can, your grace, but mark my words. Those two are trouble."

Aefric had the sour feeling she might be right.

———

THE SUN WAS STILL AN HOUR OR TWO OFF FROM SETTING, WHEN THE *Duke's Hand* pulled out of dock at Water's End, and made its way north toward the Searun River.

As it did, Aefric sat in his carved chair on the afterdeck, with Ser Beornric sitting near him, on a canvas folding chair.

Both were finishing up their dinner. Trenchers of roast beef and steamed broccoli, covered in melted cheese. To drink with it, a good red wine, that seemed to bring out more character in the beef.

The day's heat was finally diminishing, and the winds were pleasant — if too weak to help yet, though the captain swore that would change soon. Plus, there was something soothing about the sounds of the ship and the sailors going about their tasks.

Aefric found himself relaxing.

Which, naturally, was when Ser Beornric spoke up.

"I still think we should have brought a larger entourage."

"Beyond the knights of my personal guard?" Aefric asked. "If I showed up with all the soldiers of my guard as well, I'd look like an invading force."

"But you came without any advisers but me," Ser Beornric said. "Not even any lers. Looks rushed."

"Perhaps," Aefric said, "but this is one time when thinking like an adventurer is likely to help me. I show up like any other duke, I'll put Wyln on his guard. But if I show up like myself, with an urgent matter to discuss, *that* he'll know how to deal with."

"And the rest of his court might underestimate you?" Ser Beornric asked.

"It's a possibility," Aefric admitted. "And one that suits us well."

"Don't count on it," Ser Beornric said. "They've been dealing with Duke Wylyn since the time of King Colm's father. No doubt they have a handle on dealing with you adventuring types."

"Yes, well," Aefric said. "Duke Wylyn and I ... weren't exactly the same kind of adventurer."

"There's more than one kind?" Ser Beornric said in mock innocence.

Aefric chuckled. He knew that Duke Wylyn Stormsent had once been a member of the Thieves Guild of Sartis. But there was no reason to bring that up here and now. For all he knew, the man hadn't stolen so much as a coin since he was made duke. So Aefric raised another point instead.

"You weren't present at my installation ceremony."

Ser Beornric shook his head.

"Duke Wylyn didn't show up with courtiers. He showed up with bodyguards *dressed* as courtiers. If I show up with only knights at my side, he'll know how to deal with that. If I show up with a ler or two, complicates matters."

"Could throw him off," Ser Beornric said. "That would be to our advantage."

"Maybe," Aefric said. "Too many variables right now."

"Then let's talk about the person you're *definitely* offending today."

"Which one?" Aefric said with a sigh.

"Countess Briluufa. She's your neighbor and hers is the nearest port in Silverlake. But you're skipping past Redport and sailing for Alimar's Launch."

"It's a shorter, straighter road to Castle Stormsent from there," Aefric said. "Alimar's Launch is the obvious choice. Even if I weren't trying to stay away from Redport right now."

"Nevertheless," Ser Beornric said. "She'll be offended."

"Well, let her," Aefric said, shaking his head. "I can't please everyone."

"Just warning you," Ser Beornric said. "After all, threat assessment is a large part of my job."

"And is she a threat?"

"At the moment, not much of one," Ser Beornric admitted. "But that could change."

"Well," Aefric said, "depending on what we learn at Silverlake, perhaps we'll return through Redport, and give the excuse that I felt I should visit the duke before visiting his vassal."

Ser Beornric frowned. "*Might* work."

"Well," Aefric said. "If not, she can join the line of people who want to kill me, and pray that I'm still alive when her turn comes up."

"I do wish you wouldn't joke about such things."

"Sorry. But I spent years as an adventurer facing death regularly. Got well used to joking about it."

"But you're a duke now," Ser Beornric said, arching an eyebrow. "And you have no heir."

"Hey. At least I'm not flying up there on my own."

"Fair enough," Ser Beornric said, then gave Aefric an assessing look as he sipped his wine. "It's just the two of us right now, your grace."

"Yes," Aefric said suspiciously. Clearly Ser Beornric wanted to talk about something he considered sensitive. Or tricky...

"If ... if you have any thoughts about marriage and heirs, this might be a good time to discuss them. I have no agenda, save wanting to see your grace well married, with heirs, and preferably happy."

"You sound as though you have thoughts. Care to voice them?"

Ser Beornric frowned and sat forward. Lowered his voice a little, though Aefric doubted anyone was near enough to hear him speak.

"I think that, when it comes to marriage and children, you've been looking at the battlefield, but not the war."

"I'm not sure I follow you," Aefric said.

"In battle, you exchange blows with the enemies nearest you. It is ... easy to get caught up in that. To see the world around you reduced to either allies to aid, or enemies to slay, and lose track of the goals and objectives that put you on the battlefield in the first place."

Aefric nodded. He'd experienced the sensation, especially during some of the longer battles during the Godswalk Wars. Hours could pass where all he could do was struggle to keep himself and his allies alive. With no mental space to give to thoughts about where he was, what the larger goals of the conflict were, and so on.

"You think that, romantically, I'm caught up in battle haze?"

"I do," Ser Beornric said. "Right now, I suspect that when you consider thoughts of marriage and the future, you think first of Princess Maev and Mistress Byrhta, and hardly at all about anyone else. Two princesses visited your court, and while they were there, you considered them as well — whether you wish to admit it or not — but now that they're gone, I imagine they're gone from your considerations."

"Maev and Byrhta are wonderful women," Aefric said. "Princess Astrid and Princess Xenia, they're vipers."

"Princess Maev cares for you," Ser Beornric said. "There's no denying that. Byrhta as well. Any fool could see that when she looks at you."

Ser Beornric shook his head.

"But Princess Maev is off in Varondam, negotiating an alliance and a marriage. And make no mistake, she'll marry their king, if that's what it takes to seal that alliance. And Byrhta, for all she may be beautiful and intelligent, she's still the daughter of your own vassal, with hardly any dowry to speak of."

"Duchess Arinda flouted convention when she considered marriage."

Ser Beornric looked Aefric sharply in the eye.

"Duchess Arinda died without a husband to mourn her, or children to carry on her name. And for all she flouted convention, she sought an advantageous match. Don't you doubt it."

"You think I should consider the other two princesses?" Aefric asked in disbelief. "I'd have to insist on separate chambers just to make sure I wake up each morning."

"Many noble couples sleep in separate rooms," Ser Beornric said, "and only come together to conceive children or seek the bliss moment."

"So you *do* think I should consider those two."

"I think you shouldn't be so quick to dismiss them," Ser Beornric said, then drew a deep breath. "But I think you should look beyond them, too. You're a duke, and a powerful duke. You would make a good match for many princesses, and having your seneschal seek royal permission to invite a few to visit might be a good idea."

Aefric scoffed. "You think that's the real reason King Colm is coming. To push me on the marriage front. Maybe suggest a few princesses."

"I think he might," Ser Beornric said. "But there's another you should consider as well, and I don't think she's seriously occurred to you."

"Who?" Aefric asked.

"Zoleen Fyrenn."

"I thought you all considered her part of a plot by her sister to get Deepwater back into Fyrenn hands."

"Yrsa thinks that," Ser Beornric said. "But I think she served with Duchess Arinda for a long time, and Duchess Arinda never got along with Duchess Ashling."

"Next you'll be suggesting I marry Ashling herself."

Ser Beornric gave Aefric a look.

Aefric's jaw dropped. "She prefers women."

"Baron Osmaer prefers men," Ser Beornric said. "But when he took up the barony decades back, out of duty to his position he married one of the daughters of Baroness Herewyn's grandfather. By reputation, they got along well, though each, of course, had lovers. And their marriage produced four heirs."

"I didn't know that," Aefric said. "Why didn't he bring his heirs when he came to meet me in the spring?"

"Because he has outlived them," Ser Beornric said with a sigh. "And the wife, as well, who took her own life, in grief. He swore not to put himself through that again, and no one would blame him. Though it means that, when he passes, you will have to find a new baron for Havenford."

"So you *do* think I should consider Ashling."

"You like beauty and brains. She has both. And together you would be quite a force to reckon with."

"I'm not sure how the marriage would work," Aefric said. "It's not as though we could live together full time."

"You could," Ser Beornric said. "Spending half the year in one of your duchies, and half the year in the other. But you could as easily live separately and only come together to produce heirs."

Aefric thought about that for a moment.

"Wouldn't work," Aefric said, shaking his head. "Ashling and I would both want to be in charge. We'd be forever butting heads."

"Which, I suspect," Ser Beornric said with a smile, "is why she sent her sister to you."

"This is too much," Aefric said.

"I thought it might be," Ser Beornric admitted. "But all I hoped to accomplish was to start you thinking about marriage and your options in ... broader terms than you had been."

Aefric snorted. "Mission accomplished."

Ser Beornric chuckled.

Aefric cocked his head at Ser Beornric.

"Dajen mentioned that the servants would all choose Byrhta to be my wife, if they could choose. Who would you choose?"

"My choice doesn't really matter, your grace."

"Nevertheless, I would like to know."

"I would see you married into a royal family. I know you would prefer Princess Maev, but Rethneryl has three princesses who might make good matches for you. And Hatay and Shachan, on the other side of the Endless Mountains. They likely have princesses to consider as well. And then, of course, there are Malimfar and Caiperas..."

"Surely some of them would want to marry princes," Aefric said, exasperated.

"Yes, but Armyr is a rich kingdom, and it has only one prince. Killian. And with Princess Maev off in Varondam, likely to be married, they have to look beyond her too. So if any of the nearby kings and queens wish to marry their families into Armyr and an alliance, their daughters will have to look beyond our prince. And guess who that leaves."

Ser Beornric pointed at Aefric.

"There's also Duke Wylyn," Aefric said, hopefully.

"Duke Wylyn is long married, your grace. He has three children, two daughters and a son. And before you ask, his son is already married to the daughter of one of Rethneryl's more prominent counts."

"Of course," Aefric said.

"And lest his daughters concern you," Ser Beornric said, "his eldest is married already, and living off in Hatay. And I believe his youngest daughter was widowed during the wars. But I believe she's betrothed again, though I don't recall to whom."

"That's something, at least."

"But in terms of eligible Armyrian bachelors, I'm afraid that after Prince Killian, you're next in line."

Lovely. Just the sort of thoughts that would keep Aefric awake late into the night, as he tried to sleep in his cabin belowdecks.

* * *

AEFRIC EMERGED FROM HIS CABIN JUST AFTER DAWN THE NEXT MORNING, dressed in riding leathers and a quilted tunic of Deepwater gray. And as he did, the *Duke's Hand* sailed into port at Alimar's Launch.

A boulder out in the harbor was large enough to hold a small lighthouse, though that lighthouse was no longer standing. The top half of it was gone entirely, leaving a jagged stone reminder of what had once been.

Clearly the sea devils had rained havoc on Alimar's Launch, during the wars. And this had never been a big port town to begin with. In fact, from that viewpoint, Aefric was impressed that it had survived at all.

The docks were small, old, and worn. In places they badly needed repairs. There were only five piers, and from the size of the docks, there might never have been more.

The town beyond had clearly been burned out and rebuilt. The construction was almost all new wood over stone foundations, and recently painted. Mostly single-story buildings, with a handful of two-story exceptions.

Very little glass in the windows. Almost all merely shutters. In fact, the only building that looked to have glass in the windows was also the only building that stretched the three whole stories tall, somewhere about the middle of town.

A half-dozen ships spread among the three center piers, so the *Duke's Hand* joined the right-most one. Likely the captain didn't trust the vacant piers, and Aefric couldn't blame him.

"Hello, *Duke's Hand*," someone called up, as deckhands were tying off the ship.

"The harbormaster, your grace," Captain Sikel said. "Henks. May I handle this for you?"

"Please do, captain."

Sikel was a good man. He looked rough and weathered, and big enough to raise the anchor by hand, but he'd been sailing since at least Aefric's street rat days in Sartis. Possibly even before Ser Beornric was serving page duty at his cousin's castle.

While his captain handled the arrangements and his knights organized the horses, Aefric retrieved his own luggage from below, which, to his chagrin, got him frowns from the deckhands.

Apparently even here he wasn't expected to carry things for himself.

Nevertheless, he added his own luggage to Windsong's saddle-bags, strapped the Brightstaff to its sling, and was ready when Captain Sikel gave the all-clear to disembark.

"Henks says he'll have to send a rika to Duke Wylyn, saying your grace has come through," Captain Sikel said. "But he wouldn't make any fuss about searching your ship, or any nonsense like that."

"That's fine," Aefric said. "I'm not trying to hide that we're coming. Thank you, captain. Shouldn't be more than a few days, at the most."

"Well," Captain Sikel said, frowning at the town, "if you don't mind my saying, your grace, they look like they could use our custom in the meantime."

Aefric chuckled. "So long as your crew is fit to sail when I need them."

"Of course, your grace," Captain Sikel said with a smile. "But then, no one survives long as a sailor if he can't do his job hungover."

Ser Temat raised the Deepwater banner, and Aefric and his knights began their ride.

While it was true that Aefric wanted to avoid Redport while his investigation into the slavers and smugglers was underway, it was also true that this was the fastest route to Castle Stormsent.

By arriving just after the dawn, with a small group of good riders and horses, he could afford to take fewer breaks and reach Duke Wylyn's castle before sundown.

It helped, of course, that the days of summer were long.

The winds were brisk off the Risen Sea that day, keeping the worst of the day's heat at bay, and showing signs that a summer storm might be coming. A thought that made Aefric chuckle about Ler Osgood and his peppers.

The lands he rode through, though, on the road to Stormsent, were no laughing matter. Aefric had seen scarring from the Godswalk Wars before, but not like this. What he'd seen down in Deepwater and the royal lands, that had been ... normal.

The sort of devastation from fire and warfare that might follow any major conflict, albeit on a larger scale than most.

But what he saw around him that day...

There were places were everything was fine. The land looked green and hale, if a bit browned from the summer heat. Farms, and small towns, largely intact.

Other places, the kind of problems Aefric had expected. Former towns torn down, or burnt out, with no signs of rebuilding.

But none of that was what made Aefric's blood run cold on the long day's ride to Stormsent.

It was the sinkholes.

Here and there, Aefric saw sinkholes large enough to swallow a farm.

Three times, Aefric saw sinkholes large enough to swallow a town.

And once, near a river, Aefric saw what he'd first taken for a valley. But it was not a valley. It was a sinkhole, miles wide, and even more miles long.

And around every sinkhole, the land was dead. Sometimes for only a few feet. Sometimes for as much as a mile or more. Nothing but dry, flaky dirt that looked unstable, and certainly no good for crops.

This was the damage wrought by the dybbungstad and their demon twins. Those sinkholes were where their troops came through to the surface, from their homes in tunnels far below.

Which meant that ... that new valley, that had to have been the main force of their army.

It was a wonder Silverlake survived at all.

Could even priests of the Green Lord help land so ... devastated? Aefric didn't know. But once those three disciples of Baron Osmaer's finished their work in Deepwater, Aefric might offer to send them up here to help.

If clerics of Halstaffur couldn't restore this land, nothing could.

As the afternoon wore on, and Aefric rode closer and closer to Castle Stormsent, he noticed he saw fewer and fewer of those awful sinkholes.

Interesting. It suggested to him that the dybbungstad might have come to the surface in unpopulated areas.

That was his hope anyway. Though he couldn't shake the suspicion that every sinkhole represented an unprotected farm or settlement destroyed by the dybbungstad.

Especially given the number of sinkholes visible from the road.

Such thoughts made Aefric edgy and unsettled, but he felt as though turning his thoughts away would have been turning his back on the suffering those sinkholes had caused.

This Dragonscar business. It seemed so small, beside the problems he was seeing. And yet, Aefric's lands had been invaded. Spells cast. His own people wounded and killed.

He could not afford to ignore that.

If Duke Wylyn was behind it all, he would have to pay a price.

Aefric wasn't sure what that price would be. But as he thought about the devastation he'd seen that day, he hoped it wouldn't mean another war.

In heat of late afternoon, with the smell of fresh wheat in the air from nearby farms, Aefric and his knights were met among the hills about a half-hour outside of Stormsent.

Which, according to road signs, was the name of the city around the castle, as well as the castle itself. Aefric found that naming convention a touch … narcissistic.

But then, in his adventuring days, Wylyn had never been known for excessive modesty.

The party that met Aefric was twenty strong, all knights, riding with lances in hand. They rode under Duke Wylyn's banner, crossed black swords on a crimson background. But they carried another banner as well. A broad red X on a white background, which Ser Arras identified as that of Leofstan Ol'Laerallan, Baron of Mountain Home.

Dusky-hued Baron Leofstan was a stout man, who favored golds and greens. He wore no visible armor, but the rapier at his side looked well-used, and the scars on his chin and the back of his right hand suggested he'd done his share of fighting.

And he was carrying a token of magic. A bracer, on his left arm. Something protective.

Introductions were made quickly, and Baron Leofstan began the conversation.

"Your grace arrives with such speed," he said, his voice a smooth tenor, as he bowed in his saddle. "We'd only just received your grace's own rika, when a second arrived from Alimar's Launch to tell us of your coming. Is all well?"

"There is a matter of some urgency I wish to discuss with Duke Wylyn," Aefric said. "It requires my presence, as well as my speed."

"And what matter does this concern?"

"Meaning no offense to your lordship, the matter is for Duke Wylyn's ears alone."

Baron Leofstan frowned. Gnawed at his lip a moment.

"Does that present a problem for you, baron?" Aefric asked.

"Well, your grace," Baron Leofstan said. "It is only that this is ... rather extraordinary. For your grace to come with so little advance notice. To arrive with a party of knights, insisting on speaking only with the duke himself..."

"I am speaking to your lordship right now," Aefric said. "And I travel with a party of knights *as befits my station*."

He made a show of looking around himself at the seven total knights of his entourage. Looked back at the baron.

"Hardly an invading force, I should think."

"Does your grace swear that he comes in peace?"

Aefric had to check his first answer to that. It had been a long day of riding through the heat, and he was already on edge from thinking about all those sinkholes and the lost and ruined lives and livelihood they represented.

So he controlled himself through a long breath before he spoke.

"I swear two things. First, that I have come only to exchange words on a topic that I suspect concerns your liege as much as it concerns me. Second, I swear that I am losing my patience with this ill treatment. I have done nothing to merit it."

"Well, your grace—"

"My day has been long, and this delay grows tiresome. Is it your intention to put those lances to use?"

"Well—"

"I am done being challenged. Either escort me to your master, stand aside and let me ride my own way, or lower those lances and let's have at it."

All around Aefric, his knights readied weapons while he himself pulled the Brightstaff from its sling, and ignited the yellow diamond at its tip.

Baron Leofstan looked ... irritated? Apparently Aefric wasn't reacting the way the good baron anticipated. What was Aefric expected to do? Lay down his weapons?

"I came here with peaceful intentions," Aefric said. "But I will not yield to such as you."

One of the baron's knights said something low and urgent.

"There is no need for violence," Baron Leofstan said at last. "I have come to escort your grace to Castle Stormsent, and see that he is made welcome."

"Lead on then," Aefric said.

Baron Leofstan had the gall to affect a puzzled expression. "Surely your grace will ride beside me."

"Under the circumstances I shall not," Aefric said. "Nor shall I permit your knights to surround us."

"Your grace accuses me of subterfuge? Of dishonorable conduct?"

"I accuse your lordship of nothing. Neither, however, has your lordship given me any reason to trust him. You and yours may lead, and we will follow. Or you may stand aside, and we will make our own way. There is no third option."

Baron Leofstan arched an eyebrow. "I could take offense at your grace's words and implications."

"Then challenge me and have done with it," Aefric said. "For I have already borne enough insults from you for one day."

Fury blazed in Baron Leofstan's eyes. For a moment, Aefric thought the man might actually challenge him.

That knight beside the baron spoke again.

Baron Leofstan huffed out a breath. Gave a sharp bow with his head.

"Your grace will have it as he wills then," he said. "We shall lead."

He turned his horse around, while the rest of his knights did likewise. As they began riding, Aefric was certain he'd heard the baron say, "Adventurers!" as though it were a swear word.

"That was probably excessive, your grace," Ser Beornric said softly, as they started riding.

"Do you think I was wrong?"

Ser Beornric thought about that for a moment.

"No," he said finally. "Overall, you were quite restrained. The baron was more than a little rude, and everything you said and did was certainly within your rights. But you can bet he'll have his say to Wylyn before you get to."

Aefric scoffed. "Duke Wylyn knows what kind of man the baron is. He might have sent him out here, hoping I'd do him a favor."

Ser Beornric snorted. "By killing him?"

Aefric nodded.

"You don't really think that," Ser Beornric said, but doubt was all through his voice.

"Let's just say I think it was one of the outcomes Duke Wylyn considered, and it likely wasn't an outcome that would upset him overmuch."

Ser Beornric laughed aloud then, which got some of the Silverlake knights to look back, puzzled.

Well, let them look. And let *them* take offense too. Aefric was getting tired of problems he wasn't allowed to face down directly. A challenge or two while he was in Silverlake might just be a good thing.

---

Not long after Aefric and his party met their "escorts" into Stormsent, he spotted the first watch tower. Made of stonework and standing three stories tall, it perched on the last tall hill before the approach to the city proper.

"Odd that it's not farther out," Aefric commented. "From there they'll lose sightlines along the hills."

"Those sightlines won't hide an invading force," Ser Beornric said. "Scouts, sure and small parties. But you can bet that the soldiers here know every blind spot left by that tower, and their own scouts watch them like hawks."

"Let me guess," Aefric said. "They plan to draw enemies into those blind spots, where they likely have ambushes set up?"

"It's what I'd do," Ser Beornric said. "It that was *my* watchtower. Find a way to turn those hills into a killing zone."

Once through the hills, Aefric got his first look at the city and castle Stormsent, as well as Lake Silver.

Lake Silver was just south of the road, and in the late afternoon sun, Aefric though it looked more blue with hints of yellow, than silver.

It also looked more like a pond than a lake. But then, Aefric had spent the last two seasons living beside the largest lake in Armyr, and one of the five biggest lakes in all of Qorunn.

Beside Lake Deepwater, most lakes would look like ponds or puddles. This one, at least, was a pond.

Both Castle Stormsent and the city around it looked squat and wide. Smokier, too. As though the homes and inns and taverns and such burned coal and coke, instead of proper wood.

Either that, or Stormsent had more than its share of smithies, and those smithies were involved in a big project...

Speaking of projects, Aefric saw the first signs of construction just past the last of the hills. Outside the boundaries of the closest farms, a long, wide trench was being dug.

"Walls," Ser Beornric said. "It seems the duke wants a wall to protect his farmers."

"With all the rebuilding they need?" Aefric shook off that line of thought. Duke Wylyn knew his needs and his resources. His decisions weren't Aefric's to question.

Goodness knew that Aefric had enough on his plate already.

Once past the farms, Baron Leofstan and his knights led Aefric's party through the first of the already-standing walls. Stone, and twenty feet high by five feet deep, patrolled by soldiers in chainmail, carrying bows, not crossbows.

The soldiers on the wall paid little attention as Aefric's group rode through the open gates.

Inside those gates, the city of Stormsent, and Aefric's first thought was that it was dirtier here than he was used to. But then, the streets were narrow, and wound a bit as they passed between buildings full of curious eyes.

Not just from the windows either — glass here, not just shutters as he'd seen in Alimar's Launch — but many of the roofs were flat, and occupied by curious onlookers.

Some waved, or called down greetings, but most simply watched.

The baron's route did not take Aefric through any town squares or marketplaces, or near to any impressive temples or other sights. In fact, if Aefric was not mistaken, he was being taken along a military route, and some of those corner buildings billeted soldiers, whose eyes were more watchful.

Aefric could hear the sounds of a busy city. The hammering of smiths, woodworkers and other tradesmen. The hawking of peddlers. The shouts and cries and laughter and anger as people went about their days.

He could hear these things. And he could smell the dirt and sweat, and cooking and baking food, and the coke of smithies and more burning coal besides.

But he couldn't see any of those people, except for the watchers along his route.

"You realize, of course," Ser Beornric said, "we're getting the least interesting route he could possibly take us."

"The thought had occurred to me," Aefric said. "Do you suppose he considers this my punishment for ... whatever?"

"Seems likely."

"Well, I hope it's the shortest route then, so he can be rid of us."

If it was the shortest route, though, Aefric would have hated to see the longest. The sun had still been well above the horizon when he'd met Baron Leofstan out among the hills, but it seemed to be making better progress towards the Risen Sea than he was towards the castle.

Another odd thing Aefric noted about this route. All the buildings along it were two stories tall. No single story houses or busi-nesses — though he could see some in the distance, now and then, whenever they crossed a street — and nothing taller than two stories. Though Aefric was fairly certain he could spot taller buildings off in one direction or the other, as he crossed other streets.

And the sameness of the buildings around him didn't stop there. They were all painted the same dull, mud brown. They had windows and doors in the same places...

"This whole route," Aefric said. "I bet there are three or four others like it. All designed to confuse invaders."

"And here I thought I'd nodded off in the saddle," Ser Beornric said. "Glad to know it's not *my* mind that's so dull."

"Oh, I bet there are points of strategic interest along this route," Aefric said, "but good luck finding them if you don't know where to look."

"Tell me you're not thinking of doing this to Water's End."

"No," Aefric said firmly. "I don't care for it myself, but I believe I can appreciate the strategy behind it."

Finally, they turned a corner and Castle Stormsent sat in the road before them.

Aefric's jaw dropped. He'd had no idea they'd gotten so close. The narrow street, the tightly packed buildings. It had all served as camouflage for the castle.

At least he wasn't alone in his surprise. He also heard gasps from some of his knights.

"All right," Ser Beornric said after a moment, nodding. "I'll grant them that one."

The castle was of gray and brown stone, with four rounded towers at the corners, and sat behind a wall of matching stone, some fifty feet high.

And the wall sat behind a moat, some thirty feet wide, and filled with ... something that was *probably* fish. Certainly Aefric could see movement. But as the moat didn't connect to any rivers that he could see, much less the lake, he couldn't imagine fish would thrive in it.

"Baron Leofstan returns," one of the baron's knights called to the guards on the wall. "And he brings with him Ser Aefric Brightstaff, Duke of Deepwater. Lower the drawbridge."

The drawbridge chain was well-oiled, at least. It wasn't *soundless* as the drawbridge came down, but the creaking was certainly quieter than the sounds of the city around them.

Not many buildings inside the wall here. Just stables, and two smiths. A weaponsmith and armorsmith, if Aefric wasn't mistaken. Other than that, the courtyard was set with quintains, for jousting practice.

"Think he's planning a tournament?" Aefric asked Ser Beornric.

"Could be. Could also be that all those knights were carrying lances because we caught them at practice."

"I doubt we're that lucky," Aefric said.

"Unfortunately, so do I," Ser Beornric replied.

The baron led them to the stables then, and as he dismounted and gave his reins to a groom, he turned to Aefric and said, "I trust your grace will allow his steeds into the care of our grooms?"

"Is there a reason I shouldn't?" Aefric asked, dismounting.

"Of course not," Baron Leofstan said, his tone on the knife's edge of mocking. "But clearly your grace does not trust easily, and I do not know that he has time for our avener and his grooms to prove themselves to your grace's satisfaction."

Aefric turned a level look on Baron Leofstan, who met it eagerly.

"Is it the policy of Duke Wylyn to see to it that his guests are insulted at every opportunity?"

"Is it the policy of your grace to insult those who come to offer him hospitality?"

At least one of Aefric's knights hissed in a breath at that one.

"What hospitality?" Aefric asked. "I was offered only challenges and demands. I have seen nothing like hospitality since I left Alimar's Launch, where it seems that a common harbormaster understands his place and his duties better than your lordship."

Baron Leofstan's hand went to the hilt of his rapier.

Aefric allowed the Brightstaff's diamond to glow a warning.

"Your grace offers insults freely," Baron Leofstan said in what he doubtless thought was a dangerous tone. "Perhaps he would rather offer a challenge instead?"

Aefric let loose a scathing laugh.

"Challenge? An insolent nothing like you? Enough of your braying, sirrah. Send word of my arrival to your master before I simply put you in your place."

Baron Leofstan glared at Aefric. Fingers clenching and unclenching, as though desperate to pull that rapier.

That one knight, again, leaned in and whispered something to Baron Leofstan.

Baron Leofstan continued his glare.

Aefric addressed the baron's knights now.

"Unless one of you wants to explain to your duke why he has a new statue shaped like the Baron of Mountain Home, I strongly suggest you get hold of this fool."

Two of the knights grabbed Baron Leofstan by the arms and started hauling him towards the castle. Seventeen of the others covered their exit, but looked frustrated and upset about the whole encounter.

Meanwhile, that one knight stepped forward and bowed to Aefric.

"Your grace," he said. "May I escort you and your knights to the presence of his grace, the Duke of Silverlake?"

"Nothing would please me more," Aefric said, allowing the Brightstaff to dim again.

Finally, it seemed, he was getting somewhere.

* * *

AEFRIC DID HIS BEST TO GET A READ ON THE CASTLE AS HE WAS escorted in, but he didn't get to see much.

They were barely in past the portcullises and murder holes when he was led down a stone side passage, past a handful of doors and an open stairway downward, and into a decent library.

Most of his knights were required to wait in the hall, but Aefric was assured that the door was not thick, and if they were given cause, they could break it down quickly enough.

Aefric had an urge to laugh at the reassurance, but the poor knight was probably just trying to cover for the ... excesses of the baron.

Ser Beornric was allowed to join Aefric in the library, as an adviser, and even allowed to keep his sword.

The library was the first room Aefric has seen with plastered walls — painted a golden brown, and carpets of woven rushes. Fresh carpets, from the sweet smell.

The windows were little more than air slits that expanded into rectangles, and didn't do a lot for letting in light. Fortunately, there was a chandelier, with two dozen thick, beeswax pillar candles giving the room a comfortable glow.

A desk sat along the center of one wall, with a carved wooden chair behind it. Both looked like black oak. A hearth along the opposite wall was cold at the moment, for the room was comfortable enough without fire.

Three comfortable-looking couches, upholstered in a deep maroon, were grouped around it.

As for books, the library had six bookcases that came up to Aefric's waist. Their shelves filled with what looked to be histories and treatises on military theory.

A cabinet in the corner held bottles of wine and liquors of darker colors, and a small variety of glasses.

And Aefric knew all of this, because he and Ser Beornric were in that room for some time. Waiting.

Ser Beornric finally took his seat on a couch, but Aefric continued pacing as he waited. Tapping the butt of the Brightstaff on the carpeting with every step.

At long last, the door opened, and a page announced, "His grace, Wylyn Stormsent, Duke of Silverlake."

"Finally," Aefric muttered, but smiled as he turned towards the door, to see Dyke Wylyn coming in at last.

Duke Wylyn was a short man, with his chestnut brown hair kept battlefield short, and his brown beard split on both cheeks by scars.

But though he'd dyed the gray away from his hair and beard, the lines on his face and neck told of his advanced age. Still. the duke looked fit enough to take the field again today, if he had cause.

Duke Wylyn still wore a brace of wicked-looking magic daggers at his belt. Likely the same pair he'd worn in his adventuring days, much as Aefric still carried the Brightstaff.

He half-looked as though he should have been wearing armor, rather than a deep red silk shirt over black leather breeches and hard leather boots. Like Baron Leofstan, Duke Wylyn wore a protective charm. A bracer on his left arm, worn under the shirt.

Similar enchantment, though there was a difference between them that Aefric would need more time to place.

But Duke Wylyn *wasn't* wearing his coronet. And he was smiling as his page introduced Aefric.

"Your grace," Aefric said, offering his hand to shake, as was proper among nobles of equal rank.

"No, please," Duke Wylyn said, holding up his hands as though warding off a blow. "You and I, we weren't swaddled in silk with rafts of servants ready to wipe out asses, like most of the lot out there." He jerked his thumb to indicate his court. "We're self-made, you and I. So let us be Aefric and Wylyn unless time and bad decisions make us enemies, eh?"

Aefric laughed. "Sounds right to me, Wylyn."

"Excellent," Wylyn said, shaking Aefric's hand then, before dismissing the page and turning to see about the knight on his couch. "Ser Beornric Ol'Sandallas, isn't it? You used to fight for his majesty."

"That's right, your grace," Ser Beornric said. "But when his grace here was created Duke of Deepwater, I and two dozen soldiers were presented to him as an honor guard."

"And quite an honor it is," Wylyn said, turning to Aefric. "You know, this man personally saved the life of Prince Killian during the wars? I saw it with my own two eyes."

"I didn't," Aefric said, turning raised eyebrows on his knight.

"Twas smaller in the doing than the telling makes it seem," Ser Beornric said, humbly. "But I shall tell the story sometime, if your grace wishes."

"Believe it," Aefric said, while Wylyn crossed the room to the liquor cabinet.

"I should feed you first, I'm sure," Wylyn said, pouring measures of dark amber liquid into three glasses. "But I was raised to believe you greeted your guests with a toast, not a cheese."

He handed glasses to Aefric and Ser Beornric.

"To the peace and prosperity of both our duchies," Wylyn said, and all three drank.

It was strong, that liquor. And harsh enough to sting Aefric's mouth and burn a bit on the way down. But for all that, it had a rich, full taste, with hints of almond that made him raise an eyebrow at his host.

"I know, right?" Wylyn said, chuckling. "Back in my adventuring days, I carried three different poisons that had almond in their taste. When I discovered that this ishka was brewed in Mountain Home, I made it a policy to keep a barrel or three in my storerooms at all times. Just as a tribute to my old days."

"Mountain Home, you say," Aefric said with a smile.

"Yes," Wylyn said, chuckling again. "I must say, you've practically driven their baron to apoplexy."

Aefric looked sharply at Wylyn, and saw something more than humor hiding in those smoke gray eyes.

"Oh, you *gutter rat*," Aefric said, earning him an incredulous expression from Ser Beornric. "You sent that bastard to me as a *test*?"

"Well," Wylyn said, slowly. "I don't know that I'd go *that* far. But I *was* curious to see how you'd handle him."

"His lordship seemed to be angling for a duel," Ser Beornric said.

"I've no doubt," Wylyn said, shaking his head. "For all his bluster, he's not one to be taken lightly. The man is a master with his rapier and loves to prove it in duels."

"Good way to guarantee a short life," Aefric said.

"He's not a fool," Wylyn said. "He would have goaded you into challenging him, if he could, so he'd get to choose weapons. But make no mistake, he'd only want to duel to first blood."

Wylyn shook his head again. "Likely wanted to be able to tell people he'd gotten the better of Deepwater's famous duke."

"He almost became a hat rack."

Wylyn burst out laughing. "Oh, it might've been worth finding another baron for Mountain Home just to see that."

"I take it he's a troublemaker?"

Wylyn considered that through a breath. "A bit bellicose, but otherwise biddable enough. Though he did give me an earful about you. Did you really call him 'sirrah?'"

"He more than earned it."

"Lovely," Wylyn said, grimacing. "Then he'll likely continue complaining about you until Midwinter."

"Feh," Aefric said. "I suspect he cheats in his duels anyway."

"Why would you say so?" Wylyn asked, refilling their glasses.

"He wears a protective charm."

"He *doesn't*," Wylyn said, shocked.

"He does. A bracer. Same place you wear yours." Aefric patted his left arm. "Checked it out a bit while we were riding. Looks like it turns blades aside."

"Mine turns arrows aside," Wylyn said, still looking amazed. "To think, all this time he's been..." He raised one hand beside his mouth and called out, "Page!"

The door was opened and the page from before poked his head in. "Your grace?"

"Fetch Sifwyn for me."

"At once, your grace," the page said, and closed the door as he left.

"While we await her," Wylyn said, raising his glass. "Here's to *honest* duels, and the work of men like the three of us, who've seen more than our share of battle."

Aefric felt a little more hesitant to drink to that one, but he wanted to keep the camaraderie going, so he did.

"You might think of making yourself a charm like this one," Wylyn said, slapping his sleeve, where his bracer lay under his shirt.

"I suspect that his grace can turn arrows aside easily enough," Ser Beornric said.

"Ah," Wylyn said with a smile. "But it's the arrow you *don't* see coming that'll get you. In fact…"

And Wylyn told a story then from his old adventuring days, when they'd been delving into the tomb of a long-dead priest-king, whose undead guardians were said to have been leaving the tomb to drink the blood of the local peasants.

Well, Wylyn and his crew handled the tomb guardians, and staved off the raising of that priest-king. And they'd made their way back to town, to celebrate, and spread around a little of the wealth they'd found inside that tomb.

It was sometime later into the night, when the celebrations had moved in the courtyard behind the inn, with drinks and dancing and music—

And suddenly Dointas, his crew's wizard, clutched his throat and fell to the ground.

The local town watch had been chasing a thief through the streets nearby. Let loose a volley of quarrels from their crossbows.

One of those quarrels flew well wide, over the wall, and into the throat of Dointas.

"…and so," Wylyn was saying. "I commissioned this little baby with my share of the loot. And I've never regretted it."

The page knocked on the door, and announced, "Your grace's ducal wizard, Sifwyn."

Sifwyn hadn't even entered the room yet when Wylyn started talking to her.

"Sifwyn, why did you never tell me that Leofstan wore a protective bracer?"

Sifwyn was even shorter than Wylyn, but she still managed to sweep into the room, which was impressive.

Still. The woman was so short, Aefric would have thought her to have eldrani blood, save that she clearly didn't. Her face was too round for that, and her hair a very human shade of black, rather than the vibrant colors of the eldrani.

She wore robes of bright red, sewn through with crystals of different colors and shapes. She wore her hair wound tightly down to her head, and carried a greenwood staff no taller than she was.

The staff and four of the crystals were enchanted, as was an opal ring she wore, and a bracer on her left arm.

Aefric missed whatever she said in answer to Wylyn's question. Because as he regarded this woman, his thoughts all narrowed down to one.

Aefric was looking at the magic-user who'd cast those spells in the Dragonscar.

———

AEFRIC STOOD THERE IN WYLYN'S LIBRARY, STARING AT THE WOMAN who'd cast those spells in the Dragonscar. The woman who'd created those stone men.

The woman directly responsible for the needless deaths and injuries of several of his soldiers. And perhaps others besides.

There could be no doubt about this. No question. No worry over mistaken identity.

Back in the Dragonscar, Aefric had performed a ritual that brought together and sifted through the remains of the spells that had created those stone men. Analyzed their magic more thoroughly than the nose of a hound can pick apart a scent.

Every magic-user in Qorunn could be gathered together in one place, with all of them casting spells at the same time, and he would still spot the creator of those stone men in an instant.

And he was looking at her.

Right here. Right now.

Righteous anger tightened his muscles. Clenched his jaw. Sped his heart. Heated his skin. For a moment, all he could hear was the rushing of his own blood.

A dozen spells flitted through his mind...

But then a voice cut through the haze.

"Aefric?"

Wylyn's voice, and from the tone, it wasn't the first time Wylyn had spoken to him.

Sifwyn, the wizard in question, was staring back at Aefric. She looked puzzled. She moved her greenwood staff so it was between them, as though to ward off an attack.

Ser Beornric, just to Aefric's left, frowned in worry, and had one hand raised as though he might have to grab his duke.

Wylyn, just to Aefric's right, looked even more puzzled than Sifwyn. He had one hand raised, indicating that Sifwyn should stay back.

Of course, some of that caution might have been because the Brightstaff's diamond was shining bright enough to dim the midday sun.

Damn it. Aefric was angry enough to be leaking magic, and more than a little. He had to watch that. He might want to kill this woman, but this was not the time, nor the place.

And he needed a cover story for his reaction.

Aefric flared his nostrils in a deep breath, and dimmed the diamond, but thought quickly and kept up his glare.

Wylyn snapped his fingers in front of Aefric's face, and said his name again.

Aefric made a show of blinking, and turning his head to Wylyn, though he kept shifting his eyes back and forth between Wylyn and Sifwyn.

"You two know each other, I take it?" Wylyn asked cautiously.

"I have never seen his grace of Deepwater before this moment," Sifwyn said carefully. "Though I know him by reputation, of course."

"Are you sure you've never seen me before?" Aefric asked, his voice low and letting out at least some of his anger. "Are you *very* sure of that?"

"I am, your grace," she said.

"What's going on, Aefric?" Wylyn asked, but now he was glancing curiously at his own court wizard as well.

"So you are telling me," Aefric asked Sifwyn, "that you were *not* in Thunderwood six years ago?"

"I have never been to Thunderwood," Sifwyn said firmly. "I swear it."

"Six years ago when?" Wylyn asked.

Aefric frowned at Wylyn. "About Midspring. Why?"

"Couldn't have been her," Wylyn said, relaxing. "Six years ago Sifwyn was heavily involved in my Midspring Festival. Some of the finest illusion work I've ever seen."

"Illusion," Aefric said, as though pondering whether or not illusion magic fit the wizard he was making up.

Sifwyn gave Aefric a considering look, and offered a small bow.

"If my duke will give his permission," she said, "I can offer proof that I am not the wizard his grace of Deepwater mistakes me for."

"How?" Wylyn asked.

"I presume his grace of Deepwater would recognize the magic of the wizard he ... encountered in Thunderwood?"

"I'd know it anywhere," Aefric said.

"Then with my duke's permission," she said, giving Wylyn a slight bow, "I shall cast a small, inoffensive spell, and remove all doubt that I am not that wizard."

"Granted," Wylyn said. "But when you're done, I think it's best if you leave."

"Of course, your grace," Sifwyn said with another bow.

Sifwyn raised her greenwood staff, and passed it through the air, trailing in its wake a rainbow of colors that turned into a rainbow of fluttering swallows, then faded to nothingness.

That was what everyone in the room saw. But Aefric's trained eye saw more.

He saw the way she performed all the steps of casting a little nothing spell that she'd probably cast hundreds, maybe thousands of times over the years. Likely a spell she'd worked out back during her apprenticeship.

Her breathing was right. The trace way her lips moved, as though they wanted to speak words she no longer had to say when casting that spell. She likely even moved power through her body in the process.

But Aefric knew for a fact that she didn't cast that spell.

The feel of it was all wrong. Wasn't hers.

Maybe she triggered it from ... something in her staff. He couldn't be sure of that part. But he knew it wasn't hers, just as surely as he knew the stone men *were*.

But he forced a pretense of relaxation. Puffed out a breath. Made his shoulders sag a little. Shook his head, as though shaking away his anger.

Made his voice sound tired as he said, "It's not her." He shook his head harder. "Excuse me, Sifwyn. Please. You look ... the resemblance is uncanny. But I'd know that woman's magic again anywhere, and clearly you can't be her."

Sifwyn drew a relaxing breath of her own, and offered a small bow.

"Your grace has no need to offer apology. He has traveled far and wide, and met a great many people. Some will naturally resemble others, and for him to be mistaken in recognition is no crime."

She offered a small smile then, that could have been intended as flirtation.

"Nevertheless," she said with that smile, "I am grateful to have cleared up the misunderstanding. And even more so that I need not match spells with your grace. From all I have heard, such a conflict would not go well for me."

"Best if you get going, Sifwyn," Wylyn said. "I can tell you from my own experience that being around someone who reminds you of an old foe is not fun. Give Aefric here time to cool down, and maybe you two can discuss your art sometime."

"I'm sure we could," Aefric said, affecting a weak smile.

"Nothing would please me more," she said, and began to take her leave.

"Oh, and Sifwyn," Wylyn said just before she was out the door. When she turned back and bowed, he continued, "You see another one of my nobles or knights running around with magic, you tell me. Understood?"

"Understood, your grace," she said, and bowed her way out the door.

"She's a good court wizard," Wylyn said once she was gone, "but she overlooks the damnedest things. And here I was considering naming that jackass Leofstan my champion."

Wylyn shook his head and grimaced.

"Can you imagine?" he asked. "What if I had? And a real challenge came along? There'd be the formal check for magic, Leofstan would lose his trinket, and he'd probably get trounced. What an embarrassment that would be."

"I'm surprised you'd be willing to let anyone stand champion for you," Aefric said with a smile.

"Ah, I'm not as fast as I used to be," Wylyn said. "Besides, in our position, we're not supposed to fight for ourselves outside of a battlefield. Not in anything serious." He cocked an eyebrow. "You haven't named a champion yet, have you?"

"I've told him to more than once," Ser Beornric said.

"I'm not used to letting people do my fighting for me."

"Me either," Wylyn said, grinning. "But it's part of the job."

He poured them each another glass of ishka, and nodded towards the couch.

"I can almost *hear* my seneschal begging me to let you go rest and freshen up before dinner," he said, smiling, and sliding an arm around Aefric's shoulders as they made their way to the couches. "But I've just *got* to hear what happened to you down in Thunderwood six years ago that had you ready to come to spells here in my war library."

One good thing about the days Aefric had spent adventuring. He'd done a good deal of traveling and fighting, seen more than his share of wonders and horrors and other things. And he'd had to tell about them so many times that he knew all the details he needed to add, to make the story work.

And he drew on that experience as he invented the tale of the Necromancer of Thunderwood.

Aefric was given a very nice suite of rooms overlooking Castle Stormsent's central courtyard. He had four rooms to himself, and two more for Ser Beornric, with his knights quartered just down the stairs below them.

His bags had been brought up, and nothing in them disturbed, which was reassuring. Not that Aefric didn't trust Wylyn on this front, but he didn't trust that Baron Leofstan at all.

Aefric took time to wash up at a copper basin, rather than let the servants draw him a bath in the large copper tub. And after he had washed away his day's travel, he changed into a navy blue silk shirt, embroidered with silver thread to represent Deepwater gray, and a pair of sturdy black breeches.

He wore the same calf-high leather boots, though, because he couldn't bring himself to pack changes of footwear.

With the wand Garram on his belt and the Brightstaff in hand, he felt almost ready to go down to dinner.

Almost.

Ser Beornric had set aside his armor for this dinner, and changed into a forest green tunic with brown hose, though he wore his sword at his belt. And he'd combed out his graying black hair and bushy mustache.

"Ready to head down, your grace?" Ser Beornric asked.

"Not quite," Aefric said, and dismissed the servants.

Before the good knight could say anything, Aefric silenced him with a gesture, and cast a quick spell that sent a pulse of power through the room to settle into the walls, ceiling and floor, as well as filling the room's windows, doorways, and chimney.

"Now we may speak undisturbed," Aefric said.

"That tale was heartbreaking, your grace," Ser Beornric said. "That the necromancer made a zombie of your dead lover, not five minutes after killing her." He shook his head. "It's a wonder you didn't hunt her down to the ends of Qorunn."

"Yes," Aefric said with a sigh, "well, first, as I said, she didn't just flee the battle. She fled from our world to another plane entirely. There was no way I could have followed her. That's still a power I don't possess."

Aefric quirked a smile then. "Second, following the necromancer would have been impossible. Because she doesn't exist."

Ser Beornric shook himself, but before he could ask, Aefric answered.

"The lover in question," he said with a wistful smile. "Lyssandra. She died fighting necromancy, all right. Mighty skeletal warriors we faced together in the ruins beneath lost Sereth-Ke."

"But—"

"I lied to cover my reaction," Aefric said. "Sifwyn. She's the culprit. She cast those spells in the Dragonscar."

Ser Beornric narrowed his eyes, looking grim and dangerous. "You're certain?"

"Beyond the possibility of doubt."

"But..." Beornric furrowed his brows. "Then why would she cast a spell in front of you? If that alarm spell was hers, she must at least *suspect* you were involved in triggering it. Surely she knows you'd recognize her spellwork if you saw it again."

"Which was why she didn't cast that spell," Aefric said. "It was a splendid bit of deception. But those colorful swallows came from her staff, not her."

Beornric frowned. "She didn't think you'd be able to tell the difference between a spell of her casting and a spell conjured from her staff?"

"That's not quite how it works," Aefric said, trying to decide how to explain something that was a lot more intricate than he needed to make it sound.

"Think of it this way," he said. "While I am the master of the Brightstaff, and the wand Garram, magic I work with them still carries a sense of *me* to it. The spells and their results, they're not quite the same as they would be in anyone else's hands. And the difference is perceptible to those who can see it."

"But if that's true," Ser Beornric said, "how could she fake a spell?"

"She shouldn't be able to," Aefric said. "That's the point. She knows that, and she knows that *I* know that. So if she thinks I suspect her of the spells in the Dragonscar, her little display should have thrown me off her trail."

"But..." Ser Beornric shook his head. "Forgive me, your grace, but I don't follow. I still don't see how she faked that spell then. Or at least, how you could be sure she faked it."

"I can be sure because I made the opportunity for a deeper study of the magic in the Dragonscar than she could know. Deep enough that I can connect her magic to her as easily as I can connect your hand to you. I only needed one look at her to know she cast those spells."

"But... you said..."

"I know," Aefric said, and sighed. "And I'm not sure how she did it. Something in the staff, I think, but I'd need to examine the staff to know for sure. It's as though she had a completed spell prepared by someone else, that waited for her to trigger it."

Aefric shook his head. "And no doubt that's a spell everyone around here has seen her do a hundred times."

"Regardless," Ser Beornric said. "You're certain it's her, so I'm certain as well. What is our next step?"

"I'm not sure," Aefric said. "If she cast the spells, Wylyn must be involved. But if he is, he's a better liar than I've met in a long, long time. Because I can't tell."

"Nor I," Ser Beornric said.

"Well," Aefric said with a sigh. "All we can do is go down to dinner. And afterwards, I can talk with Wylyn about slavers. And maybe, somewhere in there, he'll trip up and let something slip."

"You don't sound as though you think it's likely."

"I don't," Aefric admitted. "But maybe it doesn't matter. I know for a fact that Sifwyn is involved in acts against my duchy and my people. I can bring that much to his majesty, and ... figure out the rest from there."

"I suspect you'll end up on more formal terms with Duke Wylyn, after that happens."

"If that's the worst that comes of it," Aefric said, "I'll happily pay that price."

———

DINNER THAT NIGHT WAS A MUCH MORE ENJOYABLE EXPERIENCE THAN Aefric had expected. Largely because, apart from Wylyn's own family, Aefric and Beornric were the only guests at the table.

Because that was true, Wylyn had announced there was to be no standing on formality at the dinner table that night. That all titles, graces and business were to be left at the door.

Led to easy conversation and laughter.

Duke Wylyn's wife, Onetai, was a handsome woman about his own age, and an excellent hostess.

The duke's son — Wylyn Junior, though they all called him Wylie — had his father's wiry build, but his mother's gentle features. Which no doubt stood well with his wife, Nikia. Both were about Ser Beornric's age, and had children of their own who were off being fostered down in Merrek and nearing the age of majority.

The duke's youngest daughter, Okelai, had seen about five summers more than Aefric, and apparently had her father's gift for climbing and getting into places she shouldn't.

It was unusual for Aefric to be surrounded by nobles who were all older than he was, and he found it rather refreshing.

The dinner itself was roasted venison, served quite rare, with sliced, braised potatoes and carrots, and a mixture of tossed greens. The red wine that was served with it went very well with the venison as well as the dessert, which was a thick, heavy berry compote, served with cream to lighten it.

Afterwards, Wylyn and Aefric retired to Wylyn's war library, where the duke lit up a pipe, whose smoke smelled of deep woods and moss.

They reclined on those plush, maroon couches, and sipped ishka, while gazing into a small fire that Wylyn had built more for entertainment than for heat.

"I've been thinking about that necromancer of yours," Wylyn said at last. "Did you really think I'd hire a necromancer as my court wizard?"

"I didn't think," Aefric said, shrugging one shoulder. "I saw the face, the height, the hair..." He shook his head. "I was hearing the death cry of Lyssandra all over again. I'm only glad I didn't go so far as to cast a spell."

"Yes," Wylyn said, "and don't think I don't appreciate your restraint." He chuckled. "I expect Sifwyn appreciates it as well."

Aefric gave Wylyn a chagrined look. "I do apologize for my reaction. Not exactly the act of a good guest."

"Bah," Wylyn said, waving dismissal. "Not as though you attacked her. And if I'd thought she'd killed my Onetai, let alone raised her as a zombie in front of me, well, I'd've been hard pressed not to put a dagger through her eye the instant I saw her."

Aefric raised his glass as though confirming a toast, and they drank to both vengeance and restraint.

Wylyn nodded at the Brightstaff, which stood just behind where Aefric sat on the couch.

"Bit of a tell for you, isn't it?" Wylyn said. "That diamond, I mean." He gave a breathless chuckle. "Dead giveaway that you were fighting not to strike her dead."

"It's got its good and bad sides," Aefric admitted. "Sometimes it's useful for people to know how close I am to doing something ... extreme." He shook his head. "But yes, there are times it's a hindrance."

"Unusual, too," Wylyn said, looking at the Brightstaff. "I mean, I've known a lot of wizards over the years, with their staves and wands and rods. But I've never seen..."

Wylyn turned his eyes back to Aefric. Quirked a half-smile.

"It's true then," he said, a little wonder in his voice. "You really *aren't* a wizard. Properly speaking. But you're not a warlock either."

"No," Aefric said. "I've trained as a wizard, but I frustrated my teachers. Same as I frustrated the dweomerblades I trained with, because I'm not quite one of them either. I'm something ... in between."

"You and me both," Wylyn said, then puffed his pipe and blew out a wide smoke ring. "Some people say I was a thief. Others an assassin. But I was never really either. I just made use of those skills, to further the things I wanted to do."

Aefric gave Wylyn a sly smile. "So you're saying you *didn't* steal the Coldriss Diamond?"

Wylyn laughed. "Oh, I stole that all right. A fair few other things as well. But only when there was something more on the line than my next bed and meal. I stole things, but I wasn't a *thief*, if you take my meaning."

"I think so," Aefric said. "You weren't a robber, or a second-story man or the like. You didn't steal from guilds or merchants or nobles, for the most part. Is that it?"

Wylyn nodded as he puffed. Blew an impressive smoke ring.

"I stole big things," he said, "from big places. Usually ones that were hurting people."

"And gave you a big name?"

"That too," Wylyn said with a smile. "Nothing wrong with reputation. Doing big things is what got me all this."

Aefric nodded. He couldn't deny it. He'd done the same, in his own way.

"But you didn't come here to talk about our adventuring days," Wylyn said. "And you didn't come here to duel my fool of a baron." He cocked an eyebrow at Aefric. "So why *did* you come here in such a rush?"

"Slavers," Aefric said, and told the story of how he'd fought smugglers and slavers in the mouth of the Dragonscar. Though he made it sound as though he'd been riding nearby when the smugglers were spotted. And claimed that after the battle, he and his had gone south to make sure the captives were dealt with, and the refugees taken care of.

At all cost, he avoided implying that he'd gone riding deeper into the Dragonscar.

Wylyn was a good audience. He darkened with anger at the mention of slavers, and grumbled appreciatively through the tale of the fights, the taking of the ships, and the freeing of the refugees.

"Few things in this world are fouler than slavers," Wylyn said. "How can I help?"

"This is the delicate part," Aefric said with a pained expression. "That smuggler ship. The *Swift Wave*. It had been docked in Redport that day, waiting to come down for the pickup."

"Redport?" Wylyn demanded, sitting forward and flinging his pipe into the fire. "*My* Redport?"

"It's been confirmed," Aefric said. "Through independent interviews with the captive smugglers and slavers, my court wizard, Karbin, was able to recreate the routes of both the slavers and the smugglers."

"And those routes go through Redport?"

"They have three common ports within an aett's sail of Deepwater," Aefric said. "The first is in Kefthal. The second is Wulfport. The third, alas, is Redport."

"What else have you turned up?" Wylyn said. "About Redport?"

"Nothing so far," Aefric said. "I allowed my court wizard to visit Redport to confirm that those ships had docked there, and when, but that was all. I refused to allow him any further investigation in Redport until I spoke with you."

"Good of you," Wylyn said. "I appreciate that." He cocked his head. "That's why you came here through Alimar's Launch, isn't it?"

"One reason, yes," Aefric said. "But it is a more direct ride."

Wylyn tilted his hand in a more-or-less gesture and said, "It looks that way on a map, but it's about the same in practice. The road from Redport is smoother and straighter."

"I ... wasn't sure about the reception I'd receive here," Aefric said. "So I also wanted to avoid Redport so there could be no question of *my* doing anything there."

"You thought you might be meeting a man who supports *slavers*?" Wylyn said, his voice the calm of a storm about to break.

"Not at all," Aefric said firmly. "I know your reputation of old, and I know you harbor no more love for slavers than I do." Aefric quirked a smile at him. "But I'd been warned that my installation ... might not sit well with you."

Wylyn laughed. The man seemed to shift from ready to fight to perfectly at ease with impressive speed and comfort.

"It's true that Colm promised he'd send his list of ducal candidates to Ashling and me for our opinions, and then never got around to it," Wylyn said, shaking his head. "But after I met you that day at Armityr, I knew we'd been cut from the same cloth. Survivors, yes, but only if the world stays a place worth surviving *in*."

"Just so," Aefric said, and raised his ishka in a toast.

They drank.

"So," Wylyn said, as they set their empty glasses down on the table. "Kefthal, Wulfport and Redport. Sickens me to have one of *my* ports in a list that includes both Kefthal and Malimfar."

"I hate to deliver the news of it," Aefric said. "But I knew I had to come to you myself with it."

"And I appreciate that," Wylyn said, reaching over and clapping Aefric on the shoulder. He poured them each another small glass of ishka. "Well. Kefthal and Wulfport. Shouldn't do anything about *them* without bringing in Colm."

"He's coming to visit me," Aefric said. "I was told it might be a check to see how I'm doing."

"Probably is," Wylyn said. "But you can tell him about Wulfport and Kefthal when he's there."

"That was my plan."

"Redport, I'll handle myself," Wylyn said. "And if that bitch Brilu-ufa's wantonly harboring slavers, I'll have her drawn and quartered."

"I don't know that she's involved," Aefric said carefully.

"Don't know that she's not, either," Wylyn said. "And I intend to get to the bottom of this."

He stood. Started pacing.

"I'll have four of my best agents on the road by midnight," he said. "Get them to town and in place before I arrive with a bigger party."

He turned to Aefric. "I'll want to leave in the morning to see about this. I hate to cut your visit short—"

"I have both our monarchs coming for a visit," Aefric said, standing. "I need to get back before my seneschal bursts from worry."

Wylyn reached out to clasp forearms with Aefric.

"You're a good man to bring this to me directly," Wylyn said. "I won't forget it."

"I'm just glad to find that my neighbor to the north is still the man I heard tales about when I first started out adventuring."

They drank their last glasses of ishka, and when Wylyn threw his empty glass to shatter in the hearth, Aefric followed suit.

"Go get a good night's sleep then," Wylyn said. "We'll both want to leave with the dawn. Wish I could ask you to come hunting slavers with me."

"Another time," Aefric said. "After all, we may get permission to deal with Wulfport or Kefthal."

"If you deal with Kefthal *without* me," Wylyn said, "I'll never forgive you."

Aefric laughed. They clasped arms again, and retired to their rooms.

***

ALONE, BACK IN HIS ROOMS, AEFRIC STARED OUT THE WINDOW AT THE night. The winds were gentle now, though they smelled a bit of coal smoke. The moon was two-thirds full as it made its slow ascent to join the stars above.

And Aefric felt like a bad person.

Wylyn seemed to be such a good man. Such an upfront man. He certainly didn't seem to be the sort of person who could have sent spies into the Dragonscar, then had his wizard cast deadly spells to protect that discovery.

And yet, it was undoubtedly his wizard who had cast those spells.

What if he didn't know? What if this was part of some kind of plot behind Wylyn's back? Countess Briluufa, maybe, conspiring with Sifwyn?

If so, the right thing to do would have been to tell him.

But Aefric didn't tell him. What was more, he'd lied about Sifwyn. He'd lied to the man who had greeted him like a brother, and welcomed him at his dinner table not like a visiting duke, but like long lost family.

At the very least, Aefric could have told him about the gold discovered in the Dragonscar. Come clean and discussed the issue right there. Let the two of them settle things without involving the crown.

But he hadn't even done that.

Aefric shook himself. No. In the long run, he'd probably done the smart thing. Wylyn could easily be a better liar than Aefric could ever have guessed.

Plus, retired adventurer or not, the man had been a duke for decades. And his lands were suffering, even worse than Aefric's were.

It was entirely possible that Wylyn not only knew about the gold in the Dragonscar, but also had ordered his court wizard to cast those spells. To protect the discovery until Wylyn himself was in a position to do something about that gold.

The man liked to relax in his *war library*. Clearly he was used to thoughts of strategy and tactics. And wasn't that the question Aefric was facing?

Whose strategies? Whose tactics?

No. Wylyn smiled and said the right things, but that didn't make him innocent. And Aefric had to protect his own lands and people.

Telling Wylyn the truth now about what was going on in the Dragonscar, that was probably the worst thing Aefric could have done.

Yes, Aefric decided. Tonight he'd probably dodged the arrow he hadn't seen coming. Even if that arrow was metaphorical.

Aefric still felt as though he were the one betraying a trust. Guilt played sour in his belly.

What if...

Aefric's brooding was interrupted by a soft knock at the door.

Aefric sighed, and shook his head. Tried to look as though he were just a happy, contented guest. Only then did he call to the knocker.

"Yes?"

The door opened, and in came a young serving woman.

"Your grace," she said with a bow. "I've been given permission to offer your grace *leaba*, if he would do me the honor and the pleasure of accepting."

Her smile was pretty, and her eyes both bright and eager.

In that moment, Aefric understood an unspoken truth behind *leaba*, and even behind the noble privilege.

A pretty face and a willing heart go a long way to dispelling a fit of brooding, and the cares of office.

For a time, at least.

"The honor is mine," Aefric said with a smile, "but I hope the pleasure will be shared."

**8**

———

Baron Leofstan was blissfully absent when Aefric and his knights prepared to leave Castle Stormsent the next morning.

Wylyn had an impressively large party getting ready to leave at the same time.

"Camouflage," he said with a smile, while his and Aefric's horses were readied. "If I show up for a formal visit, and do all the formal things, everyone will be looking at me. No one will notice Okelai and my agents digging into other matters."

"You taught her your old skills?" Aefric said with smile.

"Elbar's Blood yes," Wylyn said. "Not leaving the next generation defenseless. I'm not one of you wizardly types after all. I can't live forever."

"No one lives forever," Aefric said. "Not even the eldrani."

And so with fresh supplies and freshly cleaned versions of the same clothes he'd worn during his travel the day before, Aefric and his knights left Castle Stormsent.

With a soldier along, as guide through the city.

Apparently there were six routes to Castle Stormsent from the outskirts of Stormsent City. One of them was wide and broad, and included all the market squares and public gathering places, along the whole way down to the lake.

But that route didn't connect to any of the roads that led *out* of Stormsent by land.

The other five routes to the castle were all designed after the fashion of the path Baron Leofstan had led Aefric yesterday. They were dull and confusing, and intended to slow invaders down while forcing them to come through designated killing zones before they could ever reach the castle.

And that those routes led away from the more populated areas meant that these routes protected the people and the wealth of Stormsent, as well as the nobility.

Once out of the city, the road back through the Silverlake countryside was much the way it had been on the way in. All too heavily hit by those sinkholes of the dybbungstad and their demon twins.

"They've lost most of their forests," Ser Beornric said, while they were riding past the first of the larger sinkholes.

"What do you mean?" Aefric asked, plucked from other thoughts. "They cut them too deep without planting more trees?"

"No, your grace." Ser Beornric pointed to a sinkhole large enough to have swallowed a town. "You were right about those being places the armies of the dybbungstad and their demon twins came through to the surface. Sometimes through farms and towns, but not always."

"Sometimes they came up under forests?"

"Yes," Ser Beornric said, grimly. "Sometimes mere groves and copses, but that one great sinkhole we saw? The one we'll be passing again close to midday today?" Ser Beornric shook his head. "That was once a mighty forest. Some of the oldest trees in Silverlake. And now it's gone."

"That's why all the coal smoke," Aefric said.

Ser Beornric nodded. "They're facing quite a timber shortage. And because the rest of us need so much timber for our own rebuilding, the prices are exorbitant."

Aefric let out a sigh, but Ser Beornric snapped his fingers three times quickly.

"I know that look, your grace," he said, shaking his head sharply. "This is not your problem to solve. Duke Wylyn will find a way. He'll deal with it."

"All right," Aefric said, but he still considered that question as they rode that day.

The day was warm for riding, but not overhot. And the winds didn't whip quite as sharply as they had the day before. Still Aefric found it comforting as the smell of the winds shifted from carrying grasses and crops to carrying the salt of sea air.

They snacked during their brief rest periods on venison jerky, and apples.

Well, the knights snacked on apples. Aefric was still not ready to eat another apple. So he made do with the jerked venison, and some leftover honeyed oat bread from breakfast.

They rode back into Alimar's Launch late that afternoon, to the surprise of the harbormaster, Henks, who blinked so fast at the sight of Aefric and his knights that Aefric half-expected the man's eyelashes to achieve liftoff.

The *Duke's Hand* was waiting and ready, and her captain, Sikel, had them sailing out of port on the evening tide.

Aefric and Ser Beornric took their dinner on the duke's afterdeck. A good strong beer, to go with a trencher filled with a mixture of roasted meats and gravy, along with a hearty cheese, and fresh nava fruit.

They'd eaten, and settled into a comfortable silence broken only by the snap of the sails, the creaking of the rigging, the hush of the sea and the calls of the sailors at their tasks.

At length, Ser Beornric spoke. "I mean it, your grace. You cannot solve everyone's problems. *We* need our wood. Duke Wylyn can find his own."

"I know that," Aefric said, watching for the first stars of the evening to see which would twinkle first.

"So you're telling me you *haven't* been mentally reviewing Kentigern's timber reports, and trying to figure out where you can spare a shipment of wood to sell to Duke Wylyn below the current going rate?"

Aefric started laughing hard enough he had to steady his beer on the arm of his chair.

"I knew it," Ser Beornric said, shaking his head.

"How did you know?" Aefric asked.

"Your grace," Ser Beornric said, "I have known you for a little over a season now. And in that time, I have found that no matter how many problems face you, you're willing to take on more if it means helping others."

Aefric sipped his beer without comment. A little more bitter than he liked, but a good brew nonetheless.

"I admire you for it. In general. But in this case, your grace, I implore you. Leave it alone." Ser Beornric leaned a little closer. "If Duke Wylyn wanted your help, he would have said so."

"Perhaps," Aefric said.

"For certain," Ser Beornric said firmly. "You two were getting along very well. That would have been the time for him to ask for help. Instead, it's quite obvious that he never mentioned their timber shortage."

"Why did you then?"

Ser Beornric shook his head. "Because I thought it would help if you knew that the giant valley of a sinkhole had been a forest, not a city."

"Each is a special kind of problem."

"And not yours to fix," Ser Beornric said. "You have slavers and smugglers. Dragonscar gold and dead soldiers. Missing lers and smallfolk. Marriage options. Incoming monarchs. And, of course, your recalcitrant count."

"That does seem to be more than enough for any one person to handle," Aefric had to admit.

"And those are just the things I can think of offhand."

"Explains why you forgot Kivash."

"You think that the castle Duchess Ashling gave you presents a problem?"

"An entire castle, and the land it sits on, and *everything within it*," Aefric said. "That doesn't sound like a problem to you?"

"Sounds like a gift box to me," Ser Beornric admitted. "Just waiting to be opened."

"Maybe," Aefric admitted. "Maybe. But just maybe I'll also find out that Ashling surveyed the contents of each castle herself before deciding to give that one to me. Which would lead me to ask why? What's inside that she wants *me* to deal with, rather than dealing with it herself?"

Ser Beornric nodded. "You're capable of being very suspicious. When you put your mind to it." He nodded again. "I approve."

Aefric chuckled.

"I'm not joking, your grace," Ser Beornric said. "Duchess Ashling and Duke Wylyn, they've shown you their good sides so far. But make no mistake. They both have bad sides. And you'll see those too someday. So best you be ready when it happens."

"A lovely thought for a lovely night," Aefric said.

"What did I tell you before?" Ser Beornric asked.

"I know, I know. Threat assessment is a big part of your job."

"It is indeed, your grace," Ser Beornric said.

Aefric stayed on deck, talking with Ser Beornric, for quite some time. But as the hour grew late, he retired to his cabin below. And when he emerged the next morning, they were sailing into port at Water's End.

---

JUST INSIDE THE BEAUTIFUL, SHIMMERING NAVY BLUE WALLS ON THE north side of the Castle at Water's End sat a practice ground large enough to serve as a small tourney field. Assuming grandstands were brought in.

It was large enough to have two practice jousts going at the same time, while still allowing room at both ends for training at melee, and at least one target shooting range. Or three such ranges, if no one needed practice with a lance that day.

Storage rooms along the wall held everything that training might require.

On a normal morning, soldiers, castle guards, and knights would rotate through on a schedule, keeping all of Aefric's warriors in fighting shape, should they be needed.

That morning, however, the normal drilling and training stopped as those knights, soldiers and guards watched their duke take the field.

Usually, Aefric trained with one or two knights in his own small practice yard, high up in the castle.

That morning, though, the practice yard was too far away. His own sword was too far away.

No. That morning, Aefric no sooner disembarked the *Duke's Hand* than led the way straight to the practice ground and took a longsword from a storage room.

He set the Brightstaff aside for a time, and reminded all watchers that he had, in fact, trained as a dweomerblade.

Aefric was quick with that blade. And as he'd been taught, he could fight with either hand, or both on the hilt, as any given move required.

Like most dweomerblades, his style was acrobatic. Mobile. And power flared, sparked, and glowed with every spin, leap, and strike, even though he held back the true magic of those moves.

After all, this was only training.

He trained with each of the knights of his personal guard that morning, save for Ser Beornric, whose role was to oversee and critique.

Aefric wasn't as good as any of those knights he sparred with that morning. Not without using magic. But he was unpredictable enough, and mobile enough, to at least make them work.

And he had the stamina, as well. He trained hard with all six knights, all through the rising heat of morning, while Ser Beornric's implacable voice called out "too slow there," "watch your grip," "too late, the opening closed," and other admonishments that Aefric needed to try harder than he already was.

But that was fine. The sword was not his primary weapon anyway. And he switched to the staff instead about midway through the morning — a training staff, not the Brightstaff, to help avoid accidents — and then started giving back as good as he got.

Properly speaking, no dweomerblade fought with a staff. There was a reason they were called dweomer*blades*, after all. Something about the metals and edges of their swords, daggers and polearms helped bring out and focus their magic.

But then, properly speaking, Aefric was no more a dweomerblade than he was a wizard. And for him, the staff glowed, sparked and flared with power just as the sword had.

Ser Beornric's critiques were fewer during Aefric's staff work, and consisted more of comments like, "faster is better there," "drive the blade further out of line with that block," and "tighten that spin more next time."

Aefric called the halt as the sun reached its zenith, and the audience — which had grown now to include more knights, more guards and soldiers, a good number of interested nobles, and such servants as could find excuses to remain nearby — broke into applause.

Aefric dripped with sweat and panted for breath, leaning a bit on that staff now. He smelled of dirt and effort, and the sun was now baking his skin as he turned to shake his head in disbelief at the size of the watching crowd.

Feeling the need to at least acknowledge them, he gave them a wave, and then joined Ser Beornric and his knights by the door to a supply room.

Aefric felt gratified that his knights were sweating as well, and at least a few of them looked as though they'd noticed the effort of the morning's training.

"Better?" Ser Beornric asked, looking Aefric up and down as he accepted the training staff.

Aefric reclaimed the Brightstaff, which had, of course, remained where he'd left it. His people knew better than to try to touch that weapon.

"Much better," he said with a grin.

"Good way to clear the head," Ser Beornric said with an appreciative nod.

"Good way to lose it too," a playful voice said, "if your grace were any slower with some of those parries."

Aefric turned to see Ser Deirdre in her deep maroon leathers. Her arms were folded across her chest, which left her hands conveniently close to the handles of her rapier and dueling dagger.

She had her head cocked at a teasing angle, and a smile on her face and in her green eyes.

Ser Beornric cleared his throat noisily.

"Please excuse my unsought opinion, your grace," Ser Deirdre said, still smiling with her eyes, and knelt to Aefric. In more formal tones she said, "I return from Ajenmoor having completed the task your grace entrusted to me. May I present Morgard Ol'Nara."

A man stepped forward who looked as though he was walking to his execution. His lightly tanned skin was pale, and the hint of sweat on his brow looked as though it had nothing to do with the heat.

He didn't tremble, but his eyes moved as though he were trying to spot either aid or a means of escape. But he was smart enough to keep his hands away from the hilt of his broadsword.

Of course, the scabbard looked little tested, so he might never have used his blade in earnest.

He dressed like a traveling merchant, in a tunic and breeches in deep shades of blue and green, both with multiple pockets. And he didn't wear a token dagger at his belt, as nearly all Armyrian nobles did.

But he had the same pale blonde hair as Leca, and the same fine-boned features. Aefric had little doubt that this was indeed Morgard Ol'Nara.

Morgard glanced down at Ser Deirdre, kneeling on the dirt of the practice ground, and looked as though he wasn't sure if he was supposed to kneel too.

He settled for bowing very deeply.

"Your grace," he said, in a nervous voice, while a servant brought

Aefric a water bowl and a towel to clean his hands and face. "I know not of what I stand accused—"

He was smart enough to stop talking when Aefric raised a dripping hand. Aefric looked at Ser Deirdre.

"What did you tell him?" he asked, while gesturing for her to stand.

"I told him he was summoned to court," she said as she stood. "When he ... proved reluctant, I overcame his reluctance and assured him that the matter was not open to debate or question."

"And just how many strong was his 'reluctance?'" Ser Beornric asked dryly.

Ser Deirdre frowned as though trying to recall something inconsequential.

"I believe there were four guards," she said casually, then turn to Morgard. "It was four, was it not?"

"It was six," Morgard said, paling further. "And you killed them."

"Yes, well," Ser Deirdre said, as though discussing the weather, "they drew on me first and they *did* have me outnumbered. Had I taken the time to merely disable them, you might've escaped. And then I would have had to track you down *all over again*."

She clucked her tongue at Morgard, then frowned in distaste.

"Six? Really? I would have sworn I hardly needed enough effort to dispatch four. If there truly were six, you must hire a better class of guard next time."

Several of Aefric's knights had to turn away to hide their smiles.

Aefric considered all this while he dried his face. As he did, all around his group, knights and soldiers and guards filled the training ground with the clash of activity.

Aefric's stomach rumbled a reminder that he hadn't eaten yet today. But that could wait while he satisfied his curiosity.

"Ser Deirdre," he said, "how, exactly, did you approach him?"

"Well, your grace," she answered, clearly enjoying the chance to tell the story. "It took me longer than I'd intended to track the man down in the first place. And when I finally did, it was closing in on midnight, in a warehouse near the docks."

She gave Morgard a look, as though inviting him to contradict her. But Morgard looked out over the training ground at six soldiers who were drilling with pikes.

"He was clearly there to see to the completion of a business deal," Ser Deirdre said. "So I gave them time to conclude, but that time seemed to stretch and stretch and *stretch,* your grace. As though they hadn't worked the details out in advance, as proper business usually requires, but intended to see to the final details *while* they were transferring cargo."

A deal closing at about midnight? With final details only just being worked out? Aefric found himself quite curious about that cargo. But decided that question could wait for later, while Ser Deirdre continued.

"Well," she said. "At length I decided I'd waited long enough. After all, this was no idle curiosity of my own that brought me there, but a mission from your grace. Which I must, in good conscience, execute with all available speed."

At the word "execute," Morgard paled further still. At this rate he'd faint before she finished talking.

"So I stepped out into the light, announced myself, and informed all present that his grace, Ser Aefric Brightstaff, Duke of Deepwater, had sent me to collect Morgard Ol'Nara and bring him to Water's End at once."

"Arrest," Morgard mumbled just loud enough to be heard over the clashing and crashing and shouts of training.

"Pardon?" Ser Deirdre asked.

"You said you'd been sent to *arrest* me," Morgard said in a stronger voice. "Not collect me."

"That's not quite right," Ser Deirdre said with a shake of her head. "I said I came to collect you. *You* asked if I'd come to *arrest* you. And what did I say to that?"

Morgard sighed and said, "'If needs be.' Which is tantamount to the same thing."

"Not in the least," she said, then turned back to Aefric. "At that point, his reluctance required a pointed rebuttal on my part. Once that argument was concluded, I began escorting him here to your grace's presence at best speed."

She bowed.

"Excellent work, Ser Deirdre," Aefric said, which made her smile. To Morgard he said, "I summoned you to court for a reason, and I'll speak to you about that reason later today."

Aefric gestured for a couple of guards to come over.

"This is Morgard Ol'Nara. Take him to my seneschal, then see to it he is given rooms, fed and the like."

"Am I under arrest?" Morgard asked.

Ser Beornric cleared his throat.

"...your grace?" Morgard finished, wincing, as though the oversight hadn't been intentional.

"At the moment," Aefric said, "you are my guest. Anything else will have to wait."

As the guards escorted Morgard away, Aefric shook his head, and hoped he wasn't arresting Morgard after all.

---

Aefric took his lunch on the balcony of the public floor of his apartments. The sun was *almost* directly overhead, but it was *just* off enough that one of the large, round, greenwood tables could be positioned in the shadows of the Great Spires.

Between the shade and the gentle breeze, the temperature was quite pleasant. Though Aefric itched from sweat, and had had to accept a frown from Ocheda that he hadn't gone to clean up and change properly after such exertions.

But food had to come first.

And with that food, a meeting that might prove to be important.

Lunch was a thick, savory beef stew, served with fresh corn and tara, and honeyed oat bread slathered in butter. To drink, a crisp, light, day beer that made Aefric think of the pale ales he'd known a world away.

They had those pale ales here as well, but they called them "day beers."

Joining Aefric for this lunch were Sers Beornric, Yrsa, Calder and Deirdre, along with Kentigern. Though Kentigern had already eaten, so he only nibbled on the bread, to go with his beer.

Aefric, ravenous, dove into his lunch and seconds, while Ser Deirdre addressed the question Aefric hadn't wanted to ask down on the practice grounds.

"What was in the cargo Morgard had been transferring that night?"

"Well, to be honest, your grace," Ser Deirdre said. "I didn't have a whole lot of time to check into it. The manifest said the crates were full of textiles. Mostly cotton and flax. And the few crates I'd gotten to see, well, that's what they'd contained."

She shook her head through a sip of beer. "Have to say, though. Didn't look like much. Not great quality. And certainly nothing anyone would need in such a hurry that they'd have to load a ship in the middle of the night, while still working out the details."

"What if it was a replacement cargo?" Kentigern asked, drawing knowing looks from around the table.

"That would make some sense," Ser Deirdre said. "If whatever they were expecting didn't show up, and they had to do something last minute."

"Where was the shipment going?" Ser Yrsa asked.

"Wulfport," Ser Deirdre said, then shook her head. "Don't read too much into that though, your grace. Nothing short of a war will stop the normal sorts of trade, and nothing's more normal than textiles."

"Wait," Aefric said. "Cheap cottons and flax, you said?"

"That's right, your grace," Ser Deirdre said, nodding, while the others looked curiously at Aefric.

"Undyed?" Aefric asked.

"I believe they're usually shipped undyed," Ser Deirdre said, suspiciously, "but these were as well."

"Did you get a name for delivery?"

"I didn't give the matter that much attention, your grace," Ser Deirdre said. "My focus was on Morgard. The rest was only part of understanding what I was walking into."

"What did it look like to you?" Ser Yrsa asked.

"Looked to me like something shady," Ser Deirdre said, shrugging one shoulder. "But anytime Brangford Couglas is involved, I assume shady anyway."

"Was Couglas there?" Ser Beornric asked.

"Was when I made my entrance. Wasn't by the time I'd overcome Morgard's reluctance."

"What do you think?" Ser Beornric asked Aefric.

"Can't be certain, of course," Aefric said. "But it occurs to me that the refugees we'd saved from those slavers had been clothed on the cheap."

"Hardly a strong connection," Ser Calder said. "Lots of people need cheap textiles. And that includes people in Wulfport."

"I'm not saying it's a reason to make arrests," Aefric said. "I'm saying it's a point of information to add to what we know."

"With respect, your grace, I disagree," Ser Calder said. "It's speculation. If we start adding speculations to hard knowledge, we don't refine our information. We dilute it."

"Too late now to track that ship," Ser Yrsa muttered.

"And with Master Morgard's ... extraction," Kentigern said, "safe to say they won't use the same ship next time. That is, if they *are* up to something shady."

"Oh, it was definitely shady," Ser Deirdre said. "The formation. The guards. The general stress level. They were involved in something clandestine and illegal, that much is certain. I'd been assuming they had contraband hidden in the textiles, but your grace thinks the goal might've been shipping the textiles themselves?"

"His grace *speculates* that," Ser Calder said. "Hidden contraband is certainly a lot more likely."

"We could put the question to Morgard," Ser Beornric said, watching Aefric as he said it.

"I intend to ask," Aefric said. "And I hate to say it, but I need to know for certain what kind of business he's been up to before I confirm his lands for him."

"That's right, he's a ler," Ser Deirdre muttered, then nodded. "Explains a few things."

"What does it explain?"

"Well," Ser Deirdre said, "I recall that your grace told me there might be a plot to steal his lands. Discrediting's as good a way to do that as murder."

"True," Ser Yrsa said. "And an easier way to look innocent in the process."

"The *way* he'd asked if he was arrested," Ser Deirdre said. "Almost as though he'd been told that someone from the duke might try to arrest him. And the guards. He didn't order them to attack. That was Couglas. Maybe as much to cover his own escape as to protect Morgard."

"Did Couglas recognize you?" Aefric asked.

"Can't imagine he wouldn't," Ser Deirdre said. "Especially the way I leapt up onto those crates in full view of everyone and announced myself. But *I* never actually laid eyes on *him*. Just recognized his voice when he yelled 'Get her!' before the guards attacked."

"What exactly did you say?" Aefric asked. "When you jumped up onto the crates."

"I was in the moment, your grace," Ser Deirdre said with a lopsided smile. "But I believe it was, 'Morgard Ol'Nara. By the authority of his grace, Ser Aefric Brightstaff, Duke of Deepwater and Hero of Frozen Ridge, I, Ser Deirdre Ol'Miri, Knight of Deepwater and Slayer of the Ogre of Threepeaks, am come to collect you and escort you to his grace's presence at Water's End.'"

"Pity you've no flair for the dramatic," Ser Calder grumbled.

"And that was when Couglas yelled, 'Get her?'" Kentigern asked.

"No," Ser Deirdre said. "First there was a moment of stunned silence as they took in the majesty of my presence. Then Morgard asked if I was arresting him. It was after I said, 'If needs be,' that Couglas yelled, 'Get her!' and the argument ensued."

"All right," Aefric said, sitting back and pondering through another savory spoonful of stew. "We know that Mayor Brangton was in touch with his son by rika while we were in Lachedran."

"Do you think he suspected Leca would mention her brother to you?" Ser Beornric asked.

Ser Yrsa scoffed. "Wouldn't put it past him to have suggested it, to make sure. While having his son set up Morgard, to ensure he looked guilty when you sent someone to collect him."

"Why would he assume I'd send someone to collect him?"

Sers Beornric and Yrsa glanced at each other.

"Your grace..." Ser Beornric started, but it was Ser Yrsa who finished.

"There's no doubting that Mayor Brangton knew his wife would share her problems with you while she was sharing ... other things. Given your reputation for good works, of course you'd want to confirm her brother in his lands at the first opportunity. Which would mean sending someone to Ajenmoor as soon as you got back to Water's End."

Ser Yrsa nodded at Ser Deirdre.

"So you're saying I'm too predictable for my own good?" Aefric asked.

"No," Ser Yrsa said. "I'm saying that we can count on people trying to turn your known tendencies to their own ends."

"Then the plan failed," Kentigern said. And when everyone turned their attention to him, he continued. "Yes, it looks bad. But we don't *know* of any crime, or even any contraband. Hardly enough to lose a ler his lands."

"They knew we'd have to question him," Ser Calder said. "Which may lead to finding out about crimes." He shook his head. "Could be they just needed us in a suspicious mood when we took him, so we'd think to ask about what he might be guilty of."

Ser Calder cocked his head at Aefric. "Assuming it matters?"

"Of course it matters," Aefric said. "Why wouldn't it?"

"You're the one who slept with his sister, your grace," Ser Calder said, which brought immediate objections from Sers Beornric and Yrsa, as well as Kentigern.

Ser Deirdre, meanwhile, looked quite interested in all of it.

Aefric knocked on the table until he had their attention.

"The noble privilege is the noble privilege," Aefric said, "and that's all it is. I'm not going to start bending the law for a woman, just because she came to me for the bliss moment."

"Well," Ser Deirdre said with a playful smile. "That might depend on the number and quality of bliss moments she gave your grace. Just how good *was* this Leca Ol'Nara?"

Aefric tried to give her a glare, but the knight's humor was glare-proof.

Worse, it was contagious, and Aefric had to turn away before he smiled despite himself.

"All right," Aefric said. "Ser Deirdre, go over all the details of Ajenmoor with Ser Calder and Kentigern. Everything you can think of. Then I want the three of you to interview Morgard. Find out just what kind of business he and Brangford Couglas have been doing. Ser Calder and Kentigern will handle the questioning, Ser Deirdre will support as needed."

"Yes, your grace," all three said with surprising synchronicity.

"I'll take your report over dinner tonight—"

"Your grace," Kentigern interrupted, because of course he did.

"Yes?"

"Your grace has not dined with his court since returning from the Dragonscar."

"Fine," Aefric said with a sigh. "Tonight I'll dine with my court. You three report to me just before dinner. But this afternoon is my own. *Any objections?*"

Wisely, no one objected.

---

After lunch, Aefric did not go clean up and change, much to the consternation of his daytime head valet, Ocheda.

But Aefric knew that his afternoon would involve as much effort as his morning had, albeit in a very different way. So he put off a proper cleaning and changing for later, and went into his workshop.

And there, he dedicated his afternoon to his magic.

Oh, if only he could have spent every afternoon this way!

He'd have to talk to Kentigern. Clearly the Soulfists had found time for their own researches and experiments, which meant that it *was* possible to add such things to a duke's schedule without the whole of the duchy falling apart.

True, experience was probably a factor. They had been running the duchy for generations, while he was still settling into the role.

Still, there had to be some kind of middle ground. Because if he didn't get more time with his magic, well, it would start to have dele-terious effects on his mood. And that wouldn't be good for the duchy either, now would it?

So Aefric made a mental note to discuss the topic with Kentigern, as he closed the heavy door behind him, and lit the pillar candles around his workshop with a gesture.

The whitewashed walls. The twin desks in opposing corners with related diagrams tacked to nearby walls. The circles on the floor. The cabinets and closet of ingredients, reagents, and apparatus.

It really was an excellent place to work.

Normally, Aefric would have begun with some dweomerblade exercises, to get his limbs moving and his magic flowing, but after the morning he'd had, that was hardly necessary.

So instead, he shifted gears, and threw himself into an almost entirely intellectual exercise.

He sat down with the first of the Soulfist grimoires, and began to work on translating it.

Every so often, Aefric had heard non-magic-users talk about grimoires, and what they had to say invariably amused him. They always seemed to think that a grimoire was half seedy diary and half recipe book. Further, that a grimoire was written in some kind of complex system of cyphers that had only to be cracked, to have its secrets spread out wide before any given reader.

Most of them seemed convinced that grimoires were magical

objects unto themselves, while a handful insisted that they were nothing more than memory keys to secrets too powerful for a mind to hold all at once.

The truth, of course, lay somewhere in the middle of all these things.

Grimoires included records of a magic-user's experiments and discoveries, as well as their deeds and aspirations.

They were entirely idiosyncratic, in structure, in approach, and even in language. Different languages expressed nuances of ideas differently. And so a sentence that began in the common tongue might touch upon a concept that expressed clearest in High Eldrani, but required a verb from Dreykeke.

And that was only an example from Aefric's own grimoire.

Understanding the magic contained in a grimoire meant understanding the mind of the magic-user.

This was where wizards, with their logic, had an edge over Aefric. Aefric's intuition might help him grasp a concept here or make a leap there, but it didn't lend itself as well to the systematic comprehension of a grimoire the way a wizard's command of the *logic* of magic did.

But Aefric would get there. And he felt as though he was getting close.

He held that first grimoire of the Soulfists in his hands. Calmed his mind. He reached with his thoughts into the grimoire.

That was one place that many of the lay people were close about grimoires. They weren't truly magical items the way a flying carpet would be, but they were the focus point of a magic-user who inscribed his or her magic within them.

In the process, grimoires gained ... not a sentience, per se, but a coherence, aligned with the thoughts and the magic of their author. And they did not willingly or easily give up their secrets to a stranger.

And so Aefric reached into the grimoire with his thoughts, and he carried with them the seal of his office, and his personal seal.

He was the rightful Duke of Deepwater. And this grimoire had once belonged to a rightful Duke of Deepwater. That connection would assert to the grimoire both that its author was dead, and that the grimoire was now rightfully the possession of Aefric Brightstaff, current Duke of Deepwater.

When Aefric felt a sort of ... harmonic chime in his head, he knew that the grimoire had acknowledged him and his right to read it.

The acknowledgment came fast this time. That was good. Perhaps before long he wouldn't need that step at all. By then the grimoire would *want* to yield its secrets, and assist Aefric in interpreting it.

But he was not at that stage yet.

And so, Aefric opened the grimoire to its first page, took out his notes from last time, and spent a good deal of time continuing his efforts at understanding what he was reading.

He continued working on that for some time. Filling four pages with notes and ideas about that first, single page.

He was getting closer. He was sure of it. Circling the ideas in that first page, with each pass bringing him nearer to understanding.

Soon. It would happen soon.

Once he had gone as far as was profitable in his work with the grimoire that day, Aefric moved to the circles, and practiced the methods of raising and channeling power. After that, he worked through a series of spells designed to test his efficiency with that power.

This was a trick he'd learned from Kainemorton. To develop a series of spells that did the same thing, each differently.

In this case, it was to bring a single pillar candle down from the wall, move it around the room in a pattern, change the color of the flame four times as the candle progressed about the room, and then return the candle to its holder.

One trip used more power to hold and move the candle. The second focused on the wick. The third on the flame itself, and the fourth on the air, and the pattern of the movements.

Each spell accomplishing the exact same thing. But each spell requiring different foci, and differing amounts of power.

As Kainemorton had taught Aefric, once he could cast all four spells with the exact same amount of effort and power, he would have mastered the techniques involved, and should develop a new test.

He had just run through those spells the third time, when there was a knock on his door.

He sighed. Stretched. Called the Brightstaff to his hand and went to the door and opened it.

"Your grace," Ocheda said with a bow as severe as everything else about her, "instructed me to knock when the time had come for him to bathe and dress for dinner. That time has come."

"Thank you, Ocheda," Aefric said, and closed the door on a good afternoon's workout.

---

In the world where Aefric had grown up as Keifer McShane, a "bathroom" was pretty any room with a toilet.

That was not the case here in Qorunn. Such a room was called a "privy" or "garderobe" or something similar.

A bathroom here was an entire room set aside for bathing. And like most of the rooms in Aefric's ducal apartments, his bathroom here at Water's End was larger than it needed to be, and had a window with an impressive view of Lake Deepwater.

Taking in the view, it seemed, was considered part of bathing, for a duke. Apparently, past dukes and duchesses of Deepwater had used bath time to ruminate or meditate on the problems they faced.

No one was ever surprised if Aefric wanted to simply sit and soak in the tub for a time. In fact, on those rare occasions when he did so, the servants even offered light snacks to nibble on, or wine or sharabi to drink.

But then, that was as much as he would allow his servants to do for him, when it came to his bath. Apparently he could have had servants scrub him, wash his hair, and dry him off, had he chosen. But that ... that just seemed wrong.

He allowed them to prepare his bath for him, bring him towels, robes and dressing gowns, even provide snacks or drinks, should the occasion call for it.

But when it came to the actual bathing, Aefric handled matters himself.

Bathing here still felt decadent.

The tub was pure luxury. White marble, veined with silver and gold, like the rest of his bathroom. Large enough that Aefric could have invited seven others to join him in that tub, without it feeling crowded.

Not that Aefric could imagine bathing with seven other people. A special someone such as Maev or Byrhta, certainly. But even the thought of the two of them joining him at once, he knew, was nothing more than a fantasy that would never actually happen.

And probably *shouldn't,* for that matter.

But *seven* others? That just sounded unwieldy.

For the moment, though, his priority was on soaking tired muscles in water magically heated to his perfect temperature, and scrubbing his way to a cleaner, better smelling self.

In this case, he would come out smelling like cherry blossoms, which made Aefric chuckle.

The cherry blossom scent was Byrhta's favorite for him. That the servants had chosen it was likely intended as a subtle reminder of her, which meant that they were worried he might get serious about Zoleen.

Everyone had an opinion.

His body servants picked out Aefric's evening wear, led by Vafar, an elderly kindaren man whose straw-colored hair seemed to resist all efforts at brushing.

Vafar selected for Aefric a quilted silk tunic of deep sunset red, slashed with a wide cloth-of-gold belt, over navy blue hose. Soft leather shoes with turned down cuffs that had been dyed to match the shirt.

As a nod to Zoleen's family — since he would see her at dinner — Aefric wore the sapphire-studded gold brooch that Ashling had given him.

As he came out of his closets, Ocheda was waiting. She arched an eyebrow as she looked him over. Even her nod of approval looked severe.

"Your grace's seneschal and castellan await him in his meeting room," Ocheda said. "Along with ... Ser Deirdre."

Ocheda's distaste for Ser Deirdre dripped from her words like tar.

"You don't care for Ser Deirdre, I take it?"

"Her manner is unseemly, your grace. Smirking and preening. Kneeling to a duke as though your grace were a king."

"She is ... unconventional," Aefric allowed, "compared with many knights. But her skills are indisputable, as are her results. Besides," he added with a smile. "She's a dweomerblade, and that art only draws the eccentric. I should know."

"Your grace has worked hard to present and comport himself as a proper noble following his ... adventurous upbringing," Ocheda said. "It is my opinion that Ser Deirdre's company could ... have a deleterious effect on your grace's hard work."

"I shall keep that in mind," Aefric said with a laugh. "Reminds me, though. Did she kneel to Duchess Arinda that way?"

"No, your grace," Ocheda said, her expression sour. "To the best of my knowledge she did not."

Something more to think about, as Aefric went to see what his knights and seneschal had learned.

⸻

When Aefric entered his meeting room, his seneschal, castellan and knight were bent over a map that had been spread out across the round, blackwood table. Though they quickly came to attention and bowed their greetings.

Well, two of them bowed. Ser Deirdre dropped to one knee, and might have stayed there if Aefric hadn't immediately gestured for her to rise.

"I like the darker colors better on your grace," Ser Deirdre said then, as she looked Aefric over with a critical eye. "The dark blues and blacks. Especially with silver embroidery. Lends an air of mystery. Though the sapphires in the brooch do bring out your grace's eyes."

Kentigern frowned and Ser Calder rolled his eyes, but Aefric couldn't help chuckling.

"Are you suggesting, Ser Deirdre, that you could do a better job as my chief body servant?"

"*Body* servant, your grace?" Ser Deirdre said with a smile. "I might blush."

"I doubt that sincerely," Aefric said, approaching to look down at the map.

It covered the northwestern quadrant of Deepwater, from the lake to the sea in the west, and to the Dragonscar in the north.

"What have we learned?" Aefric asked, then quickly added to Ser Deirdre, "And I don't mean about fashion."

"Morgard seems quite puzzled about his being brought here," Kentigern said. "Seems to have no idea about why your grace would want to see him."

"He *does* know he stands to inherit his family's lands?" Aefric asked.

"We didn't ask that, specifically," Ser Calder said. "Didn't want to tip it, just in case your grace decides against confirming him." He shook his head. "I confess though. I did expect him to ask."

"Yes," Kentigern agreed. "Especially since we know he works closely with Brangford Couglas, and Brangford had been in touch with his father around the time that your grace was in Lachedran. It would stand to reason that Mayor Brangton would have told his son to expect Morgard's recall to Water's End."

"So if the mayor told his son," Aefric said. "The son didn't tell Morgard. Which begs the question, why?"

"We'd have to ask Brangford Couglas that," Ser Calder said.

"Shall I retrieve him, your grace?" Ser Deirdre asked.

"Not at this time," Aefric said.

"For whatever it's worth," Ser Deirdre said, "I don't think this Morgard thinks of himself as a ler at all. Doesn't carry the dagger.

Doesn't comport himself as a noble. Acts like a merchant, if you ask me. And a low one at that."

"In what way, low?" Aefric asked.

"The company he keeps. Wasn't a high-end warehouse I found him in. The goods were cheap. The deal, sketchy. Nothing respectable about it."

"But he did speak as though this were unusual. An opportunity that fell into his lap," Kentigern said. "That a request for cargo came along just hours after he'd learned about another merchant who'd found himself stuck with an excess of cheap textiles. A quick deal for a sure profit."

"And none of that seemed suspect to him?" Aefric asked.

"Deals do happen that way sometimes," Ser Calder said. "Not as though merchants all wave their business in front of everyone. Instead, you happen to overhear one conversation in a tavern, that connects with the laments you heard from another merchant only hours earlier."

"They do say that merchants do more business in taverns and inns than their offices," Kentigern added.

"Still," Aefric said. "Why didn't he just introduce the two merchants and take a finder's fee? Why put himself in the middle?"

"Higher profit," Ser Calder said. "He does the one a 'favor' by taking the excess off his hands cheap, then does the other a 'favor' by helping her fill her hold with the cargo she needs. She has to pay a little more, but meets her deadline. Decent profit margin for Morgard, at the cost of only a few hours' work."

"So *you're* saying it sounds legitimate," Aefric said to Kentigern and Ser Calder. He turned to Ser Deirdre. "But *you're* saying the deal was sketchy."

"I'm saying the look and feel of it was sketchy," Ser Deirdre said. "That doesn't *always* mean the deal is too, but it's the way to bet."

"So the questioning turned up no answers?" Aefric asked.

"Please excuse us, your grace," Ser Calder said. "We're presenting out of order."

"Not my fault," Ser Deirdre said, answering Ser Calder's pointed look with a blasé expression.

"I'm not looking to blame anyone," Aefric said. "I just want to know what you learned from Morgard."

"All right," Ser Calder said. "Kentigern, would you care to start?"

"Thank you," Kentigern said, then pointed to the map, indicating a series of farms around Lachedran. "According to Morgard, the flax and cotton were grown and harvested here, then a local trading company in Lachedran — Riverborne — had arranged for them to be shipped to another company down in Merrek."

"Via Ajenmoor?" Aefric asked.

"The sea route is faster this time of year," Ser Calder said. "When the storms aren't as big a problem. Wintertime, they'd ship down the Haven to the Tainfyr, and go from there."

"According to Morgard, the Merrek company's ship left Ajenmoor almost an aett ahead of schedule, two days before Riverborne's cargo even arrived. Which meant that cargo sat eating storage fees for several days, while Riverborne tried to find a buyer who wouldn't pay them coppers on the silver."

"Morgard had heard about the cargo," Ser Calder said. "And according to him, Brangford Couglas had heard about a captain whose shipment of pipe weed had never shown up, and needed something to sell down in Wulfport. Between them, they made the arrangements, cutting themselves in for a profit."

"A missing shipment of 'pipe weed,'" Aefric said suspiciously.

"That's what Morgard said," Ser Calder said, "and we have no *knowledge* to contradict it."

"He claims the deal went down when and where it did," Kentigern continued, "because that was the only way to make sure both the money and the cargo got where they needed to go, in time for the captain to leave on schedule with the morning tide."

"It's a believable story," Ser Calder said. "And suggests there might not be any contraband at all."

"Of course it's a believable story," Ser Deirdre said, as though Ser Calder were a dullard. "What did you expect him to tell us? 'Yes, ser

knight, everything we did was above board. Oh, except for the shipment of stolen eldrani babies?'"

"Now see here," Ser Calder started, but Aefric raised a hand to
stop the argument before it caught fire.

"It may be a believable story," Aefric said, "but do you believe
*Morgard*? Or do you think he's lying? Kentigern?"

"I believe him," Kentigern said. "In my opinion, he is holding
back information. Not about that shipment, but about something ...
bigger."

"Ser Calder?"

"I agree," Ser Calder said. "He seems puzzled that we were
concerned about the shipment. As though he was expecting us to ask
about something else."

"Ser Deirdre?"

"Oh, he's covering something up. No doubt about that." She
sighed. "But yes, I believe he's sincere that the textiles shipment was
just a textiles shipment. At least, as far as *he* knows."

"So what does that tell us then?" Aefric asked.

"It's safe to say," Ser Deirdre said, "that the textiles deal isn't what
brought him and Couglas to Ajenmoor, nor was it the reason they
stayed around. Could be I caught him during his only legitimate
deal."

"Speculation," Ser Calder said. "We don't have any proof that
either of them have been involved in anything illegal."

"Do we know what they *were* doing in Ajenmoor?" Aefric asked
before Ser Deirdre could give voice to the rejoinder on her lips.

"They were there for trade deals," Kentigern said. "We didn't press
for details of their business beyond the textiles shipment."

"Your grace thinks we should?" Ser Calder asked, dubiously. "Do
keep in mind that, whether your grace confirms Morgard in his family's title or not, he *will* be leaving Water's End. *And* talking about his
time and treatment here."

"You're saying we don't have enough to press," Aefric said.

"I'm saying we don't have *anything*," Ser Calder said. "We've been
given no reason to suspect any illegal activity. He could be hiding a

lover he's ashamed to admit to, for all we know. Or maybe he made some inadvisable joke about your grace in a tavern."

"My gut says he's been up to something shady in Ajenmoor," Ser Deirdre said.

"Fine then," Ser Calder said with a sigh. "We have no reason to suspect wrongdoing, beyond Ser Deirdre's gut."

Aefric looked at Ser Deirdre. Saw the same confidence in her eyes that he got himself, when his gut was telling him a truth in defiance of all other senses.

He nodded to her. She gave him a fierce smile and nodded back.

"All right," Aefric said, "this is how we'll play it. Kentigern. After dinner you'll go to Morgard. Tell him why I had him summoned to court. But tell him I'm worried about what my 'lost lers' have been up to since the wars. I'll be looking into his background before I'll confirm him, so if there's anything I'm going to find, it'll go better if he tells me himself."

"Not a bad idea in general, your grace," Ser Calder said. "Never too smart to hand someone power without knowing what kind of person they are."

"And I might make it a policy. I'll decide on that later." Aefric drew a deep breath and blew it out. "I'm still curious about the *timing* of a ship bound for Wulfport that didn't get its cargo. And just what cargo they were expecting."

"Your grace," Ser Calder said. "We have no reason to think it wasn't pipe weed."

Aefric raised an eyebrow at Kentigern. "Do you agree with that assessment, Master Seneschal?"

Kentigern frowned and furrowed his brow for a moment. "Your grace refers to the pipe weed reports from Goldenfall and Motte."

Aefric nodded, while Kentigern seemed to call those reports to his thoughts as though they'd been burned into his brain.

"Motte ships its pipe weed overland," Kentigern said, "but Goldenfall ships by water. And Goldenfall's latest report ... suggested that all pipe weed crops have been harvested and shipped for the year."

"Early," Aefric said, "because of irrigation problems from the wars, exacerbated by the summer's heat."

"We don't know that the pipe weed shipment came from Golden-fall," Ser Calder objected.

"We don't," Aefric agreed. "But as Ser Deirdre said, 'it's the way to bet.'"

"I could get the ship name from Morgard," Ser Deirdre suggested. "Go back to Ajenmoor and dig around. See what I can find out."

"Meaning no offense, Ser Deirdre," Aefric asked hesitantly, "can you do so quietly?"

"Your grace," Ser Deirdre said, with no more than a vague pretense at being offended. "I am like the sea dragon. I only disturb the waters when I wish to. But when I do..."

She grinned.

Aefric laughed. "You should take the sea dragon as your sigil then."

Ser Deirdre straightened as though he'd actually shocked her.

"Sigil," she said with a slow smile. "Truly? Your grace thinks so?"

"I see no reason why not. Assuming, of course, you live up to your word here, and bring me the information I seek without ... disturbing the waters."

She thumped her chest, then raised her fist high in salute.

"I swear on my honor that it shall be done," she said in ringing tones.

Ser Calder's eyes widened. As did Kentigern's.

"I look forward to your results," Aefric said with a smile, then took in the others. "Anything else pressing? Ser Calder, what are those Malimfari knights up to?"

"They're out hunting, your grace," Ser Calder said. "Yrsa's scouts track them, but early indications are that they're not straying anywhere they shouldn't."

"Good," Aefric said and stood. "Then if that's all for the moment" — he paused, but no one interrupted — "I'll thank the three of you for your work, and suggest we go see about dinner."

WATER'S END HAD AT LEAST A DOZEN DINING HALLS. AND THOSE WERE just the ones that Aefric had seen. They each had their purposes, and selection usually varied directly with the number of guests who'd be dining with the duke on any given occasion.

Aefric had been absent often enough of late that several of his more prominent lers, landed knights, and other courtiers had taken the opportunity to return to their own lands and homes and deal with the mundane matters they'd had to ignore while off at court.

That would likely change soon. Word was probably out already that Aefric was back. Further, with King Colm and Queen Eppida coming, it was a safe bet that Aefric wouldn't leave Water's End again, possibly before the end of summer.

Or at the very least, this was how Kentigern had explained the common view of the situation. Aefric would not have been at all surprised to find himself leaving Water's End as many as three or four times before the end of summer.

He'd learned a long time ago never to expect his life to go smoothly. Made for a refreshing change when it did. And when things went wrong, as they did so often, he was ready.

Dinner that night was in a room off the main hall that Aefric had come to think of as "the public intimate dining room." Which meant that the grand oak table in the center seated only thirty.

Its proximity to the great hall, with its dome, meant that the ceiling here was an arc of red and yellow stained glass. Light was provided by candelabras along the table, and a series of candles around the edges of the rectangular room.

The candles along the perimeter were positioned to highlight the art decorating the soft gray paint of the plastered walls. In this room, that meant tapestries depicting Lake Deepwater at sunset, ships sailing the Haven River, previous dukes and duchesses hunting, and the like.

And, of course, the Deepwater flags — the battle flag and the sigil flag — on the wall behind Aefric's seat.

The grand hearth along one wall was part of an even larger hearth in the great hall, on the other side of that wall. Though no fire burned in it that night. The heat of the day was past, but the evening was still warm enough to make a fire superfluous.

The white oak floorboards were covered tonight with rugs of woven rushes, which Aefric suspected was as much to keep the floors clean as to underlay the aromas of dinner with a sweet background scent.

Just over a season now, Aefric had lived here at Water's End. And in that time, he'd noticed that every time he ate with his court, the seats were filled and the dinner ready to be served when he entered the dining room.

This was true even when Aefric's day had grown ... complicated. It was true even when there were last-minute delays, such as an important late meeting with a knight, his castellan, and his seneschal.

And yet, so far, the diners had never been kept waiting long enough to look impatient when they stood and bowed a greeting to their duke. Nor had the dinner ever seemed to suffer for an unplanned wait.

Truly, the kitchen staff in this castle earned their pay.

That night was no different, and Aefric had no sooner been seated — allowing the rest of the diners to sit as well — when the first servants began pouring what was called the "palate wine."

This was a light, dry white wine. One quarter-sized glass was given to each diner, who was expected to finish the drink before the first course of the evening was served.

That night, Aefric thought he detected a hint of applewood in the wine, which was unusual. If interesting.

No toast would be made with the palate wine. That was considered bad luck.

Once Aefric had drunk his down, he greeted Zoleen, who — as the closest thing to a ranking noble in his court at the moment — sat at his right hand. She looked splendid tonight, with her copper hair piled atop her head in a fetching arrangement that left her long throat bare, but for a strand of black pearls.

Her gown this evening was silk, and a deep sunset red, which made Aefric wonder if she'd been told how he'd be dressed for dinner.

It looked to be a simpler design than the last gown he'd seen on her, but was no less elegant for that. Further, Aefric had been told that redheads couldn't wear red. And yet, the dress seemed to suit Zoleen just fine.

Unless there were multiple ranking nobles visiting Water's End — or someone else of sufficient social standing or personal importance to the duke — the seat to Aefric's left was filled on a rotational schedule known only to Kentigern.

In theory, this allowed every member of Aefric's court to have the opportunity to share conversation with their duke over dinner. In practice, it led to a lot of flirting from young noblewomen, and talk of hunting from young noblemen.

Tonight that seat at his left hand was occupied by Ler Cynewyn Ol'Cynthryth.

Ler Cynewyn was heavier than most noblewomen Aefric had met in Armyr, who generally tended toward slender. But she carried her weight well, in a gown of deep purple, accented by amethysts decorating her golden bracelets and thick gold necklace.

The brown of her eyes was almost as dark as her skin, and she wore her hair in tight braids woven with garnets and moonstones that clicked when she turned her head.

Aefric tried to recall where her lands were. Just outside Lachedran to the ... east? Yes. That sounded right. Just east of Lachedran, along the shore of the lake.

After greeting Ler Cynewyn, Aefric glanced down the table. He recognized every face, though he didn't yet know every name offhand. Apart from obvious ones, such as Kentigern, Elkari, Ser Yrsa, Ser Beornric, and down at the foot of the table, Ser Calder.

And, of course, the handful of young noblewomen present who'd come to him for the noble privilege. All of whom met his eye with smiles as he looked down the table.

By tradition, no one came armed and armored to the duke's

dinner table. Even Ser Beornric had exchanged his full plate for a dark green quilted tunic.

Technically, Aefric was breaking that tradition himself, by bringing the Brightstaff and letting it stand beside his seat.

That had caused some ... concern, when Aefric had first moved into Water's End. His courtiers' eyes had stared often at the Brightstaff, standing tall beside their duke's chair.

Worried, perhaps, that their duke's coming armed to the table was a statement of some sort. Some might even have been concerned that he might cast spells during the main course.

But they'd come by now to realize that the staff simply went wherever Aefric did, and most of them seemed to regard that as a harmless affectation. One that might even benefit them, if there were trouble.

"Your grace has been absent much of late," Ler Cynewyn said, once the salad of eggplant and mixed greens had been served.

"Yes," Zoleen picked up immediately, though her tone was more teasing. "And he took off so *suddenly*. I worried it was something I said."

"Really?" Ler Cynewyn said to Zoleen. "I wouldn't have thought it was *words* that got you into trouble, dear."

"A great deal has been happening of late," Aefric said, before Zoleen could reply to the ler. "And I hope to resolve as much of it as possible before their majesties arrive."

"There've been conflicting accounts about exactly where your grace took off to in such a hurry," Ler Cynewyn said. "Might I ask what was so important?"

"I don't believe it's a secret that those refugees who came through here recently were rescued from slavers," Aefric said.

"I'm sure those slavers felt naked before your grace's spells," Zoleen said innocently.

"Yes, well," Ler Cynewyn said, "few can match spells with our duke when he is armed with his namesake." She turned to Aefric. "But surely that matter has been resolved. It is well known that the slavers were captured, their ship taken, and their former captives freed to pursue meaningful lives. All thanks to your grace."

"The matter of that ship has been resolved," Aefric said. "But I cannot abide slavers, and wish to know where they were going, where they came from, and the like."

"But surely your grace has agents to handle such matters," Ler Cynewyn said.

Aefric smiled. "There are things my knights can handle for me. And there are things I must do myself."

"Is there any way I and mine can help?" Ler Cynewyn asked, tilting her head slightly, so that the gemstones in her braids clicked. "My husband Tegik travels a good deal for us on business. He knows people in many ports. I could summon him here to Water's End by morning, if your grace wishes."

"That is a gracious offer," Aefric said, "and you are kind to make it. That will not be necessary at this time, but I shall keep your husband in mind, as I plan the next stages of the investigation."

From there, with the cream of celery and mushroom soup course, the conversation moved to lesser matters. By a decree going back over a hundred and fifty years, talk of business was forbidden at the duke's dinner table.

Aefric and Ler Cynewyn had come close to violating that, with the talk of slavers, but as it involved news, and not truly business, Aefric felt it was all right.

Throughout dinner, Ler Cynewyn spoke of her lands, her grain crops (in general terms), the three noble children she was fostering for lers around Water's End, and the news of her own children who were being fostered down around Behal.

Zoleen spoke of Merrek, of the Summer's Eve Ball a few aetts back, and how she had helped test and train a number of horses for her sister this year.

In all, the conversation was good, and the food was even better. The main course was a mixture of grilled fillets of three different kinds of lake fish. On their own, each was tasty, but combined together with the right spices, they created a blend of sweet and savory that enticed the tongue.

Aefric was unfamiliar with the sliced, braised root vegetables served with the fish, but apparently they were grown in the shallows of certain parts of the lake. They were spiced with saffron, because apparently they had little flavor of their own, but were eaten for their texture.

They were crisp on the initial bite, but then airy in a way that felt like popping a soap bubble of flavor.

Over dessert, a rhubarb pie served with fresh cream, Zoleen found an excuse to lean closer and ask in a soft voice, "May I come to your chambers tonight, your grace?"

"I would like that very much," Aefric said with a smile.

But if Aefric had been considering inviting her up for a drink straight after dinner, his plans were dashed when Ser Wardius came up and whispered in his ear.

"Your grace's ducal wizard has returned, and awaits your grace in the meeting room of his apartments."

That was that, then. Back to business.

---

AFTER DINNER, AEFRIC HAD HIS GUARDS ESCORT HIM BACK TO HIS apartments, along with Ser Beornric, through the servants' backway.

While business topics were not allowed at the public ducal dinner table, once dinner was over, that rule no longer applied. Aefric had learned early that if he didn't want to catch an earful of supplications and requests, he was best off beating a swift, and concealed, retreat after dessert.

Tonight, he even had an excuse. Which appeared to frustrate Ler Cynewyn, who clearly had something she wanted to talk about.

Well, he'd hear about it soon enough. If not from her directly, then from either Kentigern or Ser Calder, whoever she spoke with first.

In the meantime, Aefric and Ser Beornric returned to the round, blackwood table of the ducal meeting room, where Karbin was not alone in waiting for them. Ser Yrsa was there too.

Aefric frowned at her, after the greetings.

"You were at dinner with us," Aefric said to her. "I saw you. Ten places down the table from me, on the left-hand side."

"That's correct, your grace," Ser Yrsa said with a smile wide enough to tug at that long scar of hers.

"And yet not only did you get here before me," Aefric said, "but you found time to grab your maces en route?"

"I felt naked without them, your grace," Ser Yrsa said with a shrug.

"You're not going to tell me how you did that, are you?"

"I will if your grace orders me, of course," Ser Yrsa said. "But I should point out that your grace only benefits by having a general who knows the ways of his castle even better than he does."

Aefric chuckled and took his seat at the table, gesturing for everyone else to do the same.

"All right," Aefric said, looking back and forth between Karbin and Ser Yrsa. "Which of you would like to go first?"

"Lord Wizard?" Ser Yrsa offered.

"Just Karbin is fine," Karbin said. "Especially among a group like this."

After she nodded acknowledgment, he turned to Aefric.

"I mentioned that I'd gotten a couple of leads I could follow up on that wouldn't take me into Malimfar or Redport," Karbin said.

"Why do I have the feeling I'm not going to like where this is going?" Aefric asked, one eyebrow high.

"Likely," Karbin said with a lopsided smile, "because you know me. Or at the very least, process of elimination tells you where I went, since it wasn't back to Ajenmoor."

"Kefthal."

"Specifically," Karbin said, "Drake's Landing, the Kefthali port I'd pointed out earlier as part of the normal route for both those slavers and smugglers. Have any of you been there?"

Aefric shook his head, as did the others.

"I'd been there once before," Karbin said. "Tracking down legends of this." He pulled the obsidian rod from his belt and laid it on the table. "It was in Drake's Landing that I'd learned of Sulkrekeep, and the haunted ruins beneath it."

"So you knew your way around already?" Ser Yrsa asked.

"Yes and no," Karbin said. "I knew already where a certain knot of scholars hides there, but they were no good to me on this trip. I had to make other inroads, around the docks."

"You weren't gone all that long," Ser Beornric said. "Couple of days."

"Not the first time I've done something like this," Karbin said with a downright roguish grin. "Aefric and I have hunted slavers more than once."

"What did you learn there?" Aefric asked.

"Mainly," Karbin said, "I eliminated Redport, on the topic of slavery. The only times the *Gull's Bride* did more in Redport than purchase supplies, they smuggled in *illegal* cargo. But not *living* cargo. No slaves. Just contraband such as Kefthali leather and the like."

"That's an odd turn of phrase," Aefric said. "Not *living* cargo. Did you choose those words?"

"I was quoting from my source," Karbin said. "An officious little weasel who gets a taste of everything that moves through Drake's Landing."

"How did you get information out of him?" Ser Yrsa asked.

"That part was simple enough, if the most time consuming aspect of my trip to Drake's Landing," Karbin said with a wry smile. "Men like him always have guilty secrets. I found out what his was, and threatened to put the word out about it, if he didn't tell me everything I wanted to know."

"What was the secret?" Ser Beornric asked.

"Believe me," Karbin said with a grimace. "You don't want to know. In fact." He drew a breath, as though to get past the taste of something. "I'll put it this way. If I didn't think we might need more information out of him later, I'd've killed him for it."

"Fair enough," Aefric said. "Though in Kefthal I imagine he needs to hide it because of identities involved, rather than the acts themselves."

"Exactly," Karbin said. "And it was he who specified 'not living cargo.' Why?" Then Karbin blinked with realization. "Undead workers?"

"Stands to reason," Aefric said. "Plenty of necromancy in Kefthal, and plenty of people who need a lot of work done after the wars. Often in places where the populace has been decimated."

"Like Silverlake," Ser Yrsa said.

"Like all of us, really," Aefric said with a sigh. "But yes, I was thinking of Silverlake. Beornric and I saw the some of the damage wrought by the dybbungstad and their demon twins. I could imagine a leader of … questionable morality taking advantage of undead help in the rebuilding process."

"Countess Briluufa?" Ser Yrsa asked. "Or do you think Duke Wylyn could be involved?"

"I hope not Wylyn," Aefric said, shaking his head. "For that matter, I hope not Briluufa, either. I mean, this is speculation." He sighed. "But I think it's speculation I might need to inform Duke Wylyn about. He's in Redport doing his own investigations right now."

"Do you think it's wise?" Ser Yrsa asked. "We don't have more than speculation about this, based on an odd turn of phrase."

"We know the slavers have sold contraband in Redport," Aefric said. "We're sure of that much, so I should inform Wylyn. And while I'm at it, I'll tell him the turn of phrase and what it *might* mean."

"I can tell you Calder will disagree," Ser Yrsa said. "He'll say we shouldn't pass on anything but known *facts*."

"I'll handle it if you like, Aefric," Karbin said. "I'm the one who went to Kefthal. I can answer his questions, and help him understand what I found out."

"That's probably the way to go," Aefric said. "Hate to ask you to do it, but—"

"I'll leave in the morning, your grace," Karbin said with a teasing smile. "But before we move on, we should consider the other information I confirmed there in Kefthal."

"Wulfport?" Aefric asked, hoping he was wrong.

"Wulfport," Karbin said. "My contact was upset that sometimes..." Karbin grimaced and forced himself to continue. "That sometimes the 'choicest' slaves had been sold in Wulfport before the *Gull's Bride* docked in Kefthal."

"That *is* damning," Aefric said. "Before you leave for Redport—"

"I'll prepare the report for his majesty," Karbin said. "Of course."

"Anything else on that front?" Aefric asked.

"No," Karbin said, turning to Ser Yrsa. "I believe you have something though?"

"Yes," Ser Yrsa said. "Earlier today our scouts spotted movement along the northern ridge of the Dragonscar. Most likely Silverlake scouts."

"And this is near the caves with the gold, I take it?" Aefric asked.

"Yes," Ser Yrsa said. "They were clearly checking the Dragonscar around those caves."

"Did they enter the Dragonscar?" Ser Beornric asked.

"No," Ser Yrsa said. "They stuck to the ridge, though they were clearly looking across at the southern ridge, and down into the Dragonscar."

"So far as we know," Aefric asked, "did they learn anything?"

"I don't believe so," Ser Yrsa said with a feral smile. "Our scouts were already in place, so the Silverlake scouts had no movement to key on. And Ge'rek and Po'rek have been quiet as stalking cats, down in those mines. Even our own scouts haven't seen or heard from them, and they know what to look and listen for."

"You know what this means though," Ser Beornric said to Aefric. "Duke Wylyn's involved. There can be no doubt now. First you confirm that it was his wizard who cast those spells we encountered, including the stone men. And now, just after we visit, he sends scouts down the check on it."

"Damn," Aefric said. "I really wanted to like him." He sighed and shook his head. "All right. Same thing here. We need all this prepared into reports, with copies for his majesty. I want all the evidence together before I say word one."

Ser Yrsa snorted. "That, at least, Calder would agree with."

"All right," Aefric said. "Is there anything else?"

"Yes," Ser Yrsa said. "The Malimfari knights have returned to their rented rooms from their hunt. They took down no game."

"None?" Aefric asked. Then he thumped his fist on the table. "Elbar's Blood I wish we could talk to them."

"Do you?" Ser Beornric asked. "It seems to me that they're probably under orders to avoid getting arrested or giving offense. Hunting is expected for knights, and pretty innocuous. And they avoided killing anything, thus not even letting us claim they were poaching on the duke's 'private preserve' or something."

"That's my point," Aefric said. "I think they're here on a mission. That they're biding time until..."

He turned to Ser Yrsa. "The king and queen. How to they usually come to Water's End?"

"By road, of course," Ser Yrsa said. "Makes a better entrance, and a better chance for them to be seen by ... their people..."

She turned to Aefric. "You think those knights are here to kill our king?"

"I think they might be. And there's nothing harder to stop than an assassin willing to die in the course of his business."

"But what we can do about it?" Ser Beornric asked. "We can't arrest, or even get close to those knights, by order of the king. And we can't tell their majesties to come by water because we fear the *possibility* of assassins."

"The answer is obvious," Aefric said. "Come dawn, I and the knights and soldiers of my personal guard will sail for Behal. Then we'll take to the road, meet their majesties, and escort them to Water's End personally."

"Smart," Karbin said. "Puts you and your best on the firing line, if there's a problem. And if not, it just looks like a grand gesture of respect for your liege."

"What about the Malimfari knights?" Ser Yrsa asked.

"I want those knights watched like the enemies they may be." Aefric thumped the table again. "And I want a squad kept nearby and ready. And if those knights *do* try anything, I want them taken down.

Alive, if possible. Either way, *I'll* answer to his majesty for the decision."

"Yes, your grace," Ser Yrsa said, offering the battlefield salute, which Ser Beornric offered as well.

"Karbin," Aefric said, frowning. "One more thing. After you get back from Silverlake — and don't let Wylyn lure you into his investigation — I want you to check around in Water's End and Behal. Just in case those knights are a decoy."

Karbin chuckled. "You remembered the first rule of illusions."

"First lesson I ever learned from you," Aefric said with a wistful smile. "Best illusions are the ones that don't need magic. Just distraction, to put your enemy's attention where you want it."

"I'll see to it," Karbin said. "If Malimfar has anything more than knights lying in wait, I'll find them."

"Good," Aefric said, then another thought occurred to him. "Have we been tracking Princess Xenia's movements?"

"Not since she left Deepwater two days ago," Ser Yrsa said.

"That was fast," Ser Beornric said.

"They seem to be in a hurry," Ser Yrsa agreed.

"Well, they're somewhere in the king's lands, anyway, so not our problem." Aefric stood. "And now, I'd better get a good night's sleep. Going to be a few days."

<hr>

WHEN ZOLEEN ASCENDED THE STAIRS TO AEFRIC'S PRIVATE SITTING room, she was smiling. She wore the same dress from dinner, but now she wore her copper hair down in long waves, playing past her shoulders.

"I see your grace didn't keep me waiting tonight," she said, teasing, while Dajen brought them glasses of a light, sweet sharabi that tasted like raspberries and was the green of summer grass. Very good for driving away the last bitterness from the nysta tea.

"Yes," Aefric said, smiling, and gesturing to the seat beside him on the maroon couch, "well, some would say I've kept you waiting ... four days since our last night together?"

"*I* would say it," Zoleen said, with a playful toss of her hair, "except that I am above such petty complaints."

"Good of you," Aefric said, and raised his sharabi in toast. "To savoring the moments of life."

After they drank, Zoleen cocked an eyebrow at Aefric.

"One could suggest," she said, "that such a toast could be construed as melancholy. As though such moments worth savoring were few and far between."

"I suppose," Aefric said, "one *could* read such a meaning into the words. Had one the desire." He touched his chest. "But I, myself, hope merely to express the pleasure I take in your company tonight."

"So you say," Zoleen said with a lopsided smile. "And yet, I suspect that your grace might be concealing bad news."

"Well," Aefric conceded. "I don't know about *bad* news. But I do have to leave in the morning."

"Again?" Zoleen asked, disbelief as plain on her face as in her voice. "I do hope the common thread here is not my company."

"Certainly not," Aefric said with a chuckle, then reached out and squeezed her hand, to emphasize his sincerity.

She hesitated only a moment before returning the squeeze and releasing his hand.

Zoleen sipped her sharabi, and gazed thoughtfully at him.

"May I at least ask *why* your grace must leave in the morning?"

"I will be going to meet their majesties on the road, and escort them myself here to Water's End."

Zoleen frowned. Whatever answer she was expecting, that wasn't it. But then she smiled, slowly.

"In that case, might I accompany your grace on this journey?"

"No," Aefric said. "I'm not traveling with any courtiers or entourage. Only the knights and soldiers of my personal guard."

Zoleen considered that through another sip of sharabi.

"Your grace expects trouble from a vassal?" she asked.

"Nothing like that," Aefric said, but before he could say more, she spoke up.

"But your grace *does* expect trouble," she said with a nod. "Trouble that might need his spells, or his knights. Or at least a few more soldiers than the royal entourage has already."

"Maybe I just want to escort their majesties here without making their entourage so large it becomes unwieldy."

"Many *would* believe that," Zoleen conceded. "But I myself do not. If that were your grace's sole intention, he would have left in time to meet them at the east end of Kerrik Forest."

She shook her head, while keeping her eyes on him. "Tomorrow morning is too late for that. Which suggests that your grace has learned something concerning. Something that makes him believe their majesties might need his aid."

"An interesting notion," Aefric said. "But surely you don't expect me to either confirm it or deny it."

"Why not?" She snorted. "Because I'm a Fyrenn? Because my family's name is all but synonymous with intrigue?"

"You must admit," Aefric said, "that certainly is your family's reputation."

"My *family's* reputation, yes," Zoleen said, and now her sapphire eyes blazed. "And *Ashling's* reputation, certainly. But what of *my* reputation? What intrigues am I guilty of, your grace?"

Aefric sighed. "None that I have heard of. And yet..."

"And yet," Zoleen finished for him, "that might only mean that I am the cleverest player of all. Is that it, your grace? Am I here because you keep your friends close and your enemies ... naked?"

Aefric hung his head. "No, Zoleen. Not at all."

"Certainly your grace knows that I have heard about Baroness Montess Ol'Nastath of Riverbreak. How she came to your grace for the noble privilege, and within days her son and heir was arrested and executed for treason. Not to mention that Montess herself, and her husband, the baron, were *exiled* for aiding and abetting this treason. Or am I to believe the one was unrelated to the others?"

"I will confess," Aefric said, "that when I was with Baroness Montess, I needed information about a knight-adviser her husband kept. But I didn't dream that her son had been guilty of treason. Much less that she and Baron Karmody knew of that treason."

"But you *did* have a motive beyond company and pleasure," Zoleen pressed. "When you took Baroness Montess to your bed."

"I did," Aefric admitted. "Although that has not been true for anyone else. Not for Byrhta Ol'Caran. Not any of the noblewomen of my court here and at Behal. And certainly not for you."

"It's easy for me to believe that about the others," Zoleen said frankly. "Especially the petty nobles. The lers. Their relatives. And surely no man living would refuse a chance to lie with Byrhta Ol'Caran. But how am I to believe this about myself, your grace?"

She shook her head. "How am I to believe that your grace takes *me* to his bed, and not just a *Fyrenn?*"

"Because I like you, Zoleen," Aefric said. "I enjoy your company and conversation. I laughed more with you a few nights ago than I had in aetts."

Zoleen narrowed her eyes suspiciously. "Truly, your grace?"

"Truly," Aefric said. "In fact, there was something I planned to tell you tonight. But now, well, I worry that you'll take it as some kind of ruse to set you at ease."

"Tell me *what*, your grace?"

"That I want you to call me Aefric."

Zoleen's eyes widened. Her mouth formed an "O" and for a moment, she was speechless.

Aefric savored that moment.

"You mean when we're alone?" she asked carefully.

"Did I say that?"

"You mean, even before the court? In the company of your knights? Even in the presence of the king? I can call you Aefric?"

"That's exactly what I mean," Aefric said.

"Oh, Aefric," she said, setting down her half-full glass of sharabi and throwing her arms around his neck. "You mean it?"

"I told you," Aefric said. "I like you, Zoleen. I enjoy your company.

I enjoy talking with you. Laughing with you." He stroked her cheek, and said softly. "And other things as well."

She smiled then, and there was heat to that smile.

"And lest you wonder," he said, "I have no ulterior motives in taking you to my bed."

"And let me assure *you*," Zoleen said softly. "I have no ulterior motives in coming to your bed."

"Good."

"And I believe I've had enough sharabi. *Aefric*."

She leaned in and kissed him. And then Aefric had to dismiss the servants, because Zoleen made plain that she intended to take things much further right there on the couch.

Later, when they were both naked, perspiring, and panting for breath between lovemaking sessions in Aefric's bed, she confessed that Aefric was the first titled noble besides her own sister to allow her the familiarity of a first name.

Of course, he'd long since figured that out.

# 9

———

MUCH AS AEFRIC WOULD HAVE ENJOYED LINGERING IN BED WITH ZOLEEN that morning — perhaps even seeking pleasure with her again — he knew he had to rise, clean, and dress as soon as the servants wakened him.

He could not even savor a pleasurable breakfast with her that morning. He had too tight a timetable to keep. So as soon as they were dressed — she in her sunset red gown from the night before, he in a navy blue silk tunic and his riding leathers — he kissed her and saw her to the door.

She stopped him in the doorway of the sitting room on the public floor of his apartments. She twined her arms about his neck and kissed him so long and slow he had to set the Brightstaff down and take her in his arms.

When the kiss broke at last, she said — not too softly — "Be safe on the road, *Aefric*. I shall look forward to your return."

"I'll do my best," Aefric said, matching her smile. "Try not to get into too much trouble while I'm gone."

"I promise nothing," she teased, and left.

Aefric turned. Apparently Sers Yrsa, Beornric and Calder were seated at his couches this morning, along with Kentigern. He'd somehow walked past them without noticing even one of them.

Ser Beornric, of course, was in his full plate. And Kentigern was in his favored quilted, royal blue velvet tunic, with silver trim, worn over black hose. Ser Yrsa was in full plate as well, that day, though Ser Calder was in a quilted dark brown tunic, over paler brown hose.

"Did I hear her call your grace by *name*?" Ser Calder asked, and from both his expression and tone, he disapproved.

"You did," Aefric said, turning to Ocheda, who answered before he asked.

"Breakfast has been arranged as a buffet in the meeting room, your grace."

"Thank you, Ocheda," Aefric said, taking the Brightstaff back in hand as he turned to the others. "Shall we?"

He led them once more to the round, blackwood table of his meeting room. Though Aefric filled his plate with a selection of sliced fruits and cheeses, along with roast beef, turkey, and honeyed oat rolls from the buffet along the near wall, before filling a goblet of water and claiming his seat at the table.

The others gathered their food and drinks as well, before joining Aefric at the table.

"Not sure I like the precedent," Ser Calder said, still harping on Zoleen's familiarity. "Next thing, any young noblewoman who shares your bed will be wanting to call her duke by his proper name."

"Zoleen only did so after I gave her explicit permission," Aefric said, tearing a soft roll in half. "In fact, I was the one who broached the subject with her."

"Enjoy her company all you like," Ser Yrsa said in a warning tone. "Marry her, should you so desire. I doubt many would blame you. But keep in mind. She's a *Fyrenn*. *Never* forget that. Because *she* won't."

"All right," Aefric said. "If that's all we need to cover about my love life this morning—"

"Not quite, y..." Kentigern said, then grimaced and checked himself from getting reminded that Aefric would not stand on formality in his morning meetings. "Not quite. There's been a rika this morning from Riverbreak. Baroness Regent Byrhta and her ward,

Mistress Vercy, request permission to come to Water's End during their majesties' visit."

"Is there any reason I should say no?" Aefric asked, glancing around the table.

"I can think of a reason you should say 'yes,'" Ser Calder said. "Vercy stands to inherit her barony in less than two years' time, and I have no doubt she'll rave to their majesties about how well you've done as duke."

"He has a point," Ser Yrsa said. "If King Colm is using this visit to check on you, wouldn't hurt to have a hero-worshiping ally in your corner."

"You refer to Vercy or Byrhta?" Ser Calder said with a wry smile.

"Vercy," Ser Yrsa said, as though the question were meant seriously. "If Byrhta Ol'Caran bows down to our duke, it won't be for *hero* worship..."

"All right," Aefric said. "Enough of that."

"Although," Kentigern said, slowly, "the sentiment does tie into my point, and a possible caution about allowing them to come visit."

"Zoleen," Ser Beornric said. "Popular as Byrhta is, no doubt she's heard that Zoleen's been making a play for the role she wants herself."

"Duchess," Ser Yrsa clarified, as though Aefric had any doubts.

"Could be a source of conflict," Ser Beornric said.

"More importantly," Ser Calder said, "could give his majesty an excuse to push you to choose one of them and marry her."

"I was also thinking about Vercy herself," Kentigern said. "Yes, she's young. But she's made no secret of her aspirations." He turned to Aefric. "That would mean three women here at Water's End, all with the same goal, while their majesties are here for a visit."

"Are you certain Zoleen wants to marry me?" Aefric asked. "She's certainly never brought it up."

Everyone else at the table laughed.

Everyone.

"During your adventuring days," Ser Calder said, running his hand over his short, slicked-back gray hair, "you sometimes had to kill and cook your own food, I know. But did you ever have to butcher a domesticated animal? Like a sheep, perhaps?"

Aefric shook his head. "Only hunted in the wild."

"A sheep comes to trust the shepherd's hand," Ser Calder said. "Shepherd's the one who takes care of it, after all. Keeps it safe, warm in the winter and so on."

"It's like that illusion rule you mentioned," Ser Yrsa said. "When it's time to slaughter the sheep, you distract it. So it never sees the knife coming."

"Otherwise," Ser Calder agreed, "the animal's fear can spoil the taste of the meat."

"And that's what you think Zoleen is doing?" Aefric asked. "Training me to trust her hand, so I'll never see the knife coming?" He frowned. "We *are* talking about marriage, yes?"

"Arinda certainly considered marriage a kind of death," Ser Calder said. "And that cost her in the end."

"I've already told you," Ser Beornric said. "I think Duchess Ashling sent Zoleen here because marrying you herself might bring too much strife between you."

"Has Ashling broached the subject before?" Ser Yrsa asked.

"Yes," Ser Beornric answered. "Back in the Indecisive River Valley, after Frozen Ridge."

"And I told *you*," Aefric said. "She was joking."

No one around the table looked as though they believed Duchess Ashling had been joking about marrying Aefric.

"I'm telling you," Aefric insisted. "She even joked about all the beautiful women who'd line up to share our bed. She was just trying to make me laugh, when I was down."

"She wasn't," Ser Calder said, shaking his head. "At least, not *just* trying to make you laugh. I've known that woman since she was a little girl, and she never says one thing unless she accomplishes two or three things in the speaking."

"Joking or not," Kentigern said, earnestly. "She mentioned the idea of marrying you. Tying your houses together."

"And?" Aefric asked, puzzled now.

"And she sent her sister here with a gift, not a full season later," Kentigern said. "Maybe she wants you to marry Zoleen. Maybe she's having Zoleen test the waters before making a play to marry you herself. Either way, I don't doubt she's looking to see you married to a Fyrenn."

"Even if Ashling wants him herself," Ser Yrsa said, "that doesn't mean Zoleen is without her own ideas here."

"I have to sail this morning," Aefric said. "Do we have anything more pressing to discuss than who wants to marry me?"

"This topic is important," Kentigern said. "His majesty made quite clear to us before he created you duke. We were to ensure that you didn't make Arinda's mistake, and die unmarried and childless."

"And if we're to discuss it," Ser Beornric said, "we really ought to revisit the possibilities of the princesses from Caiperas and Malimfar."

"Well, not Malimfar," Ser Yrsa said. "Not given what we know about Wulfport, and what we suspect about those four knights."

"I'm not convinced they were serious about marrying their crown princess to our duke here," Ser Calder said. "It's believable enough, but until we know why those four knights are here, we must assume that Princess Astrid's mission was scouting, not marriage."

"And that Princess Xenia was here to keep an eye on Princess Astrid?" Ser Yrsa asked.

"Seems likely enough," Ser Calder said.

"Enough," Aefric said, slapping the table. "This topic is now closed for today. I have a lot of miles to go, and two monarchs to guard. Is there anything *pressing* I need to address before leaving?"

"One thing I can think of, though it *might* be able to wait," Kentigern said. "I'm not sure."

"What is it?" Aefric asked.

"There was an escape in Ajenmoor late last night. Captain Brusi of the *Gull's Bride*."

"A known confederate of Nelazzi," Ser Yrsa said. "Wonderful." She grimaced. "At least Gwawl is right where we put him. I checked not an hour past."

"Any details about the escape?" Aefric asked.

"None yet," Kentigern said. "The matter is under investigation."

"Not even any idea of how he escaped from that mastless ship out in the harbor?"

"He wouldn't have been kept there," Ser Beornric said. "You gave that to the city, but he was the prisoner of that councilman."

"Galdiff Reteka," Ser Yrsa spat. "Slimy bit of filth. Probably left the keys where Brusi could find them, then got his own guards drunk."

"Speculation," Ser Calder said dismissively. "It's more likely that the pirate queen herself is behind the escape than an Ajenmoori councilor."

"What about Gwawl then?" Aefric asked. "Should we expect a breakout attempt here?"

"I shouldn't use the word 'impossible,'" Ser Calder said. "But near enough. This isn't Ajenmoor. Even our worst cells are stronger and better defended. And you put Gwawl in one of the special, wizard cells. I'm not sure anyone short of Kainemorton himself could get past those locks."

"Increase the guard anyway," Aefric said, "and watch the rotation. Treachery can be more powerful than magic, and Nelazzi's reach is long."

"I've personally trained every soldier in this castle," Ser Yrsa said. "I'll guarantee them myself."

"Then the guards themselves deliver Gwawl's food from here on out," Aefric said. "And if he was allowed any visitors, he is no longer."

"You can't just keep him there forever," Ser Calder said.

"I can keep him there at least until I speak with their majesties. I'll figure out what to do with him after that." Aefric turned to Kentigern. "Anyone else escape?"

"No," Kentigern said. "And the mayor of Ajenmoor assures us that they've doubled the guard on the remaining prisoners, and that they're trying to recapture Captain Brusi."

"Lovely," Aefric said. "Anything else? Calder?"

"Small matters only," Ser Calder said. "I can handle them myself."

"Thank you," Aefric said.

"I'm putting our warships on maneuvers near our coastal port cities," Ser Yrsa said, "and I'll be checking the readiness of our soldiers. If Malimfar tries anything big, we'll be ready."

"Very good," Aefric said. "Kentigern?"

"Nothing that can't wait."

"Good," Aefric said. "Beornric?"

"I'm just here to escort you to the *Duke's Hand* when you're ready," Ser Beornric said. "Though I do have a thought about Ajemnoor that might be worth hearing."

"Oh?" Aefric asked.

"It occurs to me that you sent Ser Deirdre to Ajenmoor. If she hears about an escaped prisoner—"

"She will," Ser Yrsa said. "Assuming she's not the one who stole him."

"—and if she can do so without jeopardizing her mission, I suspect she'll go after Brusi herself."

"Well," Aefric said, smiling. "Then maybe we shouldn't count him as having escaped just yet..."

He finally took a sweet bite of that honeyed oat roll, and realized that, alas, he'd have to rush through his breakfast.

———

THE *DUKE'S HAND* WAS CROWDED AS IT SAILED DOWN LAKE DEEPWATER toward Behal, at its southern tip.

The sun was only just rising in the east, and the overnight chill felt good. Alas, it would burn off soon enough. Aefric had been advised that, after midsummer, the days would slowly begin cooling on their way toward autumn, but that hadn't happened yet.

Made the cool of the morning a refreshing change.

Aefric sat in his comfortable, fixed wooden chair on the afterdeck, with Ser Beornric beside him on a canvas folding chair. The other six knights of his personal guard, in their full plate and their Deepwater tabards, milled about the afterdeck as well.

The ship was just too crowded for them to be anywhere else.

The twenty-four soldiers of Aefric's personal guard stayed belowdecks to keep out of the sailors' way.

A drum boomed a steady beat, keeping the oars in time until the wind could pick up and fill the sails. Captain Sikel had assured Aefric that the wind would pick up soon, and that they'd reach Behal before midmorning.

Behal the city, not the castle. The plan was to sail past the delta and into the mouth of the Haven. Aefric and the others would disembark near the bridge over the Kingsroad.

Wouldn't save *much* time over stopping at the castle. But after that morning meeting ran long — which Aefric blamed on all the marriage talk — he wanted to save every minute he could for travel.

Plus, this was an advantage to the rika system. Kentigern had already sent rika ahead to Behal. When the *Duke's Hand* put in, horses would be waiting for his knights and soldiers, and supplies would be waiting for all of them.

Aefric had considered either riding a *magaunt* — a phantasmal horse he could summon — or having a horse provided for himself as well. But it had been Queen Eppida who gave Windsong to Aefric, so he felt it would make a better statement if he met their majesties mounted on his gift.

Rikas had also been sent ahead to ease the way at their planned stops. Speed would matter here. He couldn't likely meet their majesties by the Kerrik Forest. It was too late for that.

But if he and his used their time well, Aefric could make Tafarac in Felspark that night, and meet the royal party at Norrtarr before dusk the next day.

Not as good as meeting them at the forest. But it would still be meeting them before they lodged for the night with one of his vassals. Surely that would be enough to make a good impression.

He liked the idea of making a good impression before they reached Water's End. Assassins or no, Aefric was a little concerned about this "check" King Colm was supposed to be making.

And since Aefric had given permission for Byrhta and Vercy to come to Water's End, Aefric wanted a couple of days in their majesties' presence before the subject of marriage was broached.

Seemed safer that way.

And the first day of that trip went well. The *Duke's Hand* reached the Kingsroad Bridge at Behal just before midmorning. Behal's castellan, Ser Grey, was there and waiting, with a company of soldiers.

A crowd had gathered to greet their duke — mostly with cheers, though Aefric thought he heard a couple of requests in the shouts — but the soldiers held a good line. Aefric had no trouble disembarking, and his personal guard got their horses and packs sorted easily.

Then, with a wave, a smile, and a few words for the crowd, Aefric and his guard took to the Kingsroad.

The Kingsroad was wide and smooth and well-maintained. Aefric had made sure of that. He also had begun the process of having the road bricked. The project was underway, but hadn't reached the bridge yet, which made Aefric worry that it might not be finished before the rains came in earnest.

Then they were riding the Kingsroad between the barony of Riverbreak and the county of Goldenfall. They passed mostly farms, at first, but by midday they'd passed construction on two new towns, one on each side of the road.

On the Goldenfall side, this would be rebuilding a town razed during the Godswalk Wars, but the construction was all new on the Riverbreak side.

Odd that Vercy and Byrhta hadn't mentioned it. Probably wanted it to be a surprise. As though Aefric weren't expecting something like this. Byrhta had been irritated that Riverbreak had never taken enough advantage of Kingsroad traffic, leaving most of it for Goldenfall.

Goldenfall, of course, was her father's county. No doubt the Riverbreak towns she was building along the Kingsroad were a statement to Aefric that she put the position he'd given her ahead of other considerations.

Aefric wondered, though, how well received her decisions would be by her father and older brother...

Traffic was better along the Kingsroad, now, than it had been even this past spring. Plenty of local peddlers and farmers, of course, but also merchant caravans coming and going. Local petty nobles, with small entourages about their business.

More concerning was the presence of soldiers from Goldenfall and Riverbreak, patrolling the Kingsroad as well. Aefric could only hope that they were there to deter bandits, and not because problems were brewing between his vassals.

The last thing he needed was to have his vassals start fighting one another.

Aefric had lunch purchased from vendors on both sides of the road, so he couldn't be seen as playing favorites. Lunch, in this case, was roast chicken with rosemary, along with honeyed oat bread and fresh, roasted tara.

The meal was good, but Aefric couldn't help thinking about how Dajen had been right about one thing. Aefric had gotten used to excellent fare from his chefs at Water's End and Behal. If he ever tried to return to adventuring, the hardest part would be eating his own cooking once more.

The afternoon heat was just shy of scalding. Even the dusty air of the road felt warm in Aefric's nostrils. There was a bit of a breeze, but it was gentle here, and coming from behind them. Not much good, for cooling the day.

How much worse must that heat have been for his guards, in their armor.

Couldn't be helped, though. If they were to make Tafarac before twilight, they had to push a bit. Shorter rests, and too much heat.

But the heat was the worst enemy they faced that day, and they made Tafarac just as dusk began to rise.

Tafarac sat only a short ride south of the Kingsroad. It wasn't the baronial seat of Felspark. That was Ruunkeep. Farther south, near the junction of the Tainfyr and Fyrsa Rivers.

Tafarac, though, was built around a secondary baronial castle, and both town and castle were big enough and sturdy enough to have come through the wars mostly intact.

The town was built in three ascending layers, each with its own wall. Wooden, for the newest and lowest part of Tafarac. Stone for the raised, older part of town, and more stone for the wall surrounding the highest part, the hexagonal castle itself.

Aefric's party was met at the wooden gate by Baroness Blaewyn Ol'Felruun herself, and her brother, Ler Ordnoth Ol'Felruun.

Oh, they also had a party of a dozen soldiers in livery emblazoned with the Felspark sigil — three white stars, falling to the sinister, on a background of goldenrod — but Aefric was more interested in the fact that the baroness and her brother had come themselves.

Very different, from the last time Aefric had arrived at Tafarac. That time, Ler Ordnoth had met them on the road, but Baroness Blaewyn had waited on her baronial throne, diadem in place, and challenged Aefric on every front.

It seemed she'd come to appreciate her duke since then.

Today the baroness wore riding leathers of her own and sat a white stallion. No diadem today. Her shoulder-length blonde hair was bound behind her with goldenrod ribbons. On her bright red silk shirt, a gold necklace featured three diamonds.

Her brother wore a white shirt that practically frothed with lace, bound by a cloth-of-gold sash belt over gray hose.

Both of them wore knee-high boots of leather, but while hers looked as though they'd seen several hunts, his looked as though the soles had never touched dirt.

Ler Ordnoth wore a slender rapier and dueling dagger. The baroness, herself, was unarmed.

"Your grace," Baroness Blaewyn called out with a smile so big it seemed to strip her of the five years she had on Aefric. She slid down from her horse to give him a proper bow. "It is with great pleasure that I welcome you back to Felspark."

Aefric stepped forward and kissed her offered hand. He smiled. "Thank you, your lordship. It's good to be here."

"Much as I might wish to exchange pleasantries here and now," Baroness Blaewyn said, "I'm sure your grace and his company are tired and hungry."

"They are," Aefric said, "as am I. About my soldiers..."

"They are as welcome here as my own, your grace," the baroness said with a quirked smile. "Only *foreign* soldiers are not allowed within my walls."

Aefric chuckled. She'd argued against hosting his soldiers last time, when he was newly made duke. Apparently she'd come to appreciate him more than he'd thought.

They both remounted, and she began to lead the way.

"With permission, your grace," the baroness said, riding beside him, "I would like to tell of the good done by the priest of the Green Lord your grace sent us."

"Please," Aefric said, beginning to understand her apparently complete change of heart from the woman who'd so challenged him this past spring.

Of course, back then, her lands had been so devastated by the wars that they might not have produced enough food to see her people through the winter.

Though no one was better for healing land than a priest of the Green Lord, surely his work here was not yet finished...

"Please do," Aefric said, eagerly, "I'd like to hear all about it."

---

THE BARONESS ARRANGED A FEAST FOR THEM THAT NIGHT, WITH ALL OF her lers, knights, and other courtiers present. Even Aefric's soldiers were feasted, albeit in a separate hall, with her own soldiers.

Aefric's feast took place in the main hall of the castle, just inside the main doors. A squared room in a hexagonal castle. The main hall here had seemed large, the first time Aefric came though, but after Water's End, it seemed tiny. Even though it had to have been sixty feet to a side.

The floors were stone, and recently swept. The walls had been covered in special tapestries for the feast. Ones that depicted feasting and dancing and drinking.

Very different from its usual tapestries of Ol'Felruun hunting scenes, and the Ol'Felruun family tree.

Aefric and his knights sat with the baroness and the most prominent of her lers at a table raised on a dais in the center of the hall. The other diners ate at tables that were arrayed around the dais like the spokes of a wheel.

After the salads and the soup, they were served a tender, roast venison, with a selection of root vegetables from the first crop of the season — thanks to that priest of the Green Lord — and for dessert a delicious three berry pie.

A dance followed the feast, which seemed like overkill. He was only to be here for a single night. He and his were already weary from the long day's travel.

But he could not refuse the dance. That might have insulted the baroness and her court, when she was clearly trying to make up for her rudeness that past spring.

Sixteen musicians, with drums and strings and flutes accompanied a trio of kindaren singers, who worked a kind of magic of their own, with their sweet harmonies.

They seemed to banish fatigue, and encourage dancing.

It wasn't actual magic though. Aefric checked, by reflex. No, it was just their talent, as singers, and the way they worked with their band.

Aefric had not brought clothes for such an occasion, of course. But that didn't matter. Apparently, sometime in the last several aetts, the baroness had commissioned a small wardrobe for him, to be kept on site, should he need it during a visit.

So instead of his riding clothes, he was provided a soft gray shirt that had so much lace at the cuffs and collar that Aefric felt as though his every movement rustled. A cloth-of-silver sash belt, over pale blue leggings, and soft leather shoes that felt almost as though Aefric were getting a foot rub with every step he took.

Because the fashion in Felspark allowed weapons at a dance — rapiers, for most — Aefric wore the wand Garram at his hip. And, of course, he carried the Brightstaff, which bobbed around behind him on the dance floor when he danced.

And oh, did he dance. It seemed that every noblewoman in Felspark past the age of majority wanted to dance with her duke at least once. More than once, if allowed.

Even the baroness herself took a turn around the dance floor with Aefric, and she moved with impressive grace.

Aefric did more dancing that night than perhaps all his nights before it.

Well, certainly more than he'd ever done before in Qorunn. He did remember, though, the way he, as Keifer, used to go dancing with Andi at least once a week. (Which was like an aett that lasted only seven days.)

This was back when they were in college, and for a while after graduation.

Andi did love to dance, so. Enough that dancing again gave him a touch of heartache for the woman who had died in an accident, and shattered his life a world away.

Perhaps the most impressive element to the feast was that no one brought up business. Not the baroness herself — even though she likely needed *something* from her duke — and not any of the guests.

That was downright strange. In Aefric's time as duke, he'd yet to see lers gather without finding some pretext to at least *hint* at things they needed from their duke. A business connection, money, seed, soldiers for one thing or another, aid with construction, *something*.

And yet, no one said a thing. Not during the feast. Not during the dancing. It was as though all such topics had been forbidden for the night.

Instead they all, women and men alike, either tried to impress Aefric with stories of their deeds or details of their own lands, crops, or what have you. Or they plied Aefric for stories of the Battles of Deepwater and Frozen Ridge, or for tales from his adventuring days.

Aefric indulged them. Listened to their stories, and told his own. Laughed and joked with them as well.

He avoided recent topics, of course, but had more than enough tales from his travels to satisfy their curiosities.

Overall, it was quite a pleasant party, if unexpected.

Towards the end of the evening, as he finished his second dance with the baroness, she was slow to release his hand.

"Must your grace leave us in the morning?" she asked. "I could arrange a hunt, or some jousting. I would very much like to host your grace properly."

"I am sorry," he said, giving her hand a squeeze, which she returned, but didn't let go. "But I am meeting their majesties on the road."

"Even so," she said. "Would not Tafarac be the finest place to do so? It's older than Norrtarr, and more impressive, if I say so myself."

"I'd prefer not to compare the holdings of my vassals," Aefric said. "But in any event, I'd rather meet their majesties on the road itself."

She gave a slight frown, and Aefric could tell she was wondering why he wanted speed now, even though he was too late to meet King Colm at Kerrik.

"Is there anything I and mine might help with, your grace?" she asked carefully. And quietly, Aefric noticed. "I know my soldiers and knights would be as happy to ride to your aid as I would myself."

"And I am grateful for it. But there is no need for such," Aefric said softly. "I would have preferred to meet their majesties at Kerrik, true, but business prevented it. Now I would at least meet them on the road before they're hosted by one of my vassals."

Understanding spread across her face.

"Have no fear, your grace," she said, so softly now he could only just hear her over the music and conversation going on in the hall around them. "I've no doubt that Herewyn will speak as well of you as I will, should his majesty ask."

"I thank you for that too," Aefric said, matching her volume. "Nevertheless, I think I'll make a better impression, meeting them on the road."

"As your grace desires, then," she said, and pressed her forehead to the back of his hand, before finally releasing his hand. "No formal breakfast in the morning. I'll have food brought to your rooms, and your horses readied for an early start."

"Thank you, your lordship," Aefric said.

"I do have one request, if I may, your grace."

"What would you have of me?" Aefric asked.

"I know your grace's morning comes early. But if your grace would be so kind, choose one of my ladies for the noble privilege tonight."

She glanced around the room, and following her gaze Aefric noticed that at least a dozen women were watching their conversation avidly.

"They all think I intend to claim the noble privilege for myself, which, assuming your grace approved, would be my right as hostess." Baroness Blaewyn gave Aefric a slow look up and down with a small smile. "I confess, I'm tempted. Your grace is quite pleasing to look upon, and I'm curious to see more of that scar I spot now and then beneath his collar."

She shook her head. "But I think letting one of the ladies of my court have that pleasure in my place would be wise politically."

Aefric snorted a soft laugh. "Truly?"

"Truly," she said with a nod. "That priest you sent us has done wonders, praise Halstaffur. But I will still have to make a few hard decisions as winter approaches. Some of my lers will benefit, others ... will not. This feast, and another I have planned for the fall, will help maintain good relations and make those decisions easier."

"And my going to one of them for the noble privilege..."

"When I could claim it for myself?" the baroness said. "Oh, they will remember that as well." She chuckled and patted Aefric on the shoulder. "No pressure, your grace. I ask only that your grace satisfy the goodwill of my lers. Assuming your grace is willing."

Aefric chuckled. "Well, I must admit, this was not the sort of request I expected, but I think I can accommodate you."

He raised a warning finger quickly.

"I'm not going to let you choose for me."

"Of course not, your grace. I would never dream of doing so."

"With that in mind," he said, "are there any you'd ask me to avoid? If the noble privilege is truly a *privilege* in this instance, I might as well not be seen to reward someone who's been giving your lordship problems."

"Your grace is most kind," she said with a small bow. She lowered her voice a little further, and nodded toward a small, conversing crowd. "The one in the complicated, low-cut gown of red chiffon. That's Ler Sineas. She's been a thorn in my boot all year."

She nodded to another group. "The blonde woman, holding the diamond-studded faux wand. That's Martret. She's the rumormongering wife of Ler Cormananth. Together they've been sowing dissent among the lers about my recovery plan."

"Then I shall choose neither of them," Aefric said with a smile.

———

By noon the next day, Aefric and his company were making good time east along the Kingsroad toward Norra.

Recovery efforts were visible on both sides of the road. They'd even passed one new town on the Goldenfall side of the road.

Well, properly speaking, they'd passed what would be a town by sometime this coming autumn. Hopefully before the rains came. Right now, it was a town in progress. Houses and buildings were being built in something like an organized process, and over a third of them were finished.

It looked as though they were using recovered stone from the remains of towns destroyed in the wars, along with new-cut wood.

Among the finished buildings nearest the road was an inn, where Aefric had sent soldiers to purchase lunch. Strips of baked turkey, with a wheel of sharp cheese to share, and several loaves of a dark rye bread. Along with a cask of a good, crisp day beer.

It might have been Aefric's imagination, but the day seemed cooler than yesterday. If only just barely. And the fields along the sides of the roads were in much better shape than the last time Aefric came through.

The hot summer hadn't been kind to those fields, but they still held onto some of their green, and their smells were much more what he was used to, riding past farms and pastures.

They were making good time, and once they mounted up and started riding again after lunch — with Aefric and Ser Beornric riding in the center of a circle of his knights, half the soldiers in front and half in the rear — Ser Beornric finally brought up the subject he'd clearly been holding onto all morning.

"That wasn't the baroness I chased out of your room this morning."

"I'm not sure 'chased' is a fair descriptor," Aefric said. "She was already dressed, and kissing me goodbye when you knocked. But you're right. She wasn't the baroness."

Their horses clopped along the road. Ser Arras sniggered into her hand, pretending to cough.

"Oh," Aefric asked. "Did you want to know who she was?"

"Your grace spends *one night* in Felspark," Ser Beornric said, "and chooses a woman other than the baroness for the noble privilege? How can I be anything *but* curious?"

"It's hardly mandatory that his grace sleep with the baroness," Ser Temat said. "Or that the baroness sleep with him, for that matter."

"Did the baroness ask, and get refused?" Ser Vria asked.

"That's not what I heard," Ser Wardius said. "The way I heard it, they were ... in close conversation after a dance—"

"I can confirm that," Ser Arras said. "I was watching."

"—but that she asked his grace to choose another."

"Odd, that," Ser Micham said with a frown. "With *leaba* coming back into fashion, I would have thought the baroness might've steered his grace that direction. Saves possible political complications."

"*Leaba* was never a popular practice in Felspark," Ser Arras said. "And I suspect political complications were the point. Did you see who his grace chose?"

"Obviously not," Ser Beornric said, talking over the other knights. "And I would be very curious to know."

"Ler Idrina Ol'Teyruun," Aefric said.

"Lovely girl," Ser Vria said. "Such a pretty face, with those cheekbones and chin. Soft brown eyes that looked almost shy. And all that long blonde hair. Like a halo of sun."

"Young for a ler, too," Ser Temat said. "Only a handful of years past her majority. I'm not even sure she's as old as our duke."

"She inherited early, unfortunately," Ser Arras said. "Her parents and older brother were killed in the wars. Her younger brother is training as a page in Castle Ruunkeep."

Aefric raised his eyebrows at her.

"As your grace's second dance with her ended, I noticed the way her hands lingered whenever she found a pretext for touching. I decided she was worth asking about."

"Fair enough," Aefric said. "And since you're all so curious, it's like this. Baroness Blaewyn asked me to choose one of her ladies for the noble privilege. I asked her who her troublemakers were, so I wouldn't accidentally choose one."

"Very thoughtful, your grace," Ser Beornric said.

"Ah," Ser Arras said, as though the rest made sense now.

All the other knights looked the question at her. She pretended not to notice.

Aefric finally started laughing. "Oh, tell them. You've obviously figured it out."

"Ler Idrina is a charismatic woman, and a vocal supporter of the baroness' recovery plan. A plan that some of her lers oppose."

"Did your grace ask what that plan is?" Ser Beornric asked.

"No," Aefric said, with a one-shoulder shrug. "From what I understand, the Ol'Felruun family has done a good job with this barony for a long time. Far be it for me to come in and start questioning the baroness' decisions, unless she gives me a reason not to trust her."

"A policy that should make your grace's vassals very happy."

"One can only hope," Aefric said. "Although Ser Arras forgot to mention the other reason I chose Idrina."

"Second reason, your grace?" Ser Arras asked.

"Yes," Aefric said laughing. "Idrina is not only *very* pretty, she's also an excellent dancer and a charming conversationalist. I wanted to help her lordship, but I'm not a saint, either."

"A saint, your grace?" Ser Micham asked, and Aefric saw that the question was echoed on the faces of the other knights.

Oops. That was an expression from his life on Earth, in Oregon.

Apparently it wasn't an expression here in Qorunn.

Odd that it should have come to his lips that morning. Something about this conversation — being teased about a lover — must've echoed his experiences as Keifer.

Of course. Keifer's college days, back before he met Andi. Or maybe it was late high school...

Not a topic he needed to sort through right then.

"Don't you have saints here in Armyr?" Aefric asked instead, affecting surprise. Looked from knight to knight. "I suppose not. I ran into the concept at a monastery down around the Cape of Teeth. A saint is someone who do devotes himself or herself to the precepts of their god so completely that they forgo all ... worldly pleasures. They eat only simple food, wear only simple clothes, and forgo the bliss moment entirely."

More than one of his knights shuddered at the thought, though it was Ser Vria who said, "Any god who asked me to forgo the bliss moment would find himself short a worshiper."

There was a general chorus of consent to that.

"I do believe our good duke here is distracting us from the most important question about this Ler Idrina," Ser Beornric said with a sly smile. "Just how pretty and charming do you find her? Should we add her to your grace's growing list of potential wives?"

"Stop. Right. There," Aefric said with a chagrined smile, raising a warning hand. "We'll have no marriage talk on this trip. None!"

He grimaced. "Well. None unless their majesties bring it up. But in the meantime, *none*. Am I understood?"

"Yes, your grace," the knights all called out in unison.

Aefric looked at them suspiciously. He was met with innocent expressions that he didn't believe in the least.

---

ONCE AEFRIC WAS CONVINCED THAT HIS KNIGHTS WOULD DROP THE subject of potential wives, he turned his attention to the ride and looked over the recovery efforts around him as they made their way east toward Norrtarr through the steadily warming afternoon.

Felspark was definitely further along the road to recovery than Goldenfall — at least, from what could be seen from the road — though neither was as far along as Aefric would have liked.

He could still spot the areas where burned out towns and farms had been cleared away, but rebuilding had not yet begun. And even more sections where the land had yet to recover, especially on the northern, Goldenfall side.

Still. There were definite signs of progress and hope, as they rode through the late afternoon heat.

Traffic was encouraging as well. More local traffic along here, and still more merchant caravans and parties of traveling nobles. A fair amount of it was clearly related to construction, but not all of it.

Aefric and his party arrived at Norrtarr well ahead of the setting sun.

Unlike between the baronies of Riverbreak and Felspark, which were divided with border markers, a clear physical feature divided Felspark from the barony of Norra, and Goldenfall from the county of Motte.

A cliffs' edge. About five hundred feet high.

The Kingsroad, leaving Felspark, descended smoothly down a pass cut between the east edges of Goldenfall and Felspark.

Norrtarr lay only a few miles down the road, the first settlement east of the cliffs. On the Motte side of the road, now, were swamps and marshes, making for the least pleasant part of the ride, in terms of smell.

Sometimes, while traveling, Aefric had passed through forests burned out by wildfire. Sometimes, among the burnt husks, he would see individual trees still whole and hale. Untouched, even while their closest neighbors burned to cinders.

The town of Norrtarr reminded Aefric of those lone, healthy trees.

Norrtarr had no wall. And yet, the Godswalk Wars had passed it by completely. As though all the armies involved had conspired together to simply let it stand.

Even from the road, Aefric could see the granite of the older buildings, and the wood or wood over granite of the newer buildings, without spotting a single demolished or burnt ruin.

Life bustled in Norrtarr. He could smell their cook and work fires, and the aromas of some of that cooking. He could even hear smiths hammering and other such work sounds in the distance.

Fortunate, those people. And fortunate their baroness, whose castle sat a hill just a hair south of the town.

But the baroness was not in that castle. As Aefric approached the town along the Kingsroad, he saw her sitting a palomino horse in the road ahead of him, accompanied by a half-dozen knights in full plate.

One of them held the Norra banner high: a white horse, rampant, on a sky blue background.

Baroness Herewyn Ol'Norette had seen only about five summers more than Aefric, but she held herself with such poise and confidence that for a moment he felt like an awkward teen again.

She wore a forest green tunic over dark, reddish-brown riding leathers and high, hard leather boots. She bore a short sword at her belt, and just enough gold at her wrists and her pale throat to catch the sun. Though her shimmering, waist-length red hair did an even better job of that, worn loose and flowing down past her shoulders.

"Your grace," she called by way of a greeting, before anyone could announce either of them. She hopped off her saddle to land effortlessly on the road.

Baroness Herewyn bowed deeply. "It is with great joy that I welcome you to Norra once more. Would that I could offer your grace the hospitality of my home for a time, while we await the arrival of our king and queen, though I suspect that will not be possible."

"Why not?" Aefric asked, swinging down from the back of Windsong, and approaching so he could kiss the baroness' hand.

"The rika from your seneschal made clear that your grace intends to meet their majesties on the Kingsroad." She shook her head. "My scouts tell me that will not be possible today, nor perhaps tomorrow."

"They can't be moving that slowly," Aefric said, running calculations in his head. "But if they are, maybe I can meet them by Kerrik after all."

"Alas," Baroness Herewyn said, "speed is not the problem."

Cold suspicion ran down Aefric's back.

"Your lordship is trying not to tell me something," he said carefully. "But I think it's better if I'm told."

"I merely wished to prepare your grace, rather than spring the bad news on him."

Her mouth flattened into a line of distaste.

"Their majesties were met along the Kingsroad this morning, as they reached the town of Drywood."

Aefric sighed. "You don't mean by your people, do you."

It wasn't a question, but she answered it anyway.

"No, your grace. Their majesties were met by Count Ferrin of Motte, who escorted them north into his lands to host them for the night."

Count Ferrin of Motte. The vassal who had actively worked against Aefric this past spring, and now was the vassal most likely to try to make Aefric look bad.

"I wish I could stay," Aefric started but stopped as Baroness Herewyn nodded.

"I understand completely, your grace," she said, and gestured for someone to approach.

Apparently there was a seventh rider back behind the knights. The woman who approached who could only have been a scout. And not just because she wore brown and green leathers instead of full plate, carried a bow, and rode a light, swift-looking brown gelding instead of a warhorse.

She just had the look of a woman who was more at home alone among the trees than she'd ever be at any court. Or perhaps even in a house.

"This is Payoom," Baroness Herewyn said. "She followed where Motte led."

Payoom nodded. "King Colm's entourage was too big to go far. I can get your grace to them before full night, if we leave at once."

"Thank you," Aefric said, then kissed Baroness Herewyn's hand again. "And thank *you*, your lordship."

"My pleasure, your grace. Happy hunting."

---

AEFRIC HAD ONLY EVER ENTERED MOTTE ONCE, AND HE HADN'T BEEN ahorse then.

No, this was back when Aefric was first settling himself as duke. He hadn't even been to Water's End yet, instead taking care of business from Behal.

Count Ferrin, in his arrogance, had thought himself safely ensconced in his Castle Kirandai when he threatened to take up arms against his rightful liege.

Aefric had used the Brightstaff to transform himself into a bolt of lightning. He flashed across the intervening miles, blew open the doors of Castle Kirandai and humiliated the count in front of his court.

But they couldn't be riding for Castle Kirandai. It sat at near the northeast corner of Motte. Easily two days' travel from the Kingsroad, for a group the size of the royal party. Possibly three.

They were met this morning. Turned somewhere north, but were someplace that Aefric could reach with only a few hours' ride...

Of course, they had to push their horses a bit for that ride. Fortunately, Aefric had been free with the rests earlier in the day, believing they would easily outpace the royal party to Norrtarr.

The path Payoom led them clung to the Kingsroad just long enough to get clear of the last of Motte's nearby marshes, then cut an angle northeast across the drier plains.

Motte had never built much near the Kingsroad to begin with. And since the wars, they hadn't rebuilt any of their lost towns and farms close to their southern border.

So far as Aefric knew, the only town Motte had along the Kingsroad was Drywood, back at the western edge of the Kerrik Forest.

So it was across plains and hills that Payoom led them through the last dregs of the afternoon. But as evening approached, Aefric decided he didn't like what he was seeing among his horses.

Too much effort. Too much spittle. Too much sweat. Eyes that looked less and less settled.

Aefric called the halt while the burning red of the western skies hadn't quite reached the blue above the Kerrik Forest to the east.

"Your grace," Payoom said quickly, "if we take time to rest the horses, we'll never make that castle before full dark."

"We won't," Aefric said. "If we try, we may well lose at least one of these horses. There's a better path here."

"Your grace," Payoom said hesitantly, looking around as though trying to see a road where there was none.

"This is what we're going to do," Aefric said. "The soldiers will stay here with the horses. Camp for the night. When they do, you're welcome to join our camp, or return to Norra."

"But," Payoom said slowly, "I thought it was important that your grace reached their majesties tonight."

"It is," Aefric said. He dug his backpack out of his saddlebag. Dug through the backpack for a gift he'd gotten from the king. Something that looked for all the world like a little toy coach.

He set the toy coach down, and whispered its keyword. "*Arcoa.*"

The coach sprang into the air and changed into a full-size, enclosed carriage with an audible *pop*

The coach was ebony, trimmed with gold leaf, and bore the Deepwater sigil on each of its two doors, and on pennants that flew from each corner.

Aefric knew from experience that the two bench seats within were padded and upholstered in pale gray silk, with the Deepwater sigil embroidered on the backs of the seats. The floor was likewise carpeted in pale gray.

"Your grace," Ser Beornric said softly. "As I recall, there's room enough inside for the two of us and all six of your knights, leaving seats for four on the outside. Should your grace wish to bring any soldiers."

"I do not," Aefric said, quietly. "I'd rather leave them here as a unit, and traveling as a unit." He turned to Payoom. "What is the name of the place Count Ferrin took their majesties?"

"He calls it Forest's Edge, your grace," she said. "It sits at the northwest tip of Kerrik Forest. The fastest way there—"

"The carriage will know," Aefric said confidently.

Payoom bowed. "Then, if I may, I shall remain with your grace's soldiers tonight and lead them to Forest's Edge in the morning."

"I would appreciate that," Aefric said. "Thank you."

Then it was just a matter of getting his soldiers started on setting up camp, with full instructions about how to handle any contact they received.

Once that was done, Aefric boarded the coach, while his knights strapped their luggage to the top, before joining him inside.

Once all eight of them were seated, Aefric addressed the carriage. "Forest's Edge."

The carriage shot forward as though pulled by a team of speeding horses.

Aefric knew from experience that the carriage would follow the road by preference. But as they were not on a road right now, it simply took the most direct, available route.

"This is spooky," Ser Wardius said, gazing out a window. It felt odd to hear a man as scarred as Ser Wardius call anything "spooky." Especially something as familiar to Aefric as magic.

"I can see how uneven the land is beneath us," he continued, "But..."

"But the carriage seems to smooth it out," Aefric said. "Wonderful design, this carriage. A good deal of subtle magic to it."

They sped across the countryside faster than Aefric would have pushed his horses if they were fresh. As though the carriage had sensed his urgency, and was trying to make the trip as short as possible.

The skies ahead of them were just darkening towards night as Ser Temat, who had been angling out the window to keep an eye on the road ahead of them called out, "Lights ahead. Has to be a castle."

A speculation he shortly confirmed, as they closed the distance.

Finally the carriage rolled to a halt. Sers Temat and Vria leapt out first, checking the surroundings.

Aefric moved to join them, but Ser Beornric shook his head. Said softly, "We've likely reached the castle walls. Better your grace doesn't step out until we're past the gates. Looks better."

Aefric nodded and sat back, drumming his fingers impatiently.

He did, at least, look out the window to his right. In the rising night, he couldn't see as much as he might have liked, but he could see the beginnings of Kerrik Forest. Here he saw mostly beeches, elms, and oaks.

"Ho! Gatekeeper!" Ser Vria called out.

"Who calls?" came the response. A male voice, but not very deep.

"I am Ser Vria Aldellac, and beside me stands Ser Temat Ol'Lazenac. We are knights in service to his grace, Ser Aefric Bright-staff, Duke of Deepwater, Baron of Netar, and Hero of the Battles of Deepwater and Frozen Ridge, who awaits entry into your castle."

Silence.

For a long moment, Aefric could hear only the buzzing of night insects. The cries of a few birds. The impatient rustling of the knights around him on the seats.

Aefric wondered at the hesitation. Was the gatekeeper staring at the beauty of Ser Vria's eldrani heritage? The pure orange in her hair? Or was he perhaps wondering about the wicked scar across the dark skin of Ser Temat's neck?

Or was it worse than either?

Were they considering denying Aefric entrance?

"Is there some problem with your gate?" Ser Vria asked. "That you must keep your rightful overlord waiting in this fashion?"

"I have no standing orders about the unannounced arrival of his grace," the gatekeeper called back. "I have sent a runner for instructions."

"How can there be any question in this matter?" Ser Vria asked, now letting impatience show through in her voice. "Count Ferrin Ol'Nylla rules here, yes, but he rules in the names of Duke Aefric Brightstaff and King Colm Stronghand. One of whom is being kept waiting, even as I speak."

"And I do apologize for that wait," the gatekeeper called down. "But this is not my decision to make."

"Refusal could be taken as an act of insurrection by your count," Ser Vria said sharply. "I ask again. How can there be any question of admitting his grace?"

"I'm sure it won't come to that," the gatekeeper said. "But I have been given instructions that today I may only admit those whose names are on a list in my possession. His grace's name is not on that list."

"An obvious oversight," Ser Vria said. "And the sun is setting. If it sets fully without his grace being offered proper hospitality, the consequences for your master could be profoundly unfortunate."

"Oh, she's good," Ser Arras said softly, admiration in her hazel eyes. "Just the right tones. Just the right timing."

"Duchess Arinda taught her personally," Ser Micham said, toying with the half-ear he'd lost to a borog's spear during the wars. "Back when she was a page."

"One moment," the gatekeeper called. And then another voice replaced his.

A male voice that affected a world-weary tone.

"Ah, Ser Vria is it?"

"I am," she answered. "And beside me stands Ser Temat. With whom am I now speaking?"

"I am Ler Tanaron Ol'Yorett. And while his excellency would normally be most pleased by the ... sudden and unexpected arrival of his grace, I'm afraid that admittance tonight is not a possibility."

"You dare refuse your overlord?"

"Such an accusation is most unwarranted," Ler Tanaron said. "It isn't a matter of refusal, my good knight, but a matter of practicality. His excellency's castle is full to bursting with royal guests. There's simply no room for his grace, to say nothing of more knights."

"This is unacceptable," Ser Vria spat.

"Yes, I know," the ler said. "But what can be done? At least half of their majesties' entourage will be camping in the castle courtyard as it is. There's hardly enough room to walk about. Admitting another guest, even one as ... important as his grace, is simply not an option for us."

Within the carriage, the yellow diamond atop the Brightstaff in Aefric's hand began to glow.

Aefric realized then that his grip on the staff had gotten white-knuckled, and that he could feel anger roil in his stomach, and tense his arms and shoulders.

"Your grace," Ser Beornric said urgently. "You mustn't. Not with their majesties present."

"I know," he said through gritted teeth, while outside Ser Vria continued arguing with Ler Tanaron. "Ferrin's probably trying to get me to do something violent, flashy and magical. Probably even ... warned ... their majesties..."

"Your grace," Ser Beornric said in a warning tone. He raised his hands as though ready to grab Aefric, if Aefric tried anything.

But Aefric smiled. Started laughing, low and apparently menacingly enough to disturb his knights. They all gave him concerned looks.

But the diamond atop the Brightstaff dimmed.

"I know what to do," he said.

"Your grace," Ser Beornric said again. If anything, he sounded even more cautious.

"Have no fear, Beornric," Aefric said. "I won't do anything violent."

As a gesture of trust, Ser Beornric sat back. But he ran his fingers over his bushy salt-and-pepper mustaches nervously.

With but a few words and a quick pulse of power, Aefric cast a spell that would carry his next words to the ears of the king.

"Your majesty. I apologize for not meeting your party at Kerrik. But apparently my count reached you first. I would join you at Forest's Edge, but it seems my recalcitrant vassal intends to refuse me entrance. I shall find a place to camp and meet your majesty in the morning."

With that, Aefric felt a sense of closure, as the spell completed and those words were whisked through the aether to the ears of King Colm.

Aefric smiled at Ser Beornric. "Give Ser Vria another minute or two to argue, then call her and Ser Temat back over."

"We're going to camp, instead?" Ser Beornric asked dubiously.

"I doubt that a great deal," Aefric said, smiling even wider.

---

It was never necessary to call Sers Vria and Temat back over to the carriage. Ser Vria had hardly exchanged another dozen arguments with Ler Tanaron before Aefric heard the creaking and grinding of something being raised or lowered.

Raised, if it was a portcullis. Lowered, if a drawbridge.

Sers Vria and Temat mounted the seats atop the carriage that would normally have been used by the driver, and the carriage began to roll.

No bridge to roll over, so it must have been a portcullis being raised. They rolled through an arched, torchlit passage of pale granite and into a courtyard by twilight.

Sers Vria and Temat leapt down from their perch, and opened the doors of the carriage.

Aefric allowed the knights of his personal guard to precede him out, gathering their baggage from the top of the carriage before forming up on the right-hand side.

The left-hand door was closed as the last of them left through it to join the formation.

Ser Beornric exited next, through the open right-hand door, and stood to one side. He called out in a ringing voice, "His grace, Ser Aefric Brightstaff, Duke of Deepwater, Baron of Netar, and Hero of the Battles of Deepwater and Frozen Ridge."

Thus announced, Aefric stepped out, whispering the word, "*Arcoa*," as his boot touched the dirt of the courtyard.

There was a slight sucking sound in the air as the carriage resumed its toy form once more, which Aefric called to his hand with a gesture, and tucked into the backpack which waited at his feet.

The torchlit courtyard was large enough to host a decent tourney, though tonight it was full of tents and pavilions. So that much had been true, at least.

Surrounding the courtyard on three sides was a reasonably tall castle wall, with a series of towers spaced along it, and crenellations facing outward.

On the fourth side of the courtyard, directly ahead of Aefric, was the keep itself. Two wide stories of pale stone, with small towers at the corners, and a half-size third story in the center.

The tents and pavilions were abuzz with activity, but closer to Aefric — just on the other side of his wedge of knights — were about three dozen Motte soldiers. All in chainmail, all with spears. And all with those spears held ready, albeit not actively menacing.

"Your grace," a familiar voice called down from the wall. "Their majesties shall be out to greet you shortly."

It was a young woman's voice. And Aefric knew that voice, but had not heard it for some time...

He looked up into the smiling green eyes of a woman who looked very much like Duchess Herewyn must have, when she was no more than a summer past the age of majority.

Her cousin, Sighild Ol'Masarkor.

Aefric had met Sighild on the day he was made duke. She had been attending on Countess Faenella Darkwalker at the time. He then got to know her a little as Faenella and Aefric had ridden back into Deepwater together.

But Aefric hadn't seen Sighild since he briefly visited Faenella's county, Fyretti, toward the end of spring.

"Sighild," he said. "I didn't know you'd be here. How lovely to see you."

She suddenly seemed very shy, but was saved from replying when a commanding voice boomed across the courtyard.

"Your grace! Good of you to join us."

The crowd over by the pavilions parted, and King Colm Strong-hand approached. The rich black of the king's hair and mustache might have touches of gray, and his ruggedly handsome features might show a few lines when he smiled, as he did now, but his powerful frame still moved like a jungle cat as he crossed the courtyard.

His majesty was dressed in a velvet doublet of rich, quilted purple, over a briskly white tunic, belted with a sash of cloth-of-gold, over dark leggings.

Keeping pace with the king came Queen Eppida, also smiling. The pace kept her long, golden curls bouncing on her shoulders. Her silk gown matched the purple of the king's doublet, and was embroidered in golden thread at the cuffs, along the bodice, and forming the Armyrian royal oak tree on the skirts.

And, of course, she wore that golden torc at her neck. There was something familiar about the magic of that torc, but Aefric had never taken the time to investigate it.

Queen Eppida was King Colm's second wife, and much younger than the king. In fact, she was about the same age as the royal twins, Prince Killian and Princess Maev.

King Colm had not yet lost all of his battlefield tan from the wars — which made Aefric wonder if the king made some effort to maintain it — but Queen Eppida was fashionably pale.

In the wake of their majesties followed a variety of courtiers and knights, some of the latter of whom were rushing to get out ahead of their monarchs, for their protection.

Three of those knights stood out. The breastplates of their full plate had been etched with the golden oak tree of Armyr, marking them as Knights of the Crown. A dozen knights, said to be the finest in all Armyr, who were tasked with protecting the king and queen.

The Motte soldiers in front of Aefric looked irritated, but parted quickly for the oncoming royalty.

Aefric's knights parted smoothly, as though this were something they practiced.

"Your majesties," Aefric said, passing the Brightstaff to his left hand, taking a knee and offering his right to his liege.

King Colm kissed Aefric's hand. Rather than stand immediately,

Aefric then offered his hand to the queen.

She looked surprised by the offer, but pleased, and made a point of kissing Aefric's hand before saying, "Please rise, my good duke."

"Good to see you getting some use out of my present," King Colm said. "Do you travel by that carriage often then?"

"I save it for special needs," Aefric said. "We covered many miles by horse today, but to reach Forest's Edge before full dark, I either needed to switch to the carriage, or risk killing a horse or two."

"A fine choice then," Queen Eppida said. "Neither of us would see your grace kill horses on our account."

"Your majesty is most kind," Aefric said with a small bow. "Our horses remain with the rest of my entourage, the soldiers of my personal guard, where they camp for the night before joining us tomorrow."

"So you *did* make a personal guard of those soldiers I gave you," King Colm said, nodding approval. "You are pleased with their service?"

"Most pleased," Aefric said. "And the knight you sent to lead them, Ser Beornric Ol'Sandallas," — Aefric paused so Ser Beornric could bow to their majesties — "has become one of my most trusted advisers."

"Wonderful," Queen Eppida said. "While dear Beornric here prefers to be known for his skill at arms, he is of an *old* noble family. No doubt his guidance has been most useful."

"Most useful," Aefric agreed, and while Ser Beornric tried to affect a straight face, Aefric could tell the knight was pleased.

"And I must say, that was a *wonderful* spell you used to contact me, your grace," King Colm said, smiling. "I would have sworn you were standing just to my left, speaking in a clear voice."

"Yes," Queen Eppida said, arching an eyebrow. "Quite disconcerting, I can tell you, to have him facing me and speaking to your grace."

"Forgive me, your majesty," Aefric said, "But that form of the spell did not allow for a response. I hadn't expected that your majesty would be familiar enough with such magics to time his response correctly."

"I have no experience with such spells at all," King Colm said, shaking his head. "I just assumed response was an option. So you didn't hear me tell you that I'd see about this business of your camping outside?"

"Forgive me, majesty," Count Ferrin said, pushing past the courtiers to join the conversation.

While Aefric considered Ler Ordnoth a fine example of a fop, the ler was still a student beside the master of foppery who was Count Ferrin.

His long brown hair was streaked with dark blonde. His skin was even paler than the queen's. The clothes adorning his slender form seemed to have more brocade and lace than base material, and their reds and yellows were ... well, had Aefric been well-disposed toward Count Ferrin, he might have thought of them as eye-catching.

As it was, he considered them garish. And that was without considering that Count Ferrin wore more gold and jewels than both the king and queen combined.

The count, at least, was unarmed in the presence of the king and queen.

"But as I said," the count continued, "this is only my secondary castle. Hardly more than a hunting lodge. And with so many guests there's simply nowhere to lodge his grace, let alone more knights."

"Nonsense," King Colm said with a dismissive wave of his hand. "Room could be found for his grace's knights in our own pavilion. And as for his grace—"

"I have a thought regarding his grace," Queen Eppida cut in. Mischief danced in her eyes, which were the same sapphire color as her sisters'.

"Yes, my dear?" King Colm asked, though from the smile in his smoke gray eyes, he already knew what she'd say.

"I see a quite agreeable solution regarding his grace's lodgings for the night," she said with a small smile. "Assuming my little sister hasn't stolen his grace's heart so thoroughly that he has become immune to the charms of all other women?"

The noble privilege with Queen Eppida herself? The idea had

been suggested, back when Ser Grey first explained the practice to Aefric.

But he never expected it to actually *happen*...

"I can assure your majesty," Ser Beornric said quietly, "that his grace enjoyed the noble privilege just last night, with Ler Idrina Ol'Teyruun of Felspark."

"Marvelous," Queen Eppida said. "Then unless your grace has any objections to *me*, I believe the matter of his lodging tonight is settled."

"But, your majesty," Count Ferrin objected. "I believe I mentioned that I intend to have both your majesties offered *leaba* tonight."

"And I look forward to it," King Colm said. "It's been ages since anyone offered me *leaba*. But I think it's clear that my queen has other plans for the evening, assuming his grace is willing."

Aefric knew he was free to accept or refuse, but he still found himself feeling a little cornered...

He shook that feeling away. The queen was undeniably beautiful, and that she wanted to spend the night with him was likely one of the highest compliments he might ever receive.

"*More* than willing, your majesty," Aefric said with a smile and a bow. "I can think of nothing I would enjoy more."

"Then it's settled," King Colm said, clapping his hands together, then rubbing them. "And now, I think our good count here said something about dinner?"

Count Ferrin almost missed his cue. He was too busy trying to set Aefric on fire with his glare. But Aefric had been glared at by far better men and women than the count, and met that glare with nothing more than mild amusement.

It took one of his courtiers clearing her throat to prompt Count Ferrin into saying, "Of course, your majesty. Dinner should be ready even now."

THE GREAT HALL AT FOREST'S EDGE WAS ABOUT THE SAME SIZE AS THE great hall in the castle at Tafarac, in Felspark, which Aefric found an odd coincidence.

Tafarac's castle was far older than this one, so likely the same builder didn't design both. Was it simply that secondary castles were expected to have squared great halls that measured some sixty feet to a side?

If so, Behal was an exception. Of course, Behal might've been the original ducal seat of Deepwater. At least, if there were any truth at all behind that song Aefric had heard about the dragon that had come out of Lake Deepwater, and the man named Behal who had placated the dragon with songs.

The walls of Forest Edge's great hall were covered in tapestries that featured battle scenes and hunts, no doubt highlighting famous deeds by past counts and countesses of Motte.

Aefric had his troubles with Count Ferrin, certainly, but clearly the Ol'Nylla family had held these lands for a long time.

The stone floors of the great hall were entirely covered in rugs of woven rushes, but there'd already been so much movement in the hall that when Aefric entered, they weren't all lying flat anymore.

The hall was packed with rectangular tables, with benches for seats. A dozen or so of the tables at the far end of the hall from its tall, arched double doors had ... passable white linen tablecloths. But most of those tables lacked both tablecloths and placemats.

And some of the uncovered tables at the back had visible gouges and scratches on their pale wood.

The three wheel-shaped chandeliers that hung down from the ceiling didn't cast enough light for all the tables, so tables closer to the edges also had candelabras.

It was clear that Count Ferrin had put this "feast" together quickly. And that he'd saved his best of everything for the royal table.

The royal table sat atop a dais at the far end of the hall. Also rectangular, but it had individual chairs with seating for six, all along one side, so that the diners would be facing the room.

The table, and the chairs, were covered in cloth-of-gold. More gold for the candelabras, plates, goblets and utensils.

No space was made for Ser Beornric at the royal table, but Aefric raised no objection. With only six seats available, Aefric was already bumping one diner off that table, and bumping a second, well, would have been difficult.

Obviously their majesties, the count, and Aefric had to be there. Which left two remaining chairs. One of them going to Ser Beatritz, Captain of the Knights of the Crown, and the other to Karna Duisdottir, Count Ferrin's fiancée.

Unseating either of those two would have been petty.

As it was, the queen herself rearranged the diners before they took their seats. The king and queen remained in the place of honor in the center of the table.

Originally, the count would have sat between the king and ... whoever Aefric replaced. Likely an important counselor of the count's. Karna Duisdottir would have sat between the queen and Ser Beatritz.

After the queen's rearrangement, Aefric sat between the king and Ser Beatritz, and Count Ferrin sat between the queen and Karna Duisdottir.

The count's fiancée was taller than he was, though she was about as slender. She had the palest blonde hair Aefric had ever seen on a human, styled into ringlets. She wore a red, taffeta gown, that showed yellow silk beneath the slashes of its sleeves and skirts.

She wore a necklace of amber, and a trio of golden bracelets on each delicate wrist.

The gown style, the hairstyle, the name ... it seemed the count intended to marry into a Malimfari noble family. Interesting. Especially considering that Malimfar had manipulated him into rebelling against Aefric this past spring.

Although, at the time, Count Ferrin had been led to believe that Merrek was the source of his "support," not Malimfar.

Had Aefric ever gotten around to correcting that misbelief? He couldn't remember...

He must've. He must've told Ser Beornric to reveal the truth to the count, when he sent Beornric with a company to make clear Aefric's reclaiming of the mines in the Threepeaks.

Ser Beatritz was shorter than anyone at the table except the queen, and dressed in a tunic and leggings of the royal colors, under a tabard bearing the Armyrian royal sigil of a golden oak tree on a background of forest green.

Her graying chestnut hair was bound in a braid that passed her shoulders. Her body was thick with muscle, and her hands were scarred and calloused from her years in the field, much as those of Sers Beornric and Yrsa were.

Ser Beatritz had a scar along the right side of her jaw that looked as though an arrow had skimmed her face and taken off an earlobe. Apart from the Brightstaff, she carried the only weapon at the table, a greatsword strapped to her back.

Their majesties sat, allowing the rest of their table to be seated, which allowed the rest of the diners to sit as well.

So many people were crammed into this great hall that the rustling of their clothes as they sat sounded like a brief gale force wind across acres of overripe corn.

The count didn't serve a palate wine. Instead, his servants poured a sweet white wine to compliment a salad of spiced greens and tiny river shrimp, under a mustard sauce.

Too much sauce and too much spice, which made Aefric question the quality of both the greens and the river shrimp.

He'd barely gotten his first taste when both the king and Ser Beatritz leaned in closer.

"Your grace did not rush all this way simply to meet me in the road," the king said quietly. "Had you suggested it, Ser Calder would have raised a fuss, and that seneschal of yours — Kentigern, is it? — would have given you five or six sound reasons why it was a bad idea."

"Neither of them uttered a word of complaint," Aefric said, but before he could say more, Ser Beatritz cut in.

"Yes," she said impatiently, "because they knew most would attribute the move to the restless feet of a retired adventurer. But I only needed one look at your grace to see the lie in that, and I believe the same can be said of his majesty."

"It can," King Colm said. "So, my dear duke, where is the danger you've come to save me from?"

"In truth?" Aefric asked quietly, with a sigh. "I don't know."

He explained about the Malimfari knights, and his suspicion that they were the obvious threat, suggesting that an inobvious threat would strike somewhere along the road.

"Interesting that his grace suggests this," Ser Beatritz said. "Considering the high standing of our host's intended."

"I'm not familiar with her," Aefric said.

"She's a third cousin to Crown Princess Astrid," King Colm said, "and part of the royal family. A real prize, for a mere count."

The three of them shared a significant look. The king, of course, knew all about the work of Malimfar's agents in Deepwater this past spring, as well as that kingdom's attempted assault on Armyr's southern border.

"One of the knights in Water's End right now is a Duisson," Aefric said. "Could be her brother."

"Could be," King Colm said, then turned to Ser Beatritz. "Find out."

"I shall have the truth by sunrise, your majesty," she said with a slight bow of her head.

"Excellent," King Colm said. "And because I do not believe our duke prone to panic, we shall have to adjust our route and timetable for the remainder of the trip, to throw off any plans made by our enemies."

"Then stopping here was to our advantage," Ser Beatritz said, and she sounded a bit disappointed. "It wasn't what we planned."

"True," King Colm said, "but that may depend a great deal on the innocence or guilt of a certain guest."

"Not necessarily," Aefric said.

"Whatever could be so troubling you three?" Queen Eppida asked with laughter in her voice. "I haven't seen such serious faces since we told Killian that he couldn't go hunting with his friends because we needed him to sit regent for a time."

Before any of them could respond, she said something softer that Aefric couldn't hear. In fact, if he hadn't seen her throat move, he might not have known she'd spoken at all.

King Colm laughed loud enough to draw attention from nearby tables.

"Forgive me, my love," King Colm said, still laughing, before turning to Aefric. "Please, your grace, I ask your forgiveness as well. It was a small joke, and one Beatritz and I planned to spring when we reached Water's End. But as you came to us, I could not resist playing it early."

Even Ser Beatritz was smiling now, though Aefric wasn't sure that smile reached her eyes.

"No forgiveness is needed, your majesty," Aefric said, but before he could continue, King Colm spoke over him.

"Now, your grace," he said, shaking one finger at him. "Don't hold a grudge. I'm not *actually* insulted that you haven't visited Netar yet. I just couldn't resist making you think I was."

"Your majesty," Aefric said, affecting a troubled smile, "was most convincing."

King Colm laughed again, and shook Aefric's shoulder.

"Come, come," King Colm said. "Even if I *had* been offended, your grace's reasons were all quite valid. Please. Say you forgive me."

"Of course I forgive your majesty," Aefric said, slowly, as though he still felt unsure. "And I am grateful that your majesty thinks highly enough of me to play such a joke on me."

"Much better," King Colm said, and clapped Aefric on the back. "Now, let me tell you all about Netar, and perhaps whet your appetite to visit it before the rains come."

And with that, they stuck to smaller topics for the rest of the meal. Which made Aefric more and more curious just what Queen Eppida had said under her breath.

Dinner was over. Aefric had seen to his knights, and made sure that they were squared away in the pavilion for the night.

It was an impressive pavilion, some forty feet across, and made of the royal gold and green. Though it wasn't the pavilion of the king and queen themselves.

This was the pavilion set aside for the Knights of the Crown.

If any of them were offended that they had to share space with Aefric's knights, they had the good grace not to say so.

Once that was taken care of, Aefric donned his pack and followed a page through the surprisingly cold stone hallways of Forest's Edge, up two flights of stairs, and finally to a room guarded by two women in plate armor, whose breastplates had been etched with the golden oak tree of Armyr.

It seemed that at least two of the Crown Knights would not need their space in the pavilion that night.

Both women wore their hair cut so short Aefric couldn't tell the color. They both carried longswords naked in their hands, though with points down as Aefric approached.

They regarded Aefric with hard expressions.

One of them extended her hand. "The wand."

"I beg your pardon?" Aefric asked.

"Her majesty says that stick of yours" — she nodded at the Brightstaff, held in Aefric's right hand — "goes everywhere with you, so by her order you get to hold onto it. She said nothing about your coming into her royal presence with a wand."

"I wore the wand to dinner as well," Aefric said. "Didn't even think about it. Forgot I was wearing it. It's the wand Garram, a gift from his majesty."

"Then we will take good care of it for your grace, and return it promptly when your grace departs. But your grace will not pass us, armed with that wand."

Silliness. Aefric knew a great many spells that needed no wand, nor any other object.

But this was not a fight worth having.

He undid his leather belt, removed the wand and its sheath, and handed them both to the demanding knight before refastening his belt.

She bowed. "My thanks, your grace."

Her partner knocked on the door, then opened it a crack and announced, "His grace, Ser Aefric Brightstaff, Duke of Deepwater, has come in response to your majesty's summons."

"Then by all means admit him." Queen Eppida's voice, and she sounded amused.

Shock slackened Aefric's jaw as he entered the room and the knights closed the door behind him.

Count Ferrin had provided Queen Eppida only a single chamber, for her use.

A bed. An armoire. A copper basin and ewer. A small couch, beside an unimpressive bookshelf. Fresh rugs of woven rushes, at least, filling the room with a sweet smell.

And, of course, the requisite tapestries depicting the heroism of past counts and countesses of Motte.

There was a small window, past the bed, though the shutters were shut fast. And there was a fire in the hearth, which must've been necessary, because the room was pleasantly warm, but not hot.

"I'd like to think *I* put that look on your grace's face," Queen Eppida said, still sounding amused, "but I believe I made the same expression myself when I saw the 'accommodations' provided for me."

She looked about and shook her head.

"At least his excellency showed no preference, providing a similar chamber for his majesty. Still. I cannot believe he has none better. Which is enough to make one wonder just how good an impression your Count Ferrin truly wishes to make."

Aefric was still looking around at the furnishings. They weren't even of greenwood or blackwood, let alone calinwood. Nothing more than red oak, or maybe cherry. Passable, but hardly appropriate for royal chambers. Which would suggest that the count — or perhaps a predecessor — had been foolish enough to assume he'd never host the king and queen.

No. It was impossible that he had *nothing* better than this. After all, this room would be an inadequate offering for Aefric, and it simply wasn't possible that the designer ignored the possibility of hosting the count's liege.

Which suggested—

Her majesty gently cleared her throat.

Aefric turned his attention to the queen, and found himself much more pleasantly stunned.

She had unpinned those of her long golden curls that Aefric hadn't realized had been bound up earlier. Because now her locks fell past her smooth, pale shoulders both in front and back.

She'd changed out of her gown, and exchanged it for ... well ... it would have looked like a simple peasant's dress. But white linen of the clinging gown looked soft, and was so thin that Aefric found himself getting a very good idea of just what the queen would look like once she disrobed.

And oh, she would be a sight to see. Slender, yet shapely, there was no denying the woman's beauty of form, as well as face.

And then there was the complete show of trust she gave Aefric, by forgoing her golden torc and its protective magics.

"Much better," she said, clearly enjoying his reaction.

"Your majesty is beautiful beyond words."

"You are sweet to say so," she said. "But I am all too aware that you have seen Byrhta Ol'Caran in all her glory. Beside her I must seem positively mannish."

Aefric shook his head.

"Every morning at Water's End," he said, "I get the delight of seeing the sun rise above shimmering, glorious Lake Deepwater. And every sunrise is so beautiful it makes my heart ache. How, then, could I ever say one day's sunrise is more beautiful than that of the day before it?"

Queen Eppida gave Aefric a small smile that made her look more beautiful still.

"I thought you were a wizard," she said. "Not a skald."

"Beauty inspires us all, your majesty."

"No," she said with a firm shake of her head. She sighed. "Hazard a guess. How many times do you think I've sought the noble privilege since I married Colm?"

"Three?" he said, picking a number at random, aiming for the low side.

"Tonight included, one," she said, raising a single index finger to emphasize her point. She lowered it as she began to cross the room toward him.

The shift of her hips was mesmerizing.

"I am a woman of exacting tastes," she continued. "A handsome face is not enough to thrill me. Nor is a scar or two, nor long list of deeds."

She stopped just out of arm's reach. Looked Aefric up and down.

"I require a man to be both handsome enough to please my eyes, and exciting enough to make me *burn* for him. Colm has so much of both that most other men leave me cold."

She closed that last gap. Aefric dropped his pack. Set the Bright-staff to stand beside him.

She put her hands on his chest. Ran them slowly over the silk of his navy blue tunic.

She spoke looking up into his eyes.

"You tempted me even at Armityr on the day you were made duke," Queen Eppida said. "Still, I wasn't sure. I thought I would play with the notion of seeking the bliss moment with you as we rode across your lands, and decide at Water's End."

She quirked a smile. Reached up and stroked his cheek.

"But here, you rode to our rescue from some threat we didn't even see."

"I—"

She shook her head. "Don't bother denying it. I saw it in your eyes the moment you stepped out of that carriage. The concern. The readiness to bring your many powers to our aid."

She cocked an eyebrow. "You started telling my husband all about it at dinner, even though doing so would have made clear to even the most foolish that something dangerous was afoot."

Aefric nodded. "There are—"

She put her fingers to his lips to stop him.

"Tomorrow," she said. "Tell me of the threat tomorrow. Tonight, I know you will keep me safe."

Aefric nodded. She lowered her fingers.

"So tonight, let us dispense with titles and formalities. Until the morning demands that we resume our roles, let us be only Aefric and Eppida. A man and a woman, come together for a night of passion."

Aefric opened his mouth to speak, but she put her fingers to his lips again.

"Don't tell me yes, Aefric. *Show* me yes."

He grabbed her in his arms and kissed her hard and deep. He could taste the dregs of bitter nysta tea on her tongue, but by now that taste was coming to excite him further.

Eppida made small sounds of approval as she kissed him back with equal fervor. When that kiss broke, Aefric began nibbling along her neck, taking in her sweet, vaguely citrus scent as she whispered, "Harder. Bite harder."

When he did, she shuddered, and began yanking at his belt. He moved back to give her room.

Seams tore as she ripped off his clothes and left him standing naked and ready before her.

"Oh, yes," she said breathlessly, looking him up and down, circling him to take in the whole view. "Yes. Those scars. Those muscles. Perfect."

Aefric moved to grab the thin material of her gown, but she deflected his hands and shook her head.

"No," she said, voice low with desire. "Use *magic*, Aefric. Rip this gown from my flesh with your spells."

He almost cast the same spell he'd used to disrobe Zoleen, but Eppida had said *rip*. So instead, he made fists, using magic to grip the collar of her thin gown.

He yanked his hands apart, the gown tore in half with a loud ripping sound. He cast the rent halves of the garment aside, leaving Eppida gasping and wonderfully naked before him.

"Come, Aefric," she said, turning her back. "Catch me and take me."

She led him on a short chase, but made no effort to get away. Really, Aefric was sure she just wanted to get them both to the bed quickly.

Well, and perhaps she wanted to feel him *grab* her. Because when he did, she made a sound that could only have been pleasure.

Then, on that soft bed, they came together in earnest.

---

WHEN AEFRIC AWOKE THE NEXT MORNING, HE FELT AS THOUGH HE'D been through a strangely enjoyable skirmish.

Eppida was a wild woman in bed. Both giving and demanding at the same time.

His muscles ached, but in a good way. As though he'd spent hours on the training grounds. And she'd left scratches all over Aefric's back, his shoulders, and his posterior. She'd marked his shoulders and his scars with hickeys, as well.

Aefric had left similar marks — hickeys, not scratches — in several places on her body, too. Receiving them seemed to heighten her pleasure, at critical moments.

Of course, he'd left no marks where they would show, once she was dressed. She *was* the queen, after all.

Her golden curls were as messy as the sheets around them, but her eyes were bright.

"Good morning," Eppida said with a warm smile, and leaned in for the first slow, soft kiss she'd given him. "I must say, that was exactly what I needed. We may have to do this again sometime."

Aefric reached out and stroked her cheek.

"Anytime, Eppida."

She flicked her tongue across his lips. Grabbed his wrists and pinned them to the bed while swinging one leg over him.

"No time like the present," she said. "Might as well have a little more fun before we must resume our roles."

She leaned down to bite … his neck, most likely. That seemed to be her preferred way to start. But her descent was interrupted.

A soft knock sounded on the door. Three times, a pause, then once, a pause, and twice.

She frowned. Sighed.

"Alas," she said. "Morning beat us to it." She dismounted. "Do you know any spells that could replace a bath?"

"Yes," Aefric said. "I think they're critical when adventuring. But they don't feel as good as soaking in a tub."

"No," she said, getting out of bed to pose naked with her arms out wide. "But I can bathe myself anytime I want." She wiggled her fingers. "Let me feel this spell of cleansing."

Aefric knew that spell well enough that he didn't need words. But then a wicked idea occurred to him.

He got out of bed and came around to stand behind her. Placed his hands on her head, threading his fingers into her soft, golden curls. She made a small, interrogative sound, but he said, "Shhh."

She accepted that, and stilled.

Instead of using the spell to clean her all at once, as he would normally have done, he ran his hands all over her body, cleaning in his wake.

When he finished, he was standing in front of her. Her lips were parted, her breaths heavy, and her eyes got that wild, hungry look again.

"Was that … how you always cast that spell?"

"No," Aefric said playfully. "Just the most fun way to do it. I could have cast it without getting out of bed."

"Mean," she said, shaking a finger at him. "Very mean. Starting something you don't have time to finish."

"Perhaps I could—"

The knock came again.

Eppida blew out a breath and shook herself.

"Another time, Aefric." She looked as though she considered coming in for one last kiss, then changed her mind. Shook her head. "In fact, make that 'another time, your grace.' The hour has come for you to be on your way, and us to resume our proper roles."

"Of course, your majesty. At once."

Aefric cleaned himself with the same spell — albeit much faster — then realized he'd brought his backpack, but nothing else of his luggage.

He had no clean clothes to change into. For that matter, her majesty had torn the seams of his tunic and leathers in her haste the prior evening.

So Aefric grimaced, cleaned and repaired his clothes with magic, and re-donned his midnight blue silk tunic and riding leathers from the day before.

"I had a delightful time, your majesty," Aefric said.

"The pleasure was mine, your grace," she said, giving him a smile. "But if your grace does not get moving, we shall both irritate his majesty with our tardiness."

Aefric accepted that as a formal dismissal, took up his pack and the Brightstaff, and slipped out the door.

The same two knights stood guard. The one gave him back the wand Garram in its sheath. Aefric replaced it on his belt.

"I believe a page awaits your grace at the end of the hall," her partner said, pointing. "She wanted to wait closer, but we don't allow anyone to linger outside the rooms of their majesties."

"Good policy," Aefric said with a nod, then allowed the page to lead him to breakfast. Which turned out not to be downstairs at all.

Breakfast was served atop the second floor of the castle. Apparently Count Ferrin used it as a giant balcony sometimes.

At the door, the page took Aefric's pack, with the promise to deliver it downstairs to his knights.

Old habits almost made Aefric refuse. But every one of his advisers had made clear over and over again — he had to let the servants do their jobs.

Really, he shouldn't have even used magic to clean and repair his clothes. And he wouldn't. Had he had anything else available.

So Aefric released his pack to the page, and stepped out into the yet-cool early morning sunlight.

He immediately spotted the breakfast table. A round table surrounded by six chairs. Again the cloth-of-gold tablecloth and chair coverings, as well as gold for the plates and the rest.

The table was empty of food as yet — though three servants in Motte livery stood by, waiting — and the four of the other diners stood some ten paces away across the grayish stone.

King Colm and Ser Beatritz were in conversation with Count Ferrin and his fiancée, Karna Duisdottir, out near the western ledge, where they could overlook the tents and pavilions in the courtyard below.

King Colm wore riding leathers of forest green, trimmed with gold, a pale brown quilted tunic embroidered with gold thread, and a green cloak that featured the Armyr oak tree, also embroidered in gold thread.

Ser Beatritz wore a dark brown tunic over her riding leathers, but on top of it she wore the Armyr tabard.

Count Ferrin wore so much lace and brocade, Aefric wasn't sure he could spot any tunic underneath it all. Either way, the color was sky blue, over black hose. While Karna Duisdottir wore a complex taffeta gown of sky blue, replete with ruffles and frills. Her so-pale blonde hair was bound up in a knot atop her head. She wore that amber necklace again, but only one gold bracelet on each arm that morning.

At the sound of Aefric's boots on the stone of the roof, Ser Beatritz turned, then said something to his majesty, who nodded and turned to look at Aefric.

"Your grace," King Colm said with a smile. "Walk with me."

Aefric joined the king in walking away from the others, towards the southern edge, which would give a good view of Kerrik Forest, instead of the marshes north of the keep.

Ser Beatritz shifted to discourage either of Count Ferrin or Karna Duisdottir from trying to follow.

"*Leaba* is a wonderful practice," King Colm said with another smile, as Aefric fell into step beside him. "I'm glad to see it coming back. I understand you've been instrumental in that."

"Well, to be fair," Aefric said, "I first encountered it when her lordship, Baroness Herewyn, allowed one of her serving girls to offer me *leaba* in Norra. Though I have continued the practice since then."

"Norra never stopped offering *leaba*, even though others let the practice fade," King Colm said. "It's *your* use of it that has brought it back into fashion."

He pointed at Kerrik Forest with one hand, while with the other he slipped Aefric a small jar.

"An excellent remedy for scratches," King Colm said quietly. "I suggest you use it before we leave this morning. You don't want to ride without treating what I suspect Eppida has left on your back and haunches."

Aefric accepted the jar and slipped it inside his tunic. He wasn't sure if he should say anything, but King Colm winked at him.

"You were right," King Colm said then. "That Karna is the sister of a Ser Tohr Duisson. I believe that's the knight you mentioned last night?"

Aefric nodded. "Does she know we asked?"

King Colm snorted. "Don't ask that around Ser Beatritz or she might take it as a slight worthy of a challenge."

Aefric chuckled.

"Your grace!" Eppida's voice, from behind them. He turned to see that she too wore riding leathers of forest green and brown, with a riding cloak that matched the king's. And, of course, that golden torc resting on her collarbone. "I must insist you return my husband at once. I'm *famished*, and we can't eat without him."

WITH THE THIRD, HALF-STORY OF THE KEEP BETWEEN THE BREAKFAST table and the rising sun, by all rights, breakfast should have been pleasant.

The air yet carried a ghost of its evening chill, just brisk enough to encourage waking up, and the slight breeze came from the south, across the forest. A good, woodsy smell, to accompany the traditional

Armyrian breakfast of sliced fruits and meats, served with honeyed oat bread and spring water.

The problem, of course, was the count.

During breakfast, Count Ferrin took every conversational opportunity to find some way to ask their majesties to stay in Motte a little longer.

King Colm asked something about Kerrik Forest? Count Ferrin bragged about the hunting and offered to take them.

Queen Eppida asked about rebuilding efforts? Count Ferrin offered to give their majesties a tour of the towns he'd been rebuilding, *despite* a "distinct lack of support from his liege."

At that line, Aefric finally felt compelled to say something.

"And yet," he said, "I'm the one who reduced your military costs by increasing my own patrols through Kerrik Forest. And I've kept your miners employed in the Threepeaks."

Count Ferrin turned on Aefric then, eyes blazing. Opened his mouth, probably to complain about those mines. Likely something ill-advised, given that Motte had never had any right to claim them in the first place, and that Aefric had only reasserted proper ducal claim.

Before Count Ferrin could speak though, Aefric calmly finished his thought.

"No, your excellency's problems come not from me, but from seeking outside support *against* me, before I was even created duke."

Karna Duisdottir's sculpted eyebrows rose at that, as though honestly surprised.

Count Ferrin, however, had a rejoinder ready.

"I—"

"*Count Ferrin*," Queen Eppida said, with impressive steel in her voice. "His majesty and I have heard more than enough of your complaints about his grace. We are well aware of *all* the facts in these matters. And we feel that his grace has acted appropriately."

She leaned a little closer to him. "The topic is closed. Do not open it again."

Karna Duisdottir watched that exchange impassively. Aefric

wondered how much of Count Ferrin's anger was his own, and how much had been stoked by Malimfar, whispering in his ear.

Through the rest of breakfast, Count Ferrin found another excuse or two to try to inveigle their majesties into staying longer, but King Colm made quite clear that the whole of his party was leaving that morning.

When breakfast finally finished, Aefric asked Count Ferrin to linger with him on the roof, while the others went inside.

As the others left, Count Ferrin glanced at the Brightstaff in Aefric's hand. "Will I require a guard?"

"Your excellency," Aefric said with a sigh, "if I wanted you dead, you couldn't stop me, and neither could your guards."

Count Ferrin gave a twisted frown. Narrowed his eyes. "If an 'accident' befell me, my brother would avenge me."

"I didn't know you had a brother," Aefric said, trying for a softer tone. "Tell me about him."

Count Ferrin still looked and sounded suspicious as he said, "His name is Godric. He's only just come of age, but already he excels with all the knightly weapons. And his puissance with bow, pike, and lance must be seen to be believed."

"Has he been knighted yet?"

"Not yet," Count Ferrin said, walking closer and keeping one hand near the hilt of his rapier. "I offered, but he wants to be knighted for a deed, not his bloodline."

"I can respect that choice."

"Meaning your grace thinks I insulted him."

"Not at all," Aefric said. "Were he my brother, I would have offered too."

Count Ferrin nodded, slowly, then frowned. "There was no need for your grace to rush here. Their majesties were in no danger in my lands, much less my keep."

"It isn't you or yours I questioned," Aefric said, then smirked. "Not this time, at least."

"But your grace won't tell me what occasioned his haste," Count Ferrin said, plainly insulted. "Any more than his majesty or even Ser

Beatritz will."

"Pressing information for his majesty's ears. And if his majesty says it goes no further, far be it for me to disagree."

Count Ferrin grimaced and shook his head.

"I have duties to tend to before their majesties depart. What is it your grace wishes of me?"

There were a number of things Aefric would have liked to say. He would have liked to ask why the count moved against him before even meeting him. He would have liked to have made some kind of overture. Perhaps invited the count to Water's End for a visit.

Something to begin building better relations between them.

But given what Aefric *had* to say, there might not be much point in any of those other things. Not here and now, anyway.

Aefric drew in a deep breath.

"The troubles between us, this past spring."

Count Ferrin nodded, his eyes narrowed again.

"I know you were led to believe that Merrek supported you in … your actions. But I forget. Do you know the truth about that?"

"What truth?" Count Ferrin said, exasperated. "That Merrek would have let me dangle? *Yes*, your grace. I figured that out once Duchess Ashling started sucking your … I mean, once Duchess Ashling started making overtures of friendship towards Deepwater."

He didn't know. He had a Malimfari fiancée, and he didn't know that Malimfar, not Merrek, had been behind his supposed support.

And Aefric couldn't tell him. Not now. Either Count Ferrin wouldn't believe him, or he'd do something stupid, trying to prove his fiancée's innocence.

Either way, Karna Duisdottir would find out.

But wait.

Aefric had laid all these things bare to Princess Astrid. So Malimfar knew Aefric knew. Hells, they might've figured it out a season ago, when Armyr's armies showed up ready to defend their southern border.

But Aefric had just come riding to Forest's Edge, at speed.

If Aefric then warned Count Ferrin about Malimfar, and if Karna

Duisdottir was involved in the plot against the king...

No. Aefric couldn't risk saying anything. Not now. Not until all this was finished.

But he had to say something. Count Ferrin was losing his patience.

"You do know then," Aefric said, hating himself for playing into the deception. He sighed. "Good."

"I'm not a fool, your grace."

"Please let me finish," Aefric said, and the "please" so surprised the count that he nodded without thinking.

"I want you to know that I understand," Aefric said. "You're of an old noble family. The Fyrenns are an old noble family, and powerful. And here I come, just some jumped-up adventurer."

Count Ferrin nodded slowly, possibly trying to agree without insulting Aefric in the process.

"Given that," Aefric continued, "I can understand why you'd worry about how I'd handle running the duchy. Maybe even seek outside allies, to ensure your own safety, and that of your people."

Count Ferrin said nothing, but he looked pensive.

"But let us be clear," Aefric said, hardening his voice a little. "I do not in any way *approve* of what you did, and I believe the punishments I meted out were appropriate. Arguably even gentle."

Count Ferrin's mouth hardened into a line.

"But I want you to know that I *understand*," Aefric said. "And I am willing to work towards our getting past ... the events of this spring. For better or worse, I am your liege, and you are my vassal."

"What does your grace propose?" Count Ferrin asked. "What would be my part in this?"

Aefric cocked an eyebrow. "Can your excellency truly think of nothing he might've done differently over the last day or so, if he wanted to prove himself a good and true vassal?"

Count Ferrin quirked a grin. Chuckled a little. "I suppose I could think of a few things."

"Start there, then," Aefric said. "Perhaps I'll come for a visit in the fall, and we can put a few of those ideas to the test."

"Of course, your grace," Count Ferrin said with a slight bow that Aefric didn't believe was sincere.

Aefric cleared his throat.

Count Ferrin's narrow nostrils flared in a sigh. He took his hand from the pommel of his rapier and offered it to Aefric.

Aefric kissed that hand, then nodded.

"Better," Aefric said.

"I'm not ready to press my forehead to your grace's knuckles."

"One thing at a time," Aefric said. "And now, I should go prepare to leave."

He stepped over to the edge of the roof, above the courtyard below.

The tents and pavilions had already been struck, and packing was well underway. By Aefric's estimate, they'd be leaving within the hour.

Aefric stepped off the roof, and with a small, simple spell, floated down to the pavilion grounds below as gently as a leaf descending on an autumn breeze.

———

As Aefric realized the sheer size of the royal entourage, he found himself feeling a little pity for Count Ferrin. Between knights, lers and other petty nobles, servants and retainers, there had to be a hundred people traveling with their majesties.

Of course Count Ferrin couldn't have accommodated them all within a smallish keep like Forest's Edge.

Then again, his doing so had never been part of the plan. The count had inserted himself into the royal itinerary. So Aefric found his pity had little weight to it.

Aefric and his knights were ready to go quickly enough, and Count Ferrin even volunteered to provide Aefric's party with horses, to get them back to their own steeds.

Aefric chose to hope that was a good sign.

Of course, if it *was* a sign of goodwill, that goodwill might be dashed when Aefric told the count the truth about Merrek and Malimfar and how he'd been deceived.

Couldn't be helped. Telling the count was not worth risking the lives of their majesties.

One problem with having an entourage this big, though — it traveled *slowly*. Aefric's estimate that they'd be ready to leave within an hour of breakfast had been woefully ambitious.

That hour had passed, and Aefric still found himself in the dusty courtyard of Forest's Edge, waiting with his knights for the call to mount up and ride.

All around them people were still packing and preparing. Noisily enough that conversation was only possible just this side of a shout.

As such, Aefric avoided sensitive topics while catching Ser Beornric up on the discussions from the royal dinner table — not to mention taking a small amount of teasing from his knights about sharing the noble privilege with the queen — when a familiar face approached.

"Sighild," Aefric said, delighted.

Sighild wore riding leathers under a cream-colored tunic that had been tailored in a most becoming fashion, with a short sword at her belt, and high boots of pale doeskin. She wore her long, shimmering red hair bound with ribbons down her back.

She smiled as though the sight of Aefric was the apex of happiness itself.

"Your grace," she said with a bow, and offered her hand for Aefric to kiss, which he did.

"I'm sorry I didn't get to speak with you last night," Aefric said. "It was you who got the portcullis raised, was it not?"

"That was me, your grace," she said, smiling even wider. "By order of his majesty, of course."

"Of course," Aefric said. "Though he must think well of you to give you the task."

"I've been visiting Armityr for the last three aetts," she said. "The queen and I are distant cousins, and she invited me out for the Midsummer Festival."

Aefric enjoyed listening to Sighild regale him with tales of the entertainments of the Midsummer Festival. In fact, it was a pleasure just to listen to her talk. When he'd seen her this past spring, she'd barely spoken in his presence. She'd seemed ... intimidated by him.

Sighild was just describing some of the dancing when another familiar face arrived.

"Nyorngyth!" Aefric said.

Nyorngyth was a priest of Ulna, the Goddess of Travel. He hadn't changed much since Aefric saw him in the spring. Same short-cut dark brown hair above his light brown skin. And same brown traveling robes, split in the front, with brown leggings underneath.

As far as Aefric could tell, the only thing the man loved more than travel was food. He'd been portly when Aefric first met him and, if anything, he looked a little heavier now.

"Your grace," Nyorngyth said, bowing, while Sighild's story tapered off. Though she looked displeased with the interruption.

Nyorngyth noticed her reaction, but continued rather than let the moment become awkward. "A pleasure to see you again."

"I'm sorry," Aefric said, turning to Sighild. "You were telling of the dancing?"

"Yes, your grace," she said, bright smile back on her lips. She raised her arms high to illustrate a move—

"Mistress Sighild!" An older woman's voice, from some distance away. "Mistress Sighild Ol'Masarkor!"

Sighild sighed dramatically. "I do apologize, your grace. I am summoned."

"I understand," Aefric said, "and will forgive you. So long as you promise to finish your story later."

"Happily, your grace," she said with that smile again. "I dine with her majesty at breaks, but perhaps she will permit me some time during the trip."

"I don't doubt she will."

"Mistress Sighild Ol'Masarkor!" More voices had joined the calling now.

"I think you'd best go," Aefric said. "Until later."

"Until then, your grace," she said, and gave Aefric one more smile before running off like a deer chased by wolves.

"I don't believe she's on the list," Ser Beornric said, stroking his mustache and side-eying Aefric. "But she really ought to be, I think."

Aefric whirled on Ser Beornric. "What did I say?"

"Your grace said there was to be no marriage talk on the trip to Motte."

"I *did not* specify Motte," Aefric said. "I said *this trip*. That includes the return trip."

"I wish your grace luck with that," Nyorngyth said. "Talk of potential noble marriages is a popular pastime. Your grace should have heard all the speculation around Armityr about Prince Killian."

Aefric chuckled. "Good to see you, Nyorngyth." Aefric scratched his chin. "Let's see. The last time I saw you, you were heading into Fyretti with Countess Faenella."

"I was," Nyorngyth said. "I was going to join her in the border investigations your grace authorized. But the events of the Indecisive River Valley changed those plans."

"They did," Aefric said, nodding. "So what did you do?"

"I went with the army to Kivash, of course," Nyorngyth said. "That much travel? How could I not? Once matters were settled in Kivash — and I'd blessed those who'd needed it — I made my way east along the Indecisive River. I'd never seen much of its length, nor visited the towns along it."

"And how did you find the river?" Aefric asked.

"Oh, your grace," Nyorngyth said dreamily. "It doesn't so much *twist* its way along as *cavort*. Seemingly at random. A true delight of travel, Ulna be praised."

"I'll have to make time to see it, when I can."

"Your grace should indeed." Nyorngyth adjusted his bulk. "When I reached that new branch of the Kingsroad, I considered going south into Malimfar, southeast into Caiperas, or following the road north to Armityr." He shrugged. "I rolled dice, and asked Ulna to guide their fall. She led me back to Armityr just in time to join a royal procession all the way to Water's End!"

He smiled and rubbed his hands together. "Truly, I am blessed."

"Will you bless us, for this journey?"

"Of course, your grace," Nyorngyth said. "It would be my honor."

"Gather about me, my knights," Aefric said, and they formed a line with Aefric and Ser Beornric in the middle.

"Form a ring around me, if you would," Nyorngyth said, and at Aefric's nod, his knights did so. "Thank you. Far easier this way."

Nyorngyth brought his hands together in front of his belly. Bowed his head and closed his eyes. Whispered a few words too softly for Aefric to hear.

Nyorngyth knelt then in the hard dirt, and scraped together a handful.

He held that handful, palm up, in his left hand, and covered the dirt with his right. He muttered a few more words, then stood.

He stepped up to Aefric then, and there was something different in the aspect of the cleric. Normally, he seemed ... so casual. Whether he was telling jokes or stories, listening or advising, he always seemed to be relaxed. At peace.

But now, in this moment, he looked a warrior. Balance in his posture. Purpose in his eye.

A breath of power surrounded him. Not the kind of power Aefric knew so well, but power nonetheless.

With three fingers, Nyorngyth took a pinch of dirt and threw it at Aefric's feet.

With those same three fingers, Nyorngyth sketched the symbol of Ulna — the crossroads — in the air in front of Aefric. And as he did, his fingers seemed to sizzle the air behind them. For a moment, it was as though that crossroads hung, reddish brown, in the air.

Nyorngyth took another pinch of dirt, threw it behind Aefric, and boomed words in a language Aefric didn't recognize.

*"Ulna nistish vra Aefricasti Brightstaffasti ell cul natath."*

Comfort and peace washed over Aefric. He felt much better about the coming journey. As though all the little things that could go wrong on the road, would not.

Nyorngyth went around the circle, performing the blessing for each of Aefric's knights.

By the time he finished, the call came for everyone to mount up and ride. A bit of timing that Aefric found he could not consider coincidental.

---

THE ROYAL ENTOURAGE TOOK LONG ENOUGH TO GET READY THAT morning that Aefric's soldiers arrived at Forest's Edge and had time to rest their horses before leaving again.

Aefric didn't need to borrow those horses from Count Ferrin after all.

Just as well. Aefric was happy to see his glorious young black stallion, Windsong. And Queen Eppida seemed quite pleased to see Aefric riding her gift.

As the royal party set out at last that morning, the entire company fell into the formation they would use for the trip to Water's End.

The soldiers and knights of Aefric's personal guard rode out front, carrying both the royal banner and the Deepwater banner.

Next came thirty of the knights who were traveling with the king. Then the royal party itself. First, six of the Knights of the Crown. Sers Beornric and Beatritz came next, followed by King Colm, Queen Eppida, and Aefric, and then the other six Knights of the Crown.

That morning, it was only Aefric riding beside the king and queen. Although, as the days passed, other nobles would be allowed to ride with the three of them, as well as occasional others such as skalds, or Nyorngyth.

After the royal party itself came the nobles, then the soldiers, then the other servants and retainers. Finally more soldiers to the rear, carrying the royal and ducal banners.

The whole of the royal entourage seemed to stretch for nearly a quarter mile.

That morning, during the ride, Aefric finished briefing the king and queen about what he knew and what he suspected, regarding a threat from Malimfar.

"So Ferrin is still in the dark about Malimfar?" King Colm asked, when Aefric finished.

"So far as I know," Aefric said. "I'd meant to have Ser Beornric tell him the truth this past spring, but— Beornric!"

"Your grace," Ser Beornric called back, then slowed his horse to join the royal party.

"When I sent you to Motte to explain my ruling about the mines, did you tell Count Ferrin that it was Malimfar behind his ... poor decisions, not Merrek?"

"I wanted to, your grace, but his excellency was not in a receptive frame of mind."

"No, I imagine not," King Colm said with a sigh. "The boy is too hot-tempered." He nodded dismissal to Ser Beornric, who rejoined Ser Beatritz a little further up.

"And to tell him now would seem to be a move against his intend-ed," Queen Eppida said. "Nevertheless, he must be told before he marries her."

"But not yet," Aefric said.

"No," King Colm agreed. "Much as I would like to tell him now that he may be sharing his bed with an adder, we really can't. Not until the question of this coming assassination attempt is settled."

"Your grace is positive the attack will come?" Queen Eppida asked, and she sounded hopeful that Aefric was wrong. "I hardly see how it could take place."

Aefric had to admit. He agreed with her. He found it hard to imagine anyone trying to assassinate the king along the road. Not with so very many knights and soldiers about him. Especially as there were few, if any, good places for a bowman to hide near the Kingsroad.

And unless Aefric was very much mistaken, knights and soldiers were checking every place that *could* hide an assassin.

And then there were the royal magical protections. Both the king and queen wore blade-turning enchantments. The queen in the torc she always wore, and the king in a bracer worn under his tunic.

Not to mention that a cleric of Ulna herself had blessed the journey. Surely such a blessing would keep them safe from assassins.

Nevertheless, he stayed vigilant as they made their way first south across Motte — staying well clear of the tree cover provided by Kerrik Forest — to the Kingsroad, and then west towards Water's End.

Their majesties were originally supposed to stop at Norrtarr and Tafarac, but spread the word that they were needed at Water's End to resolve an issue involving seabound problems between Malimfar and Caiperas that risked affecting shipping.

This gave them an excuse to change their itinerary. Sleep in their pavilions, with plenty of knights and soldiers standing guard.

And all seemed to be going well along the ride.

The blessing of Ulna seemed to dominate the trip. The days were pleasant. The weather was good. The heat finally seemed to be giving way a bit. Losing some of its edge. The ride was smooth. The entourage even seemed to fall into a rhythm that required less time to stop and start, despite the number of people involved.

It began to look as though they might make it all the way to Water's End without a problem.

In fact, by the end of the second day of steady vigilance, Aefric could tell that doubt had crept in about the imminence of an attack on anyone at all, let alone the king and queen.

But then, on the third day of riding, the attack came.

# 10

---



ON THE THIRD DAY OF AEFRIC'S TRAVEL WITH THE ROYAL ENTOURAGE, the skies were filled with slightly smeared white clouds fleeing the Risen Sea on winds that didn't touch the ground.

Down by the road, between the recovery efforts of Goldenfall and Felspark, the summer heat seemed to be staging a comeback.

By the time that great centipede that was the royal entourage called the halt for lunch, Aefric doubted there were any among them who weren't tired of the smells of dirt and their own sweat.

And they still had half a day's ride ahead of them.

The soldiers found a good-sized clearing on the Goldenfall side of the Kingsroad. The procession had been going for over an aett now, so it seemed that everyone already knew their roles and their places, when it came to taking a break.

Or perhaps everyone was simply ready to stop for food and something to drink. Because the whole of the procession seemed to leave the road and settle down for lunch faster than they had either of the two previous days.

On that third day, Aefric and their majesties were joined for lunch and conversation on the wide, forest green blanket by three others. Sighild, Nyorngyth, and a ler Aefric hadn't met before.

His name was Ler Mildric Ol'Ornalla. He was a stout fellow, of middle years, though already showing more gray than soft brown in his short hair and well-groomed beard. He dressed in the colors of mustard and rust, but his silk tunic and hose looked good on him.

In fact, he was rather handsome, in a roguish way. Maybe it was that smile of his, that always seemed to imply he knew more than he let on, but didn't mind keeping secrets.

Nyorngyth, of course, was in his brown travel robes. The king wore a pale red silk tunic over his riding leathers, and the queen wore a tunic that matched her eyes over hers. Sighild's tunic was lemon yellow over her own riding leathers, while Aefric wore soft, Deep-water gray silk over his own.

This many days on the road, though, and Aefric was beginning to see Dajen's wisdom in trying to bring back hats. Aefric could feel the sun on his scalp, and the sweat was matting his hair.

Plus, the shade of a hat's bill would have been welcomed by his eyes, which were growing tired of the daylong glare.

The royal lunch party was just enjoying an herb-roasted pheasant with a light, white cheese and honeyed oat bread — along with a dry white wine — when the hue and cry of rapid hooves approached from the east.

Everyone turned to look. A single rider, in Motte livery, pushing speed out of a horse that could not take much more pushing.

Orders were shouted. Knights leapt to their feet. Soldiers grabbed weapons. Even those who weren't standing guard at the time hurried to posts around the huge entourage, intent on scanning all directions at once, for threats.

But most eyes were still focused on the oncoming rider.

As the royal party came to their feet, King Colm gave Aefric a significant look. As though the rider could only portend bad news.

Aefric tapped the butt of the Brightstaff on the ground and caused white lightning to play along its length. To reassure their majesties of his own readiness to defend them.

Which reminded Aefric. He didn't know *everyone* he ate with that day...

He turned to make sure Ler Mildric wasn't an assassin, ready to take advantage of this distraction to end the life of his majesty.

Ler Mildric only stared toward the rider, lips and eyes wide with excitement. Beside him, Sighild looked more curious than worried or excited.

But from the corner of Aefric's eye, he saw Nyorngyth. Standing in the king's blind spot. Feet balanced like a skirmisher. A reddish, flame-shaped dagger in his hand. A dark look in his eye.

No. Not *him*.

Nyorngyth saw Aefric turn. Made his move. His hand leapt forward with the blade, aiming for the back of the king's throat.

Barely a handspan from murder.

No time to call lightning. No time for a spell. No time even to grab that hand with magic. That would take too much focus.

Aefric did the only thing he could.

He focused a burst of raw magic and *shoved* Nyorngyth. Right in the center of mass.

That was a blow that would have smashed open an unbarred castle gate. It should have knocked the portly cleric to the ground.

But not Nyorngyth.

Perhaps he was that well balanced. Knew how to use his weight right. Kept his center of gravity low. Perhaps he'd even anticipated the strike.

Whatever the reason, he stumbled backward only two steps and never lost his footing.

The king whirled. Reached for a sword he wasn't wearing.

"Down, sire!" Aefric shouted above the rising hue and cry, all around them.

The king's battlefield reflexes stayed true. He dropped to the blanket, dragging Queen Eppida down with him.

Just in time. Nyorngyth threw that dagger.

Aefric caught its handle with magic. Right above where the king crouched. It would have taken his majesty in the belly.

Aefric threw the dagger back at Nyorngyth.

The shot went wide. Nyorngyth didn't even have to duck.

He pulled two stilettos out of his sleeves and crouched to spring at the king.

But Aefric's throw had done its work. Bought him the moment he needed.

Before Nyorngyth could leap Aefric froze him with magic. Made a human statue of him.

Knights and soldiers rushed in.

"Bind him," the king ordered, coming to his feet and helping Queen Eppida to hers.

Two Knights of the Crown grabbed Nyorngyth's wrists, but couldn't budge him except to tip him forward.

But more knights and soldiers came to help. Once Aefric was convinced that Nyorngyth was sufficiently surrounded, he released the spell and left them to their work.

He turned to the king and queen.

"Were you hurt, sire?"

"No," King Colm said. "Thanks to your quick action, your grace."

Queen Eppida, breathless and clinging to her husband as though to reassure herself that he still lived, turned wide eyes to Aefric.

"Forgive me ... your grace ... for doubting..."

"You were right to question," Aefric said, shaking his head in disbelief at the assassin's identity. "Even I would never have suspected Nyorngyth."

"We traveled with him that whole way to Fyretti. To Castle Siarhal," Sighild said to Aefric. She looked even paler than normal. Almost lost. "I never... I spoke so freely around him."

"We all did," Aefric said, sighing, and looking at the assassin, whose eyes still moved as though seeking escape or opportunity. "We all did."

---

SORTING THINGS OUT AFTER THE ASSASSINATION ATTEMPT TOOK SOME time.

As soon as Nyorngyth was secured and under guard, the knights and soldiers — Aefric's, as well as the king's — made sure the rest of the area was clear.

What was more, they began a search of every member of the entire entourage. Searching for unexpected weapons, in general, but specifically for any more reddish, flame-shaped daggers.

Aefric inspected the one Nyorngyth had carried. Its reddish hue was highlighted by something smeared along its length. And from this range, he could tell there was magic in the blade that was exceptionally difficult to detect.

Holding the hilt, though, Aefric quickly determined that the blade seemed to eat magic. Not even the king's blade-turning magical bracer would have stayed that dagger.

Was that why Aefric's throw went so far wide? Was he losing his magical grip as the aimed?

Apparently such daggers were known to be used by assassins of the Order of the Severed Dream. But this was the first Aefric had heard of them.

Even his memories as Keifer, of the *Torn Kingdoms* sourcebooks from Earth, didn't seem to include the Order of the Severed Dream. They must've been new. Or newly known of.

But both Sers Beornric and Beatritz knew of them.

"They're said to be based out of Malimfar," Ser Beatritz said. "To have a guild hidden somewhere in the town of Dyrhellir."

"I'd heard they were an independent group, though," Ser Beornric said, tugging at his mustache. "More likely to work with other guilds or criminals than nobles."

"I've heard the same," Ser Beatritz said. "In fact, when we were in Kivash this past spring, word around there was that King Eadred put a bounty on them. That their work was behind instability among Malimfari shipping concerns."

"If that's true, why didn't the king just order the shipping companies to stop assassinating each other?" Aefric asked.

"The Order of the Severed Dream isn't just assassins," Ser Beornric said. "They're said to serve as spies, as well. Last I'd heard, they did more spying than killing."

"Odd, though," Ser Beatritz said, frowning. "If Nyorngyth is from Severed Dream, why should he pose as a cleric? I'd think the first time he failed a blessing, he'd be found out."

"He wasn't posing," Aefric said. "I've been blessed before, and Nyorngyth's blessing in Ulna's name was the real thing."

"But how?" King Colm said, waving off a pair of his knights who stood ready to search even Aefric for another telltale dagger. "How could he be both a holy man and a paid spy and murderer?"

"We'll have to ask him," Aefric said.

"Not yet," King Colm said. "I don't want to question him until I've calmed down. Right now I'm too ready to order his death, and that might not serve me well."

Servants came up, to offer more food and wine. Apparently those in charge of the food would try not to let a little thing like a royal assassination attempt spoil lunch.

No one nearby seemed to have any stomach for more lunch, though. Aefric and the king, along with Sers Beatritz and Beornric, were focused on dealing with the problems before them.

The queen seemed to be calming herself and Sighild by drawing the younger noblewoman into a conversation about Aefric's magic.

Ler Mildric tried to insinuate himself into that conversation, but the queen shooed him away. Which caused Ser Beornric to give Aefric an amused look that Aefric tried to ignore.

"We'll have to deal with Nyorngyth before we get back on the road," Aefric said.

"And we will," King Colm said grimly. "But first, I want to know what was so important that Motte's rider was ready to push his horse to the brink of death."

The rider was brought into a circle of soldiers. Half those of the king, and half those of Aefric's personal guard.

Waiting within the circle stood the king, Aefric, and Sers Beatritz and Beornric.

The rider was a wide-eyed lad who looked even worse for wear than his horse, after his speedy ride. He was searched thoroughly before he was allowed to approach.

The moment he was in the middle of the circle, he dropped to his knees and raised both hands to offer a scroll to his majesty.

King Colm took the scroll. Spoke in a gentle voice. "Have you any message beyond this scroll?"

"Only that I am to return with any reply your majesty sees fit to give."

"Fine," King Colm said. "Go tend your horse, and find some food. I will summon you when I'm ready."

"Yes, your majesty," the rider said, bowing his way out of the circle.

King Colm broke the seal, unrolled the scroll, and skimmed its contents. Made a humming, thoughtful noise.

Aefric checked himself from asking what the scroll said. One did not rush a king, after all. He felt somewhat gratified, at least, that Ser Beatritz shifted impatiently while the king read the scroll a second time, hummed thoughtfully again.

Then a third time.

Finally, his majesty rolled up the scroll, frowning, and tapped it on one palm. He turned to a nearby Knight of the Crown.

"Clear an area of one hundred feet. No one within but myself, his grace, Ser Beatritz, Ser Beornric, and..."

He turned to the queen. "My dear. Do you wish to join us?"

The queen considered that while frowning at whatever she saw as she looked over the rest of the temporary encampment.

"No," she said. "One of us should move among the people and settle them down. I'll handle that. Assuming, my love, that you tell me later of this conversation?"

She was smiling, now, as though this were some inside joke.

The king smiled back at her the same way. "Assuming you remind me, my love."

They both smiled wider for a moment ... but then the moment passed, and they both turned to be about their duties.

Soon, in the rising midday heat, Aefric found himself seated on the royal, forest green blanket again. This time his company was the king and Sers Beatritz and Beornric.

More of that herb-roasted pheasant, along with the light white cheese and honeyed oat bread sat nearby, in case any of them still hungered. And each had been provided with a skin of day beer.

Each of them took a little of the beer while the king looked over the message from Motte one more time.

"It seems that a member of Karna Duisdottir's entourage was caught sneaking out after we left," King Colm said, rolling up the scroll again. "Count Ferrin's men were hard pressed to find him, but when they did they found in his possession a reddish dagger shaped like flame."

"I take it Karna Duisdottir proclaims her own innocence?" Aefric said.

King Colm nodded. "Pretends fury about it. Claims the false retainer was sent by her uncle to spy on her. To ensure she wasn't 'so besotted with love that she'd give away too many Malimfari secrets.'"

Both Sers Beornric and Beatritz scoffed.

"I agree," King Colm said. "Obviously the Order of the Severed Dream sent a team of two assassins. Motte may have caught the prime, with Nyorngyth as a backup. Or perhaps it was the other way around. We won't know for sure until my justiciar digs out the truth. Either way, I have trouble believing that Karna Duisdottir was ignorant."

"She might be," Aefric said. "The more who knew of the assassins, the more who might tip their presence. Safer to slip the assassin in with her entourage without telling her."

"Seems clumsy either way," Ser Beatritz said. "The king was already at Forest's Edge. Why not make the attempt there?"

"And risk spoiling the engagement to Count Ferrin?" Aefric asked.

"Interesting thought," King Colm said. Cocked his head to one side. "How do you see it, your grace?"

"I think your majesty has the right of it. I think the assassin from Karna Duisdottir's entourage was to come to us on the road, well away from her and well away from Motte. Somewhere between Motte and Water's End he'd provide a distraction, allowing Nyorngyth to strike. Then if Nyorngyth failed, he'd make his own attempt."

"So you think Nyorngyth was the prime," King Colm said.

"I think it makes the most sense," Aefric said. "If all went to plan, Nyorngyth would have completed the job, likely dying in the attempt. The secondary, unseen, would then have fled back to Malimfar to carry word of Nyorngyth's success, and leave us with no one valuable to question."

"While Karna Duisdottir spins whatever story she wants about the escaped member of her entourage."

"I think she'd stick with the spy story," Aefric said. "Whether she believes it or not."

"And if Nyorngyth failed, the secondary was to make the attempt?"

"I believe so," Aefric said.

"That would have put Karna Duisdottir at risk," Ser Beatritz said. "She can claim innocence all she wants. But if a member of her own entourage made the attempt, she'd still face the penalty."

"If she was kept ignorant," Aefric said, "which I suspect she was, then our royal justiciar would bear out that innocence. And I suspect that the trauma of suspicion would either bind her and Count Ferrin closer, or infuriate Count Ferrin about the accusation."

"Or both," Ser Beornric said.

"More dissent," Aefric said.

"Why did Nyorngyth strike early?" King Colm asked. "That rider was obviously not the secondary assassin."

"The rider wore Motte's livery," Ser Beatritz said. "That meant there was a chance that his partner was caught. Better to strike now, with such distraction as he had, than miss his chance."

"What about the assassin caught by Motte?" Ser Beornric asked. "Does he yet live?"

King Colm checked the scroll.

"No," King Colm said with a sigh. "Died in the capturing."

"Likely as Nyorngyth was supposed to," Ser Beatritz said.

"So we can only speculate that there was a secondary at all," Aefric said, thumping the ground in frustration.

"The justiciar should still uncover the truth," King Colm said, though he didn't sound confident.

Even one working under the auspices of Taesark had only so much power to seek truth.

"All right," King Colm said, standing, which led the others to stand as well. "I'm ready to talk to the cleric."

At Ser Beatritz's call, a pair of Knights of the Crown dragged Nyorngyth into the circle.

The cleric looked sweaty and dirty, but surprisingly calm.

"May I ask something before we begin, your majesty?" Aefric asked.

King Colm nodded.

"The Order of the Severed Dream breeds spies, as well as assassins," Aefric said to Nyorngyth. "How do you reconcile that with Ulna's demand that you keep what secrets you learn on the road?"

"I have never violated a single precept of my goddess," Nyorngyth said. "But your grace should recall that I told him I must be asked to keep something in confidence, for me to be required to do so. Such a request is rarely made, but always honored."

Aefric grimaced and looked off toward the horizon. Tried to remember just how many secrets he might've let slip without realizing it along that trip.

He could only remember asking for secrecy once. That conversation at Towerkeep...

"Let us begin simply," King Colm said to Nyorngyth. "How long have you been in the employ of Malimfar?"

A pulse of magic made Aefric whirl, hands raised to cast.

He was too late.

Nyorngyth's head lolled on his shoulders, already purpling. The two knights who held him shook him, but he was clearly a corpse.

But how? No spell could...

"Reyorisalis," Ser Beornric whispered, and Ser Beatritz grimaced, but nodded.

King Colm and Aefric looked at each other, puzzled. Aefric recognized the name of course. Reyorisalis was the goddess of death. But Aefric had rarely even seen a priest of that goddess...

"Why do you invoke that name?" King Colm asked.

"Is she even still a goddess?" Aefric asked, shaking his head. "She raised no army during the Godswalk Wars. I heard no tell of her at all. Can't even recall the last time I saw a temple dedicated to her."

"She was everywhere during the wars, your grace," Ser Beornric said reverently.

"Forgive us, your majesty, your grace," Ser Beatritz said. "I don't know how much time either of you spent on the battlefields of the wars, once the battles were done."

"None," Aerfic said, while the king shook his head. "I was always rushed onwards to what came next."

The two knights looked at each other. Ser Beatritz nodded for Ser Beornric to speak.

"When the battles were over, we were among those who moved among the wounded, trying to ensure that those who could be saved, would be saved."

"Clerics were few," Ser Beatritz said, "as they always have been. But usually there were at least one or two nearby who answered the call of Nilasah, and could aid in healing those who would recover."

"And among those who would not, moved the Death Walkers," Ser Beornric said.

Death Walkers. A title Aefric hadn't heard in many years. It still sent a shiver down even his spine. They were said to be clerics who served Reyorisalis, and were said to be able to cause death with a touch.

"There can't have been many," Aefric said. "I've never even seen one, let alone met one."

"They ... do not draw attention to themselves," Ser Beatritz said. "Except when they're working."

"I saw at least one Death Walker after every battle," Ser Beornric said, and Ser Beatritz nodded agreement. "They walked among the wounded who would not recover. Blessed them with swift and pain-less death."

"And those who received that blessing," Ser Beatritz said, "pur-pled in the face, tongue extended, even as our assassin does."

"But there's no Death Walker among us," King Colm said, which brought helpless shrugs from the knights. "And certainly none who took his life. We were all watching. I think we'd've noticed."

"Conditional," Aefric muttered, which got him curious looks. "There are spells that will not take effect until predefined conditions are met. I didn't know clerics possessed the power to do likewise, but..."

He gestured to the dead assassin.

"So as soon as he was asked about Malimfar," the king said, "he died?"

"Or as soon as he was asked about his employer," Aefric said. "Sure way to keep the order's secrets."

"Unless his spirit could be called for questioning?" King Colm asked hopefully.

"Not by me," Aefric said. Early experiences with necromancy had turned him away from the art completely.

"Well, perhaps—"

But his majesty was interrupted by cries of another approaching rider.

<hr>

Aefric was beginning to think this lunch break along the road would never end. Already the sun was past its zenith, and the rushing clouds high above were beginning to leave nothing but blue sky in their wake.

And the summer heat was growing again.

A messenger from Motte. An assassination attempt by a man Aefric had come to like. Even taken advice from. And now, another rider approaching?

If they stayed out here much longer, the cooks would start talking about dinner...

This rider came rushing along the Kingsroad from the east, wearing Felspark livery. Nevertheless, the rider was met by armed and ready soldiers and knights.

Once the rider was searched and disarmed, she was brought into the circle where Aefric and the king were discussing how unlikely it was that Karbin — or indeed, any nearby wizard that Aefric knew of — would know the spells needed to call up the shade of a dead man and require it to answer questions.

Meanwhile, Sers Beornric and Beatritz insisted that the spirits of those slain by the blessing of a Death Walker were beyond raising. That such spells were anathema to Reyorisalis.

The discussions stopped as the rider arrived.

She was a dusky young woman who looked troubled by all the weapons about her, yet confident in her duty.

She dropped to her knees among the dusty dry grass and bowed to the king.

"You come bearing a message?" King Colm asked, while Queen Eppida and Sighild entered the circle, looking eager to hear the news.

"I do, your majesty," the rider said. "We received a rika at Tafarac midmorning. An attempt was made yesterday on the life of Prince Killian."

"*What?*" King Colm shouted.

"An *attempt*," Aefric said quickly. "So the prince survives?"

"He does," the rider said, visibly fighting not to squirm under the scrutiny of her king. "The attempt was made by an attaché of the Doraga Trading Company, using a red, flame-shaped dagger. Prince Killian spotted the attempt in time to twist away, turning a stab into a slash across his chest. The prince slew the assassin himself, with his longsword."

"Was the dagger poisoned?" King Colm asked urgently.

"Your majesty, it was," the rider said. "But the royal physician was near at hand, and has cured the wound. The prince will lie abed for three or four days, but will make a full recovery."

Three or four days? That must've been some poison. Aefric knew well that the royal physician — like Bebara, his own physician at Water's End —was a cleric of Nilasah.

"And the assassin died," Ser Beatritz spat.

"I fear so," the rider said, bowing her head.

"The Doraga Trading Company," King Colm said, shaking his head. "They're based on the other side of the Risen Sea."

"Likely the assassin was a recent addition to the trading company's party," Ser Beatritz said. "We'll have to find out if they stopped in Malimfar before coming here."

"That would be a little obvious, don't you think?" Aefric asked.

"I didn't mean *just* before coming here," Ser Beatritz said with an arched eyebrow.

"It's just that it seems more likely to *me*," Aefric said, "that the assassin was already ensconced in his position. An attaché to a merchant representing a major trading company travels a good deal, carries a lot of information, and can get close to many important potential targets."

"Did the rika say anything else?" King Colm asked.

"Your majesty, there was no room for more information on the message," the rider said apologetically. "The baroness did not wish to wait for more news to get word to your majesty."

"And she had the right of it," King Colm said. "Good work. Rise, refresh yourself, and when you are ready, carry word to your master that I am grateful for the swift news."

The rider was only just leaving the circle when the same thought seemed to show up on several faces at the same time. Though it was the king who gave that thought voice.

"Maev," he said. He turned urgently to Aefric. "A rika from Varondam might not reach Armyr for several days."

"I'll find out right now, your majesty," Aefric said.

He gathered together his sense of Maev. Quickly assembled a message spell that would not only carry his words to her ears, but her next words back to his.

"Maev," he said. "Please tell me you're safe. Assassins came for your father and brother, but were defeated. Likely one comes for you. Tell me you're safe."

A moment later, he heard Maev's voice. And true to form, even facing death she sounded sure of herself.

"I'm safe, dearest Aefric. Sylkanis smelled the attempt before the assassin struck. My love to you, Father and Killian. How much more can I—"

Aefric sighed with such relief that everyone around him followed suit even before he spoke.

"She's fine," Aefric said. "Her great forest lynx, Sylkanis, detected the assassin before the strike came. She sends her love to your majesties and Prince Killian."

All right, *technically* Maev didn't send love to the queen. But pointing out the omission seemed petty.

Although, honestly, from the look on Queen Eppida's face, she didn't believe for a moment that she'd been included in Maev's good wishes.

Were those two not getting along then?

"How is she?" King Colm asked. "What else did she say?"

"The spell only allows for about two dozen words," Aefric said. "She tried to say more than I told you, but the spell finished before she could."

"Really?" Queen Eppida said. "Your grace makes it sound as though he's never spoken with Maev by spell before."

"I haven't, your majesty," Aefric said. "Doing so would have felt inappropriate. We communicate through letters."

She nodded, looking pensive.

"I want to speak with her, your grace," King Colm said. "I want to hear her voice, as you did."

"I'm sorry, your majesty," Aefric said. "I know of no spells I could cast that would allow you to do so. Even those that allow *me* to are really quite limited."

True, Aefric could bind such a spell to an object, such as a ring, that would allow the king to cast the spell. But pointing that out seemed like a bad idea.

"Could your grace reach my sister Ashling by means of that spell?" Queen Eppida asked.

"I believe so," Aefric said. "Although I haven't tried. I do not use the spell often, because there's the risk of interrupting someone about an important task. Not to mention that letters provide less margin for error. A misheard or misremembered word could be dangerous."

"True," the king muttered.

"And yet," Queen Eppida said, "you both were able to reach my husband by that spell, and did so. Only a few days past, at Forest's Edge."

"I felt that the need merited the risk," Aefric said. "And in truth, contacting his majesty that way was difficult, given the limited time I had spent in his presence, to that point."

"I see," Queen Eppida said, then quirked a small smile. "What about my sister Zoleen? Has your grace spent enough time in *her* presence to speak with her by means of his marvelous little spell?"

Sighild frowned thoughtfully.

"Enough of that," King Colm said, anger through his voice, though Aefric didn't think it was directed at the queen.

"Bad enough they try to kill *me*," King Colm continued. "They also try for my *wife and children*? This means war."

"But we haven't proven Malimfar is behind the attempts," Ser Beatritz cautioned.

"She's right," Aefric said, quickly. "Don't we need proof before going to war?"

"I will get that proof," King Colm said darkly. "And when I do, I will *crush* Malimfar for this."

<hr>

THE KING'S DARK MOOD DID NOT LOOK TO LIGHTEN SOON. AS HE MOVED about in the afternoon heat, giving orders, Aefric saw the man who had led the armies of three kingdoms during the Godswalk Wars.

His own, of course, along with those of Rethneryl and Caiperas.

Interesting, when Aefric thought about it, that even the Godswalk Wars had not been enough to see Caiperas fighting alongside Malimfar.

Soon the company that had been traveling together along the Kingsroad was split in two.

The vast majority of that company would continue to travel as they had — slowly, and in as much comfort as could be found or provided along the way to Water's End. Taking another several days, perhaps an aett, to get there.

But the smallest part of that company would now proceed ahead at speed, bound for Tafarac before full dark.

That party included the king, the queen, Aefric, Sers Beatritz and Beornric, along with the Knights of the Crown, and the Knights of the Lake, which was how Aefric was coming to think of the knights of his personal guard.

In truth, Aefric had wanted to bring the soldiers of his personal guard along as well, but the king made quite clear that that was too many.

And so, shortly after the messenger from Tafarac was sent off to carry word of imminent royal arrival, twenty knights, a king, a queen, and a duke took to the road.

The king was armed now, carrying the longsword Aefric had seen him wear during the wars. And the queen was armed as well, carrying a rapier that looked as though it had seen its share of fighting, as well.

Aefric wore his own longsword, as well as the wand Garram, and, of course, the Brightstaff rode in its sling, for easy access.

Oddly, as they rode in silence through the still air and afternoon heat, Aefric found himself wondering about the blessing of Ulna.

Was it still in effect? Because the Kingsroad ahead of them was clear that day. What few travelers they passed cleared the way for them without requiring so much as a pause.

They reached Tafarac, where Baroness Blaewyn met them quietly, as ordered. No big feast. No dancing. The king hardly took food before he rushed to the rookery to begin sending rikas.

Aefric sent a couple of his own, to make plans for a speedier trip to Water's End than was originally intended.

The king ordered them all to bed early that night, to ensure they were all rested and ready for a long day's ride before dawn the next day.

Which meant no *leaba* that night. No visits from noblewomen. Likely just as well. Aefric doubted he would have been good company. He had far too much on his mind.

Malimfar, of course and the possibility of war. While his duchy — indeed most, if not all of the kingdom — was still recovering from the Godswalk Wars...

But also matters he'd yet to bring before his majesty.

The gold in the Dragonscar. The slavers. Nelazzi.

And then there was the question of the assassins.

Something about those assassins felt ... off. As though blaming Malimfar was too easy. And yet, who else could be behind the attempts? Who else *would* be?

Thoughts such as these kept Aefric awake well after he should have been sleeping.

Nevertheless, as dawn broke the next morning, they were already clear of the town of Tafarac, and riding hard along the Kingsroad.

The wind was in their faces that day. Cool against the summer sun, but harsh all the same. And traffic was worse. At times, the royal party had to leave the Kingsroad to pass a caravan, or an argument of farmers whose carts managed to block each other.

Whatever blessing Ulna had given them, it had clearly lapsed by that day. Aefric was sure of that much.

And yet they rode on, as hard as they dared without risking the horses.

It was late afternoon, though the sun was not yet setting, as they reached the bridge over the Haven River, at the southern edge of the city of Behal. There the *Duke's Hand* dominated the small dock meant for fishing boats, awaiting the royal party's arrival, per Aefric's order.

Captain Sikel saw them fed as they rested while the *Duke's Hand* sailed north across Lake Deepwater, bound for Water's End. They dined on trenchers of mixed roasted red meats, well spiced and dripping with melted cheese, along with a hearty red wine.

Aefric shared his afterdeck with their majesties, of course, along with Sers Beornric and Beatritz, while the Knights of the Crown and the Knights of the Lake found other accommodations out of the sailors' way, for their own rest and refreshment.

Sailing across the lake provided a break from the day's heat. The winds helped, but also the light lake spray that seemed inevitable when the winds were as strong as they were that day.

Strong enough, in fact, that they made excellent time up the lake.

The sun was setting on the other side of the Castle at Water's End as the *Duke's Hand* slid smoothly past the harbor traffic, through the reef, and into its reserved spot on the duke's own pier, which looked to have been fashioned and smoothed out of raw green coral.

"I always forget just how beautiful your palace is," Queen Eppida said, wonder in her voice, as she regarded the shimmering, deep lake blue of the castle and its walls. "It truly is a triumph."

The king was too distracted for such thoughts. At the queen's words, he glanced over the castle and walls, but turned his focus back to the pier, where Kentigern and Ser Yrsa waited, along with a formation of knights and soldiers.

Aefric could tell that Kentigern was practically shaking with nerves, but doubted anyone else besides himself and Ser Beornric could tell.

The key was the stiff, ramrod straight posture. Kentigern always had good posture, but not *that* good.

He was dressed to impress, though. His padded doublet of royal blue, trimmed in silver, with dark mustard hose, and those low, soft leather boots he loved so well, because they had silver thread among their black, turned-down cuffs. His heavy, dark brown beard had been recently trimmed, as had what Aefric could see of his thick hair, under that black velvet cap of his.

Wait. He was wearing the black velvet cap. Did he have bad news?

Ser Yrsa looked as calm and confident as ever, though she'd clearly had her full plate polished to meet their majesties. And she'd clearly washed her hair before braiding it, because its blood red high-lights seemed almost to glow.

Aefric could practically feel Queen Eppida studying Ser Yrsa's major scar. The long one, that came down across her now-red left eye.

The ship was still settling into dock and being tied off when the king called down, "What news, seneschal?"

"Your majesty," Kentigern said in his best, loud, clear voice, "I fear there have been attempts on the lives of both Prince Killian and Princess Maev—"

"An assassin managed to slash Killian before Killian gutted him," King Colm said impatiently. "And Maev's pet stopped her assassin before the attempt was made. Or have there been other attempts?"

"No others I know of, your majesty," Kentigern said, and Aefric could tell he was rallying against his surprise that the king already knew his news. "Though I should add that Princess Maev's assassin yet lives, and the princess is en route here to Water's End with the assassin."

"Has she questioned it?"

"Your majesty," Kentigern said, "I do not believe so."

"Tell her, your grace," King Colm ordered in tones so strong Aefric almost flinched. "Tell her *now*."

"Yes, your majesty," Aefric said, and quickly cast the spell that would carry his next words to her, then her words to him.

"Maev, do not interrogate the assassin. Doing so may kill him. We are at Water's End now, awaiting you. You may answer with twenty-five words."

"Twenty-five?" Maev said, sounding puzzled, but determined. He could just imagine her shaking off other wasted words. "I allowed no interrogation. Insisted on our justiciar. Negotiations on hold. Attack happened at palace. King Dalius investigating too." Her tone warmed with her last words. "Can't wait to see you."

"She's allowed no questioning," Aefric said. "She insisted on taking the assassin to your majesty's justiciar. The attack happened at the palace, though, so negotiations are on hold for the moment, and

King Dalius has begun his own investigation into the assassination attempt."

"On hold?" Queen Eppida said, sounding almost offended. "Surely she doesn't think we'd blame Varondam for this."

"It's the right move," King Colm said. "King Dalius just proved he can't keep Maev safe. Elbar's Blood, her *cat* did a better job of protecting her than all his knights and soldiers."

"And your duke did a better job of protecting *you*," Queen Eppida said archly, "than all *your* knights and soldiers."

"Yes," King Colm said levelly. "*My* duke."

"And what of Killian?" Queen Eppida said. "An assassin came for him at *Armityr*, and he had to dispatch that assassin himself."

"We don't know the full story there," King Colm objected.

"Nor do we know the full story in Varondam," Queen Eppida insisted. "And yet, your daughter has just put on hold *important* negotiations with a *key* potential ally. At least, if you intend to *win* this war."

King Colm shook his head. "Varondam will be more eager than ever for the alliance, if only to make clear their own innocence. Perhaps even to help protect themselves from Malimfari knives."

"But we cannot negotiate that alliance with Maev coming here to Water's End. She's costing us critical time."

"Those negotiations couldn't continue until the truth of the assassins is out," King Colm said. "King Dalius knows this. And that he conducts his own investigation works in our favor. Keeps his appetite whetted for the alliance. Meanwhile, the loss of Maev's company will work *its own* kind of magic on him."

"Meanwhile," Queen Eppida said flatly, "Maev comes *here*."

She gave Aefric a look that matched her tone.

King Colm's glance flicked to Aefric, then back to the queen.

"We'll continue this discussion later," he said.

"I concur," she said, and Aefric had the impression that this was just going to be the latest part of an ongoing conversation, that might just be about himself and Maev.

Of all the conversations to be left out of...

ONCE THE *DUKE'S HAND* WAS SETTLED AND TIED OFF, AND THE gangplank lowered, their majesties, Aefric, and their twenty knights descended to the smooth, green coral of the pier, where Kentigern, Ser Yrsa, and more of Aefric's knights and soldiers awaited them.

"General Yrsa," King Colm said, "what is the status of those Malimfari knights?"

"Your majesty," she said with a bow, "they have overpaid when shopping, and hunted without taking down game."

"But they remain here? At Water's End?"

"Your majesty, they currently remain ensconced in their rooms in the Red Branch Inn, just outside the castle gates."

"I want them arrested, in my name. See to it at once."

Ser Yrsa's eyes flicked to Aefric, who grimaced, but nodded. He hated the idea of arresting anyone without a proven crime of *some* sort. And one of those knights was the brother of the fiancée of one of Aefric's vassals...

Ser Yrsa frowned, looking at the golden oak trees etched onto the breastplates of the Knights of the Crown.

"Your majesty," she said slowly, "properly speaking—"

"Properly speaking," Ser Beatritz picked up, more authoritatively, "as your majesty is present and has his own knights available, anyone to be arrested in your majesty's name should be arrested by your majesty's knights. Though the knights of his vassal could, of course, act in support, if needed."

"Fine," King Colm said, and his words had all the calm of a storm about to break. "See to it yourself then, Beatritz. Take as many Knights of the Crown as you see fit."

She called over eight, leaving four to guard their majesties for the nonce. As she did this, Ser Yrsa called over a soldier, and ordered him to act as guide for the Crown Knights.

"Any more signs of Malimfari trouble?" Aefric asked. "Has Karbin found anything?"

"He reports in each night," Kentigern said, "but as yet, has found no more evidence of Malimfari trouble here in Water's End."

"There is another matter, though," Ser Yrsa said.

"What?" King Colm said, which got Queen Eppida to give him a nudge and a meaningful nod.

His nostrils flared in a sharp sigh. He turned to Aefric.

"Excuse me, your grace," King Colm said. "These are your people to question. Not mine."

"Your majesty," Aefric said with a bow, "Water's End is yours. If your majesty wishes information, he has only to ask."

King Colm snorted, a mere puff of amusement. Gave Aefric a wry look.

"Your grace sounds very much the duke," he said. "And here I was starting to think of your grace as an adventurer again."

"From what I have come to understand," Queen Eppida said, "he has filled both roles well so far." She arched an eyebrow at Aefric. "Though he yet leans a little toward the latter."

King Colm bowed and gave Aefric a go-ahead gesture. "I placed these lands in your trust, your grace. I shall leave the questioning to you."

"Thank you, your majesty," Aefric said. "But we need not see to those questions here on the dock."

"Your grace," Ser Yrsa said, "the matter I speak of should not wait."

"What's happened?" Aefric asked, worried now.

"Silverlake is gathering troops and miners on the northern ridge of the Dragonscar."

"How many?" Aefric asked.

"Five hundred troops, encamped. Thirty miners gathered so far, but more are inbound. And their equipment has not yet arrived."

King Colm looked as though he were dying to ask the questions.

So did Queen Eppida, for that matter.

"How recent is this information?" Aefric asked.

"Mid-afternoon. At the first sign of trouble, two days past, I increased our number of scouts watching the Dragonscar, and set up more waystations between here and there. If anything happens, we'll hear about it within a handful of hours."

"A lot can happen in a handful of hours," King Colm said quietly.

"Your majesty, I agree," Ser Yrsa said. "Which is why, while I was increasing our scouting, I began sending troops to muster south of the Dragonscar, outside the line-of-sight of Silverlake."

"Cold camp?" Ser Beornric asked.

"Of course," Ser Yrsa said. "So far, I do not believe Silverlake knows we're watching. I wouldn't risk them seeing our fires." She turned to Aefric and their majesties. "If Silverlake tries anything, our response will be timely."

"How many troops?" Aefric asked.

"I've been making sure we maintain a hundred more than they have, so far."

"Siege engines?"

"We haven't seen any on their side. I've sent up one trebuchet," she said. "Not for personnel, but to take down any mining equipment."

"Good thought," Aefric said, then turned to King Colm.

The King arched both eyebrows. "Something your grace wishes to tell me?"

"Your majesty," Aefric said, "I've wanted to tell you about this since before I knew of your visit. But with your majesty's permission, this is not the place to discuss it." He turned to Ser Yrsa. "Unless there's a need for immediate action?"

"None I know of, your grace," Ser Yrsa said. "I merely wished to ensure that your grace was told of the situation at the earliest available moment."

"As *I* should have been told," King Colm said archly. "Including the *reason* for this tension between two of my dukes."

"Be fair, my love," Queen Eppida said. "His grace has been rather distracted keeping us safe from assassins."

King Colm let out a heavy sigh.

"Fair enough," he said. "I believe the length of the day is wearing on me."

"Kentigern," Aefric said, "see that their majesties and their knights settled and refreshed." He turned to the king. "Shall we reconvene at your majesties' convenience?"

"Let us say an hour," King Colm said, though Queen Eppida frowned. "We can dine together. As I recall, there's a balcony in your ducal apartments private enough for a conversation such as this one, is there not, your grace?"

"There is, your majesty," Aefric said, and bowed. "Until then."

Kentigern called forward the senior page, a young woman who, by her poise and bearing, looked ready to graduate from her page training.

"Your majesties," Kentigern said, "with your permission, Meliflua here will see your majesties installed in the royal chambers, and provided with anything your majesties might need."

At the king's gesture, Meliflua led their majesties and their four guardian knights past the assemblage and towards the castle.

Once they were a safe distance away, Aefric began walking that direction himself, with the others falling in around him.

"Where is Ser Calder?" Aefric asked. "I expected him to be here."

"Arguing with Ser Deirdre," Kentigern said. "Last I saw of him."

Aefric got as far as frowning before Ser Yrsa chimed in.

"Your grace gave Ser Deirdre her task, and she refuses to give her report to anyone but you. This ... displeases Calder."

Aefric chuckled. "I imagine so. Any actual *word* from Duke Wylyn? What did Karbin hear from him in Redport?"

Kentigern answered that one.

"The way Karbin spoke, it sounded as though Duke Wylyn was entirely focused on finding any who aided and abetted those slavers."

"When told of the troops massing on the northern border," Ser Yrsa said, "Karbin sounded surprised. Remarked that the duke seemed to have no attention at all that direction. But that could have been deliberate deception."

"Could be," Aefric said. "Wylyn's tough to read. He certainly had a reputation for trickiness, when he was an adventurer. I doubt he's lost *that* edge."

"Likely not," Ser Beornric said. "The man still looks as though he were hammered out on a forge."

"What news of Ajenmoor?" Aefric asked. "Any update on Captain Brusi's escape?"

"Deirdre might know something," Ser Yrsa said wryly. "No one else seems to."

"There is the matter of Morgard," Kentigern said. "He's been guest here for close to an aett now."

"Right," Aefric said with a sigh. "Morgard. Did he come forward with anything he wanted to tell us?"

"Only that he has, in the past, made some deals he is not proud of. Says they were done when he was younger, and more desperate for money. He insists that since he's been working with Brangford Couglas, his deals have been entirely legitimate."

"I think we all know what Deirdre would say to that," Ser Beornric said with a chuckle. "'Anything involving Brangford Couglas is questionable at best.'"

"And what Calder would say to *that*," Ser Yrsa said. "'No evidence.'"

"You did tell Morgard that we might have to investigate him ourselves?" Aefric asked.

"I did, your grace," Kentigern said. "He seems to accept that."

"Likely a dead end investigation, though," Ser Yrsa said. "Unless he's been sloppy."

"There's a better way," Kentigern said.

Aefric stopped walking, just shy of the nearest door into the castle. A private door, that had been enameled and enchanted until it matched the shimmering colors of the castle around it. A door Aefric might not have spotted, had he not known it was there.

Aefric raised his eyebrows at his seneschal, who was smiling.

"We have those two eldrani, practically aching to be of service," Kentigern said.

"The soul thieves?" Ser Vria said, from nearby. "Your grace, they are not to be trusted."

"I'll keep that in mind, Ser Vria," Aefric said. "But it might be a good way to test their skills, and save us a good deal of time and money investigating Morgard."

"The cost may be a different coin, your grace," Ser Vria said.

"Ser Vria, stand down," Ser Beornric said.

She frowned hard, but bowed and backed off.

"I've been speaking with them, your grace," Kentigern said. "I believe they do mean well, and I believe their skills could aid us here."

"Fine," Aefric said, with a sigh. Happy to get at least one more thing off his desk. "Tell Morgard he may either remain as he is while we complete our investigation, or he can submit himself to a test by the *Sinflissacta*."

"Yes, your grace," Kentigern said, smiling.

"And Kentigern," Aefric said. "I want you watching, when the *Sinflissacta* do their work. Along with Karbin, studying the magic, and Bebara, in case her skills are needed."

Aefric turned to Ser Vria.

"I want you there as well. Observing only. Do you know what to look for, if they are, in fact, soul thieves? Rather than testers of ... destiny and character I think it is?"

"I believe I know what to look for, your grace," Ser Vria said, though she sounded uncertain. "I know what the stories told of."

"Well, if you spot anything that you believe to be dangerous, point it out to Karbin and Bebara."

"I will, your grace," Ser Vria said softly. "And thank you."

"I *am* listening, Ser Vria," Aefric said. "And I *do* value your input." He looked around at his other five Knights of the Lake. "*All* your input. But I will make my own decisions. Always."

"Yes, your grace," they all said, and slapped their hilts in agreement.

"What about Gwawl?" Aefric asked. "Has he been any trouble? Have there been any attempts at a breakout?"

"None," Ser Yrsa said. "Guards report that he seems to accept his incarceration. Though he does ask to have his pendant returned."

Aefric scoffed.

"Yes," Ser Yrsa said. "I told him not to expect that."

"Tell him the worthless thing has been destroyed," Aefric said, with a wicked smile he shared with his knights. That lie might serve him well.

He turned to Kentigern. "Has Byrhta arrived yet?"

"Unfortunately," Kentigern said, "Baroness Regent Byrhta Ol'Caran and Mistress Vercy Ol'Karmak have been delayed in River-break. Some business involving complaints from a group of lers, according to the official letter. Though Mistress Byrhta sent along a private letter for your grace, as well."

Pity. He would have loved to have seen Byrhta that night. Talked with her.

Though perhaps it was for the best, with Maev coming...

And with his head full of thoughts like these, Aefric set about seeing to his own rest and refreshment.

***

Meeting again in an hour turned out to be too ambitious a plan. Queen Eppida insisted on a bath, and from the sound of things, she may have insisted that his majesty join her.

Aefric took that opportunity for a short bath himself, though he suspected his own was far less entertaining.

After the bath, he changed into silk. A black, quilted tunic, embroidered with both gold and silver threat, over dark blue hose. His soft leather shoes had been dyed black to match the tunic, and stitched with both gold and silver thread as well. A leather belt, also dyed black, held the wand Garram, but no sword.

And, of course, he carried the Brightstaff.

He received word from Dajen that their majesties had food brought to them, so Aefric finally settled on dining alone on his small, private balcony, while he waited. A simple meal of grilled lake salmon with rosemary, potatoes baked with garlic and cheese, and a small variety of roasted green vegetables.

More important, he had some time to himself. Simple peace and quiet, for a time. Nothing but the gentle breeze coming off the lake, and the distant sounds of workers, far below.

Peaceful. Meditative. Aefric knew there were things he could have done with that time, but he let all those matters wait for a change.

Three hours passed that way. Night rose, sprinkling stars across the heavens. The moon, just past full, made its slow, lazy way up the northern sky.

A pleasant evening. Still a touch of warmth to the air, but not too much.

Finally the meeting came together, on Aefric's large public balcony. King Colm, Aefric, Kentigern, and Sers Calder, Beatritz, Yrsa, and Beornric.

The queen, it seemed, had foregone this meeting to have her own meeting with her sister, Zoleen.

The king had changed into silks as as Aefric had. A quilted, dark red tunic, embroidered with gold thread, over soft brown hose.

Kentigern had not changed his clothes, and the knights all wore their full plate.

King Colm spotted that Ser Calder was the only knight present not bearing arms, and raised his eyebrows at Aefric, who nodded, trying to convey that this was by his order.

King Colm mimed whistling.

Ser Beatritz began the conversation.

"Your majesty, the four Malimfari knights have been arrested, and given four strong cells here at Water's End."

"How did they handle their arrest?" King Colm asked.

"Well enough," Ser Beatritz said. "They seemed to expect it."

"Well," King Colm said, "the justiciar is coming at speed. We'll have truth from them soon enough."

With that, they were all seated, and served a good, rich dark beer.

Aefric began the tale of the Dragonscar. He didn't get very far into it before his majesty stopped him.

"Do I understand this right?" King Colm asked. "You not only unbound those borogs, and let them live, but brought them with you into the Dragonscar? As though they were part of your company?"

"I asked the same question, your majesty," Ser Calder grumbled.

"They *were* a part of my company," Aefric said. "Their names are Ge'rek and Po'rek, and they played a critical role in the events that followed."

"Your grace *does* remember that it was an army of borogs we faced together?" King Colm asked. "Just there, on the other side of the lake from where we sit?"

"Your majesty," Aefric said as patiently as he could, "during the Godswalk Wars those borogs were under the influence of the Flayer. The wars are over. The Flayer has returned to His hell. And the borogs are only people again. As we are."

"I doubt very much that the people of your duchy will be as ... welcoming of them as your grace."

"I said that as well," Ser Calder grumbled.

"Ser Calder," Aefric said, "did his majesty *ask*?"

"No, your grace."

"Consider that, next time." To the king, who looked curious about the exchange, Aefric said, "You majesty, the wars are over. Part of healing our people involves getting them past prejudices that crept up during the wars."

"That may be. But convincing those whose families were killed by borogs may not be so easy," King Colm said. "There are still those who harbor resentment toward Malimfar from our last true war with them, decades ago."

"The healing must begin somewhere," Aefric said. "Let it begin with me."

"Very well," the king said with a nod. "I won't overrule you in this. For now."

Aefric frowned. He hadn't considered that possibility...

"Do continue, your grace."

"Yes, your majesty." Aefric spoke then of how they traveled into the Dragonscar. How they'd camped for the night, and then faced the late night skirmish with the stone men.

"And you say the borogs fought alongside you?"

"Eagerly, your majesty," Ser Yrsa said. "It's quite clear that they regard his grace as their chief. They fought to preserve his life, and now they labor in his name."

"Labor?" King Colm asked.

"We're getting ahead," Aefric said, and told instead of the injuries and deaths his soldiers suffered against the stone simulacra, and the spell he'd worked to analyze their magic.

Once he was certain that his majesty understood the gravity of those losses, and Aefric's confidence in his ability to identify the caster behind that skirmish, he went on to explain about the borogs smelling gold.

"Truly?" King Colm asked skeptically. "Even the na'shek can't do that."

"Not only can Ge'rek and Po'rek smell gold," Aefric said, "they can mine it without anything we think of as proper tools."

Aefric set one of the large, clean round nuggets on the table in front of his majesty.

King Colm picked it up. Hefted it. "They dug this out of that cave?"

"And several others besides. All within the course of a few hours," Aefric said. "And they presented it just that clean. It seems to be a holy task for them."

"And you say they smelled gold from the north side as well as the south side?"

"Not as much, and only from one cave, but yes, your majesty."

"So your question is whether that's your gold on the north side?"

"That's one question, your majesty," Aefric agreed. "And my historian has been researching possible precedents."

"There's no need for that," King Colm said casually, handing the gold nugget back to Aefric. "Your grace is entitled to mine one hundred feet outward or downward from the natural borders of that cave, but no farther into Silverlake than that. Anything beyond a hundred feet is Silverlake's."

Aefric was pleased his wasn't the only confused expression at the table. Of those in that meeting who were *not* the king, it seemed that only Ser Beatritz understood that ruling.

King Colm chuckled. Clapped Aefric on the back.

"It was a planning game my father used to play with me, as his father did with him, and I have with Killian." King Colm smiled. "I never thought to see it come up in my lifetime, but the question was simple enough. A vassal finds a gold mine on her lands, that extends into the lands of her neighbor. How much of that gold mine is hers?"

"Why one hundred feet?" Aefric asked. "Not complaining, your majesty, just curious."

"Because one hundred feet was the answer chosen by my great-great grandmother, when she came up with the question. It's been the official answer ever since."

"I'll inform my historian," Aefric said.

"If she's come up with a different answer," King Colm said, "I'd be interested to know it."

"Your majesty," Kentigern said, "she has not. At least, not as of lunchtime, when I last spoke with her."

"Continue, your grace," King Colm said. "How did you come to believe that Silverlake was behind those spells?"

Aefric went on to explain about his trip into Silverlake, and his complete certainty that Duke Wylyn's court wizard, Sifwyn, was responsible for both the detection wards in the Dragonscar, and the attack of the stone men.

"And there's no possibility of error here?" King Colm asked.

"None, your majesty," Aefric said. "And I shall happily swear such to your majesty's justiciar."

King Colm nodded. Turned to Kentigern. "You said Wylyn is in Redport?"

"I believe so," Kentigern said. "If he's left, I haven't heard."

"Send a rika. He is summoned to me here at Water's End. At once. He is to bring his wizard, and any others he brought along to Redport."

"Yes, your majesty," Kentigern said, and then got up to fulfill the order immediately.

King Colm turned back to Aefric.

"Tell me more about these smugglers and slavers."

And so Aefric told him the rest. The strange events in Ajenmoor. The possible ties in Lachedran. The more certain ties in Redport, and the definite ties in Wulfport and Kefthal. Everything he knew, everything he suspected, leaving out for the moment only those details that pointed to Nelazzi.

"Malimfar is buying slaves?" King Colm said, his voice quiet and dangerous.

"*Someone* in Malimfar is buying slaves," Ser Calder said. "We don't know for certain that the nobles or royal family are involved."

"Nor do we know that they aren't," King Colm said, turning back to Aefric. "How certain are you of this?"

"As certain as I can be," Aefric said, "given that your majesty ordered me not to investigate Malimfar."

"Did I?" King Colm asked.

"Your majesty was quite clear that I was to take no actions regarding Malimfar."

"That sounds more like me," King Colm said, shaking his head. "I was thinking mostly of their crown princess. But I am pleased to know your grace erred on the side of caution. I take it this is also why you'd done nothing more with those Malimfari knights than watch them?"

"That's correct, your majesty."

King Colm nodded. "Anything else I should be made aware of?"

"We have compelling reason to believe that Nelazzi stands behind both the slavers and the smugglers," Aefric said. "I would like permission to hunt her down and put an end to her."

"Denied," King Colm said, then shook his head. "I'm sorry, your grace. I have no more love for pirates than you do. But war against Nelazzi is like to be as great a task as war against Malimfar. And I cannot have one of my most important vassals fighting on two fronts."

"But when the Malimfar question is settled?" Aefric asked.

"Perhaps," King Colm said. "I will promise this much. We shall revisit the topic once Malimfar is dealt with. Until then, defend against Nelazzi as you must, but *do not* pursue her. Not yourself, nor through your agents."

He leaned forward and tapped the table in front of Aefric.

"Am I understood?"

"You are understood, your majesty," Aefric said, chagrined.

"Your grace is a man of action, as I am," King Colm said. "I know this burns at you. But you and I both have cares beyond our own need for revenge."

Ser Beatritz cleared her throat.

"Something you wish to say, ser knight?" King Colm asked.

"Only to observe that, were she present, our queen would say that your majesty pursues revenge in regard to Malimfar."

"And I would tell *her*," King Colm said, his voice now low and dangerous, "that I will allow *no one* to strike at the royal family with impunity. Malimfar made the attempt. Malimfar shall pay the price."

"If it *was* Malimfar," Ser Beatritz said softly. "Which, alas, we do not yet know for certain."

"And we shall find out," King Colm said. "Soon."

---

ONCE THE ROYAL MEETING WAS OVER, AEFRIC LINGERED ON THE LARGE balcony by starlight. Not alone, though. Accompanied by Sers Beornric, Yrsa, and Calder, and joined shortly by Kentigern.

"I've sent for Ser Deirdre, your grace," Kentigern said, "and I've left word for Karbin to join us as soon as he arrives."

"Thank you," Aefric said, and took another sip of that strong, dark beer. He was still working on his first tankard, but he was alone in this. Ser Calder was on his third, and Sers Yrsa and Beornric seemed to be competing to see who could drink more without letting it affect their work.

Aefric wasn't sure how much Kentigern had drunk, but he suspected the seneschal was on his second tankard.

"I took the opportunity to speak with Li'sheneesha, as well,"

Kentigern said. "She and Li'nasachal would be pleased to perform the soul test on Morgard."

"Did you ask Morgard if he's willing?"

"Yes, your grace," Kentigern said. "Once the eldrani agreed, I asked him which he would prefer. Our investigation or a test by magic. He acceded to the test by magic. Even apologized for putting us through this."

"Yes," Ser Calder said. "I spoke with the boy earlier. He truly does seem to repent some of the ... misjudgments made in his younger days."

"Easy to say," Ser Beornric said, "when under the noble's arrest."

Aefric almost asked about that, but realized he knew the answer. Morgard had guest chambers, not a cell, but he was hardly free to move about, much less leave Water's End.

Dajen knocked lightly to announce himself, then stepped out onto the balcony.

"Your grace," he said, with only slightly less distaste in his voice than Ocheda would have had in his place, "Ser Deirdre Ol'Miri has arrived. Shall I make her wait? Or perhaps, ask her to leave her news with me?"

"No need for that, Dajen," Aefric said with a quirked smile. "Send her out. And bring her some beer, if she wants some."

"Yes, your grace," Dajen said, not trying to hide his disappointment, which made Sers Beornric and Yrsa chuckle.

Ser Calder, though, frowned hard enough to grind his teeth.

Ser Deirdre sauntered onto the balcony, wry smile in place, and for once, she wasn't wearing armor. Instead she adorned a flattering tunic of maroon silk over black hose, a dark brown leather belt with her rapier and dagger, and soft leather shoes.

As she so often did, she dropped to her knees before Aefric. And her eyes roved approvingly over his outfit.

"Your grace," she said, "I have returned from Ajenmoor triumphant. I have learned a great deal on your grace's behalf. And in so doing, as I swore on my honor, I disturbed the waters not a ripple."

"And this can be confirmed?" Aefric said, half in jest. Something about her manner just brought out old adventuring habits, where humor was concerned.

"I can confirm it, your grace," Kentigern said. "I keep in touch with friends in Ajenmoor who would notice, if Ser Deirdre caused problems in the course of her investigation. I've heard from two of them in the last three days, and both make it sound as though all is calm in Ajenmoor. Or at least, that the only disturbance of note since your grace's own visit was the escape of Captain Brusi."

Triumph flashed in Ser Deirdre's green eyes. Her smile widened.

"Stand, Ser Deirdre," Aefric said. "Join us at the table. And for Kalinda's sake, don't let anyone from his majesty's party see you kneeling to me."

"Of course not, your grace," Ser Deirdre said as she sat. "That would be unseemly."

The growl that came out of Ser Calder then reminded Aefric of the way a volcano rumbled when threatening to erupt.

Ser Deirdre only looked amused.

"*Report*, damn you," Ser Calder barked.

Ser Deirdre, smile still in place, gazed at Ser Calder through a long, slow blink, before turning to Aefric.

"Is your grace ready to hear my report from Ajenmoor?" she asked innocently.

Ser Calder thumped the table with a fist.

"Stop taunting my castellan," Aefric said.

"Must I, your grace?" Ser Deirdre asked. "I have so little fun."

"That's a lie," Ser Yrsa muttered, which made Ser Deirdre chuckle.

"Very well, your grace," she said then, and turned to Ser Calder. "Please excuse me, good castellan, if I have given offense in my efforts to obey my duke while not letting another usurp his authority."

"*Usurp?*" Ser Calder demanded, coming to his feet. His hand reached for a sword he wasn't wearing. "How dare you?"

Ser Deirdre didn't move. Not that Aefric could tell. And yet, there was a subtle shift in her posture. All the humor went out of her.

All at once, she looked the very definition of quiet and deadly.

Sers Beornric and Yrsa both shifted, ready to intervene if needed. Kentigern seemed to shrink in his chair, trying to stay out of the way.

"Enough," Aefric said, reminding them all that he could be quiet and deadly as well.

Ser Calder shook with the effort of restraining himself from going after Ser Deirdre.

"Your grace," Ser Calder said through clenched teeth. "This insult cannot be borne. I will have satisfaction."

"I will be happy to provide it," Ser Deirdre said softly.

"I. Said. Enough," Aefric said. The Brightstaff, standing beside his chair, began to glow softly from its yellow diamond. "I will not have my knights coming to blows in my own apartments."

"The practice grounds would suit far better," Ser Calder growled.

"Name the time," Ser Deirdre said.

"Ser Yrsa," Aefric said.

"Your grace," she said, coming to her feet.

"Escort my castellan to our morning meeting room, where he is to calm himself. See that he remains there, under guard if necessary, until I summon him. When you are confident that he *will not leave that room*, return."

"Yes, your grace," Ser Yrsa said.

"No guard will be necessary," Ser Calder said. He gave Aefric a sharp bow. "Your grace."

He turned and left the balcony, Ser Yrsa following in his wake.

"While we wait for Ser Yrsa to return," Aefric said, "I would like to know why you chose the word *usurp*. I know that you and Ser Calder have your problems, but you must know that word is a heavy accusation."

"Your grace," Ser Deirdre said, her tones as serious as Aefric had ever heard from her, "I did not choose that word to be flippant. When in the presence of your grace's trusted advisers, Ser Calder behaves as befits his station, more or less. In their absence, however, he speaks and acts as though he considers himself the true Duke of Deepwater."

Aefric sat back in his chair, frowning. "And yet, he displays this behavior before *you*? A knight I have personally assigned more than one mission?"

"My zest for life gives me an unconventional reputation, your grace," Ser Deirdre said. "It also has the advantage of bringing revealing behavior out of those who live by pretense."

She looked past the balcony, toward the meeting room. Nodded.

"Ser Calder is just such a man," she said. "And, in my opinion, he represents a danger to your grace."

"One you wish to eliminate?" Ser Beornric asked.

"I would eliminate all threats to his grace, if permitted," Ser Deirdre said, casually shrugging one shoulder. "I have seen many leaders, but few worth following." She nodded at Aefric. "Your grace, I am pleased to say, is one of the few. And I would follow him into each of the thirteen hells and the Abyss."

Ser Yrsa came back onto the patio then, followed by Dajen with more beer.

"Calder will be some time in calming," Ser Yrsa said, as she took her seat. "He's insisting on a duel for his honor."

"I'd be happy to fight it, your grace," Ser Deirdre said.

"Tell Ser Yrsa why," Aefric said, then gestured for Dajen to stay. "I want you to hear this too."

Ser Deirdre laid out her accusation against Ser Calder in clear terms.

"Opinions?" Aefric asked.

"I don't want to believe that's true," Ser Yrsa said. "But I can't deny it's possible. It certainly seems to fit him."

"I agree," Ser Beornric said with a sigh.

"I can surreptitiously check with our guards and soldiers," Ser Yrsa said, frowning. "Get their gauge of his behavior. If your grace wishes."

"I do," Aefric, said, then looked at Kentigern.

"I'm not sure I'd go so far as to use the word *usurp*," Kentigern said, slowly. "But I cannot deny that he's been more ... aggressive in his role as castellan since Duchess Arinda died."

Aefric turned to Dajen. "I would like you to survey the castle staff.

No leading questions. Just get their impressions of Ser Calder's behavior, and report back to me."

"I shall see to it at once, your grace," Dajen said. "I should have an answer before noon tomorrow."

"Good," Aefric said. "Thank you."

Dajen took that as his dismissal, and left.

Aefric turned to Kentigern.

"In the morning I want you to meet with Elkari about Ser Calder. Go over the books and records. See if there's anything there I need to know about."

"Should I look for anything specific?"

"Money," Ser Deirdre suggested. "And land. In the wake of the Godswalk Wars, a good deal of both may have gone missing. Perhaps some of it found its way into his pockets."

"Your grace's 'lost lers?'" Ser Beornric asked.

"Disturbing notion," Ser Yrsa said.

"Let us not jump to conclusions," Aefric said. "We don't know that he's guilty of anything beyond an attitude problem."

"Attitude is the beginning of a great many crimes," Ser Deirdre said.

"Which is why we're checking," Aefric said. "Not on the assumption of guilt. But to determine guilt or innocence."

"I'll meet with Elkari after the morning meeting," Kentigern said. "And between us we have enough assistants to finish the task ... perhaps by evening?"

"Good," Aefric said. "Officially, this is part of that 'lost lers' investigation, coming from the angle of land and money, instead of family names. No one is to know of any accusations against Ser Calder until I say so."

"What about his majesty?" Ser Beornric asked.

"His majesty noticed that I'd disarmed Ser Calder," Aefric said. "So he'll already suspect. But if anyone tells him, it will be me."

That brought a general round of agreement.

Pakel, the heavyset night servant, knocked gently and stepped out onto the balcony.

"Your grace," he said, "your ducal wizard has arrived."

Good. Perhaps Aefric could finally get his reports.

If he was lucky, he might even get to sleep that night.

---

KARBIN LOOKED TIRED WHEN HE JOINED AEFRIC AND THE OTHERS ON the wide, public-level balcony that evening. And he gratefully sank onto a comfortable, greenwood chair and gulped down his first tankard of that rich, dark beer, while the others caught him up about the accusations made by Ser Deirdre.

Once that was finished, Karbin rolled his lips around in thought, then nodded.

"You've noticed something?" Aefric asked.

"Small things only," Karbin said. "Nothing I would have considered worth mentioning. Little details of behavior I'd written off to his resenting the degree of trust and faith you show me."

"I've known you most of my life," Aefric said, incredulously. "And I've fought beside you more times than I care to count."

"But like you," Karbin said, "I am not born to nobility. Most court wizards are."

"He's right," Ser Beornric said. "The first offspring inherits, but after that, any who show potential get tested for talent at wizardry, in hope of gaining the family influence in another court."

"Not that many show the aptitude," Ser Deirdre said, philosophically.

"Regardless," Aefric said. "Before this business with Ser Calder came to a head, I believe you were ready to report, Ser Deirdre?"

"I was and I am, your grace," Ser Deirdre said with a smile.

She cleared her throat. Took a long pull from her beer, then set her tankard down heavily. She rubbed her hands together.

"My mission was to investigate all questions surrounding the shipment of textiles that Morgard arranged to fill the hold of the *Arcturus*, left empty by some problem with their expected shipment of pipe weed. To learn what I could about the missing shipment, the

*Arcturus*, and everything else related, without making waves in the process."

She paused there, as though seeking confirmation, so Aefric nodded.

"Morgard Ol'Nara supplied the ship's name before I left Water's End, and I made my way to Ajenmoor by stealth, in the hold of a fishing vessel whose captain owed me a favor."

Ser Beornric opened his mouth as though to ask about that, but changed his mind and clamped his mouth shut.

"I first investigated the *Arcturus* herself. In going through the harbormaster's reports—"

"The harbormaster gave you access to his reports?" Kentigern asked, shocked.

"If silence can be regarded as consent," Ser Deirdre said with a twinkle in her eye, "then he consented. Though I did not do him the honor of asking. After all, I would have had to explain my curiosity, and word would have gotten around about who I was, what I was doing, and why, all of which would have violated my orders."

Aefric tried to fight down his smile and lost. "Do go on, Ser Deirdre."

"Of course, your grace," she said, appearing to enjoy his smile. "As I was saying, according to the harbormaster's reports, the *Arcturus* had not docked at Ajenmoor at any time in the five years prior to its recent visit."

"Five years?" Aefric said.

"At least, your grace," Ser Deirdre said. "Though it may have been longer. I was required at that point to cut short that branch of my investigation."

"Pity," Ser Yrsa said. "I would have liked to hear what the harbormaster's office had to say about that pipe weed."

Ser Deirdre frowned. "General Yrsa, did I say I learned nothing about pipe weed?"

"But if you had to cut short your time at the harbormaster's office..."

"The order in which I report my information to his grace is not the order in which I discovered it, but the order that makes the story clear."

Ser Yrsa bowed her head for Ser Deirdre to continue.

"As I was saying," Ser Deirdre said, turning back to Aefric. "The *Arcturus'* visit to Ajenmoor was the exception, not the rule. Through my investigations of those taverns favored by sailors and dockworkers, I learned that—"

"*You* passed as a sailor or dockworker?" Ser Beornric asked in disbelief.

"Not in the least," Ser Deirdre said easily. "But there are those who regard my appearance as pleasing" — which Aefric knew was an understatement — "and rare is the inebriated man who will not talk freely to an attractive woman."

"You wore a dress, didn't you," Ser Yrsa said, sounding more amazed than questioning.

Ser Deirdre arched an eyebrow, but shifted to a playful expression as she turned back to Aefric.

"I could model the gown sometime, should your grace be curious."

"I'll keep that in mind," Aefric said, chuckling. Damn if this woman couldn't make him laugh. "But please continue your report."

"I live to serve, your grace," she said, bowing her head. "From the sailors and dockworkers I learned that the *Arcturus* usually docks at three other ports along this coast during the summertime. Would anyone care to guess which three?"

"Redport, Wulfport, and Drake's Landing," Karbin said, naming the three known stops of the slavers.

"Those very three," Ser Deirdre said, approvingly. "And the *Arcturus'* sailors were a cantankerous lot, apparently worried about their pay."

"Makes sense," Ser Beornric said, "if they were missing an expected shipment."

"Especially if that shipment would include expensive cargo," Ser Yrsa said. "Which pipe weed is not."

Ser Deirdre sighed dramatically. "You simply *must* hear about the pipe weed now?"

"Indulge my general, if you would be so kind," Aefric said.

"Of course, your grace," Ser Deirdre said, sounding a touch mollified, at being asked. "According to both the reports in the harbormaster's office, and the word around Ajenmoor's taverns, no pipe weed had come through in at least three aetts, and none was expected."

"The last shipment," Kentigern said. "Was it from Goldenfall?"

"It was," Ser Deirdre said, smiling brightly enough at Kentigern that he flushed slightly. "Very good, Master Kentigern. In fact, almost all the pipe weed shipped through Ajenmoor comes from Goldenfall."

"So what *was* the *Arcturus* expecting?" Aefric asked.

"That, alas, no one seems to know," Ser Deirdre said, before raising an index finger. "*However.* I know that they arrived in Ajenmoor the day before your grace fought the crews of the *Gull's Bride* and the *Swift Wave* at the Dragonscar. And I know that the *Arcturus'* crew did not evince worry about their funds and their cargo until *after* word reached Ajenmoor about those fights."

"How can you be certain?" Kentigern asked.

"I can read a calendar," Ser Deirdre said, shrugging one shoulder. "Though making the connections required me to check dates in the harbormaster's office against information I learned in the taverns."

"So how was this supposed to work?" Aefric asked. "The *Gull's Bride* brings the cargo of slaves to the Dragonscar. Trades them for the *Swift Wave's* cargo of stolen goods. Then the *Gull's Bride* departs, and the *Swift Wave* rendezvouses with the *Arcturus* in Ajenmoor to transfer the slaves? No more than a hundred miles from the Dragonscar?"

Aefric shook his head, trying to make sense of it.

"You're forgetting something," Karbin said softly, which got everyone to turn to him. "The *Swift Wave* was pressed into this job by Nelazzi. Why would she do that?"

"They're smugglers, not slavers," Ser Beornric said, starting to see where Karbin was going, though Aefric wasn't sure yet. "And she wanted to make them carry slaves."

"Just so," Karbin said. "Nelazzi is a businesswoman first and foremost. And with so many refugees displaced by the wars, and so many places in need of cheap labor, she's likely moving more into slavery than she has before."

"Which means she needs more ships willing to carry slaves," Aefric said, understanding now. "So she tried to force accomplished smugglers, the *Swift Wave's* crew, to carry a cargo of slaves."

"But she wouldn't trust them to carry the cargo far yet," Karbin continued. "Nor would she trust them to handle the market. So she planned to have them carry the shipment to a nearby port, where a more established crew of slavers would take over."

"But if it worked," Aefric said, "then she'd've gotten them to carry slaves once. Which would mean they'd put up less of a fight against doing so the next time."

"And soon," Karbin finished, "she'd have a new crew of slavers. One that knows all the tricks of smuggling, and is welcomed in more ports than her usual slaver ships."

"So where does the shipment of cheap textiles come into it?" Ser Yrsa asked.

"Doesn't," Ser Deirdre said, sounding almost disappointed. "I tracked all the details. Riverborne shipping, out of Lachedran. That was their usual shipment, arriving at its usual time. And sure enough, the ship they were supposed to meet — the *Salty Tears* — departed port a full aett ahead of schedule, without giving a reason. And Riverborne did indeed have those textiles sitting in a warehouse, eating fees every day."

"A full aett ahead of schedule," Aefric said, thoughtfully.

"I checked, your grace," Ser Deirdre said. "The dates don't line up with the activities in the Dragonscar."

"Worth checking," Aefric said. "Is your report complete?"

"Not yet, your grace," she said. "I was in Ajenmoor when Captain Brusi made his escape. To all appearances, it was an outside job. But would your grace care to guess what ship was said to have been spotted in the harbor that night?"

"The *Arcturus*?" Aefric guessed.

"Very good, your grace," Ser Deirdre said with a smile. "It did not dock, did not register with the harbormaster, and was gone before dawn. And yet, several night workers on the docks claimed to have seen it. They knew it by the figurehead — a sea devil with its spear raised."

"That means he's gone then," Aefric said.

"Alas, I believe so," Ser Deirdre said. "As a final note, so far as I can tell, Morgard Ol'Nara was not personally involved in any illegal activity while in Ajenmoor recently. Even the business with the textiles was clean from his end."

"But not necessarily from Brangford Couglas' end," Aefric said.

"No," Ser Deirdre agreed. "I could not confirm this, but he appears to have been known to the crew of the *Arcturus*."

"Well," Aefric said with a sigh, "we'll have to keep an eye on him and his activities then."

"And *now*," Ser Deirdre said, "my report is complete, your grace."

"And an impressive report it is, Ser Deirdre," Aefric said, which made her preen a little. "I'd like you to write up a copy for my historian, and for the eyes of his majesty."

"I would be honored, your grace."

"Karbin," Aefric said. "How do things look around the city? Any more Malimfari problems expected?"

"I have checked all through Water's End and environs," Karbin said. "I believe the knights were all the Malimfari influence in this area."

"Less of a surprise," Aefric said, "given the assassination attempts. But thank you for making sure." He stood. "All right, my good people. On that note, I'm calling it a night. I will see you all in the morning."

As they filed out, Aefric held Kentigern back for a private word.

"One more thing," Aefric said to his seneschal. "I want master jewel smith Tayor Sizen to fashion a golden brooch in the shape of a sea dragon, with tiny emeralds for eyes."

"Yes, your grace," Kentigern said with a smile. "Shall I have a sea dragon seal fashioned as well?"

"Yes, please."

"Certainly, your grace," Kentigern said with a nod. "I think she'll be most pleased with the results."

"I hope so," Aefric said. But with that, he was ready to end his long day. Perhaps read Byrhta's letter before bed.

---

AFTER DISMISSING KENTIGERN, AEFRIC LINGERED A MOMENT ON THE balcony. He looked out over the lights of the docks below, as well as those he could see on ships out in the lake.

Nelazzi. It was all coming back to Nelazzi. Pressing smugglers into service as slavers. But what did it mean that Captain Brusi was her "known confederate?"

Was his *Swift Wave* chosen to carry slaves because of his relationship with Nelazzi? Or despite it?

Gwawl had been aboard the *Swift Wave* too. And that Mavash, who'd been so ready to talk. So quick to blame his captain...

Unless Brusi wasn't the usual captain?

What if Mavash had been the *Swift Wave's* usual captain? What if Brusi and Gwawl had been planted aboard to ensure their cooperation? Perhaps intending to transfer to the *Arcturus* along with the slaves...

An interesting notion. Captain Brusi was gone, and beyond the reach of questioning. But Gwawl, *he* was down in Aefric's cells. Aefric could go down there and ask.

Or better, he could wait a scant handful of days until the king's justiciar came. Let the justiciar ask, then—

"Your grace?" Pakel's voice. Had he knocked?

Aefric turned to see the hefty night servant standing on the balcony, which meant he must have knocked and gone unheard under Aefric's musing.

"Yes?" Aefric asked.

"Her majesty awaits in your public sitting room," Pakel said.

Her majesty? Why would ... the noble privilege? No. She must be here to ask about something. A sales pitch for marrying Zoleen, perhaps.

But Pakel was still talking.

"And Ser Calder yet remains in your morning meeting room."

Ser Calder. Aefric had almost forgotten. He sighed heavily.

"Please," Aefric said, "escort her majesty to my private sitting room upstairs, see that she is offered food and drink, and tell her I will be with her as soon as pressing business allows. Then, once she's settled, bring me Ser Calder."

"Yes, your grace."

Aefric tried to return to his previous line of thought as he gazed out over Lake Deepwater by night, but it was no good. He was too busy worrying about Ser Calder, Ser Deirdre, and his own potential marriage plans.

It was almost a relief when Pakel announced, "Your grace, Ser Calder is here."

Aefric turned, and saw that Ser Calder was flanked by heavily scarred Ser Wardius and tall, striking Ser Arras.

At Aefric's questioning glance, both Knights of the Lake glanced at Ser Calder, then nodded at Aefric as though they thought they might be needed.

Ser Calder looked offended by their presence, but restricted his objections to a sigh.

"Your grace," he said with a small bow, "I have calmed myself."

"As you see it, Ser Calder, what is the nature of your disagreement with Ser Deirdre?"

Ser Calder's eyebrows raised. He scoffed.

"I should have thought that obvious, your grace. The woman may be a knight, but she has no sense of propriety or decency. And she offers respect to no one but your grace."

Aefric considered addressing that. Instead, he let silence stretch, to see what else his castellan might say.

"The obsequious way she kneels to your grace is disgusting. I struggle to believe that your grace does not censure her for it."

True, Aefric wasn't fond of the kneeling. But he suspected he and Ser Deirdre were engaged in a game of wills, to see which of them would break first. Would he order her to stop? Or would she grow tired of the game?

"Tonight, though, she went too far," Ser Calder said, tension singing through all his muscles. "To dare call me *usurper*. I have served as castellan at Water's End since before that whelp's *parents* were born. I know more about knighthood and honor than she can *conceive* of."

"Why do you think she chose that word?"

"To bait me, obviously," Ser Calder said. "To offend me all she could, before hiding behind your grace. Though why your grace tolerates her at all, I cannot fathom. Unless it pleases your grace to have a pretty girl fawn over him so. Though if that is the case, I can suggest a number of—"

"*Ser Calder,*" Aefric said sharply.

"Excuse me, your grace," Ser Calder said. "If I have overstepped, I apologize."

Aefric almost — *almost* — made a comment about how easily overstepping seemed to come to Ser Calder. But he didn't want to get distracted from his point.

"And you truly intend to challenge her to a duel?" Aefric asked.

"Your grace, I do," Ser Calder said.

Aefric looked at the many lines on the knight's face. The gray of his hair.

"I assure your grace," Ser Calder said proudly, "I am still knight enough to put that puppy in her place."

"And what does 'her place' involve?" Aefric asked. "A duel to first blood? To capitulation? To the death?"

"I would not deprive my duke of even the least of his knights," Ser Calder said. "I will be satisfied with first blood and an apology."

"And if you lose?"

Ser Calder straightened as though struck.

"I am not so young as I was," Ser Calder said, voice low, "but I am far from feeble, your grace."

"Nor do I do accuse you of *being* feeble, Ser Calder," Aefric said. "But I have seen Ser Deirdre fight. I'm not certain that I've seen her match."

"Your grace has never seen *me* fight."

"True," Aefric said, then sighed. "Nor shall I anytime soon."

Ser Calder started objecting. Aefric had to talk over him.

*"I will finish, ser knight."*

Grinding his teeth in fury, Ser Calder nodded for Aefric to proceed.

"The king and queen of Armyr are here," Aefric said. "*My* lieges. Here at Water's End. And I will *not* have their memory of this visit include a duel between my castellan and one of my knights."

"But your grace—"

*"Am I understood?"*

Ser Calder bowed. "You are understood, your grace. May I speak?"

"You may," Aefric said cautiously. "And I hope you don't make me regret this decision."

"Your grace," Ser Calder said. "I am not a young man. My wife has passed. My children went off to seek their fortunes long ago. All I have left are my position and my honor. If your grace allows some knight to insult my honor, without allowing me to respond, I..."

"I never said I would not allow you to respond," Aefric said. "Only that I would not allow you to duel one of my knights during a royal visit. Once their majesties are gone, I'll make the arrangements for your duel myself, if I need to."

"Your grace believes the whelp," Ser Calder said, wonder on his face. "All I have done in the service of Water's End and Deepwater, and your grace trusts to the word of a pretty young knight over my own."

"That's not true, Ser Calder," Aefric said, though it was closer to the truth than he liked to admit.

Still. He *was* at least requiring corroboration before acting on Ser Deirdre's accusation. Even if Ser Calder didn't know this.

"Your grace swears to this? I know I am not the favorite among his vassals."

"You spoke of overstepping," Aefric said. "Something that seems to come too easily to you, Ser Calder. Which is the source of the difficulties between *us*."

"With respect, your grace," Ser Calder said, "I could as easily say that your grace treats me and my position with ... less regard than I have grown accustomed to."

"Perhaps," Aefric said. "But I am not a Soulfist. And the way I rule my duchy will necessarily be different from the way Arinda's family did."

"With respect," Ser Calder said carefully, "one might observe that your grace is new to his position, and might do well to heed the advice of those who have more experience."

"Advice is not at issue," Aefric said. "I have never failed to seek advice from my advisers, yourself included."

"With—"

"*The issue*," Aefric said, "is judgment. You seem to feel that, because you have held your position for a considerable length of time, I should trust your judgment over my own."

"My judgment has been tempered with a good deal of experience, your grace."

"That may be," Aefric said. "But his majesty chose *me* to rule Deepwater in his name. Not you. Which means that, when all is said and done, the responsibility for Deepwater is *mine*. Therefore the decisions shaping Deepwater must be those *I* agree with."

"Surely your grace could ease into the position—"

"Enough," Aefric said. "It is my judgment that will steer Deepwater. You are castellan. With my seneschal, you share responsibility for Water's End itself. And — to the degree that I allow you and *no further* — you may stand for me in my absence."

"The Soulfists preferred—"

"I did not ask," Aefric said. "They handled Deepwater their way. I shall handle it mine. Your task as castellan is to adjust to the difference."

Ser Calder frowned in thought.

"Can you do that, Ser Calder?" Aefric asked.

"I ... don't know, your grace," Ser Calder said, with what might have been more honesty than Aefric had heard in his voice ... possibly ever. "How old are you, your grace?"

"This is my twenty-fifth summer," Aefric said, although he knew that was approximate. Because the start of his life here in Qorunn was ... unusual.

"I have been castellan here for more than twice that many years," Ser Calder said, shaking his head. "The changes your grace speaks of ... they will be difficult adjustments."

"I understand," Aefric said.

"Forgive me, your grace," Ser Calder said with surprising gentleness, "but I don't believe you could. You are far too young to understand."

"Fair enough," Aefric said. "I empathize, then."

"Perhaps," Ser Calder said slowly. "Perhaps. You didn't offer me retirement, which shows you have some wisdom." He shook his head. "Retirement would kill me."

"That I believe," Aefric said. "Retirement kills many knights and adventurers."

Ser Calder nodded.

"Think about it," Aefric said. "And let me know if you think you could adjust to being castellan of Water's End, as the position will become."

"Your grace would be willing to let me try?"

"So long as you do try, and don't fall into old habits."

"There's the hard part," Ser Calder said with a grimace, then gave Aefric a thoughtful look. "And if I cannot?"

"I could find a new role for you," Aefric said. "I've been considering asking his majesty for permission to create a new baron to look after the land around the Dragonscar. That could be you."

"Baron Calder," he said, with a small smile, then shook his head. "His majesty will never allow it. Not unless a ler is already in that post, proving that it needs more than a ler's hand."

"How long would that take?"

"Last one I heard of needed a decade." Ser Calder shook his head. "Too long, for a man my age. Besides. My children are gone, so your grace would need to find a new baron after I passed anyway."

"It was worth a thought."

"It was a kind thought," Ser Calder said. He bowed. "With your grace's permission, I shall retire for the evening, to think."

"By all means," Aefric said. "I'd like to retire soon myself."

Just before leaving the balcony, Ser Calder turned. "Oh, your grace?"

"Yes?" Aefric asked, not three steps behind him.

"No matter which way I decide, I still want that duel."

Aefric sighed. "And you will have it. *After* their majesties leave."

"Very well, your grace."

And speaking of their majesties, Aefric had to find out what Queen Eppida wanted.

---

DESPITE WHAT AEFRIC HAD BEEN TOLD, QUEEN EPPIDA WAS NOT waiting in the sitting room when he ascended the stairs to the private floor of his ducal apartments.

A chill crept up the back of his neck. She hadn't left. So where had she gone?

He checked the door of his magic laboratory. Still sealed. No one had been in there since he last was, himself.

Relief puffed out of him. All this talk about the many plots of the Fyrenn family—

"In here, your grace," Queen Eppida said, and her voice came from his bedroom.

Because of course it did.

So much for reading Byrhta's letter and turning in early...

Aefric entered his bedroom, to see her majesty standing at the enchanted glass windows that overlooked Lake Deepwater.

She was distractingly naked. Her golden curls trailing down her back, and not so much as her golden torc to cover a fingerspan of her smooth, supple skin.

Aefric's pulse quickened at the sight of her. He suddenly realized he wasn't *nearly* as tired as he'd thought he was...

"Ah," she said, turning to him with a smile, completing his delightful view. "This time I *know* I caused that reaction."

Aefric swallowed. "You did indeed, your majesty."

The queen arched an eyebrow at him.

"Aefric," she said. "I'm standing before you, naked as the day I was born. Tell me, is this a situation where you expect me to stand on formality?"

"I'm sorry," Aefric said. "I'm just—"

"Surprised?" Eppida laughed softly, and started walking towards him with a sway that seemed to heat the room more than a fire in the hearth could've.

"You shouldn't be," she continued. "I told you. Exacting tastes. And watching you take down that assassin. Your spells. Your manner. Saving Colm's life. Possibly saving mine as well..." Her pale skin ripened with heat from the chest up. "I knew I had to have you again at the first opportunity."

She made a show of glancing over at Aefric's immense, soft, ducal bed. She turned her eyes back to Aefric, and his breath caught.

"I like that outfit on you," she said softly. "But if you're still dressed by the time I reach you, I'm tearing off your clothes."

Aefric smiled. Set the Brightstaff aside. Cast the spell that had disrobed Zoleen, to strip himself this time.

Eppida's eyes widened in approval as she took in the sight of him, naked and ready, and her breaths came faster.

"Yes," she said, wetting her lips. "Can you pick me up with magic?"

Aefric nodded, and did so.

Suspended in the air before him, she shuddered.

"Yes," she breathed. "Yes, Aefric. Now. Pin me to the bed with your spells..."

Later, as they rested, perspiring and breathless and cuddled together on disheveled sheets, Eppida was gnawing gently on Aefric's shoulder when she spoke.

"May I offer you a word of advice?"

"Oh," Aefric said, embarrassment flooding his face. "If I did something wrong—"

"Not about that," Eppida said, laughing softly. She kissed his shoulder, and licked across a small scar left years ago by the glance of a thrown dagger. "No, if you needed advice in that area, I would never have come back for more."

"Oh," Aefric said, settling down and stroking her side with the light touch she seemed to approve of. At least, that she approved of between times. "Good. About what then?"

"Maev."

Nerves prickled along the back of Aefric's neck.

"What about her?" Aefric asked cautiously.

"Believe me," Eppida said, running her fingers across Aefric's chest. "I understand your interest in her. Not only is she quite pretty, and a princess, but her personality seems well suited to a retired adventurer such as yourself."

"I see," Aefric said, still as tentative as he might be if he expected her to announce his death sentence.

"And she certainly adores you. I couldn't name the last person she allowed to call her Maev for a full aett. And she's let you do it for more than a season now."

"I hear a 'but' coming."

"Very good," she said, and flicked her tongue across his nipple. She looked up at him, sympathy in those sapphire blue eyes. So like Zoleen's and Ashling's it was a little creepy.

"She must marry King Dalius," Eppida said softly. "You must accept this. *She* must accept this. That marriage is what's best for Armyr. And to help you *both* accept this, I strongly urge you to deny her, if — or rather *when* — she comes to you for the noble privilege."

Strongly urge? Oh. Of course. She couldn't *order* him to refuse. That would be a violation of the whole noble privilege system.

"That will be difficult," Aefric said.

"I know," Eppida said, patting Aefric's hip sympathetically. "You want her. She wants you. It seems like the kind of circumstance the noble privilege exists for."

"It's *exactly* the kind of circumstance the noble privilege exists for," Aefric said. "The opportunity to slake desire without letting it interfere with politics."

"Normally I would agree," she said, and shook him gently. "But it won't be just the bliss moment. There's too much feeling between the two of you."

She sat up. Leaned against several pillows. Pulled his head onto her lap.

"Consider us," she said. "I find you immensely desirable. I'd like to think you feel the same way about me."

Aefric leaned up and licked a bead of perspiration from her nipple, making her shiver.

"Good," she said. "Now, if we didn't have the noble privilege, our mutual desire might grow and twist into something dangerous to Armyr. Might even lead to an illicit affair, of the sort Armyr hasn't seen in centuries. The sort that causes *rifts*."

"And if Maev goes away to marry King Dalius? Without us ever satisfying *our* desires?"

"She'll be off in Varondam," Eppida said. "You'll be here at Water's End. Distance alone will be enough to keep anything ... untoward from happening." She shook her head. "That's not my point anyway. You two ... what you have might not be love. Not yet. But it's certainly more than simple desire. And so, if the two of you come together for the bliss moment, what you'll share will be *more* than bliss. And that will only make what follows harder on you both."

"And what remedy do you suggest?" Aefric asked.

"Zoleen, of course," Eppida said. "She's nearly as pretty as I am, and she's filled out quite well." She chuckled. "And if Zoleen isn't enough to satisfy you, Sighild Ol'Masarkor will arrive in a few days, and I know she'd be *thrilled* to share your bed."

"You could as easily be suggesting any of the noblewomen of my court. Why do I think you're talking about more than the bliss moment?"

"Am I?" Eppida said, smiling. "Well, then by all means. Let us return our attention to the bliss moment at once!"

She pounced on Aefric, and pursuit of the bliss moment kept them busy for quite some time.

Later, as they rested again, sharing glasses of a sweet, minty sharabi, Eppida said, "You're right, of course."

"About what?" Aefric asked.

Eppida snuggled in, pillowing her head on his shoulder. She sipped a little more sharabi before speaking.

"Of course I'm concerned about more than whom you share the bliss moment with." She shook her head, and her hair felt soft against his skin. "I am the queen, after all. I worry about the future of all my vassals."

"So you *are* talking about marriage."

"Of course," Eppida said, patting his thigh, then squeezing the muscles there. "Colm and I can't have you dying childless, as Arinda did. We must find a bride for you."

"Which is why you want me to forget about Maev."

"Maev is not an option for you. She *must* marry King Dalius. Our alliance with Varondam depends on it."

"And if she secures the alliance without marriage?"

Eppida sighed. "A fool's notion. And you are not a fool."

"I take it your choice for me would be to marry Zoleen?"

Eppida's eyes sparkled. She took Aefric's glass from him, and set both on the nightstand. She spun, facing him on her knees. She looked feral, the way her hair hung forward, covering much of her face.

Aefric thought of Maev's forest lynx, Sylkanis.

"Of course Zoleen would be my first choice for you," Eppida said softly. "Mine is the oldest noble family in all of Armyr. Marrying a Fyrenn would raise your standing in the eyes of not just every titled noble, but every ler and knight as well. And not only in Armyr, but in all the surrounding kingdoms."

Aefric sat up. Tried to distract her by making a show of gazing slowly over her glistening flesh. But she wasn't to be distracted. Not then.

"And if Zoleen displeases you," she said softly, "consider Sighild."

"The daughter of one of my countess' barons?" Aefric said. "She isn't even directly *my* vassal. She's the vassal of a vassal."

He reached out to move Eppida's hair so he could see her eyes more clearly.

She grabbed his hand. Nibbled on his wrist, and oh, she was good at that.

"She's a cousin," Eppida said. "And I'm fond of her. And she's positively smitten with you. I'd rather you married Zoleen. But if you prefer Sighild, I'll see her well dowered."

She moved to pounce. Aefric intercepted her. Spun them so she came down on bottom, with him holding her to the mattress by her shoulders.

"Yes," she said softly, but then focus came back into her eyes. "I'll even give Sighild a better title of her own than baroness, if you need me to."

The way Eppida moved her body against his demanded attention. For him to move events on to the next natural step.

But he made her wait.

Aefric smiled down at Eppida. "Suppose I prefer Byrhta Ol'Caran to both of them?"

"A beauty for the ages to be sure," she said. She tried for a kiss, but couldn't reach. Licked her lips instead. "But no title. No impressive pedigree. Not even a dowry to speak of."

She reached for another kiss, but Aefric held his lips just out of reach.

Eppida growled softly. "She's no fit bride for a powerful duke."

"So you wouldn't give her a title, to see me move on from Maev?"

"Byrhta Ol'Caran is no kin of mine."

Eppida cheated their game then. Brought her hands together, stroking him someplace he couldn't ignore.

The time for conversation had passed again.

Aefric kissed her hard, and she whimpered into his mouth. He moved one hand down from her shoulder—

Someone knocked urgently on the door to his bedroom.

Dajen's knock?

Dajen's voice, muffled by the door.

Dajen's words were unclear, but Aefric's ears picked out one very dangerous word...

Eppida, her expression much more serious, said, "Did your man just say someone *escaped*?"

Aefric nodded, stomach sinking. "I trust you'll excuse me—"

"Go," she said.

Aefric dismounted the queen and leapt off the bed, calling both a dressing gown and the Brightstaff to his hands, by magic.

He ripped open the door as he yanked on the gown.

Dajen stood there, perspiring for the first time that Aefric had ever seen.

"Forgive me, your grace," he said with a slight bow. "I would not interrupt—"

"What's this about an escape? Those Malimfari knights?"

"No, your grace," Dajen said. "It's the wizard Gwawl. He's gone."

---

A SHORT TIME LATER, AEFRIC WAS DRESSED IN HIS BLACK SILKS AGAIN, and flying around the outside of his castle, on the hunt for a missing wizard.

Water's End was entirely lit up. Aefric could see guards and soldiers rushing around the grounds. No doubt searching for signs of the missing prisoner.

Aefric made a sweep of the docks and looked out over the lake. Trying to spot any sign of an escaping ship or boat.

Of course, any boat or ship escaping by night would be unlit...

Aefric pulled the wand Garram from its sheath. He whipped up a spell that created a chain of fires across the night sky that spread into a broad net of fires, widening over Lake Deepwater. Fires that could scarcely have singed a swallow, but shed more than enough light to turn the dark night into a semblance of dusk for leagues around Water's End.

But he saw no sign of any waterborne escape taking place.

"Nothing over the water, Aefric," Karbin's voice, shouted.

Aefric turned to see his ducal wizard soaring through the air toward him. Aefric let the fire net dissipate as Karbin approached.

"He didn't escape by water," Karbin said. "I've already checked."

"Have you checked the roads?"

"There's little point in that," Karbin said. "Is there?"

Aefric sighed. Was it his imagination, or was the night air cooler than it had been for some aetts now?

"Only if he's escaping by *magaunt*, which he won't. Too easily spotted."

"And too easily detected," Karbin said. "He's not just a wizard, remember. He's a criminal. He's used to thinking like one. Which means he's likely used illusion to disguise himself several different ways by now."

"Then he might be hiding nearby. Somewhere in the city."

"If so," Karbin said, "we must assume he already has scry wards in place, to keep us from tracking him. I certainly would."

"As would I." Aefric shook his head. "Let's check the reports."

Together they descended to the ground before the great double doors of the castle. More than forty feet wide and sixty feet tall, those doors stood open now as soldiers and messengers ran about.

In the middle of the chaos stood General Yrsa, giving orders and listening to reports. Ser Beornric stood beside her, apparently in an advisory role.

"He's coming down!" someone called. Ser Micham? Yes. All six of Aefric's Knights of the Lake were gathered. Glaring up as though...

Oh. Yes. Aefric had taken off "without regard for his safety" again, hadn't he?

The bustle of soldiers, knights and pages parted as Aefric landed. He immediately held up a calming hand.

"I know what you're going to say, Ser Beornric. But I had to join the search personally, the way I best could."

"Of course you did, your grace," Ser Beornric said. "Which was why I suggested that your ducal wizard keep an eye out for you. My thanks, Karbin."

"Anytime, Beornric," Karbin said, landing beside Aefric.

So many torches and lamps in the courtyard that it looked almost like midday down here. And even though this part of the courtyard was tiled, the knights and soldiers had kicked up plenty of dust in their haste.

"Ser Yrsa," Aefric said. "What's the status of our search?"

"Your grace," she said, "I have teams going through the castle right now, and more searching into the city. I've sent word ahead to guard posts to keep eyes peeled, though I doubt that will help."

"And if he's hiding by magic?"

"The Soulfists left us a supply of potions that allow even the dullest to sense the presence of magic and illusions. We've broken into that store for the search."

"Good," Aefric said.

"I don't believe Gwawl would remain in the castle," Ser Yrsa continued, "but we'll know for certain by dawn."

"Karbin and I have determined that he hasn't escaped by water."

"Nor is he among the ships in port or out in the harbor," Karbin said. "First place I checked."

Making matters worse, the king approached. He too had redonned his black silks. Ser Beatritz and ten of the Knights of the Crown accompanied him.

"What is our status, your grace?" King Colm asked, on arrival.

Aefric had Ser Yrsa catch him up.

"How did he escape?" King Colm then asked.

"Just what I was wondering," Aefric said, looking at Ser Yrsa.

"I don't understand it, your grace," Ser Yrsa said. "The locks were intact."

"And the spells untampered with," Karbin added. "I checked."

"And yet," Ser Yrsa said, "when the midnight shift change came, the guards immediately reported the missing prisoner."

"When was the last time he was known to be in his cell?" Aefric asked.

"Two hours prior," Ser Yrsa said, frowning. "But it shouldn't have been more than *one* hour since he was last checked. I haven't had time to look into the discrepancy."

"Your grace," Ser Arras said, stepping forward. "I enquired, and was told that the last check before shift change was skipped because Ser Calder deemed it unnecessary. He himself had just checked on the prisoners."

The night suddenly felt colder.

"And where is Ser Calder now?" Aefric asked.

"He retired for the evening, your grace," Ser Yrsa said, though her eyes too were narrowed suspiciously. "But he should be here by now. I sent a page to rouse him some time ago."

The high-pitched shout of a page's young voice cut across the tumult of the search.

"Your grace!"

Aefric turned toward the castle. A page came running at speed.

Anger burned through Aefric. He suspected he knew what that page would say.

"Your grace," the page said, skidding to a stop. The poor youth was breathing hard and sopping with sweat. He bowed. Then spotted the king. Bowed deeper. "Your majesty."

"Go on," King Colm said. "What news?"

"Ser Calder would not answer my knock. I tried the servants' backway, but that entrance to the castellan's chambers was barred."

"Barred?" Aefric asked. "There's no bar on those doors."

"No, your grace," the page agreed. "I had to seek out Meliflua and her keys. She unlocked the castellan's door."

"I take it he wasn't there?" Aefric said.

The page blinked as though stunned that his duke already knew his news.

"Yes, your grace," the page said. "I mean no, your grace. I mean, he was gone. His person. His clothes. His armor. His weapons. All gone."

Aefric turned to Karbin. "You know what we need. Go."

Karbin took to the air, zooming toward the castle. He passed Kentigern, who was on his way out.

"He'd blocked the door to the servants' backway with his armoire, your grace," the page said. "His bed had not been slept in."

"What about the chamber servants?" King Colm asked. "Were they dead or missing?"

"Your majesty, they were missing," the page said, paling. He turned to Aefric. "Might they be dead, your grace?"

"I hope not," Aefric said. "But I think we know how Gwawl escaped."

"Your majesty, your grace," Kentigern said, bowing as he joined the group. "I've sent rikas to Ajenmoor, Lachedran, Behal, and Fyretti. The search won't end with Water's End."

"Your grace," King Colm said. "I think perhaps you should tell me of your problems with your castellan."

"Yes, your majesty," Aefric said, and then gave his majesty a quick summary of the conflicts he'd had with Ser Calder since coming to Water's End.

"Calder's horse is missing," Ser Deirdre said, approaching from the stables. "As, I fear, is Windsong, your grace."

"They stole my horse?" Aefric said.

"I fear so, your grace," Ser Deirdre said. "And they left the grooms all in a magical sleep. I roused them easily enough, of course, but they witnessed nothing."

"Of course not," Aefric said, thumping the butt of the Brightstaff against the tile of the courtyard. "Gwawl would cast the spell from an unseen spot."

"Surely your grace's horse is easily spotted," King Colm said.

"Certainly," Aefric said. "But they didn't need it at all. I can't believe Gwawl wouldn't know how to call up a *magaunt* to ride. So they didn't want Windsong for their escape. Just to hurt me."

Karbin came flying back down and landed beside Aefric.

"No good," Karbin said, bitterly. "Decades of working with the Soulfists taught Calder well. He's burned everything we could use to track him. I did find his chamber servants. Unconscious in his privy. Didn't even see who hit them."

Aefric turned to Ser Yrsa. "Did your guards tell Gwawl we destroyed his pendant?"

"Yes, your grace," she said, frowning at the subject change. "I believe the exact words were, 'his grace had the worthless thing melted down for scrap.'"

"Good," Aefric said. "How did he respond?"

"Guarded his reaction," Ser Yrsa said.

"All right," Aefric said, turning to King Colm. "At this point we can only conclude that Calder broke Gwawl out of that cell tonight, and the two of them fled together."

"Agreed," King Colm said with a grimace. "Though it sickens me to think that such a noble knight has fallen so far."

"He can only mean to join Nelazzi," Aefric said, and at King Colm's puzzled frown, Aefric continued. "Gwawl is a known confederate of Nelazzi's. If all Calder wanted to do was leave, he could have done so alone. But by breaking out Gwawl, he must intend to use the wizard as a bargaining chip to get himself a good position with her organization."

"I struggle to imagine him leaving..." King Colm stroked his beard thoughtfully. "But he couldn't adjust to working under your grace, could he?"

"I don't think so," Aefric said. "And he couldn't retire either."

"No, he wasn't the type," King Colm said. "Still. To choose piracy instead. It seems unlikely."

"Kentigern," Aefric said. "I'll need you to rouse Elkari and all your assistants. Get started on that project we spoke of. I need to know what else Calder might've been up to."

Aefric turned back to the king. "I believe your majesty has the right of it. I don't believe an honorable knight would do what Ser Calder has done tonight. But I fear that Ser Calder wasn't as honorable as he let on."

# 11

---

Aefric got little sleep following Gwawl's escape and Calder's disappearance. It was late that night when he returned to his bed at all, and he did nothing more than toss and turn for an hour or two before it was time to get up.

He had that hour or two to himself, though. Queen Eppida had not been waiting when he returned to his room. Which was just as well. He hadn't been in the mood for either the noble privilege, or for more discussions of marriage.

A hot bath helped. And the hot breakfast pastry brought to him by Ocheda — while the sky was not yet beginning to gray with the coming dawn — helped even more. He ate it beside the window, in his private sitting room. Hot melting cheese along with bacon and broccoli in a flaky crust, washed down with good, clean water.

One thing Aefric had not yet started taking for granted, as duke. That water was no longer something to be rationed, while traveling. Nor did it come to taste of its leather bag, but was always fresh and clean as though right from the spring.

"Your grace," Ocheda said, as he finished his pastry. "I have word from Dajen about the question you put to the castle staff."

"And?" Aefric asked.

"Ser Calder was not popular. The staff considered him arrogant, abrupt and dismissive. Anything beyond that, none felt comfortable saying."

"Fair enough," Aefric said. "Has my staff gathered for the morning meeting?"

"They have, your grace," Ocheda said. "And their majesties have joined them."

Aefric jumped to his feet. Checked his clothes. A navy blue silk tunic, over dark red hose. Leather belt with his wand sheath. High, hard-soled boots leather boots dyed black.

"You look good, your grace," Ocheda assured him.

"Why didn't you tell me their majesties were waiting on me?"

"Forgive me, your grace," she said, "but they told me to say nothing until asked."

"Wonderful," Aefric said, taking up the Brightstaff and hustling down the stairs to his meeting room.

When he entered it looked as though the meeting were already underway.

Their majesties already sat at the round, blackwood table, along with Karbin, Kentigern, Elkari and Sers Yrsa and Beornric.

Their majesties were in dark yellow silk that morning. A gown for her majesty, and a quilted tunic for his majesty, over matching hose.

Kentigern wore a maroon silk tunic over dark brown hose. Elkari wore a dark brown quilted tunic over lighter brown hose. The knights wore their full plate.

Karbin, of course, was clad in his colors of sand and dusk.

And on the table before them was spread a map of Deepwater.

"Good of you to join us, your grace," King Colm said with a smile.

"Your majesties," Aefric said with a bow. "Please excuse my tardiness. My—"

"I told Ocheda to say nothing until you'd at least eaten," Queen Eppida said. "And I'll hear no talk of tardiness."

"Yes, your majesty," Aefric said, bowed, and joined them at the table.

"It's your meeting," King Colm said. "We didn't start it without you. Just went over a few things about your duchy."

Aefric tried not to wonder what those "few things" were.

"Yrsa?" he said. "Would you care to start?"

"Of course, your grace," Ser Yrsa said. "We know now with certainty that both Gwawl and Calder are gone. What's more, the remains of Windsong were found on the shore beside Behal's bridge."

"Remains?" Queen Eppida asked, paling. "They slew his grace's horse?"

"Stole," Ser Yrsa said, "and slew when they were done with it."

"Any witnesses?"

"Ser Gray is handling the investigation," Kentigern said. "She promises a report by midday."

"They took to the river, then," King Colm said, pointing at the map. "At the docks there, by the bridge. Why else kill the horse?"

"They killed the horse to hurt me," Aefric said. "It's no secret I was fond of my steed. But I don't think they took to the river."

"I agree," Karbin said. "If they tried, whether they stayed with the Haven or took the Tainfyr, they'd be trapped there. Easily enough found by a flying wizard."

"Will you check anyway?" Aefric asked. "In case they count on our thinking that way?"

"Of course, your grace," Karbin said. "Soon as the meeting's done."

"Problem is," Aefric said, "we lost so many coastal towns and villages during the wars, that we don't have eyes on our whole shoreline right now. Too easy for Gwawl and Calder to head for the coast and rendezvous with a boat in one of our many blind spots."

"How could they make the arrangements?" King Colm asked.

"Gwawl is a wizard, your majesty," Aefric said. "Safe to assume he knows the message spell."

"Oh, of course," King Colm said. "And there's no way to trace that?"

"None," Aefric said. "Although there *is* a way to trace *him*. The wizard, I mean. We have a pendant that was special enough to him that, using it as a focus, I might be able to break his scry wards."

"Then do so," King Colm said.

"There's a problem with that path," Aefric said. "That pendant holds the key to a set of wards. Likely more than one set."

"Keys?" King Colm asked. "As in for doors?"

"Spell keys that allow the bearer to pass unharmed through some pretty nasty magical defenses. Possibly taking a whole ship with him, in safety."

"You're thinking of Nelazzi again," King Colm said.

"I am," Aefric said. "That pendant may be allow me to take her unawares, someplace she feels safe. Someplace she'd let her guard down."

"But he knows you have it," King Colm said.

"We've led him to believe we destroyed it," Aefric said. "The spells on that pendant were cunningly hidden. It's believable that I could've missed them. So I let Gwawl believe I did."

"Ah," King Colm said, slowly. "So if you use it to track Gwawl now, you fear it will become useless to get you past those wards."

"I know it will," Aefric said with a nod. "He'd know that pendant was the only thing I could have that could help me break his scrying wards. Nelazzi would know to change the keys, as it were."

"Your grace *does* recall he's been forbidden to pursue Nelazzi?"

"Of course, your majesty. And I also recall that your majesty said we'd review that question after Malimfar was dealt with. I rather thought the pendant might help persuade your majesty to let me go after her then."

"It doesn't have to be his grace," Queen Eppida said. When the king looked curiously at her, she continued, "His grace has acquired a tool that will be quite useful in taking down Nelazzi. Naturally, a man of action such as his grace wishes to be the one to do so. But even if the task is assigned to another, the tool remains useful to the task."

"True," King Colm said. "Very well. We'll have to let them go, for now, so that your grace's pendant retains the potency of its purpose."

"Anything else, Ser Yrsa?" Aefric asked.

"Forces continue to build on the northside ridge of the Dragon-scar," she said. "I've continued to make sure the numbers favor us."

"If I may," Kentigern said. At Aefric's nod, he continued. "We've had a rika from Redport. Duke Wylyn and his party set sail last night for Water's End. They should be here sometime this afternoon."

"All right," Aefric said. "Unless they press the matter in the Drag-onscar, we'll continue to hold there for now."

"Nothing more from me, your grace," Ser Yrsa said.

"Kentigern?" Aefric asked.

"The king's justiciar passed Behal during the night. He'll arrive late this morning. The remainder of the royal entourage, at its current pace, is three days behind him."

"Seeing more of Deepwater than we had time to, no doubt," King Colm said with a sigh. "But it couldn't be helped."

"The princess' ship was sighted late yesterday off the coast of Havenford," Kentigern continued. "She should arrive late today."

"Perfect," King Colm said, rubbing his hands together. "Our justi-ciar will get the truth out of that assassin."

"There's also the matter of what Elkari and I learned overnight," Kentigern said. "Elkari, would you care to speak about it?"

She nodded distractedly. Arranged a number of papers with her ink-stained hands.

"Much of what can be learned through the study of history involves asking the right questions, and making the right connec-tions," she said, frowning. "Your grace asked us to look into questions of land and money. But those questions are really one question. Is Ser Calder a thief?"

She shuffled a few papers and lifted one. It looked like a ledger sheet. "Thieves steal. It's what they do. And rarely can a thief be put in a position to handle money without appropriating some."

She set that ledger sheet on the table tapped it firmly with her index finger.

"The numbers on this page represent a spot-check of three dozen random intervals in which Ser Calder was placed in charge of money. None of them yielded any kind of questionable results."

"So he's not a thief," King Colm said.

"Not by nature, no," Elkari said, then quickly added, "your majesty."

King Colm nodded for her to go on.

"Land, however, is not the same as money. And must not be counted as identical. A man who might not stoop to steal a bit of gold, might wish to acquire land. For himself, or for his family."

"So you checked the records regarding land?"

"Your grace, with the aid of Master Kentigern and our assistants, I did. And while I have a good deal to report about lers and land, when your grace has time, I found nothing that connects any land issues with Ser Calder."

"So you didn't find anything," King Colm said, and turned to Aefric. "What were you expecting to find?"

"I didn't know," Aefric said. "I only wanted to be certain. Some were saying he acted as though he were duke. That might involve misappropriation, or—"

"Please excuse me, your grace," Elkari said. "But my report was not yet finished."

"Oh," Aefric said, blinking in surprise. "I hadn't realized. Do go on."

"Circumstances changed between the time that your grace assigned us this task, and the time when we began it properly," Elkari said. "I took into account the disappearance of Gwawl."

She shuffled about her papers, and drew out another. It looked like a list of dates.

"Gwawl is known to have connections to the so-called pirate queen, Nelazzi," Elkari said. "And Nelazzi harassed our coastline a few years back, before the Godswalk Wars."

"I remember hearing about that," Aefric said.

"With that in mind," Elkari said, "I reassessed the question about Ser Calder from 'Is Ser Calder a thief?' to 'Has Ser Calder been working against Deepwater?' Your grace, I presume, understands how that is truly the question underlying the task he set me?"

"I do," Aefric said, his entire self now focused on his historian. "What did you learn?"

"Well, your grace," she said. "When considering the modified question, I had to take into consideration that Ser Calder was castellan during the time when Duchess Arinda struggled with Nelazzi's ships. I went through those dates thoroughly. There was little to find, save that Duchess Arinda was a more active duchess, at that time, than she had been during the three years prior."

"Ser Calder mentioned that Arinda gave him more authority in handling duchy matters," Aefric said.

"And so she did," Elkari said. "Except during the war, if you will, with Nelazzi."

"And what did you learn about Calder from this?" King Colm asked.

She tapped the sheet of paper.

"Not before, but once the war — for lack of a better term — with Nelazzi was ended. Ser Calder began traveling to Ajenmoor several times a year on a basis that looks irregular and coincidental, at first, but follows a very clear pattern, when viewed through the right lens. Always around the time of some significant decision regarding shipping or the movement of Deepwater sea forces."

"You don't mean..." Aefric said, as the implications chilled him.

"Your grace," she said, "I believe that Ser Calder has been spying for Nelazzi since before the Godswalk Wars. I believe further that he actively aided and abetted her work in the greater Deepwater region. And I've gathered evidence to support my claim."

"Aefric," King Colm said, thoughtfully. "Once this business with Malimfar is resolved, talk to me again about Nelazzi. I may just let you go after her."

Aefric felt a vicious smile spread across his face. "Yes, your majesty."

"That is all I have to report, for now," Elkari said.

"Exemplary work, as always," Aefric said. "Anyone else?"

"One more thing, your grace," Kentigern said. "The eldrani have requested that you be present this morning, for the testing."

"Testing?" King Colm asked.

"A kind of eldrani magic that's all but lost," Aefric said. "They call it soul-testing." He explained about Morgard.

"Marvelous," Queen Eppida said. "I'd like to see that as well."

"As would I," King Colm said.

So much for a break this morning. Aefric was starting to think he'd never get to read Byrhta's letter.

---

KENTIGERN FOUND FOR THE *SINFLISSACTA* A SMALL BALLROOM, UNDER A colorless part of Water's End's glass dome. The room was square shaped, and no more than thirty feet to a side. The sky above the dome was a rich blue, lightly sprinkled with clouds.

The ballroom's tapestries had been stripped from the walls for this, leaving them bare plaster, painted soft gray. Furniture had been cleared out as well, leaving uncovered white oak flooring.

Li'sheneesha and Li'nasachal had been in here since before dawn, preparing. And Aefric could tell they'd been working magic the moment he stepped into the room.

It wasn't that they'd warded the room, or enchanted it. No. Nothing so obvious and overt as that.

It was more that ... they'd tuned the magical acoustics of the room. Its feel was different. He wasn't sure quite how, as he walked in there that morning. He'd need time, if he wanted to figure out exactly what they'd done.

But this was not the time for that.

He was accompanied, as he entered, by their majesties, as well as Kentigern, Sers Vria and Temat, and two Knights of the Crown, who lurked behind them.

Meeting them there was Bebara, Aefric's ducal physician, and cleric of Nilasah. She was a vibrant older woman, wearing the yellow robes of her order, complete with the hand-shaped symbol of her goddess.

Originally, Karbin was going to attend. But since Aefric was requested, Karbin instead flew over the Haven and Tainfyr rivers, trying to find Calder and Gwawl.

And Calder was no longer "Ser Calder." Before Aefric had left his morning meeting, he'd given the orders to strip Calder of all titles, moneys and lands, as well as formally issuing the order for his arrest.

And, as their majesties were present at the time, King Colm personally augmented Aefric's orders with his own signature and seal.

Whatever else Calder Ol'Ulith might be, he no longer had the right to call himself a knight. Not that that would probably stop him...

Aefric shook himself, and brought his attention back to the ballroom, and the rite he was about to watch.

The two eldrani faced each other in the exact middle of the chamber. They looked enough alike to be fraternal twins, and not just in their matching beauty. Both with that skin, so very dark, and looking darker still beneath their simple white robes. They shared the same long hair, the purple of late sunset. The same flame-yellow eyes.

Their hands were raised, fingers spread and palms facing each other's palms. They traced different patterns in the air with their palms, and though a hint of magic followed the movements, they weren't truly casting a spell.

It was closer to accurate to say that they were adjusting the room slightly, to account for the recent arrivals.

They paused. Turned as one to look at those arrivals.

"You honor us with your presence, *Kalifnia,*" Li'sheneesha said, approaching Aefric, then switched to High Eldrani. *"May I ask that you refrain from applying your Art until our work is complete?"*

"Of course," Aefric said, in the common tongue. "There's no need for me to do any spellcasting during your ritual." He turned to the king and queen. "Your majesties, may I present Li'sheneesha and Li'nasachal. The *Sinflissacta* I spoke of. Li'sheneesha, these are my lieges, King Colm Stronghand and Queen Eppida Fyrenn."

Li'sheneesha bowed smoothly. "Your majesties honor us with your attendance."

"I have never witnessed the work of a *Sinflissecta* before," King Colm said. "I am eager to see."

"*Sinflissacta*," she corrected gently. "And few of your race have, your majesty."

Aefric had a sneaking suspicion that Kentigern had coached them about addressing royalty.

She returned to the center of the room then.

"Bring in the ... *negala*," Li'nasachal said.

"Candidate," Li'sheneesha said. "Bring in the candidate."

Aefric nodded, and two guards escorted in Morgard Ol'Nara, who was dressed in the same kind of simple white robe as the *Sinflissacta*.

"Here," Li'sheneesha said. "Stand between us. The acoustics are best."

Morgard frowned, but did as they bid.

"Now," she said. "Disrobe."

She and Li'nasachal removed their robes in a single smooth motion, and dropped them to the floorboards.

Morgard flushed bright red, and wasn't nearly so smooth in his movements. Once his robe joined the others on the floor, he shook nervously and put his hands down to cover his genitals.

"You took the bath?" Li'nasachal asked.

"I did," Morgard said. "Used that smelly stuff, too."

"We know," Li'sheneesha said. "Had you not, your smell would be broken."

She frowned, as though she didn't like her choice of that last word, but shrugged, and abandoned the common tongue.

"*Naked are we born,*" she said. "*Our destinies inscribed into our blood and bone by the stars of our birth. And yet our choices, our will, focuses what is written into us to into what reaches our skin and exudes to suffuse the air about us. Together, our stars and our wills make up our truth, which swirls about us, waiting to sing.*"

Li'nasachal intoned a low note that seemed to slither through the room, with a wisp of power flowing in its wake.

Li'sheneesha keened a note as high as his was low. A tone that seemed to float and dip its way through the room. Counterpoint to the low tone. An opposing direction, but somehow harmonizing where they crossed, creating a third note.

The two eldrani began a slow dance around Morgard, mirroring each other's movements through slow steps and quick hops. Sudden spins and drops and leaps. Their palms always facing one another, pressing and receding. Pressing and receding.

And as they danced, they held their notes.

And yet...

And yet it seemed that more notes joined the chorus. As though each of the two eldrani voices somehow began layering in additional sounds. Forming chords. And those chords had undertones and overtones and...

Was that a third voice?

Morgard stood there between the two eldrani as they worked their art. He shivered. Looked about, caught between uncertainty and fear. Not to mention embarrassment at standing there naked before the small crowd.

His mouth was closed. And yet, Aefric would have sworn he could hear, just at the edges of his hearing, a third voice coming from Morgard.

It didn't sound like his speaking voice, either. There was a hollow, aethereal quality to it. And it never seemed to settle on a note, but shifted and ... twisted somehow. Almost hiding in the overtones and undertones of the eldrani voices.

And suddenly, the two eldrani stopped mid-step.

Li'sheneesha's left palm barely a handspan from Morgard's chest, right above his heart. Li'nasachal's left palm mirrored, just behind Morgard's torso.

Li'sheneesha looked into Morgard's eyes and made a high-pitched sound that sounded kind of like, "Tah!"

Li'nasachal, staring into the back of Morgard's head, made the same sound, octaves lower.

Then it was done. Aefric felt the release of their raised power — which he then realized had built to a significant amount, even though he hadn't noticed them raising it — even before they stopped mirroring each other.

"You may dress," Li'sheneesha said to Morgard, while she and Li'nasachal shrugged on their gowns.

Morgard quickly snatched his gown up and pulled it on.

Li'sheneesha walked up to Aefric, and spoke in High Eldrani.

*"That one lacks confidence. Until he has it, he will follow any stronger will, even down a dark path. His heart is wounded by past misdeed, but retains a good core. For now. If you give him confidence, Kalifnia, he will be strong for you."*

*"Thank you,"* Aefric said.

*"It is no more than our calling and our pleasure,"* she said. *"I hope we may serve again soon."*

"Morgard," Aefric said. "I will meet with you later today to discuss your future. For now, if you swear you will behave yourself, I will rescind your guard."

"I swear to obey your will, your grace," Morgard said with a shaky bow.

"Excellent," Aefric said. "Then you are dismissed for now."

"My High Eldrani is a bit rusty," King Colm said. "I didn't quite follow what she told you."

"He'll make a good ler," Aefric said, "if I can give him some confidence first."

Kentigern moved off to speak with Li'sheneesha and Li'nasachal. A page approached.

So many pages at Water's End. Aefric couldn't believe how many sometimes. He only knew perhaps a dozen by face and name, and this young man wasn't one of them.

"Your majesties," he said, with a smooth, deep bow, then gave Aefric a slightly shallower bow. "Your grace, I am to inform you that the royal justiciar has arrived, and that lunch is ready."

Lunch? Just how long was that ritual? It felt as though it couldn't have—

Aefric's stomach rumbled.

"I agree, your grace," King Colm said with a smile. "Let us make lunch our priority. Beatritz already has my orders regarding the justiciar."

But as Aefric turned to follow the page, he saw Ser Beatritz enter the room with a hurried step. The hard soles of her leather boots tapping the wooden floorboards like drums.

Ser Beatritz, like the other knights around them, wore her full plate today. And she wore her greatsword strapped to her back.

"Your majesties, your grace," she said with a quick bow. "Duke Wylyn's ship docks in the harbor even now."

"Already?" Aefric asked, and nerves made his heart pound. He knew so much about what was going on, but what if he'd gotten some key element wrong?

No. He knew that Duke Wylyn's wizard Sifwyn had cast those spells in the Dragonscar. So the duke had to be behind an attempt to seize the gold.

Didn't he?

"It seems the winds blow south over the Risen Sea," Ser Beatritz said crisply, bringing his thoughts back to the moment.

"Or they hurried things with magic," Aefric muttered.

"Either way," Queen Eppida said, "it seems that lunch with our good duke's court will have to wait. Pity. I'd wanted to meet more of his courtiers today."

"You still can, dear," King Colm said to her. "I don't think we're both needed for this meeting."

She frowned. "It's not the meeting I'm thinking of."

"Oh," King Colm said, arousing Aefric's curiosity. "Well, I'll still meet them at dinner."

Their majesties' eyes met, and something unspoken passed between them. Both nodded.

"Page," she called. "I'm ready to be escorted to lunch. The others will not be joining me."

Aefric almost interrupted her. After all, surely Bebara and Kentigern would want lunch. But then, they knew how to find lunch on their own.

"The justiciar?" King Colm asked Ser Beatritz.

"I gave Ser Ober handle of the matter," she said.

"Good enough," he said, and turned to Aefric. "Shall we?"

---

DOZENS OF MEETING ROOMS IN THE CASTLE AT WATER'S END. EACH with a different use and purpose. The one Aefric sat in now had been chosen for several reasons.

It was close enough to the kitchens for lunch to be served hot.

It was down on the first floor, making it quickly available at times like this one.

It was considered one of the most secure rooms in the castle. No windows. Not even arrow slits. No entrance from the servants' backway. No spy holes. The walls were thrice as thick as those of most of the castle, all but guaranteeing that scrying on any meeting in this room would be nearly impossible.

Generations of Soulfists had warded the room heavily, in their best attempt to remove "nearly" from the equation.

From what Aefric had been told, if Water's End ever came under serious bombardment, this was one of four rooms he could expect to be taken to for safety.

Assuming he allowed anyone to "secure" him with his castle under attack. Which didn't strike Aefric as likely.

The room was round, and about twenty feet across. No tapestries on the walls, but a single immense mural had been painted over the soft gray paint on the plaster.

The mural depicted Armyr in detail, as well as about two hundred miles beyond its borders in all directions.

Opposite the mural, only two other adornments on the walls. The flag of Armyr and the flag of Deepwater.

In the center of the room sat a dark red, calinwood table. Round. Eight feet across, surrounded by a dozen chairs, designed to match the scrollwork along the table's edge.

The Deepwater seal had been artistically burned into the center of the table, and the backs of the chairs.

Above the table hung a calinwood chandelier, though no candles burned in it. It lit the room with magic provided long ago by the Soulfists.

A small buffet had been set up on a curved, calinwood table under the flags. Smoked lake marlin topped with slices of nava fruit, a salad of mixed greens, and honeyed oat bread, along with pitchers of crisp day beer.

Aefric sat beside his majesty at the round table, with Ser Beornric on his right, and Ser Beatritz on King Colm's left. Opposite the king, and frowning, sat Duke Wylyn, flanked by his wizard, Sifwyn.

She was a slight woman, but looked even smaller at that table.

Sers Vria and Temat stood by the door, flanked by two Knights of the Crown. A third Knight of the Crown, naked longsword in her hand, stood behind Wylyn and his wizard.

No others were allowed in the room.

Wylyn and his wizard did look as though they'd been called here in a hurry. Neither had bathed recently, though that showed more in the limpness of their hair and their slight stench than any visible dirt.

Their state of their appearance had to be a message, though. Aefric didn't doubt that, back during her apprenticeship, Sifwyn had worked out a spell to handle rapid personal cleaning.

Every other wizard he'd met had done so.

Wylyn wore his leathers, with those wicked daggers of his at his belt. Sifwyn wore her favored bright red robes, sewn through with crystals of different colors and shapes. Her long black hair, missing its usual luster, was braided and wound down tight to her scalp.

Her greenwood staff leaned against the table beside her. Mirroring the position of the Brighstaff, which stood beside Aefric's chair.

Aefric noted that Sifwyn had added a fifth enchanted crystal to her robes, to accompany her magic opal ring, and the bracer on her left arm.

The food served them for lunch was well spiced, and excellent as always. Aefric was sure of it. The cooks would never have provided less, especially with his majesty dining here.

Though to be truthful, Aefric hardly noticed the taste of his food while they ate. And they all ate first, before coming to business, because the king insisted.

The conversation to that point had been stilted. Of weather and the seas, travel along the Kingsroad. Nothing of consequence.

But now the food was finished. And Aefric had cast the *wizard's valet* to keep everyone's tankards full without the need for a servant's presence.

The king began the conversation.

"Wylyn," he said gently. "Obviously I haven't called you here to discuss travel. Is there anything you'd like to tell me?"

Wylyn frowned at Aefric.

"I'm not sure what your majesty has been *told*," Wylyn said sharply, "but I hate slavers as much as any in this room. I only just found out they've ever *docked* at Redport. And I've taken steps to put a stop to any hopes they have of doing business in my duchy."

"No one has tainted your name with accusations of slavery," King Colm said gently. "In fact, I would like to hear more about the steps you've taken. Later. But I have not asked you here to discuss Redport, or slavery."

Did Sifwyn's eyes narrow slightly?

"Then I confess," Wylyn said with a shrug. "I'm at a loss to know what your majesty refers to."

"You are certain?" King Colm said, his voice still gentle. Though now it held an edge of disappointment. "You can think of nothing I should know about?"

"Your majesty," Wylyn said with a sigh. "I can think of nothing. Though perhaps this is because Aefric here turned my focus to Redport and slavery? I've had little else on my mind for the last aett."

King Colm turned to Aefric. "Your grace?"

"Wylyn, before I came to visit you, I made an expedition into the Dragonscar."

Yes. Sifwyn's eyes *definitely* narrowed a touch that time, before she caught herself and schooled her expression. Aefric adjusted his grip on the wand Garram, held under the table and pointed at her.

"The Dragonscar is yours," Wylyn said with a shrug. "Build a castle in it for all I care."

"Someone cares," Aefric said. "Someone cares very much. Enough to cast wards that would only be triggered by a large group of riders. Enough to assault those riders with deadly simulacra fashioned from stone into the semblance of living, fighting men."

Aefric could see tension in Sifwyn's posture now. But Wylyn sat forward eagerly. As though this were a tavern, and Aefric telling of his latest adventure.

"Golems, we used to call those," Wylyn said. "In my day. Nasty things to fight."

"I agree," Aefric said. "They slew some of my soldiers. Wounded several others badly."

"I don't understand," Wylyn said. "Why would someone go to such lengths to protect the *Dragonscar*? I rode its length once with Arinda's father, Duke Arallan. *Years* ago. Apart from the bones at the end, it's nothing but rock."

"You truly can think of no reason?" King Colm asked, voice still so gentle it was a bit disturbing.

"Aefric," Wylyn said suddenly. "Surely you don't think *I* had anything to do with those golems."

"I don't want to," Aefric said. "But I have no choice."

Wylyn scoffed. "Why? Because mine is the duchy next door? You're smarter than that."

"I am," Aefric said, turning to look at Sifwyn. "Smart enough to recognize the wizard behind those spells when I saw her in your war library."

"Preposterous," Sifwyn said with creditable disdain. "I haven't been *near* the Dragonscar in over a season."

"The spells were cast between last winter and last midsummer," Aefric said.

"Wait," Wylyn said, raising a hand. "If you believe she's behind those spells, why didn't you say something at Stormsent?"

"Because those simulacra were *lethal*, Wylyn. And since she cast the spells, I had to assume you knew. Which meant that saying something while in your castle might have been signing my death warrant."

"I'm not sure we've established that she *did* cast the spells," Wylyn said slowly. "Even if she *had* been to the Dragonscar in the right time frame..."

Wylyn rolled his lips in and tilted his head, narrowing his eyes at Aefric.

"That business you told me about a necromancer and Thunderwood. Lies?"

"Mixed with some truth, yes," Aefric said. "Sorry."

"It was a good story," Wylyn said, dismissing that part before continuing. "But it was an excuse to see her cast? To get a feel for her magic?"

"This is pointless and insulting," Sifwyn said. "I did not cast those spells. I don't even know how to *make* stone simulacra."

"I didn't need to see her cast," Aefric said. "I already knew."

"Your majesty," Sifwyn implored now, on the verge of standing. "This man may be a duke, but I've had enough of his lies."

"Careful with that," Wylyn said, easing her back down into her chair with one hand, while his other slipped below the table. "Give him cause to challenge you and I'm likely to be short a wizard."

He turned to Aefric.

"You say you knew without seeing her cast. *How?* Every wizard I've even known would need to see that, to check the feel of her magic."

"I didn't, because I'd already studied the magic of those simulacra. In depth."

That got Sifwyn's attention. Her whole focus was on Aefric now, as he laid on the table the piece of parchment he'd embedded with his sense of her magic.

"Your majesty," Aefric said. "On this parchment I captured the essence of the spellwork that created the simulacra I fought in the Dragonscar."

Sifwyn interrupted. "That looks nothing like—"

"*My technique*," Aefric said, louder, "is based on the one taught me by the Iron Wands. Their method would have produced a sort of ordered sigil, encapsulating the essence of magic they studied. My own methods vary from that, as your majesty can see, but the result is the same. Any magic-user studying this parchment would identify Sifwyn as the wizard it depicts."

"Your grace," Sifwyn said to Wylyn, "how many more of these insults must I bear? He has only his own word about this. Or must I now tolerate his ducal wizard coming in and repeating these baseless accusations?"

"She has a point," Wylyn said, though Aefric couldn't tell who the older duke believed. "It's your word against hers, and your ducal wizard is an old friend. He'd say whatever you needed him to say."

"He wouldn't," Aefric said, "as you'll understand if you come to know him. But that point is moot. Karbin is off on business."

Sifwyn snorted exasperation.

"However, as I said, *any* magic-user will suffice. Including a dweomerblade." He turned to Ser Vria. "Call in Ser Deirdre."

"At once, your grace," she said.

"Honestly," Sifwyn said. "*His* knight?"

"I know Ser Deirdre," King Colm said. "She spent two years at Armityr. If the woman has a greatest fault, it's honesty."

"I've heard that," Wylyn muttered, frowning.

Aefric almost sighed with relief. If Wylyn didn't dispute Ser Deirdre's honesty, this matter might yet be resolved without further bloodshed.

But they weren't out of the woods yet.

---

THE MOOD AROUND THE CALINWOOD TABLE WAS TENSE. MIGHT'VE helped to open a window, but the security of the meeting room meant it had no windows to open.

Aefric had his *wizard's valet* pour another round of day beer, but only Sers Beatritz and Beornric took any. It seemed that neither King Colm, Aefric, Duke Wylyn nor his wizard Sifwyn had been in the mood for refreshment while Aefric had leveled his accusations at Sifwyn. And through her, Wylyn.

The Knight of the Crown behind Wylyn and Sifwyn kept her bare steel pointed towards the floor, but Aefric could see readiness in her posture. If either the duke or his wizard tried anything, they wouldn't get far before she cut them down.

Just in case, Aefric kept the wand Garram pointed at Sifwyn under the table.

The other guardian knights stood at the round room's door, behind where Aefric and the others were sitting.

Aefric was tempted to call for a servant to take away the rest of the fish, salad, and honeyed oat bread. It was clear that none of them would eat anything more, and the smell was starting to turn a bit.

Or maybe that was just the nerves in Aefric's stomach.

Finally Ser Deirdre entered. She wore her maroon leathers, but it seemed she'd been disarmed of her rapier and dagger before being allowed to enter.

Though to look at the confidence in her step, Aefric would never have guessed that she was unarmed. Of course, as a dweomerblade, she was never *entirely* unarmed.

She wasn't wearing her dark red hair in its traditional long braid down her back today. Instead it hung loose and a bit wild. A more fetching look than Aefric expected.

She smiled when she saw Aefric notice. Her smiled gained a bit of mischief, and she knelt to the king.

Of course, she'd first positioned herself so that the king was between herself and Aefric. No doubt her way of managing to kneel to Aefric without appearing to do so.

That odd little game of hers.

"Your majesty," she said, "your grace, how may I serve?"

King Colm gestured for her to rise, then held up the enchanted parchment Aefric had made back in the Dragonscar.

"Do you recognize this?"

She looked it over slowly.

"The colors and patterns are interesting..." she said. "Such depth. But... Oh! Is that..."

She frowned, reaching for the parchment.

King Colm handed it to her.

Something shifted slightly in her aspect as she regarded it.

"I see," she said, smiling. "Clever. Not a style I've seen before, but intriguing."

"Then you know what that is?" King Colm asked.

"Yes, your majesty," she said, offering back the parchment. "Though I don't possess the skill to do so, I know that when a wizard encounters the magic of another wizard, he can bind its dregs with his sense of that magic into a sort of sigil, for future identification."

"And this parchment holds such a magical sigil?" King Colm asked.

"It does, your majesty," she said, "though I've not seen it done quite that way before."

"So *you've* never seen that parchment before?" Wylyn asked.

"No, your grace," she said.

King Colm nodded. "And would you recognize the magic of the wizard this parchment identifies?"

"Certainly, your majesty," Ser Deirdre said confidently. "Though I'd have to see some of that wizard's magic to do so."

"Your grace," King Colm said to Aefric. "Cast a spell. Something small and innocuous, if you would."

"My *wizard's valet* is functioning even now," Aefric said, and gestured. The invisible force of the spell hefted an empty tankard from the buffet and brought it, along with a pitcher of day beer, to the table. "Do you thirst, Ser Deirdre?"

"Not at the moment, your grace," she said, studying the unseen force that carried the tankard and pitcher. She shook her head. "The magic of his grace is not depicted on that parchment."

"Sifwyn," King Colm said. "Cast a spell. Something innocuous."

She reached for her staff.

"Without the staff," Aefric said.

"Oh, *really*," Sifwyn said. "I hardly think it matters—"

"Do as he says, Sifwyn," Wylyn said, his voice hard and his hands low. "Or is my ducal wizard so very reliant on a *tool*?"

She began to stand.

"Remain seated," the knight behind her said.

"Will this never end?" she asked with a huff. "Fine."

With a single pass of her hand, she scoured her lunch plate clean.

"That's her," Ser Deirdre said.

Sifwyn's hand with the opal ring came up—

The knight behind her moved forward—

Aefric started to cast a spell—

Before any of those actions finished Duke Wylyn had both his wicked-looking magical daggers crossed at her throat.

"Do anything I don't like and you're headless," Wylyn said, then addressed the knight behind Sifwyn without looking. "Ser knight, if you would be so kind as to kick away her staff, then remove her opal ring and the bracer from her left arm."

"Several of the crystals on her robe are enchanted as well," Aefric said.

"Please identify them, your grace," the knight behind Sifwyn said, while roughly yanking off Sifwyn's opal ring.

Aefric pointed them out. The knight cut them off Sifwyn's robe with her dagger, then removed the bronze bracer.

"Anything else?" the knight asked.

"Nothing," Aefric and Ser Deirdre said at the same time, which made her smile at him. Aefric couldn't help smiling back.

"What have you done, Sifwyn?" Wylyn asked, his voice almost casual.

But the knight who'd disarmed Sifwyn turned her attention to Wylyn.

"Your daggers, your grace," she said, though she didn't move the tip of her sword from behind Sifwyn's throat.

Wylyn sighed heavily and said, "Yes. I suppose this looks bad for me."

He set the daggers on the table and gestured to Aefric, who had his *wizard's valet* move them to safety with Sifwyn's items.

"My justiciar is here," King Colm said simply, addressing Sifwyn. "I will have him confirm everything you tell us. So not only do you gain nothing by lying now, but I swear your punishment will be all the harsher for each lie."

Sifwyn hung her head, looking defeated.

"It was one of the last days of summer, last year," she said. "Baron Leofstan told me he'd discovered gold. A lot of it, and easily taken. But he needed my help to get it."

"Leofstan," Wylyn grumbled, but was shushed by the king.

"Go on," King Colm said to Sifwyn.

"He took me into the Dragonscar then. To three caves, two on the Deepwater side, one on the Silverlake side."

"Into the Dragonscar," King Colm said.

"That's correct, your majesty."

"So you knew you had left Silverlake and entered Deepwater while looking for this gold."

"Yes, your majesty. Leofstan said that the regent and castellan were off at a festival, and no one would ever know we were there."

"Go on," King Colm said

"He showed me the caves. Showed me the gold. I said that it didn't look so easily taken. He said he needed a year to gather resources, and then he could take it all within an aett."

Aefric doubted that, given what Po'rek and Ge'rek had smelled on the south side. But then, the baron might've been lying to secure Sifwyn's aid.

"What did he need from you?" King Colm asked.

"He needed me to make sure no one took the gold before he could. Had me cast wards that would not alert for anything smaller than a mining company, coming down into the Dragonscar."

"Was that *all* you did?" Aefric asked sharply.

"No, your grace," Sifwyn said, shaking her head. "At his order, I created the stone simulacra your grace spoke of." She looked up and hurried to add. "But I didn't think anyone would trigger the spell. No one knew about the gold but us. And—"

"We'll worry about your motivation later," King Colm said.

"And about your sense of duty," Wylyn grumbled.

"It was all supposed to be done and finished by the end of spring," Sifwyn said. "But the early spring was wetter than usual. And Leofstan was having money troubles…"

She sighed and shook her head.

"For a while, I didn't think it would happen at all. But then, just a few aetts ago, Leofstan said he'd found a new source of cheap labor."

Wylyn whirled on her, eyes blazing.

"Your grace," cautioned the knight behind Sifwyn.

Wylyn nodded and forced himself to sit back.

"But then Leofstan came to me, complaining that the duke of Deepwater had gone riding in the Dragonscar. And then I felt the wards trigger, and…"

She shook her head, expression glum. "I'm afraid everything after that has concerned trying not to get caught."

"And what of your liege lord?" King Colm said. "What knew Duke Wylyn of all this?"

"Nothing, your majesty," Sifwyn said. "I swear it."

"As though your oath still has meaning," Wylyn said, then turned to King Colm. "Your majesty. *I* swear that I knew nothing of any of this. Not the gold. Not the spells. And certainly not the treachery of my vassals."

King Colm nodded slowly.

"Your majesty," Wylyn said, "as a show of good faith, may I volunteer for confinement until your majesty sees fit to have the justiciar confirm my innocence?"

"You may," King Colm said. "And I appreciate the gesture. I'll not keep you waiting any longer than I must."

"Thank you, your majesty."

"And now," King Colm said, turning to Sifwyn. "About you."

The knight behind Sifwyn raised her eyebrows, as though asking permission for a killing stroke. King Colm shook his head.

"Your grace," King Colm said to Aefric. "You have cells that can contain a wizard, I believe?"

"I do, your majesty," Aefric said, though those cells felt less secure now than they had before. At least Calder wasn't here to free *her* too.

"Then she shall be confined to one until the justiciar has seen to her, and I have rendered final judgment. In the meantime, her magical trinkets are now yours, your grace, as the first step towards recompense."

"My thanks, your majesty," Aefric said.

"Your majesty," Wylyn said. "Once my innocence is established, may I have the task of bringing Baron Leofstan to justice?"

"Assuming the justiciar confirms your innocence, you may," King Colm said. "So long as you bring him to me here at Water's End."

"Your majesty," Wylyn said, voice hard, "I shall."

At the king's gesture, more Knights of the Crown came in and bound Sifwyn tightly, for escort to a wizard cell, guided by Ser Micham.

Under the circumstances, Aefric's own castle guards were considered sufficient to escort Wylyn to his rooms and keep him there. Though before he left, he turned to Aefric.

"I'm deeply sorry, Aefric," he said. "I had no idea. And rest assured. I will personally guarantee any punishment and recompense his majesty metes out in this matter."

"Thank you, Wylyn," Aefric said. "I'm glad to know you weren't behind it."

Wylyn and Sifwyn were taken away.

"And now, your grace," King Colm said, turning to Aefric, "I wish to see what my justiciar has learned about those knights. Care to join me?"

"If I might, your majesty," Aefric said, "there's a personal letter that's been waiting days for my eyes."

"From my daughter?" he asked.

"No, your majesty."

"Then by all means," King Colm said with a knowing smile. "Go see what Baroness Regent Byrhta Ol'Caran has to say."

"Thank you, your majesty. I will."

But first, Aefric had to see his new enchanted items safely to his magical lab, for future study.

---

AH. A MOMENT OF ALONE TIME IN AEFRIC'S STUDY. THE COOL BLUES and greens of the walls. The black walnut floorboards, and the soft gray rugs. The scent of lilies on the air.

A haven amidst the chaos.

Today the navy blue curtains stood open, and the wide windows showed a beautiful afternoon over Lake Deepwater.

For once, the day was not so hot as to make him sweat just sitting around. And yet, the tension of that meeting had Aefric sweating.

That would never do. The meeting was over and done.

A quick spell cleaned Aefric of that perspiration.

He drew a deep breath. Let it out slowly.

He was alone. He could stand still, just inside the closed door, and listen, hearing nothing more than his own breathing. His own heartbeat.

No knocks. No cries for his attention.

Alas, though, this moment of peace couldn't last. If he wanted to read Byrhta's letter, he needed to do so quickly. Before chaos intruded once more.

Aefric took up the letter from the large, calinwood desk in the center of the room. Inhaled the spicy, exotic scent of Byrhta's perfume. Took the letter with him over to the navy blue couch beneath the huge tapestry map of Deepwater, and eased back into comfort.

He broke the blue wax of the harp seal, and opened the letter.

*My sweet Aefric,*

*I should be at Water's End with you right now. Perhaps in your arms. Or, if you are reading this late at night, perhaps in your bed.*

*Oh, that I could be there in the warmth of your embrace.*

*Alas, though, it seems the fates conspire against me. Vercy and I had made our plans for the trip. I'd briefed our castellan about everything needing care during our absence. Vercy had even assembled a series of reports to show you how well her future barony was thriving.*

*Poor dear. She seems even more frustrated at having to cancel our trip than I am. If that's possible.*

*I swear, Aefric, we were all but ready to board our ship when suddenly Ler Flizan Ol'Orvash came marching in with his cronies and*

*Forgive me, Aefric. I won't bog you down with baronial business while writing as your frustrated lover. Suffice to say that the ler has ... abused an established baronial policy intended to maintain equity among the lers.*

*And now, instead of sailing to Water's End, spending time with you, bragging about you to their majesties, and oh, so much more besides...*

*Instead of all these joys, Vercy and I must remain here. At Karmakhall. Spending days in meetings with dull lers, reviewing matters that we'd already settled and agreed to.*

*Honestly. I may need to see that policy amended, to avoid this sort of abuse in the future. It isn't as though Ler Flizan will gain anything by this nonsense of his. If anything, he's creating ill will with both myself and Vercy, and that can only cost him in the long run.*

*Not everything we do is subject to that policy, after all, and*

*Forgive me, Aefric. I've started ranting again.*

*It's just...*

*It's bad enough that I'm here in Riverbreak when I thought I would be there with you, at Water's End. But I know already that these lers will add insult to the injury they've done my heart. I know well that they'll try to wheedle and cajole — perhaps even lie — in their efforts to gain small edges over each other, or over their liege.*

*Even now they underestimate me, and oh, how I will make them see the error of their ways.*

*Perhaps I am too angry to write this letter. Believe it or not, Aefric, when I sat down, I intended only to describe exactly what I want to do with you the next time we're alone. In such detail that you might almost feel my touch.*

*Perhaps, if I did it right, my words alone would be enough to bring you to your fulfillment.*

*I like that idea.*

*But it seems that Ler Flizan has ruined even that for me.*

*Please forgive me my absence, sweet Aefric. And I hope that none of the eager noblewomen of your court are displacing me in your affections.*

*I am pleased, at least, to know that you are well. Especially after such troubles in the Dragonscar! Slavers and smugglers and more. Oh, Aefric, I know how brave you are, but please don't go getting yourself killed.*

*Have you made any progress in finding out who was behind those awful stone men? I shudder just to imagine them.*

*And what of those borogs, Po'rek and Ge'rek? Are they settling in well?*

*I've never met a borog. I've heard the horror stories from the wars, of course, but you and I both know what it is to be judged by appearance and reputation. If you wish to make Deepwater a safe haven for borogs, then I'll do all I can here in Riverbreak to make that work.*

*When next I see you, after we've tended to the obvious matters, we should discuss Ajenmoor. I know a good deal about that city, its businesses, and its major players. After all, I've traveled there for Father on Goldenfall business, as well as with Duchess Arinda, on Deepwater business.*

*I would be only too happy to share with you what I've learned about dealing with their businesspeople, their council, their mayor, and more.*

*And now, Vercy is knocking. I must meet with her before we convene with those damned lers. So I must end this letter before I would.*

*Farewell for now, my sweet Aefric, and know that I will be in your arms again as soon as I am able.*

*Yours,*

*Byrhta*

*P.S. I'm so glad you like my new sigil. I'm still looking forward to playing my harp for you.*

---

By the time Aefric was done reading Byrhta's letter, the afternoon was growing late. And yet, the king was still busy with the justiciar down in the cells beneath the castle.

And so, Aefric gathered his advisers at the blackwood table in his private meeting room, to go over what Elkari had learned about the lost lers, and a few other things.

To Aefric's surprise, Karbin joined them. The hour must've been later than he thought. Which meant...

"Has Maev arrived yet?" Aefric asked Kentigern, by way of starting the meeting.

"Not yet," Kentigern said, and Aefric could hear the hitch in his seneschal's voice, as he held back the habitual honorific.

Good. That these meetings were to be casual finally seemed to be settling in with him.

Though he wasn't done speaking.

"I've been expecting a rika from Ajenmoor, when her highness' ship sails past. But nothing as yet, which means she may not arrive until after dinner."

"Ah, well," Aefric said, pouring himself a goblet of water. "It was worth asking. Karbin? Any luck with finding Calder and Gwawl?"

"None," Karbin said with a tired sigh. "I flew the lengths of both the Tainfyr and the Haven, twice. Searched at least a dozen ships. I can only conclude that our first instincts were right. That they fled overland to the coast. Most likely they're somewhere along our coastline right now. Hiding. Waiting for nightfall, when a boat will row ashore to take them out to a ship and away."

"And we simply don't have the resources right now to find them." Aefric thumped his fist on the table. "Thank you for checking, all the same."

"Of course," Karbin said with a weak smile. "Though, with your permission, after this meeting I'm going to rest and meditate for the rest of the day."

"Of course," Aefric said, and caught Karbin, Ser Yrsa and Kentigern up about the meeting with Wylyn, Sifwyn's confession, and where the king was now.

"Where does that leave us with those forces massing at the Dragonscar?" Karbin asked.

"That was my next question," Aefric said, turning to Ser Yrsa.

"There's been a lot of activity on the north ridge today," Ser Yrsa said grimly. "Word must've reached them about Duke Wylyn's summons. Though I can't imagine they've heard about the results of today's meeting."

"Think they'll try to start early?" Aefric asked.

"I've left standing orders to repel them if they cross the border," Ser Yrsa said. "Just in case."

"I'm tempted to go take care of it myself," Aefric said.

"Please don't," Ser Beornric said. "We must assume they'll be ready to lob arrows or worse at flying wizards."

"Beornric's right," Ser Yrsa said. "I would be. Especially when my neighboring duke has a habit of flying into the hazard himself."

"That's why I said it instead of doing it," Aefric said. "Though the gods know I want to."

"Right now they haven't crossed the line," Ser Yrsa said. "They might even be intent on digging straight down for the north side gold. But your presence might spook someone into doing something stupid."

"You don't think for a moment they intend to try to burrow all the way down from that ridge."

"No," Ser Yrsa said. "I don't. But it's a believable story. And one they'll tell if prompted into sudden combat."

"I won't do it, all right?" Aefric asked.

Sers Yrsa and Beornric studied Aefric closely.

"What do you think?" Ser Yrsa asked Ser Beornric.

"He means it," Ser Beornric said, then nodded. "Should be all right."

Aefric almost said something, but he could see the way Ser Yrsa watched him. Waited for him to give her the chance to remind him exactly how many times he'd done *just* what he said he wouldn't do this time.

He held up his hands in surrender. "I'm trying to be good."

Ser Yrsa nodded.

"And as long as my being good doesn't get my soldiers killed," Aefric said, "I'll have an easier time being good next time."

"Border squabbles will come," Ser Yrsa said. "They're almost inevitable, over a long enough span of time. And when they do, soldiers will die before you have a chance to cast a single spell. That's the nature of the world. Your job as duke is to *minimize* your losses. Not foolishly try to eliminate them all together."

"She's right," Ser Beornric said. "And you know this. You're an intelligent man, and this is all part of the same conversation you and I have been having for aetts."

"Think like a duke, not like an adventurer," Aefric said.

"The next step, actually," Ser Beornric said. "*Act* like a duke, not an adventurer."

"Fine," Aefric said. "I've agreed. Can we move on to the next topic now?"

Yrsa and Beornric looked at each other. Nodded.

Karbin fought a losing war against a smile.

Aefric drew breath to make a snide remark, but Kentigern cleared his throat.

Oh. Right. The meeting.

"The justiciar has finished with the Malimfari knights," Kentigern said. "They have committed no crimes, nor made any attempts to violate the sovereignty of either Armyr in general or Deepwater in specific."

"Did he find out what in the hells they *are* doing here?" Aefric asked.

"They were told to expect Caiperas to try something intended to discredit either Princess Astrid or Malimfar or both. And so, they've been waiting and watching. Ready to intervene, if needed, or simply to report back."

"Did they say what they expect Caiperas to do?" Ser Beornric asked.

"No," Kentigern said. "Only that they had their orders from Princess Astrid herself."

Aefric frowned, trying to figure out what kind of game Malimfar and Caiperas were playing now.

"The king has ordered their release," Kentigern continued, "and they have returned to the Red Branch Inn."

"How did they take their arrest and questioning?" Ser Yrsa asked.

"They claim to harbor no ill will. That nothing we did was unexpected, and that, under the circumstances, they consider their treatment respectful."

"They do?" Aefric asked.

"'In light of the recent conflict between our countries,'" Kentigern said, "was how one of them put it."

"All right then," Aefric said. "Keep an eye on them all the same. That they've done nothing wrong so far doesn't mean they won't in the future, if given an excuse or an order."

"Already done," Ser Yrsa said. "When the king had them arrested, I gave the order to have them watched on release."

"You expected them to be released?" Ser Beornric asked.

"I believe in being prepared for as many eventualities as I can foresee," she answered.

"Which is why you're an excellent general," Aefric said, "Elkari, you said you had more for me about those 'lost lers.'"

"Yes," Elkari said, also clearly struggling not to add Aefric's honorific. "I defined the research question as 'What nobles have gone missing since the Godswalk Wars?' With that in mind, by tracing family names and cross-referencing with the last survey of lands controlled by lers and knights, I've compiled a list of three dozen noble families from among ducal lands alone."

"Three dozen?" Aefric asked in disbelief.

"Three dozen," Elkari said confidently. "Each family missing either in whole or in part. Now, the next step will be to cross-reference those names with the known dead from the Godswalk Wars, as well as the list of those who have died since the wars. This should give us as accurate a final count as we could make currently."

Oh. That number included the dead. That made more sense.

"Have any of them been found so far among the living?" Aefric asked, not holding out much hope.

"Too soon to find many," Elkari said. "Obviously Morgard and Karaleca of the Ol'Nara family, and Edric of the Ol'Nia family. Beyond that, I've received word by rika from Lachedran that Karaleca

Ol'Nara claims to have discovered four more. But I await her full report, for details."

"So we might have found as many as six so far," Aefric said.

"Yes," Elkari said. "Assuming that I can confirm the identities of those found by Mistress Karaleca."

"Good work," Aefric said. "Keep me updated."

"Yes, your grace."

"Speaking of Morgard," Ser Yrsa said. "He should be waiting in your sitting room by now, if you want to give him your decision."

"He can wait a little longer," Aefric said. "Is there anything else going on today that I need to know about?"

"One thing," Ser Beornric said. "Duke Wylyn asked that I deliver these to you."

Ser Beornric set Wylyn's wicked-looking magic daggers on the table, in their scabbards.

Ser Yrsa whistled appreciatively.

"His grace said that he offers these to you as a gesture of good faith, in case you believe he could successfully lie to the justiciar."

Aefric snorted. "If anyone could, it's Wylyn Stormsent. But no, I don't believe even *he* could lie to a justiciar of Taesark."

"A powerful gesture, though," Ser Yrsa said. "Those are his old adventuring weapons, are they not?"

"They are," Aefric said. "And they'll be his again as soon as he's cleared. In fact, there's no reason for me to take them upstairs."

With a few gestures, Aefric opened a cabinet on the far wall, then sent the two daggers floating across the room and onto a shelf.

He closed the cabinet with a snap of his fingers.

"It may not be that simple, your grace," Kentigern said. "They're a gift. Returning a gift from another noble is bad form."

"Those aren't a gift from one duke to another," Aefric said. "They're a statement from one old adventurer to another. He's swearing his innocence. And once his oath is proved true, I won't deprive him of his favorite weapons."

"Your grace knows best, of course," Kentigern said, hesitantly.

"If that's everything," Aefric said, "let's adjourn, and I'll go talk to Morgard. Kentigern, I'll want you along for this."

"Of course, your grace."

"Karbin, go get some rest."

"And food," Karbin said, standing. "Food would be good."

Aefric chuckled as his old friend left, then went over his plans for Morgard with Kentigern and his knight-advisers.

***

Morgard wasn't waiting in Aefric's public sitting room, as it turned out. He'd asked to wait out on the balcony, and Ocheda hadn't seen any reason to refuse him.

So Aefric, Kentigern, and Sers Yrsa and Beornric walked out into the late afternoon sun, to find Morgard Ol'Nara standing at the rail of the balcony, staring down at the lake beyond.

The winds were light today, but had the fresh, warm scent of summer.

Morgard was dressed as Aefric had first seen him. Tunic and breeches in deep shades of blue and green, both with multiple pockets. His pale blonde hair was freshly washed and combed, and his delicate features freshly shaven.

Ser Beornric cleared his throat.

Morgard had to shake himself to look away. Bowed deeply to Aefric.

"Your grace," he said, coming up from the bow with an expression of childlike wonder. "The view from this balcony. I'd seen Water's End in the distance, at times, but never did I dream of such a *view*."

Aefric chuckled. "I confess, I take it for granted. Too much time spent flying even higher than this."

He stepped up beside Morgard, and looked down over the busy harbor, and the many ships sailing to and fro on the Deepwater.

"I can appreciate the view's beauty," Aefric continued, "but it doesn't steal my breath, as it might another's."

"Your grace, I'm amazed I have enough breath to speak." He shook his head. "And those towers." Morgard looked up at the seven spires that stretched high into the skies above. "Dizzying just to think about."

Aefric chuckled again and turned to face a man who seemed so young, but was actually a few summers Aefric's elder.

"They're called the Seven Great Spires of Water's End," Aefric said. "And the mightiest there, alone in the center, is the Spike."

"The view from there must be like looking down from the heavens themselves."

"True," Aefric said, "but we aren't here to discuss my view." He looked Morgard over more seriously. "Thank you for allowing the *Sinflissacta* to work their magic this morning. They confirmed for me something I suspected already."

Morgard opened his mouth to speak. Kentigern cleared his throat noisily, and Morgard, chastened, closed his mouth again.

"You have had to do a great deal to survive after the Godswalk Wars," Aefric said. "Both for yourself and your sister, Karaleca."

Aefric could see the question in Morgard's eyes, and answered it.

"Yes," he said. "I've met your sister. It was she who first told me about you, and how the two of you are the children of Ler Boury Ol'Nara. Which my historian has confirmed. Making you, the elder, the heir to the Ol'Nara lands."

"Oh, your grace..." Morgard started, but Kentigern cleared his throat again, so Morgard stilled.

"Now," Aefric said. "A person desperate to survive, especially with a sibling to watch out for, may ... bend a great many rules and laws. Over time, such actions can become habits that ... twist one's view of the world."

Aefric looked Morgard over again. His merchant-style clothing.

"I'm aware that your plan has been to amass enough of a fortune to rebuild and restore your family's lands. And I have reason to suspect that not all of what you've gathered has been done by means I would approve of. Has it?"

Morgard hung his head the way he probably thought he was

supposed to, but there was a touch of defiance to his posture. Interesting.

Aefric let his question hang.

"You may answer," Kentigern said.

"No, your grace," Morgard said at last. He looked up at Aefric. "I … have not always placed considerations for what was right and legal ahead of what would keep my sister and me fed and clothed."

Aefric considered saying something then, but Morgard drew a deep breath, so Aefric let him speak.

"But I understand your grace spent many years as one of those itinerant adventurers the skalds love to sing about. If so, may I ask, did your grace always place what was legal ahead of what was necessary?"

"I always placed what was *right* ahead of other considerations," Aefric said, one eyebrow cocked. "Can you say the same?"

Morgard considered that through an expressive frown.

"Your grace," he said, "I … I will not deny that I have not always done what was right. But I would swear before Taesark Himself that I have mended my ways, and in my business dealings try to do what is *right*, as well as what is profitable."

"And how has that fared for you, on the profitable front?"

"Not so well as I'd like," Morgard admitted. "I've amassed a small sum. But I doubt it's enough to restore my family's keep and grounds. Let alone aid our people in rebuilding farms and vineyards and more."

"And now we have come to the crux of the matter," Aefric said. "The two points that make me hesitate to simply confirm you in your lands and send you on your way. You don't have the money to do what needs doing with your lands. And the temptation to seek a faster means of gathering that money might pull you back to old ways."

Morgard knelt before Aefric. "Your grace, I am yours to command."

"Stand," Aefric said. "You're not to kneel to me until the time comes to swear fealty and take up your lands."

Morgard stood, hesitantly.

"In the interim," Aefric said, "you will remain here at Water's End. You will serve as an assistant to my seneschal. He will test you in the things you should have learned as a page, and make sure you are ready, when the time comes to take up your lands."

Aefric smiled. "And as for your funds, he will help you invest the money you have, while you earn more in my service."

"Thank you, your grace," Morgard said, sounding uncertain and more than a little amazed.

Had he expected to have the family lands stripped from him? Interesting. Made Aefric wonder just what Morgard *had* done for money.

But that mattered a great deal less than setting him on the right path from this point forward.

"You will also train with weapons, according to General Yrsa's assessment of your talents and needs." Aefric raised a cautioning finger. "You are not being trained as a knight. But the discipline of martial training will serve you well, over time."

"Your grace, I am at a loss for how to express my thanks."

"Express them by working hard, learning well, and when you're ready, ruling your lands well in my name."

"Your grace," Morgard said fiercely, "I shall do my best."

"Good," Aefric said. "Kentigern?"

"Come with me, Morgard," Kentigern said.

"Master Morgard," Morgard corrected absently as he stepped up to Kentigern.

Kentigern gave Morgard an evil smile and said, "Not while you serve as my assistant."

Kentigern began a lecture about position and propriety as he led Morgard off the balcony and into the castle.

Aefric watched them go. "Think he'll be all right?"

"With Kentigern riding herd on him, and Yrsa cracking the whip?" Ser Beornric chuckled. "He may become the best ler you have."

"I can only hope." Aefric rolled his shoulders. Perhaps it was just the summertime, but his days lately had felt much longer than normal. "Suppose I should see how his majesty and the justiciar are doing with Sifwyn."

"First," Ser Yrsa said, raising one hand to slow Aefric's exit, "there's something I need to tell you."

Aefric looked the question at her.

"I know that your grace is fond of Zoleen Fyrenn," Yrsa said cautiously. "But given her family, I have had … an eye kept on her."

"Part of your role as my general is to assess and watch for threats," Aefric said. "And you're telling me that you consider her a threat in need of watching?"

Ser Yrsa nodded. Once.

"And I take it you saw something I need to be made aware of?"

"A correlation that, in this instance, implies causality. Your grace gave permission for Byrhta Ol'Caran and Vercy Ol'Karmak to come here to Water's End during their majesties' visit."

Aefric nodded.

"Well, not long after you gave that permission, Zoleen Fyrenn sent rikas to Riverbreak. A short time later, we received word that Baroness Regent Byrhta and Mistress Vercy were obliged to cancel their visit."

Aefric drew a long, slow breath. The implication was obvious. And yet...

"Do you know whom Zoleen contacted in Riverbreak?"

"Three lers. Ora Ol'Panya, Ilsk Ol'Arente, and Flizan Ol'Orvash."

"By all the thirteen hells," Aefric muttered, then said louder. "In Byrhta's letter to me, she made clear that she and Vercy were almost ready to leave when Ler Flizan Ol'Orvash and a few unidentified 'cronies' made demands she couldn't ignore. Something to do with a Riverbreak policy for maintaining equity among the lers."

"I take it this seemed unusual?" Ser Beornric asked.

"Byrhta was furious. Called it pointless. Said it was an abuse of the policy, to go once more over ground already covered."

"Your grace now understands why I mention this?" Ser Yrsa asked.

"The implications are that Zoleen somehow pressured the lers into keeping Byrhta — and perhaps Vercy — away from me."

"Thus keeping her competition at a safe distance," Ser Yrsa said, "while she continued to make her play for you."

Aefric's guts roiled at the thought that Zoleen would do something so ... calculating. After professing such innocence in the ways of intrigue.

"Great," he said. "I'll need to talk to her later, then." Another deep breath. "Ser Yrsa, obviously you were right to watch her. Know that I appreciate your vigilance, and hope you will continue to watch those you think might threaten me. Even if I myself do not see the threat."

"That is my role, your grace," Ser Yrsa said. "And I shall always do so to the best of my ability."

"And knowing that helps me sleep soundly at night," Aefric said. "Come now. Let's see how their majesties fare."

---

THE CELLS IN THE CASTLE AT WATER'S END WERE A LONG WALK FROM the ducal apartments. Getting there took Aefric and Ser Beornric — as well as Aefric's current guards, Ser Leppina with her tanned skin and long braid and Ser Arras with the noble beauty and bearing of her rumored mother, Duchess Arinda — down a great many flights of stairs.

So many stairs that Aefric was reminded of descending sheer mountain sides on the edge of the Southern Wastes.

This was a much more comfortable setting, at least. The duke had a private set of stairs here that led from his apartments down to behind the great hall on the main floor. So he and Ser Beornric could make the descent undisturbed by even the passage of servants, among plastered walls painted a soothing, icy shade of blue. The floors and stairs were covered in panels of cherry wood.

The air had a pleasant floral scent from the vases of fresh zinnias at every landing.

Rather than use the enchanted light of these passages and stairs,

Aefric simply lit the yellow diamond atop the Brightstaff, to guide them.

For the first few brief, blissful flights, Aefric thought he would make his way down all those smooth, well-shaped stairs in silence. Without any new cares being layered onto his brow.

He really should've known better.

"So," Beornric said before they were even halfway down. "What did her majesty offer you to marry Zoleen?"

"What makes you think she offered me anything?"

"Didn't she?" Ser Beornric asked with a knowing look.

"She pushed for Zoleen," Aefric said, "but didn't try to bribe me."

"Damn," Ser Beornric said. "I was sure she would."

Aefric chuckled. "Another of your bets with Yrsa?"

Beornric nodded. "Figured I'd ask while she was off getting the most recent news from the Dragonscar." He sighed. "She's going to taunt me with my own gold."

"Her majesty did say that if Zoleen 'displeased' me, she'd give Sighild Ol'Norette another title and 'see her well dowered,' if I wanted to marry her."

"Why would..." Ser Beornric shook his head. "That's right. Sighild is her majesty's ... third cousin, I think? Possibly fourth."

"It's less about Sighild than about getting me to forget Maev."

"Don't kid yourself," Ser Beornric said. "It's both. She wants the princess married to Varondam, and she wants a Fyrenn married to Deepwater."

"Sighild's an Ol'Masarkor. And just look at her. She's obviously closer kin to Baroness Herewyn than to her majesty."

"Nevertheless, she has Fyrenn blood. That's all they care about." Ser Beornric nodded his head back and forth. "Though, of course, she'd rather see you wed to Zoleen. Tighter tie to the bloodline."

"Well, Zoleen shot that one right out of the sky."

"Are you certain?" Ser Beornric asked. "Over a few rikas?"

"This time it's a few rikas. What will it be next time?"

"Intrigue is part of a noble's life," Ser Beornric said gently. "Any woman of sufficient standing to make a good match for you might have done the same. She would expect Byrhta to recognize the maneuver, and counter. Which she may have done by giving you a name you could trace to Zoleen's handiwork."

"You make it sound like a wargame."

"It *is* a wargame. One of the oldest. *And* one of the oldest causes of war."

They lapsed into silence then, though the cool color of the paint seemed less soothing now, and more ... lonely. As though Aefric were adrift in a sea of ice, that somehow smelled like zinnias.

If only Andi hadn't died. If only she'd been around when, as Keifer, he'd backed that Jumpstart. They could have come here together and become duke and duchess.

Aefric felt a pang of the heartache he'd known so well, a world away. It was faint, compared to what it once had been. He'd learned to move on, the way she would have wanted him too.

But now and then, he still missed her. Her playful smile. Her casual grace. Her laugh. Andi's laugh always had this way of perking him up, no matter how lost and blue he felt.

Memories of her laughter put a sad smile on Aefric's face as they left the stairwell for a tight side passage, skirted the great hall, and took yet more stairs down two levels underground, to the cells.

Here, he passed guards at every level. Spears at the ready, and short swords if needed. Well-oiled chainmail, coif and hauberk.

Down here the halls and stairs were brightly spell-lit at all times, so no flame could be available as a weapon, should a prisoner fight to escape.

The halls were wide enough for two to walk abreast comfortably, but the ceiling was low enough to remind Aefric just how much weight of castle was above his head.

Reminded Aefric of his adventuring days when he sometimes delved deeply beneath the surface of Qorunn.

No plaster or paint on the gray stone walls down here. No floorboards either, or flowers to chase away the smell of dust.

The cell doors Aefric passed were simple oak, but strong, thick, with iron bars, and small windows to pass food and words.

Those cells were all empty now, their doors standing just a little bit open.

Down at the end of the hall, a wider, thicker door.

Aefric knew that on the other side of that door was another short flight of steps, and the four wizard cells.

Normally, that door would be unguarded. Largely because enchantments graven into the door frame would not only give it the appearance of bare wall, but represented the first layer of scry wards that kept anyone from looking past — in either direction.

Today, of course, with their majesties and the justiciar down below, the door was visible. And guarded.

Four soldiers did that duty today. Two with spears and two with loaded crossbows.

Aefric didn't have to say a thing to the guards. They saluted, one fist high, and one of them opened the doors for Aefric, Beornric, and Aefric's knight-guardians.

One more flight of stairs.

———

AT THE BOTTOM OF THAT FINAL FLIGHT OF STAIRS WAITED AN octagonal room full of magic.

The very air down here tasted of dust seared by the presence of so much magic. The stone walls, floor, and ceiling were all inscribed with powerful sigils, in shades of black, red and blue.

This room, and the four cells around it, were even more heavily warded than Aefric's magic laboratory. And that didn't include the magical traps which would punish those who tried to escape, or aid another's escape.

That reminded Aefric. While wards such as these would no longer open for Calder — once he was removed from his post as castellan, the wards of Water's End would no longer acknowledge him — but the *mundane* locks all needed to be changed. Just in case.

King Colm and Queen Eppida looked quite out of place here in their dark yellow silks. They stood outside one of the four cells, which had to be the cell where the justiciar interrogated Sifwyn.

The two Knights of the Crown — both strong-looking men and their majesties current guards — suited the environment much better.

King Colm looked through the cell door's rune-graven glass window. He was flanked on either side by guards who bore both the sigil of Armyr and the three-edged greatsword symbol of Taesark.

"Your majesties," Aefric said, by way of a greeting, "how goes the questioning?"

"The knights were innocent," King Colm said, absently, "if you can believe that."

"How can there be any question?" Queen Eppida asked. "The justiciar confirmed it."

"There's no question," King Colm said, sounding irritated. "It's just ... unexpected."

"I'm not surprised myself," Aefric admitted. "The best distraction doesn't know it's a distraction."

"Adventurer wisdom?" Queen Eppida asked with a small smile.

"No," Aefric said. "Just part of basic illusion theory."

"The justiciar appears to be finishing up," King Colm said. "He's got that three-edged sword of his held high, and is making some kind of proclamation to Sifwyn."

"*Is* it a he?" Queen Eppida asked. "For the life of me, I can't tell. I never can with a justiciar."

"I'm not sure a justiciar is male or female," Aefric said. "I wouldn't be surprised if they're either neuter or both. More balanced that way."

"Doesn't matter either way," Ser Beornric said. "Families, children, even sex. The justiciars leave all such cares behind when taking up their calling."

"Whatever the justiciar is," King Colm said, "approaches."

They all stepped back from the door.

There was no knock. No indication of any kind. And yet, one of the guards reached over and pulled open the door just in time for the justiciar to emerge.

Neither tall nor short, neither heavy nor thin was the justiciar. Nothing of the justiciar's size would call attention. Nor would the clothes. All simple roughspun, dyed brown. Tunic and breeches, gloves and boots, and hooded cowl, worn so low and deep that nothing could be seen of whoever lay beneath it.

The only distinction to the justiciar was the triple-edged greatsword naked in their hands. A simple iron hilt, but a gleaming blade, held point up, as though in salute.

Cold power radiated from that sword. Aefric found himself hoping he hadn't committed any crimes, because if he had, the justiciar might know them all with a single glance.

Behind the justiciar, a guard closed the door.

The justiciar spoke, in a voice that sounded almost hollow. Eerily empty of all emotion, or anything like humanity.

"I have completed my questioning of Sifwyn Rikassa on the topic requested of me. Would your majesties hear my findings?"

"We would," King Colm said.

"Her guilt is certain, of the following crimes. The murder and injury of several soldiers in service to his grace, Aefric Brightstaff, Duke of Deepwater. Conspiracy to mine without permission on the lands of his grace, Aefric Brightstaff, Duke of Deepwater. Conspiracy to steal a significant amount of gold from his grace, Aefric Brightstaff, Duke of Deepwater. Unprovoked scrying and lethal magic wielded against the person, soldiers, and knights of his grace, Aefric Brightstaff, Duke of Deepwater. Spying on—"

"Yes, yes," Queen Eppida said, "on his grace, Aefric Brightstaff, Duke of Deepwater. Can we skip that part?"

"Your majesty, we cannot. The justice of Taesark demands precision in all things. I was asked to determine the crimes of Sifwyn Rikassa in regard to the gold in the Dragonscar, and those crimes cannot be listed without naming those most harmed by said crimes."

"We understand," King Colm said. "Please carry on."

"Yes, your majesty," the justiciar said, and even that was said completely without inflection.

"Spying on the lands, people, and person of his grace, Aefric Brightstaff, Duke of Deepwater, without the order or permission of her proper liege lord, his grace, Wylyn Stormsent, Duke of Silverlake. Taking up arms and making war against his grace, Aefric Brightstaff, Duke of Deepwater, without the order or permission of her proper liege lord, his grace, Wylyn Stormsent, Duke of Silverlake."

"Can't say Taesark isn't thorough," Queen Eppida muttered.

"Usurping the authority of her proper liege lord, his grace, Wylyn Stormsent, Duke of Silverlake."

"How is that one?" King Colm asked.

"Spying and making war are the province of her liege lord. By undertaking these actions without seeking his permission first, she usurped his authority."

"Hadn't thought about it that way," King Colm said softly.

"Your majesty, may I continue?" the justiciar asked, although Aefric wasn't sure it sounded like a question.

King Colm nodded.

"Conspiracy to use slave labor, in violation of the laws of Armyr in general and Silverlake and Deepwater in specific. Prevarication under the questioning of her overlord, his majesty, Colm Stronghand, King of Armyr. Unjust accusations made against his grace, Aefric Brightstaff, Duke of Deepwater. Intent to directly assault and harm his grace, Aefric Brightstaff, Duke of Deepwater."

"Directly harm?" Aefric asked. "When was this?"

"During the questioning by his majesty," the justiciar said, and the direct regard of the justiciar sent a chill through Aefric. "When her guilt became undeniable, she intended to loose a ball of fire at your grace, and would have done so if not stopped by the actions of his grace, Wylyn Stormsent, Duke of Silverlake."

Aefric nodded. He'd been mid-cast himself at the time, though only his majesty and Ser Beornric had known that Aefric had a wand in his hands...

"Your majesty, that is the total list of the crimes of Sifwyn Rikassa, in regard to the gold in the Dragonscar. I should note that my investigation indicates that Baron Leofstan Ol'Laerallan of Mountain Home carries at least equal culpability. Perhaps an even greater share."

"And you'll get to investigate him as well," King Colm said.

"Thank you, your majesty."

"What about Duke Wylyn?" Queen Eppida asked. "How much guilt does *he* carry in all this?"

"None, your majesty," the justiciar said. "All of the crimes committed by Sifwyn Rikassa in regard to the gold in the Dragonscar were committed without the knowledge or consent of his grace, Wylyn Stormsent, Duke of Silverlake."

"You're certain?" she asked.

The justiciar said nothing for a moment. Merely gazed back at the queen from the privacy of deep inside that brown, roughspun cowl.

The justiciar turned to face King Colm. "Shall I inquire of Sifwyn Rikassa about any other crimes?"

"Is she guilty of others?" King Colm asked.

"Your majesty, her guilt suffuses the air about her."

"By all means then," King Colm said. "Though I'll need you to question one more later."

"Yes, your majesty," the justiciar said. "The inbound assassin was mentioned by my guards."

"Very good then," King Colm said, nodding. "Carry on."

The justiciar turned and went back into the cell. The guards of Taesark closed its door.

"He didn't answer my question," Queen Eppida said.

"The question, well, could have been taken as an insult," King Colm said. "I know you don't have as much experience with them as I do, but believe me. If a justiciar has any doubts, they're expressed clearly. For a justiciar to make any kind of definitive statement means that all doubts have been eliminated."

"Surely even a justiciar can make mistakes," Queen Eppida said.

"I'm not sure they can," King Colm said.

"Your majesty, a justiciar can err," one of the guards said. "But Taesark cannot. It's why the justiciar holds up the triple-sword while speaking. If the sword is shining, Taesark blesses what the justiciar says. If it's dull, something's wrong."

"Thank you," Queen Eppida said.

"Shall we see about dinner?" King Colm asked, to general assent.

As they left, Aefric turned back for one more glance at the guarded cell. Sifwyn was alone in there, under the scrutiny and emotionless questioning of the justiciar.

Despite everything she'd done, Aefric found himself pitying her.

THE PLAN THAT NIGHT HAD BEEN TO HAVE DINNER WITH THE FULL court. Give all the local nobles a chance to see their majesties. Perhaps even speak with them a bit, either before the meal began or after it ended.

Maev changed all that.

She arrived while Aefric, Ser Beornric, and their majesties and guards were just coming up from the wizard cell level.

Two dozen soldiers in chainmail and tabards bearing the seal of Varondam: a triangle of ships, sailing to the dexter, on a background of pale green.

Their majesties' two Knights of the Crown moved to stand between the soldiers and their charges, much as Sers Beornric, Leppina and Arras did for Aefric.

"Stand down!" Ser Beatritz's voice, from behind the soldiers.

To Aefric's surprise, the Varondam soldiers took her order. They parted, to stand along the wall, their spears at rest.

Behind those soldiers, Aefric now saw Maev.

There were others around her. A bejeweled older woman in a gown of red and orange silks. Ser Beatritz in her full plate. A slight man with his arms and legs in chains, and a sack over his head. And, of course, Sylkanis. Maev's reddish-brown, great spotted forest lynx, padding along at her side.

But Aefric's attention went to Maev, and his heart leapt to see her.

She was wearing her buckskins, and they hugged her form and

bared her forearms in ways the queen likely disapproved. Her boots were high, and made from soft doeskin. And Aefric knew that every fingerwidth of hide, every sinew used as lace and ties, they'd all been put together by Maev herself from her own kill.

And yet, she kept her skin fashionably pale. How she managed that, while she clearly spent a good deal of time riding and hunting, Aefric didn't know.

She wore her shining mane of black hair down and free. Rapier at her hip. And the moment she saw Aefric, her wide, soft gray eyes smiled even before her lips could.

That was a perfect moment. Their eyes meeting across the hall. So many others around them, busy, while the two of them focused only on each other.

By all rights, such a moment should have been followed by Aefric and Maev talking and laughing together. Catching each other up on their lives. Perhaps boring everyone around them at dinner with the way they spoke only with one another.

But that wasn't what happened.

What happened instead was a whirlwind of activity. People moving back and forth by royal order. Several minutes of so much chaos that Aefric could only puzzle it back together once the hallway was cleared again.

Ser Beatritz had taken charge of the prisoner. Gotten him into a cell, where he was guarded by soldiers of Varondam and Deepwater, as well as two more Knights of the Crown.

But the royal family — as well as that Varondam noblewoman — were gone.

Aefric was about to ask *where* they'd gone when Ser Beatritz stepped up to Aefric and bowed.

"Your grace," she said, "their majesties will take their dinner in private with Princess Maev and Lady Zhila, Queen Mother to his majesty, Dalius Swiftblade III, King of Varondam."

Lady was a title in Varondam? Huh. But Ser Beatritz was still talking.

"Your grace's seneschal and cooks have already been advised of the changes. Their majesties extend their apologies for the sudden shift of plans."

"Thank you, Ser Beatritz," Aefric said.

Ser Beatritz bowed and left.

The stone hallway was suddenly quiet. Only the soft chatter of the various guards at the assassin's cell to be heard.

Aefric shook his head and turned to Ser Beornric.

"They're not going to let me see Maev at all, are they?"

"Not if her majesty can help it," Ser Beornric said.

A page came down the hall so fast that Sers Leppina and Arras both interposed themselves by reflex.

The page, sweating and short of breath, bowed.

"Your grace," she said, but her next attempt at words came up short of air.

"Take a moment," Aefric said. "Get your wind back."

She nodded gratefully, gulping down air. Nodded again, more certainly.

"Your grace," she said. "I bear a message from Master Kentigern."

She handed a scroll to Aefric, and Aefric grimaced as he took it. He didn't need to say anything, though. Ser Beornric beat him to it.

"You didn't need to talk to hand over a scroll, girl. You'd better hope the needless delay isn't costly."

Aefric skimmed the scroll.

"Time wasn't of the essence," he said, chuckling. "Kentigern anticipated that Maev's arrival would send the royal family into seclusion for dinner." He held up the scroll. "He'd already canceled the large dinner, and sent word to my nobles about the delay."

"Good thing he was right," Ser Beornric said.

"His family's been doing this a long time," Aefric said. "Wish he'd warned *me* though."

"What's the plan then?"

"Wylyn," Aefric said. "We have good news for him, after all."

THE EARLY STARS OF EVENING SAW AEFRIC TAKING HIS DINNER ON THE greenwood furniture of his large, public balcony again.

It seemed to be becoming a habit. No doubt Kentigern would encourage Aefric *against* this habit, in general, but certainly he couldn't object that night. After all, Kentigern himself had canceled the large, public dinner.

Still, it was a nice night so far. Warm, but not excessively so. A light breeze, but not too windy. Who knew how many more nights such as this one there would be, before the rains returned?

Aefric was joined at the round greenwood table that night by Wylyn and his daughter Okelai, as well as Ser Beornric.

Okelai made a strange contrast with Maev. Both led quite active lives, considering their stations. Both, when they could, dressed against the expectations of their ranks — right now Okelai wore a simple, black cotton tunic over leathers, rather than fancier materials, much less a gown.

But while Maev was every inch a princess — and oh, how Aefric would like to complete an inspection and confirm that — Okelai had a roguish air to her. The way she moved, the way she held herself, she looked more like someone who'd help Aefric get past the traps of a long-forgotten tomb than someone looking to marry into another noble line and expand her family's sphere of influence.

But then, Wylyn still wore *his* black leathers, as though expecting to go adventuring again himself. So perhaps this was simply the way of the Stormsent family.

No sooner were they all seated around the table than Aefric set down Wylyn's vicious twin daggers with a decisive *thump*. With a gesture he slid them across to their proper owner.

"Thank you, Aefric," Wylyn said, immediately standing and replacing them in their familiar posts on his belt. "I felt naked without them. Much as I imagine you would without that."

He nodded to the Brightstaff, standing beside Aefric's chair.

"I don't doubt it," Aefric said. "And I shouldn't have doubted you."

"No," Okelai said frankly. "You shouldn't."

"Now, now," Wylyn said, cautioning his daughter. "What have I told you about grudges?"

"When they're righteous, clutch them to your last breath."

Wylyn smiled. "Exactly. When they're righteous. In this case a grudge would be unfair. I might've drawn the same conclusion in Aefric's place."

"The evidence didn't look good," Aefric said. "Though maybe I should've asked you a few more questions about Sifwyn. Maybe something would have clicked into place."

"Sometimes," Wylyn said, "that click is a trap, dropping a ceiling on you." He shook his head. "You were right to play it safe."

Okelai frowned, as though unsure she agreed, but nodded.

A rail-thin older servant — Aefric knew this one, his name was Papenn and he had a terrific sense of humor — brought out the dry white palate wine then, one half-size goblet each. They were tossed down so quickly that Papenn was barely done handing out the goblets before he took them away again.

"Papenn," Aefric said, stopping him before he left the balcony, "a moment. What will we be dining on?"

"Aged stag, beer-roasted, and spiced with sharp yanna root. It will be served with a dark rye bread, and a medley of roasted vegetables."

Aefric turned to his guests. "Would you prefer wine, beer or ale with this?"

"You have to ask?" Wylyn said, smiling so wide he nearly doubled his wrinkles. "Ale! The darker the better. The stronger the better."

"You heard his grace," Aefric said to Papenn, who bowed, and carried the news to the cooks.

"Now," Aefric said, turning back to his guests. "If I may return the courtesy you showed me, let's forgo all ranks and courtesies for this dinner."

"Now you're talking!" Wylyn said, hands moving as though he wanted to toast already with some the ale he did not yet have. Instead, he said, "What of that fierce general of yours? Will she be joining us? I was hoping to introduce her to Okelai."

"No," Aefric said. "Ser Yrsa's dealing with that business in the Dragonscar."

"Wait," Wylyn said, seriously. "Sifwyn and Leofstan went beyond planning and warding?"

Aefric slapped his forehead. "I'm sorry, Wylyn. In all the confusion over Sifwyn, I haven't had a chance to tell you. Soldiers have gathered on the Silverlake side of the Dragonscar, as well as miners. Last I heard, their equipment was incoming."

"I will flay that man alive," Wylyn said. "I will string him up by his toes and make him watch while I peel every inch of skin, starting with his thumbs—"

"Father," Okelai interrupted, and when Wylyn stopped she turned to Aefric, looking almost as serious and deadly as Wylyn himself. "What, exactly, have they done?"

Aefric briefed them, including telling of what Ser Yrsa had been doing to counter.

"Of all the nerve," Wylyn said. "I actually gave serious consideration to naming Leofstan to my advisory council."

"Father," Okelai said. "May I ride to the Dragonscar and deal with this myself?"

Wylyn considered that. Ran fingers over the scars on his cheeks that split his short beard. "What do you have in mind?"

"Someone there has to have command," she said simply. "That person should awaken with my dagger at his throat, while I explain in simple, direct language the depth of his or her error."

"By order of the king," Wylyn said, though his eyes were twinkling with pride in his daughter, "Leofstan is to be brought here for the question."

"I won't kill anyone without your leave, Father," Okelai said, and the fake innocence in her voice sounded disturbingly like an older Maev. "But by Elbar's Blood I'll take command and make sure that Leofstan has all the company he deserves on his trip to the gallows."

"You expect to hang him for this?" Aefric asked.

"I expect to flay him for this," Wylyn said simply. "But I doubt his majesty will let me do it. I'll settle for hanging. If I must."

Aefric frowned, considering.

"You think Sifwyn's going to get anything less?" Wylyn asked. "At least three of the crimes you mentioned carry a death sentence."

"It just seems to me that there should be some way for her to repair the damage she's done. Her death won't bring back my fallen soldiers. But her life and her service might aid their families."

Wylyn laughed, loud and boisterous. He clapped Ser Beornric on the shoulder.

"You've done it, man! You've gotten him thinking like a duke, not an adventurer."

"You've been a duke decades longer than I have," Aefric said.

"And the lesson never truly took with me," Wylyn said. "No matter how many times my advisers begged me to change my ways, I never really did." He chuckled. "Oh, I manage my duchy just fine, thank you. But at heart, well, I'm still the man I always was. And I have just as much tolerance for betrayal now as I ever did."

"I hate to say it," Ser Beornric said, "but even if you want to find some alternative punishment, his majesty won't let it happen."

"Why not?" Wylyn said. "If Colm has a fault, it's that he can be *too* flexible about these things. What do you know here that I don't?"

Ser Beornric looked at Aefric. Aefric answered.

"The justiciar said that Sifwyn's guilt 'suffused the air about her.' That she was guilty of more than just her crimes related to the Dragonscar. His majesty gave the justiciar license to question her further. The permission looked pretty open-ended."

"That's her then," Wylyn said, shaking his head. "At least I'll get a full accounting of her crimes, before they take her life."

Papenn returned with the ale then. And Aefric doubted that Wylyn could have asked for anything richer or darker.

With the ale flowing, and dinner on its way, they moved onto more casual topics. Telling stories, singing songs. Even Beornric got caught up in it.

Felt much more like dinner with friends in the old days, before Aefric had become duke, than any kind of formal meal with a peer.

Good food, and good relaxing fun. Aefric was actually sorry to see it come to an end.

---

WHEN AEFRIC THOUGHT ABOUT IT, HE SHOULDN'T HAVE BEEN SURPRISED that Wylyn and Okelai retired early that night. Wylyn had had a rough few days, and wasn't as young as he used to be.

Though he was certainly still fast enough with those daggers of his. He'd proved that admirably.

And Okelai, she wanted to borrow a horse in the morning and head for the Dragonscar.

So Aefric was alone on his balcony, sipping some of the slightly sweet, yet quite strong ishka they'd shared over that lemon pie dessert.

At least, he was alone until Dajen knocked and announced the arrival of his invited guest.

Zoleen Fyrenn was smiling as she stepped out onto the balcony. Her copper hair was down and bouncing with each step. She wore a flattering, low-cut dark blue gown covered in dozens of straps and ties.

"Aefric," she said, arms spread wide, "do you like my dress? I bought it with you in mind."

Aefric didn't stand to meet her. And he didn't gesture for her to sit down. Two things that were not lost on Zoleen. Though perhaps his serious expression was a factor there.

She stopped just out of arm's reach. Frowned, and Aefric wondered how much of her pout was exaggerated, for effect.

How much of everything she did was exaggerated, for effect?

Had he even met the real Zoleen Fyrenn? Or was every word he'd heard from her pretense, trying to create the image of the woman she believed he would fall for?

"What's the matter, Aefric?" she asked softly. "What ever could be troubling you so? Tell me. Let me help you."

"I'm the wrong person to ask," he said.

"Who is?"

"Ler Flizan Ol'Orvash."

Aefric thought he could see her making connections, behind those sapphire eyes.

"That I sent him a rika?" She gave him a slow smile. "Are you *jealous*, Aefric? I assure you it was just family business. A little something my sister asked me to take care of."

"You're good," Aefric said, nodding. "You're really very good."

"You should know," she teased.

"Family business," he said. "Something your sister asked you to take care of. Words calculated to make me think you were doing a favor for Ashling. Maybe something trade related."

"What makes you think I wasn't?"

"Oh, it might've been Ashling who put the idea in your head," Aefric conceded. "Or it might've been the queen. Either way, the family business in this case wasn't trade, was it? It was the business of joining families."

"What have I done to displease you, Aefric?" she asked. "How can I make it right?"

Aefric had to admit, she both looked and sounded sincere.

But did that mean anything?

"You must know that Byrhta Ol'Caran and I write each other regularly."

"I do, and I freely admit I'm jealous that…" She closed her eyes with a small "oh" sound. Grimaced. "Ler Flizan is in Riverbreak. And so is Byrhta Ol'Caran. But … no. I'm afraid I'm still not sure what you think I did to wrong you."

"Very well," Aefric said. "If you will make me say it. I think that as soon as word got around that Byrhta and Vercy were coming to visit, you took to the rookery to use family connections to keep your competition for my affections at bay."

"Well, really, Aefric," Zoleen said, drolly. "In her most flattering dreams, Vercy Ol'Karmak could never compete with me. And Byrhta Ol'Caran, well, properly speaking she's no competition either. The impoverished daughter of your own vassal?"

Zoleen laughed softly and shook her head. "Still. The woman is so *damnably beautiful* that she could be a dangerous distraction."

"Dangerous?"

"Of course, Aefric," Zoleen said, as though surprised she understood something that Aefric didn't. "Your choice of brides is one of the most important decisions you will make as duke. It will shape Deepwater for generations to come. You really can't afford to be distracted from your duty here simply because that woman was gifted with a face and body that the gods themselves would envy."

"So you don't deny using your connections to keep her away?"

"Deny it?" Zoleen asked, still looking puzzled. "Of course not. Why would I? How could I ever spend any time with you, prove that I'm the right woman for you, if I let Byrhta Ol'Caran keep you busy chasing the bliss moment with her?"

Zoleen cocked her hips and an eyebrow. "I hope I've at least proven myself a worthy candidate in *that* regard."

"This isn't about the bliss moment," Aefric said, shaking his head. "What it's really about is the fact that I liked you."

Zoleen clearly heard his use of the past tense. Her eyes widened with worry. "Aefric," she started, but Aefric kept talking.

"I did. I enjoyed your company enough that I looked forward to spending time with you. But the problem is, you've proven I can't trust you."

"No," she gasped. "You can't mean that."

"Whatever else they may be," Aefric said, "Byrhta and Vercy are my vassals. And they asked my permission to come for a visit. To see me, yes, but also to see their majesties. Not everyone has the queen herself for a sister or cousin. Not everyone can visit their monarchs anytime they want."

"Oh, Aefric," Zoleen started again, but Aefric still wasn't finished.

"You went behind my back. Applied *pressure* to keep them away. And in so doing, you have denied them a rare opportunity for an audience with their majesties."

Tears welled up in those sapphire eyes.

"And you hurt *me* in the process," Aefric continued. "You yourself pointed out that King Colm is using this visit to check on me, as a duke. Well, now two of my most fiercely loyal vassals won't get to speak on my behalf."

"I'm sorry," she said, voice raw with emotion.

"I believe you," Aefric said gently. "And I would like to think you will never do anything like this again."

He held up one hand to stop anything she might say.

"Don't," he said. "Don't try promising me you won't. Not right here and right now. I wouldn't be able to believe you."

"What can I do?" she lamented.

"I don't know," Aefric said, shaking his head. "What I do know is that right now I can't trust you. Not after that. And trust is too important to me."

"There must be *something*."

"Perhaps," Aefric said. "Perhaps not. I honestly don't know. But right now, it's too soon for me to forgive you, much less *consider* trusting you again. I'll be too worried that you're covering. Just doing better at hiding those intrigues you swore were not your way."

Those tears began sliding down her cheeks now.

"Will you at least let me *try* to make up for this?"

The pain welling within him wanted to say no. But that would be going too far.

"Yes," Aefric said, though the word tasted bitter. "I will let you try. But not now. And not soon." He drew a deep breath. "Tomorrow morning, I want you to leave Water's End."

"No! Don't send me away, Aefric. *Please*."

"I need distance from you right now," Aefric said.

And he did. The sincerity in her eyes and her aspect was making his heart pound with doubt. As well as the desire to take her in his arms and wipe away those tears.

But he had to be strong.

Everything she was doing could have been an act. Even the tears.

"So," he continued. "You will leave Water's End with the morning tide. And you will not return without my permission."

"But what about tonight?" she asked, almost begging now. "Give me tonight, at least, Aefric. One more night in your arms."

"Tonight you return to your rooms." He shook his head. "I don't want any company at all tonight."

"One last kiss, at least?"

Aefric shook his head. "If I kiss you again, I want it to be out of joy and desire."

"Then I shall do everything in my power to resurrect those feelings in you," she said, with so much determination that Aefric was reminded of *both* her sisters.

"Until that day," Aefric said, heart beating even heavier now, "I think it's better if you address me as 'your grace.'"

She sobbed aloud, and fled from the balcony, crying.

Aefric let out a long, deep sigh.

He felt terrible, but knew he'd done what he needed to do.

"Wow. That was rough. *Deserved*. But rough."

Maev's voice?

Aefric turned to see her clamber up onto the rail of his balcony — from the outside.

She smiled.

"Are you sure you won't accept *any* company tonight, Aefric?"

---

AEFRIC COULDN'T BELIEVE HIS EYES, BUT THERE SHE WAS.

Maev. Clad in her buckskins. Silhouetted against the starry night sky. Her long black hair flying wild behind her, even though the breeze wasn't all that strong.

She crouched on the rail of his balcony, not a dozen paces from where Aefric sat on a greenwood chair. A swallow of that sweet, strong ishka still in the small glass he held.

Joy sang all through Aefric's system. He felt as though every nerve in his body were dancing at the sight of her. As though he weren't just smiling with his lips and eyes, but with the whole of his body, and maybe more besides.

After the complex feelings he'd had, dealing with Zoleen, to feel such pure, strong joy was dizzying.

Maev smiled back like he was prey she'd finally managed to corner after a long hunt.

"*How?*" he asked, torn between delighted laughter and pure confusion. "How could you possibly have climbed here from your rooms?"

He pointed down and to the right along the shimmering dark blue castle walls, nearly glowing in the moonlight.

"There's at least a hundred feet of castle wall between our balconies. All of it smooth as glass."

"You're right, of course," she said, silently hopping down onto the balcony and striding closer. She was taking so much pleasure in all this she was practically glowing.

"Impossible, isn't it?" she teased. "I mean, unless one is a wizard, or a dweomerblood or something. Perhaps I have secret magics you—"

Aefric couldn't take the delay another second. He crossed the distance between them and took her in his arms.

Then they were clutching each other like shipwreck victims, clinging to a floating bit of deck amid stormy waters.

She still smelled of honeysuckle.

"Gods I've missed you," he whispered in her ear.

"No more than I've missed you," she said. "Gods, I feared I might *never* see you again."

And then they kissed, and everything else went away. They just sank into each other, in that kiss. Aefric felt as though he'd been frozen in ice, and now the spring sun had come out to free him.

How long that kiss went on, Aefric couldn't begin to guess, but when it finally ended they were both laughing in each other's arms.

"The look on your face," she said, then licked her lips, picked up Aefric's glass, and finished his ishka with a small sound of approval.

"I still want to know how you did it," he answered.

"Well," she said playfully, setting down her glass, "I *could* ask you to let a girl keep her secrets..."

Another wonderful laugh burst out of her.

"Kindaren scouts taught me," she said, still laughing. "During the wars. It's a trick they use to scale sheer rock face, but it works just as well with your castle walls."

Aefric shook his head, amazed. "The kindaren are said to guard their secrets even more jealously than the eladrani."

"What can I say?" she asked nipping at his neck, and nuzzling. "I am beloved by all."

"You're beloved by me," he said, and kissed her again.

Oh, the wonder of that kiss. It was as though that kiss were a whole universe, born in a blaze of fire and shared only between the two of them.

The kiss might've gone on forever, but somewhere in there Maev pulled back.

"Come on," she said, taking Aefric by the hand and leading him across the balcony. "Sooner or later they'll realize I'm gone. And before they do, I want a lot more from you than kisses."

"You and me both," he said, hurrying his own steps while the Brightstaff followed at his heels like an eager puppy.

They entered his sitting room to see Dajen admitting her majesty, Queen Eppida.

---

Aefric and Maev stumbled to a halt in his public sitting room. Only a few short steps from the spiral stairs up to the private level of the ducal apartments.

Their smiles died on their faces, as they took notice of the unexpected visitor.

Strangely enough, Queen Eppida was still dressed in her yellow silk gown. But then, Aefric hadn't changed into eveningwear either. It had just been that kind of day.

For a moment, all three of them simply stood there. Aefric and Maev, staring at Queen Eppida, and the queen staring right back.

And the queen did not look happy.

Dajen, who had admitted her majesty, quietly slipped away.

The queen made a show of noticing that Aefric and Maev held hands. And where they were obviously going.

"Well, well," Queen Eppida said softly.

Maev drew a tight, deep breath as though girding herself for battle.

"I confess," the queen continued. "When I left my sister, *crying*, in her rooms, I didn't expect your grace to have replaced her company so soon."

She looked over at Maev, who returned a haughty expression, as though the queen were amusing her.

"And really, your grace," Queen Eppida said. "Not only am I left wondering at your dismissal of my sister, but here I find you hand-in-hand with the one woman I asked you to forebear."

She clucked her tongue. "I must admit I'm disappointed."

"Jealous that *I'll* be the one sharing his bed tonight?" Maev asked.

Queen Eppida turned her attention to Maev.

"Oh, dear Maev, really," she said. "Didn't we discuss this? Didn't we agree that this was a bad idea?"

"*You* agreed it's a bad idea," Maev said pointedly. "*I* think it's one of the best ideas I've ever had. And I'm not convinced Father disagrees with me."

"She really can be quite willful," Queen Eppida said, turning to Aefric now.

"Don't talk about me as though I'm not here," Maev growled.

"Then I shall revisit a few of the points from our discussion earlier. As you seem to have forgotten them—"

"I've forgotten nothing," Maev said casually. "I merely disagree."

"—and as his grace is intimately involved in the situation, it seems only fair that I revisit the major points."

"Can we do this later?" Maev said. "I want to bed this man before the snows come."

"We shall do this *now*," Queen Eppida said, snapping off that last word so hard that Aefric almost bowed.

Maev, however, didn't look impressed.

"You are promised in marriage to King Dalius of Varondam," Queen Eppida said.

"I am negotiating an alliance between Armyr and Varondam that *might* include marriage," Maev said, sounding as though she'd repeated these words a thousand times before. "No promise of marriage has yet been made."

"In the last *five hundred years*, Varondam has forged no alliances without marriage," Queen Eppida said.

"Which means that when I accomplish it," Maev said with a smile, "I will be proven the best negotiator in at least this half of the millennium."

"Varondam does not practice the noble privilege," Queen Eppida continued, as though Maev hadn't spoken.

"Which explains a lot about their nobles," Maev replied, and then muttered to Aefric. "I swear, they all tried to ravish me with their eyes."

"And Varondam does not care for *our* practice of the noble privilege," Queen Eppida continued.

"And when in Varondam, I shall do as the Varondami do," Maev said. "Fortunately for me, I am not in Varondam. In fact, I, an Armyrian princess, stand in a castle in Deepwater, an Armyrian duchy, with Aefric here, an Armyrian duke." She turned to Aefric. "Tell me, Aefric, does Armyr practice the noble privilege?"

"Yes, I believe it does," Aefric said, and Maev was getting him to smile even over the disapproving glare of her majesty.

"And do you personally practice the noble privilege?"

"I have been known to, on occasion."

"And do you have any objection to me, personally?"

"You know I don't."

"Excellent." Maev turned her smile on Queen Eppida. "I believe that settles the matter. I, a member of the Armyrian royal family, am going upstairs with Aefric, an Armyrian noble, intent on asserting the noble privilege and seeking with him the *most intense* bliss moments of our lives. See you in the morning."

"*Maev, do not take one step toward those stairs.*"

Maev whirled on the queen, fire in her eyes.

"Your majesty," Aefric said, keeping his voice low. "I have not forgotten our conversation from before. But you yourself must admit, you have no right to deny us the noble privilege, if we choose to seek it together."

"What conversation was *that*?" Maev asked the queen.

"The conversation that would not be necessary if you were a dutiful daughter to your father, and a responsible princess."

"You go too far this time," Maev said, dropping Aefric's hand and clenching her fists.

Someone knocked on the door.

"I will not let you destroy an alliance we need," Queen Eppida said, matching Maev glare for glare and tone for tone.

Both looked ready to go for weapons.

Dajen answered the door.

"Please," Aefric said. "Surely we can discuss this."

"No," King Colm said from the doorway, "I'm afraid talk won't settle the issues between these two. Not here and now, at least."

King Colm strode into the room to stand between the queen and Maev.

"One of these days one of you will kill the other," King Colm said. "And whichever way it goes, I'll be quite angry at the survivor."

"But she—" Both the queen and Maev started at the same time.

"*Silence,*" King Colm ordered.

He glared back and forth between the two of them until he was certain they wouldn't interrupt.

"Eppida, return to our rooms. I'll deal with this."

Queen Eppida looked very much like she wanted to argue, but finally flared her nostrils in a harsh sigh, and nodded abruptly.

She turned and stalked out of the room.

Aefric had no doubt their majesties would have a harsh conversation later.

"Now, Maev," King Colm said, then held up a hand to stop her from objecting. "I know. I know what's between the two of you, and I know that tonight has been a long time coming."

"Father," Maev said, "she has no right to order me away from Aefric's bed. And no right to ask him to deny me."

"Ordinarily, you would be right," King Colm said. "But this is an unusual situation."

"But this is *our way*," Maev objected. "And has been for—"

"Let me talk," King Colm said.

Maev shut her mouth tight, and nodded.

"Believe me," King Colm said. "Nothing would make me happier than to see the two of you together. For a night, at the least, for longer, if possible. As a father, I think you're perfect for one another."

King Colm shook his head. "But as king, I have Armyr to think of. I know this is our way. But *Varondam* knows that as well. And they don't like it. Which is why they sent along their king's own mother to keep an eye on you."

"I hardly need a chaperon," Maev grumbled.

"I have a dozen of the best knights in the world who would disagree," King Colm said with a smile. "None of them know how you got past them, and they'd like to know. Very much."

Maev smiled and fluttered her eyelashes.

"An alliance with Varondam is important to Armyr. They expect that to mean marriage. And they expect that their king's prospective bride won't be found in the bed of another man."

Maev opened her mouth for another objection. King Colm stilled her with a raised hand.

"I know," he said. "It's not fair. And I know. It's possible that we'll have this alliance without a marriage. Eppida doesn't believe that, but Dalius himself admitted it, before I ever sent you to him."

"Then where is the problem?" Maev asked.

"The problem is that, right now, the marriage is expected. By the people of Varondam, and by their king. Which means your behavior must fit *their* customs, not just ours. So, no, my beloved child. I cannot let you share Aefric's bed tonight."

Maev made a sound of longing. Aefric might well have as well.

King Colm chuckled.

"Think of it as incentive, my dear," King Colm said with a smile. "I want this alliance. Marry Dalius if you must, to make it happen. But if you can arrange that alliance *without* marriage. Well."

He looked Aefric over, then back at Maev.

"I'd say that opens a *world* of possibilities for you."

"Truly, Father?" Maev asked, excited now.

"Truly," he said. "*But.* Not until I have my alliance."

"And have it you shall," Maev said, turning to Aefric.

King Colm placed a hand between them.

"Until then, alas, you must forebear."

"But—"

"No, Maev." King Colm took her by her reluctant shoulders and turned her away from Aefric. "For now, *I'm* going to escort you to your rooms. And *see to it* you're kept out of mischief." He turned to Aefric. "Good night, your grace."

"Good night, your majesty," Aefric said with a small bow.

"Good night, my dearest Aefric," Maev said, and might've said more, but the king covered her mouth.

The king raised a warning eyebrow at Aefric.

"Good night ... Maev," Aefric said, and watched in frustration as they left.

Still. There was hope.

---

Sleep came in fits for Aefric that night. He tossed and turned, alone in that immense ducal bed.

That business with Zoleen. Wrenching. It left him hoping he'd done the right thing, yet hating the obvious pain he'd caused her.

Still. What could he have done differently?

She truly didn't seem to understand how what she'd done was wrong. Hadn't even considered the *possibility* that it was wrong, until Aefric had reminded her about King Colm's visit and that she hadn't just been keeping away "a dangerous distraction," but two of his most avid and vocal supporters.

Either way, Aefric didn't trust her. *Couldn't* trust her. Not after that.

Keeping her around would only cause problems.

And yet...

She seemed so sincere in her regret. Maybe it was a one-time mistake? Maybe she would learn from it? Maybe even find a way to make up for what she'd done?

No. There was no way for Aefric to know that. Not for certain. And having her around right now would be the wrong kind of distraction.

And not just for himself. If he kept Zoleen here, Ser Yrsa would have to pay attention to her. Keep eyes on her. Resources that could be watching for other threats.

And after that business with Calder and Gwawl. Aefric needed to worry about real threats to himself and his duchy. Not just political threats.

That thought was enough to make him scoff. Even alone in his bed, he could hear *every one* of his advisers taking him to task for that phrasing.

After all, political threats were just as real and could be just as deadly as physical threats.

Then there was Maev's arrival.

What a roller coaster that had been. And Qorunn didn't even *have* roller coasters. They didn't have anything here in this world that brought the kinds of highs and lows that the roller coasters of Earth did. Not in such rapid succession.

That perfect moment of her arrival. When her eyes met his, across that crowded hall, and the whole world seemed to vanish.

That was a moment that set his heart to pounding for the *right* reasons.

And then to have her just *show up* on his balcony. That was so Maev. Doing what no one else could possibly expect her to do, and making it work.

Doubtless that was why King Colm allowed for the possibility of Maev managing to forge that alliance without marrying Varondam's king.

It sounded impossible. But Maev liked to do impossible things.

Oh. The two of them had been *so close*. If only they'd gone another dozen steps before the queen's arrival.

Aefric found himself running his hands over his soft sheets. Imagining for a moment that Maev was there with him. He could almost smell her honeysuckle...

But no. Queen Eppida ruined all that.

Had she known Maev would be here? With Aefric?

No. He didn't think so. It seemed more likely she'd come to complain about Aefric's dismissal of Zoleen.

So the timing was only bad luck?

But then, how much worse would the timing have been had the queen *not* been there?

King Colm had not come to Aefric's apartments to talk about Zoleen. He'd come looking for Maev.

If the queen hadn't interfered, Aefric and Maev would already have been upstairs.

They'd likely already have been naked.

But they wouldn't have...

Well, likely they would still have been kissing and exploring each other. Still heating things up, as it were, rather than already reaching a boil.

How much worse would *that* have been? To have the king come charging in when Aefric and Maev were naked in bed together, but before they'd had a chance to *really* begin the evening's activities?

Oh, the frustration then would have been so intense that Aefric might not have been able to *walk*.

But those kisses. Oh, those kisses.

It was lying there, thinking about those kisses he'd shared with Maev that night that finally settled Aefric enough to sleep.

Though if he dreamed that night, he didn't remember.

**12**

———————

Aefric bathed early that next morning, and dressed in a quilted tunic of soft gray, over navy blue hose. A black leather belt, with the wand Garram in its sheath, and calf-high boots to match.

He was just heading out to his balcony, Brightstaff in hand, to breakfast alone with the dawn, when a page came rushing up the stairs, with Ocheda on his heels.

"Your grace," the page called urgently, waving a scroll.

As Aefric took the scroll from the sweating young man, Ocheda gave the page water, which he guzzled gratefully.

The scroll was a terse message from Ser Yrsa.

*Silverlake into the Dragonscar overnight. Fighting underway.*

Aefric turned to the page, who coughed gently and forced himself to stand at attention.

"Where is my general?"

"Your grace, she awaits you near the docks. She instructed me to tell you that she has sent a runner to their majesties, and to Duke Wylyn as well."

"Perfect," Aefric said to the page. "Well done." He turned to Ocheda. "Cancel my breakfast, and tell my guards I've gone down to the courtyard."

He stepped out onto the balcony and zipped up into the brisk morning air.

The sun was only just beginning to dawn in the east. White fluffy clouds yet lingered over Lake Deepwater, and weren't giving any sign that they intended to move.

Down below, Aefric could see soldiers. Lots of soldiers. Some in formation. Others moving about. Runners as well. And in the eye of that storm, Ser Yrsa in her full plate, giving orders.

Aefric dove like a striking raptor to stand beside her.

"Your grace," Ser Yrsa said, apparently unsurprised at Aefric's sudden appearance.

He realized then that Sers Leppina, Temat and Vria were also right there, apparently expecting their duke to arrive just as he did.

It seemed his knights were getting used to their duke's reactions.

"Status," Aefric said.

"Sometime during the night, Silverlake forces moved down into the Dragonscar. This was discovered just over an hour ago. Per my standing orders, that means our forces have moved to intercept. We must assume fighting is underway."

"How did we get word so quickly all the way down here?"

"The waystations, of course," Ser Yrsa said. "When our scouts spotted Silverlake's invasion, they fired off a flaming signal arrow. Every waystation between here and there did the same, as soon as they saw the next station's arrow."

"Good work," Aefric said, but Ser Yrsa dismissed the compliment.

"Almost as old as warfare," she said.

"What are your plans?"

"Get more forces out past Lachedran as soon as possible. Get myself moving toward the Dragonscar as soon as my ship is ready. Take control of the situation when I get there."

"You realize I'm coming," Aefric said.

"With their majesties here at your castle?" Ser Yrsa shook her head. "I advise against it, your grace. Let me handle this."

"Beornric inbound, with the Duke of Silverlake," Ser Temat said.

Aefric looked up to see Ser Beornric running with admirable

speed, for a man wearing full plate. Beside him, loping along with long strides, was Duke Wylyn. Who looked about as happy about all this as Aefric felt.

They were trailed by a dozen soldiers in Silverlake tabards.

"*He* may have to come along," Ser Yrsa said, with a sigh. "Though if it weren't a *justiciar* declaring his innocence in this, I'd want him arrested."

"I heard the justiciar's report myself," Aefric said. "There can be no doubt of Wylyn's innocence."

Wylyn and Ser Beornric arrived then, both streaming sweat and panting for breath.

"I'm ... going..." Wylyn said to Aefric. "Don't ... leave ... without me."

"Our ship's almost ready," Aefric said, including Ser Yrsa in a look that left no doubt he was coming.

Wylyn sucked in a deep breath and blew it out. Got his wind back.

"You're not taking a flying chariot thing? Sifwyn would, in a situation like this."

"Don't know the spell to call a *magari*," Aefric said.

"Neither does she," Wylyn said with a snort. "Always fingers one of her crystals when she casts that one."

"I'll be right back," Aefric said. "Bring him up to speed."

Aefric took to the air again. Soared back to the private balcony of his apartments.

Swift steps took him inside, and into his magic laboratory, where the items that had been Sifwyn's sat waiting on the big, heavy desk in one corner, where he did his spell research.

Five crystals of different shapes and colors. A bronze bracer. An opal ring. That greenwood staff.

Aefric scooped up the crystals. Two were white like quartz, though one was triangular in shape, and the other almost cubic, but longer than it was wide or deep. One was red and round. Another was blue and faceted like an insect's eye. The last was amber in color, and shaped like an "S."

No clues from the color or shape then. They all felt like magic, but only a moment's study wasn't enough to determine what type of magic went with each, to say nothing of which specific effects they could produce.

Aefric sighed. Normally, he would have taken each of them into the right meditative state. Projected his awareness through the magical atmosphere of Qorunn and into each crystal in turn. There, he could learn *all* their secrets.

But that would take time he didn't have.

He needed to know what these crystals did, and he needed to know *now*.

The adventurer's solution then.

He stood the Brightstaff beside him.

With a gesture, Aefric called forth what he needed from a reagent drawer in the desk.

A flawless pearl. Very expensive.

It had to be a pearl, because pearls were forged by a process as long, painstaking, and involving as that of crafting an enchanted item.

It had to be flawless, because the slightest flaw in the crafting process could ruin an item's enchantment.

The cost, well, that was incidental to the kind of reagent needed.

Aefric spread the crystals on one scarred corner of his desk.

He cupped the pearl in his hands.

Through a single breath, he drew power from both within himself, and from the world around him.

Through the next breath, he focused that power down...

Down...

Between his hands...

Into the pearl...

Into the heart of the pearl...

Deeper still, into the truth of the pearl within its heart.

When he felt his power touch that truth, he spoke a word so harsh it seared his throat.

The truth within the pearl evaporated its physical form, leaving only a colorless cloud of truth.

Aefric inhaled that cloud.

It smelled of two things that didn't fit together, yet somehow did.

It smelled of the summertime beach in Oregon, on Earth. Warm and salty and sweaty and slightly of decay. Like the air that day in Lincoln City, when Keifer and Andi went looking for those glass globes hidden by local artists.

But it also smelled of the streets of Sartis, from Aefric's youth. That spring day, when the skies looked endless. When he was running and laughing with his friends through the marketplace. A thousand smells of perfumes and cooked meats and more. But the smell that stuck out most in young Aefric's nose was sugared flake bread.

Aefric had almost forgotten sugared flake bread. A fried confection he hadn't had in years. He'd loved it so, as a boy, though he rarely got to taste it.

All these smells came together, and Aefric found himself smiling without even thinking about why.

He picked up the first crystal his fingers found.

The amber one, shaped like an S. It held a shape-changing magic. The power to make the bearer shift into the form of a rika bird, or back into that of a human.

His fingers next found the oblong squared-off white crystal...

This. This held the secret of the *magari*. Calling it. Dismissing it. As many as three times each between risings of the sun.

The other items tempted him. While he still felt the haze of that pearl's truth, Aefric could learn the secrets of all the items he'd gotten from Sifwyn.

Not their deeper mysteries, true, but the basics. They were all there, for the asking.

But he didn't have time.

With a loud exhalation, he blew out that last of that truth, so it couldn't distract him from what he needed to do next.

Aefric dug a pouch out of one of the many drawers in that desk.

Slipped the shape-changing crystal and the *magari* crystal into the pouch, and tied the pouch to his belt.

He took the Brightstaff in hand once more and flew swiftly back down to the coral docks, where activity seemed to be settling down. Soldiers and knights were boarding ships, though a small crowd still surrounded his knight-advisers and his visiting duke.

"Your grace," Ser Yrsa said as soon as he landed. "Mistress Okelai took a horse this morning and left before dawn."

"I know," Aefric said. "She had my permission." He addressed his next words to Ser Beornric and Wylyn as well. "Ready to go?"

"Your grace..." Ser Yrsa started, but trailed off when Aefric shook his head.

"Clear a space," Aefric called out, gesturing for the various knights and soldiers around him to move.

Once he had enough room, Aefric slipped one finger into his pouch. Touched the oblong crystal and called forth its power.

A flaming chariot sprang into being, pulled by two *magaunts* — magical horses. These were flame red, from mane to hoof.

Aefric boarded the chariot, followed by Wylyn and Sers Beornric and Yrsa. More knights of his own guard, and a few of Wylyn's soldiers, looked as though they wanted to follow as well.

"I think we're full up," Aefric said, and before his Knights of the Lake could object, added, "and I think Ser Beornric and General Yrsa can keep me out of trouble."

"I'm not sure *anyone* can keep you out of trouble," Ser Yrsa said.

Aefric smiled and wiggled his eyebrows at her, then launched the *magari* into the air.

---

AEFRIC THRILLED TO FINALLY be guiding a *MAGARI* of his own through the air. He wasn't sure even Karbin knew the spell to call one.

Of course, Aefric didn't know the spell either. But having an item that would let him do it was almost as good.

High over Lake Deepwater and into the morning skies they soared. Wylyn whooping with pleasure. Ser Beornric shaking his head and hanging on tight. And Ser Yrsa watching every direction at once, as though they might take catapult fire at any moment.

They flew over Lachedran, and its farms and foothills. And over the lands north. The groves of trees. The waystations Ser Yrsa had set up for the quick relay of information between the Dragonscar and Water's End.

At one point, Wylyn even swore he saw his daughter, riding along at speed. Aefric had to remind him that they really didn't have room for one more.

It was midmorning when they at last approached the Dragonscar and Aefric began the *magari's* controlled descent.

Lots of activity on the southern ridge. There were two trebuchets, launching missiles at hastily assembled towers on the north side.

The towers never stood a chance.

There weren't that many soldiers up on the north side. Couple of hundred, perhaps. Not as many as Aefric was expecting.

Easily four hundred on the Deepwater side of the Dragonscar, funneling around the likeliest route down for troops trying to move with speed and safety.

Shouts came. People pointed at the *magari*.

Aefric steered for descent into the Dragonscar itself. Which got them targeted by arrows from Silverlake bows.

"Damn your eyes!" Wylyn shouted loud enough to hurt Aefric's ears, though he wasn't sure how far Wylyn's voice would carry over the brisk winds. "You're shooting at your own duke!"

The arrows fell short, though, into the Dragonscar itself...

...where the action seemed to be halted.

Hundreds of dead bodies on the hard stone ground. Some from wearing Deepwater tabards, but many, many more wearing Silverlake colors.

Deepwater seemed to control the ground down there. Aefric could see Silverlake prisoners — perhaps two score — but the free soldiers seemed to be all his.

And they were all gathered around a south-side cave mouth.

That was the cave Ge'rek and Po'rek had gone into, when Aefric left them here. Had the Silverlake forces retreated into that cave? If so, what had become of the borogs?

Aefric landed and dismissed the *magari*.

"Deepwater!" Ser Yrsa yelled. "Your duke is here!"

The soldiers parted. Some of those closest to the cave looked uncertain, but they all raised their right fists high in salute and bellowed out, "Deepwater!"

"Report!" she next yelled, and a half dozen soldiers — undoubtedly officers, trotted over.

Ser Beornric drew his sword and positioned himself to guard Aefric's back.

"I'm going to check on my people," Wylyn said to Aefric. "What do you want as ransom for my prisoners?"

Aefric shook his head, while Yrsa took the officers to one side and spoke with them in low voices.

"I have to ask for *something*, don't I?" Aefric asked.

"That's how it works," Wylyn said.

"Then consider this a show of trust, Wylyn," Aefric said. "Assess the prisoners. You know their worth. But I want that ransom paid by Mountain Home."

"Believe it," Wylyn said, then shook hands with Aefric.

Aefric whistled over a soldier.

"This assault was done without the approval of Duke Wylyn," Aefric said. "He is not our prisoner, he is a guest. Escort him anywhere reasonable that he wants to go, and by my order, see to it he isn't hassled."

"Yes, your grace," the soldier said with a bow, then turned and escorted Wylyn away.

Aefric and Ser Beornric stepped over to where Yrsa was taking report.

"What's the situation?" he asked.

"Unclear," Ser Yrsa said, and she was angry enough about it that her long scar was purpling and the red of her left eye had darkened at least two shades.

"What's clear is this," she said. "Silverlake brought miners down here late last night. Lots of soldiers, too. They didn't head for the north side cave, though. They headed for the first cave they came to on the south side."

"Ge'rek and Po'rek's cave," Aefric said.

Ser Yrsa nodded. "They'd figured out we were here and watching. Created a diversion to hide their descent. A mock signal fire." She glared at one of the officers. "At least, we're *assuming* it was a mock signal fire."

"No reinforcements have been spotted inbound," the officer, an older man with drooping mustaches, said. "And we've had the scouts watching for them."

"Which was why they missed the move into the Dragonscar," Ser Yrsa said. "They didn't find out until they heard the sounds of battle."

"Battle?" Aefric said. "How much fighting could there have been?"

"Sounded like a lot, your grace," that officer said. "Could have been the echoes, though. This place echoes unto madness. Might only have been a skirmish, but it sounded like out-and-out war."

"Our soldiers hurried down," Ser Yrsa said. "Made the most organized assault they could."

"It was like Silverlake was fighting on two fronts," the officer said. "That's when we found out we had a problem in the cave."

"What problem?" Aefric asked.

The officer hesitated.

"Answer your duke," Ser Yrsa said.

"Well, your grace," the officer said, wincing as though in pain. "The scouts told us that was the cave your borogs were in. And we're certain as we can be that no one *else* snuck in there."

"How is this a problem?" Aefric asked.

"Well, your grace," the officer said, still looking pained. "We were given clear orders not to harm those borogs. So we couldn't just charge in there, weapons in hand. They'd attack us, my people would defend themselves, and your grace would be short a pair of borogs."

"You're suggesting that Ge'rek and Po'rek ... what? Slaughtered a bunch of Silverlake soldiers by themselves?"

"No, your grace," the officer said, tugging on his mustaches with one hand. "Based on the testimony of our prisoners, at least *two hundred* Silverlake soldiers went into that cave, along with at least a score of miners. No way two borogs did all that. Borogs were that tough, we'd've lost the wars."

"So you think someone *else* is in there," Aefric said.

"Someone or some*thing*, your grace," the officer said. "Seems to me that those mining borogs must've dug out something that did 'em in. And whatever it was, it's tough enough to take down a company of soldiers, too."

"Your grace," Ser Yrsa said. "Don't."

"She's right," Ser Beornric said. "An adventurer would go in there, but a duke wouldn't."

"Thing is," the officer continued. "We didn't have any orders about a situation like this. Our last orders were to leave that cave alone, because your grace's borogs were in there. And I didn't want to issue any orders against that. Even though those borogs *have* to be as dead as those Silvelake soldiers and miners."

"So you and your troops have been holding the line at the cave mouth," Aefric said.

"That's right, your grace," the officer said. "And if I may say so, we're mighty glad to have your grace and our general here to make the call."

"We need to send in scouts," Ser Yrsa said. "Smart ones. Good runners. Have them move in a dozen feet at a time. Slow. Cautious. Overlapping. Ready to break at the first sign of trouble."

"That's one approach," Aefric said nodding, then began striding toward the cave.

"Your grace, I object!" Ser Yrsa said, falling into step beside him.

"I agree, your grace," Ser Beornric said, keeping pace. "Going into that cave would be completely irresponsible of you."

"You're right," Aefric said cheerfully. "It would. Which is why I have something else in mind."

Elsewhere it was likely a warm summer morning. But there in the Dragonscar, the whipping wind made the air almost feel like autumn.

But though it may have *felt* like autumn, it smelled like blood and death. Too many had needlessly lost their lives that day.

There was nothing Aefric could do about that. But there might've been something he could do to prevent *more* death.

All around Aefric, his soldiers buzzed with wonder about what their duke was doing. Perhaps wondering if he'd lost his mind. Or perhaps just hoping to see the kind of miracle he'd pulled off at Frozen Ridge.

A thought that made Aefric grit his teeth. Even *he* was starting to think of that day above the Indecisive River Valley, the magic he'd wrought against thousands upon thousands of Malimfari troops, as *Frozen Ridge*.

The skalds always won in the end, it seemed.

Ser Yrsa, walking on Aefric's right, quietly fumed. Doubtless at what she thought was her duke's idiocy.

Ser Beornric, walking on Aefric's left, was watching all directions, as though expecting sudden attack.

Both knights had their weapons naked in their hands. Much as Aefric had the Brightstaff in his.

Aefric stopped at the cave mouth.

The sunlight didn't stretch very far inside. The angle was wrong. But even so, Aefric could see at least another dozen dead. Eight of them soldiers, bloodied Silverlake tabards over their chainmail, and four poor souls in simple roughspun.

Probably some of the miners Baron Leofstan had sent down here.

Aefric thumped the butt of the Brightstaff on the hard rock, and caused the sound of thunder to echo up and down the chasm.

*"Ge'rek! Po'rek!"* he called out in Borog. *"Clan chief call you."*

At first, there was no noise but the wind, and the hushed conversation of Aefric's soldiers.

But a borog silently stepped forward, just to the edge of visibility.

A borog who wasn't *either* Ge'rek or Po'rek. This one was larger than Po'rek, but smaller than Ge'rek. And this one had a heavier jaw, and smaller nose horns.

This borog was also armed. Held a large iron maul in one hand.

"*Who say chief call?*" the borog said in a grinding voice.

"*Chief say,*" Aefric said, and stomped the ground hard. "*You challenge?*"

The borog snorted. Narrowed his eyes — at least, Aefric thought this one was male. The borog looked long and hard at the Brightstaff. Snorted again.

"*You thunder stick?*" the borog asked.

Aefric stomped his foot. Caused another thunderclap with the Brightstaff, and in the process let white lightning play along its length.

"*Chief,*" the borog said, ducking his shoulders in submission. He turned back into the cave. "*Thunder stick. Chief call.*" He turned back to Aefric ducked his shoulders again. "*Ge'rek and Po'rek come.*"

"Check me on this," Ser Beornric said softly. "When we left the Dragonscar, we only left *two* borogs behind. And that isn't either of them."

"No," Ser Yrsa said, frowning. "That's a borog we don't know."

Minutes passed. Silence from within. The new borog simply stood there, waiting.

Finally, Ge'rek and Po'rek emerged.

Each of them carried a hollowed out brown rock two feet wide, and at least that deep.

And each of those hollowed out rocks were filled with gold nuggets.

A nearby soldier whistled appreciatively.

Ge'rek and Po'rek set their rocks full of gold on the stone ground in front of Aefric.

"God metal for chief!" Ge'rek shouted.

Po'rek answered, and wasn't alone.

Many, many more voices echoed the sentiment from within the

cave. And unlike Ge'rek and Po'rek, all those other voices were speaking Borog.

"Us bring more," Ge'rek said, and started to turn.

"Wait," Aefric said, which seemed to puzzle them, so he switched to Borog. *"Stop."*

Ge'rek and Po'rek turned back.

*"Clan grows?"* Aefric asked.

Ge'rek and Po'rek both snorted and stomped and scraped their feet along the stone.

*"Clan Thunder Stick now eight twenties strong!"* Ge'rek shouted, and from inside the cave came the thunderous sound of many borog feet, stomping.

"More come," Po'rek said, in the common tongue. "We call. More come."

Aefric could hardly believe it. He'd been worried that Silverlake soldiers would kill the borogs, but it seemed the borogs could more than take care of themselves.

"Who was it who said they'd run off to look for others of their own kind?" Aefric asked. Shook his head. "Doesn't matter. Looks as though they've called their own kind here, instead."

*"Chief pleased?"* Po'rek asked, suspiciously.

Aefric did his best to snort as they did, and stomped his feet noisily. *"Many pleased!"*

More stomping and snorting.

Aefric moved his soldiers back then, and had the whole of Clan Thunder Stick — a clan of which he was evidently the chief — come out to meet him.

If anything, Ge'rek's count was a little short. Aefric thought there were closer to a hundred seventy borogs who came out of the caves. Every one of them armed. Some with axes or mauls, others with short swords or broadswords.

But every single one of them carried a weapon. All except for Ge'rek and Po'rek.

And those borogs brought out a *lot* of gold to offer Aefric.

Then it was just a question of organizing things.

Ser Yrsa handled how the gold would be taken back to Water's End.

Ser Beornric took care of having the Silverlake dead collected and readied for return.

Aefric explained that the borogs were now free to mine all the gold on the south side, but needed to call down an engineer explain about the hundred-foot limit into the north-side cave.

That took a while. In the end, the engineer gave them a hundred feet of cord, and Aefric explained how to use it as a guide for where to stop.

He could tell that they didn't understand *why* they had to stop digging the god metal after a cord length into the north-side cave walls. But they would obey their chief, and for now, that was good enough.

Other than that, Ge'rek and Po'rek explained that things had been pretty quiet for them, up until the Silverlake invasion that morning. That they'd just been digging and, whenever they opened into an existing tunnel, put out the call for borogs to join their clan.

Slowly at first, then faster, more and more borogs had answered the call.

It seemed that there had been as many borogs as humans displaced by the Godwalk Wars.

"All right," Aefric said, once they were done talking. And after Ser Yrsa had joined them, to help clarify some of the points where Aefric didn't know enough Borog, and Po'rek didn't know enough of the common tongue.

"*Me need chief hand,*" he said to Ge'rek and Po'rek in Borog. Pointed back and forth between them. "*Which?*"

Po'rek ducked his or her shoulders at Ge'rek.

Ge'rek snorted.

Po'rek stomped.

Ge'rek turned to Aefric. Thumped his chest.

"Excellent," Aefric said. "Humanway I name you Ler Ge'rek. *Borog way me call you chief hand.*"

"*Chief hand!*" Po'rek bellowed, and stomped.

*"Chief hand!"* the other borogs echoed, and stomped.

"You weren't kidding about the borogs," Wylyn said, walking up, then stopped and stared slack jawed at all the gold. *"They* dug this?"

"Us dig god metal for chief!" Ge'rek said proudly, and stomped.

The nearest borogs also stomped, but most of them were heading back into the caves. Likely to get back to their work.

"I get it now," Wylyn said, shaking his head. "I thought you were going mad, but I get it."

"Everything straightened out?" Aefric asked.

"Baron Leofstan took off as soon as it was clear his side was losing," Wylyn said, and spat. "I'll have to dig that bastard out of his castle."

"His soldiers should yield to you," Aefric said. "You *are* their overlord."

"And the Ol'Laerallan family has been running Mountain Home since long before I was born." Wylyn shook his head. "Might not be easy."

Aefric smirked. "You're looking forward to it, aren't you?"

Wylyn grinned wide enough to double his wrinkles. "Are you kidding? I haven't gotten to break into a castle in years. Plus it'll be great experience for Okelai."

"I'll leave you to it, then," Aefric said, clapping Wylyn on the shoulder.

"Yeah," Wylyn said. "Oh, and I gave Beornric here my estimate of the value of your prisoners, and my sworn statement that I'll pay it."

"They're yours then," Aefric said.

"Good, thanks," Wylyn said, then grimaced as he looked over his dead. "I want to get as many of them home alive as I can."

He sighed. Shook his head. Clapped Aefric on the shoulder.

"Until next time," he said.

"Next time," Aefric said.

Wylyn trotted off, yelling orders at his troops.

Ser Yrsa watched him for a moment, then said, "He's a bad influence on you."

Aefric snorted. She was probably right.

But it was nice to have someone else to talk to. Someone who knew what it was like to go adventuring.

---

SER YRSA VOLUNTEERED TO STAY BEHIND IN THE DRAGONSCAR AND handle getting the gold safely and securely back to Water's End.

Aefric suspected she was also going to make sure there were no misunderstandings between the borogs and the humans. A matter that would be helped by her command of Borog, which was stronger than Aefric's.

He'd have to ask her sometime how she came to speak their language so well.

So Aefric was joined only by Ser Beornric on the *magari* flight back to Water's End.

The big knight didn't seem to enjoy flying as much as Aefric did. He clung to the chariot the whole way, and looked slightly pale. He didn't even take advantage of the trip to harass Aefric about marriage issues.

The break from that likely topic was almost as welcome as the whipping winds and the lovely view as they soared over the lands of Aefric's duchy on their way back to his castle.

Lake traffic was busier than usual that day. From what Kentigern had told him, it would grow heavier steadily through the end of summer, then taper off a bit into autumn.

They got back shortly after midday, landing on Aefric's large, public floor balcony.

It was a beautiful day. The summer heat was finally starting to wane.

Ocheda met them at the door to Aefric's sitting room.

"Your grace," Ocheda said with a bow, apparently unperturbed at her duke's unconventional arrival. But then, doubtless the Soulfists had made a habit of odd arrivals over the years.

"Has lunch begun?" Aefric asked.

"It has," Ocheda said. "The royal family, the Lady Zhila, and most of your grace's court."

"You know what?" Aefric said. "They don't need me for this. Send for the knights of my personal guard. At least, whoever of them aren't at that lunch. They can join me here."

"Yes, your grace."

It was a simple lunch of cold cuts, honeyed oat bread, and good sharp cheeses, along with good, crisp day beer to drink. Just Aefric and all seven of the knights of his personal guard.

It was a good, casual lunch. Full of stories. Some of Aefric's, from his adventuring days. More from each of the knights. Some of those were tales of battle from the Godswalk Wars, or duels, but just as many were of strange situations they'd gotten themselves into over the years, and ways they'd worked themselves out again.

Some of those were likely tall tales. Like the one about Ser Wardius wrestling an alligator in the moat around Behal Castle. Far as Aefric knew, there *were* no alligators in Lake Deepwater.

But by tradition, the stories went unquestioned over the meal. Just enjoyed.

And finally, as the food and the stories finally wound down, Aefric stood.

His knights looked up at him. He smiled and began to speak.

"When Beornric first told me that I had local knights who wanted to join my personal guard, I had trouble understanding." Aefric shrugged. "I was only newly knighted myself, before the king created me Duke of Deepwater. I had only the life and experiences of an adventurer to draw on. I knew little of the ways of knighthood and nobility."

Aefric nodded at Ser Beornric.

"But I trusted his judgment, and I can't be happier about that decision. You six — seven, really, as I *do* include Beornric in this — have proven yourselves over and over. Your skills. Your judgment. Your honor. You are truly exemplars of what a knight should be."

They took the compliment in silence, though Aefric could see the pride in their eyes at his words.

Aefric smiled.

"As such," he said, "I feel you need a title better than 'duke's guard' or 'knights of my personal guard' or some such."

The knights looked back and forth at one another. Maybe trying to see if any of the others knew where Aefric was going with this. But even Ser Beornric didn't know.

"And that is why," Aefric continued, "as of this moment, I am creating the Order of the Lake, and naming you the first seven knights of this order."

Eyes widened. One or two knights gasped.

But then all smiled.

"You'll have to re-knight us then," Ser Beornric said, chest puffed up with pride. "Make it official."

And so Aefric did that, at the end of his lunch. Each knight, starting with Ser Beornric, knelt before Aefric and renewed their vows, before each was told, in turn, "Arise, Knight of the Lake," and given the salute of a noble to a knight. One hand making a fist, the other grabbing its wrist.

When Aefric finished the ritual for the last of them, Ser Wardius, he called Ocheda out onto the balcony.

"Send word to Kentigern," Aefric said. "At my expense I want the image of Lake Deepwater etched into the breastplates of these seven, my new Knights of the Lake."

"Of course, your grace," she said, and bowed. "But I must inform your grace that the king summons you. His justiciar is ready to report about the assassin."

---

AEFRIC, ALONG WITH SERS BEORNRIC, TEMAT AND WARDIUS, descended the many long, private stairs down from the ducal apartments to just behind the great hall, and from there down below the castle to the cells.

Down here the air smelled of dust and sweat. Down here there was no hardwood covering the gray stone floors, or plaster on the gray stone walls and ceiling. And yet all was brightly lit, evermore, by magic.

The hall had been cleared of guards and soldiers save two Varondami knights, guarding Lady Zhila, four Knights of the Crown, guarding their majesties — five, if Aefric included Ser Beatritz — and two soldiers bearing both the sigils of Armyr and Taesark, guarding the justiciar.

Maev wasn't down here, which made Aefric frown, though he didn't dare comment on it.

Especially since Lady Zhila was giving Aefric the kind of look that might've been assessing, and might've been ready to pass a very lethal judgment.

The queen mother of Varondam was dressed almost as well as their majesties, in a silk gown with a high-cut, dark yellow bodice and a skirts of burnt orange. She wore a ruby studded gold necklace, and matching bracelets.

King Colm was in a wine-red quilted tunic, embroidered in gold threat, over dark brown hose. Queen Eppida wore a low-cut gown that was an even darker shade of red than the king's tunic, and embroidered with silver thread, rather than gold.

The justiciar, of course, was clad in all brown roughspun, cowl to gloves to boots. And he held his triple-edged greatsword before him, as though in salute.

"He has arrived," Lady Zhila said archly. "May we now proceed?"

King Colm looked as though he'd been expecting to formally introduce Aefric to Lady Zhila. Clearly, though, she was uninterested in the introduction.

Aefric kept his mouth closed, focusing on the lingering taste of sharp cheese and good beer from the much more pleasant company of his lunch.

King Colm turned to the justiciar. "All are present. In Taesark's name, begin your report when ready."

"Yes, your majesty," the justiciar said in that eerily neutral voice. "Would your majesty first like the complete report about Sifwyn Rikassa?"

"That can wait for now," King Colm said. "Tell us about the assassin."

"The assassin is of the Order of the Severed Dream," the justiciar said. "He was contracted in the Malimfari city of Wulfport, to infiltrate the royal palace of Varondam at Vaaran Tir and take the life of her highness, Maev Stronghand, Princess of Armyr. No additional funds were provided to ensure suffering, or any specific kind of statement in the process. Simple death."

"There's nothing 'simple' about the idea of my daughter dying," King Colm growled.

"I speak not of the concept of her death," the justiciar said. "Only of the contract, which was, in fact, that simple. Death was paid for. Not suffering or torture or any of the additional services the Order of the Severed Dream might offer."

"Oh, enough of these details," Lady Zhila said. "Bring us to the crux of the matter. Who hired the assassin?"

The justiciar did not look towards her. Addressed the king instead.

"Does your majesty wish to hear of the crimes and murders committed to make possible the attempt at Vaaran Tir?"

"Later," King Colm said. "For now, I agree with Lady Zhila. We need to know who's behind this."

"The assassin believes that payment, through channels, came from the royal family of Malimfar."

"I knew it," King Colm growled.

"Wait," Queen Eppida said. "'Believes?'"

"That's correct, your majesty," the justiciar said. "That is what the assassin believes. He is mistaken. He was led to believe this, by subtle enough means to make it seem true. But truth does not ring out in it. Malimfar is not behind the attempt to take the life of her highness, Maev Stronghand, Princess of Armyr."

"You're *certain*?" Lady Zhila asked. "But it *has* to be Malimfar, doesn't it?"

The justiciar merely stood there, holding up his shining greatsword.

"He's certain," King Colm said with a sigh. "See how brightly his sword shines?" He turned to the justiciar. "Then who *is* behind it, if not Malimfar?"

"I can provide the name known to the assassin," the justiciar said. "But the name is false. Meaningless."

"Who *is* behind the attempt?"

"There is no way for me to tell," the justiciar said. "The threads hang too loose. I cannot pull them tight enough to see that pattern. Without more information, all I can swear to was that the order to take the life of her highness, Maev Stronghand, Princess of Armyr, did not originate from the royal family of Malimfar, nor with the decision of anyone native to Malimfar."

"But it has to be the same hand behind the attempt on us," King Colm said, including his queen and himself with a gesture. "And behind the attempt on Killian."

"I sense an echo to those words," the justiciar said. "There is truth to them. Connection. But the extent of that connection, I cannot swear to."

"What does that mean?" Queen Eppida asked.

"It means that the events connect, and that the hands behind them have at least touched. But I do not know, here and know, if the same hands are behind all three attempted assassinations."

"Is there more you can get from the assassin?" King Colm asked.

"There are no further questions worth asking him now," the justiciar said. "But that may change, if new information arises."

"Then he lives for now," King Colm said. "And he comes back to Armityr with us. Today."

"Today?" Queen Eppida asked, complaint plain in her voice. "The royal entourage isn't even here yet. They're only just reaching Behal."

"Then they'll have a shorter trip back to Armityr," King Colm repeated. "We leave today. At once." He turned to Lady Zhila. "You may come with us, if you wish, but I would rather you and Maev return to Vaaran Tir and continue the negotiations."

"I would rather that as well," she said. "Too chilly up here for my old bones."

"Eppida, Beatritz, make the arrangements," King Colm said. "Aefric, find us someplace private. I'd like a word before we go."

SO MANY MEETING ROOMS IN WATER'S END. SO MANY PLACES THAT Aefric could have taken the king for a quick, private chat. But Aefric could tell from King Colm's manner that speed was of the essence.

Instead of any of those meeting rooms, Aefric led King Colm out of the hallway among the cells...

...and into a cell.

The cells at Water's End were much nicer than most of the cells Aefric had seen during his adventuring days. But then, most of those had been the decrepit remains of old cells, while exploring one ruin or another. Or sometimes while sneaking into the castle of some evil wizard or despot.

There had, of course, been a cell or two that Aefric had *occupied* ... against his own wishes. But he preferred not to think about those ... simple misunderstandings.

The cell Aefric led the king into was more or less clean gray stone, if a bit dusty. No mortar in here. Or, really, anywhere in Water's End. The stonework was fitted together so tightly along the walls, ceiling, and floor, seams were nearly impossible to find.

The smell of fresh straw from within the roughspun of the corner mattress, and the less pleasant odor of old waste from the midden hole in the opposite corner.

"Close us in," King Colm said to his knights. "But I won't find it amusing if I hear that lock turn."

"That lock couldn't hold me anyway," Aefric said.

Amusement flashed through King Colm's eyes. He shook it away.

The cell door shut with that sense of finality inherent in all cell doors.

King Colm gave Aefric a serious look.

"I erred last night," he said. "I shouldn't have let you hear what I told Maev about that alliance."

"I can keep the secret, your majesty."

"It's not that," King Colm said. "It's no secret I want you married with children on the way. Arinda only ever had the one, and she never acknowledged the poor girl."

"It's true then?" Aefric asked, even softer. "Ser Arras is Duchess Arinda's daughter?"

"Doesn't matter if she is or isn't," King Colm said pointedly. "Duchess Arinda never acknowledged a bastard child, so the point is immaterial."

"I understand," Aefric said, but his heart went out to his knight. To have come so close to becoming a duchess...

But the king was still talking.

"The point is, how can I expect you to pick a wife while you hold out hope that Maev will manage the Varondam alliance without marrying King Dalius?"

"I confess, your majesty," Aefric said. "In my heart of hearts, she is a leading candidate."

"*A* leading candidate," King Colm said. "Not *the* leading candidate?"

He didn't give Aefric time to answer.

"Ah, of course. That's why Zoleen took such steps to keep Byrhta Ol'Caran away from you." He shook his head. "Don't blame you for sending Zoleen away for what she did. But bear in mind, she's young. Only just came of age over the winter. She'll learn from her mistake."

"But will she learn the right lesson?" Aefric asked. "Or will she just try harder next time to conceal activities I'd disapprove of."

"Too early to say," King Colm said with a shrug. "I'll say this about Fyrenn women, though. Individually, they can be delightful people. And clever enough to see things you miss, which can make them great partners. But when it comes to *Fyrenn* matters, they're as single-minded and relentless as werewolves."

He shook his head. "Loving a Fyrenn can be difficult at times. But worth it."

"I'll ... try to keep that in mind, your majesty."

King Colm laughed. "I know, I know. Your heart is already full of

Maev and Byrhta. Hardly any room left for poor Zoleen. But I do advise you to give her another chance."

"So long as I get time and space first."

"Fair enough," King Colm said, and nodded. "Not that Zoleen is the only other candidate you should consider. Nor is Maev the only princess."

"Does your majesty refer to Princess Astrid or Princess Xenia?"

"Neither of them," King Colm said with a grimace. "Malimfar might not be behind those assassination attempts, but I can't believe Eadred doesn't have *something* in mind, after his failure in the spring."

King Colm shook his head, as though shaking away that line of thought.

"And as for Xenia, it occurs to me that Caiperas might've been behind the assassination attempts, hoping to push us into war with Malimfar. That would be extreme, for them. But I can't rule it out yet."

"What about Varondam?" Aefric asked.

"What *about* Varondam?"

"How much better terms could they have gotten for this alliance if Armyr felt an urgent need to strike back at Malimfar after attempted assassinations? Or worse, if one or two attempts were successful?"

King Colm frowned as he considered that.

"Doesn't track," he said. "There was an attempt on Maev, and I have no other daughter for them to marry."

"That attempt was stopped before it started," Aefric said. "They might've planned to be ready when the strike came, to either foil it, or quickly save Maev's life. But Sylkanis might've foiled the plan, by sniffing out the assassin before he struck."

"A devious thought," King Colm said. "I hope you're wrong."

"As do I," Aefric said, only half-honestly. After all, if he were right, Maev wouldn't likely be marrying King Dalius.

"I'll have to keep it in mind, though," King Colm said. "Mention it to Beatritz. Get her opinion. I'll also have to discuss the possibility with Maev. See what she thinks." He gave Aefric a half-smile. "And yes, I'll tell her you suggested it."

"Thank you, your majesty."

"But I was referring to other princesses. Rethneryl has a few. Hatay has one as well. Crown princess, I believe. And Shachan ... I forget. But now that Malimfar and Caiperas have sent princesses to see you, you can believe that other nearby kingdoms will as well."

"I will be happy to receive them, your majesty."

"That's half a lie," King Colm said with a smile. "But do your best. And consider them seriously. While I may agree, as a father, that you and Maev would make a great match, as a king I'd rather see you married to someone else's princess."

"Yes, your majesty."

King Colm laughed. "That's not an order, your grace. Just a point for consideration. And if it turns out you can't have Maev as your bride, and none of the other princesses suit you, I just might be willing to provide an appropriate dowry for Byrhta Ol'Caran."

"Really?" Aefric asked, more than a little surprised.

"Really," King Colm said, with a smile. "Do you know what Beatritz has been doing since we crossed into Deepwater?"

"Checking up on me?" Aefric asked.

King Colm laughed. "Very good, Aefric. She has indeed. Not with your vassals. They'll bring anything good or bad they have to say directly to the queen and me. No. Beatritz has been checking with the *people*. Your staff, your vassals' staffs, your citizens. Seeing what they have to say about their new duke."

"And?" Aefric asked tentatively.

"Reports have generally been quite positive." King Colm smiled at the hesitation on Aefric's face about the word *generally*. "You'll never get better than that, Aefric. It's never true that all of the people are happy with their rulers. Someone always has complaints. Sometimes even justified complaints."

"Shouldn't I look into those justified complaints?"

"When you can," King Colm said with a shrug. "But 'justified' can mean many things. One family may have their fortunes hurt deeply by your policies. Doesn't mean those policies are wrong, especially if they help far more people than they hurt.

"One example would be those priests of the Green Lord you sent to help save your vassals' farms, pastures and ranches." King Colm clapped Aefric on the shoulder. "A fine bit of work. And most of your vassals love you for that. But the merchant families who stood to build fortunes importing food? They're not so well pleased.

"A better example, though, is this borog matter," King Colm continued. "When news spreads that you have allowed literally hundreds of borogs to live in the Dragonscar, you'll get a lot of scared people. But I don't doubt the gold those borogs mine for you will help those scared people's lives."

"You've already heard what happened in the Dragonscar this morning?" Aefric asked. "*I* haven't had a chance to tell you yet."

"Very little eludes Beatritz."

"Did she tell you I named Ge'rek a ler?"

"She didn't," King Colm said, giving Aefric a considering look. "I take it he's the borog leader?"

"Technically I'm their clan chief. But he's what they call my 'chief's hand.'"

"Then it sounds as though you have a good handle on things, for now. Try to keep it that way."

"I will."

"Have you picked a replacement for Calder?"

"Not yet," Aefric said, through a sigh. "I was considering bringing Ser Grey up from Behal to serve as castellan here."

"I recommend against it. That would be a demotion, of sorts."

"How so?"

"Down in Behal, she practically lives as a baron," King Colm said. "You spend most of your time here, so she has a lot of work and a lot of respect as castellan. Bring her up here, she'll have a lot less of both."

"Good point," Aefric said. "I'll find someone here."

"One more thing," King Colm said. "I want you visiting Netar before winter." He shook Aefric's shoulder. "Have a look at your new barony, man."

"I will, your majesty," Aefric said, then sighed. "I have to get down to Kivash, too. Ashling gave me a castle down there, and everything inside it."

King Colm chuckled. "I'm not surprised. She gave me one as well. One might almost think she expects Malimfar to try to retake Kivash."

"You don't?"

"Not soon. They know we'll be watching for it. No. If they want to try to hit us again in the next year or two, they'll strike somewhere else."

"Speaking of which. Since Malimfar isn't behind the assassinations—"

"No, your grace," King Colm said firmly. "You may not have permission to go after Nelazzi. Something serious is afoot, and I don't want your focus split when I need you. Talk to me of Nelazzi again in the spring. Not before."

"Yes, your majesty."

"Anything else before I go?"

"A question," Aefric said. "Did her majesty mention that she offered to provide both a dowry and another title for Sighild Ol'Masarkor, if I wish to take her as my bride?"

King Colm laughed. "No, but I should have seen it coming, the way those two kept conferring privately on the road. I'm telling you, Aefric. When it comes to Fyrenn matters, they turn into werewolves."

"Does that include Sighild?" Aefric asked. "She's only a cousin to the Fyrenns."

"Might not," King Colm said a slight shrug. "She seems a dear enough girl. But I haven't seen her deal with a Fyrenn question."

He tilted his head as he looked at Aefric. "Is she a likely candidate to be your bride?"

"I don't honestly know," Aefric said. "Seems sweet enough, but I barely know her."

"Well, if you get to know her, find some way to see her reaction on a Fyrenn matter. See if she sprouts claws and starts howling."

"I'll keep an eye out for that," Aefric said, chuckling.

"And now I must get moving. We have many miles to cover before dark."

"Yes, your majesty," Aefric said, offering the king his hand.

King Colm kissed Aefric's hand, and Aefric pressed his forehead to the king's knuckles.

And then they left the cell together.

---

As Aefric and the king emerged from the cell and into the hall, Ser Beatritz was there to meet them, along with two Knights of the Crown and Sers Beornric, Wardius and Temat.

"Our ship is packed and ready for departure," Ser Beatritz said, flanking King Colm and Aefric as they strode rapidly toward the stairs. "The ducal seneschal provided us with the *Swift Wave* to carry us to Behal. Rikas have been dispatched to ensure that the royal entourage meets us there by late afternoon."

King Colm made a low sound of objection. "We'll have to spend the night in Behal, won't we?"

"It's the smarter way to go," she said, as they emerged from the stairs to a far more decorous hallway, where Aefric took the lead to see them quickly to the back of the castle and the docks.

"Staying in Behal tonight will see us better organized when we depart in the morning," she continued. "Your majesty knows what will happen if we try for today."

"We won't even reach Goldenfall," the king said.

"And I *trust* your majesty wouldn't consider sailing past Behal and making his entourage chase him all the way back to Armityr."

King Colm chuckled. "No, I suppose not. Do we have both prisoners? The assassin and the wizard?"

"We do," Ser Beatritz said. "And I've sent a rika to Stormsent, telling Duke Wylyn to bring his baron to us at Armityr."

"Good," King Colm said. "I find myself wondering if that business in Silverlake has any relation to those attempted assassinations."

They emerged from a door in the back of the castle to the coral-like docks of the Water's End port, right by the ducal pier.

Down at the end of the pier, Aefric could see the *Swift Wave* making ready for departure. Sailors crawled the rigging, preparing the sails. Even more sailors were busy on the decks.

And there. All the way aft, and watching. Aefric spotted Maev.

Their eyes met across that long distance. He felt her smile, more than saw it. Even so, that moment of connection was such that he felt the space between them begin to fall away...

Something jarred that connection, causing Aefric's heart to lurch and the world to swim back into place. Lady Zhila, standing beside Maev, had taken her arm. Forced Maev to look at her.

"I think it's best if your grace remains here," Ser Beatritz said with admirable tact.

"Why is Maev aboard that ship?" Aefric asked. "I thought she was going back to Varondam."

"She is," King Colm confirmed.

"She asked for the chance to say goodbye to her father, before she and Lady Zhila board their ship," Ser Beatritz said, emphasizing "her father" just a little, and giving Aefric a meaningful look.

Aefric sighed, and stopped walking.

"Farewell, your grace," King Colm said. "Stop by Armityr on your way to Netar."

"I shall, your majesty. And may you, the queen, Killian and Maev all fare well until next I see you."

He saluted Ser Beatritz by making a fist and grabbing the wrist behind it. She bowed in response.

"I shall pass your good wishes along," King Colm said, and then he and his knights proceeded down the docks, while Aefric and his knights remained behind.

"It's for the best, your grace," Ser Beornric said softly. "How much harder would it have been for you to say goodbye to Princess Maev from arm's length, without getting to hold or kiss her?"

"You're right," Aefric said with a sigh, watching as Lady Zhila led Maev out of eyesight. "I still hate it."

"We never had our morning meeting, your grace," Ser Beornric said, and Aefric could tell the good knight was just trying to distract him.

"And we won't," Aefric said. "Not today." He shook himself, trying to get rid of the dull ache in his chest at being parted again so soon from Maev.

"Your grace really ought not go to Behal today," Ser Beornric said carefully.

"I won't," Aefric said, steadying himself through a deep breath. "But during our hunt for Calder we went through a good many of those potions that allow the drinker to see through illusions and sense magic."

"We did," Ser Beornric agreed.

"And I am going to spend the rest of my afternoon brewing more."

Without another word, Aefric took to the air and flew up the gorgeous, sparkling deep blue walls of his castle to his smaller, private balcony.

From there, he passed through his private sitting room — offered a quick word of greeting to Ocheda — and on into his magic laboratory.

Those items from Sifwyn, still awaited his attention. But they could wait a little longer.

Aefric lit the room by magic. Set his Brightstaff just inside and closed the door.

The room smelled like vervain today. Odd, that. It probably meant something, but he didn't know what. And likely he wouldn't. Not until he understood the magic of the old Soulfist grimoires.

He crossed the permanent magic circles, within the whitewashed stone floor on his way to his alchemy desk.

He checked the worktable beside it. He'd need at least two of the mortars and pestles, he knew that much. Likely two or three of the alembics, at least one burner...

Beyond that, he wasn't sure. Potion-making had never been an area of expertise for him. But it would require a focus that he would very much benefit from at the moment.

He took down the first of the old Soulfist recipe books. It was a heavy, leatherbound thing. Taller than his forearm was long, and just about as thick as his wrist was wide.

No dust, of course. Books and magic and alchemy always seemed to pick up traces of the magic used around them, and inscribed in them. Sometimes that made them quirky to the point of becoming peculiar.

But one thing it always ensured — they repelled dust and vermin.

As he did with the Soulfist grimoires, Aefric took a moment and projected thoughts at the book before opening it.

*I am Aefric Brightstaff, rightful Duke of Deepwater and Baron of Netar.*

That latter part wouldn't likely mean much to the recipe book, but it was part of a true statement about who Aefric was. And the truth of the first part likely mattered a great deal.

After all, if he was the rightful Duke of Deepwater, then it stood to reason that he'd *inherited* this book, not stolen it.

Along with those thoughts, he projected the image of both his ducal seal and his personal seal.

He felt a sort of harmonic chime of acknowledgment. The book wouldn't object to Aefric's opening it.

He began to read.

And a short time later, he began to laugh.

The key was here. In the first few pages of the oldest alchemy book the Soulfists had left him. The answer he'd been hunting so hard for, working so hard to figure out on his own. It had been in the room with him all along.

The first pages of that old alchemical recipe book, they carried the key to the cypher the Soulfists used in recording all their recipes and formulae.

Between the book's acknowledgment of his right to read it, and the key to the cypher contained in those pages, he could read the rest as easily as though it were written in the common tongue.

Laughing, Aefric set down the book and crossed the room to his magic research desk. Pulled down that first grimoire. The one he'd been working to hard to translate.

It acknowledged him before he even sent it a thought.

Aefric pumped his fist and opened the book.

The very first spell was a Soulfist version of the same personal grooming spell Aefric used himself.

And he understood it!

Excitement thrilling through his veins now, Aefric set that grimoire back on the shelf. He ran back across the lab to his alchemy desk and skimmed through those recipe books for the potion he needed.

Then he fetched the reagents he needed, and began to brew.

# 13

---

An aett after the king and queen departed Water's End for Armityr, Aefric boarded his *magari* with Sers Yrsa, Beornric and Micham, heading for the Dragonscar.

The day was bright and clear. The late summer's heat had resurged a bit, but Kentigern kept promising that this was a temporary thing that happened every year, and that the days would be cooler soon enough.

Of course, Kentigern also said that by Midwinter Aefric would find himself missing the summer heat, but that seemed unlikely.

Still. Up here, flying high above Lake Deepwater, the temperatures were milder, and the winds were strong, and smelled cool and clean.

Ser Beornric was taking his fourth ride on the *magari* now. Though he still held tightly to the chariot's sides, Aefric noticed that his grip was less white-knuckled than it had been. He was even willing to look over the side from time to time, though he wasn't yet much for conversation while flying.

It seemed, however, that Ser Yrsa intended to make up the difference.

"Your grace has spent a great deal of time in his lab, of late," she said. "Not avoiding Sighild Ol'Masarkor, I hope."

"Why?" Aefric asked, standing the Brightstaff beside himself, so he could handle the reins with both hands. "Do you like her?"

"She's pretty. She's charming—"

"Understatements, both," Ser Micham said. "She's the prettiest and most charming suitor your grace has. Excepting Byrhta Ol'Caran, of course. But it's hardly fair to compare anyone to her."

"As I was saying," Ser Yrsa said. "She's pretty. She's charming. The staff all like her. If your grace *must* marry a Fyrenn, she'd be my pick."

"Well, I'm not avoiding her," Aefric said.

"She's been at Water's End for four days and you haven't bedded her yet," Ser Beornric said.

Thus proving that Aefric's marriage prospects were a topic powerful enough to overcome even Beornric's problem with heights.

"And I told her why," Aefric said. "As she wants to be considered a potential bride, I want to get to know her *before* I sleep with her."

"That's not how it's usually done in Armyr," Ser Yrsa said. "Your vassals won't like it."

Aefric chuckled. Maev herself had once told Aefric she wouldn't show up at his chambers if she were only after the bliss moment. That she found him "far too handsome and interesting."

So even in this, royalty played by slightly different rules than the rest of the nobility.

"I never thought that being a duke would have so many people concerned about my sex life."

"Welcome to Armyr," Ser Micham said.

"Fine," Aefric said. "I'll sleep with her tonight. Happy?"

"*She* will be," Ser Micham said. "Every time she looks at your grace, I fear her gaze will set fire to your clothes."

"*The point is,*" Aefric said. "I've been in my magic lab so much because I've finally cracked the Soulfist grimoires. I've been working on learning their magic."

Ser Yrsa whistled appreciatively and said, "All objections withdrawn. I'll cover for you myself, if I need to."

"Be easier," Ser Beornric managed, "if you named a castellan."

"I'll have to before I go to Norra for the Feast of Dereth Sehk. But I still haven't settled on who."

"Can we ... talk about that ... later?" Ser Beornric asked.

"Happily," Aefric said, and gave his focus to steering the *magari,* while Sers Yrsa and Micham continued discussing Aefric's marital prospects. Which were growing even more complicated, now that word had come that Rethneryl, Hatay and Shachan would all send princesses to meet Aefric in the autumn.

And Rethneryl would send more than one.

Of course, Aefric's thoughts still turned more often to Maev and Byrhta than to any other.

Maev was back in Varondam, where letters told Aefric that the heat was oppressive, negotiations were going slowly, and she missed him.

Byrhta, though, Aefric would see soon. She and Vercy were coming along to Norra for the Feast of Dereth Sehk.

It would be good to see Byrhta again. And this time, no one would be working to keep them apart.

Pleasantly distracting thoughts as Aefric steered the *magari* over Lachedran and points north all the way to the Dragonscar.

But Aefric didn't land there, nor stop to visit the borogs of Clan Thunder Stick.

Instead, Aefric turned east, whisking through the air above the Dragonscar as the miles fell away beneath him.

His knights now were discussing the Dragonscar, the borogs, gold, and the like.

Finally, shortly after midday, Aefric reached the end of the Dragonscar, and eased the *magari* down out of the sky to land on the hard brown stone of the chasm floor.

He took the Brightstaff in hand, and he and his knights left the chariot of the *magari.*

Aefric dismissed the magical flying chariot, and looked up at last at the sight he'd hoped to see, oh so many days ago, when he and his knights and soldiers came riding into the chasm.

The dragon's skeleton.

It was tremendous. Huge. It filled the very end of the Dragonscar. Its ribs were so big that the spine they held up was at least level with the ridge above.

The bones of its six legs were longer and wider than many tree trunks.

The skeleton showed no yellowing or browning with age and weather. The bones were still as bright a white as though they'd just been denuded of their flesh.

Aefric could see the frame of the great wyrm's wings, folded down tight along the spine. Even in that state, they looked so very thick. Each of those wings, when spread, must've been wider than the flight of an arrow shot by a master archer.

The dragon's skull was large enough to serve as a house or pavilion, and faced the sea. And every tooth in that immense jaw was still in place. So many teeth that...

Wait...

"It faces the sea," Aefric said.

"It does," Ser Micham said. "If your grace wishes to climb the skeleton, I can show you the route I took."

"You don't understand," Aefric said. "The dragon's skeleton faces the sea."

Ser Micham frowned, perhaps still not understanding.

"Your grace refers to the legend," Ser Beornric said. "That the dragon was dying as it flew, and crashed here, digging out the chasm in the process."

Aefric nodded.

"Perhaps it tried to turn?" Ser Micham suggested.

But Ser Yrsa's eyes widened in understanding. She looked back down the chasm, then at Aefric.

"You don't think..." she said.

"I hope not," Aefric said. "A dragon that could do all that. What could kill it?"

Ser Beornric looked down the chasm, then back at Aefric.

"You think the dragon *made* the chasm? With its breath?"

"Some of it was probably the dragon's cave," Aefric said, looking around. "But maybe. Big enough dragon, letting loose everything it had in a final death blast. Maybe."

"What could kill a dragon like that?" Ser Yrsa said. "For that matter, what could survive the blast? Not like there's another skeleton here."

"Just a theory," Aefric said.

"Could be that the breath was enough to incinerate the great drake's killer," someone else said.

And Aefric knew that voice.

"Kainemorton?"

"Of course," Kainemorton called down from atop the dragon's skull. Even from there, Aefric could see the old mage's periwinkle eyes twinkling. "Who else?"

Aefric flew up to meet him.

"Good to see you," Aefric said.

"And you, *your grace,*" Kainemorton said with a wink. Kainemorton was the only person on Qorunn who knew that Aefric had once been Keifer McShane. But then, it was Kainemorton who'd taken Keifer here to become Aefric.

Aefric still didn't know how exactly that worked...

"You seem to be settling in well," Kainemorton said. "Making friends with borogs, and enemies with pirates. Plenty of rich, lovely women vying for your hand in marriage."

Kainemorton's gaze grew penetrating then.

"How fare you on that front?" he said softly. "Ready to marry again?"

"I think so," Aefric said, just as softly, with a nod. "It's what Andi would want, which helps."

"Good," Kainemorton said, then nodded at the skeleton. "You weren't thinking of taking a bone or claw, I hope."

"Considered it," Aefric said.

"Leave it be," Kainemorton said. "You don't know what purpose it serves here."

"Purpose?" Aefric asked.

"Ah, lad," Kainemorton said. "You've learned so much, but have so much more to learn. When you figure out how to sense beyond magic itself into the very essence of Qorunn, you'll begin to understand features like this skeleton, and the sacrifice this dragon made for us all."

"Sacrifice?" Aefric asked.

"Of course," Kainemorton said with a chuckle. "A dragon like this majestic wonder doesn't die just because something tries to kill it."

Aefric chuckled. "First lesson you ever taught me. Look beyond the obvious."

"In all things, my dear Aefric. In all things."

Aefric scoffed. "You're talking about my marriage prospects, aren't you?"

Kainemorton didn't answer, though his eyes twinkled a little harder than normal.

Aefric looked away down the Dragonscar toward the Risen Sea, which was so distant now that Aefric couldn't even smell the sea on the nonstop wind that whipped through the Dragonscar.

He turned back to Kainemorton, but the old mage was gone.

"I hate when you do that," Aefric grumbled, and flew back down to the ground.

"So what would your grace prefer?" Ser Beornric asked. "A tooth or a claw? I'm not sure it can be done, but if anyone can loosen one enough to remove it—"

"Neither," Aefric said, looking back up at the great skeleton. He shook his head. "Let it remain intact, as a monument to the wondrous beast it once was."

"I thought your grace wanted a souvenir," Ser Micham said. "I couldn't manage it myself, but surely with your grace's magic—"

"No," Aefric said. "The most important thing was seeing it. Taking a moment to admire the creature that those bones once formed."

All four of them took some time then to gaze up at the dragon's skeleton, each lost in their own thoughts.

"Come on," Aefric said, finally. "I have a castellan to pick, and a duchy to run."

And with that he summoned his *magari* and they took to the air, heading back for Water's End.

# SIGN UP FOR STEFON'S NEWSLETTER

Stefon loves to keep in touch with his readers, and loves to keep you reading. The best way for him to do both is for you to sign up for his newsletter.

Sign up at http://www.stefonmears.com/join

If you sign up for Stefon's newsletter, you get...

- Monthly updates about his publishing and travel schedules
- His latest news, in brief, and answers to reader questions
- A free short story for signing up
- List-only offers and occasional specials
- Plus a free short story every month!

# ABOUT THE AUTHOR

Stefon Mears has role-played Ge'rek under a different name. Stefon has more than thirty books to his credit, and he never stops writing. He earned his M.F.A. in Creative Writing from N.I.L.A., and his B.A. in Religious Studies (double emphasis in Ritual and Mythology) from U.C. Berkeley. He's a lifelong gamer and fantasy fan. Stefon lives in Portland, Oregon, with his wife and three cats.

*Look for Stefon online:*
www.stefonmears.com
himself@stefonmears.com